17

Kathy
Frias

Rumors of Eden

300 years after the flood . . .

God was a rumor . . .

A fading whisper . . .

Published by White Feather Press. (www.whitefeatherpress.com)

ISBN 978-0-9831751-0-0
Printed in the United States of America

Cover photo ©iStockphoto.com/ James Steidl

White Feather Press

Reaffirming Faith in God, Family, and Country!

Dedication

For my husband, Robert, and our children, John, Paul, and Jared,
Laura and Danielle.

Acknowledgments

My sisters, Janice and Debbie, my brother, Jimmy and friends, Teresa and Gina who read this book in its roughest form.

My brother, Billy, whose life experience inspired part of this story.

Glennis and Sylvia Boatwright, my parents, who taught me to seek God.

Skip Coryell for being brave and publishing *Rumors of Eden*.

Mary Mueller for fastidious editing and genuine hospitality.

Robbie of The Antares Rock Shop in Evanston, WY for sharing his love of fossils and who has questions of his own.

Dr. Carl Baugh for his studies on the earth before the flood.

Bobbie Bedient Photography for erasing 10 years with an airbrush.

Rumors
of
Eden

Book One

Madai

- 1 -

The belly of the whaleskin boat hit the valley of the wave with a crash. No sooner was it dumped into the chasm, than it vaulted back into the air on the wings of a surging, roaring sea. The man inside held the rudder against the hands of the wave to aim his craft at the gale. Water battered him at every side, salt etched his face, and the wind howled. His name was Madai, and he was an agony of straining, aching flesh upon the Great Brine Sea.

His vessel dropped, smashing onto the iron surface of the water again. Madai lost his grip, shaken as by a mighty beast and hurled against the bottom of his boat. There he scrambled in the sloshing seawater to regain his feet, caught with the red fish and lej dumped inside by indiscriminate waves.

The sea fish thrashed and beat their tails against the bowels of Madai's ship, pumping their gills to strain a breath in the air, only to be washed back into the sea by the next coming wave. Madai's leg, lashed by a length of cord to the mast, was all that saved him being from carried away as well.

"What have I lost?" was his thought. It did not occur to him that he might die. Perhaps it would not have mattered to him much if he had. But all his panic was for the star map, and The Family's spear... and he would reach out to find them safely strapped against the side, but for another groaning of the boat that signaled his next rise and coming fall upon the Sea. It was a moment that signaled itself to him that he should not give way to despair, though it was a quiet thought against the furious storm.

He wrenched his leg free, feeling the boat hapless against a pitiless foe. It was a mammoth effort to regain his feet, fight with the waves for the steering shaft and prevent himself from turning broadside into the gale.

Still, the typhoon screamed... an indifferent carnivore. It ate the sun and moon and stars, and Madai had ceased to know whether it was night or day, or how long he had battled it. But he set himself to battle it again, starved for sleep and fresh water and a moment's reprieve. He knew it had been too long since he had slept and shook himself in a panic each time the howl of the wind grew quiet or his head banged against the steering shaft or his eyes closed of their own accord.

When he heard her voice speak, "Madai," it frightened him, because he knew she could not be here, and he snapped his eyes open. A dream... where the sound of her voice was fresh and perfect. How long had it been since he had heard her speak? The beloved voice. He must not sleep, yet how kind it would be to just drift away and chase it... But he was shaken by a primal fear, proving himself very much a living man. He pushed back his shoulders to take a lungful of air and shook himself. He forced his eyes wide and let them burn in the endless icy rain.

In the end, it was not his will that failed him, but rather the sheer passage of time. And he was not warned of sleep's coming, for he began to feel it possible that, indeed, he flew with the wind, rising above it to be greeted by a gentle, twinkling heaven, calling him to peace. Soon, he heard her speak again, and he tumbled back to earth. And somewhere between flying and waking, he tied the rudder against the storm.

In his vision, the voice started as a whisper...her... calling his name. This time he followed the sound, adrift and past controlling, till he could just see her; and he felt himself smiling as he was restored to the best of times. Then he was part of his own vision, and he watched as his own hands reached out, trembling slightly. He watched his fingers touch the silky head of his little boy; he could feel him, alive and warm...wet and sticky, red and screaming. She was smiling, offering him a son.

How had he once thought this tall, good lass plain...this stalwart wife? He lifted his hand to touch her face again, and she whispered, "Take him, Madai." Madai wanted to, but suddenly the very palpable feel of her skin was lost, and he was starting to drift away, till her image was gone and finally her voice was lost in a roar. He tried to bring her back, but he felt himself falling away as he fought with his breaking heart to deny what it knew.

His heart pounded, even as he slept. His wife was lost in dream as much as life, with the babe, too... and then suddenly... Madai was the child...

In his dream, standing with his own father, Madai heard his voice, able and strong, always dependable, telling him how to hold his breath just before he let the arrow fly. Madai felt himself a boy, full of confidence. He looked up at his father, eternally old and very tall, able to keep the world in place.

Such a world, living in summer along the mighty stream that was his ever-constant music in waking and sleeping, a backdrop of roar that the ice of winter could not silence. The river had been his first adventure, his hunting grounds and swimming hole. It cut through the mountain, taking a course down from the heights that Madai's clan should take in winter, escaping into the sea. It tumbled over new black rocks, scraping the earth raw, that and the wind.

Sometimes the wind brought fierce storms with it, and cones of water dancing in the bay. Trees followed the stream all the way to the sea, massive terebinths that brought them shelter from the storms; and large boulders tumbled down from some quake of times past.

It had been a grand life for a boy, chasing through the forest, through a maze of granite monoliths, to hidden azure pools and secret wells of fish. The Family followed the river down, then up, in season, a life of practiced effort. And it was all they knew, save the rumor of times past...

ঙ্গ ঙ্গ ঙ্গ

The next day his boat was still a tiny spot on the endless ocean, a sea pitting itself against an insignificant. It was wrought with a skin of whale and by hands of perfect maritime skill, tried and true, learned at a time when men ran away from other men because their tongues were suddenly strange. The skill was honed in the advance westward, across a dangerous plain, across a Brine Sea; and it defended Madai against the storm, even as he slept strapped to the mast and riding through the heart of the typhoon.

The boat rose and fell, and Madai was insensible to it, living his own story again through his dreams. And in his dreams he was once again a child, his hands black, his nails ragged and crusted with dirt the color of soot. He was on his knees wedging up a rock whose edges were sharp as flint and tore his skin, to which he was oblivious, for the sake of the cold and his own excitement.

"I have it!" the little boy cried to his friend, and then he struggled, yanking and pulling and digging around the edges. With a mighty last tug, he lifted the sharp, black rock up and out of the ground.

His childhood friend, Tiras, was watching, catching his breath after giving up on his own unmanageable rock. "Good," he panted with a grin missing a tooth just right of center.

A young Madai, squatting with the rock clenched in his hands, straightened his legs, back bent, to lift the stone. It just cleared the ground, and Madai shuffled like a crab to move it toward the pile of similar rocks, heaped as high as they could reach. The other little boy squeezed his hands between Madai's to help, and their crab appearance was complete now, with four legs. Together they shuffled toward the stacked stone and, grunting, hefted it up to be the crowning of their altar. They shoved it into place, maybe not as straight as their fathers would, certainly not as high, but, in their eyes, perfect. It was a mound of black lignite, the prefered stone for altars, always ready to burn.

They stepped away to admire it.

"Done," Tiras proclaimed.

Madai scratched a place on his neck.

"Is it high enough?" he asked his co-builder.

Tiras studied it a minute more, then, with the serious expression of a boy one year older, nodded, 'Yes.'

Madai grinned, and all his reservation vaporized at the assurance of his indomitable friend. Tiras was, after all, the natural leader of the two, as his nature was both confident and resolute. Togarmah, Tiras father, demanded it.

Madai was the inspiration. He had the secret inkling that The Great God was just past the clouds, and watching. He leaned toward Mighty God in an uncommon way for a boy of ten, as though a longing sprouted in him from his start.

But it was late and it was getting dark. The long night would soon claim its long, winter hours. There was a white fox lying in the snow, very stiff, frozen in a crimson pool. The boys had been excited when they came upon her on the trail, trying to hide against the snow. They took it as an omen that she should carry their smoke to God. But the building had taken a long time with the snow fight included and sliding on the ice beside the river. The coming dusk surprised Madai, who had lost all worry of time. He glanced at his friend to see if Tiras was worried, too.

Tiras was also looking at the fox. "Let's hurry," he whispered.

Just what he hoped to hear! Madai bent down for the frozen carcass while Tiras piled the altar with sticks they'd had the foresight to bring from camp.

The little vixen was, in Madai's estimation, the perfect sacrifice, of purest white but for where she was lanced through with the arrow. There her hair stood stiff, frozen red. Madai held her just slightly extended from his body for God to have a perfect look at her. This he did circumspectly; even Tiras might not understand. But it was going to be a truly sublime offering of their own, to Mighty God, Who would be highly impressed.

It could not all go as planned, which was a great disappointment. It just wasn't right that there should be a struggle with the fire. It always seemed to extinguish itself just when the flame had started well, when the ice itself, affixed to the fox, began to melt and drown out the flickering part. But they were dogged, and too embarrassed to let it go to failure now.

So it was only a matter of time, perhaps too much, until the altar finally licked like a torch into the dusk, hailing their devotions up to heaven.

Madai and Tiras backed away. They watched the flame spatter in triumph. Just as Elders did, they lifted their arms to make of their bodies arrows, aimed at the sky. Neither boy spoke a word aloud. It was a frightful and awesome thing, to speak to Great God; and besides, they were both suddenly shy with each other. But Madai spoke in his heart and vowed himself bound forever.

The fox was not, in fact, Madai's first offering. When he had been very much younger he had laid a blind mole before The Great God and voiced aloud some of what The Elder spoke at the altar, running words together by rote, not understanding, but altogether sincere. And he had set it afire with a stick he had brought from under his mother's cooking pot. There had also been a grouse and a painted lizard. But this fox he and Tiras had planned in route, and it was more worthy indeed than a blind mole.

Deep in the boy's spirit was a longing after the God of his world. The One Who lifted the mountains with a shout, Who spoke a mammoth to life, Who lit the night sky with stars. Such a God!

That first star had already lit its place in the sky. Madai knew exactly where the others would appear, and in what alignment. They were, after all, as explained by his father, divine communications, God's very own intent, telling of things yet to come, though he could only guess how it should all be done. He felt his eyes fill with tears that trailed a cold path down his cheeks. It sometimes happened when he felt seen by God. Of tears he would be ashamed except on this occasion. And besides, it was dark.

"We better go," Tiras whispered.

Madai heard him as from a far distance, but the words punctured the atmosphere, dropped him back to earth, where the air was considerably chilled and the meager winter light was fading. As if in emphasis, a wild saber cat yowled. It truly put a trail of fear down his back; and a look at Tiras's face said he felt something similar. Their flight to the sublime had been squelched to earth, confirmed by a prowling, hungry lion.

"Get a torch," he whispered.

They pulled at the fire first. Madai took an end of pine, only to have its flaming half crumble back into the fire. Tiras snapped a low bough from a drooping cedar and finished it with his knife. He set the green part ablaze.

"Get one of these," he ordered, grabbing for his bow.

Not intending, of course, to return in darkness, they had come away with only their bows, smaller than the long-bows they would one day carry. But it was an effective weapon if they could see the target, which was, of course, a condition requiring light. In the day, it was not so very far home, but danger prowled after the sun sunk behind the mountains and stretched the way back by frightful degrees.

Tiras scanned the tree line, waiting for Madai. He was not just afraid of the saber cat, or whatever else hid in the forest; he was afraid of his father, who would only care now that Tiras had been foolish enough to stay away too long.

Madai did not think about his father or his mother. He thought only about that narrow part of the way home where the shale was covered with snow and very treacherous - the slowest part. Even as he chopped off the limb, he was planning how to cross the slide and dreading it.

"Let's go!" Tiras's voice was jumpy.

Together they abandoned the altar, slipping and stumbling through the snow, but with the remarkable speed of terrified rabbits. There was a tickle of lion canines between their shoulder blades, scooting them along.

Besides the lion, there was something else, at least for Madai... phantoms in the forest at night. They were The Banned, chased away long years ago, but rumored to haunt their woods at night in search of careless boys. Madai was singularly afraid of The Banned. Fear sprung up unbidden, especially at night, and even in his own bed. Sweat was turning frosty against his skin.

It was a long way home on a moonlit night across the twinkling snow, as they panted and wheezed, marking an easy trail to follow. But the saber cat had taken advantage of the white fox, knocked from its higher purpose to the ground by two frightened boys looking for torches. When the lioness finished the fox, Madai and Tiras were already making the clearing that ringed their village.

It was fortunate they did not know what finally became of the fox, as they would have seen it a profane affront that would surely be their doom. Instead, on the morrow, Madai remembered the night in a convenient, amended version. Dismissed was the scare and undignified flight. He lay on his back under his night covering and remembered how the fox had felt, how her hide was pristine; and he felt that surely Mighty God reserved special favor for boys like himself.

He listened to what his mother was doing. She did the same thing every morning. He knew that the world was good, and he would grow to be strong as his father. He smelled the stuff his mother was boiling when she added a handful of savory. Mammoth. His mouth watered and his belly growled. Some day, his Patta would take him after mammoth. But today, he would be nearly as happy just to eat his mother's morning stew.

- *2* -

It didn't rise like the hulking creature it was. Instead, it shot like a firefly straight up from the blackest, coldest depths, up past frightened fish, up past the quiet to where the sea was heaving with the fury of the storm. It had spied a piece of flotsam bobbing and dipping and thrashing around. And it was going to see it.

It rose with its muscled, cylindrical body, up vertically, straight into the air, and crashed back down a safe distance away. Still, Madai's little craft held its balance on the waves. So the sea creature dived back to the depths, then in a serpentine motion advanced again toward the surface. It swam just below, all around the boat, and opened its gills to try to sniff it. But the craft didn't smell of any sort of blood that the creature knew, so the thing flicked its tail at it, a communique of retreating disappointment, and rolled away from the spot to try out something else.

But as its tail curved back over the boat, it touched a soft, warm thing. A thing that was likely full of blood. The creature had started back toward it when a kipper swam past, a really fat kipper, so the sea serpent chased after it.

The kipper was in a race for its life, and it knew it. It used all the skill its Maker had given it and drew the creature far away from the craft, to be sacrificed in the end. It was a fitting task for the kipper.

But... there is a thing about monsters. They remember.

ଓଞ୍ଚ   ଓଞ୍ଚ   ଓଞ୍ଚ

Lives lived on the edge of time, at just the start of a new age may be perilous; but they are magical to little boys who are immune to either migrating glaciers or marauding wolves, especially if their tribe is successful. And Madai's was a prosperous clan that kept the First Ways as best they remembered and sang tales passed down by ancient fathers... come down from the father of the Second Earth, or so it was said.

The seasons to Madai were eternal, as to any other child, a winter that seemed a thousand nights and spring that slipped fast toward autumn; an eternity till he was man enough to go after mammoth. It was his ambition in the entire, though the scouts said that mammoth were increasingly hard to find, which would certainly be the calamity of his lifetime.

Madai had watched his father mark their 'story pole' with a long notch and his mother paint it red each season of color. That was when she had squatted on the birthing stool and brought him out. It measured the slow passing of years till he should finally be allowed to step forward into that most admired society - men of The Family clans.

There were fifteen long red marks now. His foray into the cold with a white fox seemed far ago, a child's thing. Today would come what he had been waiting for. He woke up when it was still dark, even before his mother, and he laid there with his skin dancing... and waited.

Mineo knew what day it was. Even on a cold morning they would go. She prepared their breakfast and their ration for the day - or perhaps two, though she hoped not two. And then she waited for him to announce it, as if Ashkinaz had not already told her.

He made it until the moment he sat up in his bed. And then he called, "Mamam!"

She smiled. He was never able to contain himself at times of pure joy. Not a boy any more, but acting like one, her last live son calling her with the old endearment. It was what he had called her when he was a little boy, and it reached into her soul. She was a fierce mother, a fine woman and brave, a necessary quality in such a time. Without it, one would not love, for fear of broken hearts, nor cross the sea, nor bear children. She had scraped every skin of their lodge and kept the fires day and night. She kept a bow at ready for any red hyena or lion come near while the men were away. And though she had buried all but her second son, there was light in her eyes.

"Yes, Madai?" she replied, looking up.

"I am to hunt!" he exclaimed. "Mammoth!"

"O?" she glanced at her husband as though surprised.

Ashkinaz nodded. "He is fifteen. Look at that arm!"

Madai leapt out of bed, his mouth stretching in a wide grin, and he thrust his shoulder forward for his mother to approve.

She turned her shining eyes from her husband to her son, who nearly reached the height of a man full grown. "Hmm, yes," she answered with unrestrained admiration.

Ashkinaz was proud of her. She did not betray herself by wince nor hesitation. He loved his wife and one son, and grieved the others privately, and never thought his God unkind. It was only the age and the land that was wild. Ashkinaz kept the First Ways and did not take a second wife. He taught his son the holy ways of the Ancients. No one sang the sacred songs better than he.

Madai was eager after his mother's face; he only knew that she was proud of him and did not guess what fears she hid.

They ate their breakfast standing, with Madai already dressed, as he had slept that way.

"Will we seek favor of Great God?" his father asked when they were finished, as if it were really a question.

Madai nodded, but with a racing heart dancing all the way to his stomach and tingling legs that scarcely held their place. He kept himself still as his father started what he knew would be an eternity of praying. In his impatience, he could not close his eyes, but trained them on the ridge line of their lodge and restrained himself from huffing when he heard the others just outside.

Madai had not grown indifferent to the Great God. Indeed, he learnt his father's teachings with a steady will. He was, in fact, uncommonly dedicated to regular and earnest prayer. He asked the Unseen One for a proper reckoning of fact... not to be confused or drawn aside with fancy... but held steady on a rock of truth. It was a less than common concern for one so young, a matter that would one day see him troubled, disenchanted and undone. But today, he was a lad on a first mammoth hunt, and every part of his body clamored for it.

C３C３   C３C３   C３C３

It was cold, with ice in the air. Madai felt the frozen hairs of his nose poke like sharpened spikes. If he turned his eyes down, he could see a crust of white affixed to the top of his lip, where the first of a mustache was started. His boots were stuffed with the fleece of a wild rock ram - the same that his father found tasty. His hands wore the ram's soft belly. A heavy cape of bear weighted him down. Madai was a red wooly creature, shouldering a cape of color rare, tipped with silver where the animal's high shoulders rose to a hump and warned he was the fiercest of his kind. Madai wore it proudly, this beast slain by his able father, who carried its teeth under his shirt. That it was a like beast which had taken his last brother was a proper and just revenge.

The flap that covered his ears was tucked inside and beginning to freeze stiff. Madai was anxious for the sparse chin sprouts to thicken, to cover his face like a seal, to make him warm and show him a full man at last. He kept his eyes on the back of his father and angled his own shoulders to match. Ashkinaz was close, though scarcely more than a silhouette in the misty air, which was crystalline with ice. Madai prayed a blizzard would not start. He mimicked his father, turning his ear to the distance, listening. He tensed his muscles as he walked, to fill them with warm blood, and followed his father, setting his feet into the tracks of Ashkinaz's long stride. It was not so simple a task, as his father stood a full hand's breadth above seven feet. Madai's lips bent in a smile that cracked his lip, recognizing that it was not so hard as last year to stretch his legs across the expanse.

Madai suddenly felt a quick though cushioned smack between his shoulders. He heard a choked laugh, but did not slow his pace nor show a sign save that first surprised flinch. All his ponderings on manhood happily fled away as he suddenly recognized a diversion: Laeden, an arm's reach behind him. But there was Ashkinaz, an arm's reach before him, and this an immediate need of mammoth meat. He gripped his bow tighter, as though to stop his impulse to reach for Laeden's ankle and drop him to the snow. Madai only allowed a glance across his shoulder at the red-faced boy, his green eyes wet with mirth and cold.

Scarcely discernable came a sharp, aggrieved grunt - Reoan, Laeden's father. Madai looked beyond his friend to the swarthy face of a grey-haired man wearing the scruff of a wolf whose worn snout curled up under its empty eyes, with its legs tied across the old hunter's chin. Madai instantly turned to the front. He was not afraid of Reoan, only loath to be admonished by the kind man who walked with one stiff leg from an old snakebite.

"He can hear it snow," Madai heard Reoan whisper, meaning mammoth with its hairy, wide ears.

Madai was entirely glad he had not disrupted the silent march after mammoth, glad he was not the aim of Reoan's crinkled, stony glare. And he was sorry for Laeden, who had disappointed his father. What Madai did not see was the furry paw Reoan rested - just a scant moment, on Laeden's shoulder.

Ashkinaz had heard the chortle. He felt Madai's absence behind him, and felt it when Madai caught up, breathing in short, quick, huffy gasps. He smiled. So his lad was still the Little Hunter; time enough to be a man in a season hence.

Madai felt a bit of snow melting down his back, having found its way past the bear. This was why you did not scuffle in the snow. Madai knew it was dangerous to be wet against the skin, and he hoped they would not spend the night on the tundra. It was a long distance they had come, a far way to retrieve meat that would freeze to a stiff hulk even as he carried it. But he could manage a good weight of it and make his father proud.

The mist began to lift as the day carried on. Madai watched the sky begin to part, to show the sun a faint bright sphere in the white winter's dim. It was an illusion of warmth, but an encouragement. Madai watched the steam rising from his mouth toward the brightening sky, from where the Most Great God could certainly see him. He felt a tingle run slowly down the length of his skin, starting with his scalp. It was good to go with the Great God Who sat upon the crown of the earth.

Perhaps they would find mammoth after all, though his impatience had come to doubt it. Perhaps it was a sign that he had been touched by the sun and seen by God. So he began to rehearse the first shot he would take and ran his father's instruction through his mind again, that he would not fail him. Toban was here, the Elder, and Madai should not want to disgrace his father before such a one as he. He looked at Ashkinaz, moving through the knee- deep snow with unwavering strength. Madai sniffed; his nose was dripping and he rubbed at it with his frozen mitt.

He hunched his shoulders, beginning to feel an ache. He released the tight grip he kept on his long-bow. The air was so silent, save the rhythmic crunching of brittle snow. It seemed not even Eagle had come to hunt today. The sun's cheering was fading quickly, the way monotonous, and Madai was thinking about Laeden again. He looked back across his shoulder at his friend. They grinned. But Madai glanced Reoan, as well. So he looked away, determined to concentrate. He rehearsed his first shot and let himself imagine driving the finish lance into the great heart. He was occupied by such pleasantries a long time - till he felt his feet begin to go dead, and he tried to curl and wiggle his toes, grateful that most of his body was still warm. 'Thank you, Bear,' he thought, even as ice ringed his nostrils.

The plain around them was a white landscape that rose toward a white horizon. It was almost possible to imagine that the earth was one with the sky, except where the sun turned the ice crystals to tiny prisms of colored light. The plain rose toward a hill country, which they steadily neared. His legs felt the ground begin a climb as he caught the scent. It carried like a sharp lance in the frigid air. He smelled musk. It was like a stirring potion and woke every lanky limb of his body.

Suddenly the ground rose just in front of his father, throwing off shards of snow. Madai's heart jumped to his throat as he started for an arrow, then immediately eased his arm back down, recognizing the scouts and slightly embarrassed. He glanced nervously at Ashkinaz, glad he had not seen it. He ducked his chin into the fur of his robe and hoped no one had noticed.

The scouts pointed and signed with a crackle of ice that had froze in a thin tomb all around them. Madai forgot his misstep and wondered that their hands worked at all.

"Beyond the crest of that hill," their fingers told him.

His heart was slowly climbing up his throat again. The hunting party, as one, crouched low and spread out toward the hill. Madai's chin just skimmed the snow. They looked like animals themselves, all covered in skins. Madai tried to calm himself, to remember he needed a steady hand. But his stomach was twirling, and even in the cold, he was starting to sweat. He plowed his knees through the drift, up the east side of the hill, and smelled the mammoth. All the distance behind them forgotten, Madai advanced the rise in a thrill, until finally he put his eyes just above the crest, and gazed into the basin below.

There was the foraging creature, swinging its tusks slowly back and forth, musking, marking the patch of ground it claimed, where the fires from the depth of the earth opened up the ground in iridescent, odorous pools. And if the beast came too near the edge, it should be soon boiled... and lost to them. Madai's mouth suddenly tasted exactly like the smell.

The scouts pointed where they should skirt the beast and drive it out of the little valley, and mind the ground was not a crust to swallow them in the process. Madai was a little frightened of the place, with its bare ground ringing the pools, thawed of snow by an inner fire.

He followed close at his father's heel, fanning west. One should think the stench rising in the steam would cover theirs; perhaps it was the creature's persistent ears, but it raised its head, more defensive of its ground than its life. The men lifted their frozen arms and set up a howl, enough to back the animal up, a first step in seeing it off the dangerous plain. But it shook its tusks at them and lifted its trunk to set off an irritated trump.

Madai felt his stomach fall from its place. There were tusks heaped up at their winter's camp, arching high enough to clear the head of the tallest among them. They were frameworks that withstood the seasons, built long years ago. Though sunk in a living skull, wrapped in a heavy hide; these were fearsome weapons indeed. Animated by the most thunderous of stomping, they seemed to shake the earth, and Madai too. Moreover, there were men in The Family who had suffered those tusks. They were dead, except the poor cripple with the twisted spine. He would die before summer.

Madai's fingers pinched the arrow already on the string of his long-bow. The bow was made of the thick heart of yew and stood six feet tall. It was tapered to the sapwood which gave it its spring, coated with fine tallow for repelling the damp, and deadly in the use of a practiced hand. Madai was practiced. But he was awe-struck. He felt his heart galloping in his chest, and his mouth gone dry.

Next, they were a blur of fur-coated men, launching themselves into the valley, at the mammoth and the rising steam. Only a seer could know if the beast would turn or charge. It had better not charge; its head was a rampart of bone, preceded by two deadly prongs. And it could stomp a man to death, and cut a swath with its trunk... or back them into the stinking, scalding pools.

It ran.

Madai found himself yelling with the men as they chased the mammoth away from the boiling pits. All his first paralysis was gone. A shrill, excited sound was chasing the beast beside him, startling Madai to find that it was himself, making all the noise of an excited child. Then he heard sharp whistling ahead of him – flint-tipped arrows flying to their mark. He fumbled with his own, and dropped it into the snow. It was all such a scuffle of sounds and running that he was not even ashamed of his lost arrow, and he put another to the string.

It was amazing that these stone points could pierce a hairy winter hide, but they were dispatched by a field of long-bows, the masterpiece of war work, put to air by muscle-hard arms of magnificent men. Madai watched the animal bellow and lift its trunk at the sky, a sight like a giant porcupine, with six-foot arrows wobbling as it moved. The wounded beast plunged up the opposite hill, waving its quills and wavering near the top. It bent at the knee with a grunt and finally knelt on the frozen ground. Madai could only hope that one of the arrows had been his own.

All his frozen parts forgotten, Madai watched Toban approach the animal slowly. He carried The Family's Sacred Spear and drove it from behind, between heaving ribs and into the great, beating heart. It was the honor of his place in The Family, and dangerous. The dying mammoth had just to turn a tusk across his shoulder to take a last man with him off the earth.

ᘓᘗ   ᘓᘗ   ᘓᘗ

Madai had had a haunch of the beast, cut between himself and Tiras and Laeden, far more weighty and burdensome than he had even guessed. First, it smelled strongly of blood when it was hacked warm off the bone. They had moved quickly, to finish the task in the light before the flesh could freeze solid. And then it did not smell to human noses any more. They had left the towering hulk of skeleton for the pack of wolves that were waiting, ringing the kill at so near a distance that Madai could hear the rumbling in their bellies.

The way back was by the light of stars; fitting it should be the constellation Bowman. They heard was the din of wolves fighting each other behind them. They would walk for miles across the tundra in the dark with marathon legs and mighty hearts. And so Madai walked, until his muscles drained of excitement, till by and by, he just managed to stumble behind his father across the frozen distance. He had wanted to tell his mother all of it when they returned. He wanted to sit at the fire with his father and recount every step, only leave out his fumbling... but he could not even quite remember getting home, nor curling himself inside his bear robe beside the fire.

When he slowly opened his eyes, he was on his bed, out of his robe and nestled in his night covering. He did not move. He smelled that savory aroma, the mighty beast mammoth his mother would stew for two days with cammron root and tea willow. He would not admit it, but it was better than hunter roast, which he had been allowed...had it been just yesterday? He slowly stretched, to find that his body was restored, only mildly ashamed that Ashkinaz must have carried him like a babe to his bed.

The lodge was smoky and dim. Only that his parents were awake told him it was day. His mother was serving his father a bowl of broth, and they were aware of each other alone. His father had emptied his bowl, his mother filled it, and their hands touched. A look passed between them and Madai scowled. And they so old! He had heard once, when Ashkinaz recounted their lineage, that he was one-hundred-two; it was just half a lifetime. Pity to live half a life already old. Madai looked away.

He closed his eyes again, to wait a later moment when he would recount to his mother all that he had done. And he thought about that daughter of Tiptri. She was lively and ready always for a round of fun, perhaps he would tell her as well. She did, after all, linger round the lads. He supposed she found woman's things dull. Well, so they were. Except his mother, of course.

He heard his parents whispering then, not their night whispers when his Mamam thought he was asleep, but something that was troubling her.

"Will it begin again, then?" she was quietly asking.

Madai opened an eye to look at her; there was worry in her voice, and he didn't like it. Well he remembered other nights and mornings when he had heard her from his bed. He never saw her cry, but in the dark he heard it. At nine, his eldest brother, Javan, had gone into the marsh to chase a bear and had not come back. Madai thought he had got eaten by it, or something worse. But he did not tell his mother that. He did, however, ask his father why the Great God had not saved him; but Ashkinaz had given no rightful answer. It was his last brother, and a terrible thing. He felt his nose sting with the thought and wiped his eyes.

"Will we neglect it, and Madai be turned aside?" his father whispered.

Madai's body prickled at the sound of his own name, and he lay completely still.

"No!" his mother answered, grit in her voice and louder than she would have wished. Both his parents looked toward him, and Madai squeezed his eyes shut.

"It may be that I am hasty," his father replied, in so low a tone that Madai's young ears strained to hear.

He opened his eyes, one at a time, seeing Ashkinaz put his hand on his mother again.

"When Palteel left, I thought it would be over," Mineo whispered, bringing her voice back low.

Ah, Madai understood. His phantom... the quake in The Family, when the accursed were chased from the clan... chased toward the East, from where the corruption was born... forever banned. He was suddenly annoyed that such a thing should occupy them on this most auspicious morning after his first hunt with a great abundance of meat, and reminding him of his old fears.

"Tell me what he said," his mother asked.

Ashkinaz glanced toward Madai again, and back. "That good mammoth was detained by the stars to fall by our arrows."

Mineo caught her breath with a quiet gasp and put her hand to her throat. Ashkinaz did not move, but to put his bowl down.

"What will you do?" she asked, so quietly Madai needed his eyes as much as his ears to tell what she said

"Give the Provider's Portion," Ashkinaz replied simply.

"Of course..."

Madai sneezed, and quickly shut his eyes.

"Are you awake, Little Hunter?" his father asked in a tone as common as any morning.

Little Hunter... an endearment no longer appropriate. He rubbed his eyes, to conceal that he had heard them, and sat up.

෬෯ ෬෯ ෬෯

Even at all that, it was a glorious morning, and Madai could not conceal his pride. He was part in the getting and giving of the sacrifice. Laeden was first beside him, a shiny face with red ringing his eyes and wide smile and crooked teeth. Tiras stood silent and tall beside his own father. Madai was proud of them all. He scanned the crowd for Yamma, but it was early and cold.

The altar was never disassembled. It kept its place in the valley, waiting for their return every winter season. It was black, of stacked precious stone, the scraps of which he and Tiras had used those years before, the sort that burned in their fires when at its purest and was therefore of great value. Most of these stones were not so pure as that and did not consume themselves in the heat, perfectly suitable for the sacred altar. It was the full height of a man's chest, as near heaven as could be lifted a heavy shank of bone. And it was carving out itself over the years, as the fires slowly ate it, one offering at a time.

Madai watched fat run down its black surface and ignite. He would enjoy it, swell his chest and think on the smoke rising to Great God's enormous nostrils and say to Him, "This is for You."

He would not share in his parent's worry, but he would take special notice, watching the men, looking for the one who had dared look to the stars for their good fortune. He studied their faces, marked with evidence of a long night, though of high spirits, grouped tight around the altar with steam rising from their mouths. They were all watching Toban, waiting for him to address the Most Great God. It was a moment that always sent chills down Madai's back, a moment when the smoke of the earth touched the realm of the heavens. A better sacrifice, he was sure, than any attempt of his childhood. Toban moved the fire to the back quarter. They would burn one portion in the entire and eat the rest.

Not a one betrayed himself. All, with arms raised, thanked the Most Great God of the Second Earth for their life and livelihood, and for the mammoth. And Madai, also; he forgot the morning's whispered concerns and turned his face up to the sky and smelled what God was smelling.

☍☎ ☍☎ ☍☎

It should have ended there. Madai thought so at least. For what could be said to the God of Heaven that He did not already know? Their thanks was given, and the Portion burning, but Toban began his long, ponderous oration, which always outlasted the thrill of smoke rising to God, Madai had to admit it, and he felt the cold in his feet again. He deliberately stomped at the ground, thinking something had better hurry the Elder, or they should all freeze, and the whole sacrifice turn to ash ...until finally, as though in deference to Madai's feet, Toban stopped speaking.

Madai felt a poke in his side and whirled around, prepared to take Laeden to the ground; but it was that daughter of Tiptri. So, she was here, after all. Yamma had a half-smile and a light in her eyes, and Madai felt himself go as red as a summer fish. Then she laughed at a thing Laeden said, and he was the one who chased after her.

"She is a shameless one," Tiras commented, suddenly beside Madai with dripping slices of meat. He offered one to Madai.

Madai took it, feeling his face go brighter. He did not reply to Tiras's judgement, knowing his friend a mild legalist, very like his own father. It disturbed Madai quietly to find his friend of stalwart and true nature so ill-disposed toward the lively daughter of Tiptri.

"Take it, Madai," Tiras insisted, giving him the other piece. Then Tiras grinned, and Madai recovered himself. He was in the moment again and felt a thrill chase up his arm from the meat of the mammoth to his lips as he took the first sweet bite of Provider's Portion... one that he had hunted.

"Toban was long today," Tiras whispered. "Father says he has a dangerous leaning... as Palteel."

Madai's pleasure fled away.

"Palteel is gone," he answered in a voice equally low.

"Yes," Tiras spoke quieter still. "Perhaps they are returned."

Madai looked at his friend. It was long since The Banned had been chased away, when he was just a very young lad, ancient history, really.

"Toban is no idolater," Madai snapped, watching his father come to help the Elder, an honor in itself.

Tiras turned to follow Madai's eyes. "There are rumors," he insisted.

Madai reached down for a fistful of dirty snow. "Rumors," he laughed. He would have used the snow on his friend, had not Laeden returned. He had been ambushed, as his wolf head was askew and his back pelted with grimy, wet slush.

Tiras showed Laeden his piece of meat. "Get some," he ordered, "before it's gone."

Madai was glad Tiras did not chastise him more than that, or complain of Yamma. Laeden only grinned and went for his piece of mammoth offering. Madai dropped his snowball. He took another bite, and this time he tasted the musk, a sharp witness of the animal's last strength, but not altogether tasty. He must confess that the morning of his greatest pride had been tainted, first by the dawn's conversation and second by Tiras, his own worrisome friend.

He watched his father give what was a hearty portion of sacrifice to Laeden, and was glad for it. Ashkinaz gave the lad a look of import, one he would give any worthy hunter. It made Madai sorely proud of his father. He watched as the rest of the meat slowly disappeared, being portioned to any of The Family willing to brave the cold. He watched the hunters return to their lodges, warm and smoky, with boiling stew like his mother's. The greater number of them were headed there to eat, and sleep, and wait for spring.

ᘓᘏ ᘓᘏ ᘓᘏ

To the mammoth had been added caribou, kept in a bank of snow. Madai had helped with that, and then it stormed again for a fortnight. Winter was most tiresome. Only when it did not blizzard would Madai be spared the stuffy inside of their lodge. Sometimes he dreamed that they were all trapped in the bowels of the very animal whose hides kept them warm - fur side out. If not for his father's teaching, which he had learned to perfection, it would have been unendurable, suffocating monotony.

"Keep the First Ways as taught by the Ancients, my son." Ashkinaz would say, "Remember what came of the First Earth and those who did not.

"Always give the Provider's Portion... and watch for the coming Warrior.

"Be not deceived by the fire serpent that speaks a human tongue and would turn you aside. Worship the Most Great God alone. There is none other. Remember that."

That was how his father always ended the tales of The Family, directives slightly less compelling than the fabled voyage of Ancients across a vast sea. His father had told him about that too, and battling creatures of the deep and typhoons... and the enormous quakes that were once in very great numbers, dividing land from land. It was how their histories were remembered - by mouth. The Family had, as yet, no written chronicles, neither of their own migration nor of the two earths, nor more importantly, of an unraveling of divine importance. It was spangled across the heavens in the stars of night... an enigmatic promise telling of a mighty Warrior to come, to slay the Scorpion and the Serpent. A fine story, even if Madai did not understand it. But it was the way he endured the long. dark winters, listening to his father and dreaming of what the star stories all meant.

Indeed, it had been an honor for Madai to take a mammoth hunt at fifteen. He should have endured another year for it, when The Family would, by tradition, have called him a man. But Ashkinaz was as impatient as Madai, and he had seen all his sons dead but one. The span of a man's life, moreover, had shrunk to a scant 200 years, less than Ashkinaz's own father's father, and many less than fabled forebearers who told their years in many hundreds. But the times were changed, so Ashkinaz hurried it along a bit, and all had ended well.

Ashkinaz had plied Madai with all his knowledge, willing him to prosper, his only son from a troupe of six. How to find green edibles in the forest and smell a yap rat if that is all the meat to find, or staunch a flow of blood, or lash together cypress for a sea vessel and cover it with whale and read the moods of the sea. Ashkinaz had done his best.

Madai was altogether confident in the forest. He had learned his teachings well, all of them, and had the indestructible body of youth. His nose and ears were trained for the hunt, and what else did one need? He listened to the well-worn star story with nearly as much zest as when he had first heard it. But this winter would be his last cocoon. He should have prized it more, had he known.

Ido

- 3 -

Snow chits called him to a sky coming lighter each dawn. The dark little birds flitted from tree to tree, first to announce the spring. Madai came to recognize their voices as what would precede the snow's beginning a trickle toward the river. He opened his eyes and stretched, never surprised that his mother was ready with a porridge of something warm.

"It's early." His mother's voice held that certain something when she spoke to his father.

"Yes," he answered.

Madai sat up; perhaps something would happen today. He had heard the snow chits, after all. He started to speak, as he was feeling guilty to hear his parents again in secret.

"You are certain that is what Toban meant?" he heard his mother ask, so she was not talking about the early hour of the morning.

Ashkinaz nodded. Madai watched him in the dim of the firelight and knew that his father was not pleased. He swallowed his words; now it was too late to announce himself.

"I think I heard him the night of the high moon." Ashkinaz looked up at Mineo.

"O?" she asked.

"Divining," Ashkinaz whispered, and the fire snapped as though to underscore that single illicit word.

Madai watched his mother's face drain of color. She began to whisk the porridge roughly. "You did not see him?" she asked.

"No."

"Surely not Toban," he heard her murmur softly, then she scooped the brown mash into a bowl and blew on it. She swirled her finger in it and put it to her mouth. "It's spring," she announced, and looked back at her husband with a hopeful eye. "The clams are sweetest now. That is all." She handed Ashkinaz the bowl and smiled at him. "That is all," she repeated.

He took the bowl. Madai watched his father watch his mother. He watched the crease between Ashkinaz's eyes slowly disappear and knew what look they would have, looking at his mother. The graying whiskers of his father's face furrowed around his lips, where a soft smile was forming. Madai relaxed; if Father was satisfied, then Madai would be satisfied, as his Patta was always wise. It was a good moment to feign waking. He stretched and made a loud yawn. He threw back the night covering and immediately fumbled with his boots. He knew they had heard him now.

"Any later, lad, and the crow would have your bowl," his father called from his place at the fire.

Madai laughed, hearing the old threat.

"Come, Madai," his mother added. "We shall thank the High God for what we will eat today."

Madai stood up.

"We shall follow the river," his mother told him with a smile.

He heard the words with a skip in his heart. At last! An end to the mud wallow of their camp. He ate his mush with a gleam in his eyes for his mother, as though she alone had banished the long monotony.

&#x0 CE03;&#x0 CE12; &#x0 CE03;&#x0 CE12; &#x0 CE03;&#x0 CE12;

Madai was laughing and tugging at the snow skiff. It would be their last slide of the winter. They should all be needed tomorrow, even the smallest, to disassemble their village and move it out of the valley and to the sea. Tiras and Laeden slapped their hands together, shaking snow from their mitts and harassing him for the good loss of day as they waited. But it had been weeks since they had used the sledges, and his was banked with snow.

He heard a voice behind them and his stomach banged down to his feet.

"Are you coming?" it asked with a laugh. Madai did not have to look to know the voice of Yamma. But he did look, over the bend in his arm, to see her edged up to Laeden. His friend was turning scarlet and his green eyes were wide as the high moon.

"Where is your skiff?" Laeden managed to ask, a rise in his voice.

"Guran took it," she complained, her lips forming a soft, round pout which Madai suddenly found altogether appealing.

"Ride with your brother," Tiras complained, looking at her with a cold expression.

She turned her sweetest appearance on him. "Already away," she smiled. Madai watched her eyes glitter. "Take me, Laeden," she continued, watching Tiras with a pout.

Laeden replied with a thin laugh, one that embarrassed Madai for him.

"Go with Uke." Tiras would not let Laeden answer.

Madai glanced over at Tiras with surprise. They all three knew what he implied, as Uke was a wild sledger, and a boy had slid into a blue crevasse riding with him two winters before. Madai thought Tiras had stepped too far. But Yamma only smiled at him with the truest of smiles. She slid her shoulder forward, a sumptuous effect, even under her winter's cloak.

"Perhaps I shall," she replied softly, and left them standing there.

"You did not have to say that," Laeden mumbled, his wolf cap fallen to his back, and his ears tipping with red.

Madai and Laeden watched her go. "Old Tiptri does not mind her ways," was the answer Tiras gave, and no other. He began pulling at Madai's sledge.

They did not hear a timid approach till a shadow fell across them. Madai turned his head, hoping perhaps it was Yamma returned and thinking better of riding companions. And for a moment, head obscuring the sun and in silhouette, the form might have been hers. But she bent and asked with a warble in her voice, "Have you got it?"

At the sound Madai wrenched the last bit of frozen runner free. His sledge was last season's, with an underside of mammoth ribs fixed to a poplar frame; a speckled deer pelt was its coat, tight and seamless.

"Ido!" Tiras greeted the little girl. "Come ride with me."

Ido had a thin scrap in her hand, pulling a battered sledge that had seen two brothers before her. Its covering was ripped, edges frozen and gaping. It rattled when she pulled it, with a tattered fox's tail hanging from a willow pole like a sail. She let the straps fall to the snow and grinned.

Madai watched her leave her little skiff and go to Tiras. Her smile showed that she had lost another tooth, and her face was pink with cold.

"Will we go very fast?" she asked him.

Tiras grinned at her and took her hand. "Come on and see," he answered. He picked her up and dropped her inside. Then Tiras pulled his skiff across the top crust of snow as though it held no weight at all. She turned around and waved at Laeden and Madai.

"Hurry on," she laughed.

Madai watched them go. The sun was well high, a definite sign that they had taken too long.

CЗCЯ   CЗCЯ   CЗCЯ

It was just cold enough still that the snow was deep, and warm enough by day that the top was part ice. The ice pelted his face in a shower of sharp and cold, a minor nuisance, even part of the thrill. Their sledges skimmed the crust, rounded bellies lifted just enough with long ribs of bone, parallel from front to back. Madai leaned left and the skiff veered left. It gave him a feeling of controlling the wind, chasing it like a bird. He laughed. The wind blew his cap off, turned his ears blue with cold till he couldn't feel them, glorious! Snow blew back into his mouth, melted on his tongue and tasted a little like dirt. It blinded him and made his face numb - and lasted far too short a time.

At the bottom of the hill, he ended in a flurry. a short sliding turn where he braked just ahead of the river. He had been practicing that. The ground was packed and dirty where they had all ended their snow-sailing a score of times already. Tiras was just behind him, and Madai jumped aside to pull his sled out of the way. But Tiras veered right, and Madai heard Ido squeal with delight.

The morning air was dancing with laughter. It rolled across the valley to tell all its creatures that the children of humankind had borne another season. Madai wiped his face and started eagerly for the top again, leaning into the hill and dragging the sledge behind him. He sniffed. The top of his lip was suddenly warm from a drippy nose. Even in the crisp cold, he was starting to sweat. He thought about shedding his coat as Laeden suddenly pulled along beside him. They faced each other with a grin; Laeden's speckled face was blotchy-red, with a scant sprouting of fur above his panting lips. They instantly started to run, panting and slipping up the hill to be the first to reach the top. Tiras followed more slowly behind, pulling little Ido in the sled like a queen.

Madai and Laeden stopped their race only once, to watch Uke fly down past them, spraying snow like frozen little stones, leaving them pelted with envy, with just Yamma's merry yelp singing back to them. Madai watched Uke aim his skiff at the snow bank to finish their catapult downward, and Yamma rolled out laughing. She bent and put her face up to Uke's.

Then she started the climb with her winter's cap hanging by a leather strap. Her hair was braided, pushed under the furry collar of her cloak but golden in the morning sun. Of all the laughter on the slopes this morning, it was hers that chimed the brightest. He saw that Laeden was watching her, too, and for the first time in his short life, Madai would challenge a friend to something more than a race.

෨෬ ෨෬ ෨෬

They raced and careened and showered each other with snow. They laid strips of caribou across a huge fire at midday, and Madai watched Yamma bite tiny bits between her straight white teeth. He watched her feed Uke a bite too hot and whisper to him softly that she was sorry. Then Madai saw her glance across the smoky fire at himself, not one time but thrice. He was certain of it, and was more than certain of his first and glorious new obsession.

- 4 -

"The way is blocked." A voice echoed through the granite canyon back at them. Madai glanced at his father to see his lips form a tight, straight line.

"It is too early," he heard Ashkinaz complain in a low mutter.

They disentangled from the leather straps that bound them to the loaded skiffs and made their way to the head of the trail. Indeed, great boulders of ice carried down by the river had piled against the single narrow passage out of the valley. The river cut its way beneath the unstable, frozen dam, but they could not.

"Are we trapped?" Madai asked quietly.

Ashkinaz did not answer, but only stared at the impasse. They were slowly and silently joined by Reoan and Togarmah and Tiras. They gathered along the west side of the gorge, where the afternoon sun lay a strip of thawing earth, to look at the blockage with a bleak quiet. There was only a tinkling trickle of dirty water trailing off the topmost pile of ice, melted at a pinpoint where the sun was touching it.

"A week," Togarmah grunted.

Madai thought that was optimistic.

Toban stood in the lead. Madai watched him slowly turn away from the ice flow to look at them. Toban's face was as impassable as the trail. He looked beyond them and down the length of the gorge. Madai followed his gaze. The sight behind him was a scattering of snow sledges, piled with skins and lodge poles and weapons and pots and children. The valley narrowed here, flanked by high, craggy cliffs. But there was no land wide enough to resurrect their village.

Ashkinaz and Reoan passed him, moving silently to Temah's sled, where they briefly conferred. Reoan pointed up the side of the mountain. Madai followed his finger to a spot of shadow where the sun revealed a cave with a wide, oblong mouth - a place for sleeping bears. Madai was not enthused.

A late spring storm ended the matter.

ೞೞ ೞೞ ೞೞ

The cave was not a terrible place. It was dry. It was large enough for them all, at close quarters, and very smoky when the women started their fires. A consideration of bears was moot, as the fires drove out no sleeping mother with her cubs. She had, in fact, long since found the spring inviting and was introducing her twins to the wide world and chasing warm meat for her empty belly.

The cave was quite convenient, really, as Madai could watch Tiptri's little family through the smoky haze. There was just Tiptri's ancient first wife, as his second wife was dead by childbirth, and Guran... and Yamma. Madai followed Yamma secretly with his eyes across the entire expanse of the cavern, for Ashkinaz and Mineo had chosen a spot with Temah and Reoan. Why they must be so far back, Madai could not imagine. Tiptri had a very favorable location, nearer the cave's entrance, beside Toban.

The first night might have been in dead of winter for the frigid wind that chased down the river, licking its tongue into the cavern and pushing back those who had chosen a spot at the front. It reminded Madai again that his father was wise; and it did not matter, after all, as Tiptri's little family had to move and found a place very near. Mineo helped the old mother rekindle their fire before they all lay down, exhausted at the end of day. The wind cackled outside the cave, a lone wolf complained of the stubborn winter, and The Family tried to go to sleep.

Madai turned with his back against the unyielding rock. He kept turning, cold where he touched the stone and warm everywhere else. He listened to the sounds of men sleeping after arduous toil, and those other few, like him, who were not so fond of their hard beds. When he turned on his left side, he was able to watch Yamma's shoulder rise and fall in sleep. It was all that recommended their arrangements to him. Morning light would not come soon enough.

"Madai?" he heard a whisper. It was his father, sounding tired.

"Hmm?" he responded, surprised that his own voice sounded as though he was answering from sleep.

"You will wear a trough in that rock."

Madai raised on his elbow to look at his father. Ashkinaz lay on his back, cradling Mineo in the crook of his arm, looking most uncomfortable.

"Sorry, Patta."

Ashkinaz answered by sliding Mineo carefully aside. He sat up slowly and rolled his arms up toward the cavern's craggy ceiling. Madai sat up also, and silently they looked across the dim, hazy cave at all of The Family, rolled in animal skins, sleeping and trying to sleep.

"This was a mistake," Ashkinaz muttered.

"The cave?" Madai wondered.

"No," his father answered. "We left the valley too soon."

And Madai did not answer. He heard an edge in his father's voice, and he did not want to know a thing that seemed as though it could shake his faith in things.

"The stars are not for divining," Ashkinaz continued, speaking as though his son were a man.

"No, Patta."

Ashkinaz looked round at him, feeling surprised that he had spoken his thoughts aloud. He smiled. "You are a good boy," he said. Then he looked out through the mouth of the cavern into the black night sky, where the stars were all in their assigned places. He stared at the pole star, silent, caught by its faithful, constant light.

"A time is coming, you know," he whispered.

"Yes, Patta. I know."

Ashkinaz turned again to look at his son and was flooded over with love for him, knowing the lad did not know what he meant but would always strive to please him.

"I am looking at the great dragon," Ashkinaz explained.

Madai was surprised. What comfort would his father find there? And yet, Madai could see that Ashkinaz was finding hope in the stars and hope was not divination. Hope was believing the tale carried from that far place in the East, believing it was God that set the patterns in the sky with a promise to men in a dangerous world.

"Is not the pole star our guide, especially on the seas?" Ashkinaz asked.

"Yes, Patta."

"We are bound to it, captive to it, and the great dragon is coiled around it."

Madai nodded.

"The dragon winds around the north sky," Ashkinaz continued quietly. "His tail commands the territory of a third part of the stars." He slowly shook his head. "Even now, with a mystery promised by the Most Great God, it slithers amongst us."

"What do you mean, Patta?"

"The constellation."

"Yes?"

"A sign of the enemy."

"Yes."

"But there, Madai," Ashkinaz said, pointing to the sky.

"Yes, Patta, the Bowman."

"His time must come soon, Madai." Ashkinaz turned to look directly into the eyes of his son.

"Who is the Bowman, Patta?" Madai whispered, never before daring to ask.

Ashkinaz looked surprised, and then his lips formed a wry smile. "That is the question..." his father's reply was low, conspiratorial. "Yes, that is the question."

They were quiet.

"But he will rout the serpent," Ashkinaz finally added. "Do you believe it, Madai?"

Madai nodded.

Ashkinaz looked at his son with compassion. He saw that Madai did not perceive the times, did not know the dangers. "The perversion is among us already," he whispered sadly. "Divining by the stars, and other things."

It was said, and Madai was unhappy by it. "But The Banned are gone," he quietly insisted.

"Yes, Madai... but their lies are left behind. We are here in this cave for it."

"Who is divining by the stars?" Madai ventured a challenge.

Ashkinaz shrugged, the gesture scarcely visible in the waning firelight. "They may yet be persuaded," he finally answered. Then he smiled again. "I remember when you were a lad, Madai, and you loved that bow your brother made." Ashkinaz blinked. "Javan," he murmured. "Too brave a boy."

Madai was being pulled into his father's humor, melancholy for the cold restless night and for the lost brother and for the pernicious threat of which his father warned. He shivered.

"I would like to have had it for that mammoth hunt." Madai pulled his knees up to his chest to rearrange his cold parts, and to banish the mood.

Ashkinaz laughed quietly. "It was a great bow," he agreed, reaching out his hand to lie across Madai's shoulder. "But that was not my point." He looked out at the sky again, though a cloud was slowly snuffing out the stars one by one. "You played at being the Bowman."

Madai chuckled, slightly embarrassed at being recalled to a childish game where he had always wanted to be the hero.

"No, I was proud of you, Madai," his father continued, knowing the every tone of his son's disposition. "It is our greatest duty to watch for Him." Ashkinaz circled Madai with his burly arm. "Humankind has waited for Him since the Most High God garnished the sky with the promise, that evil would be destroyed."

Madai felt himself smiling, sharing with his father an excitement for an inscrutable time to come, a riddle not seen nor understood... for how does a hunter put evil to flight, or the seed of a virgin ripen? Old riddles, though tonight it was enough to be approved, to be loved by such a man as his father. And what could be better, than to look into the heavens where the constellations, no matter what they spoke, held their places against a shifting earth. What better refuge than the arm of a father in a shelter of rock against an unexpected storm?

"There is something, Patta," he ventured.

"O?"

"Yes. It is... the Virgin."

Ashkinaz smiled. "Indeed," he answered. Then he chuckled. "So the little hunter is thinking of such things."

Madai felt himself go crimson.

Ashkinaz let him squirm. He tightened his arm round the boy's shoulder and finally asked, "What about the Virgin?"

"Only that none are come by a virgin."

"No."

Madai turned toward his father. The man faced the moon with a wrinkly look around his eyes. "So?" Madai persisted.

"So how is the Bowman come from the Virgin?" Ashkinaz articulated.

"Yes."

Ashkinaz shrugged and tipped his head to the side, grazing the flesh of Madai's neck with his grey beard. "Only God knows," he said simply.

Madai faintly nodded, accepting the only answer he would receive tonight. He fixed his gaze to the part of the sky that held the Virgin, sheaf of seed-grass in her hand.

"It is another cause to leave a maid alone till you are wed," Ashkinaz suddenly asserted, dropping his arm and looking at Madai in a purposeful way.

Madai felt his tongue go to mush, and a great rush of blood shot up to his scalp.

"Who can tell who the virgin may be?" his father finished. Then he pulled away from Madai and scooted back to his place beside Mineo. "Try to sleep," he said and laid down. He pulled the bear skin back over himself and inched his side against his wife. He looked at his son, grinned and winked at him and closed his eyes.

Madai sat fixed to the spot, feeling his head pulse and wondering at his father's quick wit. How did he know? It was smelling like snow now, as clouds began to curtain over the stars. Madai pulled his coat together and moved back to his bed. He felt the hard bumpy surface of the cave against his back. He pulled the night covering over his face and did not one more time glance across the fire at Yamma's perfectly rounded shoulder.

- 5 -

The storm was like a blustery child, kicking before going off to bed, making certain the valley suffered its leaving and pelting it a last time as it passed. The dawn was announced with clouds streaking across the sky, racing to follow the storm and unfetter the sun. But it was cold, with a padding of fresh snow reducing the rocks to an endless ocean of white, crystalline mounds. A beautiful sight; almost a crime to mar it.

Of course there was a trail of human prints already this morning, threading up the river in search of meat. Mineo watched her little fire and shrinking supply of wood. Ashkinaz was right; they should have waited. She felt responsible for the old mother's fire, also. Tiptri was gone with the hunters, though his sight was unsteady and he would be no use to them. Guran was also away. It would fall to her to get wood for their fire, as well.

She looked across at the women of Tiptri's family: Old Mother, the only name Mineo knew of her, and Yamma, a girl as beautiful as a painted evening sky, with a certain swagger to her step. Yamma rolled over onto her back. Mineo would have to wake her, surely, as their fire was gone long since. But she watched the girl sleep, soft, silent breathing making a little cloud in the chilly air as she breathed through parted lips.

Mineo shivered, suddenly glad Madai had left with the men. She moved quickly to their meager little camp and shook Yamma's shoulder.

"Wake up, lass," Mineo whispered. "Your fire is out."

Old Mother opened her eyes first. They were moist and red. She coughed.

"Yamma and I will bring you wood," Mineo told her, and the woman smiled. Her face was craggy, with skin that had been old friends with the sun. Yamma sat up, pulling her robe up to her chin, and blinked, surprised that Mineo was beside them.

"Your fire is out," Mineo told her again.

Yamma looked at the pile of ash and back at Mineo, and out at the lighting sky with its white earth.

"I will help you," Mineo encouraged the girl.

Other women of The Family were beginning to forage for wood. The clean, fresh blanket of snow was soon pocked with little trails. Mineo and Yamma put their own in it, breaking off brush that grew along the river with frozen fingers made bloody by the thorns that ran up the stems.

One by one, the women retrieved the wood to the cave to rekindle their fires. The whole of the cavern was soon billowing smoke again, sending a steady stream into the valley and hanging like a shroud above the river. Mineo's eyes streamed as she readied a place to broil the meat she hoped Ashkinaz would bring her. She worried that their source of fuel would not last them a week here on this mountain of bleak granite.

Yamma had set a pot of snow on their fire, watching it turn to water. She dropped crumbly, dry cammron into it, making a tea for her mother, perhaps the last of their supply. Mineo was struck again by her beauty. When had she grown up? Then Naru, Mineo's cousin, called to her, inviting her to share a drink of hot tea before the men returned. Mineo gave the girl a last studied look and moved across the cavern to her cousin's camp.

Naru, mother of Ido, who had been a surprise, was quite a bit older than Mineo, She had a plentiful supply of brush heaped up against the cave wall and Mineo glanced at it with a certain degree of longing.

"Tiras brought it," Naru explained. "Early, before the men left. He is vigilant toward us."

Mineo nodded. Good Tiras, thinking of the little family, bereft of sons now, having lost three to an avalanche and one... the cruelest of all, with The Banned now these many years. Naru and Temah had Ido and they, Madai. Madai was a great comfort and help, but Ido was only a little girl.

Naru handed a cup of tea to Mineo. It was a lopsided piece of clay-ware, but painted with a fanciful design. Mineo could almost see the little indentions of Ido's fingers in the soft clay before it was baked. She tasted the hot brew.

"I will surely be happy for the spring," Naru said, sipping her own cup carefully. "Our honey is used up."

"You may share ours," Mineo replied, thinking how good it would taste this morning.

"You have some left?"

"A little."

"I used our last on Temah's wound."

"That is a better use of it, then," Mineo approved.

"Well, yes," Naru looked at her sheepishly. "Though I do love it."

Mineo smiled at her cousin, who had been very beautiful, an artist married to Ashkinaz's uncle, making them twice family. Ido came to sit with her mother, gold hair fanned across her robe of spotted lynx. She smiled up at her mother and drank from her own little cup, quiet and suddenly shy.

"Toban has been ill-advised, do you not agree?" Naru's abrupt change of topic startled Mineo and her soft tone belied her serious expression. "What do you suppose he thought, bringing us away so early?"

Mineo looked at Ido cautiously. "We must pray that God will keep us," she answered.

"Yes, certainly," Naru agreed, and looked from Ido to Mineo with an inscrutable look. "There is nothing amiss with him, surely..." she began.

Mineo looked out toward the sky, not at all certain what she thought.

"Bring Mamam another pot of snow," Naru asked Ido, and the little girl popped up, glad to have a mission.

Mineo watched her go. "Ashkinaz is afraid," she muttered.

Naru was quiet, waiting for Mineo to finish. She was not so fanciful as she seemed, and she knew a thing was very much amiss.

"Someone was brewing sorcery the night of the mammoth hunt after the Provider's Portion, when we all were in our beds," Mineo whispered. "And Toban searched the stars for the time of our leaving."

Naru had known it somehow. It was the way that Mineo had looked at her when she asked the question. She had somehow known it even as she asked. There was a thing afoot in the atmosphere that was not as it should be, a turning. It felt as it had before, when poor Sru had left them, sucked up by The Banned. She could not shed the shame that they had failed their son and lost him to the great deception and should never see him again. A tear born of old sorrow found its way down her face.

Mineo took her hand. "Ido is coming," she whispered.

Naru swept the tear aside and looked out across the smoky expanse for Ido. The little girl grinned, and when Naru bent to take the pot from the child's hands, she had her composure back.

- 6 -

One week was optimistic. But in the second week, the sun pushed back the chill and began to melt the ice flow.

The man with the twisted spine felt the last spring sun before he died. He could not come out of his skiff an more and had to be dragged like a bit of baggage, so Madai thought it was best that way, after all. It was no strange occasion for Madai... death... nor for any of The Family. And still they did not discard him, but laid him on his back, and crossed his arms, and covered him with stones. He would welcome the bear next winter at the back of the cave. His wife found snow crocus, and put them in his hands before they entombed him with rock, and Ashkinaz said that he would walk upright again in the heavens. And Madai believed it.

The sea welcomed them with its sweet, abundance. Mineo was comforted by that, persuading herself that Toban had only been impatient for the clams.

ଓଞ୍ଚ ଓଞ୍ଚ ଓଞ୍ଚ

Snow is a happy playground when you are young... for a time. It is a challenge when you are old... but it sweeps the air and starts the green things fresh. When its time is ending, you are speeding for the sea, with all its chasing wind and fleshy creatures, and colored shells and gravelly earth. It is like another life altogether. It reminded The Family from where their fathers came. After the arduous march down, along the river, the shore seemed a long-awaited paradise.

Madai and Ashkinaz set up their lodge in the old spot, the one they always chose. It was a favored spot, as Ashkinaz was, by merit and tradition, an important Elder.

Their summer lodge was still lined with felt for its warmth against the cold wind that would blow across the sea for another month. And then Mineo would pull down the felt and hang it in the sun to rid it of smoke and other unpleasant smells. The felt came from wooly down that grew beneath the coarse, dark hair of mammoth. It was best if the animal were killed in winter, when its supple wool was heavy. It was prized and valuable and dangerous to hunt. Bison felt would do, but it was not so thick or so warm.

Mineo often watched the mountain sheep, great herds of them, smaller certainly, and less good wool, but white. She had ambitions of taming one each of male and female, and providing herself with both milk and wool, though she had yet to devise a way. As often as she soaked the wool of mammoth in ashes and brine, it was never enough; and her lodge was dark in winter, the worst time for darkness. She sorely coveted the ram's thick, white pelt.

She had weavings, of course, gleaned from sheep that Ashkinaz killed for meat, dyed with berries and yellow earth. But they were not enough to dispel the dreary grey of insufficient bleaching. So she often removed the linings a bit early and kept her fires heaped up. And when the spring was fully arrived, she pulled up the bottom half of the skins to let the fresh breeze blow through.

Spring was her favorite season. When summer came, she knew the winter was approaching. They seemed to be growing longer now, the winters, with summer a short prelude to the cold. So she pulled all her robes out into the sun to beat them free of dirt and muck as early as she dared. She harvested reeds at the marsh edges while they were green and wove them into new baskets. This spring, she would weave a whole section for her walls.

Naru had her skirt hiked up to her waist, scandalous if not that the men were away at the ocean. Mineo looked up from the muddy root she was cutting to watch her. She smiled, slightly envious that Naru possessed such daring. Ido was cutting reeds beside her, up to her knees in murky water. The girl was not so unconventional as her mother, but she had the same artist's bent. She would make a good daughter. Mineo felt her eyes water, looking at the child. So young, and yet coming nearly as tall as her mother in a surprisingly short time.

The morning sun glistened on her yellow hair, braids looped around her neck lest they hang all the way to the marshy water. She was thin and straight, with the body of a child. Mineo hoped Madai would be patient. He was three years Ido's senior and feeling it, she knew. They needed to tell him she was set aside to be his. He had noticed Yamma, that was certain... and Yamma noticed him. Mineo bent back down and cut the reed off. She would talk to Ashkinaz tonight, and they would tell Madai tomorrow, no later than tomorrow.

And then Mineo felt the silt tremble under her feet. She froze, watching the water ripple and glisten in the sun. She heard the earth groan, and women screaming. Her body reacted before she could tell herself to run, as she felt her feet splashing through the reeds toward the dry land.

Trees were lurching wildly, as in a typhoon come ashore from the sea. But it was not the sea; it was the ground. Mineo fell to her knees and crawled across the pitching earth to Naru. Naru had her face buried in Ido's hair, body flung across her child, scarcely free of the marsh. Mineo threw her right arm over Naru and the three hugged the earth. Time stopped its regular march. Mineo felt each grain of sand slowly roll beneath her left palm. She felt the trail of marsh water down her leg. She felt the wild pulse of her own heart and listened to the earth release itself. She heard a woman's short, startled yelp, carried in the wind that had sprung up and was screeching overhead. Trees were snapping in it, branches making a whooshing sound. It always seemed to last forever.

But they were not in the valley where it once had been more terrible. Mineo felt tears dripping off her nose onto Naru's arm. When the ground shifted, or a boulder loosed in the shale, she was always brought back... No length of time, it seemed, was enough to make her forget that last frantic look she had seen on Lamak's little face. It was forged inside her heart, her son forever trying to scream, but too terrified, and dropping out of sight, swallowed by an earth that opened its rocky mouth in what would ever be a boundary-mark in time. Before the great quake; after it. Though for Mineo, it would always be before Lamak; after Lamak. He was the first of her sons who died, when it seemed the world changed forever, when terrible things came to their fire as to any other. And they did not even fold his arms a last time, or wash the mud from his face, or lay him on a downy mat.

The crevasse was deep. They looked for him, but he was gone. Mineo could not even find the place now, as the earth was ever changing, shifting with each new quake.

It slowly came to Mineo that it had become absolutely quiet...no birds, no twirping frog, no rushing wind... just the blood coursing past her ears. She felt Ido and Naru beside her and was glad for it. Those first days, with Lamak suddenly vanished away, she had thought she would go mad. And even now, when she remembered it, it put a jolt in her spirit that she was nearly afraid of.

She carefully lifted her head. Naru lifted hers and they looked at each other. Ido came up on her elbows. Two wide blue spheres looked at Naru from a muddy face for a moment. Ido's lip trembled only just a little bit.

"It was not so bad as some," Naru whispered.

"We had best get up to the others," Mineo heard herself say.

Ido followed. "I hope Patta is all right," she called, looking back across the marsh and to the east, where the sea was still atremble.

ೞಬ ೞಬ ೞಬ

Ashkinaz came running. They had only just brought their ship up the river and fixed it to the shore when he made a straight rush to his lodge. Before he reached it, he knew she was well; there was smoke coming from its peak.

Mineo turned. She recognized the sound of him, and she was caught up in his arms to his thrashing heart. He put his face into her shoulder and crushed the wind out of her. He smelled of fish and sweat. She would ever be captive to him, and he held her a long time. They did not hear Madai.

"Mamam!" he called. There was a trace of fear in his voice.

At the sight of him, tears sprung to her eyes; in that moment she knew they both were safe, and she pulled him against her and kissed his bristly cheek.

"Are there any hurt?" Ashkinaz asked her.

"No," she answered. "And you?"

"We couldn't feel it in the boats, Mamam," Madai answered. "Not a bit."

Mineo nodded. She smiled at him.

"There is nothing changed," she continued. She looked up at Ashkinaz. The hard line between his eyes was going away. She wanted to run her finger across his mouth and make him smile, but she saw that he had been greatly worried. She was suddenly seized with happiness and wanted to wrap them both with her arms. The melancholy fled as it had come in her very great relief.

The fish Ashkinaz brought was wondrous sweet. It was not just the fresh change from mammoth and caribou; it was that they were safe. Mineo had nearly forgotten what they should tell Madai. But she needed a time alone with Ashkinaz first, that he would agree the time was proper. Perhaps they should wait for Naru and Temah... but Mineo had a trouble in her heart about it. When Madai asked if Yamma and Old Mother were well, she was ever more determined. And Madai's bristly cheek felt like a man's. It was all happening so quickly.

When Mineo called for Ashkinaz from behind their curtain, she saw that certain look in his eyes. What was he thinking, and Madai still awake? So she quickly quelled the look with what was really on her mind and found to her wonderment that Ashkinaz had noticed it, too. When Madai cut his eyes to the side, there would be Yamma in his sight. Ashkinaz had seen it more than once. He had seen the swell in Yamma's breast and the swing of her hips, and he knew old Tiptri did not watch her well enough.

So they would tell Madai tonight.

ʊꙅ☘ ʊꙅ☘ ʊꙅ☘

Madai looked up from the fish spine pinched between his fingers. He was wondering if any of the bones were stout enough to save for his mother to use when she quilled wool for felt, a tedious task for which he pitied her. When he saw them coming back from their sleeping quarter, he dropped the bones into the fire.

He was vaguely disappointed; he had planned to go back to the common fires to look for Tiras and to see if Yamma were there. Then he noticed they had each an inscrutable look in their eyes. His father took up a cold fish and asked his mother for a draft of ale. It was a pretense at normalcy, and greatly piqued his interest.

"What is it, Patta?" he asked.

Ashkinaz took the earthen cup from Mineo. "And one for Madai," he said to her.

ʊꙅ☘ ʊꙅ☘ ʊꙅ☘

Madai laughed. It put one dent in his cheek, that extra emphasis that his smile was complete, and Mineo glimpsed the lad he had been for a fleeting moment. He laughed a good bit till he saw that they were not laughing with him.

It was like watching a bird fly against the wind, slowly his smile fading, with his mouth and eyes agape, an expression frozen with disbelief.

"What do you mean?" he stuttered.

"It is time to think of such things," Ashkinaz told him.

"Yes..."

"Ido is your kinswoman. Well brought up, devoted," his father continued.

"She is ten," Madai gasped.

"She is twelve," Mineo corrected, "nearly thirteen."

Madai only looked at them. He still could not believe it. "She is a baby," he nearly laughed.

His mother did not look amused, and he did not see concession in her eyes. That it was utterly preposterous stifled all other feeling...

Ashkinaz put a hand on his shoulder, noting when he did that Madai nearly matched him in height. "Not right away, lad," he offered, as though it would amend the sting.

"But she's a little girl," Madai repeated quietly.

"Not forever," Mineo whispered, with the first look of compassion in her eyes.

Madai heard the subtle change and looked at his mother hopefully. "Mamam..." he coaxed, putting a touch of coercion into his voice.

She smiled at him, knowing the tone and knowing as certainly that it only hardened her resolve. He was a precious place in her heart and would be protected at any cost.

When she did not answer, it began to feel as though they meant it. Madai looked from one to the other, his world suddenly tearing apart. And then he thought about Yamma.

He watched her from his mind, bending over Uke on that last day of snow- sailing, and then her eyes looking across the fire at his own. He felt her poking his side and laughing. He watched her breathing softly in sleep those nights in the cave when the blessed storm had locked them in together. He felt himself go hot and his face turn crimson. His hands began to sweat. He quickly looked down.

"I do not love her," he whispered, hoping his father did not remember their talk of virgins.

He did, of course. It was what Ashkinaz needed to carry him purposefully to the fire and take a long, slow drink of ale.

"Sit here," he ordered his son.

Madai was watching his father bleakly. He looked down at his own cup and took a drink and went to the fire.

"You are nearly grown, Madai," Ashkinaz began. "It has been proved on many a hunt, and I am proud of you. You will prove it again in the way that you command yourself, and in the esteem that you will grant Ido."

Madai only stared at his father. "Why?" he muttered.

"She has been set aside for you from birth," Ashkinaz answered smoothly.

"I did not know that."

"You did not need to know... till now."

Madai slowly shook his head. "But, why Ido?"

Ashkinaz smiled slightly. "They are kinsmen. They serve Mighty God. They follow His ways."

"Ido is a sturdy, delightful girl," his mother added.

Madai only looked at her with stony disbelief. She was asking the ridiculous of him, and he slowly began to feel the weapon of anger awake in himself.

"Love comes," his mother insisted.

"You will have time to prepare," Ashkinaz continued, undeterred by his wife's compassion. "Plenty of time."

Madai looked back at his father, feeling a slow, hot wave rise up his throat. He wet his lips. "Then why tell me now?" he challenged, feeling the roots of his hair stand up, unaccustomed to speaking in such a way.

"That you will not be persuaded elsewhere," his father replied with a potent look of his own.

Madai was first to let his eyes drop. He knew the matter was ended, that somehow his own passions were laid bare, and that his fate was decided. The only light in his darkness was his father's words, 'plenty of time.' "When?" he asked.

"I will talk to Temah tomorrow," Ashkinaz answered. "But you will surely wait till she is fifteen, at least."

"Still a babe," Madai dared mutter, forgetting that he was yet to turn sixteen himself. He quietly calculated the years and slowly began to encourage himself. There was time. A lot could happen in two or three years. A lot could change.

Tiras kicked the side of Madai's foot. "What has you looking like a bleached fish?" he laughed. "Look there at Laeden." Tiras laughed harder this time.

Laeden had his chest poked out and chin pulled in, stomping the ground around the fire like a rutting moose. His face was red and drippy with sweat.

"He plays a fool," Madai muttered.

"It is his 'marking day.'"

"You do not see the others like him."

"O, you do not?" Tiras chuckled. "Look again."

Madai looked up at the newly marked. Yes, they were all stout as yearling stags, scraping their first horns against an aspen for any passing she-deer to see. Madai looked away. It was well enough for Tiras. His marking was one year past, and he was newly pledged. Keillet. As flaccid as an old woman perhaps, but Tiras was pleased!

Madai decided to tell him.

"I am bound to Ido," he whispered, feeling the words like sand in his throat.

"Madai!" Tiras enthused, roughly shaking him. "What excellent news this is!"

Madai gawked at his friend. "She is a baby," he muttered.

"Ridiculous," Tiras answered with a smile that showed all his teeth. "She will make a good wife and bear you a flock of children."

Madai glared at him now. "It is Ido. How can you even think of that?"

The tone and look of his friend registered for the first time, and the smile on Tiras's face faded by degrees. "She is thirteen, Madai... at least."

"Twelve."

"She is strong and spirited. She will get older. You are lucky, Madai. And she will be a beauty."

"Who are you talking about?" Madai argued. "She always plays at things. She is a child. She is... boring."

Tiras laughed. "She is not boring."

"Then marry her yourself."

Tiras laughed harder. "Kiellet would not approve."

Madai heard the delicate tone in Tiras's voice when he spoke Kiellet's name, and the ready laugh, and for a moment he hated his closest friend.

"That is well enough for you," Madai heard himself saying, and could not stop his tongue. "Kiellet will sit with you and pray to God."

Tiras turned to look at his friend, not in the least offended. Madai was younger by a year and did not know the elegance of love. "You will come to it, Madai," he said. "And be glad."

Madai thought he sounded like his mother.

"Give her a year, and Ido will be soft in all the right places; you will see."

That did not sound like his mother, and Madai cut his eyes back to Tiras in surprise. Tiras chuckled and, despite himself, Madai slowly grinned. He could not think of Ido in that way, but that Tiras had such thoughts at all encouraged him. Perhaps he would understand how Madai felt about Yamma. He looked back at the celebration, and at Yamma standing on the far side patting the ground with her feet in cadence with the drum.

"Look at her," Madai ventured.

Tiras followed his gaze. "Yamma?" he asked, incredulous.

Madai heard the shift in Tiras's voice, and was not happy.

"She may as well be Banned," Tiras hissed.

Madai felt his blood run to the soles of his feet, and then he felt it rise up again and turn his face red. He whirled around to Tiras, stunned at such a maligning.

"What are you talking about?"

Tiras leaned forward, close to Madai's ear, and whispered, "Watch her, she will disappear in the forest. Things are done there."

Madai laughed. He understood it now: Tiras, always careful, always alert, afraid of the least variance. Yamma was not like Kiellet, nor Ido nor his own mother. She was courageous of spirit and beautiful. She was practically an orphan with Tiptri and Old Mother, ancient and nearly blind.

"You worry too much," Madai whispered back, and rammed his shoulder against Tiras. "I know the First Ways as well as you."

Tiras hated that tone in Madai's voice, the one that really said, 'I know it better than you because my father is Ashkinaz.' Well, he would let Madai find it for himself, what Yamma was, and he had best not hurt Ido. He felt a rise of compassion for the child. Tiras looked at the boys around the fire again and shook his head at Laeden, who was less grown than Madai. They were both fools for Yamma. Tiras watched the daughter of Tiptri, but only for a moment. She was beautiful. Then he left his friend's side in search of Kiellet.

Madai was glad when Tiras left.

৩৫ৰ   ৩৫ৰ   ৩৫ৰ

Ido had quit tugging at her mother's hand. Naru had her tight enough to hurt. She was insensible to the marking rite. So they were made men tonight; she did not care. HE was standing there, on the far side. HE was standing with him, illuminated by the fire. Ido did not bring Madai's image into focus. He was only the one to whom Tiras was speaking. He was only the friend, the friend of her beloved. Tiras.

She felt the full devastation of her heart.

That Tiras was pledged was inconsequential. It was a father's choice for his son, and Tiras did not love Kiellet, she knew, but only her. And he did not approve second wives. It should have been resolved somehow. But now...

She did not dislike Madai. Madai was a hearty boy, and son of the esteemed Elder, Ashkinaz - and friend of Tiras. That was the credit to which he rose in her estimation. But he was still only Madai.

Now the impediments were past overcoming. She was pledged as well. Kiellet and Madai were their common tragedies, and she should be forever bereft. She felt a tear rise up from her child's heart and trail down her face.

- 8 -

Madai watched the whooping circle of boys, celebrating their man-coming around the fire, suddenly revived from its heat by a breeze blowing in from the sea. He studied Laeden and for the first time saw him not merely clumsy, but silly. He was a big lad, the biggest at the circle, and essentially red all over, especially when it was hot. His mouth was agape in a ridiculous grin. It had been well enough when they were children, snatching fish up from the clear waters with their bare hands, or racing by foot or kayak. But now he was making himself a fool, especially on the farthest swing around the fire, where Yamma was standing.

Madai felt not the least pang of conscience watching Yamma. He had made no pledge to Ido; it was, in fact, the last thing he ever would have considered. He did not even know if Ido was here tonight; he had never thought to look for her. He did, however, look for Yamma - instantly. And she was still just opposite him, illuminated by the fire's phosphorescent flame, licking up into the night sky.

He was certain that he could find her laughter out of all the chorus of laughter and was equally certain of her glances through the crackling, sparking fire. He felt a wide grin stretch across his face and was not in the least afraid. He had tracked down a mammoth, after all. He would just wait till his parents had gone to bed...

ଔଋ ଔଋ ଔଋ

Madai made his way around the fire. His sweat had turned icy after the blaze had died to a glowing mound of ash. And the high spirits had waned as well, giving way as the night advanced, cooling the air and sending dancers off to bed. Madai kept his sight pinned on the darkening form, still swaying to a silent song in her own head. He wove his way through the retreating, sleepy, newly marked. He suddenly found himself blocked midway by a large form with long arms, smelling especially strongly of smoke and ale. Laeden.

Laeden's head rose a half hand above his own. He would near eight feet as a full man, Madai guessed. Madai felt his stomach churn, desperate to break free and finish the way to where Yamma had danced all night. But Laeden was happy to see him.

Madai felt himself pulled in to the boy's wide chest, a vigorous clench. Laeden said something and released him and stepped back with a spacious, wide smile.

"... a night," he was finishing the sentence, and Madai nodded at him and cut his eyes away across the dying fire.

Reoan came from behind his son. Madai was surprised to find him there still at the long end of the night. The deep crags of his face seemed deeper in the shadows, and slightly drooped. But he put his arm around Laeden's shoulder with a firm grip.

"A good night," he pronounced in a steady voice. "But the morrow will not wait." He tightened his arm around Laeden again and steered him past Madai.

"Ashkinaz will not wait for you either, Madai," he called behind.

Madai heard a soft chuckle in the old man's parting words. They would surely have scurried him away to his own lodge on any other night. But Madai's heart was beating hard, suddenly free and only a few steps more to reach her.

But the far side was empty. Any who had waited till the last were leaving the fire, and Yamma was not among them. Madai's heart stopped pounding and went dead still. It made his ears ring. He whirled in place, certain that she would be standing in the darkness, watching for him. But he was the last at the fire.

ଓଃଙ   ଓଃଙ   ଓଃଙ

Ido was sitting on a log. She had heard the last drum-beat and watched the darkness slowly reclaim the night as the glow of the fire receded. She was waiting for Tiras. She knew he would have heard the news from Madai's own lips, and they, she and Tiras, should say goodbye. It was the most obvious thing to do.

He would pass their lodge on the way to his own. He did it every night when he looked in to see that her parents did not need anything. Her father, Temah, loved Tiras as well as he should have loved a son of his own. That she was given to Madai was certainly and only because Tiras was pledged to Kiellet, a prodigious mistake, one Ido had mourned for a half year and then ignored for the last half... till tonight. She hugged herself, feeling the cold creep up from the ground to her feet and all the way to her narrow, thin chest. The flesh of her arms was cold to her hands as she started to shiver.

Then she heard a soft scuff along the path. It was His step. She was surprised that it had gotten so late before he passed by. It had only given her time to grow cold and sad. He did not see her at first, and then he stopped.

"Ido! You are not in bed?" he whispered with surprise in his voice.

She lifted her face to his looming height and scooted over; he sat down on the log beside her. She felt the warmth of him, but somehow could not lean on him as she would have on any other night. He put his arm around her and gave her a little hug.

"It is cold, Ido; you should be under a fleece."

His warmth was slowly seeping into her, but her teeth had started to clatter anyway. Her knees began to shake. Thankfully, she did not feel inclined to cry, but she was afraid to speak for the trembling.

"Is something wrong?" Tiras suddenly asked, looking at her face.

She nodded.

He watched her eyes begin to shine in the moonlight, suddenly and inexplicably filling with tears. And then he realized what had been told him, that she would surely know and what it meant for her. He hugged her again and looked into the night across the top of her head. He felt her heart beating wildly.

"Do not be afraid," he whispered. "Madai is my closest friend. He will be a good man."

Tiras felt her body grow completely still. He heard her breath catch and he quickly added, "Of course, he will wait till you are older."

Still, she did not move or answer him, and Tiras felt for her hand to pat it gently. "Madai is like my brother," he whispered. "Why... that will make you my sister, Ido." He leaned away to see her face and smiled encouragingly. "But you are my sister even now... are you not?"

Tiras thought he felt her hand tense ever so slightly under his and a curious quiver weaken the set of her mouth. He watched as two glistening tears overfilled her eyes. She was white as the moon, wide-eyed and perfectly still. "Ido?" he asked.

It surprised him that she did not answer, but slowly slid off the log to stand facing him like a startled deer. She did not tell him, 'God speed the good night,' and did not cry again, but quietly moved past him and into her father's darkened lodge. Tiras watched her go, surprised that the little girl had looked at him with devastated eyes. He had thought her sensible and brave, but it reminded him that she was young indeed. He sighed and comforted himself that she would be as pleased as he and Kiellet... in time. And he resolved to see that Madai treated her well, and gently.

৪৯ ৪৯ ৪৯

There in the wood was the sound of rustling brush. Madai smiled and leaned in with his ears. She was playing a game with him. He knew it, because he could hear her feet crackling leaves and snapping branches, moving into the forest. He stepped into the trees, eager to catch her.

But following the sounds, Madai realized that there was more than only one, and his smile wiped away with confusion. Tiras's warning, just this night, that she joined others in the forest recalled itself with unwelcome clarity. Their numbers made it easy to follow their whispers and muffled laughter, and they were moving fast, away from the village. Madai followed them quickly, without hesitation. His senses were perfectly trained for it, and they, whoever had joined her, were easy prey to stalk. He realized his feet were following a trail, one that was made by either man or beast, but fairly well traveled.

"She will disappear in the forest... things are done there," he heard again and wanted to scoff; but he began to recognize a slow-moving disquiet in himself. He felt all the hair on his body alert, standing straight up, and thought for the first time that perhaps he should turn back. As quickly as he thought it, another came to replace it: Uke leading Yamma away.

Madai had a visceral dislike of Uke, three years his senior, older even than Tiras, who commanded a certain respect with his steady ways. Uke's ways were any but steady. He had never been pledged, though his father was a worthy man, and that was curious. If there were rumors about him in that regard, Madai did not know them. What he did know was that Uke was always first to draw the bow, even if another had the better shot. He was incautious on a hunt, and his stories always took the longest to tell. Even Ashkinaz disapproved of him. Yet all that had not been relevant till now. Now, when Madai was feeling true jealousy for the first time. Uke - disagreeable Uke. Thinking about it only made him move faster, till he could see their shadows moving in the moonlight. And Yamma's form was set apart to him, trailing behind. She had a certain way of moving.

The whole group traveled quickly, with certainty, as though they had been here, in the dark, on many an occasion before. Madai was smelling the biting odor of burning wood and thought it was the common fire he had just left. But it was steadily growing stronger; a tiny spot of light began to flicker through the trees. He did not need his ears to follow now. The fire was where all of them were going, a beacon pulling them in. Madai was curious that it was here and wondered, with a sudden chill, who had made it.

಴ೞ಩   ಴ೞ಩   ಴ೞ಩

Naru lay beside a snoring Temah. There was a secret hollow in her breast that had reopened. It kept her awake, that and the knowledge that Ido was not home.

She suddenly knew.

She had watched it happen, day by day, and had not seen it; but it was obvious now. She listened to the night, and heard Tiras on the path, and heard his voice, low so not to awaken them. She had heard the unmistakable ragged breathing that was Ido trying desperately not to cry. Naru would not indulge herself with it, either. She sat up and quietly left her bed.

She heard Tiras whisper. But there was an owl calling to a mate, and it covered Tiras's words. There was quiet after that. Naru heard only the beating of her own heart until finally there were Ido's feet at the front of the lodge and the flap pulled aside. Naru walked out of the shadows to stand beside the night fire. She startled her child, standing there; and Naru extended her arms.

"My Precious One," she called softly.

Naru watched every shadow of her daughter's face, and every flicker of her eye, and the way she stood, uncertain and tragic. It entered her soul that her last child did not come immediately into her arms but stood as she was, a lone spirit with a coming independence, and already grieved.

"I am sorry," Naru whispered.

Ido found her arms then, and they sat down together beside the dying fire. Ido pressed her face into her mother's breast so that her weeping would not awaken her father.

Naru was proud of Ido. Her body shook from a quake reaching down to her heart, but she did not wail. There was no untruth of drama, only an outpouring of unexpected grief.

"I am sorry," Naru whispered again, unconsciously stroking Ido's hair. "I should have seen it."

Ido lifted her face, and its look pierced Naru through, a pain not of scuffed knee nor wounded pride but a simple first bereavement, that of the private sort, and more than a lost brother.

"Do you love him as much as that, then?" Naru finally asked.

Ido nodded.

Naru pulled her child back to her breast. "There is nothing so good as love," Naru began quietly. "It is from The Mighty God."

"I love Tiras," Ido squeaked.

"Yes," Naru breathed. "I know you do. That is my fault." She was quiet a moment, thinking what to say next. "And if he were not so far older than you, perhaps he would love you as you love him. But Mighty God has seen him born to Togarmah at such a time as He chose, and for a purpose known only to Him."

"He does love me," Ido insisted.

"Yes, child, he does. That makes it... harder." Naru drew back to look at Ido's face. Even as she thought it, she hated what she would say next, so simple, so true. "There are many kinds of love, Precious One."

But Ido did not seem to hear and looked at her with wounded eyes that were searching for comfort and an explanation. Then Ido let her eyes fall and spoke with a child's sentiment.

"Madai is stupid."

Naru caught herself from laughing. Perhaps it would not be so hard after all. "Ido," she scolded.

"He and that Laeden," Ido finished.

"Madai is the son of Ashkinaz and Mineo, our kinsmen. They are strong in the One God. That is important above all else. And Madai is a good hunter and brave... and..." Naru hesitated, "and he is beautiful."

Ido looked up in surprise. "He is?" she asked.

Naru nodded. "Undeniably.... beautiful."

Ido watched her mother's hopeful face, and then she thought about Tiras and felt herself sucked down to the depths again. "Tiras is beautiful," she insisted.

Naru sighed. She patted Ido's hand, and was not entirely displeased that her daughter could not be so easily distracted. "There are first loves," she began. "And they are sweet, and hard to forget. But there are other kinds of first loves, and they are beyond breaking." Naru looked at Temah's sleeping form. "You will find the sort of joy that will help in mending you, Ido. And you will find it with Madai."

Ido listened to her mother and tried to believe her and nursed the full weight of her broken heart.

ଓଞ୍ଚ   ଓଞ୍ଚ   ଓଞ୍ଚ

Madai crept forward, his heart pounding. A great fire was built, and a half score of men sat around it. They were waiting, and Yamma was fast approaching them with Uke and perhaps ten others. Those at the fire were clothed in streaks and patches of white paint and feathered amulets. Madai, crouching in the shadows, moved closer. He was finally able to distinguish both men and women waiting, seven of them, dotted oddly with black paint making a pattern through the white, and entirely naked. He felt himself go hot and knew in the instant that here were, indeed, the stray faction of The Banned.

It hit him like a stone, the danger of dangers, here in his forest, the pernicious lie.

He was suddenly filled with rage. That Uke! Bringing Yamma here! He started up from his hiding spot to brave the clearing for her rescue, where she stood, a bright shine upon her face, when she slowly began to sway. His feet became fixed to the ground, watching her. The neat order of things threatened to scatter in his mind. What was she doing? She, a member of The Family, borne to know the Great God... what was she doing?

She was the first who came to the fire. The first to dance, the first to make her way to them who waited, the first to run her finger through the cords that tied her dress, and the first to give her skin for painting, as she joined The Banned at their fire.

Madai swallowed. How long had he squatted here? Long enough for his ankles to start to burn. He was otherwise insensible to time, for it was the first that he had seen a woman in the entire; he was suddenly full of shock and shame, and he turned his head. But there was a malevolence stirring at the fire, and it was reaching a long claw through the forest after him.

The whole of the scene played before him one sense at a time. It was first his eyes, and then he became aware of his ears and the low song that began, and a reed harp. He felt the urge to look at them again and turned his head around. He watched , as The Family's youth, one by one, became indistinguishable from the first seven. Ah, Yamma...

His belly began to ache, and he backed away, all the while feeling a savage pull. Then he started to run, mindless of the noise he was making. He was covered by cold sweat, and as relieved as a child when he reached the quiet lodge where his parents were sleeping. He felt loud and clumsy, creeping to his bed, and did not remove his clothes, that they would not know where he had been. He lay on his back and drew his night covering up and listened to his heart. He felt as though it would leap out of him, his mind and body still aghast at what they had seen.

There was a palpable evil in his forest. He closed his eyes. He must tell Ashkinaz on the morrow. But then Madai slowly opened his eyes again and remembered that his father would know... would know that he had followed into the dark after Yamma. Madai blinked and swallowed and remembered that lust he had felt kneeling in the dirt, that second look; and he began to feel something new, his first zeal slowly giving way. He had something to hide.

ଓଔ ଓଔ ଓଔ

For Yamma's part, she knew that he had followed. Moreover, he was the son of an important Elder, who was a keeper of the old way. And Madai was so tall and beautiful. She had assured herself of his presence each time she turned a certain way and the fire's light revealed his silhouette. He was exciting because he was forbidden. His passions would be intense.., she could see that, and he would bring her power.

Mineo recognized something amiss in her son. He was quiet; his quick smile was gone. He was obedient. He did not argue his betrothal. He did, in fact, not mention it at all. He was suddenly serious, even brooding. It was as though in a night he had lost his boyhood. She was sure it was not the prospect of Ido, but something more.

It was something more. It was Madai's first betrayal, his heart struck with its first wounding. And it was his first doubting of his own worth, the least worthy sort of pain. He watched Yamma from a distance, calculating what was different in her now. There must be something different; she was a partaker of evil, after all. And yet, she seemed the same. And that frightened him.

What he had seen that night was etched in his brain. It was replayed in every detail every night before he went to sleep, unbidden, waking passions every time. He forgot what it had been to live before he had seen it. It had shaken the world. An atrocity before Mighty God, a stain amongst them. He was often at the very precipice, ready to tell what things were done, when a slow shame, even the vilest thought of all...to be one with them... nipped at him and stopped his voice.

ଔଔ ଔଔ ଔଔ

Tiras was clearly angry. It was the time of his Joining. Could Madai not put aside his gloom for even this day? And Laeden, past enduring. It was a fortnight's time since Laeden's hope had been dashed by Yamma's pledging to Uke. That Laeden mourned her was incomprehensible to Tiras. At least Madai had lost his heat for her long since.

Even little Ido did not bring her smile, and Tiras was sad for that. It was as though they were all changed somehow and did not care at all that it was the start of his true manhood, his new life. 'Well, I will only think of Kiellet,' he decided, carefully donning his new leggings.

Tiras wished his mother could have been here. She had been gone a long time. If he were honest, he scarcely remembered her. Naru was the one who had been mother to him. If he were brave, he would ask her the workings of a woman's mind, but he was not. So he relied on his own father, Togarmah, and learned very little.

It seemed his father would not forget nor forgive a wife who had chosen a different god and followed The Banned across the sea. Tiras did not forgive her, either,
though he remembered a soft white hand and gentle voice, a lost scrap of time he hid
in a cherished spot in his heart. It caused him a secret, a dual self, and determined
him to start a better life with a better choice than his mother had made. He would
keep The First Way in his own shelter with his own wife. He smiled. He thought
about her as he tied his belt: the shining spot in his life...Kiellet.

ഇൽ   ഇൽ   ഇൽ

Ido ran her hand down the length of her work. It was almost finished. She had
started on the morrow of the night Tiras had called her 'sister.' That was a season
past, as they had journeyed to the winter valley and now back again. She sat at the
very spot where she had sat with Tiras to hear those terrible words. She looked back
at the weaving and straightened a row. There were spots only she could see, where
her fingers had bled. It was not crooked and loose, the way her last effort had started.
And she would finish this one today.

It was a smallish blanket. She had altered the weave to make a pattern. It was
the constellation, a bump for every star, with a precious bit of white ram's wool for
accent. It was nearly perfect, her Mamam had said so, though she had yet been
reserved. Her Patta was proud and patted her head, slightly amazed at her talent.
It was Naru who perceived her meaning in weaving 'The Virgin.' She had watched
Ido through the weeks, as the pattern became unmistakable, and had never commented. She smiled when the last star was finished and told Ido that it was lovely.
White on black, simple and charming, the rendering of the constellation's pattern
was perfect.

Ido tied off the last stitch and sat looking at it. She knew where every mistake
was hidden, but that could not be corrected now and did not really mar the appearance. Perhaps she should have made it larger, because now she did not know what
to do. Tiras was married.

Kiellet was not beautiful, but he loved her. It was plain as winter turning to
spring.

The old sledge was left in their winter's valley, too much a shamble to move even
the lightest weight. She smiled and remembered flying in the shower of pelting
snow, Tiras at her back and very warm. She remembered it as clearly as this morning. Could it really be two winters past? It seemed so long ago with everything
changed. Ido pulled lightly at the blanket still tethered to her loom though it did
not need squaring. She had been painstaking that it would not bulge or lean and
had made up the difference with her advancing skill as the rows tightened. Her hand
skimmed her rounding chest and she grimaced. A tear sprung up; her nose began to
sting. She put her face in her hands and let herself cry.

There was a shadow moving in the forest behind her. The bough of a great fir
was parted just enough for a painted face to watch her silently. He was patient and
very, very careful.

ഇൽ   ഇൽ   ഇൽ

Madai flexed his arm to loosen the muscles. He grinned nervously at Tiras beside him. They were waiting outside the den of a spotted saber cat. She had troubled the village all spring, stalking around the rim at night. Mothers did not let their children out at dark.

Tiras was going to be a father. Madai supposed he wanted to impress Kiellet too. As for Madai, he only wanted the thrill, and one of the long canines to hang around his neck. Tiras could have the other.

There was mewing in the cave. They had tracked her here, heavy with unborn and hungry. They would take her at her weakest and not suppose themselves cowards. A man could widow a wife or cripple himself with a saber cat. And they neither wanted that.

She started a low rumble, and Madai knew she had smelled them. Tiras aimed an arrow and Madai clutched a spear. They only had to wait.

She came out of the cave like an eagle after prey. Madai had time to see an afterbirth dragging behind her. She seemed to squint at them in the sun and rolled her lips back. He thought in a flash that a new mother may be a fiercer threat than they had predicted. But she hesitated, unsure whether to leave the rim of her lair where her babies needed her. It gave Tiras just the moment he needed: her heart was bedded between her ribs and she turned sidelong. He let the sinew release with a snap and impaled it.

She swung his way with a shriek, fangs barred - and dropped. Her heart beat out its blood in a crimson pool.

Madai knew he did not need the lance. They looked at each other, startled and disbelieving. Tiras's eyes were wide and he made an odd, gasping sort of laugh. Madai prodded the cat with the pointed end of his spear anyway.

Tiras took his knife from its sheath and began to carefully remove her pelt. He first cut her head from the spine, then her paws, then a careful and shallow line down her belly. He and Madai pulled the skin away from the muscle, still warm. She did not carry much fat. All that had been for her kits.

They took her two back haunches next. She would flavor a stew, which was some less value than the skin. With that skin they would proclaim themselves brave, making a place in The Family beyond that of sons born to important Elders.

Tiras held the heart in his hands. "This is for Kiellet," he said, "if we hurry."

Madai nodded. He was glad he could be a part in giving Tiras's wife the cat's vigor. She would need it; her belly was ripe.

"You give this to Ido," Tiras finished, pushing the wet saber pelt into Madai's hands. "It will prove your love."

That surprised Madai, and it certainly disturbed him more than a little. And he was not quite ready to know a Tiras who would first think of love after such a great triumph as their kill. But he took the pelt, rolled it fur side out and lashed it to his waist. Tiras wrapped the skull and paws in a separate bag and carefully stowed the heart. Then, with the meat hoisted on their backs, they began the trek back to the village. They did not think again about the cubs deep in the den, knowing the cold night without their mother would do its work.

They were starting to feel the evening chill. Tiras was glad it was getting cold, ever conscious of the lion's heart. Kiellet would bear their first child in a month, and she would need the strength from it. He let Madai lead the way and watched him juggle the pelt with the haunch of meat. He hoped Madai was more sensible now about Ido. He felt a little guilty about that... his duty to Naru, who had been mother to him, and Ido, who would marry his somewhat thoughtless friend. He had neglected them both, but then Naru would surely understand.

"She will like the pelt," Tiras called ahead to Madai.

Madai did not slow his pace and did not answer. So Tiras hurried beside him.

"I have learned a lot in a year," Tiras continued. "A woman likes the little things."

"So what is little about a saber cat?" Madai asked with an edge.

Tiras laughed. "No, that will impress her. But that you thought to give it to her."

Madai looked at Tiras then. And Tiras thought it was a blank look. He frowned slightly. "Ido is coming four and ten," he mentioned.

Madai nodded.

"And you seven and ten," Tiras persisted. "I was scarcely older when I married."

Madai thought he said it with a certain air. "Have you seen what she is weaving?" Madai decided to ask. "A man would think she wants to be the Virgin."

Tiras laughed again, more gently. "All worthy women want to be the Virgin."

Madai suddenly thought about Yamma, and that night he had followed her. It was only last spring... and still it seemed that it had changed the world.

"But when they are pledged, and have waited the acceptable time, they are happy to come to you," Tiras was saying.

Madai glanced at Tiras and thought he saw a rise of red above his friend's new beard.

"And you will be glad for it, too," Tiras finished and nodded. Then he smiled.

Madai glanced away, which baffled Tiras. An owl hooted, and Tiras let the quiet linger a moment more before he ventured, "A woman could think you do not want her."

"Ido is still a girl," Madai insisted.

"Have you seen her?"

Madai stared straight ahead. Indeed he had tried not to see her, certainly not like that. There was still that other image which haunted him, one that he at times would chase away and at times conjure back. He could feel his face growing hot.

"I see you have," Tiras said. "She is not a little girl any more."

It was the moment to rid himself of that niggling guilt, but he somehow could not reveal it, even to Tiras. Perhaps especially to Tiras, who was pristinely devout. So instead, he would just agree, let that be the cause of his red face. Madai produced a dry chuckle. "So you say," he answered.

Tiras bumped against Madai's arm. "I know you love her."

Madai looked at his friend then. He forced his lips into a slightly crooked smile and nodded. Tiras bumped him again. "Good," he replied. "She will make a good wife."

The sun glowed burnt orange and inched its way toward the hills. It was a spectacular orb and turned the sky violet and pink. Tiras's spirit lifted; with the meat from the hind leg, and the heart for Kiellet, and with his friend to marry, life was good.

He knew Madai would love her. And they would both have sons to raise up together.

Madai was only glad the talking had stopped.

- *10* -

*M*adai's better knowledge of Yamma quelled his want at times, and yet at times it came at him like a hungry bear. There was danger in a bear... She was, to him, all that was warned against. He found himself a curious tangle, the wanting of her and the revulsion of her. When he closed his eyes for sleep, he saw her again as she had been on that night. Sometimes he caught himself watching her. It was starting to happen more all the time.

His secret, all that he had not told, had twisted inside Madai to make him think he was guilty of it, too; perhaps more so, as he claimed obedience to the One God. He wanted to watch the sun come from behind a cloud and know that Mighty God had seen him. But he did not feel it any more, or think it was even still possible. He had lost a first love and a God. He could not have one for the fault of the other... and he could not have the other, either.

He wondered who he had become. Who was he, if God did not see him?

He glanced at the saber skin - and then he thought about Ido. Was it possible that someone entirely pure could drive away his fonding after Yamma? It seemed absurd to think of Ido that way, and yet he needed to be who he had been before. He liked his old world. He pulled the saber cat down from its curing rack and ran his hands across the soft, spotted pelt. It was thick, the lioness being still with her winter coat. Madai was suddenly grateful to Tiras, who thought of all the right things and might make a bridge for him to Ido. He could have given it to his new son. That would have been fitting.

Mineo was watching Madai. She had to. What she learned of him now was not from the words of his mouth, but from his eyes. She saw that lost look in them, and it broke her heart. But when he took down the lion, he looked at it with real pleasure. And now, he was looking up at her and smiling.

"This is for Ido," he said.

And her heart soared.

ೞೞ   ೞೞ   ೞೞ

Madai came to Temah's lodge with his gift. In the space of that short distance, he was brought a new feeling, a quiver in his belly that he had not expected. It was different from cresting a hill with a mammoth on the other side, and different from racing up a snowy incline. And it was certainly different from the feeling of watching Yamma.

He reached the door. Its flap was pulled aside, and he could hear Naru talking to Ido. He called out then for a sudden fear that he might hear them talk about him - or their Joining.

"Ido," his voice sounded unfamiliar to himself.

The talking stopped. And then Ido came to stand in the doorway. She was holding a ladle full of soup.

"Madai!" she sounded surprised.

Madai quickly lifted the pelt. He tried to smile at her. "This is for you," he said.

She looked at the skin. She seemed surprised, even a little pleased.

"Why, thank you, Madai," she answered. Then she looked up at him. He saw that her eyes were wide, but a smile began to creep across her face. He also noticed the red cast on her forehead put there by the sun and the rather lovely pink on the crest of each cheekbone. Her hair was yellowish, touched with a sparkle of red.

Naru came to stand beside her daughter.

"What have you got?" she asked.

Ido turned to her then and showed her the hide. "A saber cat, Mamam, from Madai."

Madai heard a tinge of pride in Ido's voice. He could not help but see a budding in her narrow chest, and he thought for the first time since he had been tied to her that perhaps Tiras was right about her after all.

"You will come inside, Madai?" Naru asked.

Madai ducked and walked inside Ido's home for the first time. It was made of the same materials as his own, and in the same style. But it was a transport of color and pattern. Indeed, all that was said of Naru's eccentric nature was proved here.

Where his mother had spent her time in bleaching the dark winter felt of mammoth, Naru had obviously labored over hers a time long enough to turn it a pale grey. And on every surface hung something that was dyed red of yaddish-berry or lemongrass green. And there were mats woven in every shape. The surprising array for the first moments kept Madai's attention from his own unexpected timidity.

Ido returned the ladle to the soup pot. She laid the lion pelt on her sleeping mat and ran her hand across it a lingering moment. She stuck her finger in its down, up to the second knuckle. She also had a fleeting temptation to wish it had come from Tiras, but she chastised herself and stole a private glance at Madai... looking strange and uncomfortable in her house.

He was very tall, certainly more than seven feet. His arms were golden already from days in the spring sun. His hair was golden as well, tied behind his head by a leather strap. There was the start of a real man's covering on his face. She watched his eyes trail across the walls of her home. They were of deepest blue.

O, he still had the look of Madai who would need to win at all the games, and be at the front of a hunting party and rally a troupe together if there was an adventure to find. But he could be sensitive, obviously; there was the lion skin. He worked very hard when it was needed, had a true devotion to the Mighty God, and he was, as her mother said, beautiful.

It touched her that he had brought her a token achieved by courage. Perhaps she had not judged him well at first. He was Tiras's dearest friend, after all, and that was the highest recommendation. There was still a dull ache when she thought of Tiras. But Kiellet's swelling belly had done the last work needed to quell what hope remained for his regard. Ido was growing up.

"Ido, I need water," Naru proclaimed, interrupting her thoughts. "The thaw has swollen the river, Madai; would you help her?"

Naru tilted her head at him as she had done when she was a ripe maiden and smiled. It was an affectation she was not aware of. Madai did not know why he wanted to please her, but it was a suggestion he knew he would not refuse. He glanced at Ido then, watching her lift the buckets up from the ground with a rise of color in her cheeks. Then she came past him, and he followed her out the door.

The way to the river was prudently far, as a late winter's melting of snow on the uppermost peaks often swelled the waters to dangerous heights. This spring had been such a season. Madai walked a step behind Ido, not quite ready to implicitly proclaim their betrothal by walking beside her. He found himself slightly embarrassed as heads turned their way. He would surely have seen approval in all eyes but two... as Yamma watched them pass.

Yamma fingered an amulet under her dress. It hung neatly over a mark tattooed between her breasts.

CℬCℛ   CℬCℛ   CℬCℛ

They started for the river without speaking. Madai watched Ido's perfectly balanced steps find their way down the path. She held the buckets in either hand, away from her sides. Her hair was a long plait hanging down the center of her back. Her hips moved with a gentle rhythm, which was beginning to interest him; and for the second time in one day, he considered that Ido might have become something more than an irksome child.

When they reached the steep, rocky bank Madai quickly reached out his hand to put it on her arm.

"Let me help," he heard himself saying.

She looked over her shoulder at him then and he caught a pleasing, if amused, light in her eyes.

"Why, yes, Madai," she said, and gave him one of the buckets.

He took it in his left hand and gently closed his right hand around her arm. In that instant, every fiber of sensation rushed into that hand. He felt it when the sturdy muscles of her arm tensed and relaxed. He felt it when she bent her elbow to take a first step down the incline. She was warm and soft. Then he slipped, not watching where he put his foot, and it was Ido who kept him upright. He heard her giggle; it was a familiar sound, as it had accompanied him with Tiras on every adventure where girls were allowed. And it was not an unpleasant sound, though it embarrassed him mightily to stumble.

He moved in front of her then and stepped down off a high rock. He released her arm and extended his hand to her, which she took with a womanly smile. He felt the pulse in her fingers as they stood there. Perhaps it was the moment. They looked at each other, Ido standing on the rock and Madai ready to help her down. Then she laughed, with a little hop off the rock, and it was over. She stood beside him, nearly as tall. She was so close he could have leaned forward and touched her lips with his. He had seen it done, though he had kissed no one in all his years but his mother. But she quickly turned and stepped away. Then she looked at him again with a bright flush and a timid smile, and his unruly inclination toward Yamma fled away.

He helped her down the rest of the way. It was done in silence, as though they were suddenly strangers. Madai took the other bucket from her when they reached the river's edge. The water was making a powerful noise which filled the awkward silence. He positioned himself carefully, with his right foot up against a rock, and knelt on his left knee. He held the bucket under the water, fighting with the rushing current to keep it from washing away.

There was a pair of wood ducks in the eddy. Their presence somehow belied the intense cold of his hands and the raging current. They kept near the edge and kept close together, with their golden crests and the male's glistening green head saying it was spring. Madai pulled the first bucket out of the water and lowered the second. The ducks disappeared around a bend, and he glanced at Ido to see if she had seen them. But she was watching him with a faint smile. That expression nearly chased away the painful cold in his hands, but not quite.

With one hand, he held the top edge of the last bucket, and he reached under it with the other to pull it up. He lifted it out of the river; clear snowmelt water spilled over the top as he set it down beside the other. His hands were as red as summer choke-cherries.

Ido was squatting beside him, every bit capable of filling the buckets herself. That he had insisted was charming, but that his strength was effortless was eminently important. She looked at him, hands tucked under his arms. She reached out and firmly took his right hand. Then she rubbed it between her two. It was cold as ice and took a good deal of rubbing.

"Give me your other," she insisted.

Madai reached it out to her. It was not really necessary. His hands had been cold before, but he was glad to do it. Still they did not speak. Madai was afraid to. What did you talk about with women? So easily he had abandoned the description of 'child' in reference to her. He studied her as she was warming his hand. Her eyes were turned down. He had not noticed how very long and thick their lashes were, and that she held her mouth at an angle with a concentrated diligence. Yes, she looked like the Ido he had always known, but now... something more. He was also brilliantly aware of just how close his hand was to her budding breast.

"There," she said, all too soon. And she smiled at him brightly. "Thank you, Madai." And with that, they each took a bucket and carried them back up the bank. They carried them toward the village, careful not to slosh too much of the frigid water, and Madai walked beside her.

- *11* -

*I*t was winter again. But this winter would be different from any other, and Madai was literally numbering the days. There would be thirty. He had come to understand his friend's preference for Kiellet, when Tiras alone had found her beautiful. Madai was as certain that Ido had come to be more than just the little girl always at their heels, and was glad his father had seen into the future when he chose her. In fact, in regard to the thirty days, Madai had developed a certain physical urgency that stretched the prospect of a month to eternity.

Though he had built her a home, he had not enjoyed again the intimacy of that spring morning when he and Ido had retrieved water from the river. It was seen to by her father, and his own. Temah insisted the summer must pass, and Ido come to a full four and ten years. The closest Madai had been to her, in fact, was at their betrothal. He had sat across from her when Temah and Naru had brought her to his parents' lodge. They had eaten together, and he and Ido had lifted cups together to seal their pledge. She had scarcely looked at him then, but he had watched as her skin turned brightest crimson, which was for him a charming modesty. And then they were 'forbidden,' not to share company for thirty days hence. If Ido were indeed to be the Virgin, they would wait that time. Madai was beset with an unsettling jealousy that Mighty God might choose her. He wondered if Tiras had had the same fear. He had not said so, and neither would Madai, as it was utterly impious.

Madai shivered and rolled over. He was sharing a cave with nine other men, led by his father into the western valley for caribou. Togarmah, Tiras's father, led a second party after elk, or tapir if they were lucky. And Togarmah had been lucky. He, with his group, had an abundance of meat and were nearly home. Tiras had more than Kiellet to feed. Now there was little Naru, named for Ido's mother, she who had been mother to him when his mother had chased more modern and varied gods. They had brought both tragedy and disgrace to Togarmah's lodge and had made him a bitter man. Kiellet had changed that for Tiras. She had given him a daughter and a new life. He would bring her an elk.

As for Madai, he was cold and disappointed. He pulled his bear robe up over his face. A fox skin covered his head, but it was the bear that kept him warm. The fire lighted the circle they were sleeping around, their sledges strapped together. The hides were removed, as it was easier done before the carcass froze. The hides were rolled and carried in total on the last sledge, one that would have been emptied of that cargo if they could have taken a sixth animal - and they should have. Madai felt testy, trying to sleep in the cold with only a meager five animals for his trouble. He hoped Tiras had had better luck. He did not cherish a winter of starving, especially if he had to do it with Ido. Perhaps the sacrifice Toban had made before they left had not been sufficient.

But it was the last long night in the cold. That was a thing to rejoice in. At any normal time, this would have been the most thrilling of months for Madai,; but his energies were divided, and he was anxious for a wedding. He heard his father move beside him. It would not snow tonight; but that left the sky clear and left the men cold. The cave had a wide mouth and was shallow. But it was large, so they had used it every winter's hunt. They had never found a bear inside. Perhaps she could smell the men over the years, or the smoke. The walls were black with it. The cave did not keep out the cold, but it faced south and kept out the wind.

"Are you asleep, Patta?" he whispered.

"Yes," came the instant reply.

It made Madai chuckle. "Do you think Tiras and Togarmah have had better luck?" he asked.

"We are not so failed," Ashkinaz replied. "The big herds have split up. We will have another chance."

Madai nodded. He pulled his robe tighter and closed his eyes. He hoped someone would replenish the fire. It was Tiglath's watch. And that was the last he remembered till a dusky glow of sun began to rise in the east.

It was no matter that they were only coming with five cows. The night's sleep had restored Madai's optimism, and besides, they were nearing the village. And here they would rest a day, perhaps two, before they would set out again, as a whole, after mammoth on the sulfur plains. And after that, another forage for caribou... and after that... Ido.

He had to control himself. He wanted to rush ahead of the others, who were, in fact, pulling the weight of their sledges at an enthusiastic pace already. Not a man among them, save Madai, was coming to a cold bed. Madai heard the sledge runners slicing through the crust of snow, heard it bounce stiff against a rock or frozen clumps of stubborn mammoth grass, named for the valuable creatures that loved to eat it. He heard the men's straining breath, and his own, and the frozen creaking of the sleds. And he was not, in the beginning, aware that these were the only things he heard, not even a nosey crow.

$$\text{ෆ૪ෂ} \quad \text{ෆ૪ෂ} \quad \text{ෆ૪ෂ}$$

It was Ashinaz who caught Madai's attention first. He dropped the tethers of his sledge, pulled his bow off his back and dropped to his knee. The others did the same as though they shared the same brain. A stray wind sailed across the tops of the trees and showered them with a thin dusting of snow.

They kept their position a time long enough to steady their breathing and listened. On the wind there were no sounds of battle, nor wounding, nor grief. Instead, a quiet murmur. Ashkinaz nodded to Tiglath, who crept forward toward the village. Madai watched him. He could have been a white wolf, invisible on the landscape and completely silent. Tiglath disappeared behind a fir tree.

Only a moment more and he reappeared and signaled them 'ready approach.' He came back toward them with a stony face, and Madai was disturbed that the sign had not been 'nothing amiss.'

They came upon the scene dragging sleds of dead caribou, whose value was diminished, at the moment, by what they found. There lay, face down, a man... and two others lashed together. There were mothers he knew, staring at Togarmah, who stood above the dead man. The women were in little huddles, standing a way back, both curious and aghast. And they were casting glances at Toban's shelter.

The hunters had brought a silence with them, but it lasted only that moment and there was once again a low murmur passing through the scattered knots of frightened women. Togarmah looked, up only enough to find Ashkinaz. He rolled the man over with his boot.

He was not a man Madai knew, but his death had not been won easily, that was clear.

Toban, the clan's Elder, stood a way back, and protectively, beside the two who were tied together, though it seemed to Madai that Togarmah was in control. Reoan stood with Toban, which was an unlikely alliance in Madai's estimation. He looked at the captives. He felt his stomach fall as he recognized Laeden.

"Who is this man?" Ashkinaz pointed at the body and asked Togarmah.

"Banned." Togarmah spat out the word.

Madai's felt a chill run down his arms, and then a dread. Now it would all be brought out, just when he thought he had escaped the singe of that night in the forest, the idolatry, his own silence and desire. He wanted to shrink back into the trees. He was afraid to look up, but afraid not to. What would scream his guilt more? So he forced his eyes to look at his father and found, oddly enough, his father was not surprised.

Ashkinaz nodded, and with that gesture Madai was sure that his father approved the man's death, no matter his immediate crime. Still, there was Laeden. Madai could look at any face but his.

"These were with him," Togarmah continued, cocking his head with disgust.

Ashkinaz turned to the two captives and looked at Reoan. The old man stood beside his son, wearing the withered wolf head as a second scalp. He waited silently, a composite of both grief and defiance.

"What is the crime?" Ashkinaz demanded.

At this question, Togarmah's face came even more grim, were that possible. He nodded toward Toban's lodge in the center of the village. "In there," he growled cryptically.

"What are you talking about, Togarmah?"

Madai looked at the lodge. There he saw only Toban's young grandson, and Tiras standing guard outside.

"This Banned came to steal away these youth," Toban finally spoke, gesturing to the two bound up together, the one being Laeden.

"What you mean to say," there was a challenge in Togarmah's voice, "is that this Banned, with Uke and Laeden, came to steal away our maids."

Madai's head jerked back around to Laeden. The boy would not lift his eyes from the ground, but Uke looked square at Madai. Even now, it was a derisive look; and Madai became frightening aware of what he had not seen at first, that his mother was not present, nor Naru, nor Kiellet, nor Yamma nor Tain... and, especially... not Ido.

Madai started for Uke, but his father grabbed him with one great hand on his shoulder. "Wait, lad," he whispered. Ashkinaz took a step toward Togarmah, bringing Madai with him. "Tell it plain," he demanded.

"They are safe." It was Toban who spoke.

"They are safe by the Arm of God," Togarmah's voice rose with a challenge. "Had we not returned..."

"They were found along the way," Madai heard a voice that sounded a little like Reoan's, but strangely pinched, and old. "Togarmah's party came upon them. Ido," he said and looked up quickly at Madai, "Tain and Yamma... trussed up. Uke was with him," Reoan tilted his head at the man on the ground, "and Laeden." The last was scarcely audible.

Madai felt all his blood pounding, and then a heat that raised up and sat in his belly. He felt his father's fingers clench like a fist around the bulk of his winter robe. He started for Uke again, but Ashkinaz gripped him. All that followed Reoan's short speech was a palpable silence. Togarmah moved his foot and the frozen snow crackled.

"They are whole?" Ashkinaz quietly asked Reoan, speaking of the maids.

Reoan looked squarely at Ashkinaz. The blacks of his eyes were little dots, and he nodded. "They are whole."

Madai heard compassion in his father's voice toward Laeden's father and could not understand why. Laeden's position as friend had changed in an instant. He was a fool, dangerous and treacherous.

"What's to come of them?" Togarmah nearly snarled.

"There is time enough for that, Togarmah," Ashkinaz insisted and looked at the dead man as though really seeing him for the first time. "You need to take him out there." He nodded toward the woods.

Togarmah nodded. He would acquiesce in the matter for now. There was a fight to come. What to do with the living was entirely more relevant and would prove a thorny issue that he could not lose.

Madai watched Togarmah pull the dead man into the trees. He looked at the trail it dragged in the snow. Reoan took the moment to steal his son away, and when Madai looked up, Laeden was gone. Uke was gone, too, and Ashkinaz was watching Madai.

"We have the caribou," his father reminded him.

It stunned Madai, when a thing so terrible had happened.

"You and Ido will need it."

His father's voice was quiet and steady. The sleds were making a crisping sound on the snow, being dragged away. Yes, there was the winter provision. Still, it seemed ridiculous dullery in the light of so grievous crimes. Madai still felt the place on his arm where Ashkinaz had held him and assured himself that there would come an accounting... even if it had to wait.

ɔʒœ ɔʒœ ɔʒœ

Madai was raging inside, pacing because he did not know what to do and his father would not let him do what he had already thought about doing.

Mineo was quiet. She was serving them stew with a forced calm. It was absolute dark outside, the caribou packed deep in a snow bank. Her face was pale as she moved quietly about, bringing them food.

"Ido was only frightened," she had said. And she had told the story that Laeden had drawn them away with a ruse and Uke had strapped them together with the help of the stranger.

Togarmah's party had come upon them, praises to Mighty God, and the fight had been short. That the stranger had died a savage death was witness itself that Laeden and Uke were also spared at His will.

Madai was not so sure of that.

"What brought Laeden so low?" Mineo had asked.

It was one of those times that sons view their mothers as too naïve for the world as it has become. He knew the answer in a name, but would not speak it for having to explain himself. But Yamma was the spoiler, of that he was sure, and Laeden quick to scramble after the bait.

They would not let him see Ido. Naru and Temah were guarding their only living child with every vigilance to spare her curiosities, even his, and to see that she slept calm and well through the night.

"How far had they got?" Ashkinaz carefully asked after it was clear that Ido was unharmed.

"To the bend of the river," Mineo replied.

Madai listened to his parents with an energy building in his belly, thinking how mild their conversation was. "You are sure Ido is whole?" Madai finally asked, red in the face.

"Completely sure," Mineo was quick to answer.

Madai studied her face. It was reassuring and completely truthful. He nodded.

"We should have killed them all, all those years ago." Ashkinaz muttered quietly.

"We could not do that!" Mineo insisted.

"It was done once," he argued. "Mighty God did it."

"But He is God."

Ashkinaz looked at his wife and his face softened. "Yes," he affirmed. "God is God...Even so," his voice was stern, if quiet, "were they dead, they could not have come back. And Laeden..." Ashkinaz did not finish his thought.

"Was there only the one?" Madai interrupted, thinking uncomfortably of the numbers he had watched that night around the fire.

"One?" his mother asked.

"The Banned."

"Yes, I think so," she answered.

Madai slowly nodded. He looked at his parents a moment. It was time to tell. "There were others," he began haltingly. "I saw them once... last spring... in the forest."

Ashkinaz frowned and looked at him. His eyes were a very light brown, nearly yellow. They had a way of speaking every reprimand and disappointment with devastating clarity. It was the look that pained Madai, and still he kept his father's gaze as though to bear the punishment.

"Why did you not tell us?" Ashkinaz asked quietly.

Madai shook his head, feeling more chastised than if he had been laid after with a stick, yet somehow enormously glad that it was finally told. "Unspeakable things were done," he whispered.

He watched the blood rise up his father's face. "Sorcery?" his father asked.

Madai only nodded.

"You know what comes of sorcery," was all Ashkinaz replied.

Madai nodded again, slowly; his chin felt unsteady. "I don't know why..." he began.

"You might have saved Laeden."

"Laeden?" Madai asked, incredulous. "What of Ido and Tain?"

"They are unharmed; Laeden is not."

Madai's stomach began to hurt.

"But Laeden is just a boy," Mineo interjected.

"He is one year more than Madai," Ashkinaz told her grimly.

"Ashkinaz," she whispered, "it is Laeden."

Ashkinaz looked at his wife. "Choices were made." His voice was low and settled. Then he turned toward Madai. "And there are others to contend with now."

Madai clenched his teeth together. "I am sorry."

"Yes," Ashkinaz replied. He kept his eyes on his son. "I know you are sorry. But now there are things to set right."

☙ ☙ ☙

They set out before dawn. Ashkinaz led the party. They found tracks in the snow, they found the place the maids had been taken. They found where a camp had been struck. But whoever had made the camp had melted into the forest like phantoms, their trail covered in the snow that finally turned Ashkinaz around toward home. New vigilance would be needed now.

Reoan had not come on the hunt. He was guarding Laeden. He trusted Togarmah not at all.

- *12* -

er nose was cold, and Ido pulled the wooly robe back over her face. It was still dark, and she could hear her parents plainly. She wanted to be asleep. She knew a terrible wrong had been done, and she was at the center of it. And Laeden was a culprit. Poor Laeden. He had been nearly as scared as she when the horrible stranger had come out from the shadows with his face all painted and tied her to Tain. Poor Tain, younger by a year and so terrified she could scarcely stand. Yamma was the only one calm.

"How will you speak?" Ido heard her mother ask, and she squeezed her eyes shut.

There was a long quiet till her father answered quietly, "Death."

"O..." her mother replied with a tremor.

"How would you have me speak?"

Ido pulled the bear robe back from her face. Her mother's voice was low and, despite herself, Ido wanted to hear.

"They are very young, especially Laeden."

"They are both old enough to carry away our child."

"Yes..."

Ido shivered. She was glad she should have no say in what would happen to Uke and Laeden. But she believed Laeden had been drawn away by his own folly, and no real rebellion against the Mighty God at all. She slowly crawled out of bed to have something warm to eat. Suddenly, she did not want to be alone.

ଔଓ   ଔଓ   ଔଓ

Yamma took another cup of cammron tea to her mother. She arranged the old robe around the woman's shoulders and thought her mother was thinner every day. She listened to her father and brother move toward the door.

"We are leaving," her father said.

"What will you say?" she asked him, looking up.

Old Tiptri looked at his daughter trying to read what lay behind her eyes. Why did she coax him to mercy? Why should he grant mercy to them who would steal her away? Especially Uke, who was her betrothed. What sort of fellow would do that? And this son of his, Guran, who did not burn for revenge. What children had he made?

He saw her start to ask again, so he ducked out the door. The cold hit him like a fist, made his eyes water, and made him feel painfully old.

Yamma scowled. She saw in his face that he would be as sanctimonious as Togarmah. They would not listen to Guran, but Guran would guard himself, anyway. It might be the last of Uke. She was sorry about that, sorry for Laeden, too, he was harmless. She had an affection for Uke. They had discovered a lot together; they had tasted each other, and they had tasted a source of unrestrained power. It was that which she mourned the most.

The others would be afraid, after this, and no one would follow her to the secret fires. What good would she be to them then? That The Banned needed the youth of The Family did not alarm her. She could not know there was a pollution rampant amongst them, and the wombs of their women brought forth nothing that lived.

Ω Ω Ω

Ashkinaz ate the hot grain mush slowly. It was luxury food, gleaned at the season of color from the grasses that grew tall in the meadow lowlands. It was scarce. He loved Mineo for serving it this morning. It was probably their last, and it was flavored with honey. Mineo always knew when he was the most distressed.

He heard Madai making far more noise than putting on a winter robe should make and scraping his elk bone knife across the table when he picked it up, pacing across the floor with loud exhaling and ill-concealed impatience.

Ashkinaz ran his spoon around the bowl one more time and closed his eyes as the warm sweetness trailed down his throat. How do you take a boy from his father? How do you do it to the good, devout Reoan? How do you? Ashkinaz sighed. Mineo was suddenly beside him to put his heavy fur robe across his shoulders.

"Do as Mighty God has told you," she whispered.

"If He has been silent?"

She was quiet a moment. Then she closed her hand around his. "Then do as you must to serve Him best."

He suddenly wanted to be back on the sleeping mat with Mineo beside him, the night robes pulled up and only their noses cold, anywhere but where he was going.

Ω Ω Ω

"There is one price for idolatry," Togarmah insisted.

"What proof of idolatry?" Reoan persisted.

There was a change in the old Elder's voice. It was strong this morning, even commanding, and his eyes burned at Togarmah.

Togarmah turned away from Reoan, an indelicate affront. "We all see what has come of a father's mercy," he fairly growled.

Madai held his eyes on the two in the shadows, both convicted by what they intended for Ido and Tain and no matter the idolatry. Both worthy of death. He could not imagine there be doubt at all. Laeden was likely one who had been dancing naked at the secret fires all the summer last, joining himself to who knew what darkness of both spirit and flesh.

He practiced how he would articulate their fate. He could not speak in the Elder's Council, but he would be a part of the judgement, as Ido was his betrothed. His was as critical a vote as her own father's. If it were only Uke, it would not be easier. Indeed, perhaps that Laeden had been a friend steeled him more against them. He relaxed his jaw; his head was starting to hurt.

"It is not only a matter of Laeden and Uke," Madai heard his father's voice, "but what has come of rebellions before." Ashkinaz spoke the words carefully.

Madai could not but notice how his father was always able to command the Council's attention. Even Togarmah.

"What do you mean, Ashkinaz?" Togarmah asked, a soft hint of victory in his voice.

"The deluge, brothers," Ashkinaz answered simply.

Toban huffed. "In truth, Ashkinaz?" Toban looked at all the Council's faces in turn. "Perhaps it's a bit severe to judge these lads by that measure."

A low, indistinct murmur rose instantly amongst the men. Madai glanced around the room. Tension was high in the air, but he could not tell what course it was taking. Toban and Togarmah each raised their arms at the exact moment. Toban turned to Togarmah with a warning look. Togarmah held a stony challenge in his own eyes, but it was Toban who spoke.

"There are many amongst us who have losses from the times of The Banned." He looked at Togarmah again with cruel satisfaction. "Let us not speak from revenge, but from prudence, what is fitting to the crime. We know only that these lads were deceived by a cunning far past their years."

"Yes," Ashkinaz said, and again the Elders turned their attention to him.

Madai looked at his father also, seeing his face and surprised to find tears in his eyes.

"That is why we have but one choice today," Ashkinaz continued, turning slowly to Reoan as he did. He did not speak again until the old hunter returned his gaze. "If The Banned had been rightly judged at the first, this thing would not be upon us now."

There was a silence after that that even Togarmah did not interrupt.

"How so, friend?" Reoan asked quietly, as though it were only he and Ashkinaz in the room.

Ashkinaz leaned toward the older man. "The cost of sorcery," his voice was nearly gentle, "must from this day forward... be death."

Reoan kept his father's gaze. Madai could see him plainly, see his face looking as though it were stuck. But the eyes did not waver, keeping on Ashkinaz, who was to him an old friend and ally. Madai felt the rise of triumph in his own stomach. He watched as Reoan tried to speak; but Reoan's mouth began to quiver, and he was silent.

"Surely not, brothers!" Toban interjected quickly. He turned to look directly at Ashkinaz. "It is too near your fire, Ashkinaz, with Ido soon to be your daughter."

"No, Toban. It is that Mighty God rid the First Earth of corrupt men. Do we so quickly people the Second with the same?"

Toban made a scoffing sound in his throat. None in the counsel spoke, aware with a rising discomfort, that another sort of battle was brimming. Togarmah took a step toward Ashkinaz.

"Rightly spoken," he declared.

"Are we gods, then?" Toban insisted. "Do we judge today by an old tale?"

"More than a tale, Toban," Ashkinaz replied stonily.

"Yes... well, yes," Toban quickly answered.

Ashkinaz knew at that moment how dire and deep the trouble ran. But he would save that for another time. He turned his back to Toban then and looked sadly at his old friend.

Reoan was staring into the fire. He was resolved to keep his counsel till the last moment, now that Ashkinaz had spoken a truth that even he could not deny. He heard the heavy breathing of his son behind him and desperately wished they had not sent The Banned away all those years ago but had seen all of them ended. He suddenly wondered whether Togarmah could have spoken death to his own wife, or Temah, death to Sru; and he decided to use them ruthlessly to save his son.

Temah, father to Ido. father to Sru who was lost to The Banned, stood up. He cleared his throat. "I stand with Ashkinaz," he said.

Togarmah felt the shift. "And I," he quickly added.

"I do not think," Tiglath spoke for the first time, "that Uke's fate should be weighed against an ancient tale. Does a God really judge the earth by water, wipe it away save a man and his sons? Does He really? What do we know of floods? They rise and fall, and wash away a valley for a season - but not every valley. What flood is great enough for that?" Tiglath turned to look at Tiptri. "Old Father, have you in all your years seen a flood so great as that?"

Tiptri looked confused. He did not answer, but a low muttering was building amongst the men.

"This Great God, Who gives us mammoth, Who sends us all that is good... "

"Tiglath," Togarmah stopped him with a threat in his voice, "Guard yourself that you are not guilty of the same crimes as they." He jerked his head toward Uke and Laeden.

At that, the control of the Council was lost. An Elder, more ancient even than Tiptri began to shout at Tiglath in a thin voice all but lost in the din of other voices. Madai was stunned by the turn. The judgment was a simple one. How should it be clouded by questions of what was already known by all? He glanced toward the pair in question. Laeden was white as snow, trembling. But Uke stood unwavering, with an odd expression, as though it nearly brought him pleasure.

Tiras was not of an age to speak in the assembly, but Madai could hear him; and Togarmah was shouting something at someone. Ashkinaz and Reoan only looked across the fire at one another.

"Brothers!" Toban shouted. The noise began to subside. Toban blinked rapidly and took a step toward Tiglath. "Sit down, Tiglath," he said.

The young scout sat, his face ablaze with color.

"We are here to make a judgment. Will we do it with shouting?"

"Toban is right," Ashkinaz agreed.

"Let us each cast the judgment, then," Togarmah insisted. He looked at Toban, pressing the Elder to begin the vote.

Toban considered briefly. He believed the scrap of doubt that Tiglath brought was all they dared, and he looked at the oldest man of The Family. He nodded. The thin man stood. He was eight feet tall, even with a stoop in his back. He could remember what his father had told him of the voyage across the Brine Sea, and the sea serpents, even fire-breathers. He could remember what was said of the scattering and of great walled villages in the East. He was to some a sage, to others, superstitious, a bit daft. He leaned on a thick staff to speak a single word.

"Death."

Tiptri stood with a degree less vigor. "Death," he enunciated, but he was proud of himself and looked at his son Guran with what severity he could still command.

Tiptri's brother spoke next, and around the fire with each a fatal judgment until there was a long stretch of quiet. It had come to Reoan.

All the faces turned to him. Reoan stood with surprising speed, considering his lame leg, and pronounced in a clear voice, "Flogging, and let them be outcast."

A scattered mumbling began at Reoan's pronouncement. A few younger heads nodded, and another man rose to cast his judgment. One by one, from eldest to youngest, judgments were spoken. Madai was astonished that the finding was mixed. He heard his father's pronouncement with pride:

"Death," ignoring the tremor in his voice.

Togarmah fairly spat out the word.

He recognized Tiglath without looking up, "Flogging." Madai believed it might even have been less had the tide been more to his favor. Guran pronounced "Flogging" with a stiff-backed challenge. Madai did not attempt to hide the disgust he felt as he turned to glare at them both. But his turn was coming. His heart was pounding so that he began to sweat. He did not look at Laeden again, but remembered Ido as she had been a little girl, dragging a rotted old sled and whooping down the mountain behind Tiras. Then he remembered her hand in his, waiting to take a precarious step and looking into his eyes. He remembered her rubbing the cold out of his hands, as he had remembered it nearly every night, and he stood and said "Death," with a shock of pleasure.

In the end, he was only mildly disappointed that the judgment was not unanimous, for it was soundly in his favor.

The Council was silent with the last vote. They had never before required the life of one of The Family by consent. It was lost to beast or storm, but not at the hand of a brother. They had always before guarded every life, as every strong arm was needed, to speak nothing of fear of a Mighty God. It seemed they were stunned at what they had decided. That Togarmah had slain a Banned was not the same, and it had been done in heat. How should they expunge a life... and who should do it?

Reoan slowly rose to his feet. Madai had nearly forgotten him.

"I would like to speak," he said. His face was ashen. Toban was eager to let the old father plead his case.

"We have measured the fate of my son and this lad by a high standard. Perhaps it is a standard best left to Mighty God." Reoan looked squarely at Togarmah. "Will you take this boy's life, Togarmah? Would you have taken the life of your own Emni? And you, Temah, what of Sru? Could you have put the blade to his throat those many years ago?" Then, without waiting for them to answer, Reoan turned to Toban, as though asking the Elder to decide.

"Let them be banished. It is deep winter. Let Mighty God decide whether they should live or die. And to see that they do not return, let me go with them. I will bide the winter in the forest, without aid, save the will of God. Let their blood not be against you."

Reoan's plea was loud after the silence, though spoken earnestly and softly. Ashkinaz heard him as though he had expected it. Had the old hunter not raised the boy alone, his mother taken at a deep water crossing? She had been snagged by something, dark in the water, and not seen again. It was a shocking incident, and Reoan had looked for her a long time afterwards. And then the boy became the father's life. No, it was no surprise that Reoan offered himself as guard to The Family against his own son and Uke.

"You will not survive." Ashkinaz warned him anyway.

Reoan looked at his friend with a wistful smile. "Let it rest with God."

Ashkinaz thought about arguing again, but then he wondered if he would have the mettle to see his only child cut off. They would certainly not survive the winter, he was fairly certain of that, short of God's keeping. But then, perhaps Reoan would die of grief otherwise, without his son, and it would all end up the same in the end.

"Why do you think you can stop them, old man, if they try to come back?" a voice growled.

But Toban ignored it and lifted his arm. "They are banished," he proclaimed. "Their blood be lost or spared at the hand of God."

Madai was stunned. It was no more a decision than what had been done to The Banned a generation before; and here, they had come back. Except, of course, that a worthy man would probably die in the cold.

As though his father knew his mind, he leaned in and whispered, "They will first starve and then freeze." With that, Ashkinaz stood up and began to leave the Council.

But Togarmah came beside him and gripped his arm. "Let them come back, and I will kill them myself," He hissed, shamed that Reoan had used Emni against him.

"As will be your right," Ashkinaz replied, "if they do not abide by this ruling."

Togarmah nodded, still glaring across the way at Uke, wholly dissatisfied.

"Wait, Ashkinaz," he heard Toban call. "We must decide where to send them."

Ashkinaz stopped. He could feel the eyes of the Council on his back. He slowly turned around, avoiding the gaze of both Reoan and his own son.

He looked at Laeden. "You have played with the tempest, boy. You are in God's Hands now." Then he answered Toban's question in a flat voice, "Freezing is a cruel way to die; you decide."

Ashkinaz left the lodge after that, into the subzero air. A blast of winter wind entered as he left, as though to prove him correct.

⊂3⊂3 ⊂3⊂3 ⊂3⊂3

The next morning, Ashkinaz did not watch as the three men turned east, away from the village toward the river encased in a tomb of ice. Below an inch of frozen water, beneath the snow, the river was still alive, speeding its frigid black current toward the sea. There was a thin sliver, in the centermost part, still liquid, and a dangerous crossing. But the three were to do it and camp on the far side, without shelter or food and only their weapons a chance of survival at all, to be impaled upon sight, should they try to return.

Ashkinaz would not see them go, a good man to forfeit his life... and for what? He sighed from his depths. To let God decide was perhaps a cowardly notion, and yet he would see it done that way.

Madai watched Uke and Laeden test the river. They prodded the ice with their sticks all along the edge, till they disappeared around a bend. It disappointed him severely. He wanted to watch their last bitter step till the last bitter end. Not one of them looked back, but he could tell Reoan, moving slowly with a familiar limp. When Madai thought about it later, it was his last glimpse of the old man that he remembered most.

- *13* -

Ido came out of her parents' lodge. She was wearing the cape of spotted saber cat. A storm had accompanied the three exiles into the wild and lasted a fortnight. It seemed to have carried away the stain as well. Today the sun was shining. Ido looked up at the sky when she emerged, to let the sun fall on her face. The air was cold enough to lock in the winter, but it was still; and with the sun it was a beautiful day.

It was a good way to end the last days of her maidenhood. She looked in the direction of Ashkinaz's lodge, where a new one stood beside it, built with the able hands of her betrothed. She remembered his hands, red and cold, pulling her water bucket up out of the river like it was a bit of froth, so easy. She smoothed the cape unconsciously.

Today she would take Kiellet a new basket. It was Ido's secret 'making peace,' as no one knew she had been at war with the young mother. The basket was sturdy; the only concession she had made with it had been a medallion of sea conch, which in fact had been at Naru's suggestion. But it was a strong basket, made of willow, for holding clams.

Kiellet would be very happy to have it, with her new babe and little time to make baskets. Ido wondered whether Kiellet knew; women do know such things. She stopped, suddenly nervous. She felt her face grow hot; terrified to have the wife of Tiras know her old heartache, she nearly turned back.

"Ido!" she heard a musical voice calling, and it was too late. Kiellet was coming out of her lodge with a bowl for scooping snow.

Ido looked at her squarely. Always before, it had been a hasty glance, and she realized with an alarming pique of disappointment, that Kiellet was lovely. There was a rose in her cheeks from more than the cold, and kindness shone from her eyes. Ido suddenly felt the peace offering in her hands a ridiculous sham. But she tried her best smile and held the basket toward Tiras's young wife.

"What a lovely basket, Ido!"

"I made it for you." Ido's lips felt wooden speaking those few words.

Kiellet stopped and looked from Ido to the willow basket.

"Whatever for, Ido?" she asked with surprise. And then she flushed. "'Tis beautiful," she added quickly. "But you..."

"I thought, with the babe..." Ido felt her face growing hotter with each stammer.

Kiellet made a soothing 'hmm' sort of sound and took her arm and began walking back toward her door. She squeezed Ido gently. "'Tis lovely, Ido. A lovely little thing." She pushed open the heavy outer door and pulled aside the ox-hide curtain. "Let's have a good hot tea," she invited, guiding Ido inside.

Ido was momentarily blinded in the darkness, and then the fires slowly lit the inner space till her eyes came accustomed to the dim. She was heartened by Kiellet's lodge, for it was not adorned with all the little touches her mother had given theirs over the years. And then she was ashamed again, felt very young and clumsy. Kiellet put down her bowl and took the basket from Ido's hands. She held it up and turned it to every side and ran her fingers over the conch. She looked at Ido then with a perfect smile.

"I have always admired things like this," she said. "And never had the gift for it. Thank you."

It was surely the absolutely wrong thing to say. It made Ido's eyes turn a bright blue, threatening tears. She was aghast and amazed at the emotions welling up; she tightened her lips and held her breath to stop an eruption, and turned her head slightly away.

Kiellet noticed, of course. What gift she lacked with her hands, she made up for in her heart. And so she moved away from Ido, toward the fire where her baby was sleeping. She put the basket down and pulled the blanket up to the little girl's chin. Kiellet heard Ido take a few choppy breaths and gave her a moment more. It was also time she needed, considering whether to speak about IT... or leave it alone.

Ido was filled with shame, watching the young mother tend her babe, Tiras's babe. She recognized that old foe trying to steal back in her heart, but it was more than that. It was still a wound. How was she so stupid as to think it could be so easily gone?

Her hand clenched around the cape of saber cat, and she willed herself to think about Madai. She tried to recall that moment last spring when he had given her the pelt, standing in her doorway with his eyes alert and nervous. He was both beautiful and brave. And then he had touched her and guided her down the hill. It was the moment he had become more than only Madai, and it was the moment this other feeling had started to fade.

"Come see the babe," Kiellet invited carefully. She turned her head toward Ido and gently smiled.

Ido felt herself moving toward the little bed. It was made of the same willow as the clam basket, and with quite passable skill. It was lifted onto a platform of logs, lined with felt; and it held Tiras's baby girl. "She is beautiful," Ido sniffed, though little could be seen of the child wrapped in all her winter coverings.

"Yes," Kiellet agreed quietly.

Ido moved back, afraid a stray drop of tear might fall.

"I am sorry, Ido," Kiellet said, surprising them both.

Ido felt her nose tingling, a sure warning sign that all control might be lost. She coughed to ease the tension in her throat and without looking up asked quietly, "You know?"

"Tiras told me."

Horror crossed her face. "He knows?" she asked a degree louder.

Kiellet touched her arm softly. "The night Madai told Tiras he was pledged is the night Tiras found you outside your house. He was so glad his little Ido would marry his closest friend. And he was confused at how you acted." Kiellet paused. "But I was not. I watched him take you everywhere he went when you were only a little girl. I knew what was wrong."

Ido felt Kiellet's hand, curiously steadying her. "And you don't hate me?" she whispered.

Kiellet leaned forward in the dim light to let Ido see her eyes. "I know Tiras loves me, Ido. And I could never hate you."

Ido felt those untimely tears but was strangely relieved that she did not have to hide them anymore.

"Just wait, Ido. Madai will take your breath away," Kiellet finished, slipping her arm around the girl's shoulders.

Ido felt as small as a bark bug. There was nothing left of her dignity now.

"I am sorry," she managed to whisper.

"Why be sorry, little sister?" Kiellet asked kindly. "You have done nothing wrong."

Ido was ashamed in her heart again at that. Kiellet guided her to a stool and gently sat her down.

"I will get us that hot tea," she said, as though all their talk had been just a trifle. "It is dreadful cold out there."

Ido watched Kiellet pour from a clay pot beside the cooking fire. The sight had the effect of making Tiras's new life real to her. It had the effect of putting Kiellet beside him in Ido's mind. It was like a fresh cut against an old sore, but somehow, it also cut a last cord in her heart free. Ido took the tea from Kiellet's hand. Its steam warmed her face as she tried to take a first sip, and it smelled of dried spring. There was a familiar sadness she thought she had shed, back again - but not so dreadful as before. Kiellet was sipping her tea carefully and smiled at her again. And Ido could no longer deny that she was a worthy woman, and well deserving.

"I was fortunate," Kiellet leapt back into the conversation after she had taken another sip. "When I was a little girl, my mother told me, 'Kiellet, there is your husband,' and she pointed to Tiras. So I always knew. And so I always loved him."

"As simple as that?"

Kiellet looked over at the sleeping child and back at Ido. "Yes," she answered easily.

Ido was quiet a minute, thinking about what Kiellet had said and slightly amazed. "Have you always been so wise and good?" she asked.

Kiellet laughed. She was starting to feel old beside the willowy Ido. And that was not easy when she was just in the first blush of motherhood. "Ido," she said with her most instructive voice, "my mother always told me there is no good thing in humankind. What good we glean is by the mercies of Mighty God." The baby stirred. Kiellet seemed almost pleased to put her tea aside. She went to the baby, bent and picked up little Naru, named for Ido's own mother. She put the child's little lips to her breast with a smile. "This will keep her quiet a while. Now tell me about Madai."

Ido blinked. She could hear the child suckling, so intimate a sound. It brought no fresh wounding, just the lingering sadness. But the warmth in her hands from the tea was comforting; Kiellet was comforting. Ido began to realize that if she tried, she could feel a bit cheered. Perhaps it was all the confessing.

She discovered as she sipped the tea that she was curiously pleased at the prospect of telling Kiellet intimacies of her own, as though somehow, in the dark of Tiras's lodge, a true bond had been formed with his wife. And so, quite easily, really, she began to tell Kiellet about the saber cape and the trip to the river for water. She told her Madai had a clumsy, nervous side but was exceedingly strong. And she did not leave out his blue eyes, and that quick moment when it looked as though he would kiss her. She told Kiellet about holding Madai's hands when they were like ice from having drawn her water, and that she had rubbed them longer than she needed to... and that she was proud when they walked back together.

Kiellet was nodding like a conspirator. "He nearly kissed you?" she asked. "Tiras was never so bold."

Ido raised her eyebrows. "I would not have let him, you know."

"Of course," Kiellet agreed. "But he loves you, then."

Ido watched Kiellet nurse Tiras's baby a moment. "I think he does!" she announced.

"There is nothing better than love from the start," Kiellet proclaimed. "You shall see for yourself... like Tiras and me." She said the last bit carefully, watching the girl. If hurt flashed across her face, it was brief. Kiellet was one to face a trouble straight on, to get it healed thorough and clean.

"There is a fortnight left to you, Ido," Kiellet continued. "Watch Madai. Say, 'There goes my husband. Is he not beautiful?' And see how your love will grow."

Kiellet winked at Ido. Then she pulled the fat little Naru off her breast, wiped her mouth, wrapped her snuggly, and put her into Ido's arms. Ido looked at the mother with a touch of surprise, and then she looked at Tiras's child. But it was Kiellet's child too, and Ido was quickly filling with warm affection for the quiet woman. She was also happy she had brought Kiellet the willow basket and glad it had the seashell adornment.

She was suddenly anxious to see Madai again, walking out of the woods with his bow across his back and his hair stiff in the cold. What a proper time to be young... and nearly in love.

- 14 -

Yamma was hungry. And she was cold. She squatted at the edge of the river and looked out into the empty white sea of snow. No matter where she looked, there was no rising column of smoke, nor hint of human life. She pulled her cloak around herself and buried her nose. She waited what seemed an endless time and finally pulled off her mitt. Then she dipped her fingers in the cooling stew and pulled out a tough piece of caribou. She put the whole thing into her mouth, licked her fingers and slid them back into the glove. The stew was tough because she had made it in a hurry, and it was cold because it had sat out on a bed of snow that had, by now, melted all around it.

"I know it was a track," she whispered to herself, sending up a puff of steam from her mouth. She shivered. "It was a man's print." She hunched her shoulders and thought about giving up.

Yamma had discovered, in the first days of Uke's absence, that she truly missed him. He had sneaked into her parents' lodge many a cold night when they were past hearing and lost in their snores. And she had found a warm spot beside herself for him. Well, she missed that. But it also made her angry.

What right had they to send a perfectly good hunter away to freeze? They were all smug and self-righteous, grovelers to an impotent, antiquated god. And Toban was a coward. Tiglath had been the only man at the counsel. She drummed her fingers inside the mittens. She chewed the meat some more. She stared out into the white expanse again and thought about all the men around the Council fire who had judged Uke a sorcerer. Madai. He was a disappointment. She thought he was ready for something more. She could have made him ready, given time.

Yamma began to feel that surging rise of anger again. It had frightened her the first time. She had never felt such an uncontrollable rage before, but she recognized it now. Now it seemed to give her power, power over other people, power even to arrange a happening. She had never known such a thing was possible. She could not remember whether she had resisted it in the beginning, but she never thought about that now. Instead, she began to crave the way it made her feel. Foolish girl. She thought she owned it.

She stood up and looked down at the pitiful pot of cold stew. She decided to leave it. Uke had found it before, she was sure. But she would not bring another. No. There were others amongst The Family. She could rally them, and she would draw Madai away, too. His transformation would be a coup... and it would be a fitting reward to those ancients of The Family. She felt a confirmation in her soul that she was right. Her heart began to beat out an excited rhythm.

- 15 -

By the third week, as if to certify that the earth was just as happy about their joining, a warm chinook wind began to blow through the valley. Overnight, the cruel, biting cold was overrun by the almost balmy gentleness of the Chinook, enough that it could nearly be spring. Even if it wouldn't last, which it wouldn't, it was a fitting way to start a marriage, in Madai's opinion.

All the preparations were made on his part, his share of the caribou still frozen in the snow cave, the lodge complete, and better than only adequate, snug and covered over twice. His mother had assured him of that. Ido would not freeze or want for food. She would not want for protection, either, never again.

Madai managed to keep himself busy. With the intermission of winter, he and Tiras took a two-day excursion after red deer, named for the color they came when they briefly shed the winter's coat of powdery grey to glisten crimson in the spring. All they found with any sort of life, however, was a beaver dam, and that blockaded with thick ice around its hut of sticks. But it was not time wasted. Tiras plied Madai with as much advice as two days would hold. They did a boy's share of laughing and never once thought about Laeden.

When they returned, Madai's Day of Joining was fast upon him, only five days more. Just enough time for his mother to finish the new leggings intended for a celebration, just enough time to start believing the eternal waiting would really end, and just enough time to start a rush of blood every time he watched Ido, as he was doing now.

She was coming out of Tiras's lodge. She had been in there a long time. Kiellet was standing at the door and they were smiling and talking. Ido gave her a hug. Good. They would all be friends. She pulled the saber cat around herself and waved - and turned around - and saw him. Her eyes were smiling, the color of sky. They widened, and her cheeks turned a firey crimson. Kiellet must have said something, because she glanced back and then, joy of joys, started walking the distance to him.

Madai just had the moment to study her and found to his delight no shadow left behind from her stealing, nor any hint that she might be the Virgin of the stars. Though he really didn't know what that hint might be, it was all a great relief.

He was sitting on a flat rock, one of many that ringed the communal fire and would be the setting in five days of their marriage. He stood up.

"Ido!" he said. He was suddenly afraid of her. He had watched her over the month and had seen her seeing him. It was always a rush of confirmation, but this - this was the first time they had been alone again, as alone as one could be in the center of The Family. Her hands were tucked inside her robe, but the hood was fallen to rest on her back. The air was warm enough that she let it lie there and Madai could see plainly her yellow-red hair pulled back and hiding in a long, thick braid. The color in her cheeks was as red as a strawberry. Madai reached out his hand toward her before he could stop himself.

Ido looked at Madai's hand. She stopped. She decided it was perfectly proper. She let go of the cape where she had held it shut and extended her own hand to his.

"I am happy to see you, Madai," she chirped in a cheerful voice.

Madai grinned. "Yes, good." He watched the color climb to the roots of her hair. He felt her fingers pulsing in his grip and tightened his hand around hers. Then he didn't know what else to say.

෬෬ ෬෬ ෬෬

She was wearing a woolen dress, woven on her mother's loom, the golden color of wild yarrow, soft and expertly done. Naru had used all her artistry to form a perfect garment. It fell from her neck to the tops of her feet, an articulate complement to Ido's blue eyes. A wedding robe made of the skin from a white deer, a worthy garment and rare, was draped across it to keep out the determined cold. Ido carried juniper boughs in her hands. Were it summer, it would be long blades of marsh grass with their seed heads, in recognition of the prophecies, whether they were understood or not.

Madai's heart was pounding, enough to make his stomach hurt and give him the trembles. Ido looked at him with trembles of her own, and he thought her eyes were marvelous, great shining wells of virtue. Everything about her presence overcame him. She was no more the little girl of his childhood, but nearly another person altogether, a perfect creature. Though they were surrounded by all their clan, which had the effect of blocking the wind, he was impervious to all but her.

Ashkinaz gave one end of a hair rope to Ido's father, and they began to wrap the couple together, round and round. Madai felt Ido's warmth through all their winter coverings as the fathers bound them up. Her shoulder came nearly to the height of his own, and he smelled her. Tanned doe hide, never worn before, and something combed through her hair. All his right side was alive with her touch.

There was a fire, built up to a mighty pyre. It lent light to the dusk, when maidens were joined to husbands. The Joinings were always done at end of day as a kindness to the young men and in modesty's sake for young maids. But it made a winter's joining a chilly affair.

Madai felt a tug, and Ashkinaz began pulling them along with the rope. He was leading them through the assembly of Family, who were beating painted sticks together and blowing incessantly on one- note reed harps. It was enough clamor to announce to the world, and all its spirits that Madai, son of Ashkinaz, was taking Ido, born to Temah, into his own lodge.

They came to a stop beside the fire, where there would be a round of dancing if the weather allowed it. Toban the Elder was waiting. He was holding juniper boughs, too, and he lifted them toward the unseen God to present them for the cause of a fruitful union.

Madai knew this practice was not necessary, might even border sorcery, but it had been lately adopted and drew no real trouble. Juniper was unharmed by the winter, ever enduring, always producing its spikey green little berries, a voucher of sorts for living long.

Blessedly, Toban's dabbling with the new lasted only the moment. He was soon reciting the old customs, hearkening to a time long since when the Great God set a woman before a man in a place called Eden. It was the most ancient rite carried with The Family from the time of the great scattering. Then the Elder thrust his hand between them, where their two sides were pinned together, the cause of which was forgotten, and pronounced, "Her flesh is you."

He turned to Ido and said with equal mystery, "His flesh is you."

There may be some brides who do not hear what is spoken at their Joining, but Ido was not such a one. Her mouth had gone dry and she was hot all over. Madai suddenly felt like a stranger beside her; indeed, she must have been caught in a kind of spell these months to think otherwise. She glanced at him who would become the patriarch of her sons with near dread.

She realized Toban had stopped talking and the people were clapping their sticks together again, singing the 'Song of Maidens.' She had sung it herself, at other Joinings... She was starting to feel faint...

But it was done.

Their mothers began to unwind them, and Madai had to steady Ido as she was left to stand on her own. He was not sorry for it. He kept his hand on her waist as he turned to her a last time before the Dance.

He heard the melody of another reed harp. It was the tune that would begin the dance around the fire. Temah was playing. He had a talent for making a flute sing.

He leaned down to whisper in her ear before she could be drawn away to stand in the 'Maiden's Queue,' where they would all line up to dance before an opposing line of The Family's young men. He would stand at the head, have his claim to any of the girls, and chose Ido at the far end. It was always done that way, and the bride was always chosen, and Madai always wondered why they did it. But he felt inspired tonight and what he whispered was, "I would always pick you, Ido," before she was pulled away by a giggling Kael.

Madai watched her go. The last he saw of her face were her eyes. They were wide and reminded him of a child's. He smiled, watching the top of her head as Kael pulled her away to stand in the last spot at the far side of the fire. It was getting steadily darker, for which he was glad. It was also getting colder, and the line would move fast.

Ido was glad for Kael's hand leading her, because she felt all a-muddle. It gave her time to remember her part. She saw Kiellet, and Tiras, holding little Naru. Kiellet mouthed something to her and then she was past them. She heard the jangle of copper disks fastened at their ankles, and the dancing started.

಄ CஐG ಄

They stood facing each other, maids and men. Temah had finished with the flute, and drums had started, punctuated with clapping and laughter. Madai was still craning his eyes down the string of girls, barely spying Ido. She had taken some juniper boughs lying on the ground, put there by the married women, even his own mother, and was lifting her arms like all the others. She was twisting and twirling, nearly like a child playing a game, and then she disappeared in the host of other dancers.

Yamma was feeling the power again. It was making her more than only angry. It was making her feel like stealing the fire from someone's lodge or breaking a clay pot after it was dry. It was making her miss Uke again, and what they did in the dark. It was making her blame Ashkinaz the most, and Madai second most. She had been watching Madai. He was drooling like a stag after that witless child.

The thought and the dancing were starting to rouse her, and she toyed with a few of the boys as she passed them. Some had been to the secret rites in the forest, and some had not. She decided at that moment to begin again, find the bravest amongst them and fritter them back to The Banned in the spring. She felt she had more power now. She laughed aloud, looking into the face of Tiglath. He was a fine one. He leaned in as she passed him and whispered something in her ear. She could not understand the words, but it drew up her blood.

಄ CஐG ಄

Madai waited as patiently as he could. He had never thought before that there were so many unmarried girls. But he could see Ido again, coming nearer - and then the whole thing would be over. He could hardly wait.

But then he felt her. She was like a presence even before she reached him. She was not dancing. He looked down into Yamma's eyes and felt struck by her. She looked at him as the saber cat mother had looked the day Tiras shot her. Yamma chilled his blood that had been hot only the moment before.

"I know you saw me," she whispered, leaning into him. She pressed against him and put his hand on her waist. "I know you watched." She began to lead his hand up toward her breasts, but he jerked it away. She smiled at him then, but only her mouth smiled. She lifted it toward his and took his lower lip between her teeth.

Yamma was not surprised when he jerked his head away and pushed her aside. And so she only barely stumbled. That he had treated her roughly pleased her strangely. And it stirred her to revive the expectations she had once had for Madai. She licked her lips, tasting the salt in his blood, and left him with the feline smile never leaving her face. Her body felt hot all over where his hand had been.

She ran her hands over the places, and then she left for the fire to wait for Tiglath.

಄ CஐG ಄

Ido watched. It was like seeing a rabbit just before it steps onto the snare. But the rabbit had not been rabbit-like.

In the instant, it all made sense to her: how Yamma was not afraid, even how Uke had not dishonored her after all. Perhaps he had been a rabbit, too. She felt it physically, sitting in her stomach, repulsion and disgust, enough to chase away her own quaky nerves. Madai had maintained himself well. And he looked angry. Well, he should be. He had rebuffed Yamma; some had not. It was a strange time to remember Laeden. It was a strange time to feel tearful for him. It was, in whole, a very strange time.

All these thoughts carried Ido down the queue, past the last few young men, and gave no time to ready herself for the one who waited at the end. Madai. When she heard her name spoken by his voice she looked up in near surprise at his face. He looked relieved. And that was the look she needed. Certainly she had glimpsed a part of Yamma's soul, Yamma wanting most what was not hers. Had she, herself, not relinquished Tiras? Now it was Madai who would be her love, and she would defend him from all others.

ভেও ভেও ভেও

He reached for her hand. He took her juniper bough with the other, laid it across her shoulders, leaned down and rested his cheek against hers. It was the sign that he had made his choice, that it was Ido, born to Temah, that she was irrevocably his.

Thank the heavens it was over. Madai gripped Ido's fingers, not thinking he might hurt them, and turned what he hoped was a face of confidence toward her. He would trust she had not seen Yamma. No, Ido did not look angry. She looked young, though. She looked pristinely untouched in her white deer wedding robe, with warmth in her eyes. O, his father had been right.

There had come no snow tonight; the sky was clear, and lighting up with stars. It was going to be bitter cold. Still, there was a boar roasting on coals. Madai did not feel hungry for boar. And he was slightly afraid of Yamma; there had been something in her eyes. He gripped Ido's hand.

"Come with me," he whispered quickly, and started to pull her out of the light made by the fire and toward his new lodge.

ভেও ভেও ভেও

Ido knew where Madai was taking her. The Joining was not over; there was boar to eat, and the cup of mead to pass between themselves. Though, somehow it encouraged her that Madai took her hand so firmly in his and was taking them away with a strength of will. The most important part was over anyway. She had become wife to him when Toban proclaimed their flesh one. They could eat tomorrow, and drink the mead, too.

But the thrill did not carry itself inside when they came to the heavy outer door; because when Madai pulled aside the oxhide hanging behind the door, they were alone. The trappings of a party were behind them and no one would dare follow them here, here where it was just Madai again, where it was real.

Madai felt Ido's hand keenly. She was breathing rapidly, and he had heard her quietly laughing when he spirited her away. He wondered if they were discovered missing yet. Most likely. It inspired him, gave him an air of daring. He turned around, glad that Ido had shared in the rebellion, but her face stopped him cold. She looked terrified. At her look, Madai felt his coursing blood cool. He lightened his hold on her. He was disappointed in a way, and yet it suited his expectation of her, that she be more a young doe than a she-cat.

Even at that, he was not really prepared to be alone with a frightened girl and did not know what to do beyond what he hoped would eventually happen. There was nothing cooking in the fire, so they could not bide the time eating. Perhaps there was something to drink. He looked around and then, with brilliant inspiration, decided to talk.

"This," he said with a circular roll of his head, "is for you."

Her face was steadily climbing with color. She thought she smiled at him then, but she wasn't sure. She was glad for the distraction of looking at what had been prepared for her. There were his arrows and bows and lances. There was her own cooking pot, a gift from Kiellet made at no small sacrifice, and the weaving loom where Naru had trained her fingers to make a length of cloth or a wool blanket. And there was the pile of skins that would be their bed. There was the 'Virgin' weaving. It made her blush a furious red.

But she took a deep breath before she looked back at him. "It is well done, Madai," she whispered.

Even that small degree of encouragement hefted Madai's confidence a bit. He started to answer and discovered how dry his throat was; he really did want something to drink. But he was now afraid to let go of her hand, not knowing how to retrieve it later if he did.

"I am thirsty," he heard himself say. It was probably the right thing to do, because she smiled then.

"Do you have tea?" she asked.

He just stared. "Well, I don't know," he answered.

She hid her face behind her free hand and started to giggle. Madai did not know what could be funny in that, but it started to be outrageously funny somehow, and they both laughed. They laughed till there were tears streaming on their cheeks. It was precisely what was needed for their nerves and calmed them down, so that when Madai looked at her, she was again the girl he had drawn water for. Yes, he did know her. He reached out cautiously and touched her teary cheek. "I dare not ask my mother," he said.

Ido pulled her hand gently out of his. "Let me look," she answered.

Madai watched her peering into pots, looking for the dry herb that put both strength and flavor into a pot of steaming water and chased away a chill - and might ease them through this night. Or perhaps there was beer somewhere to be found. He had not thought about such things in the preface to their Joining. No, he had not thought about any such niceties at all.

He did find the night's supply of wood. He stoked the fire that had likely been started by his mother, and was certainly glad for that. Ido turned around then, her arms hanging rather awkwardly at her sides. "Nothing," she said.

Madai's mouth turned up with a roguish grin. "They expected us to stay and eat boar, I suppose," he answered.

She smiled back at him. "Yes."

"Should we go back?" he asked, cocking his head toward the door.

The question surprised Ido. She looked at him, standing in the circle of light brought by the night's fire. He did not look ready to pounce on her. He looked like Madai, strong, yes, but also kind. In their month of waiting, she had not missed the obvious, that he was also much admired by all the other girls. And here he stood, as timid as the rabbit. It made her proud again, remembering how he had pushed Yamma away, with no look of secret desire at all.

"You may be at ease," she suddenly said. "We can eat tomorrow." Her voice sounded far more shaky than she wanted. She looked at the bed with its heap of new skins. "Ignorance and inexperience are not the same." She managed to get it out. "I am prepared," she finished, before she lost her nerve.

Madai began to laugh. He saw her standing there, looking like a little girl trying to be brave. "Ido," was all he said. He came across the room to her and put his hands on her shoulders with more tenderness than confidence. "I am no unkind fellow, and no better experienced than you."

Her face felt hotter yet. Her eyes were nearly at level with his, and she kept her head up to see them. They were amused, they were large black pupils ringed with ocean blue. They were both gentle and wildly intense. She lifted her finger to touch the dry blood on his lip.

"Then we learn together," was what she said.

℮ℯ ℮ℯ ℮ℯ

Madai woke because he was cold. It was entirely dark, still the deep of night. He rolled over and reached for the spot where Ido was lying. He would not wake her; even though he was entirely awake, he would only find her for warmth. But she was gone. He sat up in panic and looked toward the only light in the room.

There she was, with an arm-load of wood, like an amateur version of his mother. Piece by piece, she was stoking the fire. She was immersed in the soft fleece of a mountain antelope, and her hair was undone, like a summer cloud in the sun.

"Come here," he said, then quickly added, "it is too cold out there."

He startled her. But she put the last log into the rekindled blaze and straightened her back. If she was not so enthusiastic as he, she did not show it.

And so it was. Cold darkness shut them in earlier each night, and Madai thought that every man should marry in winter.

- 16 -

He might actually have passed it by, if he hadn't been Togarmah. But there was a compulsion driving the man. It had started when he found the remains of a frozen stew on the east side of the river. He had chased away the wolf that found it first and then tracked it. Now he was wearing its teeth.

The pot that held the stew was indistinct. It could have belonged to any of The Family. So he began a miserable job that day, looking for a traitor.

Whoever had brought the food did not come back. But it confirmed Togarmah's conviction that there were betrayers in their midst, and that Uke had probably eaten stew and was alive. It had really started then. Now it finished at the ramshackle lean-to, all but entombed with snow. Togarmah kicked away the frozen pine boughs.

He didn't need to look at the face to know. But he looked anyway. He pushed the dry wolf snout aside. He did it gently, because he had pity for the old man.

Reoan was leaning against the base of the tree that anchored the whole shelter. He was part of the snow drift that had found its way inside. If Togarmah had been a creative man, he would have seen how Reoan's beard had turned to ice and was like a carving cut out of the snow, his craggy face really a part of the tree. But Togarmah had lifted the wolf hood, and was looking where the old hunter's skull was bashed in.

The only thing of mercy here was that Reoan had not died of cold. Maybe he had not even been hungry. Togarmah hoped he had been asleep.

No one ever found the lean-to except Togarmah, and he never told anyone. It was a ghastly thing to do, and sometimes it bothered him, but he had dragged Reoan's body out and left it for the wolves. There was no burying him, and it somehow seemed worse to leave him frozen till the spring, when anyone might find him. A true dishonor to be killed by a son. Reoan should not be remembered that way.

He later wished he had burned him, but then there was the blizzard. It occurred to him how paradoxical it was that the iconic image of Reoan had been his wolf hood, and here he was left for them to scavenge. Togarmah wished he had not thought of that. It seemed, somehow, the last cruelty.

Ido, wife of Madai, was carrying a secret. The spring was upon them with every new life.

And Madai, husband to Ido, had found hunting a new adventure in the entire, a great purpose somehow. Ido always welcomed him home at the end as though he had felled a dragon and not just a fresh stag with a sprout of horn no more than a finger's girth.

The winter was over. Madai deemed it the happiest winter of his life. The Family had all kept as well as he and Ido. Two births came in the dark months, and none were lost, which was an uncommon mercy. It somehow added to Madai's perception that his marriage had started everything new, and that his brush with darkness was long ago and could touch him never again - that life was grand.

When the breeze had only the first smell of spring, they had all started their move toward the sea, where they would make their living on the creatures there and have something new to eat: sea turtles, fish, and mussels. Fresh green sea grass for making baskets was gleaned at the marshes and had a spicy root.

The marshes supported every sort of life. Red-billed, long-legged birds lived there. Night's air chirped with frogs the color of moss, which fed on crickets and waterbugs; the frogs fed the birds, and smaller winged serpents fed upon them all.

It was a nomadic life, moving from season to season carrying their homes with them. It was a life Madai loved, especially now. The sons and brothers of Lemmek had found a place to the North and built their homes there with cold, black rock, permanent, never touching the earth where it was green and new.

But The Family had chosen to keep their old ways, learned at the time of their migration when their forebearers came a great distance, escaping other clans of men, each afraid of one another when their speech became suddenly strange. Civilization was splintered, reaching every part of the earth as far as they could walk or ride or sail. Many were lost along the way to dragon or marauder or some more random thing.

The great migration followed soon after the death of the First Earth, or so chroniclers would say. The First Earth had had the great jolt, spewing fire and gas, quaking mountains and plains, death to all in an assault of water that caused land to separate from land and float away at fractures deep inside the earth, great fragments that were even now still moving. Gone were the great forests which wept of dew, gone the gentle sky, gone the ancient beasts that spoke like men.

This second earth was started afresh. It floated on its foundation of many waters. The men who peopled it did not really grieve what was lost, never having known it, nor scarcely believing what was said of it. They were all modern children, born of one Nua, a distant son to one called, most curiously, the name for dirt. That Nua had been the only one of unspeakable numbers to survive the death of the First Earth was a matter of considerable fear and some doubt. But there remained enough fear that The Family was always diligent, offering the Provider's Portion to Great God on an altar lifted as high from the earth as they could. They were careful to lift their hands as well, and to no other gods, for fear of angering Him, He who commanded both earth and sky, storm and calm.

That was why they had chosen to diminish their own numbers by chasing from amongst themselves a part of The Family who had revived the art of soothsaying. They were scorned and loathed, somewhat feared, and called 'The Banned.' The Banned had decided there were other gods more interesting, certainly less forbidding, entirely more entertaining, and burned their altars to them. The Banned were driven back toward the East and settled where the land jutted out into the great sea. They carried with them a powerful hatred for their brothers. Certainly their loss left The Family's numbers at risk by plague or attack, but the danger of another fatal blow at the Arm of God carried a greater degree of terror.

Madai was hanging his door, thinking how soon he would take it down again and use only the oxskin to block the wind. It was still frightfully cold at night, but that would change soon enough; and they would use the door for a table and eat under the stars.

He could hear his mother. She was beating out the winter's debris from her felt linings. He needed to bring Ido the soft black wool, so that she could comb it and quill it into linings for them, because there were not enough to circle all their lodge and the cold crept in. Well, that would not be for many months more. But the thought led him to worry again about the mammoth. The best felt was made from its wool and mammoth seemed to be growing scarce. They had had to range farther and farther after them. Even the sulfur plains could not always lure in the creatures. Madai looked up at the sky. It was crisp and deepest blue. Early this year. Not that he begrudged the coming of warmth, but perhaps this was chasing the mammoth away. And what would they do without them?

He felt arms circle his waist, and Ido laid her head between his shoulder blades.

"Stop glooming, Madai," she chastised him. "I want to go swimming."

Madai grinned and turned around. He was glad she came nearly to his level, for he could always look into her face.

"We will freeze," he answered, putting his arms around her. "But we could go in there." He indicated their lodge with a look in his eyes that she had come well to know.

She laughed. "The sun will keep us warm," she insisted. "You will go with Tiras after a tapir or a bison, and then whom will I swim with?" She wiggled away from him. "We are so stale. Think how it will feel on our skin."

Madai thought about that. Yes, and they would most assuredly be alone. No one else would be so reckless as to brave the sea today.

୧୦୧ ୧୦୧ ୧୦୧

They found the water turquoise, as clear as crystal to the bottom. There was a place Madai liked, though usually at a warmer time of year, where the cove was hidden, surrounded by a rise of white cliff. There were rocks there that baked in the sun and gave a place to dry.

What still chilled the air some was a light western breeze. It played with the surface of the water and made it glisten and shimmy in the early sun. Beyond the cove, where the sea was free, there was the tide's constant surging, a rhythmic breathing of the earth itself. It was a regular, steady sound Madai loved after the stony grip of winter.

Ido was standing beside him. She was wearing a linen under-dress that he had watched her put on. Over it was a leather apron. That she would really take it off for a swim and a wash was inconceivable. So he watched her make her way to the cove, nearly afraid, despite his usual proclivity for disrobing, that he would have to follow her into the water if she did. She suddenly turned and pointed and drew his attention to the inlet, where there was a school of porpoise.

Ido headed for the water. "Come on," she called as she turned.

Madai watched her go. At times like this he remembered Ido, the little girl. She would jump right in, he knew.

The fish began to swim out of the bay, all but one. It was bright green with glistening sides of bronze in the morning glare. It chattered at Ido and leapt into the air. 'Precisely,' he thought, exactly the encouragement that would seal his fate. He started to come out of his clothes, heading for the beach.

Ido was out of her leather; her linen came next. It was more than the cold that took away his breath.

That she was swimming after a gigantic fish suddenly came to Madai, and it was clear to him that she intended to touch it. The animal seemed to wait for her in the calm before the breaking waves, and then it sprayed seawater from its spout and posed for her with a merry, smiling face.

"Ido!" he called the warning to her. "Wait!"

Of course she couldn't hear him. So he plunged in after her. Even his sudden fear of pointy porpoise teeth could not dispel the impossible cold. He thrashed his arms and legs to catch up, but she had started far ahead of him. He could only look from a distance as his wife came to face the creature, treading water, and reached out her hand. He yelled at her again, but she didn't even turn her head. Instead, he watched with horror as she trailed her fingers across its snout.

At first he thought she was crying out, but then he recognized her laughter. She was laughing at the fish! And it was backing away, gently, as though it understood the frailty of her body. It bobbed its head at her once and sank back into the deep. When it reappeared a moment later, it was a good way from her and chattered again, telling her goodbye, perhaps. It turned and raced across the top of the water then, back toward the open sea.

Ido was still wearing the smile when Madai reached her. She circled his neck with her arms and let him tread water for both of them.

"I told her to keep away when you are casting out the nets," Ido laughed.

"Don't do that again!" he ordered.

"Why not?" she asked with surprise. "There are plenty of fish."

"No," he answered with a measure of seriousness in his voice, "do not go chasing wild things."

Ido cocked her head back. "Were you worried, husband?"

She had that irresistible mirth in her eyes. She leaned her forehead against his, and his attention was instantly redirected to the warmth of her body against his own.

"Let's get out of this sea," he said, already pulling her with him toward the beach. "It is cold."

"But did you see how beautiful she was?" Ido insisted.

Madai didn't answer. He had swum so far so fast in such a chilly bay that he did not even try. But Ido was swimming beside him back to the beach, which was nearly all he wanted.

ഇൽ ഇൽ ഇൽ

They were drying on the flat sandstone where the sun had been making it warm. Madai was watching Ido wind the wet lengths of her hair into a braid. She was covered to her waist, but had left him her breast to see. He put a finger on her, and her flush was not crimson any more, but inviting.

She took his hand and put in softly on her belly. She leaned in to put her lips up to his ear.

"There is someone in there," she whispered.

He drew back quickly and blinked. It took him a moment to think what she could mean by that.

"What?" he asked.

She smiled at him, feeling very wise and womanly. And she nodded.

"Did you not know how a babe is got?" she chided.

He watched her eyes twinkle at him, eyes the color of sky. He put his racing heart against hers and loved her, right there on the sandy rock.

Japhet

- 18 -

A son born at the season of color arrived under the highest expectations. He should be clear of eye and skin, with straight spine and ready lung and hair red as sun. Red hair was known to bring abundance and good fortune. Madai listened to the fire spit, telling himself all that and more. He was reminding himself that Keillet had brought Ido all the clams in purple shells. And Naru had sacrificed all the meadow grain for Ido's last month. And he had brought the heart of a young bear. That was nearly as good as the saber cat.

He should have gone with Tiras.

He looked up at his lodge. It was quiet in there. That meant the last push had not even started. His company had been lucky, and they were the first to return, with the meat of seven good blooded antelope and a tapir. Tiras had not yet come back. They were still somewhere on the plain. He should definitely have gone with Tiras.

He jumped instantly to his feet. There was a sound coming from his shelter that began like a growling bear and ended like a she-cat. He started for the door and was overwhelmed with fear for what he might see. He considered running to the river - there might be some use for water - but he could not decide. So he stood there, waiting for the next time she wrenched out a savage sound. If it had not been the first birthing he had sat through, he would have recognized the cry as pure aggression. Let it not be said that Ido, wife of Madai, brought out the babe with anything but rigorous determination.

ଓଞ୍ଚ   ଓଞ୍ଚ   ଓଞ୍ଚ

"Take him, Madai," she whispered.

Madai could not take his eyes off the red-faced, screaming boy. He watched his own bow finger come close, with all its callous and broken nail, to touch the wet black hair.

"Do not be afraid," she coaxed.

His mother laughed. "You must cut the cord, Madai," Mineo insisted, giving him the elk-rib knife. "Here, lay him across your knees."

Mineo helped, because Madai had never touched a thing that frightened him more. There was a piece of sinew painted red tied above the cut, and Japhet was finally detached from his mother. Madai watched Mineo give the babe to Naru, who gave him to Ido. He was entirely red, all but his hair, and very tiny, indeed. Ido bared her breast as though it was no immodesty at all and put the child there. The wailing stopped instantly and his first suckling began. Madai was in awe.

捳 捳 捳

The fathers brought in a right thigh of tapir. It was charred to a crust on the outside, but red and rich on the inside. The liver and heart were already in the smoke rising to an upper realm. The fathers had been through it all before, though it may have brought Temah trouble to hear his child in pain. But it was done, and a great happiness. They were one now with a son born, the mingling of their two bloods once more at the coming forth of Japhet, named for the bygone forebearer, patriarch of their clan and revered second only to the ancient father.

They devoured the tapir and enjoyed it as though they had survived a famine, which in fact they had, a famine of children with the loss of so many between their two families. It was the reason Ashkinaz removed the small leather pouch from around his neck. He opened it solemnly and emptied a collection of little round stones into his hand. He laid them out on a square linen cloth that Mineo laid down before Temah and Naru with a deliberate and gentle hand. Temah produced a tiny red stone he had brought from the shallows and held in his palm, then laid it with care beside all the others. Ashkinaz nodded at Madai with a look in his eyes that told more than he would trust his mouth to say at such a time. Then he put his bow finger on the red stone and pronounced:

"Japhet."

Madai felt his breast swell to near pain, seeing the stones that were the chronicle of all his forebearers poured out on the linen, and now the newest red one, brought forth from his own flesh.

"Japhet came by Madai," Ashkinaz began. When he spoke their names, he touched the red stone and another and picked them up and dropped them both back inside the pouch.

"Madai was come by Ashkinaz," he continued, and the same at every next name he spoke, "who was come by Iberes, come by Sru, who was come by Easru, come by Baath, come by Jobhath, come by Javan, come by Japhet, come by Nua, saved by the Great God upon the Sea and was come by Lamak, come by Mathuselah, come by Enoch loved of God, come by Jared, come by Mahalalel well-blessed, come by Kenan, come by Enosh, come by Seth, come by Adam, come by God."

When Ashkinaz finished, the stones were all back inside the pouch. Because his other sons had died with no sons of their own, they were buried with their stones placed inside their mouths, all but Lamak, who could not be found. He would give the pouch to Madai at his own death, and then Madai would carry their generations as he had done.

Mineo thought the custom unkind, to have Lamak's stone cast from the pouch, out to be lost amongst the common dirt; she took it the night he was swallowed in the quake and hid it with her cooking wares. Probably Ashkinaz knew it when he counted them, when it was clear there would not be a body, and he did not ask after it. That was another thing she stored in her heart of love for her husband.

Temah did not have a living son, and at his death the generations of his fathers would lie with him in the earth. That he and Ashkinaz shared the blood of Japhet would be his consolation.

As for Madai, he watched as his father put the pouch around his neck again. The names, he had inked upon his memory, like a clay pot was inked with beautiful designs traced in the bile of purple sea snails. The tracing and keeping of blood history was uncommonly important to them, a fastening cord that stretched back to the First Earth and the speaking of the first life.

Madai felt tied now to all the forebearers, tied by Japhet. He got up from where he had sat watching Ashkinaz speak his son's name into the pouch and went to where Ido and Japhet were now asleep. He put his mouth on Ido's brow and smelled her in and kissed her with his lips and vowed her his ever-keeping love and safeguard.

෮෮෩ ෮෩ ෮෩

Over the months, Japhet's soft little baby hair turned completely white, like a quail chick's, and never came red. But it didn't need to. He was fat and round and jolly and utterly healthy. Madai made him little arrows. Ido painted them red. And then she tied a little tail of fur and shells to the miniature bow. She had to laugh when Madai gently tested it, and then she was surprised, though she hid it, when the tiny bent length of yew actually worked.

- *19* -

When Japhet came a year from his birth, their lives changed forever.

It was the season of color once again. The previous winter had been short; it had been kind to the caribou and to The Family. The river had scarcely slept till it thawed at its center and was engorged with melted snow. The summer was a-plenty, and they were not prepared for what was coming.

It was a man. He came into their camp minus his fingers. His head was not covered with the face of any beast's skin, nor was it covered much with hair. What hair he had was brittle, ragged, dirty and the color of starvation.

The husband of Kael found him first and brought him to sit at their fire. And then he asked that Madai keep him and Ido dip him soup from her pot, as Kael could not bear him. Ido thought it strange that her friend should turn away comfort from one who was crippled and nearly dead, till she saw the face of him.

His tongue was bitten nearly in two, and so it took much study to decipher what he was trying to say. He was asking for food, of course; they should have known. Eating and sleeping, however, was soon followed by a sudden incoherent raving. Barren silence followed that. So they sent him to Ashkinaz, for caution of Japhet, but not before they had found, through the troubled, ruined flesh, the piteous face of Laeden.

Mineo had been sent to Ido, where Naru had also come. There the three women would take the night and leave to their husbands the fate and care of Laeden, who had become both a stranger and harbinger of unnamed dread to them. Their naturally generous characters were stilled by it.

ଔଔ ଔଔ ଔଔ

Laeden was sobbing. It was a piteous sound, a lake loon cawing after the fox has found her nest, or a wolf when its mate is dead. Such sounds from a man. Madai listened to his weepings with a real variance of heart and mind, a dreadful sight, true enough, but brought upon himself. He watched Laeden's hands twitching where his fingers should be. There was a burn on the back of his skull. It was a mark with a design in it, raised and scarlet, badly healed. All Laeden's hair was gone there. Madai resolved a part of his conflict and kindly covered the ragged scalp with his own cap.

Laeden stopped then. He turned his face toward Madai; he swiped his paw across his eyes and blinked. Madai thought he saw in them a flicker.

"Mashai?" he whimpered.

Madai put his hand on Laeden's shoulder. "Laeden," he answered.

Laeden ducked his face away. Madai thought he would succumb again to more weeping, but he began in a muffled, shuffling voice.

"Fo-give... fo-give..." he pleaded.

Madai was overcome with pity at that and nodded, though Laeden could not see it, and tightened his hand on the man's shoulder. "Yes, Laeden. "

Laeden's shoulders began to shake with fresh passion. He sniffed and hunched up his back, wiping his face again, and tried to pull himself up straight.

"What has come upon you, Laeden?" Ashkinaz's voice was measured. "Where is your father?"

At the question Laeden's eyes changed again. They lost their man quality and he was gone once more in some private storm. He seemed to shrink back down and tried to pull on Madai's cap, as if he would crawl inside it... but of course his fingers were gone.

CʒCʁ CʒCʁ CʒCʁ

"What do you think?" Temah asked.

Ashkinaz grunted. "Uke," was all he said. He sighed and shook his head. "We will not see Reoan again."

"No," Temah replied. "But has Uke found The Banned, do you think? " He nodded his head toward Laeden. "Uke would not have done this - not alone."

Laeden lifted his head at Uke's name and began to whimper.

"Shey aa coming," he moaned.

The men were startled when Laeden began to talk again. Madai leaned in toward him, but it was Tiras who asked, "Who, Laeden?"

Laeden looked at his old friend with rolling eyes. It was clear that their recognition was gone. "Shey aa coooming," he crooned.

"The Banned?" Tiras prompted. "Is it The Banned?"

Laeden let his eyelids droop, and then he closed his eyes all together. He sniffed. "Shey aa coooming," he repeated, this time with a hint of amusement in his voice.

"What do they want?" Madai demanded of him.

Laeden turned his face toward the sound of Madai's voice. Madai was close enough to trace the blue veins under his dry, pale skin and close enough to look into Laeden's eyes. They seemed to be lifting from a fog with startling and sudden intensity. But they did not know him or beg forgiveness again.

Madai felt a shiver trace down his back.

Laeden's shoulders began to shake, and he began to chuckle. He turned his head like a cunning mongrel and looked at Madai across his shriveled shoulder. He didn't speak, and yet Madai watched as the eyes inside Laeden's skull shone at him with unveiled hatred. He felt sweat spring up on his palms even as cold descended down from his scalp to the root of his spine.

"Tell me what they want," Madai heard himself demand, as to a stranger.

Laeden's smile began to twist slightly, and Madai flinched. He jerked back.

"Waa shey waaam... shey wii ge," Laeden slurred and, despite his inability to clearly speak, he was still smiling.

"Kill him," Togarmah suddenly demanded.

Laeden flinched at that. His face lost its bravado and he hunched his shoulders around his head the way a turtle disappears into its shell.

"It was decided," Togarmah insisted.

"Yes," Ashkinaz affirmed. "But look at him."

"Are you a woman, Ashkinaz?" Togarmah's voice carried as much puzzlement as it did scorn.

Ashkinaz didn't answer. It was Toban who put a settling hand on Togarmah's arm.

"We need to know what Laeden can tell us," he reasoned.

"How his soul was stolen along with his fingers?"

"Yes."

Togarmah silenced what he wanted to tell, never forgetting his pledge to the old hunter, Reoan, but he did inquire, "Can It be believed?"

Madai was feeling his heart pound from the pit of his belly. That was all that he felt of himself except the cold skin of sweat that sat upon his upper half. He rose from the crouch he had assumed to back against the wall. And he, too, wondered if It could be believed; somehow he feared that It could.

೮೪೦೩   ೮೪೦೩   ೮೪೦೩

In the end, they were afraid to kill him. They wanted something of greater value than Laeden's lifeblood - what he knew. They were uncommonly afraid of The Banned, even Ashkinaz. And Togarmah came to want a greater revenge than the blood of the pawn. But Laeden seemed to sink into madness and could not tell them more of what he warned.

Though the men who had met together that night did not expressly divulge what was heard, their manner was noticed. And for a time an unsettling spread throughout the village, a fear of phantasms and specters. And the vigil that began that very night continued through the autumn.

Laeden himself eased toward the unremarkable, slowly fattened, a benign, if piteous imbecile. As It did not expose itself again, all but Togarmah and Madai slowly lost the image of him spitting out mockery with a crooning, mangled tongue.

The Family began to feel safe again with the encroaching promise of cold and snow. It had always been a fortification, guarding them like a womb inside their winter's valley. The journey to that valley began at sunrise. They left a scattering of ash and blackened bone atop the altar that had smelled up their last night on the summer coast, an incongruity of stink and perfume. Toban's portables were carried by Laeden, who had been slowly reclaiming fat and muscle in the leader's lodge. He had always been a strong boy. He had even begun to grow his hair back, all but where the brand was burned into his skull. But that was now covered by the red fox Toban had given him to ward off the cold - or to blind the devil's eye.

ഇരു ഇരു ഇരു

At the Heap Altar, they made their first camp, as they had always done, and reached that accustomed stop with commendable speed. There were already, before the fall of night two grouse and a yearling sow atop the altar to beg with their wafting smoke another day's safe travel. Then with blinding surprise the bloodletting began.

Madai knew in the instant that 'shey haa cooome.' He turned his skiff, already emptied of its nightly necessities, over on his wife and son. And then he found his spear. There was the sound of arrows through the air and a surprised yelp of pain at the camp's outer rim.

"Patta!" he heard himself cry.

Ashkinaz was instantly beside him with his own weapons, still dressed, as though he had expected them.

Madai thought at first that they were truly fighting demons. They seemed to come invisible out of the night. He scarcely had time to recognize The Family's first casualties, shot through with painted arrows and sprawled out in their own beds or slumped over their own last cooking fires. But his brain seemed to calculate without his demanding it that their own numbers had been diminished by five.

He lifted his spear and pointed it at gut level, a signal from some primal self in time to impale his first attacker. The man stumbled at his feet, and Madai had trouble tearing the weapon out of his belly. A second was at him with a hand knife. He saw his own arm opened up like he would cut a fish, though without a sensation of pain. He wrestled with his spear, a worthless disadvantage at close proximity, and dropped it. In one instant he let go the spear's oak staff and grabbed for the man's wrist in the other, a time quick enough to stop a second stabbing. But the man's momentum took them both to the ground. Madai was face to face with him, and on the underside.

Madai pushed back with the strength of an ox, never mind his bleeding arm or the stench of the man. He heard a roar come out of his own mouth and twisted the man's entire body to the side. Then he was on top, the knife wrenched loose and in the dirt. He pushed his forearm across the enemy's throat to force the life out of him.

When it was done, Madai grabbed for the knife. He spun off the body and came to his feet. But the fight was over as suddenly as it had begun.

"Patta!" he called again.

"Here!" came the answer.

They looked for each other, and then for the other men, Tiras among them, with puzzlement that it was so soon over. There were the first five of The Family dead, and none others, but only their enemy. Madai knelt down at the second man he had killed and and his question was answered. The night hid their features, but not their circumstance.

They were invisible because they were painted black. They were both naked and nearly down to the bone. So came their easy defeat. Madai stood up.

"They are wretches," he muttered.

Ashkinaz suddenly bolted back toward the center of camp. He stumbled across a body, its limbs splayed in all four directions, but it hardly slowed him. He ran till he reached what he was looking for: Mineo like a sentinel with a javelin in her hands, protecting Madai's upturned skiff. Madai was quick beside him, just a pace behind. He rolled the sled up and off in the half-beat of his heart to find, still safe, his only treasures.

"A diversion," he proclaimed, while at the same time lifting her up from the ground. He heard his mother behind him, saying something.

"What did you see?" Ashkinaz was asking Mineo.

"They were in the camp," she whispered, and she trembled.

捴 捴 捴

The night had been well chosen. A covering of cloud undulated across the sky, extinguishing the stars. Madai was sure The Banned had come to take their women again, but there were none found missing. Even Yamma was in her camp. It was not till the next morning, having kept watch through a sleepless night, that they found what had been raided - all their summer's store of meat.

What was left them was in their cooking pots. Madai was chewing a piece of antelope while looking across the smoke at Toban's camp. He was there with his two wives, their two sons and Laeden. The eldest of his wives was adding a root to her pot. Their breakfast must have emptied it. Somehow Laeden was a culprit; Madai was convinced. He chewed some more, all the while watching Laeden, who was, in fact, returning Madai's gaze with a surprisingly lucid eye.

Japhet squealed. Ido laughed at him. She put her hand on Madai's thigh.

"Are you glooming again, husband?" she asked.

Madai looked away from Laeden. He swallowed his meat.

"You will go hunting," she continued, "and we will go on to the valley. Stop your worry."

"How do we leave, and you unguarded?" he asked.

She tapped her fingers absently on his leg. "Not unguarded, Madai."

He smiled at her despite himself and looked down into his bowl again. The soup was nearly gone. He felt an unsettling, and it was not just the stealing of their food. It was, a shameful admission even to himself, that he had never before killed a man. He had felt the life go out, and that felt... more than killing an animal. Even The Banned, though they had struck first with a mind to kill them quickly and then kill them slowly.

Madai tried to recall the terrors he had heard of those banished brethren, even what he had seen himself, what they had done to Laeden, what they had made of him. It was all true, and undoubtedly more, besides. But there was something dreadful in it. He, Madai, had become a partner in a profound happening. He had not known it would make him feel so... accountable... somehow.

"Tell me," Ido whispered, leaning forward to look at his face, "what is wrong?"

She was so close. He could smell her. He reached up to touch her; maybe she could make him feel better. But she brushed her lips across his forehead and pulled away.

"Tell me," she coaxed.

Madai was not sure he wanted to tell her. It was so new to him, unexpected, really. And was self-indulgent, besides. There was a great choice to make; should they move on to beat the snows, or should they search for more meat? He decided to tell her that.

"I killed a man," he heard himself whisper instead.

"O!" The sound caught in her throat and she put her arms around him. She laid her head on his shoulder and breathed against his neck. "O."

Madai was just thinking that she would not say anything else when she sat up. There were shining tears in her eyes.

"Of course. But he would have killed you."

Madai nodded. He looked down. "I am a fool," he said.

He was ashamed to look at her, now that he had said it. But he couldn't help himself. She had a tender light in her eyes, and the faintest of smiles. "I love you so," she whispered.

Japhet was waving his arms, still strapped into his bed and starting to squeal again. It was a most inappropriate sound at such a time. But Ido turned away to untie him and lift him out. It was all the little boy needed to make him quiet and start looking for breakfast of his own.

Madai watched her, really starting to feel like a woman because it made his eyes water. She sat on the ground and supported Japhet on her knee and dropped the fold of her dress for him to nurse. It was a comforting sound for Madai as much as for the boy.

"God knows," she suddenly said.

"What?"

"That you only killed them because you had to."

"O."

"They are for Him now."

"Hmm," Madai mused. He put down his bowl of stew.

She looked away from her son with a soft, full smile. "It should bother to kill a man."

Madai slowly nodded. "I... just didn't expect..." He let it go at that. He had noticed, in fact, that he often did not have to say it all for her to understand. That helped, especially now.

"I am glad it matters to you, husband." She had a pleasing way of calling him that. She readjusted Japhet in her lap. Then she looked at him with a wise look for being not yet twenty years. "Mighty God may ease you," she said. "I will ask Him to. But likely He would not want it an easy thing." Then she smiled again. "I know you will be always kind, and never cruel." She leaned forward, squirming babe and all, and kissed his lips.

He felt stirred. O! Love is grand! What can stand against it? Of lost meat, it can be got again. Of coming winter, it can be raced and won. Of treachery, it can be fought.

☙☙ ☙☙ ☙☙

It was a pretty picture. Laeden poked a piece of stringy meat into his mouth with the stub of his thumb and watched.

- *20* -

They decided to go hunting. There were still ochre-colored leaves on the trees and warmth in the air. Even with a delay to re-supply their food, they could still make the valley before the snow. Togarmah wanted to chase The Banned, but Toban decided they could not spare three parties. One must assuredly keep watch of the women, and one must find a four-footed herd. The two-footed kind were probably on the river by now, and hunters could not catch them if they were. A deer was easier prey, and more savory, in more regards than only one.

Madai had no appetite for killing another man. It had proved a surprising trouble to his mind and to his soul. They had removed the bodies, only to find them both starving and with mottled flesh beneath the dark paint. It was pitious and dreadful. The ones staying would bury them.

Madai was anxious to go after better game. He left with seventeen others, Tiras among them.

Ashkinaz remained behind to keep watch against another attack, although it was unlikely. Toban and Temah stayed, as well, with others of the older men who could not run quite as fast after a herd but yet had a strong, rehearsed and reliable aim. Madai and his fellows left before first light, chasing the elk that were eating up the last autumn grass.

The cows were free from their nursing calves. They were anxious to rebuild a layer of fat and had noses buried in drying meadows. The herd was somewhat complacent, being disciplined through the years to a certain rhythm. They were cautious in summer, and somewhat less so in autumn, when smelly men were busy heading toward the valley. In the end, in this certain season, that very learning helped it all turn out rather well for the men.

Madai was nearly laughing at himself, that he should have been so worried. Certainly they would take another week to smoke and dry the flesh before they could move on, and they would need an especially bounteous harvest of caribou in the early winter, but by the Arm of Mighty God, they would survive. That He had already protected and provided was proof enough of that. So great was Madai's assurance that he made a secret sacrifice of his supper to Mighty God as a sign of thanks.

CRCR   CRCR   CRCR

Ido laid Japhet down. He was easy to wake, now that he was older, and especially at night when he wanted to play. It was a careful exchange from her breast to his bed, where she would tie him in for the night. Tonight he settled peacefully. She ran her finger gingerly along his cheek, moving a yellow curl. She thought she could look at him all night and never be tired of it.

They had only put up lean-tos, planning the shortest stay possible here while the men hunted. Ido sighed. It had been such a good summer, and they had had such a bounteous supply for the winter. She leaned down to graze Japhet's head with her lips. 'Why were they starving?' she wondered of The Banned. They had once been a part of The Family and knew how to survive. Perhaps it was something to do with the red welts that traced along their flesh. Or perhaps the place they had come to live across the great sea was not good for game. But they had been gone a long time, and had only now come back for thieving. She didn't understand, but she was uncommonly glad they had not come for anything else.

She thought about going to see her mother. She wished she could; she hated it when Madai was gone, especially the first night. But she certainly wouldn't risk waking Japhet. 'I should have thought of it before,' she scolded herself. 'Perhaps Mamam will come to see me.'

Then she heard a soft foot-fall. She turned with the happy smile of someone whose prophecy has come to pass.

"O!" she exclaimed.

Laeden was not really looking at her face, but at something just beyond her, as if he were shy.

"I-yo," he whispered immediately. He inched himself under the lean-to, trying to pull his eyes to look at her, but they came only as far as her shoulder. He had always been of ruddy complexion, but it seemed now that his face was aflame, kindled first by his red-tinted hair and next by the blood pounding upward.

Ido backed toward Japhet, nearly imperceptibly, perhaps enough to disguise her alarm even from Laeden who, after all, passed his days a simpleton. But she saw it in his eyes. They flinched, as she had flinched. She wanted to reach out to him, a kindly gesture, but she had other duties first.

"I-yo," his voice held a measure of pleading, "issom, issom pees. I wii yyot hurr you."

There were actual tears in his eyes that he did not try to hide. "I hurry before iii comes."

She glanced behind him, frightened of what he was frightened of, and then put a hand on Japhet's bed.

"Iii ish iii shey skiii."

She shook her head. She couldn't understand him. He pulled at the skin on his arm.

"Yes, Laeden?" she finally spoke, hearing her voice as pinched as a field mouse in a snare. "Skin?"

He nodded frantically. He closed his eyes and swallowed, tears spilling down his face. "You were goooo sho me. You aaaa goooo." He started to reach for her, but he could not avoid the look of his hand, and flinched again and dropped it back at his side.

She was relieved; a quiver ran down her spine as she took a shuffle back to touch Japhet's bed with her leg. She stood, fixed purposely between them. She thought about crying out; Ashkinaz and Mineo slept very near, but that would be foolish, surely. Laeden had lived these months amongst them, with Toban, and never bothered. In fact, he had provided a strong back all the day while the ones who stayed behind had put up these shelters. She calmed herself, and then she allowed herself the liberty of really looking at him. He had put flesh back on his bones. His face was not hollow, not even his eyes. In fact, they were the deepest pits of remorse. She felt chastised by them. She suddenly wanted to ask him why he had done it; and then, as quickly, it didn't seem to matter that much.

"What happened to you, Laeden?" The question escaped her throat full of compassion. She reached out to take the bulbous remains of his hand that had so unsettled her a moment before.

He only watched her; and the tragedy was that there was Laeden, fully aware. He only needed to chuckle and it would be Laeden of old.

"Sheeeriba, sheeeriba shings," he whispered. "Shey aaa sheeriba." He closed his eyes. "Eeeviia," he shuddered.

Ido was glad she could not understand him as she watched his eyes roll behind his eyelids. She thought he was going to lapse away from her. She closed her fingers more tightly around his hand, as if it would keep him.

"Laeden," she prompted. "Why have you come here?"

It seemed an effort for him to look at her again. It seemed as though he were afraid of her as he pulled his hand away and seemed to hug himself. That look of his eyes was back, and it frightened her again. And then she began to understand that he was not afraid to touch her; it was something else he was afraid of. If it were not so unlikely a thought, she would say he was trying to hold himself from flying apart. She reached out again and put her hand on his arm. He was trembling.

She was a mother, and she suddenly wanted to mother him. He was a true orphan, and so pitiful. So she stepped toward him to hold him. He shrunk away instantly, his eyes suddenly warning.

"Uuo," he whispered, shaking his head. "Iiii wiii come."

Ido felt a chill trail down her skin. But Laeden appeared to have brought himself back by some sort of urgency.

"Shere ish shikesh."

Ido frowned.

"Shikesh," he repeated. "Shikesh." He held his stomach and doubled over. "Shikesh."

"Sickness?" she asked him, and he nodded vigorously

"Iiii shey skiii," he added, striking his arm.

"What kind of sickness, Laeden?"

Laeden looked at her sorrowfully. He let his gaze stray for the first time toward Japhet's bed. "She shikesh wiii kiii." He finally said. "Maaaay."

"What?" she asked.

"Who shouches shem wii she shikesh wii shi, maybe yesh, maybe uuo... annn who he shouches wii shi, maybe yesh, maybe uuo. Burr boshys. Burr."

She shook her head at him. "What?" she asked.

Laeden pointed at the fire. "Burr... burr boshys." He suddenly struck himself in the chest and in the belly. He began to tap, tap the stump of his arm on the side of his head. "Burr boshys." He pleaded.

"Burn their bodies?" Ido asked him with surprise.

He stopped hitting himself. His forhead relaxed and he opened his eyes again. Then he allowed the wisp of a smile and nodded.

"Shorry, shorry, I-yo." He reached out. He touched her arm with the end of his palm. It felt soft to her.

He held his eyes on hers a goodly long time. She read the deepest of sorrow in them. Many things flashed from his depths at her in the dimness of the temporary lean-to. She did not have the experience to understand them, but they made her cry. And that made Laeden slowly back away. He allowed an ambivalent, fleeting smile again and hesitated. He let his eyes search the kind corners of the lean-to, rested a gaze on Japhet's bed a moment...and left.

Ido felt as though she should try to stop him, bring him some comfort. But she let him go and felt both a wrench and relief at the same time, watching him disappear back into the shadows. He left a heaviness behind that threatened to break her heart for him. Instinctively, she went to Japhet and picked him up, never mind waking him, and wrapped him up in her arms. She buried her face in his baby curls, not for his comfort, but for her own.

- 21 -

Once again, as it had been done in all their seasons past, they were coming home. Madai was anxious to finish the distance, bringing Ido the best of his efforts. They had been successful. It was enough, and more, to see that they would not starve.

It was the first time he had not hunted beside his father, and Tiras the same. The older men had both stayed behind to keep watch against The Banned. But there had been no sign of their doubling back. In fact, he and Tiras had followed their trail a way just to be sure and found it ending at the river, where ther were signs of boats slid from the shore and into the current. Madai readjusted the load on his back. But why had they risked it? He couldn't help but wonder. It would surely have been as easy to simply hunt their own food. No, it was not only about the meat. That was what was bothering him.

His legs burned. It had been a long trek, loaded as they were. He stretched his neck to ease his muscles. The leaves were blowing way up in the trees. He watched the way the branches moved with the wind, great distances back and forth above him. The sound was comforting. Not so great a howl as would bring the storms, but the steady reassurance that a new season was coming; life was moving on, and they were coming home. Home was always where Ido and Japhet were.

ଔଓ ଔଓ ଔଓ

There was a faint smell in the air. It was the smell of a sacrifice... nearly. It quickened Madai's feet ever so slightly, as he was the first to sight the little community waiting for them. Someone had killed something and it was offered up for their success, certainly. But when he looked aside to the Heap Altar, there was nothing on it.

He frowned.

But Ido was coming, and she was carrying Japhet. The sight never failed to set his heart racing. It made the pack on his back all the more cumbersome. Kiellet was meeting Tiras. They were back, and with good results.

Ashkinaz began to untie Madai's burden.

"Elk," Madai sputtered, slightly out of breath. "We came upon them the second day."

He stretched his back as Ashkinaz dropped the elk quarters to the ground. "The Mighty One was with us," he finished with a fast grin.

"And The Banned?" his father asked.

Madai was not ready to think about The Banned. He shrugged. "We followed them to the river. They are gone."

"Good," Ido proclaimed.

Madai smiled at her, but she did seem troubled, and trying to hide it.

"What has happened?" Madai heard himself ask. He was thinking of the smell again.

"I should help..." Ido insisted mildly, meaning the elk flesh that was long since drawing flies.

"Take him home, Ido," Mineo argued. "He needs some food and some rest." But she gave Ido a look full of question.

Ido watched as Ashkinaz took Madai's load. He pulled it as easily as a young man to the smoking racks she and Mineo had prepared. And there was Kiellet with Tiras. Little Naru had his hand, chattering away. Finding out terrified Ido. And telling her own tale was the last thing she wanted to do. Let it only be a common coming home.

୧୬୧ୠ ୧୬୧ୠ ୧୬୧ୠ

Madai took a drink out of the pot above the fire. Ido had a flavor of meat in there, saved no doubt for him. He watched her taking Japhet to the bed and giving him a colored stick.

"Let your Patta eat, my boy," she instructed.

So Japhet turned his attention to the stick with the eager gladness of boys a year old.

Madai watched her. There was something on her mind as surely as flies on that meat. But he was finding himself extremely hungry. He drained another bowl.

"What did you put in this?" he asked with juice trailing down his beard.

She smiled. "Antelope."

"Someone's vest?" he asked.

"We were not so starved as that," she laughed. "Some dried I had. And Togarmah brought a deer. We all divided it."

Madai nodded. "Good," he said. "So that is the smell in the air?"

He watched her flinch. She looked away a moment, toward the forest and back at their child. She shook her head.

"I thought not," he muttered.

She put her finger to her lips and came to stand very near him. Her look was so changed it frightened him. He wrapped his fingers around her arm.

"What is it?" he asked.

"Laeden came to me," she began, and felt his hand tighten around her. "He warned us to... dispose," she looked down, "to burn their dead."

"Ah," Madai nodded. "Yes. Was it terrible?" he asked, relieved.

She nodded. "They were, under their paint... with pestilence," she whispered.

Madai believed his heart stopped. He swallowed. "You did not touch..."

She shook her head. "They burned them where they lay. Only," she looked up at him, "you piled them up."

A gasp of air escaped his chest. "O!" he exclaimed. "Is that it? But I am fine. Look at me. Do you see anything?" He opened his vest.

She traced her hand across his skin, then took his arms and studied them.

"Would you like to see the rest of me?" he suddenly asked, chuckling.

She didn't answer. But relief instantly remade the lines around her mouth. She blinked her eyes closed, though not before a tiny shimmer of wet showed on her lash.

"Ido?"

'O, let me breath this peace,' she was thinking. But she said with an effort, "Laeden." A ghastly look was returning to her eyes when she opened them.

"What?"

"The Banned left a terrible rot on his soul." She felt the chill again. "When the fire was lit for burning them, we burned it ever so hot. He started to croon, a terrible song." She put her hands on Madai again and gripped his open shirt. "He was babbling. Toban tried to pull him away and," Ido paused. "And Laeden struck him," she trembled. "To the ground. He was babbling at Toban, looking at him laying there. We couldn't understand it, but it was a terrible sound. And then he started to laugh. He laughed like a beast, Madai, and - " She put her face against him. "And he just jumped into the fire," she finished in a whisper.

Madai was stunned.

"No one could pull him out. It was so hot."

He felt her tears on his skin.

"Terrible sounds."

He tightened his arms around her. He wanted to shield her like a baby from what she had seen. He suddenly lifted her, as light as a bird, and carried her to the bed where Japhet was jabbering. Japhet looked at him with the wonderful face of a little boy at play.

"Mamam." He enunciated the word with devotion. Madai scooped him up and put him beside his mother.

"Mamam," he repeated and squirmed, trying to get back down.

"Yes, Japhet. Your Mamam." He kissed Ido on the mouth, "Your sweet Mamam." He straightened his back. "Do you want to find your second Mamam?" he asked, speaking of Mineo.

Japhet nodded joyfully.

"No, Madai," Ido stopped them. "Make him stay here. It worries me."

He looked back at her, all the while closing his fingers around Japhet's little wrist. "You do worry," he said. Japhet began to fuss.

"No!" he said, turning to the boy.

Japhet instantly stopped. A boy learned early to heed that certain tone.

"Would that we had finished them all the winter past," Madai whispered his thought. "It has brought us... this trouble."

102

Ido was regaining her color. "Do not worry over me. I'm better, now that it is told. And you are not come home unwell."

"I am not come home unwell," he assured her. "I will show you so tonight."

She smiled at that. She gave Japhet a second stick to bang against the first one, vaguely knowing these things would not keep him entertained very much longer. And there was so much more she needed to ask. Then she smiled at Madai again, as he was watching her.

"What?" he asked.

She wished she were as settled as he was. But he had not heard what she had heard. She would never hear fat in the fire again without thinking... She shook her head.

"Laeden was not an evil man." She ventured.

"Laeden was a fool."

"But not evil."

Madai was not so sure. He shrugged. "He is dead."

"Yes," Ido breathed. "That is the trouble."

Madai only looked at her with that wonder one feels at seeing something indiscernable. 'But,' he reasoned with himself, 'she did not see the turn of Laeden's eyes.'

"Perhaps Laeden had been gone long since," he said.

That surprised her. "What do you mean by that?" Ido challenged him. There were things about men that she could not understand. "He was Laeden," she finished, her voice beginning to rise.

"He turned against the Mighty God when he followed The Banned," Madai announced.

"He was deceived."

Madai looked at her. "He was not deceived," he argued. "Laeden chose. There is terrible... power with The Banned." He watched her expression remain unchanged. "You don't know," he finished.

"Yes," Ido nodded, "I know. Tis true."

Her eyes were so blue, so much like Japhet's who did not see an evil. He touched her cheek. "It is a power that you do not know, Ido."

"Of course I know it."

He heard a touch of annoyance in her voice.

"I saw it," he continued. "Before we were joined. I saw them in the forest."

"O!" her lips formed the word more than she spoke it.

"Patta knew." Madai would not look away. "I told him after you and Kael were taken."

She didn't answer, but she watched the trouble come to his eyes.

"And I felt the power with them." Now Madai looked away. "Even after. I felt it... enter me." He looked at her then, because he had to. "The way it entered Laeden."

She tilted her head to study him. He looked as though he were caught trying to slide on the ice before it was safe, a ten year old, found out and waiting for his Patta. It filled her with such joy! To have such a husband! She took his hand and put it on her knee and fondly patted it.

"You are too noble, husband. You were stung," she simply said. She cut her eyes toward the sky. "It is marked there, is it not? A scorpion stings. Sometimes it kills, sometime it doesn't. But it leaves a welt and hurts of hell." She leaned toward his mouth. "Let me pull the stinger out," she said with a smile.

Madai would have liked to leave it that way. But it had finally been broached and he was afraid he could not do it again.

"It has been a long time since I have felt seen," he admitted.

She stopped, her lips just touching his, and backed away.

"Why, that isn't true, Madai!" she answered tightly. "It is a lie!"

She was always surprising him.

"You have killed a man, two men, and been undone by it. You have never forgot to set aside the Provider's Portion, and..." she had a growing intensity in her voice, "I have seen your face before the altar." She stopped talking and watched him. She felt a rising indignation in her own soul. "When you hear the voice of the enemy lie to you, you must recognize it."

If a voice can echo in the open air, Ido's voice echoed. He heard it come into his ears and plunge down into his belly and up again to his brain. Deception may, perhaps, carry many faces.

"The serpent carries a madness," he whispered. "Laeden was mad."

"Lies will make you mad," his wife told him. "You are a good man. You are seen of God."

He looked at her, feeling in an instant the glooming lift. Yes, he had felt seen of God. He knew he had... now. It had come back with her. He started to reach for her when he was stopped by the look on her face.

She lifted her hand, palm up. "He walks among us. I feel Him, Madai," she said.

And seeing her there, he could not doubt it.

- 22 -

The Family carried within its genes a powerful strength, a strength not yet diluted by an age after the deluge. But there are things, unnatural things, that eat away at good genes; and The Banned had feasted on them. It had left them susceptible, scooping up disease, living with it long enough to turn them into man-killers. What they carried into the camp of Toban, they did with forethought, chosing their weakest to draw away The Family's strongest. It was just this misstep that saved Madai from the pestilence, he and the other hunters who had fought them that night. Ido found a reddened rise of skin on Madai's chest and nursed it away in the short span of three days. Ashkinaz had the hide of buffalo for skin and was not afflicted, though some others of the younger men were. They recovered with as little difficulty as Madai.

Madai took it as another sign. They burned an offering on the Heap Altar for that very recovery. And then they found their winter's valley a day before the snows, with enough smoked elk to see them through. In a week's time they would journey to the Sulphur Plains for mammoth, blessed and seen of God.

But before they could leave, the cold came. It was the paralyzing kind of cold Madai remembered of his first mammoth hunt. It seemed to make the earth stop as it did the river. That very cold was just the proper antidote for plague - if it had not come too late.

Those who nursed the first sick, if they were young or weak by any measure, became vessels of warm, incubative flesh. Ido had a second son in her womb. She had known it with the first absence of monthly blood. She was saving it for just the right time to tell... and it had made her just weak enough.

ෆ൰ ෆ൰ ෆ൰

Ido was bent over the loom, just starting a blanket for a little boy who would become an eldest son and brother. She had completed a span of woolen cloth the length of her forearm. It was going to be beautiful. But the tight little rows were making her eyes hurt, and she was starting to feel what her own Mamam complained of in her back. She reached back to rub that soft part above her hip.

Japhet was piling rocks for the hundreth time, little round stones he had stowed with her pots. A heap altar. It made her smile; so Japhet would be like his own Patta, a seeker. Well, they made the best men. Only he didn't keep his first attentions very long. He was snooping around his bed now, looking for... She heard his garbling, chiming little voice say what only she could decipher, "O! Japhet's arrow."

Ido looked away from her weaving to smile and watch him. He scooped up his blunt little sticks, clutched them in fat little fingers and tried for the opening of their shelter, hoping, of course, that he would not be called back. Today, his mother would let him go.

"Can you take him, Madai?" she asked.

Madai had been watching the center of his heart with complete and perfect peace. But it could be time to put those painted little sticks to the bow and let Japhet find his aim. It was never too early.

"The cold has just come," he said, finding Japhet's wooly coat. "It will be all snow soon enough. There is the winter for weaving. Come with us." He had Japhet with one arm and put the other around her. "Come with us."

She leaned against him. It took away that dull throbbing in her head. "Maybe I'll just rest a minute," she said.

It surprised them both.

And that was how it started.

ः ः ः

Her skin was sensitive to touch that night. Madai was disappointed, of course. But he was not worried till the next day, when the first of the rash appeared. They, neither one, named it any other thing than a common sort of unwell.

The next day she was tired. They ate pottage and stew from the day before. That night, the fever started.

Madai woke, dripping with sweat. It was Ido ablaze. She was muttering in her sleep.

"Ido?" he nudged her awake and got up to go for a cup of cold water.

"I'm hot," she whispered, pushing the wooly night robe away.

"Here," he said. "Have a drink."

She took it from him and swallowed. It was cold and wonderful... and sharp, like stones cutting her throat.

He took the cup when she was done, put it beside the bed and lay back beside her.

Her hair was spread out on the ginger-colored bearskin, very like its same color. Her skin was a rosy hue, quite beautiful, really. She smiled at him. It was her last untroubled smile, but he didn't know it then. It was even an inviting smile. But he had started to worry. He reached his arm gently under her head, and she found the familiar resting place. She closed her eyes. He felt it when she went to sleep, and he would listen through the night to her breathing.

In the night, a blizzard came, blowing through the valley. Though it coated the mountains first, it spared a good amount for them. Madai got up before she woke, or Japhet. He had finally come to rest with the boy because Ido had been fitful. He looked outside. At just dawn, the world was elegant with untouched snow. He bent down to take a handful and sucked it through his fingers. He had the disturbing thought that it would be needed for Ido. He looked back at her. She was still asleep, and her face was red. When he touched it, it was dry and hot, and, as was his first intuition, he cooled her forehead with the melting snow.

It was late enough, he reasoned. He wrapped up his child and slipped out with him to remove him to his parent's lodge. Just a precaution, he told himself.

Mineo was only slightly alarmed. "Well enough, Madai," she said with a smile and took the wiggling youngster, who was only too glad to be with his second Mamam. "Make her drink," she added. "And I will come with a broth in a while to have a look."

Ido was still asleep when he came back. When he touched her forehead with the tip of his bow finger, she stirred. She opened her eyes.

"Japhet?" were her first words as she looked at Madai urgently.

"I took him to Mamam," Madai whispered, hoping she would not recognize the alarm he felt.

Instead she sighed, "Good," and closed her eyes.

He wondered if she was going back to sleep, but she started pushing at the night covering. "So hot," she complained.

When Madai pulled them off her, she was warm to the touch. But her face relaxed and she granted him a look of relief. "Better." Her voice was slightly hoarse. She tried to sit up. "Is it cold outside?" she asked.

"Yes," he answered with his hand behind her back, easing her upward.

"I'd like to see."

He could see that the pressure of his hand on her back was hurting her. Still, he wanted to keep it there, just to hold her.

She swung her legs around to touch the ground. "Help me, Madai," she asked him.

'Good,' he was thinking. 'This is a good sign.' But when she tried to stand, she slipped through his arms like a bird falling to earth. He had the instant vision of wings bent upward and useless.

"Ido!"

He was on his knees and reached under her arms. "Ido."

Her head came to loll against his chest, but she was coming awake. "Ooo," she muttered.

Madai picked her up with the uneasy sensation that she was somehow lighter.

"Show me the snow," she whispered. She sounded like Tiras after a cup too much of mead.

"You should be back in bed," Madai argued.

"Please?" she moved her head into the bend of his elbow and looked at him. Her lips were dry as they smiled.

It was easier to take her to the door than to argue with that face. So he did it. He pulled back the ox-hide curtain and pushed the outer door open. It was snowing again, with a new pile started at the bottom. He had to give it a strong push. She made a little sound when he moved with her outside, and he looked down at her.

Giant, round snowflakes were falling on her face. Her eyes were closed and he noticed, as if it were the first time, her almost white lashes thick, curling like fringe in a gentle arc. She had a look of bliss. "Mmm," she breathed.

She opened her eyes then and set them on him gratefully. "Now let's go in," she insisted.

His heart sang with joy. So, she would be better! He took her inside and laid her down. She had her arms around his neck, holding him over her. "Lie with me," she whispered.

He was nearly giddy. Why had he been so worried?

∞℘ ∞℘ ∞℘

That she had flinched a little when he touched her skin, that she had been a little languishing, and that she had wept ever so slightly at the end he put away to only a bit of weakness. His Mamam's broth would put Ido right.

It was the first time he had thought about his mother since taking her Japhet. But he realized she had taken a good while to come. He hated thinking about it. He would rather watch Ido sleep. She had the look of peaceful rest on her face, which she would need to get strong again. How elegant had been their loving, speaking the meaning of words that had not yet been wrought without an effort at all. He was left with the perception of being Ido and giving her his strength. He could will her well.

∞℘ ∞℘ ∞℘

That morning his mother brought the broth. He wondered briefly why she had taken so long at it, but it was here now. Ido sipped at the soup when she woke. It seemed to make her choke, so Madai put it aside for later. It was the last morning he was hopeful.

The fever mounted steadily through the day. Once, when she woke up the second time, a broken look was in her eyes and she muttered, "The babe is dead." Madai put it off to the fever. He would never know.

She ran her tongue across her lips - and it was brown. The water he gave her to drink slid down her chin and pooled in the hollow of her throat. When she fought with her bed clothes, he pulled them off her. Her glorious ivory skin was covered with welts like a red vine.

Madai was paralyzed. His breath caught in his throat with a groan. But he did not weep, because he still had another, last course of attack. His arms lifted without his conscious command, and he lifted his face upward.

"God of heavens," he called out. "Do You see her?" His fingers seemed to stretch, reaching for another realm. "Half that I take will be devoted. There will always be a smoke rising to Your nostrils." Madai waited. He considered that perhaps half was not enough. "All my share of mammoth," he amended. "Whatever You want. Only tell me."

He felt a hand on his shoulder and for a blessed, terrified moment thought it was The God Himself. It was Naru. She smothered a gasp at seeing Ido's body.

"She will freeze, Madai," Naru softly insisted, pulling the bearskin up.

Madai let his arms fall back down to earth. He nodded.

"Will she drink?" Naru was also asking.

Madai watched Ido's mother get a cup of melted snow. She dabbed it to Ido's lips. It seemed to work, and Ido sipped it up with her tongue. Madai had to turn away; her tongue was covered with brown fur now.

Naru nursed Ido through the next night. If she shivered, Naru covered her. If Ido burned, Naru pulled the heavy robes aside and bathed her face with melted snow. Madai let the night pass that way. It was as if a song of some unknown persons were being sung to him, and not himself and Ido at all. He prayed relentlessly, lastly abbreviated to: 'Don't let her die. Don't let her die,' like the sea's regular lapping of the shore. Over and over and over.

ଔଔ ଔଔ ଔଔ

Ido, wife of Madai, had traded places. She was sailing on the snow again. Flying, flying... pelted with ice crystals... laughing, only something hurt her throat when she laughed. The skiff was spinning, taking on wings and whirling into the white expanse of their snowy world. Glorious freedom.

And then she was too near the fire, when the playing was done and they were huddled around it getting warm. She had the most curious sensation of watching it all happen... All of them, around the fire. Tiras was there, as he had always been... Why, there was Laeden! But why was she looking for Madai, the son of Ashkinaz? It confused her. It was Tiras she loved, was it not? But when she saw him... Madai... he was looking at her through the smoke with such a look! And she was filled with such an excruciating love. It made her start to cry.

Her face was suddenly cold again. What was happening to her? All the faces vanished, and she became aware that her eyes were closed. She tried to open them, but they would not obey. She heard voices... and she remembered something about being sick.

"Ido?" From some other place, a voice was stealing through. It was a place where everything hurt. A heavy weight was on her face and cold wet. She opened her eyes to searing pain.

But there was her mother. There was Madai. Now she remembered. It really was Madai she loved. 'I think I am going away, Madai,' she tried to tell him. She remembered Japhet, but no, even he could not keep her here. 'It doesn't hurt there,' she explained. And then, 'Take care of them, Mamam.'

Her Mamam was beautiful and strong. Madai and Japhet would be all right.

Ido closed her eyes. She thought she would like to go snow-sailing again. Everything was white there. And she was lifted back to that white place...but... now there was some One else. "O!" was her last mortal thought.

Book Two

- 23 -

The boat seemed to quiver, a last realignment after the typhoon had done its best to peel away its sides. The stitching was swollen, tighter than a mother's belly, and just as safe. Indeed, it was Madai's womb against the infinite sea, or so it seemed infinite. And Madai, the helpless babe, still asleep, part by fatigue, part by a stray blow to his head, suffered somewhere in the long dark hours. He lay in the bottom of his craft, still lashed to the mast, curled up like a fist with his face turned out of the bilge.

The sea had become as still as it had been turbulent. It was glistening in the sun, a mirror broken only by the man's boat. Madai's face was cooking in the sun, his pale skin a shade of scarlet with swollen lips. There was a lash across his back where he had received a glancing blow from a serpent's tail, a tail infused with a thousand little spines, and each spine erect with a vein of poison. It was fortunate for Madai that he had been lying down and asleep, as he had not resisted, and the spines had stayed embedded in the serpent's skin. He would only feel a burning in the wound, and that would be indiscernible from all his other wounded places.

೮೮ ೮೮ ೮೮

A gull had survived the storm and had found a fortunate spot to rest. The outside of Madai's boat was squirming with sea slugs, and the bird was scurrying to make a feast of them before her other flock-mates could find them, too. If she had only known that some had found the shore already, she would have pecked them up more delicately, for she wasn't really starving.

She eyed the man. He was partly immersed in the seawater trapped in the bottom of the boat. His ankle was swollen where a cord was fixed to it, tied to the splintered mast dripping with lowered sails looking very like folded wings. She cocked her head to the other side and wondered what sort of creature he was. No matter, really; he had afforded her a meal and a place to rest. She snapped up another slug.

Then she noticed the slugs on the man. Her head suddenly tipped to the side, hearing that familiar Voice, the One that told her where to fly before the seasons changed. She would obey, of course, without hesitation, only glad to do it, even if her belly was nearly too full to fly already. She hopped down to the man's shoulder and started to pull off the slugs. Little trickles of blood trailed from every spot the squirming masses had been affixed. She carefully pulled at the leeches and found them even in hidden places, till the man started to move. Well, she was glad for that, because the Voice said she had done enough.

She started to sense the shore. She tried her wings, to find herself just barely able to fly. Then she felt a little breeze blow under her wings. It had never entered her beautiful little bird's mind to deny Him, nor to consider her own end. She only knew it was time to soar, and she smelled Him in the breeze.

Madai opened his eyes. The lids hurt, the sunburn hurt where salt crusted his face like a second scratchy skin and stung, and he was thirsty. He was lying in water, but not what he would think to drink. It stank like... He lifted his face and tried to sit up. Everything hurt. But he was fascinated by the quiet. He looked out over a perfectly calm sea.

He blinked. The day was brilliant after the storm, the sun bright and an immediate source of pain. Madai reached for something to shield his eyes, but everything was floating in a sodden jumble. What was not tied down was probably gone. And then, when he was reaclimated to his body, it hit him like a lodestone - all his dreams.

Madai was first aware of complete and abject loneliness. What had been with him through the sleeping part of the storm was just a scrap in the wind; and this, surely not worth the waking, all open and bloody, without the scab of time.

He sat perfectly still in the belly of his boat, hearing in the still the last echoes of their voices. Beautiful Ido. He closed his eyes, and her face sprung instantly before him. He gasped.

And then that other thing threatened to resurface. Thank the gods he had not dreamed about that last of betrayals. He pushed it all away and rose to sit on his heels. He threw back his head and howled at the empty sky.

ଓଃଔ ଓଃଔ ଓଃଔ

Some time later his stomach spoke to him. He tried to remember how long it was since he had eaten. He thought about the dried fish his father had given him, when something else caught his eye. The sail was limp in the still of the air and hung down pitifully. His eyes followed it up the mast. When had that broken in two? He looked around, for a moment expecting to see the top half bobbing about on the waves somewhere behind him. He blinked, ignored the feel of burned eyelids, and cursed.

That was when a gull came to rest on the splintered top. She tilted her head at him as though she would speak.

"So, I am not alone, bird," he rasped aloud and was startled by his splintery, foreign sound. It was enough to make the gull squawk and flap away. Madai watched it fly toward a distant line on the horizon. He did not stop to contemplate what kindness directed him, but retied the scrap of sail and waited for a breeze to carry him there.

The wait lasted through the day, but with the coming cool of dusk his ship began to move. First slowly, so slowly that Madai held his breath so as not to compete against it, and finally a steady gliding toward a silhouette that grew into a rocky shore.

His body was a husk of aching. And all of it shook when he finally pulled the boat from the sea. He stumbled, barely able to stand with shaking sea legs. The earth unsteadied him and he tripped. The rocks cut his knees.

That was a fresh shock. He looked down at his leggings, at where they were torn and blood was starting to bubble red. He thought for a moment whether he should get up or not, whether he should just laugh or cry, curse or bless. He decided he should save his strength.

Madai put his palms on the ground to steady himself and stood up. It made his stomach lurch, but he willed himself off the rocks onto the inland. He wondered briefly whether his head was whirling from lack of food, or from his coming out of the boat. It was, in truth, the pounding it had gotten. He spied a man-sized monolith of granite and made his way there. He sank down, leaned against the stone and looked out toward the endless sea.

He remembered the smoked fish then.

And there was other food at the shore; the gulls were pecking at it again, back from wherever they had scattered at his landing. Madai was suddenly mad with thirst as much as hunger. He cursed himself for forgetting to look for the flagon of ale. Last he remembered, there was some left. He gave himself the briefest of moments, then wrestled himself to his legs, only slightly more steady, and stumbled back to the boat. There was the star map, wrapped in seal. There was The Family's sacred spear, fastened to the vessel's ribs, and his bows. There was the goat belly, still half full. Thank the gods he had had the foresight to tie it all down.

He took a long drink. He took another drink. And then he spied a red fish twisting around in the water, trapped in the stinking bilge. He grabbed at it like a bear in autumn and beat it against the rocks. He carried it still twitching to the granite boulder, started a fire, and forced himself to let it cook. Another few drinks of beer and the fish was not quite raw.

Despite what sleep he had gotten in the storm, he was tired again. He looked at the sun, which told him it was well beyond midday. Still, what could he do without his strength? Then he remembered this was likely the shore of The Banned; he really should get the Spear and his bow and put the fire out. There was only one of him, and he remembered too well what had been done to Laeden. But the fish was sitting badly and his body felt as though it were weighted down. Maybe a little more rest would recover him. A thought struck him then and he coughed with a brittle chuckle. Reckless, he let the fire burn and dared The Banned to see it. It had occurred to him that it was perhaps as good a way to die as any.

CЗCR CЗCR CЗCR

When Madai woke, night was near upon him. He slowly stretched, finding himself for the most part whole again, except his head. There, he found a welt the size of a buffalo gourd, for which he was actually happy, as it explained the pain. He stood, reasonably pleased with the effort, and admitted an appreciation that he had not been eaten by The Banned.

He found the Spear in his boat and took the time to calculate what other of his provisions had survived the typhoon: his ax, two simple oak spears, two long-bows and his quiver. There was the painting of a mammoth hunt on the quiver, which threatened to undo him. It had always been a quality of Ido's that he could not quite fathom, to make a roll of leather beautiful when its simple function would do.

He collected the arrows floating in the putrid water. He gathered all that was left, turned his boat on its side and watched the murk empty out. Then he retied the Spear and the long-bows with their arrows. His second coat was gone, but pinned against the side was the wrapping of dried fish his Patta had given him.

Madai had an abrupt vision of his father's hands, rough and large, a web of thick veins across their tops, pulling a cord tight to close in the fish. He had handed the bundle to Madai with a determined and hopeful look. "Bring us back good news," he had said.

Madai shook his head to chase away the image. Dark would follow that colored sky in the west, and he wanted a look at the trees on this coast. His mast would need replacing. He considered taking The Family's Spear, then settled on his own oak. He turned away from the boat with a purpose.

The forest grew straighter where it was not battered by the wind. Madai chose a tree a bit inland, only not so far from the coast as to bring him a great challenge getting it out. He set down his spear and laid after the trunk with the ax. He felt his shoulder in places he had not noticed before, and a long streak burned down his back. He hacked harder at the tree. He ripped away the bark and then the white flesh of the terebinth till shadows began to command the thicket, and he could hardly see. He wiped his face and looked up toward the sea and the dimming light. The colors of the sky were down to the water, casting it in orange and red. He would have to finish tomorrow.

Madai straightened his back. He looked at the cleft he had cut at the base of the tree; not so deep, but a start. With the chopping of the terebinth, his body recalled the last exercise it had had of this sort, cutting the ridge-poles for his new lodge. That seemed long ago, and another person. He was tempted to lean on the butt of his ax and contemplate the changes, relish them as sweet poison, but he was too tired. His head was buzzing again, as well, threatening to pitch him to the ground. So he used his ax like an old man and left the woods.

He found his granite, and the fire, down now to a heap of crumbling ash. His head was throbbing in a steady rhythm. He knew he could not do a thing more but slide down with his back to the boulder. He had the briefest notion of finding a more comfortable spot, then decided it didn't matter. He would sleep here. He closed his eyes, felt himself sinking and whirling, going deeper into black with every pulsing of his battered skull.

In the night, Madai was hidden among the rocks. His fire was silent and dark. The dark covered the prints he had put on the earth, but it did not hide the boat. Waves lapped it and the rocks while silent feet stole to the water's edge. The whale-skin boat was of no interest to them, though they could see it was made by one of The Family. It was their pleasure to loot what they could find. Consider their delight at the first glimpse of The Spear! It was of greater value even than Madai, for whom they had not bothered to search. The boat was big enough for three healthy men, and they were afraid. Why bother with fleshy confrontations when their curses would do the job?

They took The Spear, and its second blade, which was tied to it. They could not know, of course, about the third one, still sheathed like a dagger and hanging on Madai's belt. Their speech was the same as that of The Family, though it had changed some, being injected with new words born of new thoughts and deeds. It was no kindness that they left the other possessions of Madai alone, leaving them where they lay, for it was these things that indwelt their curse: the skins of the boat and its stitches, the scraps of foodstuff tied in sealskins. They cursed the very water around the boat, as hatred was strong in them for their pious brothers. It was hatred born of a competing spirit. It gave them a good deal of joy to imagine a slow, cruel death for the men who would trust their lives to these things on the morrow.

When they had been driven from The Family, with their other songs and star stories, they had desired the Spear, as well. It was forged, after all, in the fires of Shinar and was bound with its tradition. But the Spear possessed all the secret power of that place, and Toban had desired it, too. His prominence was secured by its possession and its magic, and he had prevailed. It is the victor who wins the spoils in battle, after all.

Three exceptionally tall, naked men crept over the rocks in the moon's light. They reentered the forest at a point well away from Madai with their secret magic left behind. They were savoring the favor they were about to find, having reclaimed the sacred Spear - a lucky night, indeed.

挃 挃 挃

Madai awoke to a raw and undisturbed day, scarcely light. The first duty of his consciousness was to reconstruct the shamble of his life. The second was to push that all aside and the third was to evaluate his physical condition. The headache was considerably less, and the dizziness gone. His bumps and bruises were nothing to him.

He looked at the boat, instantly oriented in time and place, and was satisfied to see it undisturbed. He scolded himself, though, resolving never to leave its safety to chance again. And, he was hungry. Madai stretched. He was feeling more himself now, the sleep having done him better than the half stupor he had suffered in the boat. He decided to eat some of his father's fish. It was an easy meal and he would like to finish the tree. He also decided to examine the skins of his boat to see how they had managed the storm.

He scanned the seams and found them tight. Satisfied, he reached for the remains of his dried fish. His hand stopped in mid-air. The Spear was gone! He did not think once that he might have moved it. He knew of certainty that it was gone; and if it was gone, it was taken. A very bad omen. Just his own spear lay there, with its plain oak shaft and its single sharp obsidian point. Though he had outwardly agreed with his father that The Family's Sacred Spear was only a relic of another time and place, he had retained the possibility that it did, indeed, hold some secret power.

His belly suddenly leapt to his throat, a question of spears aside. Here he was on a far shore, with them that had been here in the night - his old phantoms.

His eyes immediately found their tracks in the sand. There were too many of them. He scanned the forest; not a shadow moved, and the birds twittered undisturbed. Suddenly he became stone still with the thought of his form here in the light and them with the Spear and its dark powers. He crouched, shrinking his visible form, and crept back to the fire for his ax and second spear. His fingers fumbled with the knot where he had tied his boat to a leaning terebinth, then he slunk back to push the craft off the shore. He pulled himself quietly inside and used a paddle to move himself into the waves beyond the coast, instantly proving by his galloping heart that he was not indifferent to his own death.

He knew he was leaving the Sacred Spear behind with every league he gained from the shore, and he was also leaving his tree. But he was afraid as he had not expected to be. He would not get the mast on this shore. He tied the sail to the stub that was left and kept his boat in sight of land, but at a distance further than a spectre can throw a sorcerer's Spear.

Madai ate what was left of his fish. He watched the coast as he ate, alarmed to be first washed up with a typhoon and then chased away by an old foe. He had not found fresh water or fresh meat. He had not got his mast or consulted the star map. He had no real estimation of the days he had been on the sea, having lost count in the storm, and he didn't know how long he had slept before he was wakened by the quiet. He could only guide the ship to hug the coast and point it eastward. At least the wind was in his favor.

He let the water and the wind take him, passing enough time to allow a full mourning of the Spear. It was clear to him that it had gained him confidence. A grim thought, to be without a High God to see him and no fabled Spear. It had been something, after all; his first touch of the relic had told him that. It had come from a legendary place where time had started again. He remembered the way Toban had looked at it on the day it passed to his own hands.

“—” “—” “—”

"The Spear of The Family, Madai," Toban had said, holding it on the flat of his palms and stretching out his arms.

It had gleamed in the light of the fire that morning, possessing no constant color, but shifting as the fire rose and ebbed... almost ethereal. A serpent made of some other thing, equally hard, coiled around it. His hands had trembled taking it from Toban.

"The forebearers brought this Spear from Shinar," Toban had said. "Its shaft cannot be made again; the skill is forgotten." He indicated its lethal blade. "And this can command the heart of a fire-breather." The long arrowhead was a burnished slate grey, thick and sharp. Not flint, not obsidian, something harder, forged in fire. It had a dragon etched on it and was barbed with five long prongs pointing backward. Madai had always admired it.

"But it cannot be pulled out," Toban continued, "or shaken off. It has bested the heart of mammoth in this place; it may best dragons where you are going." Toban had looked at him with glittering eyes when he said that, and Madai was a little surprised that he would give it up.

Toban had taken the Spear from Madai then and turned with startling speed to plunge it into the carcass of a boar lying in the dirt beside the fire. Toban tugged at it, then invited Madai to pull it out. The barbs held the arrow fast between the animal's ribs. Toban continued to smile, and he ran his finger along a deep groove concealed near the top end of the shaft. He released a latch, which gave way with a metallic sound. He twisted and pulled the shaft free, less the blade, its barbed end still inside the boar. And there was more: two other spear-heads. Toban took one and pushed it into a slot at the head of the shaft. The other he gave to Madai.

"You see," Toban announced proudly, "a secret is revealed."

Madai remembered the flush of power he had felt when he first held the Spear. And he remembered his father's face, lips tight, eyes warning, as Madai struggled to compose his own expression.

He sat alone in his boat and chuckled. Now it had all came to naught. The Spear was gone. At least his father would be pleased.

- 24 -

The girl lay on her back, on ground that was a desert in the making, though not for many years more. She pointed a stick at the clouds, directing the wind as a concert. She stood up to join the song, twirling. The dog that should have been at the water hole with the goats was suddenly licking nervously at her toes.

"Aten!" she snapped. She scolded the dog. He danced indignantly in the dust, his bristles standing straight. Then he began to whine. She waved her stick at the cur, and he dashed back a step.

The little shepherdess relented and bent to pat the dog, though her father would disapprove the petting.

"Is it a lion?" she asked the edgy beast. And she decided she had best get her rod. But Father would not send her to a lion's range, though she picked up the heavy staff and stabbed in artless defense at the horizon.

- 25 -

Madai straightened his back and quit his glooming over the Spear; he had, after all, lived a lifetime without it. A bitter chuckle found its way up his throat. He felt outside himself, still stunned at where he was and half starved with cooked skin and a throbbing head. Thank the gods the wind was calm.

Absently, he chewed on a salty strip of dry fish, rolling a long bone across his tongue. It placated his stomach but savaged his mouth. He discarded the bone and licked his lips in a futile attempt to wet them. He allowed himself a tiny sip of beer and felt like a drooling fool, afraid to go ashore again.

He spent the day that way, hunched over the rudder, letting his ship carry him away, impressed by the stunted sail and the sturdy boat. The craft was a credit to his forebearers, to build so seaworthy a vessel from the skins of great water creatures, saving him from both typhoon and the dangers of the dark deep. The skill of men was great. It struck him that all his survivals had been by his own hands. Why was it that men craved the gods anyway? Perhaps all their Provider's Portions had been to imaginary nostrils, after all. It was a hard thought, a far leap from only apathy, the character he had lately lent the God Who would take his heart away...

"No," he rumbled aloud to an empty air. "Cruel."

A sovereign God, if He lived, was a cruel God. And a God Who was not sovereign was not God at all.

Madai lifted his chin and straightened his shoulders again, carving a new posture for himself. How ironic, to come searching after the Ancients with such an outrage growing in his mind. All his first life set after vanities...

The sliding of the sun toward the sea came as a true surprise to Madai. He found he had sat the afternoon in a stupor, carried by the breeze all day. He had found it a sort of pleasure to contemplate the unthinkable, and that had brought him to sunset.

An armor was building around him, making him full of a confidence that was born of newly-wrought indifference. Madai's mouth had formed a hard line across his face. What had happened just this morning seemed an ancient past, when he had been panicked for his life. He could face The Banned now. He needed a drink and something fresh to eat. There were no scruples left in him, and he could kill another man. They had brought the sickness, after all. His mutinous ponderings had strangely heightened his spirits. They had yet to bring him to the matter of standards, where a God did not set the measure. But that would come.

ಣಞ ಣಞ ಣಞ

Madai began to look for a place to come ashore.

He chose a spot with a wide mouth and a forest that came down to greet it. He decided to make his night's camp here, find a mast, a meal and good water. Then he would wait for the stars and chart his course again.

His legs did their job this time, and Madai didn't stumble ashore like a drunkard. He found a place set in a cleft of rock overlooking both the beach and his boat. He had beside him, both his oak spear and his long-bow. He had made a fire, and he had the remains of a yap rat. It was starvation fare for a tundra hunter, but a fresh meal that had, in truth, tasted very good. Madai also had the scroll of the star map. He had waited till now to unroll it.

It would tell him what he needed to know of distance and direction. But it held the threat to restir his old self. There was a queasy feeling in his stomach, which he was trying to ignore. He shook his head, a vigorous shake in case there really was Someone watching, a tactile expression of budding independence.

"His time must be soon, Madai," came the words of Ashkinaz.

Madai jumped. He looked at the skin scroll in his hands as though it had spoken. As fresh as if it were yesterday, he remembered sitting inside the cave with his father. It was cruel to think of those days.

And there was the constellation coming out to wink at him.

"Mighty and righteous comes the Archer," went the song.
"He rises for battle.
"His arrows cleft
"The heart of the Scorpion

"His appearing brings its
"Lasting doom."

Madai's smile was thin. A God Who sees... it was a little matter beside a God Who comes. His chest heaved a dry chuckle.

Who had devised such an elaboration? he wondered.

He found the places in the sky that he needed, as easy as breathing. He calculated positions and angles against the guide star and was surprised that he was so far on his voyage.

"Storm, you did me well," he said aloud. His voice sounded small on the great empty coast and he was glad for his shelter of rock. He rolled the scroll without another glance at the constellation of the Bowman. He thought he would have a good night's sleep, being restored from his bumps and wounds. But the night stretched long.

In the dream that came at dawn, he heard his father's voice again.

"Sacred wisdom shall robe this Warrior. and all that is noble," it said. "He is the One."

Madai felt still commanded by the remains of his dream when he woke up. It was barely light; and though the rocky ground was hard against his back, he hated to move. He hated to lose the comfort that had accompanied the dream, though it made of him a fraud.

ೞೞ   ೞೞ   ೞೞ

The stone ax-head chipped at the tree. Cold and wind had made the tree hard. He knew by experience that it was not as straight and true as those sought for ships, and it would be slow work. But he was enjoying the exercise, reviving his body again.

And when he was done, he was drenched with sweat. He hacked off the limbs and top, ignoring anything of himself that complained, and dragged it through the forest one painful inch at a time. At the water's edge he leaned his palms on his knees and watched sweat roll off his face to make fat rounds of mud in the dirt. His lungs hurt, and his back was near to grievous.

He slowly drew back up to survey his work: a felled runt of a tree amputated of limbs, not so much more than the stump of his own mast and twisted, besides.

He snorted an ambiguous laugh and sat down to rest on it.

The dawn brought him up starving, so he decided to ignore the repair of his ship and went to hunt a deer, which he ate like a barbarian. He was glad his mother couldn't see him, and he ate till his belly was tight as a green plum. Still there was meat left, enough for a Provider's Portion and more. It was a thought as natural to Madai as breathing. But he leaned against his tree to rest from the exertion of eating. Instead of piling up an altar, he scrubbed his teeth with a twig.

"I have decided to leave you," he said, speaking to the tree.

He stood up and stretched and rubbed his belly. It was rumored that limbless trees grew from the sands of the East, topped with wide, spiny ferns. They would make a mast. Of course, all such tales carried from the scattering brought, as he had lately learned, shameless myths as well.

Madai was constructing a path for himself, one step at a time, testing the ice, so to speak. The sea had fed him a fish, the forest a deer. He had asked no gods for them. He had spoken to a tree of leaving it, in earshot of heaven; a god of respectable heft would perceive the duallity in that. And he had failed to leave a Provider's Portion. He would see what happened.

ೞೞ   ೞೞ   ೞೞ

The wind that sprung up was brisk. It was due east. With the doldrums he had experienced, a good wind was a godsend. He chuckled at his own joke and collected his things. He left the tree and the deer to rot.

His sail caught the breeze, and he was scooting across the water nearly before he knew it. It was the first time he had felt in command of his voyage since the typhoon. There had been hardly time to think in the first days, to evaluate the quest in the first blush of leaving, the strange excitement stirred with a pot of grief, the regrets, Japhet's little face watching him go and not suspecting that his Patta would not be coming home - not for a long time, anyway. Madai turned his face eastward with a vengeance, having remembered the boy. But the thought of Japhet mended the tether tying him back to his purpose. This was a quest for Japhet, he knew. He needed to have a truth to tell his son - a settled truth.

Madai stood up; he studied the coastline, watching for it to change. It was stretching directly east as the sun bore down on his face. How long till the peninsula disappeared to leave him in open sea? How far across the expanse was the land of his forebearers? It was somewhere there, somewhere in the distance, with all the answers.

A disciplined breeze continued him east. He decided to let the coast disappear to a thin line, because the wind was stiff farther out. The water itself was calm after the storm, flat and blue. It reflected the sky and the sun, sparkling; only his boat cast a shadow. When he noticed the shadow turn and glide away, that sat him up with a quick stab of alarm. Of all the stories he now believed, why must it be sea monsters that seemed to strike a plausible note? But there... he laughed at himself... it had disappeared.

Madai relaxed. He reached for the skin of ale. There was a thirst he seemed never able to quench. He suddenly seemed dry to the bone. He took a long, slow drink and realized he was hungry again; then suddenly, like a gnat in the wind, the breeze evaporated and the shadow was back. He stared and told himself it was a trick of the deep or a school of kipper, as it held no constant shape. But when it disappeared again, his heart was pounding, having realized a new-sprung faith in sea monsters... indeed, the hair danced on his arm. He waited, staring at the spot where it had been.

And then came...a bump at the craft's underside, and a slight jostle. The water, being calm, permitted his hand to find his man-spear. Madai cursed the still air.

He should have prayed.

To his left came the shadow again, seeming to slither, an undulating mass. The thing came near the surface. It was long and thick, and Madai was anxious to see it, to know what he would soon face. Only it dived back out of sight. Madai studied where it had vanished, calculating its rhythm and its ways. The water seemed thick, a shroud hiding danger. He had gripped the spear with so tight a hold that he relaxed his hand consciously and flexed his fingers. He bent his knees slightly, and looked over the edge into the water, not a nervous look but a look as predatory as the thing hiding in the water.

A shadow uncoiled; Madai had a glimpse of it, longer than wide, like a thick, hideous eel. It began to climb through the sea and the hairs on Madai's head stood up. It came higher and higher, growing larger and larger. The water cleared as it neared the surface, exposing fleshy gills and a serpentine snout.

Suddenly Madai fell away from the side and back to the center of the ship. The creature had blinked at him through the water and was hurling itself up, maybe all the way up into the air. But it just broke the surface. Madai watched a black coil follow its head back down as the boat rocked. He felt it bump its way down the length of the ship's whaleskin belly. There was a moment of calm before Madai felt it hit the boat again, from the other side. He suddenly knew the creature's purpose. The serpent would engage its prey only when it knew its size and strength. Madai desperately regretted losing the Sacred Spear.

There passed another agony of time as the creature seemed to be gone. Only a ruse, he knew - as the sea erupted with a roar pulled up from reptilian throat. Just to Madai's side the water boiled, and the thing exploded through the surface, raising its gargantuan head higher than the sides of Madai's boat. Its mouth unhinged like a snake's and hissed at him through its spiny teeth. Madai swung his spear at the creature's face and watched it dodge effortlessly aside. It bobbed back, and turned its snake-cold eyes at him. Madai watched the water roll down its snout, hovering in mid-air above him, every black scale glistening in the sun. The thing was vibrating its skin all down its length, causing the water to dance and the air to resound like distant thunder.

He was awe-struck, a moment that hung infinite in time, to recognize an authentic fable breathing through soft, red gills that throbbed like a scaly bellows. A film closed over the creature's eyes as it pulled higher from the sea, arching above him, hissing out a shriek. Madai was a part paralyzed, only watching as a man removed when, quick as lightning, the creature lunged like a striking viper. The unthinking part of Madai's body flinched, and he took the serpent's strike on his shoulder rather than his face. He twisted his body, the spear as a child's toy in his hand, and drove it up into the monster's panting gills. He felt its hinged jaws release slightly to leave his left shoulder pierced with a thousand little wounds. His hands threatened to go lax, but he held on by grim will and drove the spearhead deeper into the beating flap. It was all he could manage, holding it there against the creature's thick muscle.

The screech of the serpent crescendoed, and then it arched itself violently away from the boat. It took Madai's spear with it, and he fell back into the ship's belly. He watched the creature whip itself around and fling the lance away like a slingshot. It hit the water and sank. The animal hung above him, its mouth wide and dripping ooze. It turned to eye him in his little ship and came plunging down again. This time it took the side of the boat in its mouth and lifted it perceptibly, shaking it side to side. Madai gripped the ribs of his craft with one hand, and grabbed for his knife with the other. He wavered between dread of the monster and dread of the deep where the monster lived. But the animal suddenly let him loose, as though it thought better of eating wood, and lifted its head again. It was hanging slightly to the side of its damaged gill and posed that way with its longish, humpish body for what seemed eternal, and hissed again. A fountain of blood pumped through its gill-flesh. And then the serpent simply dived back below the surface and disappeared in an instant.

Madai breathed. He stood fixed in the boat, unmoving. He breathed again, and found his second spear. He did not remove his eye from the spot where the thing had disappeared. How long he waited that way was lost to him. There is something horrific in being eaten by a snake. He watched the water till his heart was quiet. And he was infinitely grateful for the wind that had sprung up again and was blowing him away.

⊗⋈ ⊗⋈ ⊗⋈

Madai did not sleep on the sea for a third night. He found a barren place where the rocks were flat and lay out under the stars. His fire was enormous. It was roasting a water otter he had stopped from trying to swim back to its burrow. Madai did not watch for the constellations or contemplate newly fledged philosophy. He was deciding, for this night at least, that rebellions may have proved dangerous. There was always the chance, of course, that all this was a random happening... which was, in essence, the whole question.

Iscah

- 26 -

The earth began to thunder. The girl, whose name was Iscah, lay still with her ear to the ground. A great herd... or many horses. She dropped the staff and scrambled to where she had left her sandals.

Aten growled and whined until he decided what his stance should be. Then his lips curled back from his fangs as he faced away to the south.

She wished the sound had been a quake. But it was a horde. Their horses were lathered and steaming and jangling with stolen gold.

The last she heard was the startled yelp that came from Aten's throat. The last she felt was being lifted up. The last she saw was her mother's scarlet veil wrapped around a barrel chest.

He clutched her tightly and drove his horse harder.

When he found his place at camp that night, he let the others count the gold. His intent was for the girl.

ೞೞ   ೞೞ   ೞೞ

This had all been done before the pestilence on the tundra. It had been done before a new red stone was dropped into the leather pouch. It had been done in a far land where civilizations are the oldest. It had been done to a simple goat-herder's daughter.

Kittim

- 27 -

Madai let the coast drift farther and farther away. By degrees he regained his confidence, until finally he set his course directly east, trusting in the old tales that there was, indeed, a land at the finish of the Brine Sea. He was tired, with crispy skin and a shrinking supply of ale. It had been ten days since he had encountered the serpent, and the wounds on his shoulder were covered over. The wind had lately been benevolent and did not veer from a determined and brisk effort to see him eastward.

At the next midday, Madai was rewarded with the first sight of floating kelp. By dusk, a flat expanse of land was visible, and near. The waters were calm that formed its undulating shoreline. The craggy cliffs and giant, serrated boulders which crushed sea crafts in the waves, were mammoths of an entirely distant land. Moreover, there were towering poles of trees, with only shaggy green at their tops.

Had he expected total and uncompromised relief at coming to this new land, Madai would have been unfit for the quest. He was already prepared with the highest degree of caution, having reasoned that if The Family's description of the trees was correct, then so would be the fierce men of strange speech...the men his forebearers had crossed this very sea to evade. And so with great vigilance Madai first set his boot from his ship to the foreign shore.

His nose was telling him many things. There was the smell of sweetness in the air, some sort of fruit. And there was the smell of rotting seaweed. There was also the smell of a burning campfire; and, already, he was not alone. But the campfire was broiling fish. He could smell that too. His stomach growled.

He crouched down beside the boat to look for the source of the smell. It was easy to find, coming from a surround of those trees, because a man was tending it and was not trying to hide himself. He was, in fact, standing with his hand raised as though in greeting. Madai actually turned to see if there might be someone else on the shore.

The man was somewhat in the distance and Madai, not knowing the dimensions of the trees, had difficulty gauging his height. But to a seaman come freshly from a far land, this stranger had the look of a Nephilim.

"Maybe not so tall as that," Madai whispered to himself. Even at this distance, Madai counted the man's fingers - only five. He breathed out relief. Nephilim were known for six.

The man was wearing a cloth of brightest color, a thing Madai had not seen before. A thing also that, in his experience, one of The Banned would not wear. Madai slowly reached for the spear, careful not to stir up any sort of needless alarm in the stranger.

.He was suddenly overwhelmed with the strongest desire to set sail again.

'You are not ready for an encounter with a peopled beach.' He nearly heard the thought with his ears.

And he wanted to follow that advice. He was nearly overwhelmed by its warning, but coming upon people of the East was precisely the point of his mission and it was sitting wrong against him to turn like a woman at the first sight of another human, be he ever so tall.

"Brother!" the man called. "You are tired? I have food and drink, and a fire, as you see."

Madai did see, indeed. And he swallowed. He thought quickly; 'He has no weapon,' which was an assumption from what was immediately visible. It was slightly more curious than reassuring. 'He is not of strange speech.' That was what actually stayed Madai from sailing away. But he would be cautious.

"I have not been far on the sea. I am well," he called, wanting to appear neither weak nor desperate.

The man turned back to his fire. He sat down. "As you wish," he said and turned his attention to something cooking over the flames.

Madai stood from the crouching posture he had kept beside his boat, immediately aware that his squatting betrayed fear to the stranger. He took a few steps forward, fighting the compulsion to turn. And yet...there was that heady smell of food.

The stranger stood again and lifted his five-fingered hand.

"Peace be yours," he called across the beach. "My name is Kittim."

A tongue with the exact cadence as his own, and Madai recognized a name from The Family of Japhet. 'Even if he is an enemy, it is better to keep him in sight,' Madai reasoned, beginning to steady his own steps on the sand. He was moving slowly so as to have time to scan the surroundings: a meager camp, surely, no visible weapons, a staff of some sort of heavy appearance. But then there was the man. Madai had never before seen a man with the look of Kittim. His hair was dark. His skin was the color of a roe deer. His height was greater than The Family's tallest man. As Madai came nearer, he saw with a degree of alarm that the man's eyes were black as night.

"Peace be yours," Madai heard his own voice greeting the stranger, glad that something inside had prompted him to speak. He could not, after all, avoid the company of humankind, even one of so peculiar an appearance, and keep his quest. But then he stopped, clutching his spear in his hand, within striking distance of the man. His mouth was dry as dust.

"My fire is yours," the man, Kittim, said simply and bowed.

Madai had not seen a man do that before, though he could not think much beyond the first curiosity of it, for in Kittim's hand was a skin of water.

"I am honored," Kittim continued. He held the water out to Madai.

Madai stretched out his hand and took the flask. Surely there was something he should say, but he took a long drink instead. Ah... the water was good.

"God reward your kindness," Madai spoke The Family's blessing.

"Drink as you wish," Kittim returned, sitting down at the fire again. "There is sweet water not far."

Madai nodded. Maybe he could trust this man who relinquished the waterskin to him like a brother. He drank again, till the smell of the fish began to tantalize him more than the water. He eyed what was roasting on the flames.

"Are you hungry?" Kittim asked, and poked a fish with his stick. He held it up to Madai with a faint smile. "I have plenty, as you see."

Of course, there was nothing for him to do but take it. Madai moved the spear to his left hand. "Thank you," he replied truly and began to eat. When one is long on the sea, tasting salt with every bite of dried fish, which is salted through, the taste of something fresh is stunning. Madai could hardly remove the bones quickly enough. And it felt ungracious to eat, still standing, but Madai finished the fish that way.

Kittim handed him another.

Madai ate it, eyes on Kittim. His impulse was now to trust this man, who spoke as one of The Family and freely shared his fire. But these were distant shores. He studied the contour and color of Kittim's face as he consumed yet a third fish. He dropped the remnants of bone into the fire and wondered whether he should sit down.

"I am Madai," he suddenly offered.

"Welcome, Madai," the man replied, looking up. He handed Madai the skin of water again and watched him drink it. "Your day has been long," he continued. "You may take the night here at my fire."

Madai didn't answer. He was completely taken aback, for Kittim then did an incomprehensible thing: he spread a white linen on the sand, turned his back to Madai, and lay down. "God speed the good night," was all the strange man said.

'Who does such a thing?' Madai marveled. He sank down to sit on the sand. He took another sip of the water and watched Kittim, expecting to see him turn at any moment to guard himself against a travel-worn stranger. Perhaps it was all a trick to gain confidence and then attack in the night. Well, it would be a foolish plan, giving Madai the first strike as he did. It was a thought unabashedly ungrateful, but he could hardly help it.

Soon, the steady sound of breathing betrayed that the stranger was asleep. Madai watched him a long time. He sat, legs crossed, at the edge of the fire and contemplated what appeared to be good fortune. The fire crackled. A thick piece of charred wood burned in two and fell into the embers. He watched it slowly disappear to ash.

He was feeling the long days, but he fought it. He was determined that his eyes not close. The night was surprisingly cold, which reminded him of his robe still in the boat. But likely that would make him rather too comfortable. Instead, he piled the fire with more wood. He calculated his position by the constellations, another of the countless times he had done so, to be gratified that it was as it should be. Then, somewhere between the guide star and the dragon's tail, he fell asleep.

∞∞ ∞∞ ∞∞

With his face resting in sand, Madai woke up; he had had a strange dream. He could see his spear beside him, but he could not remember quite where he was. He slowly stretched, testing his limbs and wiping sand from his face. He needed a drink of water. Rising on an elbow, he spied a white piece of linen lying on the sand, which announced that it had not really been a dream at all. He scrambled up. He was alone.

He spun around to find his boat. Ah... it was there. But he was slightly ashamed of himself, that for a drink and a fish he had...

"You are awake, Madai!" he heard Kittim call from somewhere in the distance. He turned around and saw the tall man coming over the crest of a dune with a bulging flask of water.

Madai squinted into the rising sun to watch him, rebuking himself. Truly his quest was safe not by his own hand. All he could think to do was raise that hand in tentative greeting.

Except he did have a talent.

"Today I will return your kindness," he called.

Kittim raised an eyebrow with a half-smile and finished the distance to Madai. He gave him the water skin.

"I am a good fisherman," Madai announced, taking a drink.

"That is excellent!" Kittim replied.

∞∞ ∞∞ ∞∞

Madai was eating his share of the speckled fish and he was looking out over the land. Sand surrounded him. It was coarse and nearly white, dotted with not a rock or sprig of grass. It spread toward the horizon, running like a ribbon along the shore and rising to dunes. Only the single-trunk trees varied the landscape, with their little islands of green. 'Their roots must drink a stream from the earth,' Madai decided, because the sand was dry as ash. He recognized the trees with their sparse foliage and mast-like trunks from The Family's songs. They stretched into the distance as far as he could see. A scorpion scurried up the slope of sand near him, leaving a little trail.

It was all so vast! Where to go from here, now that he had crossed the sea? He searched his mind for a clue from the old songs.

"So, what do you see?" Kittim suddenly asked him.

"A new land," he replied. Then he studied the man who had lent him a comfortable night. "Thank you, Kittim," he said. "I thank you for your fire." He was suddenly filled with emotion. Maybe it was the long weeks alone on the sea; maybe it was just unexpected loneliness to be adrift from family and God. "I will sing to the Ancient Ones of you," he added, part by old habit and part sincere, "offer sacred smoke -"

He suddenly stopped. It was trifling to say that Kittim did not look pleased. 'Such a lie!' Madai scolded himself, brought back from all his sentiment. 'See what it has got you.'

Kittim lifted his hand. "Offer your sacred fires to God," he insisted. His face was grim as stone, with a sound in his voice not to be opposed. He turned away.

Madai was freshly alarmed. And just when he was trusting the fellow.

"The people of this land are many," Kittim suddenly continued, with a clear tone of warning. "Some are fierce. You shall need your spear."

'Ah!' Madai thought to himself. 'So he is exposed. I will listen to the voice next time. Now I may have to kill this man.'

"The place from where I come is a land of fearsome beasts," Madai returned the warning. "I have great skill with this spear."

Kittim's expression betrayed nothing. He stood up, which alerted Madai to wrap his fingers around said instrument.

"Tell me, Madai," Kittim replied mildly, "from where do you come?" He did not look afraid in the least, though he could see Madai with the weapon and he with none at all.

Madai stood up, as well. "The West," he answered.

"So where do you go?"

Madai was confused, but at the advantage with his spear. "North and East," he replied, and thought dreadfully, 'Get on with it.'

Kittim turned his eyes away then and gazed out at the sea. "As do I," he said quietly. "Perhaps we may share part of the journey."

Madai was stunned at the turn, hearing the peaceable tone. 'Very stealthy,' came the voice again. And yet some other, quieter voice gave Madai the hope that he might leave Kittim alive.

"I know much of this land and its people." Kittim continued. "I know their speech." He looked at Madai mildly, and at his clothes. "You have come far for a purpose?"

"Yes," Madai heard himself answer. He was utterly spun about by the waverings of his own judgment. "If you are not of this people," he tested, "how do you know their speech?"

"I am not of this place," Kittim mildly affirmed. "I know of its people and their speech."

Madai didn't answer.

"So, my friend," Kittim prodded again. "Will you not tell me your cause?"

It suddenly occurred to Madai that the answer might persuade a marauder to look elsewhere, and he jutted his chin slightly forward, looking squarely at Kittim. "Only truth," he answered. 'Let him think me poor'.

But Kittim seemed, instead, duly impressed. "A worthy purpose!" he replied with relish.

Madai wondered first if he were being mocked; but there was a thing about the man: he didn't seem false, and he wasn't angry any more. Kittim picked up the white linen and shook the sand off.

"And you," Madai insisted. "What is your purpose East?"

"There is a man I seek," Kittim answered. He piled the fire with sand and looked at Madai's boat. "There is a river that flows from the sea," he pointed with his chin, "just up the shore. If you wish to take your boat further, it can be done."

"Where would its waters take me?" Madai asked.

With a faint grin, Kittim turned his black eyes to rest on Madai's face. "North and East."

Madai had watched the man's face take on a smile as a wolf gauges the intention of another wolf. He read Kittim's expression as one of complete fidelity. An unpracticed, though wholly converted cynic, Madai reasoned with himself that 'if the stranger is treacherous, he will be at my back. Either kill him now, or not...'

"Do not be alarmed," Kittim abruptly announced. "I would do you a service and gain one in return."

Madai felt his head angle to the side with a curious sensation and the image of that gull perched on the edge of his boat. 'Perhaps so,' he thought with an odd sense of reprieve. 'A skill with strange tongues is a good skill... and how has he done me any thing but good?'

Then Madai nodded, not lending his sudden decision the weight of words.

Kittim smiled, "Excellent."

With that, Kittim took a step toward Madai and reached for him. It was quick, and Madai had no time to react. Kittim pinched the sleeve of Madai's shirt between his fingers.

"You have been long on the sea, my friend," he said. "Will you refresh at the spring?"

Madai nearly laughed. He touched his beard, crusted in salt. "Do I smell so much as that?" he heard himself ask.

Kittim raised a brow.

But Madai only allowed himself a thin smile and indicated the boat with a wag of his head. "The wind blows east," he said.

ෆ෨ ෆ෨ ෆ෨

They were being pulled into a current that seemed anxious to mix its salt with the wide, muddy river. It greeted the sea craft with a steady stream, carrying Madai and Kittim as though with a purpose, from the ocean into the heart of the foreign land.

Madai had never been a lover of solitude. But his last friend had been Tiras, proved a trustworthy fellow in every regard. Tiras had been with him at every important place of his life. This Kittim was in his boat now. A man of strange appearance who spoke like The Family and looked like a Nephilim - or how Madai imagined one should look, less a finger. Kittim had offered nothing but his help and had asked for nothing but to sail in his boat. He had no weapon and he had knowledge of fearsome peoples in this land. Most peculiar. Still, the only alarm Kittim had raised was his untoward reaction to a blessing. Madai shook his head and told himself he was being a woman.

He swatted at a spearfly that was buzzing him. They seemed thick as hordes on this river.

"I would like to have left these behind," he complained, swinging his arm at the undulating mass.

Kittim snorted, "One of the worst of His creatures."

"And everywhere."

"Steer to the center of the river, Madai."

The smallest turning of the rudder moved them farther from the bank. Madai sucked one up his nose.

"They take your blood, bring a sickness. They are a curse," Kittim grumbled.

"Spearflies," Madai agreed.

Kittim looked up. "Is that what you call them?" he asked.

Madai nodded.

"It's a fitting name."

Madai nodded again. "What are they called on this shore?" he asked.

Kittim's answer was guttural, and impossible for Madai to imitate.

"How do you know this tongue," he asked, "if you are from another land?"

"I have a learned Master," Kittim answered obliquely.

Madai frowned. He fiddled with the rudder and thought that if Kittim would be elusive forever, then what good would he gain by him?

"This truth you are seeking..." the man inquired.

Madai let the insects whine in answer and sat down to watch the current carry them on. "The truths of the heavens," he finally answered with a mocking voice.

"Hmm..." was Kittim's only reply.

Madai was annoyed at that, and surprised that he was annoyed. He harrumphed at the spearflies again, knowing the while that he had hoped Kittim might have an answer for him, that there might be such an answer at all.

Kittim was watching him with a faint smile.

 C３CR C３CR C３CR

The warm, humid day stretched into the humid evening. Madai was not accustomed to it. It would have been beyond suffering if not that he had come from what seemed an endless ocean. And this place was of another sort entirely. The sounds were different, except for the water frogs which were starting up their nightly chorus. He had stopped trying to talk to Kittim, watching instead the grassy shore. A great roar suddenly broke the quiet, coming from somewhere in the reeds. It was answered by other roars - a saber cat, or a thing more exotic and fiercesome. He thought of a hoary snow bear; they could swim.

But they sailed past, and nothing troubled them. Kittim did not seem alarmed. So the evening carried on. Suddenly there were the great leaping fish he knew from the sea. They were skimming along beside the boat with all their peculiar joy, and he was reminded of Ido; he couldn't help it.

Madai looked away and at Kittim, who appeared quite entertained and far removed. There was a look in his eyes of some sweet memory, too, though they neither disclosed their secrets. Madai felt smothered with melancholy and nursed the mood despite the jubilant swimmers beside his boat.

"This truth you seek - " Kittim asked abruptly, as if their conversation had not been broken by the whole length of the day.

It startled Madai. He leveled his water-blue eyes at Kittim's black ones, inscrutable to their depths. Madai was closed, sunk in a well of angst. The smell of Ido seemed to linger in the dusk, and that in itself inspired a generous reply. "I seek truth of a sacred kind."

"That is worthy...Though it would seem a vanity to some."

Madai drew up out of his doldrums. It was a heartless thing to say when he had been so open. "Such things as living have forced me to it!" he snapped.

Kittim seemed not to notice. "And this sacred truth is of value to you?"

"I am no animal," Madai retorted.

Kittim's eyes sparkled. "No," he answered. "I see that. But not all men would sail the length of a sea. What is it you think you will find here?"

There was a pause, a stony pause, as Madai knew he hadn't any idea how to find an Ancient. "Have you sacred truths?" he asked, rather than answer.

Again Kittim's eyes flashed. "Indeed!" he replied. "There is One Holy God, Maker and Head of Days."

A frog chirped to span the silence that followed. Madai felt a prickle run up his skin as though he had stepped backward in time. "My people believe in One God," he offered very quietly. "Who spoke with men in the time of beginnings. We keep songs of those times."

The sounds of water gently drummed the sides of the boat. The stars were coming out. Kittim was watching them. "What kind of sacred truth do you need, then?" he asked.

Madai looked away. His skin laid back down, and he felt suddenly alone again. It was coming night, with the stars seeming to fall away into a great vastness. "To know if it is true," he answered.

"Ah," Kittim mused quietly. "The knowledge of good and evil."

Madai shrugged. It seemed he could not understand Kittim if he did have the answer.

"So, how do you suppose you will find out if it is true?" Kittim's question spread out like a challenge.

"If there is an Ancient still alive," Madai replied stonily, "I will ask him, here at the place of beginnings... an Ancient, or one who spoke with him."

Kittim raised his brow, slowly smiling. "I see; a witness."

Madai nodded.

"With what measure shall you prove him true?"

Madai leaned his back against the rib of the boat. He still hurt where the serpent had got hold of him, and he was suddenly drained of all his energies. Kittim seemed to delight in asking, when the precise opposite was what Madai had intended of him. "Are you tempting me?" he asked wearily.

Kittim shrugged. "You will ask it the same, when the time comes. And there will be matters decided by choice, my friend, in the end."

"Certainly not! Truth is truth."

But Kittim only looked back at him thinly, then away to where the river snaked toward the horizon. "There is one far on this river," he said. "Well- honored, a man of renown among the people of the East. It may be that he knows something of what you are seeking."

Madai watched the enigmatic man and wondered why he could not merely have said that in the first place. "So you say!" he replied, energized again. Perhaps he would not lose the full of the year after all, and he would be the one to train Japhet's first arrows at a mark. "How far on the river?" he asked, suddenly stinging for his son.

"A fortnight, perhaps a bit more... and that, a part by land."

That was sounding very far. It certainly did not take a fortnight to carry a whole village down to the sea at every season. Madai was impatient and he was wishing he had not thought about Japhet. The little boy had his mother's eyes. At least Naru said so. And he did, when he laughed. There was a thing about loving a son... Madai could never have imagined it.

The frogs had not let up their singing, or the occasional frightful beast its roaring. But Madai had forgot to listen. It was true, he was disappointed that his first promise of an Ancient would take him till the new moon. The boat was drifting now, carried along in the laggard current and around a bend, when his eyes were caught by lights across the scattered dunes. A moment more, and the lights spotted the distance, fires that carried their scent as well as the promise of a village.

"Who lives there?" he asked. "Do you have their speech?"

Kittim shifted his weight, and did not answer at first. "A dwelling of no small number," he finally replied, "though I would press you on to the one I spoke of."

"That is good," Madai interrupted. "Perhaps they have stories."

"Assuredly," Kittim answered. "Everyone has a story."

Madai cocked his head at Kittim, clearly aware that he had known the man but one day. 'And I have made costly mistakes.' He thought of his stolen Spear and looked at the distance.

"I have come for this," he said aloud. "Are these not a people of this ancient land?"

"Is that the same as an Ancient, do you think?" Kittim reminded him.

Madai knew it was not. But still... they were here, and he might want to hear a thing that they remembered. "Are they fearsome?" he asked.

It was clear to him that Kittim was greatly disinclined toward this place, but Madai knew as well as anyone that men held their partialities dear. His could be as false as they might be true.

"There are those to fear among all men." Kittim answered, "but he that I speak of - "

"I wish to speak with these," Madai interrupted, claiming his authority as owner of the boat.

He recognized the slow, differing exhale as Kittim's reply and ignored it. Madai strained his eyes toward land, wished it were easier to see into the shadows now, for he was starting to look for a place to come aground. And he was aware, once again, of all the persistent bellowing ashore. He had not yet remembered that speaking would be a difficulty with a strange people of a strange tongue.

"As you wish," Kittim replied grimly. "Shall I speak for you?"

Ah, he remembered now. He felt a bit fallen away, but he answered as casually as he could, with a nod.

There had been a cloud of fish following his boat. They were slightly irridescent in the moonlight and making a feast of the slugs and such attached to its outer skins. Madai, having taken his ground, would not lose it; so he reached for his bow as the only tolerable sign of gratitude.

"Are you hungry?" he asked.

"I can eat," Kittim replied.

Madai fixed the rudder in place. He looked into the water, feeling oddly admonished. "Are these the sort of fish for eating?" he asked.

Kittim merely answered with a nod.

The swarming cluster was making a ready target glimmering in the moon- light. Madai impaled one with his first try as the rest scattered. Arrow and fish bobbed immediately just beside them. Kittim reached his hand and grasped the catch. "Another?" He asked, extracting the arrow and handing it back.

The fish were swarming back, not so smart, perhaps, and Madai took another with as little difficulty as the first. Kittim had reached out to scoop it up from the water when great spiked teeth closed around the fish, arrow and all. The animal rolled away, as skillful as a dancer, while Kittim jerked his hand back in fright. Madai's immediate thought was the sea serpent.

"What was that?" he asked with alarm, snatching a look at Kittim's hand.

Kittim looked at it, too, grateful, his face ashen. "A great toothy beast," he gasped.

Madai peered over the edge to catch just a glimpse of dark disappearing into the depth. "Maybe we should find something ashore," he suggested, watching the blood come back to Kittim's face.

In the shallows, the grasses parted as the boat moved through. The river was wider than it looked. Madai was sailing through an ocean of reeds. He tested the depth with his pole - level to his hip.

"I'm not getting out here," he muttered, thinking about the 'toothy beast.'

They poled a while longer, stirring up things that slithered and croaked, things that flew and bit, things that splashed the surface of the water with agitated tails. They poled long enough to ease the air of their disagreement. And when they reached a depth shallow to their knees, Madai cautiously stepped out. He would have hurled a lance close range at mammoth with more ease than he took that step.

But there were quick-moving, ugly, fat fish at the shore. They had long, black spikes undulating like arms around their mouths. Madai lanced one and lifted it out of the water thrashing on the point of his spear. It tasted like mud, even though they were exceedingly hungry. They saved the glinty fish for last and shared it.

The beach here was sand, crawling with spiky vines and hungry fleas. A horde of juvenile gnats competed with the fleas and spearflies. Madai and Kittim hugged close to the fire, where its smoke was their only defense. With a trolling water-beast near by and multitudinous miniature mouths all around, Madai suffered another near sleepless night.

And he was oddly ambivalent about tomorrow. What a pity it was that Kittim had managed to sully the prospect of these peoples on this eastern shore. Try as he might, Madai could not seem to assert his own judgements with clean authority. He felt a lot like his boat in the typhoon, at the mercy of ... what? The whim of the wind? He pulled his sandy robe around himself; something tiny nipped him from its folds. He rolled onto his back to see if the stars were still falling away. It relieved him that the dizzying feeling was gone, but the bejeweling stars were slightly awry. Always before the Bowman had been... there. Now the cosmic map showed him he was but a tiny speck in a far. foreign land.

He closed his eyes.

"Is this what You did?" he muttered upward. "Were Your eyes closed?"

It felt good, at first, to say that, but Madai let the lid of one eye open just a crack, with an ambiguous hope that there might be a shift, or a sliding star to mark that he, at the least, was heard. But the sky was still. He waited, then closed his eye again. Was this how freedom felt?

- 28 -

In the first of the morning, Madai pulled his aching body upright. He might have thought that sand would be a good sleeping-ground, no rocks or bumps; but it was a haven of nipping insects, and cold. If he had slept, he didn't know when. Kittim was pinching something between his fingers and popping it into the fire. So the night had not been kind to him either.

The idea of going to the village had regained its sheen, and Madai stood up. He looked into the distance. The village seemed farther away in the light. It was an impressive sight, enormous, especially for one accustomed to shelters of poles and animal skins. It was his first city, and by the sight of it, he was suddenly certain great wisdom indwelt it.

He had grown immune to the roaring and scuffing sounds through the dark hours. He was only mildly curious at the rustling of reeds along the river, though he did find his spear. It seemed something was coming their way, or so the bending grass seemed to say. Maybe it was something to eat, something besides mudfish.

He heard the water splashing in all directions away; a pair of long-legged birds shot up out of the rushes with a semi-hysterical caw and, following that, came a magnificent roar. Madai instantly thought about 'the toothy beast' and looked toward Kittim, who was also standing now with a look of...

Kittim pointed toward the dunes. "Run!" he commanded.

Madai hesitated. He was hungry and cranky after a miserable night. He had his bow, so he would kill it from a distance. As though 'it' heard Madai's intentions, a rumbling growl starting from the abyss of a very large lung came rolling through the reeds, setting his hair up. Kittim grabbed his arm and pulled him backward.

"Run!" he commanded again.

Madai shook him off. He planted his feet with a seriously clenched jaw and waited for the thing to emerge from the rushes.

It had slowed. That gave Madai the time to reset his arrow. And then a serpent-like face appeared above the grass. It swayed slightly from side to side, wide nostrils flaring and quivering. Its head hovered above the reeds as though detached from its body. It rolled out its tongue, licked the air at them and emerged.

Madai heard the twang of the string as he released his arrow. It hit with all the ferocity of a hollow reed and glanced aside from the creature's glinty chest. Madai was stunned - and motionless. The thing was a distance from them, breathtaking, with sparkling scales in the early sun. Madai recovered himself and lifted his spear above his shoulder. Kittim grabbed his arm again and swung him around.

"We must get over that dune," he yelled. "Run now!"

The beast lifted its head, sniffed again and lowered it. Then it began a slow lope across the sand toward them. Its sound was a huff, huff and a light crunching in the sand. Its eyes were yellow. Kittim jerked Madai back around and they started to run. That running of theirs snapped something in the creature's brain, and it started a gallop. Madai heard it behind them,quickly closing the gap. There came another more terrifying bellow, and Madai smelled an acrid scorching behind them.

"A fire-breather!" Kittim cried.

Kittim was running beside him. Madai heard him breathing fast, then a prayer in an unknown language. So, dragons were no fable after all!

The beast bellowed again, and this time Madai thought he could feel heat licking his back. They topped the dune; he stumbled, spilling them both into a roll that sped them down the other side. It gave them a momentary reprieve, taking them with a speed greater than they could otherwise have managed. When he scrambled up, Madai could not restrain a glance across his shoulder to glimpse the beast. It was just cresting the dune above them. No child's tale could tell the whole of its description, or the primordial terrors it conjured, even as it stood no taller than a man. It stretched a serpentine neck and seemed to pose there with all its shimmering scales that shifted colors in the sun, brilliant green, to blue. Red streaks ran from its twitching nostrils to its yellow eyes, which were slit in two by black. Its lips curled back to sniff at their fear. Madai watched, mesmerized, as it tilted its nose to the sky and lit the air again with the torch of its breath. It filled its lungs and sent the stream of fire upward, more than half the length of its scalloped tail. Kittim pulled at Madai again. Even as they ran, it struck him that here was another part of The Family's lore proved true, as though he were outside himself and living a high tale - till the animal bellowed again.

A plain lay before them, a flat expanse and, in the distance, the walled village. It was an irony that Madai's first glimpse of eastern man should be that of little black dots in the distance scrambling across the sand, running toward the city's protection. And he was leading the dragon there by just a hair's breadth.

Madai thought Kittim a wise man, knowing the location of the city, though a dismal prophet, for the beast would not be outrun. It was sliding in the sand behind them, coming down the dune. But as they ran, the city a distant if unlikely haven, Kittim turned just east of a straight course there. He gestured with his head for Madai to follow in a direction toward the plain. Madai turned and followed, his brain composing no thought but one: he did not want to feed a dragon.

The sudden shift seemed to throw the beast off its pace, at least for the moment.

Madai's lungs were suited for desperate running, his home being set in the rarified air of higher elevations, but the sand made his feet like stones. This, and the terror of his first sight of fire-breather - with him its aim. He was breathless. He started to wonder if Kittim was drawing the dragon into the plain to save the village, and he but a grudging sacrifice, when he glimpsed a sheen of black on the sand a short way ahead. They were slogging toward it, and the air began to smell.

The beast had ignored the fleeing townsmen and turned to follow them eastward. It was at home on the sand with its webbed feet and could actually run faster than it did. It was having a game with them, like a lioness, both sated and cruel.

Kittim turned his face toward Madai so that his words would not be lost "Bitumen," he cried. "Make for it, then do as I do."

Madai did not know bitumen, but he plunged after Kittim. They came right to the edge of the black mass and stopped. Kittim grabbed for Madai's arm, so as not to lose him in the sulfury murk.

Madai dared a moment's glance at Kittim, who was supremely confident. The dragon stopped when they did, some distance shy of them and lifted its head. It flexed the muscles of its jaw into a sort of sly grin.

"Do something!" Madai shouted, gasping for breath.

"Wait," Kittim answered softly.

Madai brought his spear to his shoulder again. If Kittim had nothing better in mind...

The dragon angled its snout at them; its neck muscles seemed to swell. It was no moment for study, but Madai watched in mute fascination. The animal lifted its shoulder slightly, a bulge appeared, and slowly, delicately, wings unfurled. Madai was stunned and cold with the knowledge that he was surely being mocked by a creature. The thing could have swooped upon them at any time. He was desperately wishing for the Sacred Spear, even as he gathered his wits and lowered his own oak to brace it against his thigh. He would wait for the final assault and hope the beast might impale itself by its own weight. It was perhaps a puny defense, but all that he could rightly think of.

The dragon was assessing them with its cold yellow eyes. It refolded its wings and huffed smoke into the air, followed by a spit of fire. Then it roared, lifted a front leg, and charged the distance between them like a galloping ox.

Madai willed himself to stand, waiting the coming blow. His first confidence fled as the ground shook, but he stood his place, as there was nothing else to do. Flashes of insight left their impressions instantaneously... Ido, and sorry he could not believe in life beyond... his mother, that she would never know what came of her last living son.

Though it seemed more, it took only a moment for the armored creature to reach them. "Pop!" And Madai instantly wondered if he had turned the head of the lance at himself, for the pain that pierced his thigh. He heard the quick snap that could be his own bone. A proper reckoning of time ceased as he looked down to realize he held just the shaft of his spear in his hand now, with the broken half buried in dragon flesh. There was red ooze coming from the spot. Madai was falling away from the animal backward, toward the pit. He felt Kittim grab him with an urgent strength and pull him away to the ground.

The dragon was bellowing. Madai heard its rage, if he couldn't see it. He felt Kittim's weight come down on him to force his face into the sand. He closed his eyes and listened to the creature's wounded fury.

It was being slain by its own force as its momentum carried it on into the slick lake of bitumen. It clawed at the black tar, igniting it with the fire of its mouth, then howled with unexpected agony. It rolled, covering its brilliant scales with flaming black. Still it flailed, as the sticky soup sucked it like a twisting anchor into the pit. There was to see, at the end, just the thrashing tip of its tail. Tar burned like a torch where it had been.

Madai was still, smelling fire and flesh, now in a heavy silence. He lifted his head, spitting sand. Kittim moved and they each rolled to their backs. They were breathing in short gulps, air that was singed and sharp. If they had not seen the last terrible struggle, they had heard it. They looked at the place where it was still burning.

"I lost my spear," Madai wheezed, sitting up.

"Be glad that is all!"

Madai was dazed, surprised to be alive. "I've not seen one before."

Kittim hit him on the back. "And lived to tell it. But you need not have lost your spear."

Madai looked away from the spot and blinked at him.

"So you led him to the bitumen., he granted.

"I thought it was a good plan." Kittim grinned for the first time.

Madai nodded and lay back on the sand, looking up at the blue-white sky. His leg throbbed and he rubbed it a moment. He rolled over and got to his knees. He slowly stood up, testing his leg, and shook the sand off. He looked at the pit, wondering if he were the singular aim of malicious serpents.

"I am starving," Kittim abruptly announced, sounding victorious.

"Yes." Madai answered vaguely. He looked back toward the river with a degree of uncertainty. "Do they come in packs?" he asked.

"They are solitary, my friend."

"Even a serpent has a mate."

"Only to plant his seed," Kittim replied. "They are cold-hearted beasts and do not tend their young. The brood devours one another."

"Good," said Madai.

He limped cautiously toward the pit, where the tail of their dragon lay across the black surface. Limp, without a twitch. He bent and touched the sticky mass and brought his finger back afixed with a second skin of steamy tar.

"Bitumen," he mumbled. He looked at what was left of the animal again, vaguely thinking of Japhet and the story he would tell.

"Shall we celebrate with a speckled fish?" Kittim asked.

Madai looked at him and away, toward the distance. "I am tired of fish." He gestured at the city with his eyes.

Kittim's glow slowly faded. He shrugged. "As you wish," he said. "They shall welcome us, as we have killed their dragon."

- 29 -

Sand seemed to have found every crevice in Madai's body, scraping him raw with every limping step. He touched his beard and heard it crackle. He was hungry, and his thigh was on fire where it remembered the heel of the lance.

But the village was close now. Madai wondered at the pace Kittim had set, brisk even if he didn't want to go, and with remarkable stamina. Of course he had not suffered the end of a seven-stone spear. Madai rubbed his thigh again. His stomach grumbled as he thought about the fire-beast, a conglomerate of malice and beauty.

He shifted his third and last spear to his left hand, recalling to himself that he had lost both his others. He resettled his quiver, strapped with the long-bow across his back, having taken the time to reclaim them from the boat. Madai had insisted. He probably looked more the antagonist than a man looking for answers. That he was cloaked in crusty animal hides and had a wooly golden head of hair and beard had not occurred to him.

There was a real clamor going on in the village, and the smell of something awful in the air, carried, perhaps, in the smoke churning up into the sky, black as storm clouds. Madai had never endured such a stench; even the inadvertent slip of his knife into the musk sack of a water sow did not smell so bad. His eyes started to stream the nearer they got.

"We have started a spectacle," Kittim announced. He stopped just outside the wall and turned around to wait for Madai.

"What is that stench?"

Kittim covered his nose with his hand. "Bitumen in their fire," he answered as they approached the open gateway.

It was a strange occurence in a land of dragons to leave the passage unguarded; at least Madai thought so. He stepped first through the gate. And as he did, something dropped suddenly from above, all arms and legs and stirring up the dust. Madai coughed and didn't have time to defend himself.

But it was only a boy with big black eyes and perfect white teeth. He flashed them an energetic smile before he fell facelong into the dirt. Madai was immediately relieved and alarmed in one, wondering whether the boy had broken his leg.

Kittim bent down to touch the boy's dusty hair. He said something that sounded a lot like a kind of throaty bird; the lad looked up, seeming both awestruck and excited, and babbled back at Kittim with the same raspy sound.

"This boy watched you spear the dragon," Kittim explained, glancing toward the top of the wall, "from up there."

Kittim lifted the boy to his feet and started to talk some more. The sounds were totally indiscernable. Madai watched them a moment, listening in vain, and looked away at the first city of his life.

It was beyond all imaginings. It spread in every direction, ringed by the thick, high wall. Its earthen dwellings stood square and erect on either side of narrow lanes. It seemed a place to get lost in, with nothing to set for a landmark. It was dusty and smelly and entirely remarkable.

Its inhabitants were responsible for the infernal stench and noise of profound celebration, utter abandonment. Madai forgot his hunger and limpy thigh and looked toward the sounds, hoping the folk of this great place had something true to tell him, though they were now rejoicing in the death of the dragon, as anyone would.

He glanced at Kittim, who was fixed entirely on the boy. There was a look on his face that Madai couldn't read. It was as inscrutable as this people's tongue. Then the boy nodded, his face transformed from awe to trust. He spun around and raced away toward the heart of the city.

"He is telling them we have arrived," Kittim muttered, looking after the lad. "Good."

Kittim gave Madai another of his looks, which Madai would ignore.

In addition to the burning tar, he was beginning to smell the quiet odor of humankind exuding from open doorways. It was one reason The Family moved with the seasons. A domestic fowl skittered across the path and the sand itching at his skin rose up to plague him again. It was all that and Kittim's scowl that really pressed upon him. If not for the man's skill with tongues...

"They are coming," Kittim announced.

Madai looked the direction the boy had gone. "Good," he repeated.

෴ ෴ ෴

Madai saw immediately that they were a people of the same foreign appearance as Kittim, dusky skin and cropped black hair, though Kittim stood above them by a head. Madai could not deny that the thought of Nephilim occurred to him once again. Their clothes were not nearly so fine as what his companion wore, but altogether more elegant than his own. And, as Kittim, their men did not wear hair on their faces.

A persistent babble emanated from the approaching men, and rapt expressions. What Madai had hoped for was an Ancient, wise and noble, with empirical, original knowledge. What he got was a surge of excitable people who fell on the ground with their faces in the sand.

Madai gaped. Kittim took a step back and barked at them. They popped up instantly, startled, their eyes round. Madai knew that tone, as Kittim had used it when he insisted that sacred offerings go to The God alone.

"What did you tell them?" Madai asked.

"That we are no gods," he muttered.

Madai had thought as much. There were hoary heads in the lot, old enough, older than Ashkinaz, even Tiptri, and from east of the Brine Sea. He didn't try to stop himself, but laughed a cold, dry and disappointed chuckle. He was hungry and his leg hurt and he was feeling like a fool. He was looking at a rabble of smelly, dirty people whose ignorance exceeded his own most impious doubts. Even he knew that men were not gods. Kittim had been right after all.

A ripple ran through the crowd, beginning a slow murmur. They shuffled aside, creating a wide pathway. Madai ran his eyes down the opening toward a second, more official-looking group of men, who approached with an important air. They were passing with uplifted faces through the throng, wearing flowing robes and stiff expressions. That he and Kittim were not gods here was clearly understood by the leader of this entourage. He did not seem pleased, and Madai had seen his manner before, a man chasing power. He was hairless, with eyes that were dark and long, ringed with black, making them the only distinct feature in his narrow face. It surprised Madai to feel the hair on his back stand up. This would complicate things.

Madai had seen other kinds of men than The Family in his life; but they had been kinsmen of a distant blood. And they who made houses to the north, all hairy men and stout, as tall as he and rightly clothed against the cold. This one was also tall, but lanky as a boy though he did not have a boy's face, though it was sleek of hair. And his clothes would not stand a storm, were white, adorned like a woman's. He carried a staff worthless against any sort of beast, topped with the caped head of a serpent. What he possessed that suggested itself to the people to be of importance, Madai could not see. The half-score of men who were with him wore eely faces with sweaty skin.

What had he thought, coming here?

Kittim waited, watching them come. The crowd was bowing again. Kittim held erect. Madai watched the man come just below Kittim's chin. If he were leader to this people, Madai supposed he and Kittim were less welcomed now than they had been at first.

The fellow cleared his throat and waited a moment before he began to speak. Madai recognized the throaty quality of the language again, helpless to understand. He could, however, decipher the man's stitched mouth and his manner. When Kittim answered, Madai had to cock an eye at him with genuine amusement. If the leader's first speech had been haughty, Kittim's answer held a decided bite.

The listening crowd reacted to the exchange with considerable interest and a low, spreading murmur. Madai glanced down at them. Their faces were still on the ground, with their backs in the air, but a few were turned to the side and watching Kittim respond to their leader with an utter lack of admiration.

The man's face stiffened, with piercing little dark holes for eyes. Madai knew he would not allow such a slight as Kittim had given him. He was gripping his serpent staff as if to pose a threat, his face turning dark. It made Madai actually smile to envision this innocuous fellow in a joust with his rather more able companion. Then the man relaxed. He turned away and said something to the crowd with a derision that all could understand. His words lifted their faces out of the sand as a thin smile pulled the man's lips tight.

"He is their chief?" Madai asked Kittim.

"He is their priest."

The man looked back at the sound of their voices. His face was inscrutable, indifferent; he spoke to Kittim again, overtly dismissive, and turned away with a slight wave of his hand.

"What does he want?" Madai whispered.

"That we follow him."

"Why should we do that?"

Kittim indicated the crowd. "They will do us an honor."

Madai looked back at the people. They had more the appearance of a mob now. With liberation from the fire-beast, and an amount of strong spirits, their friendly manner could easily shift, especially if set after by their priest. Madai literally began to count the number of arrows in his quiver and assured himself that his long-bow would end a match of strength - till the arrows ran out, of course.

But a fellow scrambled up and grinned at him. He said something. And when it was clear that Madai did not understand, he came to Kittim's elbow and repeated himself. Kittim answered. They exchanged a short volley of raspy sounds before the fellow indicated with a sweeping arch of his hand that they were to follow him. He seemed a merry sort, which quieted Madai's growing apprehension. The drumming started again as the crowd remembered that their beast was dead and shifted back toward the boiling pots of tar with good cause for a revelry.

ଔଙ୍କ ଔଙ୍କ ଔଙ୍କ

"This fellow will take us to the bath," Kittim explained.

Madai thought it was a strange turn; but with his skin rubbed raw, the long drenchings from the sea, and the indomitable fleas, the thought of a cleaning took on a welcome nearly as good as a meal.

They followed behind the talkative and friendly fellow, who followed several paces behind the priest. Madai wondered where the bath should be taken, as there was no water to see but what was behind at the river. He trailed a bit behind, taking in all the sights, which, despite the priest, continued to astonish and amaze him. He wondered at the square mud dwellings with their human stench, and supposed he should prefer the mountains. They came to the fire reeking of boiling tar, from which the townsfolk lit arrows to repel the dragon, as told them by their guide. They passed through the square and the surrounding collection of what now seemed cramped little dwellings.

The lane suddenly opened to a second square, this one clean, unsullied by the town's populous and fronted by a tall, white construction made of clay bricks. Madai stared with even greater wonder than he had had at first. He had never seen a step before - sharp, precise and regular - but this building was set atop a rise that was climbed by a small mountain of them. The priest began a very regal ascent toward what was, again as told by their guide, a temple.

The immediate surrounding was paved not by dust, but by stone. Madai looked at the fitted blocks with the wonder of a dweller in forests. He had heard the tales of cities from which his forebearers had come and had come to think them high tales, a bit of fancy, given the years and natural sentiment. Well, they had been modest. He looked back at the construction, unmatched in all his experience of human structures. It made the little lodge he had made for Ido with such pride seem a hovel.

The priest had not spared them another glance, but topped the stairs to pass under a portico supported by a pillar of clay in girth the size of Madai's chest.

Their guide did not follow up the stairs. He was muttering. It had the music of a man chanting by rote, maybe a prayer, and he did not move from the place they had stopped till the priest passed out of view. Then he turned back to Madai and Kittim, his eyes veiled with a mixture of veneration and uncertainty. He waved his arm again to a building set at the side and slightly back.

This second building was not so large, and there were no steps to reach its arched entry. But it was adorned all across its front with the most vibrant of colors. It was a great panoramic of wild and brilliant blue centered with a green the color of emerging spring. In his surprise, it took Madai a moment to recognize that there were figures painted in the green. One was a great creature, his mouth sprung wide and ringed with a wealth of teeth, instantly bringing to mind of the 'toothy beast' at the river. The second figure was a man who had harnessed the creature and led him by a cord. Madai harrumphed; such arrogance! What men could do with mud and stone, they could not do with such an animal.

He was suddenly being pulled at. Madai looked down at the little man, who was plucking at his ragged sleeve to lead him forward and to make him hurry.

Together, they stepped into the shade of the arched doorway. Madai forgot all his first disparagements as they came through the outer door into the soothing cool of the inside. He had become a being of raw discomfort and ravaged skin. Here, the air seemed a kind of balm, damp and fragrant with myrrh, an odor of which he had no prior experience. Madai realized in an instant, and with his every sense, that he had come to a whole other land. He closed his eyes and allowed himself a lapse into pleasure.

When he opened them again, there had joined them in the wide and empty entry a young girl. She was standing at the back, looking almost ethereal in the misty air. They came across the tile floor toward her. As Madai's eyes adjusted, he saw that she was not a goddess-spectre at all, but a young waif, and nearly naked. A round black disk set in a hole in her ear pulled heavily at her lobe. It seemed a ridiculous offense when she was so scandalously uncovered. Instead of a vest, an amulet hung between her two tiny breasts, with a rope around her waist holding up a sort of kilt behind and before. Madai was indignant for her and looked away, as it was the only kindness he could show her, though not before he had found her eyes, which were dark and nervous.

She could be no more than ten and would have been guarded in The Family. He remembered Ido, coming to sail the snow in Tiras's sled, as innocent and free as a lark, and not despoiled by a gouged-out ear and a talisman between her baby breasts. This had been done by some ruthless, Godless fellows. The thought brought him up short - for if The God was not, then who was to set the boundary stone, to proclaim a thing not done? His lips stretched into a tight thin line, perceiving irony: that men may, in fact, all be Godless fellows, should they like it or not.

Madai was glad when she turned her back to lead them behind a curtain. The talkative fellow seemed to have disappeared, but Kittim followed the girl without a question. She brought them into a room with a pool sunk into the floor. A score of other girls just like her were filling the pool with water. It seemed the source of the mist and the myrrh, a rising of sweet vapors. Madai felt relieved when the girl was joined by the others. Somehow, a score of little maids seemed not so terrible as one... with nervous eyes.

They were asking for Kittim's clothes. That seemed the case, at least, because he stood with his arms folded across his chest while they pulled at his sleeves. He spoke to them in a kindly voice, though unshakable. It was a short contest, as they seemed soon convinced that he was burdened with a strange sort of modesty and left him alone. Kittim must have explained that Madai was the same, despite his looks, because they didn't pry at him. They did, however, study his beard and the hair on his arms at a wary distance. In any case, the girl who had met them gave Kittim a jar. She chattered at the others, and they left with her. Madai heard their twittering behind the curtain, and then fading, as if they moved a distance into another room.

Madai was glad when they were gone. It was clear that the water was drawn for them. But he waited for Kittim, as if there were some sort of rite which Kittim would know for stepping into a fragrant and steaming bath set in tiles.

"You are more salt-crusted than I," Kittim observed with a smile. "She may be back if you don't hurry."

Madai started pulling at his clothes. They were stiff as a dry pelt and harder to climb out of than he expected. Kittim pulled his over his head and stepped into the water as though he were lord of the house. Madai could only be impressed by his confidence.

Madai followed him in, setting his first foot into the warm, steamy water, watching a milky cloud form around his ankle. It was warm, like the place where the waters of the sulfur plains drained into the river, only a better smell by far. He walked down three steps and sat on the slick tiles, letting the oily water find all his bitten places. He leaned his head on a step, closed his eyes and forgot his pity for the maids. It was an excruciating bliss that he decided to savor.

"The priest will drink a libation with us and bless us and send us away," Kittim told him.

Madai slipped farther down to his chin, till his beard was floating in the water. "Hmm..." he offered. "He would be an enemy, I think."

Kittim grunted, and Madai smiled, cracking his lips in a new place. "I suppose we will leave after that."

"I think they will feed us first."

Madai opened one eye. Then he closed it again with no mention of his quest. It was quite understood by them both that nothing here would be gained save a full belly and a good wash. He sunk with his face under the water to soothe his sunburned skin. His hair floated on the surface like dry twigs, and he didn't emerge till he was desperate for air. The water tasted of his own salt. He blinked it out of his eyes and tried to pull his fingers through his tangled beard.

Kittim had the stone pot given him by the girl. He took a globby fingerful and rubbed it into his hair and all over his skin. It had the effect of washing him clean and stirring up a whole other smell of perfume. He gave it to Madai with a raised brow and that look of command. Madai took it, smelled it, and washed countless weeks of filth away. There was a foam in his hand that came from the stuff and floated in the water all around him. A bit of twig was floating with it. The foam was brown and gritty, and made his eyes burn, and smelled like hyacinth. Even Tiras, who might laugh at the woman smell of it, would not resist. He wondered if he actually moaned at the pleasure, and hoped not. It was not such as a hunter would wear, to announce himself to even the dullest nostril, but it was irresistible. When he closed his eyes, it brought to mind the lower meadow in spring.

He might have been drifting when he was startled by a most regrettable sound, Kittim coming out of the water and dripping plinks back into the pool. He opened his eyes. The water was cloudy, with a new layer of grit on the bottom. Kittim had a cloth and was rubbing himself dry.

They searched for their clothes with no success. It seemed that some silent, naked girl had taken them in the quiet and left in their place two clean, brown robes. Kittim took one and pulled it over his head. But Madai was searching the place a second time. He was not indifferent to the loss of his elk breeches; they had been sewn by a precious hand. But also missing were his last spear and his long-bow.

"My bow is gone!" he whispered, more a hiss.

Their noise brought the slave girl back. She came with another jar of fragrance, which was intended for their hair. Madai was glad of the bath, glad of the soft new robe against all his nicks and bitten skin, even glad for the oil on his scalp. But the theft of his weapons was a disaster.

"My bow!" he insisted.

Kittim seemed not concerned at all, which was more than odd. And worse, he was the only one of them who could ask. And here, he was sitting quietly, eyes closed, as the girl finished the combing of his hair. Madai could only watch in impatient silence.

೮೧೧ ೮೧೧ ೮೧೧

As they emerged from the bath, there was the same merry fellow, who appeared to have been waiting all the while. He had a countenance that said he would do them a service and be glad of it. He was slightly worshipful as he bowed. Kittim said something, which lacked that bark he had used with the priest. It brought the man's face up, bearing an anxious smile.

"We are summoned by the priest." Kittim informed Madai. "We are to follow this fellow."

"But my bow!" Madai protested again.

Kittim smiled. "I expect it will all be returned. That priest only wants us thanked and gone away."

"I will have it back," Madai muttered. He followed Kittim, who followed their guide out of the cool of the bath and into a hot midday.

ഗ്രരു ഗ്രരു ഗ്രരു

Madai was glad he had seen the priest and his protectors, and they had shown themselves harmless in strength, for all the powers of intimidation this temple possessed. It was once and again the size of the bath, lifted higher, entered by a galley of stairs as wide as his ship. And when they reached the top, the sound of their sandals, which gave Madai real trouble in walking, echoed across the portico.

A man with a wide curved blade in his hand was waiting at the door. Madai had never seen such a weapon before and kept his eye on it. This man was not a timid priest, to be sure. He had his sights on Madai, as well, but stepped aside and opened the door, a somewhat mild duty in the face of such a knife. Madai could feel the guard at his back even as he walked inside. He heard the door close, and they were left to adjust their eyes in the dim. A strong smell hung in the smoky air.

"Incense," Kittim told him.

Madai felt naked, standing in the alien atmosphere robbed of weapon and leggings and all things familiar. A man was coming toward them through the smoke, as Madai reminded himself it was only today that he had escaped a fire-beast. He had the presence to know the approaching man was not the priest, though he shared the same hairless face and head which made them all indistinct from one other. But the priest would save for himself an important entrance, Madai knew. Men like that would.

Their guide was dismissed. Madai heard him shuffle away.

Their new attendee wore a less friendly face. A slight gesture of his immaculate hand indicated that they were to follow. He led them into a second, tiny room, which adjoined the first. It was furnished with a low wooden bench against the wall and nothing else. He said they were to wait. Madai was annoyed.

"I have remembered my stomach," Kittim announced quietly, which had a way of drawing a smile to Madai's face and dismissing the dismissive servant.

"I would watch for poison," he warned

"Ah, but we are still their champions."

Kittim sat down, secure and unconcerned. And Madai went on a search for his weapons.

Straight through the little room was another door, which Madai pushed open. Windows in this room lighted a cavernous space. The look of the walls made him forget what he had come through the door to find.

"You must come here!" he called.

He was looking at the disembodied head of a dragon. It was painted with nearly the brilliance of the living creature. And there was a man, slayer of the beast, mighty in appearance. These people did love to paint and brag!

Only there was something about the man… He was holding a great spear and wearing a headdress of gold and precious stones. Madai knew gold and precious stones; they were craved after by other clans and fought for, even if they didn't feed a hungry belly. But Madai understood a thing, looking at the mural.

"I think we have impersonated their chief," he said, smiling.

Kittim grunted something. Madai turned at the sound, not having heard him come into the room; and there, behind Kittim, was a painting on the opposite wall with another story to tell. It was the same man, dark as the earth, dressed in colorful clothes and feathers, with a circle of stars inscribed above his head. It was the stars that caught Madai's attention: a well-recognized constellation of critical importance, with hints of a Bowman's claim and a Virgin's seed. Should he scoff? In such a place, Madai didn't know. And then he felt a question pose itself, as fraught with possibility as it was world-shifting.

"The King of Shinar," Kittim virtually hissed.

And for some reason, the scoffsome tone annoyed Madai.

- 30 -

Madai was finished with the food nearly before the echos of the servant's retreating footsteps died. He was, of course, thinking about his long-bow again, and the King of Shinar, and what Kittim was not saying about it all. The priest was just an unnecessary appendage, an impediment to what he was now determined to discover.

When the priest arrived, he had refreshed the paint around his eyes and donned a headdress reminiscent of the mural, and he wore a hint of red on his thin mouth. He had wine brought, and a brazier smoking with incense. He blessed them, thanked them and had them served the wine. Madai thought about poison again even as Kittim took the cup.

"He asks our honor at a festivity tonight," Kittim chuckled with wine on his lips, "and he says the tar pit was convenient."

Madai started to ask about his spear.

"He gives us lodging with our friend from the bath," Kittim continued. "And he regrets that this temple cannot abide the unclean or the foreign."

Which irked Madai yet again. He would have settled a menacing look on his face if not that the priest had swung away and was crossing the hall and out the door. Madai coughed, being robbed of even the chance to pose the threat.

ଓଔ ଓଔ ଓଔ

Hamonheb, their new friend, began a long and throaty discourse, making the sort of sounds of a rowdy gull to Madai and leading them toward his home. He was, in elaborate detail, explaining about the pots of tar used for setting an arrow to flame, once the defense of choice, though now only an old habit. They had found a more successful way to pacify the beast: a cripple or a beggar, a blood offering and quite dependably effective.

Despicable, in Madai's estimation, finishing his verdict of the place.

The people had been on the plain planting the fields when they heard the dragon, Hamonheb was telling them, and had fled away, back to the city. The boy had climbed the wall to watch. He had seen the dragon turn after two foreigners, be slain by the yellow-haird one, and fall into the tar pit.

"Like the great Nimrod!" Hamonheb enthused. He gave them a conspiratorial look. "The Priest said you were men as any others, and it was the pits," he chuckled, bobbing and smiling at Madai. "But the boy saw it all - you with the spear."

Kittim recounted it to Madai and added at the end, "The people will honor us at a festivity tonight, when it is cool, and there will be a banquet. We are expected."

"They are better pleased by us than their priest," Madai assessed.

"They are those who have fed the dragon."

It was only a short walk to Hamonheb's little house. It appeared obvious that he was not a man of great means, which delivered an indelicate and silent message. But his home was Madai's first experience with houses. That it was square struck him as unnatural, though he knew their kinsmen North had made square huts of stone. But he had never stood in one. It felt as though the roof sat on his head. The furnishings were clay, as was his house, as if it all had been hewn from a mud pit. As though to disguise what seemed an earthy tomb, benches had been draped with colorful weaving, and grass mats covered the floors.

Figures of clay were tucked away into niches which pocked the walls. They were grotesque shapes, great swollen bellies and the hidden places of men, the size of ox parts. Laughable... and something unsettling, too. There was an obvious dragon set in the highest niche, where the smoking lamps were placed, like a sort of shrine. Madai realized with a start that this kindly man had a beast for a god. It was a bitter discovery, to come so far for this, to leave his son...

But Hamonheb blustered with the honor of his guests, and he seemed a good-hearted man. He called his wife, a slightly voluptuous middle-aged woman covered in thin gauze, and was proud also to bring them his other wife. She was scandalously young, and thin. But she was clothed in a more substantial cloth, with a gaping hole in her ear where the disk of a slave had once been lodged. She seemed something of a slave still, and busily arranged sleeping places for them. It appeared the people rested at the heat of the day. Hamonheb clucked his tongue at the girl, who came from her duties to remove his sandals. She took his cloak and hung it on a peg set in the wall. He was wearing a grey tunic that just barely covered his "ox parts." He grinned at Kittim. Madai could see that he was somehow proud of his situation. He took a drink from a cup his first wife was offering him and said something to Kittim. He pointed at the mat laid out in a far corner, just as the child-wife laid a last covering on it. He bobbed his head with another grin and retreated to a back room.

His two wives clucked and tucked and pulled at Madai and Kittim until they shed their sandals and settled on the mat. They were given mugs of thin ale which was the same color as the mud hut. Madai lay with his head on his arm, remembering sand fleas. But his body was wonderously clean again and he didn't recognize his own smell. There were the first rumblings of Hamonheb's snores. And with the bread, and clean bodies, and the day's changeable circumstances, he was brought to an encroaching drowsiness, till he ceased to hear the ministrations of Hamonheb's wives.

⊱⊰ ⊱⊰ ⊱⊰

The celebrations began before nightfall. Some tame beast had been taken and was roasting over a second pit of hot coals. The priest was in attendance, seated above them as any principal should be. Madai had wakened from a sleep that had started well but had been betrayed with dreams. He had had to rearrange the face of Ido from the piteous servant girl. And he woke in the dark disoriented. He woke with a sadness again that overrode even the smell of roasting boar.

The priest was brought a first and prime part of the meat. He took it between his fingers as if it were a piece of yap rat. Perhaps his taste rose above swine on a spit. Madai watched and gladly exchanged his angst for disdain.

He was hungry again; the meat was in plenteous quantity. He and Kittim were served immediately after the priest. A servant brought them brimming cups of ale and Hamonheb beamed at the tribute.

Just after the feasting had started in earnest, a good deal of bellowing began, and the drums, beating a contagious rhythm. That started a clamor through the crowd and the beginnings of a chant. It was a reenactment, the death throe of the dragon, complete with two men dressed as the fire-beast, which set Hamonheb to another monologue telling about the whole episode, as if Kittim had not been there at all. It was a tale Kittim soon quit recounting, leaving Madai to watch the show.

It was a diminutive dragon at best, a head of skin pulled around a skull. But it was an enthusiastic dragon, and a creative reenactment, most pleasing to the excitable crowd. There was also the infinite passing of strong wine amongst the people, which heightened everyone's spirits. The battle of impersonated beast and man matched the growing mood. It even drew a smile from Madai, as he took another sip. And the show lasted a good deal longer than the actual event. Hamonheb stood up, teetering a bit, started to point at Madai and called out to the crowd to take note that the champion was here beside him.

The crowd turned their way and started to cheer with a louder swell. They were near the point of utter bedlam, due mostly to the spirits, when, as though to send a raucous mob the distance, there came a loud blast from a long, copper horn. It came from the direction of the priest.

It had the intended effect as the crowd gave him their somewhat fuzzy attention.

The priest stood up. He lifted a bowl of incense into the air and waited for quiet. An immediate hush descended, punctuated by spotty cheers and hushes from those more sober. Perhaps by habit or hope, they were waiting for their leader to speak. And so he began a long pronouncement. He took a tray filled with smoking coals and sprinkled it with incense.

The people roared at the blessing, having decided to cheer the priest as well as they had cheered the dragon slayers. Madai had the eyes of a falcon and watched the priest's expression start to glow at the praise. He wet his mouth and waved the smoking incense higher, from side to side, before replacing it on its stand. He lifted a hand to them and said something else. Three men came up beside him holding rams' horns, which they blew in short, quick blasts to announce the priest's withdrawal. But as the last echo of trumpet faded, there came from the bath house two little maids. They came wearing sea lilies in their hair, and nothing more. They came across the stone courtyard to slowly climb the stairs to the temple, to grace the priest with their gifts of self.

Such was come of the little maids.

ℭℜ ℭℜ ℭℜ

At this, the crowd considered themselves dismissed to their own pleasures. Their attentions turned, and the drinking rose to extravagant heights. Hamonheb was boundlessly good at it. There came a passing maid, whom he invited with a gesture. He leaned toward Kittim to ask him something, a glistening on his lips but did not seem to notice Kittim's responding look. Instead, he turned to the girl himself. And with just the support of a willing partner and a cup of ale, Madai and Kittim's importance was forgot.

So was Madai's first education of a people to the East. He watched Hamonheb with new eyes, remembering the second wife in his little hovel, the gaping, drooping hole in her ear and her youth. There was an unsavory stirring in the atmosphere as Madai was witness, though he did not know it, to a rising goddess cult, the origin of which had brought a tower down.

Kittim put his hand on Madai's sleeve and did not hide his words. "Time to leave," he muttered, and they rose without speaking again toward the house of Hamonheb.

It was not empty, which gave Madai a profound relief. He was glad to see the young slave-wife. She seemed surprised that they had so soon returned, but somewhat hopeful as well, and she gave them each a cup of warm goat's milk.

She explained that her master's first wife was also at the festival and that they would be gone a goodly while. Madai was glad there would be no difficulty in leaving. It would be a simple matter to slip away to the river by cover of the celebration noise.

"But you will not be meddled with here," she argued. "They will go till morning and will not bother about you at all."

"Nonetheless," Kittim answered kindly, "we would like to be away."

Madai watched as her eyes grew large and round. He was struck with a feeling nearing guilt as they glistened with unexpected tears. Then she glanced away. When she looked back, she looked at Kittim as though she would speak, then a thoughtful expression passed her face and she disappeared into the back.

"Please, will you wait?" she called from inside the little space.

Madai could hear her rummaging. It was dark in there, and he wondered that she could see anything at all. But she quickly returned, covered in a heavy cloak that couldn't possibly have been made for her, enormous as it was.

"Then I will take you to the river," she said. She leaned into the little niche again. "Your clothes and weapons were brought here." She brought them out. "I will not be missed, and you will need eyes that know the way."

Kittim bowed to her, as he would not to the priest. They scrambled into their own clothing, now a little cleaner, probably by her own hand, and followed her through a back door. The sound of revelry was slowly dying. But their passage was silent enough. They passed through deserted, darkened streets, streets that turned and twisted, and were soon most grateful for her.

She took them in a meandering route. They could not know that the lodgings had not been well planned and many paths would only take them back to where they had started. But their quiet guide led them unerringly to a small opening in the wall. A light gate of woven rush closed it. She pushed it open with one tiny hand.

"We shall cross the dunes behind the tar pit," she said to Kittim, a tremor in her voice at the mention of it.

Once outside the city, she moved like a little bird hopping across the sand; she was so slight. And they slogged along behind her. Madai was amazed they could have out-run the fire-beast at all. He knew it was some cruelty of the dragon, prolonging the game, that had saved them in the end, that and the bitumen of which Kittim had somehow known. He could smell the sulfur now; it was getting stronger. But the fire was out, and the tomb of the dragon was fully dark. Madai strained to catch a last glimpse of its tail as they hurried past. And then, retracing their way, they climbed what had been the first dune of their frantic escape.

As they crested the top, there was visible the shimmer of the river crawling peacefully across the desert eastward. Madai thought the air was fresher by extreme degrees. It was an odorous stench they were leaving behind, of the tar and of the city. He knew Kittim had been right about that place. But Madai was not fully disappointed, having gone there. At last he had a destination in mind; he would find the warrior-king, the King of Shinar.

The girl was hardly out of breath and seemed glad to have gotten them this far. They began the slide down the dune. Madai would just have asked what she knew of the man in the mural when a little bundle dropped from inside the folds of her voluminous cloak. She looked up, afraid and found out, with a terrible entreaty in her eyes.

Hers was a desperate plight. The night air was thick with its unspoken presence, and no man of the Holy God nor man of simple honor could leave her. So three put prints in the mud and then waded into the river, to find the boat quietly bobbing unmolested in the reeds. It seemed so much longer ago than just the one day since they had left it. Though here they were, returned with a little stranger.

There were also shining eyes skimming the surface all around them, red and moving forward. Madai nearly forgot the girl with an urgency which brought tingles racing from his toes all the way to his knees.

The girl ignored the eyes and preferred the boat as a kind of savior, to take her across the waters a long way. She did not cast a glance across her shoulder from the way they had come; and though she had seemed lithe and able as they escaped the city, she was tired now. Kittim picked her up with her light bundle and set her inside. He tucked her round with the cloak like a meticulous father.

Madai and Kittim poled the boat quickly away. They were anxious about the red-eyed creatures, the city, as well, and they with a stolen girl. They paddled into the current and slipped around the bend. The fire was what they could see of the city, still blazing high in the square, proclaiming an end to the dragon and the hearty embrace of a goddess cult. The city would not discover them missing till light, nor the little maid with them. Even so, Madai and Kittim were silent, the boat outlined in the moon's wake, until they had put it all behind them.

- 31 -

All the night they poled against an indolent current, making good distance with so little effort. Only the bright crimson of morning evidenced the length of their vigil. The little visitor stirred as she, too, felt the dawn. She came first as sprouting legs, stretching, coming out from the huge wool cloak. A tumble of brown hair emerged next, then wide brown eyes in a thin brown face. Awareness was immediate as she looked up at them.

"Are we escaped?" she whispered.

Kittim smiled at her. "You are safe," he said.

Madai watched her relax, and age rolled off her till she was just a shy little girl. Where before she had served in Hamonheb's house and led them away, she was now a guest of two men she didn't know. Indeed, one who spoke a strange tongue, with eyes like the sky and hair like the sun. But her smile, when it came was true, if slightly cautious. She inclined her head with a dignity born of better circumstance...

"May God bless your kindness," she whispered.

"And yours as well," Kittim replied in yet a third language.

She was startled that he could speak her native tongue and gave a quick, open smile as her last reserve evaporated.

Madai did not understand the words, but he heard the shift in Kittim's tone. He looked at the man again with new wonder. "What did you say?" he asked.

"I have told her she is safe with us," Kittim answered.

Madai nodded, glancing her way again.

"What is your name, child?" Kittim asked.

"Iscah."

He continued gently, "How did you come to that place?"

She was watching him with growing devotion. "Taken by Sabeans," she answered calmly. "While I tended Papa's goats in the hills."

Kittim put his hand on her shoulder. "How long since?"

She paused a moment, looked from Madai to Kittim and contemplated her answer. "It has been two summers past," she finally replied, absently tugging her earlobe.

He nodded. "She was captured and sold two years ago," Kittim told Madai.

With the light of morning, and the distance growing between them and the city, Madai was glad they had stolen the girl. It reminded him of a long-ago rescue, another life-time. And also that men are the same, even here, where original truth should be easily had. It was a discouraging thought...

He realized the boat had become motionless in the water. The current had disappeared. He looked at the sky, where the sun had brought the dawn, and turned his mind to eating. He took his bow, grateful a second time to the girl, as she had given it back. He propped his foot on the side of the boat, which brought Iscah's eyes wide and round.

"For fish," he assured her.

Kittim clucked Madai's words at her. "Can you see in there, Madai?" he asked.

Madai looked into the soupish murk. "Mudfish?" he asked.

"Maybe something better on the shore," Kittim suggested.

Iscah chirped an alarm as they turned inland, pointing at the reeds. Indeed, there was a thing lurking there, with grey nodules; it slowly submerged, in hopes of an ambush, perhaps. They passed the place and pushed farther up-stream till they came upon a shore where the coastline was free of hiding places. Iscah had sat, her hands in her lap, satisfied that she had saved them again when she spied a large flat turtle sunning on the sand. It had come out hoping for warmth. An ironic end, as they soon had it roasting.

Its flesh was sweet and mild, a good end to the long, sleepless night's fast. Madai had enjoyed the meat immeasurably. He stretched and rubbed his face. Already, the sweet smells and comfort of the bath seemed a time long ago. He would have tried to snatch a moment's sleep if not for the fleas once again.

Iscah knew only that she was safe and, licking her fingers, that she was fed. The taller of the two, Kittim, who was exceedingly beautiful, spoke the language of her father and looked at her with virtuous and gentle eyes. That he spoke as her kinsmen suggested that he might know how to find them. She was exultant.

She watched the two wrestling with the fleas and was afraid they should soon wish the protection of their boat. It was her purpose to delay that. She stood up and shook the sand off, careful not to fling it in their direction, and set her goal along the river toward a patch of fern that had the promise of an edible herb.

Here, she dipped the turtle shell in the river to scrub and began to feel the stir of freedom in her blood, though she was not foolish enough to cast no diligent eye round for the river crocs. She raised her head to look up its course, seeing the look of the landscape beginning to change, change to give her cause for hope. In the first terror of her capture, she did not remember well the route they had taken, nor the length of travel from that other plain of Shinar. But her papa's hill country lay up this river; that she knew. Surprisingly, the sound of Aten's yelp recalled itself to her then, and she was startled that it could still cause her pain.

There was suddenly a brush against her fingers and she jumped, thinking of crocs, but it was a minnow, nibbling at the turtle shell. She waggled her finger after it and watched it dart away. As suddenly as Aten had brought her grief, the fishling brought relief and she laughed her first free laugh.

After that, it was all a pleasure to clean the shell, carefully,so not to break it. She probed about for a casscass root, delectable in nearly every stew. And she kept her head bent, so Kittim would not call her back.

Madai had watched her leave. He saw her bend above the mud and then finally stand. She was coming toward them now with a face full of pleasure. She was holding the turtle shell, and in it, a dozen little spotted eggs.

"They are charming when they hatch," she called out before she reached them, "tiny spotted fluffs." Her lips drooped ever so slightly before she added, "But their mother will lay more, and eggs are good to eat." She opened her hand; "with these," she finished, holding a dripping white root.

Her look was expectant, so Kittim and Madai nodded. She smiled and carried them back to the boat, satisfied that their time on land had been long enough. She sat in the boat with the turtle shell in her lap and folded her hands. She thought of a reunion with her Papa and would not think of her mother's fluttering scarlet veil tied round a killer's chest.

Madai looked at Kittim, who raised his brow, and with a slight smile, piled the fire with sand and followed her. They pushed the craft back into the river, poling it up the deep, slow current, each content for different causes, happy to be fed and to watch the water bring them East.

C3CR   C3CR   C3CR

They were quiet, Iscah drowsy. With the likes of a high tale behind him, Madai could only push his boat up the river and be amazed at what had so few hours behind been his experience. It was indeed a foreign place of breathing fable. Great flat-shelled turtles lay on the shore; and with the daylight, he could see the full length of a creature, perhaps what had so cleanly snatched the fish from Kittim's fingers, certainly what was painted in mud and dye on the walls of the bath. It was as long as his ship, nobby, brown and very, very still. It had a tapered, thin snout with ferocious teeth pushing up through its nose and down over its jaw. Its eyes were closed, narrowly set at the top of its head, an arrangement Madai quickly envisioned shining red above the water at night. There was a sleek deer the size of a hyena, all spotted, with swooping horns designed like a giant's lance, large enough in appearance to topple the delicate creature over. But Madai watched it sip water from the edge of the river, lift its head in alarm and leap away with a speed near to flying. Effortless grace. He was touched by the creature's beauty and coughed to hide it.

He found himself, this fresh morning, not unhappy to be alive. Perhaps it was his joust with death - three times that he knew. It made him feel guilty, with Japhet behind, with Ido... He coughed again. He jerked the steering shaft of the boat, turning it abruptly sideways against the current and bringing Iscah up with a yelp. He righted them, remembering what dwelt in the muddy depths and looked away from Kittim, out to the surrounding plain. Kittim did not remark, and Madai did not explain.

They came by mid-morning to a village of brickmakers and fishermen. In the distance rose mountains of terraced brick, a human endeavor. As ever curious of this new land, he glanced at Kittim.

"Ziggurats," Kittim said. "Built for the gods."

"Then they are devoted," Madai responded.

Iscah snorted. She jumped up, dropping her precious turtle shell, and glared out at the men hauling nets up onto the banks.

"Idolators," she snapped. The words were indecipherable to Madai, though not the tone.

"There is a man," Kittim repeated, ignoring Iscah, "well favored, renowned among the people of the East. I would like to find him and leave this place behind."

Madai felt the heat rise in his face. It was not that he wanted to put ashore here, being so near that other town. Only it was slightly irksome to be reminded of his blunder.

"It was good to have gone there," Kittim said, understanding him, "We have Iscah."

Madai nodded, glancing at the girl, feeling the novice anyway. But he knew other men who would have begrudged him the time wasted. He studied Iscah, standing that way with a peculiar look on her face and a rigid back. She was a queer arrangement of grit and fear. She had survived a cruel kidnapping, braved a river's shoreline of crocs and had knowledge of a place called a Shinar plain. Still she was afraid of - or perhaps scorned - a distant construction. Whatever her inclination, she was still just a child; and Kittim was talking to her and sitting her back down, certain, as he seemed to know Madai's intent, that they would travel on.

Madai waited till the place was behind them and Iscah calm again to ask: "What troubled her about a ziggrat?"

"Ziggarats," Kittim pronounced it for him again.

Iscah looked up at them. "Dais to the stars," she scoffed. "But not high enough."

Kittim translated and Madai asked, "High enough for what?"

She looked at him with a degree of surprise, "His flood," she answered.

"Mighty God shall not flood the earth again," Kittim told her.

She shrugged. "Why would they believe that?"

Madai was surprised, but encouragingly so, watching the rapid changes in her face. "Ask her about the flood."

Iscah turned him an amused expression. "He does not know?"

"I think he only wishes to hear it from you," Kittim answered her.

Still, she saw Madai with renewed doubt, unconvinced. His eyes were quite pale and perhaps not very smart. She arranged her thin little garment around her knees and rested her hands in her lap, fully prepared to instruct him.

"There was a time," she began gravely, "when all the land was one, and full of people. And the men were great, evil giants, with hearts of murder and thievery. That, my own father told me. It was long, long ago." She stopped speaking and lifted her eyes slowly to the distance.

Madai watched her. She was waiting for Kittim to translate and seemed far away, and pensive. Then she looked back and nodded, as if she understood full well

Kittim's rendition of her story thus far.

"There was a tale of poetry come by way of a camel trader," she continued, "Come from another tribe of people and very," she blushed so deep a scarlet that it took a while for her to finish, "very vile in parts. Papa would not have it all sung. But I learnt the part about the flood; I remember it all. Papa..." she stopped, her voice cracking as she sniffed. "Papa let me hear that part. And I learnt it right off," she finished. She scrubbed her mouth with her hand and blinked and finally looked back at them. "I will just tell it myself," she decided. She cleared her throat.

"The Heavenly God was insulted and tired of all the cruel men, because they forgot Him, and forgot that He made all things, and especially they did terrible things to children. God was very angry about it, repented of ever making men. But He had one good man, and He wanted to keep him. So He told him He was going to flood the whole of the world, which He did, with all the animals, too.

"Only, the one good man did what God told him to do, built a great ark, and he was saved, and his children, and so were some animals. All the ones we have now." She smiled at them. "And Heavenly God washed the world. I think it was a good idea and a good end. So cruel men had better not forget it."

"It is a good story, Iscah," Kittim agreed. "And true."

"Certainly," she responded. She closed her eyes then and lifted her chin. "And this is the poetry," she announced.

> *"A dark cloud loomed,*
> *Come forth from the heavens.*
> *Brightness turned to darkness,*
> *And none see his father again.*
> *Forty days and nights*
> *A great storm doth rage..."*

She paused, and frowned, "I think I have forgotten it some," she muttered and seemed greatly disappointed by it, "but here is another part...

> *"All human kind be lost*
> *And washed asunder."*

"Washed asunder," she muttered, faintly smiling. "Do you not like that part?" she asked, peeking out of one eye, then continued.

> *"As deep as the sea, rose the waters*
> *Upon the plain,*
> *Until a great wind blew it dry*
> *And an island emerged.*
> *Upon Mount Nitsir came the vessel,*
> *And let it be not removed."*

"I like that," she said, looking at Madai. "And the man lived at the foot of Mount Nitsir with his wife and never forgot Mighty God, Who wanted him saved."

"Tell her she spoke it well," Madai asked Kittim.

Of course, Iscah knew that she had spoken it well, but it was kind of the ignorant yellow man to say so.

"But," Madai dared ask, having seen her recite the tale with a measure of satisfaction, "do you not also think it was terrible?"

Iscah's eyes grew wide. She swung her head around to Madai and stared at him and then blinked. A dubious expression crept into her eyes as she remembered her mother's scarlet scarf - and all the other things. She lifted her chin higher, and then she turned with purpose away from Madai to look at Kittim.

"There are ones who deserve it," was all she said.

But Madai was watching her, thinking he had asked a question of the child he only just dared ask himself. He should have held his tongue - a child, and abused, and no Ancient. She did have the story right, he told himself, and in so far a land. But she had looked at him in such a skeptical way, which he found distressing, having always thought himself no unkind fellow.

So he asked about the star stories. She might know them, and it would give her pleasure, as she seemed a true believer. But it was no look of pleasure she gave him; rather, a fierce and florid face. She battered Kittim with one long, unbroken sentence in her foreign tongue.

"There is a city where she was first taken," he finally related. "There they search the stars and are guided by them."

Madai was beginning to wonder whether she could be pleased at all. And he was puzzled. "The Families have always been guided by the stars," he argued.

"It was the guiding of sorcery in that place," Kittim explained. "There lives a king, a mighty hunter and evil, supplanter of God."

Iscah spoke again.

"She wants you to know they do not remember how high God can bring a water, and their trifling towers will not save them."

Iscah's look was thunderous, turned to Madai. He suspected a good impression of himself was irredeemably lost. But there was what he had seen on the temple walls and he could not ignore it at the tale of just a child. The painting did not suggest sorcery, but bravery. In fact, if there were such a man, slayer of dragons, provider and protector, perhaps.... He thought about the Bowman, knowing the while that he had decided to doubt all such legends. But they were planted deep and sometimes sprung back to life.

"Do you know the way to this city?" Madai asked Kittim, glad the girl couldn't understand.

Kittim nodded. "It is far. We cannot get there by this boat, but we pass the man I speak of on the way."

Madai slowly smiled. Perhaps it was providential that Kittim's man should be passed along the way. He would not take Kittim off his course again, and from there he could find his own way if he must.

"Excellent," he answered. "But what will I do with my ship?"

"This river shall yet carry us perhaps the day," Kittim answered. "Your boat will be one amongst many, and not meddled with. We may leave it in the reeds when the water is shallow. It is a big boat for just a stream."

"Then we will take it as long as we can," Madai replied, his blunders with Iscah aside but not quite forgotten.

Cଷଔ   Cଷଔ   Cଷଔ

And so they did. The river shrank late in the evening of the second day. Madai would not leave his boat before he unloosed the skins from its cypress frame and oiled them and rolled them. He bound them round in sealskin for that purpose and secured it with a leather cord. He had planned to carry it on his back, but it was a heavy bundle. So he relied on Kittim's assurance that it should be untampered with. They removed the mast pole, laid it inside and pulled the frame into the grass.

"The people who live on this shore build boats of reeds." Kittim assured him." They would not want this one."

So with that encouragement, Madai left his boat behind. But with it lay the means of his return across the Sea; and he left it with heavy reluctance.

Cଷଔ   Cଷଔ   Cଷଔ

The sun was still hot by day. It caused the sand to stick to them in the paste of their own sweat. Iscah was irritated. She picked her way along the blistery earth, cross that everything grew sharp and thorny, not like the fertile pastures of her father. She was vexed as well by the suspicious fellow who kept company with Kittim... who was everything good.

Madai learned that the way on foot was harder here, the air damp and thick, the ground sharp with hidden briars, the girl prickly. But he observed as well that the toothy beasts laid along the bank of what had become little deeper than a stream in the day, and did not venture far afield, though they sometimes roared as he passed, which was a mighty and fearsome sound.

But the land was home to an abundance of life, despite its challenge. And by end of the second day, it was pocked with natural springs, which erupted from the earth to carve out a fortune of green oasis. By these waters were the beasts of the land fed, and sweet fruits grown.

Their route began a rise on the third day, sand giving way to pebbly earth. It made Iscah hopeful, having a look of home. And the vegetation changed from thorny to something milder, a promise of verdance yet to come. Though it was no cooler in the day, the air was dryer; and the giant spearflies all but disappeared. The river quickly narrowed as Kittim predicted, swifter, louder, and cleaner, rushing to the sea. There was an artist's palette of small fish pushing up its course.

Now a purple outline of mountains could be seen in the distance, which Madai was glad for. It also seemed, at least to him, that a sort of truce had been struck with Iscah. He knew, in any case, to venture lightly in the realm of sacred things. She was, he learned, a child of ancient traditions very like The Family's, and devout as his own mother. She was tight with her tongue about the years spent a captive and said nothing good of Hamonheb.

He had for some time been watching a great herd of two-legged creatures, long of neck, bulbous of body. They were quite shaggy and turned tiny heads their way as they passed. Iscah warned a proper distance from the creatures would be prudent, which they carefully maintained. But Madai was taken with the odd creatures, never seeing them fly, but being assured by the girl that they were, indeed, birds.

As night approached, Iscah urged them break her own rule. The birds were dim of sight at dusk, she said, and could be deceived. It was the only way to snatch one of the creature's eggs, rich and big enough to satisfy even the greatest appetite. And she showed them how, and explained that the mother laid a large batch of them, which would be her consolation.

Thus, there were soon, after efficient chicanery, two eggs roasting, buried in the earth under their night's fire. It would be a time before they were cooked; but there had been no lack of food in this land, and they could wait. Iscah was busy digging out a root, the knowledge of which Madai admired her for, as it seemed she was good at finding such things. She was also humming a tune, both melodious and cheerful.

"This may be the plain of my people," she announced at the end of her song.

"It is possible," Kittim replied. He watched her pulling on the root. "This land is large," he warned.

The root snapped, and she fell back on the ground with only half of it in her hand. "I know that," she answered, looking at Kittim with an edge of hurt in her face. "My Papa has great herds. I took them to water, so I know it is large, only it looks like this..." Her energy was seeping away. "I think they killed Aten, too," she finished softly.

Kittim translated for Madai; it was, except for the particulars, unnecessary. Her bloom was wilting. And in so close a time to her happy song, it seemed the more tragic. He felt a kinship with her, robbed of things held dear. He watched her carefully, sitting in the dirt with her broken root and grimy hands and dusty hair. He had yet to see her cry and was proud of her for that. Just as he thought it, he watched a muddy drop fall to her lap. Kittim knelt beside her, spoke quietly and let her cry, his arm around her.

"But we will look for them," she finally insisted. And Kittim assured her that they would, which seemed to satisfy, as she had laid all her trust in him.

Madai looked away; his kindness to her was that he did not watch her weep. Instead he carefully moved the fire to check on the eggs. As he was entirely inexperienced, he dug at it cautiously, till a white orb was finally exposed.

"It is done thus," he heard Iscah, apparently recovered, though she had a muddy streak across her face from nose to ear. She leaned over him and tapped the egg lightly with a stick. Hearing a proper sound, she rolled it up and away from the fire. Then she cracked it with a mighty whack.

છાર છાર છાર

Madai was full and thought the egg had tasted strong. But it was plenti-ous and would certainly see them through the night. Iscah was sitting close to Kittim, cutting her eyes at him as though he might somehow, at any moment and to her dismay, disappear. Her face was nearly comical, a busy canvas of dry, dusty tears. But the tempest was over and she seemed content. She was scraping a last remnant of spongy white from the shell when she looked at Kittim with an untroubled expression.

"Do you want to know how I was stolen?" she asked suddenly.

The translation startled Madai, who would not have predicted the unexpected question from a face so content. But he had known only brothers and decided a young maid such as this might need to tell more of herself than less. It was a tale he was certain he knew the most of, having in his own experience seen men capable of far worse. And he wondered afresh that a Great God would make such a creature, knowing as a god should know what they would become.

"They came over the top of the hill," she was saying, "and stole me up before I could even get my stick. And he stunk, he truly did. All Sabeans do." She lifted her chin. "He rode a red stallion and sat me on it and kept on riding. He did not even slow down to do it. They came from where our tents were set," she ended thoughtfully, but said no more on that.

"How old were you, child?" Kittim asked carefully.

She held her head high. "Ten," she answered. "They took me to Shinar. The priest's man bought me there."

"Priest?"

"You saw him," Iscah answered. "En-UtuAten. Named for a false god." She twisted her mouth. "I named my dog after that god - Aten."

Kittim chuckled.

"The priest-king?" Madai asked Kittim.

"I suppose that was how she was brought to Hamonheb," he answered instead.

And Madai laughed to think the dog had been named for the false god, false indeed if it produced such a crop. But he remembered also the little maids brought from the bathhouse at the sound of the copper trump... worried for them.

Iscah was watching them carefully. "Things were done," she added brusquely. She took the turtle shell from Kittim and washed it out with sand and tossed the discarded root into the fire. "That might not have broken," she muttered. "I got just the bitter part."

CRCR CRCR CRCR

Madai was glad the talking had stopped. He had things to think about. Were there truths to learn here at all? If truth dwelt in this East, then why the ridiculous hailing of men as gods? Why the corruption of stolen maids despoiled? Why the tale of a champion born from a virgin's womb when all the world was peopled by coupling, both beast and man? Was that not a sorcery greater even than divining? He looked at the darkening sky, knowing where the constellation "Virgin" would appear and remembered Ido's woven stars. It cut him savagely, enough to remember with a bitter laugh that he had thought himself glad of life just this morning.

He could hear Iscah talking happily with Kittim. He thought it a cruel jest that she imagined herself seen of God. Seen of God and left at the whim of abhorrent men, Hamonheb with his god of the ox-parts, perhaps even the Sabeans themselves. He watched the strange birds silhouetted against the dimming sky, jealously guarding their various nests of eggs. He wondered absently whether they knew that two were missing in this world of random mishap.

A dust cloud was forming. Madai watched it spinning in the distance, hoping in his present humor that they would not be awash in it. Here was no real shelter, just a meager outcrop of boulders for their night's camp. The little twister was holding together and seemed intently approaching. He shrugged, resigned to endure the storm, when he recognized the sound of hooves beating the earth. A herd had stirred up the dust, with the unlucky, flightless birds in their path and their own camp, as well. A worse prospect than dust storm was a stampede; Madai got to his feet, waiting to see whether the beasts would veer from the rocks. But they held their course. They were oddly shaped, and he slowly realized that the animals were sat upon by men.

Kittim dowsed their cooking fire with dirt. They flattened against the boulders as Madai wedged an arrow onto his bowstring. Iscah's eyes filled with terror. She reached for a sharp-edged stone.

The men came from the direction of the mountains and were following the stream. They scattered the birds, splattering their nests as they turned toward the west in a straighter line. If they kept this course, they should merely pass them by. And so it seemed they would.

Madai was certain they were bandits, for they had the look and sound of savage men. They rode much closer, close enough for Madai to hear their animals' labored breath, close enough to tell the men were painted and they were giants. Close enough, indeed, to take his breath away, because he saw something. On the lance of one of the giants was a thing wrinkled and black, with golden hair. Gaping emptiness peered from the place where eyes should have been. Only it was not what was impaled that quickened Madai's heart, but what it was impaled upon. It gleamed in the waning light; it sprouted razor-prongs backward, fixing the head upon the lance despite the wild ride. The Family's Spear, the Sacred Spear of power.

If ever he had hoped to reclaim the weapon, it was impossible now. These men were Nephilim, surely, with wild, streaming hair, certainly as great as nine feet in height, riding great, swift beasts. They carried curved lances and seemed one creature with the horses, steaming sweat and spattered red. Madai knew there would be a massacre should they be discovered, and Iscah would be far worse off than she was before.

But the horde rode on. There was still light in the sky. Perhaps they knew a better place to camp. Whatever the reason, Madai thanked the Great God, should He live; it was a habit hard to die at such times. He watched till their dust disappeared.

"There is an oasis some distance south from where we came. I think they will stop there," Kittim offered.

"We had better not have a fire." Madai said.

Kittim nodded. Madai asked if they were Sabeans, not wanting to speak the word 'Nephilim,' and Iscah, her eyes desperately round, blinked rapidly.

"Anak," Kittim answered quietly. "A people as fierce."

Madai still clutched the arrow at his bowstring.

"How far is that oasis?" he asked Kittim. "They may return in the night. I lost a great Spear that way."

"Why should they come back?" Kittim asked. "They have already been here."

Madai considered this, "Perhaps," he said, "but I will set a watch anyway."

Kittim looked into the distance. "That is wise," he replied, nodding. "One cannot know for sure." He moved to where Iscah had curled herself somehow under a jutting rock. She was looking at the distance, a mixture of fierceness and fright, and had exchanged the rock for Kittim's staff. Madai heard him speaking to her quietly, but she did not lay down the staff. It was getting cold, and she allowed Kittim to cover her with the cloak.

രുഇ രുഇ രുഇ

Iscah's hand ached where she still held tight to Kittim's staff. He was trying to coax it from her and did not understand. So she gave it up. She closed her eyes and lay completely still, hoping kind Kittim would think she was asleep. Instead, she looked across the folds of the robe into the distance. Her heart was still thumping wildly, and she could not stop herself from shaking. What the two men could not understand was that it was not for fear alone that she shook. She knew she should have caved in the skull of a giant if it had come to that. She recognized the part of herself she most loathed... and feared. It caused her an estrangement, and she could not bear that. Where was Mighty God in times like these? He Who did not leave her to the lust of grunting old men? He Who soothed that hollow in the nights when she cried for Papa? Where was He when she needed Him most? When she wanted to kill a man?

There was an edge in her heart, and it frightened her more than giants. What worse could be done her than already had been done? She had survived it all. What she could not survive was the absence of her God.

"It is You," she moved her lips silently into the night. "I must have You." Salty tears made her face cold. "I slide away without You."

She listened. Her hand moved unconsciously to her heart, gripped like a fist. "I cannot do that," she whispered back.

രുഇ രുഇ രുഇ

Madai crouched behind his rock, more than happy to keep a vigilant watch. Another brush with mortal peril had convinced him afresh that he was not so weary of life after all. Deceitful glooming... did not Ido warn him of that? He rested his chin on his hand and let himself think about her. He couldn't conjure her voice, or even her face, any more. But he remembered what she made of him. He remembered her. The stars were blinking now, and if God was really seeing, then Madai would show him a broken, wooden heart. "See what I am?" He only mouthed the words, trusting a proper God to have impeccable eyes.

It was taking a long time for the night to pass. Long enough even for recrimination to grow dull. Madai's thoughts turned to the Spear. What chance was there now to get it back, and from where might that miserable head have been removed? Perhaps from one of The Banned who had stolen it from him, for its hair was gold. But did Anak build ships? Or was the land one long finger, spanning the whole of the seashore? Whatever the fact, they had captured the Spear. Perhaps a kinsman...

Madai heard a jackal howl, a chilling sound on a plain shared by Anak. Nights were full of the hunted and the hunter, he knew. An owl flew past, silently slipping through the air. He imagined he could hear the chit of a captured mouse. And nothing else moved in the night. Even the breeze was quiet. He thought of the Anak, wondering if they were Nephilim, only called by another name. Such stories were told of them. The night was turning cold and Madai shivered.

He hunched his shoulders. There was no one coming back. Kittim was right.

He thought about the painting on the walls of the temple, a thin clue. And he thought about Iscah's poem with its Mount of Nitsir. He could ask about that. Kittim might know where it was. Here in the cold and the dark and alone, Madai wanted a truth. He wanted a truth he could touch.

He slowly stretched, realizing he had kept the same position too long. His toes were asleep; he shifted his foot, scraping the pebbles beneath him.

Crunch.

He jumped - and steadied himself and drew down, completely still, his heart suddenly thumping with everything changed. He listened for the sound again, knowing it had not come when he moved his own feet. If it was a creature, it would scurry off at his smell. Gravel moved again, and Madai caught an odor on the breeze.

There was the sound of a two-legged someone, heavy, though he snapped no twig, a talented stalker. A cold sweat sprung up over Madai's body. He stopped breathing to listen and knew the Anak was listening, too. He reset his arrow, as smooth and silent as the master hunter he was. He heard the intruder take in a long, quiet breath and lower himself. Madai imagined him kneeling on one knee and wondered what sort of weapon he carried. He was desperate to think it not the Spear, suddenly superstitious, remembering the promise of secret powers.

And then Madai was aware of someone behind him. Kittim, Kittim with his staff, waiting and silent, as well. Madai was heartily encouraged by the quiet presence. The Anak seemed aware also and rustled the pebbly earth as he shifted his position. Madai's advantage, and all the sound he needed. He released his arrow and heard a surprised grunt in return.

The giant suddenly rose to a full and alarming height, nearer than Madai had expected, a rushing shadow lit by the moon. He was more a brute than a man, wounded at the shoulder, less wounded than Madai had hoped. The giant lunged and Madai sprung up to meet him. The Anak took him full on. Where was Kittim?

Bullish arms wrapped Madai around. He kicked, and they rolled on the ground, driving the arrow deeper, inflicting the giant with the only visible pain Madai could detect. But the man rose like a mammoth barely grazed to stand on his feet, effortless, lifting Madai with him, and squeezed again. Madai's lungs were worked like a bellows, pushing out a gasp as he grabbed for the arrow with a saved bit of strength. He heard the man gasp, startled and angry, dropping Madai to the ground.

Madai blinked to clear his vision, seeing the bull of a man in the moonlight, crouched above him... smiling. The Anak held a knife, deftly lashing out with the greatest length of arm. Madai rolled, wondering again about Kittim.

No sooner had he got clear than Madai heard a swoosh and a crack. Kittim proved himself effective and powerful as he swung his staff against the giant's head with a solid blow, breaking the wood in two, leaving the Anak stunned, though not overcome. Madai grabbed the broken piece from the ground as the man got his footing. He rushed him and got the giant square in the gut with the jagged end.

The Anak was stunned, hardly believing what protruded from him. He gripped the staff in a primal reflex and wrenched it free, watching himself spill out onto the ground. He grabbed at the wound, blood spilling through his fingers, and in the moment knew he was dead. It was not a moment to consider his soul, but to rage, and to use that rage for one last attack. But his footing was lost in his own gore and he stumbled, falling headlong.

Madai watched the giant roll slowly to his back, attempting the horrific task of stuffing himself back inside himself. He took the man's knife and buried it deep between his ribs, a mercy really.

Then he and Kittim stood above him, silent and aghast. It had ended as quickly as it had started.

"He came back," Madai muttered.

"Maybe the smoke..." Kittim answered.

Madai stared with terrible curiosity. The dead man's eyes were open, a last vacant stare, and his beard was bloody and braided. His hair was wild, and he was clothed in a girdle of hide. This was the third man Madai had killed. It was not the same as the first, as a certain crust had formed, though it did not sit upon him well, even still. He was surprised at himself, and somewhat relieved.

"There was nothing but this spear," Kittim called, coming from the giant's hiding place.

Madai looked up, expectant, to see it only an ordinary spear, though the girth and weight of a yearling tree.

"Is he a Nephilim, Kittim?" Madai dared to ask.

A dark, troubled look spread across Kittim's face, and then he shook his head. "No," he said, "but much the same."

Madai hardly heard the words, hearing instead the way Kittim said them. That his friend held a terrible knowledge of the fabled tribe was clear and, for the first time, Madai did not want to know.

"Will they come for him?" he asked instead.

"He came alone," Kittim replied, and shrugged. "I do not think they hold their brothers dear. In any case, we are a small bother, and not worth a day's loss." He touched the man with the tip of his sandal. "We must leave him for the jackals," he said. "It will not matter to him now."

There was no need to rouse Iscah. She was awake, standing rigid in the little surround of boulders with fierce eyes, holding a stone. Kittim turned her away from the sight.

"Roll your cloak," he told her. "I do not think they will come for him, but we had better be away from here. We shall meet a friend soon."

She was silent a moment, with wildness in her face. "O?" she finally asked, turning toward him stiffly with her child voice. "A friend?"

"Over those mountains," Kittim said. Noting her disappointment as she looked into the dark where he had pointed, he added, "Not so terribly far."

Madai slung a water skin round his neck and tucked his star map into his girdle. He tested the soundness of the giant's spear to find it perfectly balanced, heavy, and he looked at the girl. She was like a little statue turned to the horizon, a lean silhouette with a tangle of hair standing out around her face. She was completely rigid. Then she took her tattered sack and filled it with the turtle shell, a pair of sandals, a thin garment and a water skin. It was all she owned.

Their day's escape began well before morning's full light, and with an urgent speed. Their fear of pursuit was left unspoken for Iscah's sake. And Madai did not notice the blood which leaked from a secret wound on his chest.

The sun was up and warming the air before they slowed down. They gave notice neither to its heat nor to their stomachs, for they each knew the threat of ranging bandits. The mountains were their aim, both a place for hiding and the route to Kittim's man. But they were not hunted. Instead, the horde followed the stream to get a ransom of man or treasure from some other unfortunate place.

Daylight had freed Madai from his meloncholy. His quest was worthy again, in the light. But Iscah was silent the whole length of the day. Madai had seen her eyes wild, and now they were veiled, older. She was shifting from child to maid before them. He knew she thought her parents dead. He thought so, too. It moved him. He felt a little ashamed, as he planned to trouble her again about the painting of the Shinar King. What she knew of him, he needed to know. He tried to quicken his pace to catch up beside her - and found that he could not. There was something wrong with his legs; they felt... or rather, they did not feel. He looked down in alarm and was relieved to see them moving as they ought. He pushed the hilt of his dagger against his thigh and, with a great relief, felt that.

'I'm tired,' he reasoned with himself, "I haven't slept.' But he was beginning to notice the smallest of tremors in his muscles. He looked up at the pair in front of him. The gap had not widened, but the giant's spear seemed heavier in his hand. Then he began to feel the cut across his chest. What had seemed just a bruise had come full round to a stinging pain. He saw the blood on his vest and thought for the first time that it might be his own. He looked up at the mountains in the distance, feeling a great longing for them, where it would be cool.

"I have been done worse than this," he told himself. He took a drink of water. It was warm. His throat was raw.

He wanted a look at his chest but could not think how to manage it. He felt awkward, carrying a spear suddenly too heavy and maintaining a pace slightly too fast. He could do nothing beyond that. So he imagined a mammoth hunt, where he walked and walked and carried frozen meat on his back and could not stop at all. His body was trained by treks like that. He imagined himself outside of himself, somewhere on another shore, till, finally, evening came. They had not eaten, but Madai was not hungry. He laid his weapons with unconscious diligence on the ground, dropped his robe and then himself upon it.

CᴚᏯ   CᴚᏯ   CᴚᏯ

Iscah sat on her bundle, thoroughly spent. It should be understood, acceptable, to kill a Godless brute, a child stealer. But always, when she entertained such thoughts, God felt far away. She had been whispering with Him, begging mercy for her bloody thoughts, and she felt some small relief by it. She was ready for the night, her body not accustomed to the long march. She took a drink and glanced around. Kittim was still looking out toward the mountains and Madai - he was asleep. That was odd. She came to look at him. Only then did she see the blood.

"He is wounded!" she cried.

Kittim came instantly. He leaned above the sleeping man and touched the place where his blood had seeped through. The vest was neatly incised, a diagonal slice, and mended in part with dark, dry blood. Kittim leaned down to smell it. Madai shivered.

"We dare not have a fire," Kittim muttered.

"Is he wounded sorely?" Iscah asked.

"Not deep," was Kittim's answer, as he gently lifted the vest. But that did not seem to relieve the furrow between his eyes. He looked at the distant mountains, only a shadow in the moon's light. "There will be shelter there," he continued thoughtfully. "Another day, perhaps less, and spring water."

Madai moaned. They looked back at him, and Iscah thought his face was ghostly in the dim. The night air was cold again, and no fire. Iscah watched as Kittim put his own robe over the fevered man. By this she knew what value he was to Kittim. So she heaped her own cloak on top of Kittim's and they huddled there beneath it, on either side of Madai, through the long night.

CᴚᏯ   CᴚᏯ   CᴚᏯ

Morning brought Madai a sense of revived strength. He opened his eyes, wary of waking again the pain that had started in his head. He ran his hands down his thighs to find that they were whole. He did not see Kittim and Iscah, but he could hear them; and he was grateful he had not betrayed his wounding. 'My strength will get me there,' he assured himself. There was a stretching pain in his chest when he told his legs to stand, but they obeyed and he was confident again.

The stream they were following was narrow now, a rocky vein cut into the high desert. It was soon joined by another, coming, it seemed, from the promise of mountain heights, which encouraged him.

But Iscah was soon tired and feeling starved. Her size lent her no reserve and, beyond that, she had spent a cold, fretful night with no hope of food. Kittim knew they were not being chased, but even so, he would not take the time to hunt a meal. He knew they must reach the mountains by night, for the western man would not travel another day.

Madai's first blush of strength seemed to have leaked out of him. His wound screamed of fever and his legs were lifeless weights again. His thinking had narrowed to encompass two thoughts: that he must not stretch the gap between himself and Kittim, and that the blade of the giant had somehow been tipped with poison.

He knew there were ways to do it, but it seemed not worth his strength to remember them. To be certain, that he stayed his pace all morning was goal enough.

What he could not know was that their progress had slowed as Kittim matched their speed to his ability. It took till evening to reach the foot of the mountains, twice what it should have. Here Kittim let them rest. Madai heard him talking to Iscah; his voice came as a muffled roar. Madai closed his eyes, still standing.

They were watching him, braced up by the giant's spear, shivering, with eyes sunk in a pasty face. They saw his lips move, cracked and dry and no sound coming out. Kittim reached his arms under Madai's arms and took his weight. Iscah took his spear, and together they laid him down. Madai was insensible to it all.

"Stay with him, Iscah," Kittim told the girl. "I will find a shelter." He indicated the side of the mountain with his hand.

捲掃 捲掃 捲掃

Iscah sat beside Madai and put his head in her lap. She watched Kittim moving away, beginning a steady climb into the trees. It was certainly the last thing she wanted, watching him disappear into the forest. She sighed. Bravery was an illusion; it had not saved her before. Lost was Aten, too, who had been a brave dog.

It was not the wilderness she feared, having been a tender of goats. It was what a pack of wild men could do, and there were a horde of them in this land, she knew. Madai had killed one. And, though she trusted the word of Kittim, his assurance grew dim as she sat alone on the stickery earth with Madai, a man full grown and helpless. She was trembling now with hunger. Her head pounded, though not so much as to quell the dread of Sabeans. She scanned the horizon obsessively.

The evening began to cool; still she was alone in the desert. So she strayed her eyes to a string of ants in the dirt beside her, watching them at home in their little world. She pinched one between her fingers and put it in her mouth. It gave a sharp, unsatisfying crunch, and she scattered the rest with her hand. She checked the tree line methodically, watching for the first sight of Kittim. And she waited.

A shrill, harsh caw suddenly sounded from above. It woke the child who had slowly drooped over to prop her forehead atop Madai's. She jerked her head up, searching frantically for the sound.

It was not an eagle, but something with a call that stretched out long, piercing, shrill. It circled above, its shadow cast across the sand and its wings so wide. She had a first impression that its skin was made of scales, and she muttered a prayer. "Courage," she insisted; "he shall return." And then it flew past the trees and disappeared behind the mountain. She watched the place in the sky where it had vanished, feeling foolish. "Only a bird," she whispered as the prickles on her neck lay down. But she smoothed the place she had put on Madai's brow, searching for comfort in the weight of him on her lap.

He was heavy, and hot. She touched his head again, too warm under her cool fingers. That was not good. She studied his face. She had had no real interest in it before but now started to feel a weight of compassion. Perhaps she had formed a hasty perception of him. Perhaps he was merely ignorant, and no pagan. He had killed the giant, after all, perhaps not a Sabean, but one who needed killing. She fingered his hair, so yellow. His face was unnaturally red, next to her olive hand, but fine-boned. She felt a certainty of pity as he moaned faintly.

'Why, he is lovely,' she realized. Only Kittim, in her estimation, was more so.

She sighed again and looked away toward the foot of the mountain, knowing it had been long since Kittim had left her; and she pulled absently at the flesh which dangled from the hole in her ear, an unconscious habit. She remembered the pitiless barbary that had made her a slave, mangled her ear and healed it with a wooden disk. Her memory raced ahead of her will, down that familiar path which always led to the priest. He was surely one to loathe, with his hot, sweaty hands.

"Once only," she whispered with a smile, remembering how she had bitten a perfect circle into his flesh. He had struck her and covered her face with his hand till she thought she would die. She shook herself. 'I will think no more on that,' she told herself, as she often did.

And then, at last! Only a tiny sound, but it was Kittim coming. He emerged from the trees, sliding down the slope in the gravel toward them. He was dusty, but not tired. She watched him approaching, amazed at his stamina.

"I am so glad you are back!" she earnestly proclaimed.

"I found a cave," he answered, pointing, "up the mountain a short way. Can we carry him between us, Iscah?"

So they left their packs and carried Madai instead. Iscah took him about the waist; with Kittim bearing the most of him, they moved like a six-legged insect dragging its middle. Madai would not remember the ascent, but his body did what it could. Kittim got him into the trees, where the coolness was like a fresh breath in his face. He thought he was home again. He lifted his legs with a great effort, eager to reach the rest and healing of a mammoth-skin lodge. And then he was confused, feeling the cooler air of a rocky place. This could not be his lodge; it smelled of damp; there was no smoke. Ido was not here. No, she couldn't be... but his mother...

Instead, Kittim was here. Madai opened his eyes, though it hurt his head, and looked around the darkened place. 'A cave,' he thought regretfully. They laid him down on his own elk robe. He looked at the other face above him and remembered Iscah. Then he closed his eyes again and wished they would get him some water.

Kittim pulled lightly at Madai's leather vest where it was affixed to the wound.

"It will bleed again," Iscah warned.

"That may be good," Kittim replied, thoughtful, looking at Madai's chest. He looked back at her. "I think he is poisoned," he said. "But I do not know what they used."

Iscah's eyes widened, "Pray it was not a viper."

"Would that be mortal?" Kittim asked in alarm.

Her eyes were solemn and she did not answer him.

ങ൚ ങ൚ ങ൚

Together they cut away Madai's vest. Iscah washed him with warm water from her flask till the real damage was exposed: surrounding purple flesh and a seeping ooze.

"It is not deep," she whispered again. She put her hand on the side of Madai's face, felt it so hot and looked at Kittim. She shook her head. "A bad fever," she said. "My mother gave me the green underskin of a tree." She looked beyond the overhang of their cave. "It grows in the mountains, beside springs," she added.

"That is well enough," Kittim said. "But you shall not wander this cliff in the dark. I know the look of the tree."

"Where are you going?" she gasped.

"We need our packs," he answered. "And I will find your tree."

Iscah would rather have searched the forest for the fever tree than wait for Kittim again, but she only nodded. "Hurry," she begged him.

She was disappointed with herself again, glancing around the cave, watching now for a giant bird or what other her imagination might devise. It was that imagination she could not control. It gave her a flight if she was bored, but it could make an ill spirit of a shadow, too. So she distracted herself, scrounging for brush and piling it up for a fire, only to remember that the flint was in their bundles. Madai moaned again, which gave her another diversion. She brought him a drink of what was left, but his teeth were clenched so all the water ran down his lips and soaked his beard.

That seemed to bring him around, and he started to talk, a garble of sounds, though there was one word - "Ido" - that he kept repeating. His eyes fluttered, and closed again. Iscah fanned his face, and felt ashamed that she had kept bad feelings for him. He looked so foreign, after all, and he should not be blamed for his ignorance.

His eyes were sunken, with white lashes against the dry red of his cheeks, this strong man turned helpless in a matter of a day. The fever had come swiftly, and with a greater force than the giant had first cut him with. She remembered also that he had saved her, and not Kittim alone, and felt tears well in her own eyes. She knew a jealous God waited in the realm beyond and was not certain Madai should find a welcome there. She began to pray.

ଔଓ ଔଓ ଔଓ

Kittim's return was a welcome sound. He had their things, and a rock hare besides. Together they boiled a broth made of soft bits of rabbit flesh and strips of woody healing bark.

"I smelled wild leeks at the stream," he told her.

She looked up, a light in her eyes. "Onions?"

Kittim nodded but stretched his arm out to stop her. "In the morning," he told her.

She was relieved, truth be told, to have to wait for light. So Iscah turned the rabbit above the flames, ravenous, nearly wild for it to roast. She was also watching Kittim. He was squatting beside Madai and praying, as he so often did. He was truly a devout man, for whom she thanked Mighty God.

When at last the rabbit was cooked, she twisted off a hind leg and gave it to Kittim, licked her fingers, and got one for herself. She was surprised as the whole leg was so soon consumed. And she tested the broth, thinking about the onions.

Kittim ate, watching Iscah watching the broth. He heaped a pile of prickly brush on the fire. The smoke coiled past the mouth of the cave in a determined column, and over the edge of the cliff face, obscuring her form.

"To ward off what prowls at night," he explained.

Iscah scooted back and leaned against the rock. She licked her fingers.

"I saw a great bird," she offered. She looked up at him to emphasize it. "A very big bird."

Kittim faintly smiled and stirred the fire again. It shot up into the dark, crackling a warning to the wild forest.

Iscah watched it, brave again. Her stomach was full and she had a quiet in her spirit, having given up her dislike of Madai, having prayed for him. She glanced at the sleeping man, rolled on his side and muttering again.

"He is not like us," she said.

Kittim followed her gaze. "Not so very different," he replied.

She raised her brows, certain Kittim had spoken a first untruth. But she could forgive him that, because she knew it was for the cause of his own goodness. She watched him and considered it a sacred mercy that he had found her.

"Why did you come?" she asked. "To that terrible place?"

"Hmm?"

"When you and Madai came to the city; why did you come?"

"We journey to a man in the East," Kittim answered, "and fell upon the fire-beast..."

She nodded, and looked away. "An accident, then."

Kittim's face softened. "Perhaps to some... an accident."

At that, she closed her eyes and smiled. "Then it was for my sake," she whispered.

He looked at her with a tender smile. "One does not know the purposes of Mighty God," he reminded her.

But she was confident. "He would have me saved," she insisted.

Iscah watched the look that came on Kittim's face, what all Elders have when they mollify a simple child, but she tucked the assurance safely away. She had known the Hand of the Mighty One in the dark of the night, after all. Was it not He Who calmed her breast when she would have her mother? Did not His care keep her safe the long days of the temple; did not He rescue her to Hamonheb for the cost of a few nights in his bed? Yes, Kittim was brought to the city for her better rescue, of this she was more than certain.

She was grateful, also, for this unknown man of the East, the one Kittim would reach. He must be remarkable to bring so foreign a one as Madai to travel so far and to be known to one so grand as Kittim.

"What do you want from the man of the East?" she asked.

"His wisdom," Kittim answered easily. "This man is loved of God and well-honored among the people. And Madai is a great distance from his family. He is seeking the truth of what they were taught."

"The man of the East has taught his family?"

Kittim smiled. "Madai wishes to meet one who is wise, and who is old and knows the truth of the world and The Mighty God Who made it."

"No one may know God," she responded with surprise.

"Madai wishes to know if He is."

"If He is what?"

"If He lives."

Iscah looked at Madai's sleeping form. "Is he your master?" she whispered.

Kittim shook his head, "No, Iscah, I serve a Great Lord."

"Good," she replied, "I should not wish you to have a foolish master."

He chuckled. "'Tis not foolish to seek truth, Iscah," he said with surety. "Much is told in this world that is false."

She was silent then, watching Madai breathe. "Certainly, you are right," she conceded, her face lit by the fire, recalling her education of the world. "The King of Shinar is called god by some. En-UtuAten speaks his incantations." She shuddered.

"And you?" Kittim asked.

"The One God, certainly," she replied ardently, "He Who made us." She looked at Madai again. "If he is not your master – why, then?"

"Hmm?"

"You travel with him."

"He has need of my skills," Kittim answered. "I know the speech of many, and the one in the East knows truths of God."

"Then your master is generous."

"Infinitely," he agreed.

"And you are honored," she continued. She looked away from him, into the face of the sky, gathering her courage. "I would serve you. Will you keep me?"

Kittim turned to her gently.

"I have been a wife," she added.

Kittim reached through the smoke, took up her tiny hand in his and held it quietly. "Child," he said softly, "it is a Father you need."

He watched great, wet tears roll down her cheeks. "And if he be killed?"

Still holding her hand, Kittim gently whispered, "If your father is taken to Holy God, then he is safe." He moved and put his arm around her thin shoulders. This kindness brought a choppy sob to her throat. "We shall not leave you alone," he quietly insisted.

ᎦᏋ   ᎦᏋ   ᎦᏋ

Madai heard their voices... faintly. Sleep was not so delicious as he liked. It was clouded with danger and fearsome creatures. And though it did not rest him, sleep would not let him go. He strained to move a hand.

"Are you awake, Madai?" he heard Kittim ask, for which he was grateful, as it pushed back the fog. He opened his eyes.

Iscah came to hover above him with the turtle shell. She wanted him to drink from it.

He swallowed. It tasted a little, with a sliver of rabbit on his tongue. That was unwelcome, but he moved it between his teeth. It was work and he quit chewing.

"Only a little, and you may rest again," she urged.

"Are we in the mountains?" Madai croaked.

"At their west edge."

Madai chewed the string of meat. "The giant cut me."

"Yes," Kittim answered. He looked into Madai's eyes and saw them aware. "There was poison."

Such he had feared, and was not surprised. Somehow, Madai could not hold on to the idea, but he could feel what it was doing to him. And then his thoughts seemed to drift past his control again.

Iscah laid the broth aside and patted his head awkwardly. She smelled the filthy water that had dripped from his wound in a pool beside him.

"He needs cleaning," she whispered.

Kittim studied the congealed mass of water and blood with a frown. He rolled Madai off his elk robe and onto the cave floor with great difficulty, leaving Iscah to drain the water flask across Madai's chest again. She did it over and over, till the water ran clear. Kittim rolled up the robe and threw it away.

"Get my mat," he told her. When Iscah had stretched it out behind Madai, Kittim helped him roll slowly back.

Madai had a sense that he was falling, and his belly threatened to loose its bit of broth. That cleaning had cost him more than it was worth. Even this small effort, and none of his own really, left him as slack as a babe. He could not tell when he stopped hearing their voices and drifted away again.

Iscah tore a strip of cloth from the hem of her skirt and laid it on the gash. "It is not clean," she said.

"We have done what we can," Kittim answered. "God shall have His way now."

Iscah looked up at him, wishing she could read his expression, because she heard worry in his voice. She peeled more of the inner bark away from the willow and dropped it into the broth. She hovered over Madai, nursing a guilty conscience because she knew he was of value to Kittim. She was truly tired past standing and finally wrapped herself in her cloak. She lay behind the fire, with Kittim in her sight. He stared into the night as long as he could, but by the first hour he slept, as well.

Creatures indeed prowled the night. The fire blazed high at the entrance to the shelter, which had the intended effect upon them, a fortunate thing.

- 32 -

Kittim was first awake in the morning. He knelt at the mouth of the cave, studying the ground. A deep furrow was set between his eyes. Iscah heard him, and threw off her covering. To prove herself a useful girl, she supposed to fetch water from the stream. Kittim stopped her with a gesture and swept the dirt smooth with his hand.

"Tend Madai," he said, reaching for the flagons. "I will bring the water after I have got us something to eat."

Iscah was young, but no fool. She looked where he had wiped the ground clear.

"A precaution," he answered her eyes. And he was gone to the stream, taking the bow, leaving her with the giant's spear.

Madai slept. Dawn lit their cave, and though he slept early, he did not sleep well. The fever took him to dark, hazy places with snatches of dreams. His mouth was dry. He heard Iscah. Somehow, she seemed to know he was awake and touched him. Her fingers felt thorny on his skin. 'Ahh... water." She was holding it to his lips, and he tried to swallow. He wondered vaguely if Ido had felt this way and was instantly afraid. But Iscah brought him more broth. He was grateful, and tried to take it, anything to hold back the dreams. There were bits of inedible strips in the water. He tried to push them back across his lips with his tongue and felt her pluck them up.

Iscah was hopeful. He had taken the water willow broth again, and she was anxious to tell Kittim.

"Madai," she whispered. She watched his eyes trying to open, then she lifted the rag that covered his chest. A stench came up from it. "Polluted," she whispered, glad he could not understand her.

Suddenly there was a rustling behind her and she looked up, hoping for Kittim. She felt a streak of cold run down her back and swiveled her head in alarm toward the back of the cave. But there was only the rock. She was annoyed with herself; then in a flash of brilliance she remembered the leeks at the stream. She remembered, also, that Kittim was afraid of something on the mountain and never let the fire die. "I shall be just a moment," she whispered to herself. She piled up the fire and took the Anak spear.

"I am getting you something," she told Madai, knowing that even if he were awake, he would not understand. But she could not leave him without saying it.

∞ ∞ ∞

As in the height of the storm, Madai could not tell how many days and nights he passed in a disoriented, half-waking sleep. Often he opened an eye to see Iscah above him with water or a hot, foul paste in her hands. He heard Kittim at times, saying a single word, over and over. And Iscah, chirping back the sound like a mimic. It was a fight each time he passed through the shroud of fog, with a heaviness that pinned him just the other side of wakefulness. He dreamed of dragons and priest-kings. He dreamed of demons tugging at him, an empty, cold tomb cut from frozen earth. It brought a cold sweat that left him shivering. And there was the face of Ido, always fading to black, leaving him confused in time and place... But he could not control the visions, or find her at will, try as he may. It was the voices of Kittim and Iscah that kept him planted on the earth, and sane.

The first morning of his recovery he was aroused by a hot, caustic mass pressed just under his face and onto his chest. He welled with tears at the pungence and coughed, an aggravation to a chest ravaged by poison. He coughed again, shooting pain through him, but it was a healthy pain, one that said "I have suffered a wounding and I am mending." Madai opened his eyes.

Iscah saw them first, focused and clear.

"Kittim!" she called.

Madai heard Kittim shifting stones as he moved somewhere just beyond his vision.

"Madai?" Iscah turned her question to him. "Do you wake?"

"How long?" he asked her.

She put her ear to his lips, trying to hear.

Then he remembered her strange tongue and that she would not understand.

"Many nights," she answered, "many days."

Kittim came round his head and squatted beside Iscah. "Ah, Madai!" he pronounced with a wide smile. "You shall not die, my friend!"

"Praise to Mighty God," Iscah agreed.

Madai thought there were tears in her eyes. He coughed again.

"Which shall do him most harm?" Kittim chuckled.

"He is not dead," she returned, and laid her hand on the poultice, "as you see."

Then she lifted back the rag that held the onions, her eyes streaming afresh. Madai felt the burn in his own eyes, finally smelled the onions and knew what was done to him.

"The black is gone," she proclaimed.

Kittim saw it, too. "You are a clever girl."

Madai coughed again. He tried to lift his arm to push back the poultice.

"God has used it, Madai," Kittim protested, "this and Iscah."

Madai laid his arm down and closed his eyes. "How long has it been?" he asked again.

Kittim shrugged. "Long enough."

"It was poisoned," Madai told him.

"Colocynth," Iscah replied. "Probably. A beautiful flower with a bitter result."

Madai thought something strange... that he had understood her. But he was tired, too tired to think about it. "Water," was what he asked for.

Iscah had a flask beside her. He sputtered a little, but drank a cool mouthful. He vaguely heard them then, speaking of fish. 'I would like a fish,' he thought and went back to sleep.

ርጽርድ ርጽርድ ርጽርድ

Iscah tested what she hoped to be the last of the onions above the fire. She stood up, stretching her back and determined to wash her hands. "I shall smell for days," she announced. "It is nearly full light; may I go to the stream?"

"Not light enough," Kittim corrected.

"Is there a threat?" Madai asked. It was coming dawn and he was alert again.

"We were visited," replied Kittim.

"Anak?"

"No. A creature prowls this mountain. "

Madai tried to rise on an elbow, holding onto the poultice.

"You are stronger!"

"I'm hungry."

"O!" exclaimed Iscah. Forgetting her hands, she pulled a spike of crisp, dry fish from the skewer, where it had spent the night. She brought it to him and Madai put it into his mouth. Even that tough flesh filled his mouth with saliva. His stomach rumbled as he ground it between his teeth. He swallowed, the smallest of efforts, and coughed, and felt an explosion in his chest. He laid back down, proven not quite whole. Kittim brought him some water.

"It was a good try," he said. "The fever has left you weak, but that will not last."

Madai believed it. He felt stiff where his back had been too long on the ground. He turned with care to his side.

"Tracks of what beast?" he asked.

His friend smiled. "Not one to worry you."

Madai knew, of course, that was true. He would do them little good against a beast, but he found his bow with his eyes anyway. He noticed also that the spear had become an unlikely part of Iscah's little frame, always close beside her.

"Let me see you," she said, smiling and coming to him. She knelt and pulled back the stinking rag. She looked quite pleased. "'Tis finished," she said and stood up with the poultice in her hands.

"I once liked onions in my stew," she added.

She carried the rag to the edge of their cave and tossed it as far as she could into the brush. She flicked her wrists briskly, setting bits of mash flying. It would be a good day.

ርጽርድ ርጽርድ ርጽርድ

A great shadow swept past their cave and came again with the rushing sound of giant wings. Iscah leapt back, having seen a glinting flash. They heard an angry shriek, something like the call of an eagle.

"Kittim!" she cried.

He pulled her arm. "Get back!" he ordered.

"But, it's a bird," she muttered, perplexity in her voice.

Kittim snatched the cold end of a burning limb from the fire and hoisted it toward the opening of the cave. They heard the creature. It swooped past a third time and Iscah scrambled to the back wall where she had leaned the spear.

"It has been here before," Kittim muttered, watching the enormous shadow pass over them again.

"Is it a bird?" she asked this time.

"It's been here before," Kittim repeated. And the creature fell from the sky to perch on the lip of their cave, standing the full height of a man.

"My bow!" Madai cried.

Iscah lifted the spear instead, only staring at the thing. "Le'habat," she whispered. "But they only eat rotted things..."

Its claws were thicker than a man's finger, and as long. The giant creature had a remarkable ability to stand on one stubby leg, wings extended, and slash at the air with the other.

"Stay back!" Kittim ordered again, as she had advanced a step to point the spear at it.

"A winged serpent!" Madai insisted, calling back his strength. "Get me my bow!"

The animal clung to the outcrop of rock, wings spread for balance. It was angry, aggressive, an unlikely stance for a scavenger. Kittim could neither advance toward it nor go around it. It seemed frantic, its long, lance-like beak jabbing at the flaming limb in Kittim's hand. Though it had a bulk greater by far than an albatross, the danger was not its size, but in the claws that carried the rot of carrion. The flaming weapon Kittim employed served both to enrage and to drive the creature back.

"My bow," Madai commanded again. But Iscah was intent on the spear pointed at the creature.

It screeched and flapped at them with a wild frenzy. It had a wicked-looking beak, more a spear, and snapped at them. It tried to lift itself from the cave shelf to get at them from above, but the overhang was too low. Catching it off-balance, Kittim struck it in the face with a fortunate blow of flaming wood. It howled savagely, its tiny red eyes crushed. It blinked blindly, bewildered and backing away. Iscah held the lance above her head and took the moment to swing it down like a knife across ithe outstretched wing, breaking a bone and ripping it more than half-way through. An arrow whined through the air at its breast, as Madai had got the bow himself.

The animal's voice still echoed off the walls of the stone-faced cliffs... complaining its death. It crumpled to the dirt, its skin a patchwork of bejeweled scales. They could only stare at it shimmering in the early morning light. Madai leaned heavily against the cave wall.

"Why, it's beautiful," Iscah murmured, bending to touch the sapphire scales, cool as a serpent, and smooth, with her fingertips. "Pity." She looked up, "I wonder why..."

Kittim lifted its foot and held the claw in her sight. "It meant to do worse than charm us."

Madai put down his bow, realizing he had reopened his chest. "A winged serpent," he insisted, even as Iscah fingered the soft leather that covered its wings.

"Might I have this?" she asked abruptly.

Madai propped himself up with his hands on his knees.

"You were part in its end," Kittim answered. "It is yours."

She lifted the slack wing. "I would never have thought it was so beautiful."

"Tell her it wanted her flesh," Madai told Kittim, hearing remorse in her voice.

She looked at them with her child's eyes. "I say it was a lovely creature, made by Mighty God." She indicated a colorful crest above its battered eye. "He admires beauty, you know."

Madai was suddenly reminded of Ido and that pleasure she found at her loom, creating beauty when warmth would suffice.

"It is good that we have dealt with it," Kittim said, dragging the carcass out of the cave. "I have been watching for it." He pulled it into the forest and was gone a long time.

Iscah cleaned Madai's wound, where fresh blood had leaked. They did not speak, but Madai felt her hands gentle on him and thought perhaps their first difficulties had been somehow resolved. When Kittim returned, he brought the luminous skin of the serpent, the crest of its head, and both wings.

"Artistry is not wasted on you," he said, giving Iscah the skins.

Iscah examined the hide front and back. Kittim had peeled it well from the body of the animal and had brought it nearly clean. She lay it bloody side up and drove stakes into the earth to stretch it. Then she found a flint to scrape it as Kittim cut the leather wings loose from their scaffold of bone.

Madai watched the two working at the serpent's hide. Kittim had not brought its meat, a murky soup of scavenged flesh. But Madai's stomach had recovered from the illness and the fright and was getting desperate. He was swallowing his own spit. Iscah glanced back at him; as though she knew, she plucked a roasted fish from its skewer. She laid it in her turtle shell and gave it to Madai with a tentative smile, "Eat?" she asked.

It finally registered, and he was startled. "She spoke to me," he called to Kittim in surprise.

"She has learned much," he answered.

"When?" Madai asked as he took his first bite.

"As we tended you. Slowly, Madai." For Madai's mouth was full.

"Well got?" Iscah asked.

"Well pleasing," corrected Kittim. And she put the phrase into her good, young mind to be easily retrieved.

ঙ৫৪ ঙ৫৪ ঙ৫৪

Later, when the spit was cleaned of meat, Madai watched her working at the leather wing. He tested the diversity of her newly acquired words, to find it remarkable, and wondered, indeed, how long he had been ill. He watched her punch holes in the leather with his knife, which she called 'nif,' its proper name if slightly misspoken, and she drew a slender bone through them, joining one side to the other in an odd bowl-shape. As well, she attached the crest from the head of the serpent to the bowl's rim by another thin, slight bone. She balanced it in her palm a moment, then, to his surprise, turned it upside down upon her tangle of hair. There she pushed the disobedient coils up from her face into the golden leather cap and tied it under her chin with a dangling piece of scrap. The cap was fringed with the crest's bejeweled scales, like the brilliant plumes of a parrot.

"Well pleasing?" she asked, smiling, touching the new adornment.

"Handsome," he answered, offering her a new word. He smiled, looking at eyes that wavered between child and maid. It seemed she had learned much. He was impressed.

"Water?" she asked. He nodded to encourage her and watched her disappear in the foliage to the stream, the crest visible till the last.

ଚଙ୍କ ଚଙ୍କ ଚଙ୍କ

Madai's confinement, brought by the poison of the Anak giant, was not so long in fact as it had seemed. Meat of the mountains and scrupulous attentions and wild onions each worked a healing in his body. But in those dark days, he had met a fear he could not best by strength. It was now imperative that he find the truth, for he could not face death again without it.

- 33 -

Ocah had charmed Kittim to take her with him. They were hunting something stouter than fish, and Madai was alone. He had studied the mountain. It rose nearly to the clouds, and at a vertical pitch. He would need better strength than he had now if he was to cross it, as Kittim said they had to do. So he began to stretch himself. He felt his wound, and he felt his back where the cave had rubbed it nearly raw. He decided to find the spring and have a bath.

The way down was steep. The water was cold, gushing out of the rock with great force. He tried to wash himself but found it too cold and too difficult. So he started the climb back to the cave, and the way up seemed steeper even than the way down. He hid his heavy breathing, though there was no one to hear it but himself, and reached the cave again, his legs atremble. He was much too tired and had a sudden craving for the dark, rich meat of mammoth.

With no one watching, he lowered himself carefully to his mat and didn't mind the familiar contours of rock this time. Just a minute was all he needed, and he would see what lived in this forest. He looked for his bow. Yes, against the rock. And then... he went to sleep.

First, it was a pleasant drifting, with the sounds of the mountain giving him a chorus, slowly fading to silence. Following that came a deep, sinking sleep, the sort that sent his body falling. He tumbled, aware enough to know it was a dream of the unpleasant sort. And he was caught in the snare again, like the fever, being watched by something from the shadows. It was familiar and felt invincible and gave him the same terror as nearly dying.

As on the mountainside, he fought to crawl up and slid back down. Something was, in fact, holding him down. Something was attached to his body. It seemed another sort of trouble that started with his legs, shooting him with arcs of pain. He thought he was awake, though it was still dark behind his eyes and he couldn't move. He ordered his eyes to open. He felt a sharp poke at his chest but couldn't force his arms to beat it away. His brain screamed at flesh that would not respond: Move! Move! And then his lids flew open in a brilliant reflex.

He was seized with instant awareness, staring at a pair of serrated blades just above his nose. Narrow, unblinking eyes studied him. Claws sunk into him and flooded him with relief! A thing of flesh and blood, no dark spirit at all, but a baby replica of its dame.

He jerked his legs to unseat the creature. He reached up to grab its beak as a sharp pain streaked across his chest. He glanced down to see himself pecked at the scab, which both horrified and enraged him. He grabbed for a rock and hurled it at the thing's scaly breast. The creature squawked, released his legs and flapped its wings for balance.

The hatchling serpent, startled by Madai's attack, leapt back, using its wings to escape. It was standing on its two stubby legs and tilted its head to the side. Then it turned to sniff the hide still pinned to the ground. Madai supposed it smelled its mother there.

Despite the pecking, Madai knew it posed little danger; but he felt no pity at all. It would only grow to be a creature like its mother and sire more of the serpent brood. So while it sniffed at the mother skin, still and unaware, Madai found his bow and raised it to the level of his ear. He felt the muscles of his chest, held his breath for a better aim, and alerted the prey by the scrape of his foot against the ground. As the crested head jerked around, its tiny eyes blinked at him vacantly, and the arrow found a vital spot. The fledgling shrieked as its mother had done and flung back its head. But it did not take a step; its wings collapsed onto its back and crumpled. Madai watched a claw scratch at the ground till its last muscle died.

He went to it and grasped the shaft of his arrow, pulling it with ease from the soft flesh. He knelt beside it briefly to study the delicacy of a jointed bone trailing across the wing to become a small half-claw attached at an outermost segment. And then he wondered where the lair of the flying serpent was hidden.

He noted how briskly the smoke cleared the outcrop, blowing through the entrance to rise up through the trees. And he turned slowly in place. He ran his hand along the jutting rock, searching for the cause of a flow of air that would drive the smoke away. The cave was somewhat shallow; why hadn't they discovered such a cleft? But then, in the darkest corner, he felt the air, and with that a small crevice, no larger than his hand. He followed it down to the base of the rock, where it grew larger, large enough, indeed, for a miniature flying serpent.

He lay on his belly and put his eye to the opening. From a great distance away, beyond the channel of stone, there shone a dim and tiny source of light. He blinked his eye and looked again, straining for any movement: a tall leg or a snapping beak perhaps, even a sound. Then he tested it. He shimmied his shoulder into the opening and began a squirm into the mountain's tiny mouth.

'A passage to the other side, and with a hand's breadth to spare!' Madai realized. He held his breath, trying to shrink in size, and inched his way forward, pushing with his toes and pulling with his arm till he guessed he was fully inside the channel.

But for the distant spot of light, there would have been the darkest of darks around him. Madai's experience with caves did not include places like this. There was a strong odor in the air. It was not a bear smell, but this could be a lair. He could just imagine sticking his head through and having it bored into by another baby beak. A jagged vein ran the length of the crevice. He felt it scraping along his thigh. He was trying to protect his chest and pull himself with his right arm just as the way began to widen. He had not thought himself frantic in small places before but was discovering it now and silently cursing himself, laid out like a worm.

The light was definitely there, peeking dimly above the channel's rock floor, which had started an upward slope. Madai fixed his eyes on it, reassuring himself, till finally the crevice was wide and high enough to kneel. He bumped his head getting his knees up and commanded himself to be calm. His back was doubled over, feeling every jag along the rocky overhang.

He crawled out into blackness. The light which promised an opening on the far side of the mountain did not help here. This cavern was enormous, a great hollow, cold and damp because the source of light was a long way off. He listened for the breathing of any other creature than himself. There was only silence. Madai pressed his palm against the back of the cave just to orient himself, to feel something, and he strained his eyes. Nothing. He put his hand in front of his face, and covered the only minute source of light he had.

Surely nothing lived in this blackness. Madai whistled low; a thin, eerie strain echoed off the walls. He strained his eyes again; maybe he could outwait the darkness till they adjusted. Still only black. But he was feeling something on his leg. He snatched at it sharply, suddenly all prickles, but It was just a soft rush of wind funneling through the crevice. His skin was feeling clammy; it was significantly colder here. He kicked with his foot, pebbles or some such rubble sprawled across the ground, but he was afraid to move. For all he knew he was standing on a ledge with a chasm tumbling in front of him. He slowly lowered himself to his knees again, feeling for the crevice. A moment of panic gripped him that he wouldn't find it, when he heard a welcome call.

"Madai!" It was very faint. They had found the fledgling creature and had not found him. A rush of relief seized him.

"I'm here," he called back.

"Madai?" it was Kittim again.

"There is a cavern," he tried to explain.

"Where are you?"

He put his mouth at the heel of the rock to answer, "There is a cavern; push through a torch."

"Madai?" Now he could hear Kittim plainly, and he called again.

"At the back of the cave..." he explained.

Kittim was finding it. "Are you there?" he called.

"Send me a torch," Madai insisted. "There is a cavern, a way through the mountain."

He was suddenly blinded. The torch was pushing through. He blinked, feeling great reassurance as light began to lick across the cavern floor. He bent and took up the end of it. He held it to the side to see Kittim's face, looking alarmed, squeezed into the center of the crevice.

"Are you all right, Madai?"

"I've got a way through the mountain," he called again and stood up to see what exactly he had found.

Only an immediate few feet around him were clearly visible, with dimness and arching shadows beyond that. There was dry, crushed brush - remarkable how that was here. He brushed it into a pile and set it afire. It lit the greater space around him and showed a long, narrow expanse reaching into the distance toward the tiny spot of sun.

"What is there, Madai?" He heard Kittim reach the mouth of the channel.

"A passage through the mountain," he answered again. He noticed the scraps of bones scattered around him. "And the den of the flying serpent, " he finished, sniffing the smell of rot and offal in the burning brush.

"Give me some light," Kittim insisted.

Madai bent down with the torch. He watched Kittim unfold himself and stand inside the cavern.

Kittim looked all around, and toward the cavern's distant mouth. "It could be a long way out," he muttered.

"How far, do you think?"

"Far."

"Is it safe?" they heard Iscah calling through the rock.

Kittim bent to the opening, "Stay where you are, Iscah."

"Is there day enough to get across?" Madai asked.

"If there isn't," Kittim answered, "the way out will disappear."

"Yes."

Kittim squatted down. He was quiet, and Madai felt left alone again in the silent hollow.

"There is sun left," Kittim finally proclaimed, standing again. "With a torch for us each we will be safe, and it will save an arduous climb."

Where was that assurance found? Madai wondered. If it was a prayer, he was not so confident...

"I am coming back through," Kittim announced to Iscah. To Madai he said across his shoulder, "We will need torches."

So Madai and Kittim squeezed back to the other side. They took the skin from the infant serpent, keeping the fat with it, divided and wrapped it around six sturdy limbs.

Tutan

- *34* -

Iscah laughed. "How funny," she called with an echo. "All the while there was this lovely great cavern whilst we kept on a ledge."

Madai thought he might not have called it lovely, with the scatter of bones. Even the brush was dry, thorny skeletons, and the air reeked.

Kittim kicked at a tiny bone. "She did not like us so near her den."

Madai looked at the collection of rubble. A serpent nursery of long standing, he supposed. "Maybe she was a better mother than we thought."

In the light of her torch, he glimpsed Iscah's smug expression. "And beautiful," she added.

"We have a way to go," Kittim insisted. "We must reach that light before the sun is set, or spend the night here." They lit a second torch. "Follow behind me, Iscah."

Kittim knelt down. He collected a handful of pebbles and started tossing them ahead of himself into the dark, to listen and tell that the floor did not drop away to a chasm.

They began their traversing of the cavern that way. Madai was getting used to the smell, or it was fading as they left their great fire behind. Shadows loomed and undulated around them. He felt the skin on his neck bristle and scolded himself, alarmed and ashamed that he seemed now strangely cursed with fear.

The passage narrowed, then it widened again. Madai ran his hand along the rough walls. They were pitted, pebbled and cold. The air felt good, chilled and damp where the wound still held the slightest of fever. He began to hear a sharp drip dripping sound, the sound of water against a puddle somewhere in the distance. A tiny drop hit his head, so small he wasn't sure at first that he had felt it. But another drop fell; it was cold, also. Then the sound was steady and certain, splashing in the darkness just beyond. It was a pleasant sound, the sound of life. Then one of Kittim's pebbles tumbled into space, followed by a plink into water.

"Careful," he warned.

The light of their torches illuminated the space around them enough to find the shallow pool. The rock floor shone up through the water, water that had collected drop by drop by drop, sifting through the earth into its smooth depression. Madai watched his torchlight dance across it, snaking out and away in a stream that cut through a low channel, disappearing back inside the mountain. He knelt down to cup up the water in his hand. He smelled it, was satisfied and sucked it down his throat.

"Oooo," Iscah's voice echoed on and on.

Madai glanced up and followed her arm holding its torch like an arrow at the cavern's ceiling. There were shiny, dripping columns gripped to an arching roof of stone. The columns were white as snow, stretching down to meet exactly opposing pillars stretching up, reaching out finally to touch. Madai lifted his light higher, where ribbons of glistening white crystal hugged the rocky crags above them.

"What is it?" Iscah asked, craning her neck. "So beautiful!"

"It is," Kittim confirmed. He filled his waterskin and gave it to her.

"Has the Mighty God put such a thing here for the Le'habat to see?" she asked.

"We have seen it."

"Yes..." she mused, taking a sip. "But," Madai watched her look at Kittim with a real light in her eyes, "only here in the dark."

Kittim looked at her.

"He loves beauty too," she whispered. "Though no other eye sees it."

Madai thought about that, remembering again how his own mother and Naru and Ido had made things beautiful, things that took a long time to make. How would a God Who crushes life be also in love with beautiful things? No. He couldn't believe it. He cupped up some icy cold water in his hands and remembered another outcrop of rock where he had listened to his Patta speak of stars and gods. That had been a simpler time, a time he would never have again. He felt his stomach begin to crawl up tight into a fist.

"Are you all right, Madai?" Kittim asked.

The voice startled him. He refocused his eyes and caught a glimpse of a man's face in the pool, his features rolling and shifting with every minute droplet of water. The face wore a reddish beard that reached nearly up to its eyes, a scowling look and haggard, with eyes made brittle by a memory. Why, he looked as hard as Togarmah! Madai quickly wiped himself away with a wave of his hand across water's surface.

"Only tired," he managed to say.

Iscah wasn't listening, knowing as she knew that Mighty God did act with an artist's heart. She was working off her sandals, putting her feet into the water. She lay on her back, torch lifted to the ceiling, and begged them explore the wondrous chamber. Madai filled his water skin; he splashed his face, feeling the grime of long days in his beard and glad the girl had diverted them.

"There is no thing darker than a cave, Iscah," Kittim insisted. "We had best get to the end of it."

She rolled her head to the side with a stubborn look. "We have these torches left," she argued.

Madai tried to set his face right again, wondering that such a hardness had settled upon him. Maybe it was only the sickness. He listened to their conversation, spoken in Iscah's own tongue. It sounded like one long indecipherable word, but slightly musical, and he wouldn't have guessed there was a disagreement at all, but for Iscah's face. She was a stubborn one, looking comical with her serpent's cap and springy hair. The look of her eased the crease between his eyes; he could feel it, for which he was glad. In the end, they left the pool behind. The water disappeared into the darkness with nothing but the noise of dripping water to prove it was there.

Soon the atmosphere changed. The ground was a clutter of fallen rocks and dropping crevasses. Dry rock walls curved above them. Kittim collected a fresh handful of pebbles for use along the way and the cavern answered them with a pling as the stones skittered across the floor.

Madai was suddenly exhausted. The tedious shuffling in semi-darkness was drawing up the muscles around his wound till he started to favor his right side. The long-bow strapped to his back with his spear was pulling and catching against the ceiling, considerably lower now that they had left the large inner cavern. But the light he had first glimpsed as only a faint promise had grown in size to establish it was, after all, the way out.

The passage suddenly widened, revealing the gaping mouth of the mountain. Madai felt a warm, slight breeze from an entrance no farther than twenty arms' lengths, and they should soon have what was left of the day's sun for light. He felt the warmth begin seeping into his achy muscles, and lowered the torch he was carrying. Then he noticed evidence of campfires, and soot stains that crept up the walls.

"See this!" He heard Kittim call with excitement in his voice.

Madai looked where Kittim had leaned his torch close. In the flickering light there was the witness of a story-teller's hand.

Iscah ran her fingers the length of the stone canvas, too anxious to see it all to study anything by detail. Gazelles she knew, and especially flying serpents, but she was stopped by a thing. She was stunned. Here was a creature of red paint, with stout body, long tail and stretching neck topped by a tiny head. There stood beside it a man, looking the size of a beetle!

She twisted her head to look across her shoulder and put her finger on the animal's tiny head.

"Ooo, see Madai?" she exclaimed, as he had come to look. And then instantly followed the chatter of her own language. But the sounds were cheerful and full of energy. She nearly dropped the torch, but Madai rescued it from her hand.

He nodded, even laughed, balancing her torch with his own. He was glad for the distraction, having been genuinely alarmed by the look of the man in the pool. He watched Iscah and Kittim examine the walls, the red and ochre drawings, and tried to look engaged. What happened on his inside was shaping his outside. He knew it. More than only being poisoned... But he was tired, so soon come from the sickness, with too much to think about. So he looked at the drawings with feigned interest, which shortly turned to genuine curiosity.

"Look at that," he said, reacting to Iscah's find. Then he moved past her, tracing his hand across the rock to another place where there was a clutch of flying creatures, and marks that could have scored days, or seasons, or births, or deaths - or the tally of any noteworthy event.

"What do you think this is?" he asked, looking up to find Kittim absorbed in something else.

But his mind was suddenly engaged, thinking what band of people had arrived before them, coming from what land, going to what land... He moved his torch slowly down the wall to a senseless scrawl of lines. He studied it, wondering, little peaks circumvented by lines, till he could finally interpret what might be a sort of trail.

"Yes! This is a map!" he called out.

It wound around mountains and along streams. He felt a ripple of energy run down his back, daring not think that this might be made by an immediate son of Japhet, The Family's most ancient forebearer save Nua. Unlikely, really, but he continued along the rock face, to inspect it for a piece of the sky map. The stone lent no smooth canvas, but here... here were the familiar patterns. His heart began to thud. And then, near the bottom like a signature, was a lance, its point prominent with five prongs thrust backward.

"This is a place my kinsmen passed!" he called again, this time with importance.

Kittim looked up, acknowledged the Spear with an indifferent nod, and pointed at another drawing.

Madai was annoyed. But he looked at the place Kittim was pointing, to see only another peak design; it was a mountain made significant only by its size, located beneath the pole star. Madai would have had Kittim's full attention, but for the look on his face. That look was saying something, and he came to see what his mysterious friend had found. It was an object sitting upon the mountain.

"Ararat," Kittim breathed.

Madai only looked at him blankly, and Iscah came to stare.

"Your Mount Nitsir," Kittim elaborated, and Iscah's hands flew to her throat.

Still Madai did not remember.

"Noah," she gasped.

Madai blinked. His stomach took a leap and he forgot the Spear. Had he seen his face, he would have seen the crags around his mouth lose their sharp edge.

The three began to examine the whole of the rock face, to discover any sort of orienting sign that would point the course to Ararat. There was none save the pole star.

Madai began again, going back to the enigmatic stone map, even the constellations, searching for any possible clue. Was there a progression to the mountain? Anything? When there was no sense to be made from the whole, his first excitement began to die. He looked back at the drawing of the Sacred Spear, and at Kittim, who still lingered over the drawings like a delighted scholar.

"They were my kinsmen," Madai whispered.

Kittim glanced at him quizzically. "Why, then, are you discouraged?" he asked.

"It is only a recounting of the tale," Madai answered, "and not that they came upon the ship itself, or we would carry that finding in our songs."

Kittim smiled at him kindly. "Perhaps," he replied. Then he gestured the great hollow of the cavern with a look. "Others may have taken shelter here, as well."

Madai was not convinced, but he was sympathetic to his friend, this wise one who held without question to the same lore as The Family. 'I will not spring to easy conclusions again,' he warned himself, putting his hand on Kittim's shoulder. Madai looked at Ararat with his friend, a twinge in his heart.

಩ಚಿ   ಩ಚಿ   ಩ಚಿ

They did not notice Iscah leave them. She had finally acknowledged a loud hunger and was scavenging for dry brush at the mouth of the cave. The night was close. Her eyes strayed to the far side of the ravine and she silenced them with one sound.

"Shh," they heard her from just outside. "I see a man."

Madai was at her side in an instant, crouched down, following her finger.

"There, beside that flat red rock," she whispered.

Madai couldn't see him till he moved again. The man was alarmingly near, just on the far side of the gorge and creeping his way down. He was alone and afoot, picking his way very slowly past the boulders.

"Not Anak," Madai whispered, as the man was smallish.

Kittim came behind them. He stood watching the stranger continue his descent into the ravine. The sun was touching the earth behind the cave, and the man appeared to be seeking a safe place for the night. He was scanning their side of the mountain when his gaze crossed the cavern's wide entrance and he shielded his eyes with his hand. Then he leaned against a large boulder and rested a long time. They watched him look at the climb again and stand there, perhaps deciding whether he had the strength before he began his ascent with a weary limp.

Madai put his hand on Iscah's to silence her and studied the stranger. He supposed the man was not a threat, for he carried no weapon, and he was alone and seemed to be lost.

They watched him silently. When he had climbed midway to the cave, Kittim moved. He stretched his arm above his head and waved - to Madai's astonishment. The lone traveler's as well, it seemed, for the man threw himself to the ground.

"Peace to you," Kittim called down.

The man was lying on his belly with his face in the dirt. He lifted his head.

Kittim called to him again, and this time the man answered. His voice was thin, fighting the distance to their shelter, and it quavered; but he stood and unconsciously shook the dust from his robe.

"I shall help him," Kittim said, turning toward Madai.

"But who is he?" Madai called after him as Kittim slipped down the shale to meet the stranger.

Madai looked after him, scarcely believing it as Kittim reached the man and took his arm. He heard the babble of words again before the man leaned his weight on Kittim in a tribute of trust and fatigue. They spoke again. Kittim gripped the man's arm and slowly propelled him upward with steady progress. Madai watched in disbelief, remembering Kittim's shortage of caution, as when he himself had stumbled upon the beach to share a stranger's fire.

"He is coming?" Iscah asked, still clutching the brush she had collected for the fire.

Madai stood up and retrieved the giant's spear from the place he had leaned it. With the other hand, he took her load of sticks and piled them in a heap. He took a torch and set it ablaze and moved Iscah behind it. Then he heard the scramble of rock and frantic breathing which told him Kittim had returned with an utter stranger.

挅 挅 挅

The man leaned his weight on Kittim, standing scarcely to his shoulder. He was very nearly spent, his face glistening with sweat and deeply crimson. It seemed he could not speak for gasping, but he bowed at the waist. Then, as though something frightful were recalled to him, he shot a frantic look across his shoulder and spattered a few words at Kittim. They moved deeper inside the enclosure.

"This is Tutan," Kittim told them simply. "He has come over the farthest mountains of the East by way of a caravan."

Tutan's clothing had been entirely drenched in blood but was now dry; and Madai supposed him victim rather than culprit. His robe was torn, though it had once been very fine. He was no warrior. His eyes were gray and lined, and his face was neither pale nor dark. He could have been an Ancient or not.

Iscah dropped her hands, which had drawn in panic to her mouth, and scrambled to bring the stranger a drink. Her kindness was clear, and her impulsive trust. The man took it from her gratefully and drank as though it were days since he had last tasted water. He bowed again before Kittim moved him to a low, flat rock and urged him to sit.

"May the favor of the Mighty One rest upon you," Kittim proclaimed.

Tutan turned weary eyes to him with gratitude. "And you, as well," he answered.

Kittim did not translate their exchange, and yet Madai imagined that he had understood it. It was only the lilt of the stranger's tongue that was foreign.

Rather than Madai's caution being lessened, it was increased. "Blessings be yours," he tested.

Tutan looked at him quizzically, and with a certain fatigue.

"He has come over the mountains," Kittim began to explain. "A swarm of bandits has attacked a caravan."

Iscah looked up with alarm.

"Giants?" she asked.

Kittim nodded. "I think we may have met them before," he continued, "as they rode great horses."

Her face drained of color.

It took an effort for the man to speak, but he seemed immediately inclined toward affection for the girl who had brought him water.

"They have left," he assured her.

"And you escaped?" Madai asked, impervious to pity.

"He crawled under a dead camel," Kittim explained. "Till the Anak found the caravan's wine."

"Fortunate," Madai replied skeptically.

Tutan looked up at Madai from his seat on the ground. He spoke slowly, realizing, as had Madai, that their language was shared. "Not fortune, my young friend, mercy."

Madai wanted to smile. Another believer; the East seemed full of them. What he would grant was that the stranger posed them no pressing danger. He put his lance aside and joined Tutan on the ground.

"Are you well?" Iscah asked.

The man nodded, an ironic look in his weary eyes. "I am not injured," he answered, "Only... it was a grievous butchery. Such things..." He trembled. "For a silk... a piece of gold." Then he reached a graceful hand to her, immediately regretting his candor as she blanched white again.

"You must not be afraid," he amended.

Iscah, who kept his eyes with her own, found little assurance in those few words; but she began to relax beneath the comical leather cap, as it appeared that his was a kindred spirit.

"You were not followed?" It was Madai who inquired after their safety.

Tutan moved his head wearily from side to side. "They slept," he answered simply. "Drunk."

"Will they come this way?" Madai pressed.

Tutan looked at him, then answered slowly. "A bag of silver was tied to the camel that hid me. I lay very still, to see stout legs come to stand a hand's breath from my nose and a man take that bag. Another came with the wine. Later, they spoke of a route east. To their village and their women."

Iscah turned to him severely and mouthed the words, "Stop, Madai."

Tutan noticed this, and it brought the first glint of vigor to his eye. He began to fumble about, searching for something first in his vest and then, with a worried look, in the deep pocket of his trousers. He finally withdrew his hand. In it he held a smooth, round pebble, slightly pink, the size of a quail egg.

"A pearl," he said and put it on Iscah's palm.

She gasped as she held it and lifted it in the light to see that it was a perfect sphere. It recalled to her the slender necks hung with adornments at the temple, adornments such as this, though this pearl was not defiled, having come from a good hand. She turned it between finger and thumb.

Tutan drank the water again, finding he could not quite get enough. Kittim replenished the fire.

"Dare we?" Tutan asked in alarm.

Kittim offered him his steady gaze. "You yourself have heard to which direction they are aimed. And I have no desire to pass the night without a fire."

Madai watched the smoke, amused, knowing a good amount was drifting in the breeze that blew through the cavern. But then, Tutan was nervous, not one acquainted with heathen hordes; and Madai would have trusted his rather timid face, had it not been that he knew such other speech as the marauders', if his telling were to be believed.

Tutan had settled in a weary posture on the floor of the cave. He watched Kittim a moment, that concerned look in his eyes. And then he sighed, nearly inaudibly, and turned his attention back to Iscah. She held the pearl with an admiring smile.

"It comes from the sea," he explained, "the land of the Miao."

"Miao?" she asked, finding the sound amusing.

"The land of my people."

"Ah," she breathed, not knowing what else to say. She reached her hand back to him, but he put his finger on the pearl.

"You are a lover of marvelous things," he said looking at her cap of le'habat wing. "It is for you."

"I cannot."

He only smiled at her and patted her fingers closed before he turned to Madai, who did not know, in annals of The Family, a name "Miao."

"Then you are from a long way?" Madai asked.

"A long way," Tutan answered with his lilting cadence.

Madai did not need Kittim's skill to understand the stranger, and yet he did not recognize such a face in The Family. A puzzle.

As though the stranger perceived the same curiosity, he inclined his head in a gesture which denoted a humble bearing. "I am Miautso, the lineage of Go-men, of the primary son, Jah-phu. From the scattering we moved East, to a land of green steppes - Miau."

At the name of Jah-phu, Madai was all attention, that and the speaking of a scattering. Even so, Madai could scarcely grant himself to believe the stranger could be of The Family, he with a face so unlike his own, and covered with blood.

"Scattering?" he finally asked

Tutan ran his tongue across cracked lips and raised the water to his mouth again. He closed his eyes and drank. There was a streak of blood dried across his nose, which troubled Iscah. As he had finished drinking, she eyed Madai with a warning.

"Thank you, child," he told her.

Madai narrowed his eyes, scarcely believing that in all of this wild East should come to their very cave one with knowledge such as he was seeking – and of the lineage of Japhet.

"Let him rest," Kittim called from the fire, smaller than he might have kept at another place.

Madai would not be shamed, but he would give the man an evening. He was feeling his own weakness again. He nodded at Tutan. "Welcome," he said slowly. "I have shared a stranger's fire before."

- 35 -

Madai opened an eye. Kittim was gone again, probably praying. He opened both eyes to peek at the dawn and remembered his own injury. It was unavoidable, as his body was stiff and needed a careful stretch. He heard the new sounds of the stranger, still asleep, and Iscah. He raised his head to watch her dig in their pouches with a disappointed look. She glanced up and saw him.

"No more rabbit," she whispered.

He laid his head back with a tiny grimace, his chest pulling with a dull pang. But he thought instantly of Tutan, the supposed kinsman gone east from the scattering. He could hardly wait for the man to wake.

৪৩৫ ৪৩৫ ৪৩৫

"It is recited at every marriage," Tutan explained. "And every birth."

Madai nodded thoughtfully.

"The primary lineage," Tutan began:

> *"The Patriarch Dert begat Patriarch Se-Teh.*
> *The Patriarch Se-Teh begat a son Lusu.*
> *And Lusu had Gehlo and he bagat Lama.*
> *The Patriarch Lama begat the man Nuah*
> *His wife was the Matriarch Gaw Bo-lu-en.*
> *Their sons were Lo Han, Lo Shen, and Jah-phu. "*

Madai listened, recalling the same custom amongst The Family - his own wedding, in fact, and the birth of his son. He recognized a genealogy with like names as The Family... exceedingly strange.

> *Jah-phu begat Go-men," Tutan continued.*
> *"Go-men begat Tutan, for whom I am named.*
> *Tutan begat Gawndan Mew-wan*
> *Whose son was Jenku Dawvu*
> *Whose son was Tutan."*

At this, the man of this lineage reverently bowed, indicating himself.

"Tell me what you know about the scattering," Madai insisted, "and Jah-phu."

"Shall we not have food?" Iscah asked quietly. But Tutan lifted his hand.

"I am a stranger, brought to safety by your kindness and Heavenly God," he assured her. "It is little to answer." And he turned back to Madai:

"The scattering comes after the generations of Lo-han," he continued. "That begat Cusah and Mesay. Likewise, Lo-shan that begat Elan and Nga-shur. And Jap-phu, of whose lineage I am," and he bowed again. "Their offspring became tribes and peoples who built cities and encampments, the same in which to dwell, despite the command of Heavenly God that bade them people the farthermost parts of the earth.

"Likewise a tower they wrought to rise unto the highest heaven, there to make foreign and unclean devotions. Heavenly God smote them with strange tones and voices, and they were scattered by this cause to every part of the earth, as was their first instruction."

Madai watched the man skeptically, but with a glimmer of possibility. And, despite himself, his heart was beating faster. Only there was some... thing in the way. It was bringing out impediments, old sores and old grievance.

'How can you forget, Madai?' it seemed to ask. "Was she so little to you after all?'

"And you, Madai?" Tutan was asking.

"I am come from Ashkinaz," Madai told him quietly. "Who was come by Sru, who was come by Easru, come by Baath, come by Jobhath, come by Javan, come by Japhet, come by Nua... Are we kinsmen, then?" he finished, verbalizing what Tutan had implied. "How can it be? The tribe of Japhet crossed the Brine Sea, to a far land, far west."

Tutan shrugged. "I am from the East," he answered simply.

ᎧᏣ ᎧᏣ ᎧᏣ

Iscah, who was hungry, still held the disappointing pouch, from which she retrieved a bit of dry and shriveled rabbit flesh. She started it to boil. Madai confused her; what was to be gained from a tale known to all, she wondered. She wanted more meat, or some green thing for the soup, but Madai was leaning on his elbow, listening to the good eastern man. She looked out the mouth of the cavern, supposing Kittim would bring something.

She had a taste for a vegetable, though, and left the cave to search after something, noting that neither Madai nor Tutan watched her go. There were the signs of edibles, wedged deep in the rocky earth. She wondered whether they had been planted by those who drew on the cave. Well, she thanked that woman's hand. It was surely a woman who had heeded such ordinary things.

Here was a patch of cleaned earth, save a recognizable twining vine. And in its forgotten depths should be long, yellow tubers. Her mouth watered. Yams. She dug them till her fingers were sore. The root smelled of dirt, but there was saliva in her mouth at their very thought. And then she heard Kittim. He came with empty hands. Well, she could forgive that; he had been praying.

She followed him into the cave and set the tubers roasting above the flame, beside the watery rabbit soup. Madai and Tutan talked on. She was mildly annoyed, but she would take the moment to study this new Tutan. His face was entirely benign. A thin plait of hair lay down his back, dark and coarse and streaked with silver. His hands were fine; she supposed they did not wield a weapon at all.

Iscah adjusted the tubers and stood up. They would tend themselves. She quit the fire to come beside Kittim, where he was studying the cave wall again. It was exciting - ancient pilgrims, forefathers - Noah? She watched Kittim run a finger up the mountain of Ararat.

"Is it there yet, do you think?" she asked, startling him.

"It is possible," he answered.

"After so long a time?"

"It should have been invincible against the waves," he replied.

She smiled. She could imagine it.

ଔଔ   ଔଔ   ଔଔ

"What is this?" The Eastern man asked, having come to see.

Iscah turned with a start. "Mount Nitsir," she answered. "Noah's mount."

Tutan's eyes widened.

Madai noticed and was not surprised at all that Tutan's expression was full of belief. "So, you know the deluge," he said.

"Certainly he knows," Iscah proclaimed. "Who does not know?" She raised her brows, eyes warning.

"Indeed," Tutan replied. "The second beginning."

Madai was suddenly nervous looking down at Tutan's dusky face.

"Are you an Ancient?" he asked quietly.

Tutan answered with a hearty laugh.

"Madai is seeking the truth of beginnings," Kittim explained. "He is come East to find an Elder, one who knew the first ages."

Tutan seemed to approve.

"I am not so old as to know the first times in my own years," he answered. "But our poetry is old, written first by honorable fathers. We have a telling of the deluge..."

Iscah clasped her hands at her throat. "As do we!" she exclaimed. "I so love poetry." She smelled the yams but let them alone and charmed Tutan for just one verse.

He began slowly, careful that the cadence of his words would be understood. He spoke of the earth filling with tribes and families who came not to love their Creator. He told of their fist-raised defiance and the ultimate Wrath. Wrath was manifest in sheets and torrents of water, a great flood that showered down from divine Eyes and broken divine Heart. It was forty days of destruction, the same as Madai's Family told, and – from those so far away – the same.

Tutan's speech echoed in the cavern when he had finished. It gave the effect of a profound and true thing and put a tremor down Madai's neck. When the echo had finished, Iscah scrambled back after her yams. They had the unmistakable smell of something burnt. She pulled them off the fire with a yelp.

The three men were hungry and did not discuss Tutan's poem. Madai was glad they did not. He was oddly uncomfortable now with declaring his doubt. Iscah handed him a charred vegetable, which Madai bit too quickly. He sucked cool air across his tongue and they all drank the soup, which tasted faintly of rabbit.

Kittim was cautious with his yam, and then with his next question. "Will you tell us about the caravan?" he asked.

Tutan looked up from the blackened root. "It should be told," he said, "I suppose." But he savored the yellow pulp a moment more, remembering just then how long it had been since he had eaten. His gaze strayed to his bloodstained tunic and the rip in his trousers.

"I traveled in their company nearly the whole of my journey," he began. "They carried spice and silk to the great city of Shinar." Then he set the yam to rest on his knee and looked past their faces at the opposite mountainside. "I think the barbarians knew its route," he began again, "and were upon us before we could even beat the camels. It was... a massacre.

"My pony threw me, and I crawled under a camel, God be praised, and lay there until I heard them find the cache of wine. And I saw none else that happened, though I heard men die. I shall not forget the sounds."

Kittim and Madai listened silently. Madai swallowed, grateful for the mountain that separated them from marauders. He was wary to travel there without knowing to which direction they were gone, or whether they were gone at all.

Iscah wished they might have waited to ask such questions. "Must we go that way?" she asked.

"They are surely gone," Tutan repeated his assurance.

"Our course lies across those mountains and through the valley," Kittim answered her.

Such was her dread, and it spoke in her face as she peeled the crust away from her yam.

"They have what they came for," Tutan encouraged her. "I heard them planning; they will go farther East."

"How?" Madai asked, "How do you know their speech?" He asked it as his eyes traveled up the gorge.

Tutan was looking there, too.

"Kittim is able," Iscah defended him.

But Tutan was not offended. "I have spent my years in study," he explained. "It is the second passion of my life." His face colored ever so slightly. "My third," he amended quietly.

"Madai's passion is questions," Iscah inserted, lifting her eyes askance at Madai. She did not miss the scarcely discernable color rise in Tutan's face, but she would shield him from unkind curiosity and did not ask what his true second passion was, knowing of certainty that Mighty God was his first.

Madai merely raised his brow with a wry smile. Iscah had just that shine in her eyes that softened her tongue.

"Can we see the caravan from a hidden place?" he asked of Tutan.

"From the crest of that mountain," Tutan answered, pointing across the gorge. "I can show you," he offered. "I rode a good pony. He carried me from my home and if he is alive, I should like to find him."

⊰⊱ ⊰⊱ ⊰⊱

At a distance, the precise savagery was not visible. Early morning, in fact, lent the place nearly an idyllic view. The valley was lush; birds circled over-head... it was just that they were scavengers.

Madai surveyed the scene from the objective perch of the mountain top to decide their route. A stand of aspen between its base and the caravan would provide them cover and a closer look. He was pleased by this as Iscah reached them. He heard her breath catch in her throat, and then a hush. In the valley below, he heard the whinney of a horse.

"Are they gone?" she finally managed.

Kittim put his hand on her arm. "We had better see," he answered gently.

So they left her there behind a sticker bush with instructions to watch for their sign.

"Grievous," Tutan had whispered before following them. Iscah watched them go with a knot in her throat, determined to be brave.

⊰⊱ ⊰⊱ ⊰⊱

They made their way slowly down the mountainside, slipping on shale, weaving round rocks, and keeping the caravan in wary sight until the tree tops blocked it from view. Madai would have used his ears to find the sounds of men, but for the noise they three were making. But Tutan would not be left behind, even for Iscah's sake. He led them into the shelter of the trees. A mat of composted earth at their feet was soft, silent; it belied the massacre just beyond.

The way to the outer edge was not far, and they reached it quickly, stopping as one in the shadow of the grove. Here they watched a few of the animals milling aimlessly. Tutan spied his pony.

The image of men crumpled in ruins was terrible and claimed all their attention at first. Some had been in flight when they were cut down, their bodies pointed toward the aspens for refuge, or spun round in a tangle. Even from this distance, there was a perpetual hiss of buzzing flies, and stench carried on an unkind breeze. Dead animals hopped at the persistent tugging of black buzzards - and winged serpents, too, the master scavengers. One had the leg of a man in its grip, trying to fly away with it. Madai watched as the creature spread its leathery wings and lifted into the air. But the baggage was too heavy, and the scavenged leg tumbled back to earth.

Madai inched forward to verify that there moved no Anak giant in the scene. He pinched the arrow at his bow, having given Kittim the spear. And then he signaling them to follow. They crept carefully from one brush or tuft of grass to the next, until they finally reached the first dead camel, swelling on the ground. It was surrounded by sundry spilled and pillaged packs.

The foraging birds ignored the live men; they did not scatter or threaten, as the feast was plentiful enough. Just beyond, a two-wheeled cart was toppled, its contents slashed and tumbled out. It was a distraction, the array of colorful items flapping around. The breeze strengthened, and a wisp of scarlet cloth swirled up with the dust to catch on the stiff leg of the camel, pointing at the sky. And still, no man moved. They lay at awkward angles, the dead men, some without arm, even head; and looking as though they were still running away, parallel to the ground.

It had been a wealthy caravan. There were several overturned carts, many bundles still tied to the packs of dead animals. It appeared the pillaging had been done thoroughly, if not efficiently. Spilled cloth and spice lay everywhere. Madai began to walk amongst the wounded animals, slitting their throats, ending mournful wails, for which they all were grateful.

Tutan had captured his pony and held it tightly by the rein as Kittim growled, "Butchery."

Madai was sprayed with camel blood. He looked up from the task to see Tutan and Kittim near, above the form of a young man. The boy was slashed across the chest; his face, an ear missing, was covered with black blood. Kittim knelt in the dust and closed his eyes. Then he looked away. Madai knew Kittim had gone to that place he often went; so he moved beyond the pair to inspect a pot emptied of its treasure. He lifted it to his nose, as a wondrous scent remained. The odor was strong, warmly pleasant, even in the growing stench. He dropped the pot and looked round for another, one that might still be full of the intriguing stuff.

Reaching a second camel, Madai found its pack still bound up and unspilt. He slit the ropes with his knife to find two bundles inside. In one was a pouch of fragrant, earth-colored spice. He pushed the bag into his vest and looked into the second. Here was folded soft, shiny cloth such as Tutan wore. This cloth was not, however, plain. Its colors were brilliant. He pulled a length from the pack and unfurled it. It was a garment, crimson like the sash he had watched blow in the wind, covered with birds and flowers.

"We have forgotten Iscah," Kittim said, coming behind him.

Madai turned, still holding the cloth. He looked up toward the mountain and, though he could not see her, knew that she could see them.

"So we have," he answered. He took another cloth from the bundle and handed it to Kittim, who tied it to the spear and waved it, facing the mountain. They saw her tiny form then, just a speck, rise and begin to come down the mountain.

"This will please her," Madai said, holding the crimson garment for Kittim to see. "She tore her robe to the knees making bandages for me."

Kittim ran his finger down the silky cloth. "Splendid idea," he agreed.

They began pulling others from the stash. All the cloth was as richly colored, meant for a wealthy court. Kittim moved on to another pack lying open. It was torn, most of its contents taken. He looked until he found a garment as fine as Tutan's must once have been.

Tutan joined them. He had been searching the remains of packs, also, a panicky horse in tow. It didn't like the smell of death, and had given Tutan a difficult time till he covered the creature's eyes.

"Savage," he muttered.

Madai looked at him, suddenly ashamed of the silken cloth he held.

"For Iscah," he explained.

Tutan nodded. He looked kindly at Madai. "A fine thought," he agreed.

They both turned to look at the mountain again. She was lost from sight. "She is in the trees," Madai assured them.

"There is something I seek," Tutan said, shifting his thoughts. "It shall be black as ash. It shall be like sand."

"I have found it," Madai said, taking a handful of the rich-smelling powder from his vest.

Tutan smiled. "Ah, pirum seed. But, no, rather darker than this. It is black."

He began to look into broken earth vessels, leading his blinded pony behind him. He tied the animal to the shaft of a cart and looked into the pots there.

Madai had found a second leather pouch of spice. This he tied to his girdle. Kittim had found some leggings of linen and put them in his pack. But the stench was terrible, and the sun was making it worse. Madai looked around again, was disgusted afresh and ashamed again. He was full of an urge to leave it behind. He moved to the edge of the trampled ground to search for the path the raiders had taken. He was looking East when Kittim came behind him again.

"She is long coming," he said.

Madai looked up quickly.

"In truth," he answered.

They stared at each other a silent moment and turned back to the trees, hoping to see her. But she was not on the mountain, and she was not in the valley. Madai and Kittim did not speak. They turned as one and began to run.

*M*adai followed fast behind Kittim. He found himself gasping to breathe, having been so long convalescent, and tried desperately to quiet himself. He needed quiet, hoping to hear something of the child. But all was silent, it seemed, even the birds. An empty feeling shared space with cold fright inside him. He could not insulate this abduction from what had befallen Ido. And he could not forget the tiny hand that had soothed him through his fever. All the innocence lost or befouled by vilest of men.

"She was here!" he heard Kittim cry from inside the grove.

Madai found him crouching on the ground above hoof-prints and broken branches.

"Anak?" He looked at Kittim, confused. "How did we miss him?"

"He must have hidden here, waiting for us to pass." There was deadly calm in Kittim's voice. "Can you track him?" he asked.

Madai was already studying the ground, following just the slightest of depressions made in the years' worth of composted leaves, and places where a horse's hoof had cut through to the earth. It seemed the Anak had taken her and left at his leisure while they had gathered the last of the plunder.

Madai stood up to follow the faint trail with his eyes, determined to rescue the child as Togarmah had once rescued Ido for him. He caught sight of something just beyond them and bent to pick it up. It was Iscah's cap. He put it in his vest.

"It was only one of them," Kittim muttered.

"Yes." Madai stood up.

"I will get Tutan," Kittim said, starting back for the caravan at a run.

Madai looked through the trees, following what was now to him a discernible trail out into the open, through tall grass and into the distance. The grass was high in the valley, bent over to form an indelible mark.

Kittim returned with two camels and Tutan on his pony. They showed Madai how to bring the camel to his knees. He stepped into a sling attached to a leather seat and sat for the first time upon the back of a beast.

He learned the ways of a camel quickly. They followed the trail of the Anak through the evening and into the night, always miles behind, and they stopped to check the earth in the moon's light when the grassy swath gave way to forest. Each heaped blame upon himself. And they were silent, hoping to come upon the man unsuspecting.

CR&CR&CR

The Anak were a confident breed, being masters of war, and heady with plunder and wine. Their raid had cost them not a man. There were trinkets for their women and new camels for themselves and gold and spice and absolute success.

Magshir had rejoined the horde early in the night. He brought with him a ragged little scrap of she-flesh, hardly worth the trouble, though he was intent to keep her for himself. They might have opposed him for her, had they not already set after the wine again.

The encampment was a noisy rabble full of drinkers and snorers and occasional fights. Even Madai, at a distance, recognized the universal sound of cursing. And he soon discovered that men were not so different a herd from deer or elk or any number of prey he had stalked in his life. Neither their noses nor their ears kept so vigilant a watch, and he was greatly relieved that his apprehensions were more terrible than true. And it did not hurt that wine was plentiful in the camp.

He had left Kittim and Tutan in a stand of dense rush just south of the camp, and he was on a scouting mission. A few were asleep, but there were still unsteady figures roaming, silhouetted in the dark against the fire's light. They were of an enormous size, and a great number. So Madai moved around the camp carefully, just beyond the light and, like a lion, downwind.

At this distance he could smell Anak. He was glad in part that he could not understand their words, as he was afraid he would not restrain himself if something were heard of a stolen girl. He made a mental map of the slumbering men, like gigantic terebinth logs felled in a quake, tipped in every direction. He knew where the greater number of them were sleeping. He had already counted them, in groups of twenty. There were half and two such groups. It was their unassailable advantage. And so his rescue of Iscah would, of simple necessity, be made by wit.

In the middle of the camp, there was a kind of tent set up, and two men were lying across the doorway, the only sort of guard he had yet to see. Their weapons were lying at random in the dirt, if not providential, certainly a happy lack of vigilance. Madai thought it a stroke of fortune, and he crept forward for a better look. He had feet as silent as an owl on wing and he hunched behind a tree to look inside. There were bags of grain, and sacks of cloth such as he and Kittim had found. There were bangles and trinkets, but no Iscah. He looked again, just to be sure, and then retraced his steps. He had awakened no one.

He certainly had not thought it would be so simple a matter to find her in the dark, and he carefully made his way around the camp's perimeter. He stopped to study any likely silhouette, any shadow half the size of her keepers. He passed their animals, all hobbled in a group on the far side. The horses kept a better watch than the men guarding them. Madai was cautious of the guards and kept on them his second eye. As he tried to back away, he noticed a third form. It seemed affixed to a tree and was not nine foot. A prisoner. Madai could not restrain his stomach from jumping at the early signs of success, even as 'it' became 'she' in his mind.

She was covered entirely in a blanket, head against her breast. Madai braved a better look, coming up behind the animals. The two Anak were making a fine job of snoring. The captive was sleeping, too, and Madai's heart was beating fast. Iscah! One of the men threatened to wake up, grumbling something before he readjusted his position. Madai pulled himself back into the dark of the surrounding forest.

"Do nothing alone," Tutan had whispered with a hand on his arm.

And Madai had no intention of it. He would not fail her now by haste; if he and Kittim were cost their lives, then she would suffer, indeed.

෴ ෴ ෴

Kittim and Tutan knelt together, facing the camp. With a blade, they cut a long length of a completely dry stalk of rush and quartered it, and then again. The rushes were hollow, into which spaces Tutan poured a substance. They prepared a substantial number that way.

Kittim helped Tutan, keeping his eye on the dark camp and knew it had been a long time ago that Madai had left them.

"He will not act alone?" Tutan worried again.

An answer came by way of Madai himself, crawling back through the rushes. He put his hand over his mouth as he joined them. "Shh," he warned.

Tutan swallowed his impulse to speak. They showed Madai their pieces of reed, which he did not appreciate to any degree. Instead he commanded their attention with gestures, pointing to the distant camp. And then, as he had learned in ambushes of other beastly herds, he used his hands to show them the places of the guards, the camels, and Iscah. To Kittim he gave his bow and showed them the place they should wait and watch while he crept round the far side to cut her free. The plan was simple: use stealth to accomplish all of it - with the aid of extravagant drinking and an arrow from Kittim if the quiet approach failed.

Kittim nodded firmly. Madai had not expected the glint of supreme confidence in the man's eyes. As well, Tutan, neither reluctant nor fearful; he took the spear, and they three crept to the outer ring of the sleeping giants.

All was as he had seen it last, sleeping lumps of men and waning fires. He exhaled slowly. It was time to move.

Madai's was once again a quiet stalking, his eyes trained on Iscah and her watchmen. The guards were slouched against the trees with their heads resting on their chests. What danger they supposed from Iscah, Madai did not know, but the Anak closest her held a spear slackly in his hand. Madai became an apparition, slinking at them on his knees. They snored heavily, a horse whinnied, and all else was still. One of the men grunted, then abruptly moved. Madai froze. But the giant was only shifting his head before he snored again. Even so, Madai was immobile, fixed on the man's every aspect, even to the spear that had tipped its point to the ground. It was a five-pronged spear... and Madai's heart leapt.

The Spear of The Family, powerful in mysterious ways. Rid of the head of him who had stolen it second, slack in the hands of him who had stolen it next, and guarding a helpless girl. "How can I get them both?" was his unexpected and immediate problem.

And now, she stirred. She stretched, her leg awkwardly coming out from under her cloak. A very long leg.... Madai froze, horrified. In the second it took for him to blink, everything was changed and Iscah was failed again. This figure was a man; in fact, an enemy who had somehow become enemy to his fellows. Madai felt the blood drain from his face, his hands turn icy. He sat back on his haunches, the Spear forgotten, darting his eyes frantically around the fires for her once again. In their dimming light, nothing but mounds of sleeping forms were discernible. His mind raced. Where could they have taken her? Could he creep around to every shadow? He calculated what was left of the night. He would wake someone if he searched about now, and he thrashed himself for his first presumption. They should have to watch the men by day to find her.

He did not spend another moment's precious time, but backed away into the shadows. He would have to bring the news to Kittim. A camel huffed, shifting its bulk as it rested, attracting Madai's attention. He carefully circled the beast, to use the forest as his shield.

Just then he heard soft breathing, and a little whimper. Certainly not come from the camel. He closed out all other sound as he made that breath his absolute obsession, listening as he did for something familiar in it. 'Where is she?' he wondered. There were only the three Anak and this camel. He looked closely at the animal for the first time, and the burden on its back, an unusually sloppy pack. Slowly, a form emerged, a tiny human form.

Madai made out her body now, a dark shadow laid forward, arms draped on either side. Only her legs were tied, one to the other on either side of the camel with a rope slung under its belly. She stirred and lifted her head enough to turn her face away from the animal's neck. Madai took that moment to put his hand on her mouth.

"Sh," he breathed. "Iscah."

She was immediately awake.

"Iscah," he whispered again.

She sat straight up, her face stark and eyes wild. "Iscah," he repeated, "It's Madai." He pushed his knife between the hide of the camel and the rope and sawed till it snapped. She shied back away from him and he whispered again, "Iscah."

"Madai?"

He heard a feral roar, and a great weight of giant fell upon him. He felt his breath forced out through his mouth in a wheeze and himself lifted high and spiked back at the ground. He felt his bones rattle and was struck blind for the breadth of a moment. When his vision cleared, he saw that he should die by The Family's own Spear.

The whole of the camp responded to the giant's first cry like restless jackals. But Madai's concentration was bent on the lethal lance-head. He rolled frantically to the side, feeling a course of wind peel back the air beside his cheek. The Spear bedded itself in the earth, pinning the unfortunate camel to the ground.

Madai leapt up... Iscah! But she had tumbled away. He spun back around and there was a high-pitched whine as an arrow pierced the soft center of the giant's neck.

The Anak were drunk and did not know the precise cause of the disturbance, only that there was some sort of trouble. They were unsure at first where to start the fight, which lent Madai the scant moment he needed to find Iscah. She was crouched wild-eyed behind the stricken camel. He lunged past the animal and scooped her up. With his other hand, he found the latch on the Spear shaft. He tripped it, releasing the point still lodged between the camel's ribs.

By some divination, the Anak spotted him and counted him the intruder. Madai saw them coming, nine-foot hulks, and he flung Iscah over his shoulder just as another rushing sound - but this, a flaming arc whistling past his head. He jerked around to see a streak of fire racing back at him, some magic weapon of the Anak! Another and another vaulted into the night. They hissed like serpents, spattering the dark with sizzling light. In that one eternal moment, he calculated for the second time the cause of his own death, and Iscah's and could not; in his darkest dreams, decipher what it was.

What he first overlooked, was that the giants were running, too, equally terrified. They were not upon him, but in a mad panic, wailing and shouting, groggy men stumbling over each other, cursing wildly, leaving their treasures behind. Whatever danger this was was meant for them all.

Madai slunk low, afraid to look up, and stumbled straight across the camp. Naked, terrified giants rushed past him, away from the source of the attack, as Madai hurdled toward it. Still the night sizzled; wild catapults, flaming lances, careened and whistled above them, leaving a tail of fire.

His grip on Iscah was savage; her head bounced against his back and she screamed right along with the giants. The air was full of a biting stench that burned his lungs; his eyes ran. A flake of fire settled on his beard with a singe and sizzle. And all the panic afforded their escape. The camp was emptying of men, filled instead with screeching, mysterious pikes of fire.

"Kittim!" he shrieked as he rushed at him. Kittim ripped Iscah from his shoulder and plunged back toward the rushes. Madai scrambled behind. Whatever had been the magic, it was over now, leaving smoke and an acrid smell.

They threw themselves into the rushes. Tutan, with their mounts ready, leapt like a youth to the back of his pony. Madai did not remember diving for his camel, but he was next galloping behind Kittim, his eye on Iscah as she hugged Kittim's waist. Together they galloped in the direction opposite the fleeing bandits.

ෂ ෂ ෂ

Madai was still astonished and absolutely numb, except for the tingling expectation of wild giants or mysterious fiery projectiles finding him again. His camel was stretching its knobby legs like wings across the ground. He felt a wet smattering of camel slobber slap him in the face. They covered the same ground again, from where they had started at the caravan, needing the sense of their mounts to carry them back through the dark. He would have liked to run till dawn, but Kittim gradually pulled his camel back. Even then, the animals were long in slowing, perhaps as terrified as their riders.

"What sorcery was that?" Madai cried as he threw himself to the ground. His knees nearly buckled as he swung his head around, looking for pursuers.

Kittim, ever calm, took his camel to its knees before he got off and lifted Iscah down. He chuckled. "I would not call it sorcery."

Tutan slid off his pony, only just visible in the moon's light. He took something from his pack and handed it to Madai. It was a tube of rush, stuffed at one end with mud. "Fire ash," he proclaimed. "Used by the Hsai to frighten the enemy."

Madai held it curiously.

"The black sand I got from the caravan," Tutan explained.

Madai looked from the benign wood in his hand to Tutan's expectant face.

"You set it afire," Tutan explained.

- 37 -

They reached the caravan. Much had been accomplished through the night by wind and scavengers. Iscah buried her eyes and nose in Kittim's back, but she couldn't stop the smell. Here, they turned north, putting the carnage behind them as far as the dawn would take them. And Madai was confident at last that they were not being followed. What prize Iscah had been to the Anak might be traded for their lives, as their fright had been as great as his own. He expected they would reclaim their treasures only after a time long enough to dull their fear.

So with night given way to dawn, and dawn to midday, they reached a pleasant place to rest on the banks of some unknown river. The frantic energy born of mortal peril had long since vanished.

Madai was hungry, and for fare richer than roasted tubers. He was just reaching for the satchel of arrows when Tutan brought a thick fingerling of sticky fruit out of his pack and handed them round.

"Sweet as honey," Tutan proclaimed with a weary smile.

"Dates!" Iscah approved.

And Madai put one into his mouth.

They ate voraciously, reminded by the safety of distance that they had passed a full day and night with only the fruit of a scorched yam.

Madai carefully rolled to his back, having remembered the fine powdered stuff inside his vest. He loosened the string closure, smelled it again, and dangled it in the air before Iscah. "Smell this," he insisted.

She sniffed it with a bright look, for which he was pleased: only a small thing, but good to make her smile.

Kittim was pulling something out of a bundle, billowing white trousers and a vest. "For you," he told Iscah, holding them out to her.

She blinked as Kittim put the garments in her hands.

"Clean and whole," he explained.

Her mood was instantly changed, holding the stark white cloth, an extreme contrast to her own, where her leg came through by a long tear, nearly to the hip.

Madai watched as great droplets of tears traced their way down her face. He was enormously thankful that he had not offered her the ornamented crimson cloth, which was more beautiful, by far.

"I'm going after a deer," he announced, in part to divert attention from Iscah with his voice uncommonly loud. He was up quickly and retreated to the river before they could respond.

രുന്ദ രുന്ദ രുന്ദ

Madai brought them pig. A mother sow had only twelve piglets now. Along the way back with his prize, he had passed a still portion of the river, where he had heard a sound. Thinking first it might be Anak, he stole a look, to find there only Iscah. She knelt in the center of the river, bathed in moonlight. That his seeing her would cause her shame, he had the sense to know; and he would have turned away but that he saw she wept...and was less child than they all supposed. Seeing her there aroused great pity, and he no longer doubted what had been done to her by the giant.

രുന്ദ രുന്ദ രുന്ദ

"Swine must be thoroughly cooked," Kittim was saying as Iscah came out of the forest. She was wearing the clean, white clothes of the caravan. She was as she always was, delighted, a stomach as demanding as Madai's and happy for the pig, thanking Kittim for the clothes. Had Madai not seen her at the river, he should never have guessed her angst.

She was laughing and telling Tutan about the really marvelous creatures at the river. And the sow she had startled with her piglets, and that it was a tremendously fortunate meeting, for Madai had killed one. She showed him she still had his pearl, and her voice was guileless; thankfully, she was a child again. It was, in fact, turning into a peaceful night, with an evening air that did not smell of danger.

Madai was happy to find that Kittim had clean clothes from the caravan for all of them. After a bath of their own, they settled beside the fire like members of a family listening to tales. Tutan told the story of the pearl, acquired from great depths in the Eastern Sea. He told tales of bright coral reefs and fishes a multitude of colors, shapes and flavors. He explained the fleshy parts of an oyster, a lumpy, inauspicious animal, that the mussel was a prize in itself which offered a pearl from time to time. He showed them a pouch of grain, which he called 'rice', and promised them a feast.

Madai told of mammoth hunts and the sulphur plains. He showed Iscah the saber tooth, still tied around his neck. And she talked about goats and dogs, fathers and mothers, and something called whey, a delicacy, it seemed. He didn't expect a delving into her most recent life, and he was proved correct.

Only Kittim kept his secrets close; and when it was his turn to talk, he asked instead, "Tell us Tutan, what has brought you here."

Tutan was pleased to tell them.

"To gain a place," he answered. "The river, Pishon."

"O?" Iscah asked, wondering what a simple river might bring a man who was afforded such a sea of coral and pearls.

He nodded. "It is across those mountains," he answered with passion in his voice.

"I have traveled far to be here."

"What would bring you so far," Madai asked, "a man of your years?"

Tutan chuckled. "The barely old are ancient to the very young," he answered.

Madai raised his yellow brows and Tutan grinned, wrinkling his wrinkled eyes.

"I took the merchant caravan at Gomen, traveling west." His face clouded with the memory of what had come of it. "And still, I am glad to be here." He looked at them, a little ashamed to have said it, knowing full well what an irony can be made of life. "But I am seeking a worthy thing."

"What?" Iscah asked.

"My child," he was only too happy to answer, "The Maker " he lifted his arms to his sides, " of all of this."

Her eyes were wide.

"Precisely," Kittim responded with surety.

Madai had stopped being surprised. He watched Tutan silently, fond of the man, who was all that is kind but surely a dreamer. Even Madai, unlearned as he was, knew that God, should He live, would not be found by a human man. Finding God, and finding knowledge of Him were certainly not the same. But he would hold his tongue, as Tutan's confession had brightened Iscah's eyes, which was, for Madai, worth a good deal. She leaned forward expectantly, waiting for him to tell her more.

But he did not. He looked at her kindly and patted her arm.

"At the Pishon?" she asked faintly when she had waited as long as she could.

He slowly smiled, his eyes still as bright as hers, and he wanted to tell her. But he was also most aware that there were more here than just the child. "There are many who call me fool," he finally replied.

"We shall not!" Iscah exclaimed, glancing at Madai.

The words, spoken with such a force, persuaded Tutan. Had he not seen her trusting, abundant soul, a lover of Mighty God who suffered and cast no blame? If there were one who should benefit from what he had learned, it would be Iscah.

He looked just at her. "Shall I tell you, then, what burns my heart?" he asked.

She nodded.

He nodded in return. "There is a people," he began slowly, "who are not of the Miau as I am. Though we live amongst them, we are two tribes. They have an ancient skill, which I have learned, the skill of painted words."

Iscah wondered that this should burn his heart. A fold creased between her eyes. "We have painted stories," she said.

He nodded his head once, "Exactly so, though these are more than stories; they paint each word." His face clearly expected that she should be impressed, though she stared blankly.

Madai hadn't expected such a thing. What a great trouble, he supposed, to paint each word when a picture would do.

"Why would they do that?" he asked.

Tutan looked at him, resolved to patience. He tried again. "To tell their thoughts," he said, "to keep all the histories of humankind."

Madai thought of The Family's songs, confident it was the easier way.

"There is a painting for the Name of the Mighty God," Tutan resolutely continued, having once started.

Iscah put her hand to her mouth. "They know His Name?"

Tutan nodded, satisfied at last that she seemed to grasp the significance. "It is Shang Ti," he answered solemnly. He took a stick and scratched two symbols in the dust. "This," he said, indicating the first, "is the mark for 'heavenly,' and this is 'ruler.' It is spoken 'Shang Ti' by the Hsia."

He waited again. Madai leaned forward to see the scratches Tutan had put in the dirt.

"There are other symbols of other words," Tutan continued, overtaken by his own story. "There is a symbol which speaks the knowledge that you possess of the deluge, Madai. It is the sign for boat." He put his stick to work again. "This is the mark for vessel, this is eight, and this is persons. These three marks make the painting for 'boat.'"

He looked at them, triumphant; but when they did not seem to grasp it, he prompted them with a question. "What of the first ship built in this world do you know?"

"Eight were saved," Iscah breathed.

Madai studied the ground skeptically.

"My people live amongst the Hsia," Tutan continued. "We are not of the same speech, but that can be learned. We have shared knowledge of beginnings. And I have a great friend amongst them, a scribe who is truly patient. From him I have seen their parchments, and many signs... He has given me the learning of many written words."

Kittim slowly nodded. Iscah and Madai only looked at the marks made in the dust.

Tutan continued, "My people, the Miao, came away from the confusion of tongues into the East. The land there is gentle, though there are great mountains inhabited by ice and white leopards. Beautiful creatures." Leaning toward Iscah, he murmured, "My mother is a lover of magnificent things. She tends the flowers of the meadow and the valleys and the mountains. Even now, that she is old, she keeps her gardens."

Tutan watched her eyes soften, thinking of mothers. It touched his heart, and yet he was still cautious to reveal a thing about himself that should surely be mocked by some. Though, as he looked into the dark pools of her eyes, he wanted her to understand, to know there was a place indeed where God should be found. He waited a moment longer, smiling at her.

"I loved the gardens," he said. "Not for the sake of beauty alone, but for the One Who put them there, He Whom I loved." He whispered the last words. "I loved Him even then, when I was not so tall as to see above the peony heads. I came away to my mother's garden and sang to Him. Very long, till I was missed." Tutan's voice was very quiet. "He smiled at me there."

Then Tutan looked up, nearly ashamed, remembering Madai and Kittim, sharing his most dear remembrance. He looked at Kittim. "Pray, do not think me proud, nor mad."

"It is scarcely mad to seek the Maker," Kittim replied.

"He is all I seek," Tutan declared quietly.

Iscah was filled with a sharing of emotion with Tutan, longing to smell a fragrance of sweet peonies, though never having seen such a bloom. And she had to know.

"How do you seek Him?" she whispered. "Can you fly?"

One corner of his mouth twitched a smile at her. "Well, I can't do that," he said. "One does not fly at heaven by determination." He leaned toward her with a twinkle in his eye. "I have tried it," he whispered.

Her own eyes rounded even as she nodded knowingly.

"When I was no more than this," he continued, holding his hand at waist height and serious again, "perhaps six, I went to the garden, as that is where I talked to Him, and stretched my arms high up to the sky, waiting for Him to reach down and say 'Yes' and take me. I waited a long time, till my arms hurt. But nothing moved in heaven; He would not be persuaded. In the end, I went back to my mother. She gave me sweet curd and plums; I remember that...."

"I love Him, too," Iscah whispered.

Madai looked at them, all silent save a twittering bird. Tutan's story was sentimental, a foolish child's tale. He resolved not to think of a time when he was a boy and felt seen of God. Instead, in the still, Madai recalled his own good mother with her busy hands, the way that she soothed him and gave him from the prized parts of elk. And despite his strongest efforts, that last look, that last promise... "He does go with you, my son." And Madai was annoyed with himself, feeling his eyes mist. He looked back at Iscah, who had spoken last, her quiet whisper, young and motherless. Still, she loved a god.

It was she who broke the silence, "So," she asked practically, "how will you find Him, then?"

Tutan picked up his stick. He began to scratch on the ground again. He traced a square in the dust and intersected it north and south and east and west, with a curving, graceful line beside it, and two smaller ones. "The sign for border," he explained. "Amongst the Hsia, a yearly sacrifice is made to Shang Ti. It is called a Border Sacrifice, made by their Imperial King. It has been so from ancient times, even before the flood."

Iscah watched his every mark, trying to understand.

Madai wondered, of course, what proved these Hsai true; but he restrained himself from asking, thinking it somehow unkind at the moment and not immediately urgent.

"Their sacred words are written upon parchment and are spoken in a rite, the Border Sacrifice, made each year by the Imperial King." Tutan continued. "I have witnessed it myself, a very great honor, as I am not Hsai. The words are highly auspicious, as I am certain you will agree."

He raised his head toward the sky and closed his eyes. He lifted his hands slowly, likely unconsciously, and he began to recite a tale of order from chaos and the birth of heaven, of earth, of men.

His voice was solemn, and Madai guessed they had been forgotten by the Eastern man as he finished the ancient words.

It was like a song spoken to a great God, Shang Ti, a God Who had made the world and all those in it. A God regarded as Father by unenlightened children. A Potter God working with dirt. It was a song of gratitude to a Sovereign Whose goodness was infinite, His care enduring. It was a blessing meant to woo back a lost love.

There was only the sound of a lark answering Tutan when he finished, and the constant running of the stream. Madai supposed it was the man's own reverence that granted the moment its gravity.

Tutan opened his eyes then and looked at them each with expectancy.

Iscah pursed her mouth. She cocked her head to the side. "It is lovely," she affirmed. Then she took on a repentant look. "But where is God to be found?"

Tutan was disappointed again. "Border sacrifices," he answered patiently. "This blessing is made by the Hsai Imperial King at the Border Sacrifice. It has been so since Adam was cast out."

Tutan continued to watch their faces. "Ah," he finally perceived, "I have not been clear. Another written word."

They waited as he traced the same intersected square on the ground below the first symbol he had made. He looked up smiling. "Garden," he read with importance.

Then he pointed to the sign above it: "To come before Shang Ti… at the border."

"Yes?" Iscah encouraged.

"This," he pointed to the second square, "the mark for 'garden,' divided by four rivers, the Pishon, Gihon, Tigris, and Euphrates." He was triumphant. He leaned forward. "Adam and those after him came to the place closest to God, the boundary of the Garden." His eyes were full of fire. "This garden they could not enter, but only the border, guarded by fierce angels. The Hsai retain that detail. Can you not see? What is written cannot be forgot or changed."

Still, they looked at him blankly.

He eyed them shyly before he spilled the last. "I seek Eden," he finished.

Iscah could suddenly see it! Her hands flew to her throat as she envisioned strange men who looked like Tutan bent before a terrifying angel at the edge of Eden.

No one spoke. Madai recognized quickly every logical reasoning against him. But it was Kittim's voice that finally answered in the quiet.

"Might it survive the deluge?" he asked softly.

There was a long, heavy pause, while Tutan's face paled perceptibly. "That is a consideration," he replied. "But the rivers exist, do they not?"

"Indeed," Kittim replied.

"And we near the Pishon. I know, for I have made trade with a map maker."

Kittim nodded again but did not speak.

"I can not wait," Tutan said abruptly. "The life of a man is great, beyond 200 years, and I am not half there. It is too long a time to wait for God. "

"Why did fierce angels protect the garden?" Kittim asked.

Tutan would not answer at first. "Life grows in the garden," he finally acknowledged. "The Tree of Life, and holiness of God." He looked at Kittim bleakly. "We are separated by the evil of our own hearts, and none can undo it." He sighed deeply. "So I must come as near Him as I can. I must make sacrifice for reconciliation - there."

There was compassion in Kittim's eyes. He put his hand on Tutan's shoulder. "Come with us," he urged. "We are on a sacred quest, as well. We seek Heavenly God by the Ancients who knew Him, and to whom He spoke."

Madai, who had listened with two minds, was immediately struck by Kittim's assurance that there were indeed Ancients, and that they had word from the Great God Himself, should He live. And he was moved by Tutan himself, sorry that Tutan would certainly fail.

"I can not leave my search," Tutan argued.

Kittim nodded, having a look of both disappointment and admiration. "What will you do when you find the Pishon?" he asked.

"I will follow it," Tutan answered stubbornly. "I do not know its length, but it flowed from Eden."

Kittim's voice was pleading now, "It is the mercy of Almighty God that brought us together, for our journey east is ended, and we go north from here." He watched Tutan closely. "Perhaps the Holy One proposes that you join us."

"Or you join me..."

Kittim smiled at that. "The man to whom we travel is well favored of God. He has wisdom to offer. I fear Eden is lost."

Tutan would not hear it. Surely the garden of the Mighty God was mighty as well, with roots sunk deep and held fast. Their timely meeting, fortunate as it was, did not usurp his cause. His had been a private quest, known only to his aged mother, and he had not considered meeting other pilgrims.

"Give me a map to the man you speak of." Tutan conceded. "When I have followed the Pishon, I may return that way and bring you good news."

"As you wish," Kittim finally assented. Then he took a stick and drew in the dust as Tutan had done. In it, he scratched the river and mountains that separated them from the fields and herds belonging to the man of renown.

Tutan watched; and when Kittim was finished, he drew one identical, to fix it in his mind.

And after this, the course seemed set. Tutan went to the stream and Kittim followed him. Madai watched Iscah, who was watching them. She sighed and fingered the last of the pig, crusted and completely black above the embers.

Madai got up and stretched, "How can it be that I am hungry?" he asked, to brighten the mood.

"If you are not hungry you are asleep," she quickly replied.

- 38 -

Tutan reached for his pack. They had all awakened and taken breakfast. The morning was bright, a good day to travel, with everyone rested and the danger of barbarians somewhere behind.

He was not embarrassed by his evening confessions, though he had not expected to reveal the whole of his heart to his little-known companions. He hummed a tune under his breath, digging round his bundle for the rolled parchment. He spread it out carefully on the ground and squinted at it.

He was aware of Madai watching him. "The barbarians took us here," he said, pointing at the scroll with his finger. "We are north from the caravan, that is correct?"

"I am a seaman, Tutan. The stars do not change, and we traveled north from the caravan, as I am sure you know," Madai answered.

Tutan grinned, "Precisely. But corroboration is prudent, think you not?" He looked back at the map and squinted at it again. "The Pishon is beyond that hill, Madai," he finally continued. "Or the one just further."

Kittim and Iscah were silent, looking down at him. He coughed and rolled the parchment, putting it carefully inside his pack. "So..."

Madai shrugged and began collecting his possessions, disappointed that Tutan had not been persuaded. And he was amazed that the Eastern man, who had been nothing but a hindrance and a caution before, had somehow become a friend.

They secured their bundles onto the camels, all a bit subdued, reminded that Tutan would leave them, though Madai was not so sure it would be allowed. As true as he knew Kittim, he knew they would not watch Tutan ride away on his little pony. Tutan should not journey alone, be it toward the Pishon or to Kittim's man. If he would not be persuaded, and it seemed he would not, they would have to go along. Madai saw no other way, but only wondered how long it would take.

ଔଓ ଔଓ ଔଓ

The morning stretched on. Madai was grateful for his camel, thinking how he had gotten used to easy travel astride a beast. It coughed and complained and was generally a disagreeable animal; it smelled, but it took long strides and was sure-footed. It carried him without effort through the valley. It carried him to the foot of the mountain and began a lumbering climb. It gave him a high perch from which to survey their surroundings. He was accustomed to its amble, and his muscles had not complained in a long time.

He was anxious to look on the other side of the mountain, to see what was there. He was living the parts of a new song, the tales of which stretched past the days of Ido. He was storing up the story of the cave paintings in his head: its mythical creatures, even the prospect of Nua's ship itself! And indeed, it excited him. That his life carried on was, for Madai, a terrible discovery.

The camel huffed. It seemed to know it was reaching the end of its great effort up the mountain. Madai watched as its head came silhouetted against the sky. A moment more and they would reach the top.

CSCR   CSCR   CSCR

It took her breath away. Iscah gasped as she and Kittim joined Madai at the crest of the mountain. Below them twisted a long silver cord of river. It sparkled in the sun and watered a valley of brightest green. She watched great birds, looking white against the blue sky, soaring on the drafts of the wind above giant, gently swaying trees.

"The Pishon," Tutan declared. His eyes were brilliant. "It has been a long journey here."

He would not be delayed. There was shale mixed in the vegetation, and they slid as much as stepped. Holding on was worse at the downhill slope, but there was no stopping Tutan. Cedar grew thick the further down they slid and mingled with aspen, its white bark peeling like a shaggy goat.

They gained the river through the grassy plain. The valley was ancient remains, the path of a river much grander in earlier times, fertile, with rich soils carried down from other places. The Pishon that remained was wide and slow and clear, skimming across a rocky shallow. Bright pebbles sparkled in the sun just under the water: green, amber, red, peafowl blue. When Kittim let his camel drop its head for a drink, Iscah was first to the ground. She scooped the stones in both hands, delighted.

"There is a fire mountain near here," Tutan explained, looking from his map to the rocks. "It spits them out."

She looked up at Tutan and asked him how he should know such a thing, holding her hand just under the water to watch the pebbles begin to sparkle again. Kittim chuckled. He held the rein of his camel loosely, its nose buried, sucking up the river.

Madai was on his knees beside his camel upstream, having a drink. "It's not so grand a river," he observed, looking at Tutan with water dripping from his beard. "This Pishon."

"'Tis the tail, no doubt," Tutan responded, undeterred.

Iscah dropped the pebbles. "You won't let him leave us."

Kittim was cupping water up to his mouth. "It flows north and west," he said, looking at the horizon.

"Precisely as shown on my scroll," Tutan agreed.

Madai, squatting beside his camel, looked between its legs at Kittim. "You know he can't go alone."

"What will be done for it?" Kittim asked.

Madai was surprised. "We will have to go with him."

"It may be a long way," Kittim warned.

Madai took another drink. "Even still..."

Kittim watched as his yellow-haired friend stood, moved past him and came to stand alongside Tutan, who was rolling up his map. "You will not come with us?" Madai asked again.

"My friends, I owe you very much. Should it be any other thing...."

"God does not live in a garden," Iscah pronounced.

Tutan sighed, patting her head. "I shall miss you," he said.

"Two days," Kittim announced abruptly. "We will follow this river with you two days."

Tutan stammered, "I have not asked..."

"You have not," Kittim agreed. "But we shall."

"I cannot allow it."

Kittim turned away casually. "Two days," he repeated calmly. Then he lifted Iscah to their camel's back and remounted, drawing its head upward, out of the water. The animal grumbled about that, water dripping from its lips, but it started its long legs moving to follow the river.

Madai and Tutan hastily remounted. Tutan was anxious, attempting to visualize his map, trusting two days' journey would be enough to get him to the river's head. He hoped Kittim would not count this as the first, for it was nearly midday. No, surely he would not.

Madai was less perturbed by the detour than he would first have thought. He believed he had gained a great deal of information from Tutan, all that supported the old lore. His father would be glad of that. And it was a good day, the sun bright, the air cool, the flies mostly bothering the camels. They had not seen a flying serpent in a fortnight. And the Anak traveled in a direction opposite their own. He watched Iscah's back as she bounced along behind Kittim. Her cap was gone and her hair was one great hive of black.

 C3C3 C3C3 C3C3

The river slowly grew wider. It was deeper, too. Madai wondered how far they had come. No more than a few hours, he determined, looking at the sun. His stomach rumbled and he remembered they had not eaten past the morning's first meal, but he hoped they would keep their pace till dark. Poor Tutan, how anxious he must feel to watch the sun climb to its height and begin to draw downward. Madai turned to get a look at the man, knowing his pony had short legs. He slowed his camel, letting Tutan catch up.

The pony trotted uncomfortably. "I am ever in your debt," Tutan's voice bounced with each step.

"Debt is not marked by family - or by friends," Madai answered.

Tutan looked grateful. "I ever thought to go alone."

From his higher perch, Madai looked down, his eyes reflecting the green of the grass with a friendly glint. "Your painted words intrigue me," he said. "There is no debt."

Tutan was grateful. He looked out across the river and back at Madai. "Do you believe Eden is lost, as well?"

Madai shrugged. "What beyond old songs do I know? Or you? Only what we are told."

Tutan was quiet at that, then slowly twisted his back. He turned his neck, easing it gently back and forward, and briefly closed his eyes. "All live by trust," he muttered. "More than you know."

Madai heard him but did not respond. Instead, he busied himself with the view of the river snaking through the long valley. It had become much deeper.

"Tell me about your green steppes," he asked Tutan.

The man was glad to do it. He nodded with a sentimental smile. But he also noticed Kittim's camel was stretching a distance between them and hurried his pony.

"As this," he began his description, "though the mountains are higher, steeper. We have terraced the hillside slopes where there are great deposits of mud, baked by the sun." He looked up again with a spark in his eyes. " In the deluge, we presume."

Madai threw back his head and laughed. The sound caused Iscah to turn around with envy in her face. She found it ever boring, staring into Kittim's back or just to the side of their way.

"You are as determined as a badger, Tutan."

"You flatter me."

And both men laughed again.

"So, Madai... why have *you* come here?" he asked. "Kittim says it is a holy quest."

Madai squinted at the sun in the west. He nodded. "It is to seek knowledge of the Great God, should He live."

Tutan studied him shrewdly. "So you have a question about that."

Madai stared straight ahead. It was not distrust, it was not an ill favor that held his tongue. He knew his face, perhaps even his voice, would betray his emotion - and he did not like the prospect of that.

"A private matter," he muttered.

"Yes," Tutan assented. "It is usually so."

Madai had not been trained to deny grief, only to endure it, because life on a frozen waste was full of danger. They spent more than half their days on the tundra, prey to saber cats and quakes.

"I lost a wife," he answered abruptly.

Tutan did not look at him, but only asked, "And you blame the Holy God?"

Madai shrugged. He looked purposely at Tutan. "And...does He live, Tutan? Truly?"

They rode in silence. A bird chortled near them. They could hear the rush of the river and the soft swoosh of the grass. Madai's face was set, betraying nothing.

"All live by trust in the end," Tutan repeated vaguely.

Madai had a stark look in his eyes. "As I feared," he replied.

Iscah rested her head between Kittim's shoulder blades, catching their words on the breeze.

C3CR   C3CR   C3CR

The remainder of the day passed quietly. A stag startled and rushed ahead of them through the grass. They watched it bound across the river and into the rushes, its pointed hoofs splashing through the water. A doe drank water on the far side and raised her head, ears forward. Her fawn peeked from behind her flashing white tail, and that was all. They traveled till dusk.

When Kittim supposed they had come far enough, he tugged the cord that fastened a thorn to his camel's nostril. The animal stopped, immediately munching at the surrounding grass, and Iscah slid off, hopping once as she landed. She disappeared into the meadow, her head just visible above its tall grasses. She was making her way toward the river, bending, disappearing, moving forward and bending again. Then she raised up and lifted her hand in the air, filled with lacy yellow blooms. Her face was lit with delight as she waved her bouquet at them.

Kittim looked over his shoulder. "She has been begging to stop for miles," he explained.

Tutan dismounted. He bent at the waist and flexed his back. "Exquisite timing," he remarked, leading his pony to the river. "If this counts a half day only, I suggest we boil a pot of rice."

C3CR   C3CR   C3CR

The first full day of their journey up the Pishon began before full light. They had passed the night comfortably beside the ancient stream, molested only by a ground rodent which had gorged itself on their leavings of rice. Iscah left her bouquet beside the stream, stems cupped between stones at the water's edge, not to watch it droop and die.

The volume of the river was increasing steadily. It deepened, disguising the true force of a strong current. They passed roving herds keeping near the banks. As the river grew, so grew the pitch of the land, if ever so slowly.

Even Madai was finally troubled by monotony, though he did not hope to find an Eden at the head of this Pishon. He watched his camel's floppy jaws as it chewed its cud in display of a similar mood.

Tutan's pony abruptly began to dance. Madai glanced at it, then past it to a movement in the deep center of the river. But the sun was bright on the water, where its brilliance shielded a ... thing.

The pony shied and Iscah was suddenly pointing excitedly. She squirmed behind Kittim for a better look. Then Madai saw it as well, a long serpentine neck above the water's surface. He did not share Iscah's glee, instantly recalling the dark serpent of the sea. But no, surely nothing like it could swim its way up this river.

Tutan had not seen it, trying to hold onto his pony's back. He held his knees tight to his skittish mount and called, "What is it?"

"A serpent, in the deepest center of the river," Madai answered, sharp with concern.

The camels had stopped and they began a low rumbling aimed in the direction of the beast.

"No, Madai," Iscah called back.

Madai frowned; and as he watched, the animal began to move toward the far shore, seemingly indifferent to their near proximity. It was a massive creature, brilliant green, slowly moving into the shallows. It churned the water to little whirlpools as its great, wide back rose from the river. The neck, towering gracefully above, supported a surprisingly benign, tiny head. It lifted its nose into the air. Was it sniffing them? Whatever scent it caught did not disturb nor hurry its climb. With slow elegance, it turned its head in their direction and posed there, motionless. It seemed to huff through its nostrils at them, then resumed its placid retreat from the river. A long, thick tail followed behind it, lazily swaying back and forth in the water, creating little riplets that reached to the near shore. Madai watched, astonished, as the beast emerged fully from the water, larger by far than even the great mammoth. It moved noiselessly into the meadow, turned to look at them again, and made a deep whistling sound. Then it slowly, even gracefully, arched its face down into the grass. When it raised its head again, it chewed a great mouthful. Madai remembered the cave painting.

Even Iscah did not speak. They waited, watching the creature for a long time. Then, with far more delicacy than its size suggested, it moved away, down through the valley. Its neck and back were ever visible, with the swaying grass betraying its great, wide tail.

"Behemoth," Kittim finally spoke. "We are near."

"Is it fearsome?" Iscah whispered.

"A graceful giant," he answered. "The Maker's power in evidence."

"Then it is not fearsome?" she asked again.

"But for defending her young, she is harmless."

Iscah nodded solemnly. Then they sat atop their mounts watching till behemoth had disappeared.

A moment longer, for Iscah's sake, and Kittim nudged his camel with a willow switch, intent to gain a long distance on Tutan's first day of only two. Iscah was twisting round, wishing for a second look at the beast that was, sadly, gone from sight.

"We will come this way again," he assured her.

Madai watched where behemoth had gone, knowing of a certainty that such things were surely made by a god of some sort, the details of which he only had to reason out.

They continued their slow ascent away from where the beast had gone. A mountain rose in the distance, and it was clear that the Pishon came from there. It was a mountain of spectacular heights. Snow clung to its upper parts and shone with brilliance in the sun.

೮೩೮೩ ೮೩೮೩ ೮೩೮೩

It was well past midday when they finally reached the foot of the mountain.

Iscah had watched at every bend for another sight of behemoth, or some other exotic thing. But there had been nothing to see save the transformation of the river. The Pishon, which had been silent and deep in the valley, was starting to roar.

The mountain was formidable, with massive boulders half-erupted from the earth. Madai's camel was beginning to struggle. When it became more difficult to press them forward than to walk, they went afoot. They hobbled their animals and retrieved weapons, cooking pot and rice, robes to guard against the cold, and Tutan's parchment map. Iscah especially was pleased to be on the ground. She made her way with agility, exercising cranky muscles. It gave her time to study a rock squirrel or follow a bird with more than her eyes.

The higher they climbed, the more treacherous the way became along the river. So they came away from the bank. The Pishon was soon lost from sight in the density of the forest, but her roar was a constant presence. The climb became real work, even for Madai and Iscah. They started up a sheer of rock, only to turn back for an easier route, and had to slow down for Kittim and Tutan often along the way. The sound of the water intensified like thunder, and Madai knew the Pishon had found a rocky edge and was tumbling off the mountain somewhere.

Iscah scrambled past him, back toward the river, and was first at the precipice, first to see what spilled from a great height to a great depth. No less than two rainbows hung in the prism droplets of the falls. It was an enormous fountain, pulled across the jagged edge of the mountain, tumbling and smashing the rocks below. She stepped back involuntarily, her stomach dancing nervously. A perpetual wind reeled in the spray, dashing her face with a mist icy cold.

She spoke an exclamation in her own tongue, but the sound was lost in the roar. Madai was there a second later, immediately wet by the spray. He gripped her wrist to pull her back another step.

"It is very far down," he shouted into her ear.

She was laughing, blinking the water out of her eyes, bobbing her head at him. "It puts a queer feeling in my stomach," she yelled back, and they stepped back again. "Wondrous, is it not?"

"What wonder?" Tutan called as he and Kittim reached them.

"A mighty falls," Madai yelled above the roar. "Mind the edge," he finished ,still gripping Iscah's arm.

Tutan nodded vigorously and turned his face to the mist.

Kittim pointed to the rainbows. "His oath is spoken even here." And Tutan nodded a grinning face toward him, hearing not a word.

It was a cool shower on a hot day. They let the falls drench their fronts and listened to its power till, fully soaked, they retreated from the edge. Iscah found a spot where she could see the top edge of a perpetual rainbow in the mist. She was deliciously cool, and thinking about food again.

☙☙ ☙☙ ☙☙

Tutan was looking up the side of the mountain. "Still a great height," he muttered. His mind had already returned to his purpose. He gauged the placement of the sun to be yet hours from dark. He sighed, "What more time do I have, Kittim?"

"Next morrow's end will be the second day."

Tutan nodded slowly.

"But we are near the summit," Kittim continued. "We shall know something soon enough."

Tutan's heart was banging a drum in his chest, and it was not from exertion. He could not decide whether it was excitement or dread. How shortly would the goal be reached! His aged mother had not encouraged his journey, counseling him by the same reason as Kittim. But the paintings of the Hsai were ancient, brilliant; and his longing great. They had got it all so splendidly exact, matching what he knew of first and second beginnings. He looked up. They were all three looking down at him.

"Are you well?" Iscah asked with concern. She moved to sit beside him.

"Merely resting," he assured her. "It is a long climb still."

She looked back at the height from which the river poured. "Not so great; we can be easy at it."

He patted her hand.

So after a short rest, they began to climb again, though more slowly than before. Tutan did not seem ashamed that he needed assistance, which Madai found amazing. But Tutan was gracious as ever, and merry, and thankful. He seemed even to prolong their ascent, fairly despising the journey's end. About this, Madai was not so unclear, and he pitied the man's dilemma. For surely the deluge had changed the terrain of the old earth, surely washed away its life, both plant and beast. Perhaps this was not the Pishon of old at all. It was good that Tutan should know.

They climbed till they found a level spot, with the river more tame. There Iscah boiled the rice and they washed their feet and hands in the icy water. Tutan was content, even insistent, and they made their night's camp at the spot, for he was tired enough. They could see the sky through the trees at the top a good distance away and suspected a morning's trek would take them there.

ෆ෪ ෆ෪ ෆ෪

They slept the night with the river sounding them a crashing lullaby. But Tutan, tired as he was, could not sleep. He waited for first light, anxious as a cat, and thought of his mother, that he should like to tell her he was here. And he thought of Enico, wishing it were possible to speak to her, also, if only a word. Then he trained his thoughts from her, a habit born by fear of grief. Though tonight he was not troubled by that. Indeed, he recognized an old communion, as old as his first recollections. Heavenly God, Who brought the sublime Presence, the bursting heart, the palpable assurance.

'I Am here,' he almost heard it with his human ears. And Tutan was overcome with peace.

In the end, Tutan must have slept, for it was morning's first light that woke him. He felt his body revived, grateful that he was not so old a rest could not restore him. A faint light flickered through the trees, making dim outlines of his good friends. He rose as silently as he could, looking toward the summit and the promised source of the Pishon. His ambivalence of the previous day was replaced by rugged confidence.

Whatever he might find here, he would deny nothing. Still, he had his hopes.

He bent to fix his boots to his feet, then began what his eyes had found to be the clearest path to the top. He soon had the forest at his back, hiding his companions. His advance was not graceful. He slipped, cracked branches, muffled a cry as he cracked his shins, though ultimately he made his way slowly forward, always training his eyes on the morning sky which drew him up. More than once he had to retrace his steps, finding an obstacle of boulder or climb too steep. But he was bent on a course.

He did not hear the others following, respectfully distant, for his assault on the mountain was not a silent one.

ଔଓ ଔଓ ଔଓ

Morning songs by the mountain's birds were Tutan's companions as he topped the summit to greet the end of his long journey. He gazed with awe at the mirror which reflected the sunrise in its azure depths. A snow-fed lake.

"Ah," he breathed aloud and stood rooted to the spot. Turning eyes to right and left, squinting toward the far side, he felt his mouth tremble slightly. Here were no flaming broad-swords brandished by mighty angels, no splendid tree of life, guarded by cherubim.

There were no divine footprints.

Finally, he put his hands on his knees and bent at the waist, breathing raggedly. He closed his eyes, hearing his own blood as it pounded in his ears. All else around him was elegant silence. Then he slowly lifted his head, feeling a fresh breeze cross his face.

The lake was not large. It reflected the masterpiece of sunrise and gave life to a ring of snow crocus - really quite ordinary, though a lovely, site. He filled his lungs with the aroma of crisp spring. And, as he had his breath again, he quietly sang the childhood song, so low he himself scarcely heard it. There were his eyes filling... He blinked and tears escaped to wet his cheeks.

"I am no different than before," he whispered; and he looked up to the sky and lifted one arm in greeting. The heavens did not part, the sun did not shine a brighter gleam. 'What is this but defeat?' he wondered, as the world was as it had been before. Only, he was surprised by himself, that he was not undone; and then... he felt The Father smile.

All that happened at the mouth of the Pishon was another touch such as he had felt before. And Tutan surprised himself again with a chuckle.

ଔଓ ଔଓ ଔଓ

Kittim, Madai and Iscah waited below him in the tree line. They watched him mouth words and heard an odd laugh. Madai would have stopped her, but Iscah slipped away and scrambled to stand beside Tutan. She looked at him with concern. Not knowing what other comfort to give, she slipped her hand into his.

Tutan only looked at the lake a little while longer. "He has no limits," he answered Iscah's unspoken question. "So simple. I should have known." He looked down and smiled at her. "I think He must sometimes laugh, foolish as I am."

"He is pleased by you," Iscah answered quickly. "It is your heart He loves."

Tutan looked at her serenely. Then he sat down on the grass and beckoned her sit beside him. Together they watched a fish leap near the center of the lake, snatching an insect in its mouth.

- 39 -

They remained the rest of Tutan's second day, exploring the boundaries of the lake and extinguishing any remaining ember of hope. Madai was surprised by the manner in which Tutan accepted supreme disappointment, for he was entirely content. Iscah surprised him, as well, as he had heard her gentle encouragements. How were they both so certain of a God Who was kind?

In truth, Tutan was relieved. His long-planned journey was completed. There was no longer cause to fear that he should not find God in the garden, for God had come with him.

Kittim was solicitous. "You are well?" he asked, scratching the mark for 'Shang Ti' in the dust as Tutan had shown them.

"My good friend," Tutan assured him, "it could not be better." He smiled broadly, "One can not trek to Eden each time he needs Holy God."

Kittim chuckled and put down his stick with a twinkle in his eye.

"What of the paintings of your Hsai then?" Madai could not help himself.

Iscah glowered at him but by some faint sense held her tongue.

"Our own father's fathers knew the deluge, Madai. Doubt you that?" Tutan asked quietly.

He shook his head slowly. "Forgive me, Tutan. It is not the place now."

Tutan turned his palms up, lifting his arms from his knees. "What better place?" he asked.

Madai was ashamed of his own words. He would not disturb the peace of Tutan's face, and he thought himself unkind for the first time. But he had started it, and Tutan was watching him expectantly, with crinkley eyes.

Madai scratched his head. "The story of the flood is widely spread, I know that now," he said, glancing at the girl. "Your people have it, and the Hsai, Iscah and Kittim. That is a truth I will take back with me." He shrugged and looked at the ground, and then he said more than he had expected: "I don't want old songs, or star stories. I want... more," he whispered.

Iscah squatted carefully beside Kittim, not trusting what she had heard Madai so quietly confess. Kittim held her hand firmly, and she knew it was to stop her tongue, though she had more sense than that.

Tutan listened and waited. A moment more, and he answered, "I do not doubt the Hsai writings. I know they tell of a time before the deluge. I know that ancient ones worshiped there, at the boundary between Holy God and rebellion. And now I know Eden is washed away." He looked directly, purposefully, into Madai's face. "This I know. I know. And this knowing is not enough."

Madai frowned.

Tutan smiled.

Madai would have laughed at Tutan before - a child's faith in a man's world - but there was a great confidence inside him. "What is enough, then?" he finally asked.

"His Presence," Tutan answered simply.

ଔ୧ଔ   ଔ୧ଔ   ଔ୧ଔ

That Eden had not been found did not distress Iscah. There was Adamah and the first mother, and there was the garden. But it was the first earth, and drowned by a disappointed God long ago. That Tutan had born it well alleviated all else that would have troubled her.

What concerned Iscah was today, and that her legs hurt where they straddled the camel, and that the lake was cold and beautiful. Tutan, her kindred spirit, would stay one day or two. But they would be away, that she knew, Kittim and Madai. So when the morning came full on, she stubbornly searched the shoreline, busying herself with matters that should not be interrupted. She discovered white scalloped shells, opened like little wings and empty, and clams, tightly closed, only to learn that what makes great pink pearls would not be found at a mountain lake. Still, she stretched their morning, daring the icy water with her toes. She stalked river rodents just to watch them swim away. She let the cold air turn her cheeks red and chap her lips, and she dreaded riding the camel again.

At midmorning the men had done all they could to bide the time. Even Tutan, who was better inclined to patience, kept a stern face when Kittim went to fetch her. She would need to be obedient, a good daughter and no trouble at all.

They went back the way they had come, past the roaring falls to their animals, hobbled and rested and clipping grass with their teeth. They rode down the steep and crumbling slope of the mountain to the enigmatic Pishon, its past a secret still.

They passed the place where they first had seen behemoth and followed its same path through the high grass that could not grow tall enough to hide it. And though Iscah craned her neck, sadly, she did not see the beast again. She removed her sandals to glide her feet across the tips of the grass, whose stiff whiskers brushed along her soles.

It seemed to her the plodding was endless. Surely they had ignored the noon meal. The sun was full on her back, putting a wet place between her shoulders on the lovely white tunic Kittim had found for her. Her sleeves were dingy now, where they hung too low on her hands, and they made her hot. It was sometimes hard to be an obedient daughter. O, for a breeze!

"Will there be water soon?" she finally asked.

Kittim handed her back the water pouch. The liquid was hot, and her stomach rumbled.

Finally Kittim looked over his shoulder. "There is a good place waiting us," he encouraged, "Or we may see the beast again."

She knew that tone, a tone just to quiet her.

"And yet," she cajoled, "it has been long since we ate."

Kittim's reply was jovial. "Will we eat grass?"

"There is rice..."

Kittim looked at the sun and felt where Iscah's forehead had dropped hopelessly against his back. He tweaked the cord which commanded his camel's head and brought them all to a stop. Iscah felt no guilt at all, but only sublime relief.

It seemed they all were hungry, and they consumed what was left of their morning meal.

She was better when they had traveled a bit longer then, to end the day at a second little lake, amethyst in the evening light. This was not fed just by snow, but by a spring that bedded below in the endless grass of the lowlands. Indeed, the whole of the country was green, enjoying a drink of water that would vanish, rising in the heat of later days.

Tutan was not so weary as he had been, nor so stiff. And the air carried the coming night chill. It surprised him that his "Eden" lay just a day behind them, a quiet end to his years of learning Hsai writing. Such were the ravages of flood, he knew all too well.

It had been a long ride, a hot sun, though now the night air was chilled; and this little lake was a welcome sight. Iscah disappeared instantly. Madai supposed she must be bathing again. He and Kittim would see to their meat-gathering. Tutan busied himself with what remained of their rice. He dipped water from the lake into his pot and set it above a flame.

There, leaning against a pine, was Madai's favored Spear. Tutan had not studied it before, as Madai had it always near. So Tutan lifted it and found it perfectly balanced and heavy. When he had reclaimed it at the camp of the Anak, Madai had taken his peculiar knife from its sheath and replaced the missing spear point. It had fitted exactly and lodged fast inside the shaft. Excellent skill in that. It had been a talisman of some sort, so Madai said, of his Family, from the scattering. But Tutan was not pleased by it, though it was a fearsome weapon. There was a carving, perhaps gold, likely bronze. Unearthly creatures, nearly enchanted. He frowned and hoped the value Madai lent it was just its deadly, perfect utility. Tutan leaned it back.

He looked to the lake, where Kittim was kneeling above the water cleaning fish. He supposed his rice would tend itself and left it boiling to join his friends. There were two fish, already cleaned, lying on the rocks gutted and twitching; Madai was hunting a third. He held an arrow trained at the water and was utterly still. Tutan heard a swoosh, and Madai leapt after it. Then he lifted a fish into the air, pinned through the gullet.

"Ha!" Tutan exclaimed. He touched a fish on the grass with his toe and grinned at Kittim.

Kittim grinned back.

"Where is Iscah?" Tutan asked, looking round.

"Bathing, I expect," Madai answered, bringing his latest catch.

Tutan rubbed his arms, as the night air had arrived. "Hmm, remarkably cold, I should think."

Madai laughed. "Maids are hardy when dirt is concerned."

Tutan smiled wryly at him. "So you say."

"You don't know the ways of maidens?" Madai asked with a chuckle.

Tutan looked at Madai with a rare ironic smile, considering his answer, "The Creator's eloquence is woman," he said with more importance than Madai had asked. "And we are tamed by her."

"I did not think you had a woman, my friend," Madai replied.

"Once," Tutan answered. "As did you, though more years ago." Tutan tapped at the rocks with his foot. His smile changed to stoic calm. "She was taken by the river in the spring rains…"

It surprised Madai that this man who was very nearly old, gentle and without passion, looked back at him with a memory lit hot as coals. He read an old grief there, and then it passed.

"I am consecrated," Tutan suddenly announced.

Iscah, who had wrung out her sleeves and pulled her shirt back on, came from behind the rock, mostly dry, but with muddy feet. "I am sorry you are consecrated," she said, as she had heard Tutan's short tale.

Tutan smiled. "Consecrated means to be pledged to God."

"O! Then I, as well," she responded with a bright face. "Consecrated."

He shook his head. "I shall not marry again," he clarified. "I am a 'devoted one.' I have renounced the carnal."

She did not understand all he said, but she knew what it was to marry.

"Then I shall certainly be consecrated," she pronounced.

Tutan patted her wet hair a bit awkwardly. "You are still a child," he suggested. "There is more of life to be had before such as this is decided."

She let him pat her and hid the truth behind a calm face, well trained, knowing precisely what she wanted… and did not want.

"Did the Holy One ask this of you?" Kittim asked Tutan, taking their fish back to the fire.

"He would not?" Tutan responded, following, having always before felt inspired by it.

ଔଔ ଔଔ ଔଔ

Madai let them walk away. He wiped his arrows and laid them on the rocks to dry. His mood had suddenly changed. He felt a slow heat rising, his chest suddenly hollow with an old shame. His easy fall… His was no renouncing of the carnal. He wondered how he should ever have thought it could be other; certainly he did not outrun his guilt, and redemption was lost. It always came to that.

It had been weeks from that cold, bitter day when he had left Ido in the frozen earth. He had not wanted to leave, because when he did, she would stay behind. They had burned the earth to thaw it, though some would wait till spring. He could not have endured that.

And on a night when he was freshly wakened from a dream, a spectre had come dressed in the flesh of Ido. She had found him impassioned by the dream. She had made a place for herself beside him in the dark and he had granted himself relief there. But not before he heard her voice, crooning from above him, a visitation not of spirit, but of flesh - Yamma.

Ah, betrayal is worse than grief. Ido betrayed, and he the culprit.

Madai squeezed his eyes shut, remembering his once-held assurance of a God Who sees. What could be worse, to betray a love so true as Ido, who lay as pure as winter snow in the eternal earth, or to be Seen by God doing it?

Then he shrugged and remembered with a spark of relief that there was no proof of God, great or no. From whom, then, to claim redemption?

છ૪ર   છ૪ર   છ૪ર

Iscah was pleased to let the silence grow, watching a half moon make a smooth sheen on the lake. The three men were staring at the fire, watching the fish curl. She studied their faces, now lit more by the fire than the sky. She thanked God for them, and for her rescue. Her shirt was still damp, putting a bit of chill in her from that relentless bathing and that indelicate knowledge that she was not, nor ever would be, wholly clean.

The night was quiet, where each kept their secret thoughts and, in separate ways, wished for a help that should satisfy insatiable need.

Long after the fish were eaten and the men asleep, Iscah stared up at the stars and thought she heard a distant whistle and a rustling in the grass on the far side of the lake. She allowed herself a smile for the harmless, awesome beast and diligent mother. She took comfort in that and dropped away to sleep.

Kittim was still, but did not sleep so quickly as Iscah had thought. He read the signs of the countryside, glad that the land of his man was near. He sought instruction of his Master and waited daybreak.

- 40 -

The morning brought them up early. Kittim was an inexhaustible guide. And so began a near fortnight's journey north and east. It took them through and past the fertile valley, up and over the rising hillside and to another surging river, which it was their course to ford. But the way was not frightful, for this land was planted with many streams, which fed an abundance of trees and plains. It was only its unremitting vastness; and Kittim, who was by nature serene and unhurried, had become relentless.

Madai could not reproach his eagerness, as the quiet man had twice veered from his course, once for himself and again on the Pishon. He was, in truth, glad of the hurried pace, for he knew Kittim sought the famed man of the East, the one who was pledged to know ancient secrets.

Iscah seemed to suffer most, though it was only monotony. But slowly, and with growing excitement, the girl began to perceive a greater tameness to the countryside, recalling cultivated fields. She hoped Kittim's great man lived near.

The once-beautiful garments brought her by Kittim were stained and torn; she longed after something clean. Her neck ached perpetually where she had craned it to look round Kittim at the horizon. Only today was the effort rewarded, for there, to her eye's welcome, were hills to the east, conclusively marked with the pattern of a tended field, bordered by still another.

"Is this the place?" she asked hopefully.

"We are near," Kittim answered.

"What name has this place?"

He turned his head toward the fields on the slight hillside. "It is Ur," he answered.

"Is it a great city?" Her questions spilled from her. "Is it wicked as the place you took me from? Is it the place of your man?"

She heard patience in his voice; "It is a great city, the royal city of the Chaldeans."

"Are they wicked? Are they fiercesome?" she suddenly shuddered.

"They serve many gods."

"And the man you seek?"

"Lives beyond Ur, not far."

She sighed and relaxed, then stiffened again, "They are not fiercesome?"

Kittim looked at her over his shoulder. "They are busy building their temples. They will do us no harm."

She was satisfied and determined to study the nearing habitations of a city named Ur, to recall them to herself when the way was dull once more.

The rise of a brick ziggurat came to view. It was only just being constructed, as its top was unfinished and asymmetrical, the height just more than half what its designers intended. The city's wall was complete, however, with a great wooden gate that stood open. But they did not pass through it. Kittim took them round the north side of Ur and away. Iscah could smell the smoke of their cooking fires and had to please herself with only that glimpse through the gate.

Tutan recognized the marks of a caravan route, bringing him soundly back to a civilized world. They followed the road many miles. Past the unmistakable sound and smell of goats. Past stone pillars etched with half-moon shapes and wedges and other odd markings. Past small huts of mud, reeking of wood-smoke and fat. Past booths, little more than racks, from which sheepskins and earthenware hung. Iscah caught the sheen of a familiar skin, iridescent in the sun. As the road carried them further past the city, the pitiful mud shanties disappeared, until the evidence of a human hand was seen only in the patchwork fields.

The road was easy to travel, and a morning's time brought numerous more fields to view, traversed by ditches of water and an eternity of waving, seed-topped grass. The road stretched ahead of them to meet the foot of a small hill. To their west was a ribbon of green, coiling and winding, flanking the fields, a river supplying water to tiny canals.

"We are arrived," Kittim announced.

Iscah, who knew the signs of wealth, was heartily impressed; and when they came to the foot of the hill, she recognized an ancient orchard. The stalks were as thick as her arm; and though the time for fruit was not come, she knew that when it was, the sturdy vines would hang with grapes. They wove between the plants, trellised by skillful hands, to the top of the hill.

They stopped at the crest. Kittim was pleased to let them see from this height, the lands of his 'man of renown.'

ଔଔ ଔଔ ଔଔ

The orchard draped both sides of the hill. At its base was a protective boundary built of sun-baked bricks. Iscah judged it not high enough to hold back the goats she saw dotting the pasture beyond. It seemed the earth itself moved, for the number of odorous beasts feeding upon it. Still to the northwest twined the river, spawning a forest of giant trees that spread up and down its length. A familiar sound reached their ears, sporadically carried on the breeze: a herd of asses, obstinate desert creatures, an impressive number of them.

There in the distance was a sprawl of buildings painted white against the sky, and wondrous. And she was surprised that Kittim should know such a man, for he had seemed always humble. Iscah had known such as this in the city of Hamonheb, but they had been not dwellings of men, but of gods.

Madai commanded his camel forward, following Kittim. All such constructions continued to astound him. 'Surely,' he thought, 'this is not the lodging of one man's family, but a village.'

They descended through the orchard to come upon the brick wall. Kittim found the way through, and they rode amongst the herd. The goats did not scatter, but continued their business with scarce a look. A he-goat, enormously shaggy, with one broken prong, began to charge them, thrusting its one belligerent horn at the ground. Kittim merely looked its way, which arrested it at the spot.

And then Kittim slowed their pace. He would allow, Madai assumed, those who kept this village to know them harmless.

The nearer they rode, the more curious became a certain side-building. It was earthen bricks mortared in a circle, twice the height of a tall man and open to the sky, save a tangle of vine which grew a great deal higher and seemed to cling in mid-air. It was, at closer inspection, growing to a woven mat. The mat arched above the whole, supported as much by the vine as by its own structure. The building was quite large, fully enclosed, attached to the main building by an undulating stone path. Madai could not imagine its purpose; and there was scant time to consider it, for the massive door of the largest building swung open on its silent brass hinges.

There stood a man of stature, an effusion of health - of bearing, merry -with a generous beard and a generous smile. He was dressed modestly in an unbleached tunic which covered trousers of the same, finely woven though unadorned. He did not reside in the shade of his porch, nor send a servant, but came to the place where they were just arrived, spreading out his hands.

"Greetings," he effused with genuine eyes. "May the Grace of Mighty God be yours."

"Peace to you, Excellency," Kittim replied.

The big man smiled and bowed. He spoke over his shoulder to one standing behind him, whom Madai could not see well within the shadows of the portico. Before Madai could evaluate even this, two finely dressed men arrived at their sides, reaching for the reins of their camels.

"You are dusty and hot," the Excellency surmised, stepping aside, extending his arm in silent invitation. "What Almighty God has given me, may I offer you."

Kittim approached the man and spoke a good while to him. The man continued to nod and smile and looked at each of them. Madai supposed Kittim a frequent guest of the great house, but he marveled at such fearless hospitality. Surely The Family would have offered the same; but they would have, as well, reserved a guard.

Iscah came behind Kittim into the perfect cool of the great man's house. Glowing candles and oil lamps assisted her eyes in the dimness. A profusion of colors and textures, patterned rugs, rubbed and glistening walls drew from her throat a quiet gasp. Surely not even in the temple of En-UtuAten had she beheld a glory such as this!

Along the walls of the narrow room were benches, covered over with the finest of cloth, dyed a profusion of colors. Long fringes were sewn at the edges, touching the floor, which was made not of the same brick as the walls, but of hewn stone. Her eyes trailed from the floor to the walls. Here was another wonder, neither white-wash nor a simple mural, but a relief, a long parade of camels, molded in clay af-fixed to the plastered bricks, marching across the plain of this man's long hall. Each carried a rider clothed in colored brilliance, the riders each from some exotic land, each differing one from the other. The rendering exaggerated a wild eye or crimson mouth. It pronounced with a flourish every artful textile or jade-hued parrot. They breathed life. The hand, which had molded and painted these men and beasts had lent them a splendid story.

She was startled then by a tall young girl who tugged at her sleeve and chirped a strange sound at her. She was holding a silver bowl filled with water. She clearly wished Iscah to sit upon the woven tapestry benches with her dusty clothes and sur-render her feet for washing. Like maidens commanded the same of Kittim, Madai and Tutan. It became clear that they would take her sandals, broken and muddy as they were. Instinctively, Iscah looked at the lobes of their ears, to see no great disk embedded there, and grew conscious of the gaping hole in her own.

And then the girl put Iscah's feet into the bowl, one at a time. Had she not washed better at the lake than this? Iscah was bitterly shamed and closed her eyes as she leaned against the coolness of the wall, feeling the lump of a camel in her back. She had often done such as this to another, but never had it been done for her. 'What kindness has this man to a shabby girl such as I?' she wondered. She opened her eyes then, at the arrival of a second bowl and a silver pitcher. The girl placed her feet in the empty vessel and poured them over with water from the pitcher. Never had Hamonheb instructed a second washing!

When the maids disappeared, a small man arrived with new leather sandals, which he instructed, by way of dropping them at their feet, that they wear. Thus shod, they followed him to the end of the hall, where a flourish of his hand beckoned them behold the grand room beyond, as though it were his. There, lit by other lamps. was the Excellency, seated beside an enormous stone fireplace. At their appearance, he rose instantly and came to greet them again.

There he bade them sit and spoke through Kittim to explain that a lamb was roasting at the very moment, and water being drawn for a full cleansing, and cham-bers prepared for their needs. He explained that there was much of the world to learn from such travelers as these and presented his hospitality in gratitude, which was a modesty, apparent even to Madai. Kittim, who was ever restrained, responded to the Excellency with a respect Madai had not witnessed before of his friend. He thought of himself for the first time, standing in the fair opulence of the man's house, wondering whether he were smearing bits of muck into the elegant couch.

"Sabta," the nobleman spoke. "You will show our guests their chambers." And the little man who had shown them in began to lead them out of the room.

෨෬ ෨෬ ෨෬

Within the separate rooms of the house were bathing pools sunk into the floor. One meant entirely for Iscah filled the room with a pleasant, scented mist. Lemmeri, the girl who had washed her feet, was now asking for her clothes.

Before ever she felt it, she knew the water would be warmed, an extravagance she would not have dared to dream. Even Hamonheb did not possess a cleansing pool; and had he, he should not have granted even his first wife such a pleasure as clean, warm water. Only the temple, and her preparations made for En-UtuAten, recalled such as this. She had delighted in that first bath, a dizzy fragrance rising in the mist, and she an uninformed shepherdess, only knowing she must be come to a better place than the wild Sabeans. Not often did Iscah recall the night with the priest, the offensive man who had scraped her raw and stolen her childhood. This had cost her tears once, but it would not today.

Lemmeri, who had left while she undressed, returned with a jar of fragrant soap. Iscah sat rigid in the water, watching her. "Awk," she complained, as the girl immediately began tugging at her hair and reproving her in an incomprehensible tongue. When Iscah, who could not know what the girl wanted, did not obey, Lemmeri pushed her head under the water. Iscah came up gasping. A smell of wet dirt and sweat clung to her scalp. Clearly she would have her hair washed, as the servant dropped a large puddle of soap onto her head. Iscah thought it could be done with less abuse. The maidservant began to scrub and pull and build a mound of foam that crept down Iscah's temples. She made continuous noises that communicated frustration, till the roots of Iscah's hair began to throb.

When she was finished at last, Lemmeri pushed Iscah by the shoulders into the water again, till only her face was left, looking up at stars painted on the ceiling. There, her hair floated and gave rise to a new odor. And Iscah's benevolent assailant was satisfied.

She would bathe her body then, a thing Iscah had done to her that once, and she made it clear to the servant that she could do it alone. The girl left Iscah a cloth by which to dry and bowed and left the room. Iscah leaned her head against the wet, cold stone and looked at the stars on the ceiling. Save the temple slaves, there was only one other who had gently washed and combed her hair, a mother. Well, she would not think of that. She splashed soapy water at all her dirty places and blessed Mighty God, Who would see her clean.

A fine garment was brought her shortly: pale blue, adorned at the hem with a scarlet cord. It slipped effortlessly over her jutting ribs and thin legs. The maidservant was immediately at her side with another disapproving look. She pushed something other at Iscah - an unbleached linen garment which would reach barely past her knees. Iscah, by way of hand signs, surmised this second garment was to be worn beneath the first, which was a new experience for her, though it pleased her: a house of modesty.

When that was finally complete, Iscah tied the new sandals to her feet and glanced at the servant girl, who stood there with a shell comb in her hand. A less gentle hand firmly took her hair and pulled at the wet tangles. Iscah had admired the girl's own hair a moment before, shiny, gleaming black, straight as a horse's tail; and she suddenly understood that her own curly mane was undesirable.

The tangles would not be undone. Too many days had passed in wind and stream, upon a camel and upon the ground. Iscah felt tears stinging her eyes at the pulls, but this she would not allow before such a haughty one. So she clamped her teeth together and waited till the servant girl tired and finally stuffed her hair into a thick, untidy braid.

Iscah stood, at the end of these ministrations, a young maid in a blue garment, mildly scented, with a fat dark braid down the center of her back. Her hair pulled back, revealed large brown eyes rimmed with curling lashes in a thin, olive-skinned face. At times of excitement, her cheeks flushed with scarlet. Now, having lived with the sun, a sprinkle of unexpected freckles spotted the bones of her cheeks and the ridge of her nose.

Delicious smells floated in the air and began to waken her stomach. It was rumbling when Lemmeri led her away toward a dining hall where a large table was prepared and three men she knew and scarcely recognized were seated.

Their surprised faces brought an uncomfortable flush over her, and a mild annoyance that they should be so amazed at her civilized appearance. She took the seat indicated for her. She watched as Lemmeri left the room, glad the girl was gone.

The Excellency gave her a welcoming smile, then turned his face upward. His eyes were open as he praised and thanked his God for the bounty and the unexpected guests and the good wife beside him and the children elsewhere and the provision of food. Iscah thought it never would end. Though she also loved a Creator, another time would be better for such an enthusiastically thorough prayer.

Substances reminding Iscah of her father's table were heaped onto her plate, one portion at a time, and good wine in a silver cup. She watched her hands tremble, trying not to spill the wine from a goblet of more worth than she had brought the Sabeans from the city of Shinar. She heard the grateful pleasantries of Kittim, and polite questions from Tutan, and carefully sipped her wine. She tasted the plump dates, ever more than enough for all, and more, besides. Sweet curd and pomegranates. It was bliss.

When she put her empty wine cup down, it was filled again. She glanced at Kittim, who scarcely ate but talked with the Excellency at great length. There was a mild dizziness creeping into her head, and she left the wine alone after that. Her plate was empty. When had she finished it all?

The others were speaking amongst themselves. The "man of renown" was speaking words in a halting way and smiling at them all. It seemed he had a friend, one who rode the caravans and studied in far lands and taught him the languages of many peoples. He was not as adept at learning new speech as she, but he had an exceedingly merry, kind expression. His eyes were wide black orbs in a lined, dark face much the color of her own. His beard was black, just slightly graying at the chin, and his hair was thick and curling. A woman Iscah deemed to be his wife sat at his side. She was undeniably younger than he, and beautiful. Her hair was drawn away from her face and covered with a violet-colored veil as fine as gossamer. Her robe was as white as her husband's, and carefully decorated with shining beads. When Iscah looked at her, she saw that the woman had been gazing at her, as well, with a smile.

They were next taken on a tour of the Excellency's favorite places. His wife quietly disappeared; and Iscah, who would not be left, took her usual place at Kittim's elbow.

☙☙☙   ☙☙☙   ☙☙☙

Madai had hardly listened to the man praying. He was smelling Iscah, like a purple snow bloom. He could see her in his periphery, her with nearly a woman's shape in her new clothes. He was surprised by himself but could not quite put it off to just the new surroundings.

☙☙☙   ☙☙☙   ☙☙☙

The first room was a gallery of frescoes, furnished with a long, low table, a clay fire-pit, seating for twenty-two, and a wall lined with scrolls. Iscah was to learn that this room provided dining for the entire family, sons and wives, and a place of learning. The scrolls contained knowledge of legal matters, certificates of property, and historical tomes. The frescoes, as well, were monuments of history. The wall of one, a glorious rainbow, painted the entire length, one end to the other. It was accomplished in brilliant colors, these against an azure sky. Another might have been a family portrait, as she recognized the owner of the house and his wife standing proudly with ten others. The third wall was the scene of a river, surrounded with a thicket of giant trees; the fourth housed the scrolls. These frescoes were done with a precise hand, faithfully executed and exacting. But they seemed to lack the passion of the caravan in the entry hall. The ceiling was a painting of the night sky, as in her bath chamber, its constellations lightly outlined.

She heard the halting words of the Excellence, then Kittim's faithful translation when it was just easier for the man to speak in his own tongue. His language was familiar to her ears, just of a slightly different cadence. Still, the voice of her native tongue was welcome, having been forbidden after her capture. A bright hope sprung back into her heart that perhaps her kinsmen were near.

"A great pity," the man said, and looked at her kindly.

"And you, Madai?" he was asking.

So Kittim told Madai's tale.

As the unfamiliar words expressed his familiar purpose, Madai studied the man Kittim had brought them to. He was not so old as Ashkinaz, perhaps the age of Tutan, certainly no Ancient. He was stroking his beard in that absent way, listening, nodding, smiling - and earnest. The man clasped Madai at his shoulders when Kittim was finished. His hands were strong and shook him with exuberant energy.

"My young friend, God be praised!" the Excellence spilled his words from whiskers that smelled of wine. He released Madai and fanned his hands in the air toward the largest fresco. "'Tis true; The Almighty, praise His Name, has left us this promise, that never shall He end the world again by flood."

Kittim asked him to retell the flood, as he knew it, and the animated man did the telling with a faint gleam in his eye.

"Tired and grieved of making man, Mighty God swept him from the world by way of the deluge, a cataclysm which covered all that lived, save, of course, the man, Noah and all his sons. It was grievous indeed. There is a favorite place of mine," he added, "and it has to do with the deluge." The man cleared his throat. "So at the behest and design of the Almighty, Noah built a great ship in which he and all his were saved. I have heard it told by those who know that the ship rests to this day atop the great mount on which it last came after many months afloat." He waited impatiently for Kittim to repeat his speech, then rushed ahead, "From which time God, again grieved at such loss, swore in oath, testified by that which is painted upon my wall, never to so destroy the world again."

Madai was nodding as Kittim translated, no longer surprised to hear the familiar tale. And there was the mention of the great ship's resting place! He leaned toward their host, hoping for more.

"But come, there is something else to see," their host continued. "We shall speak more when the night has come. For there is more yet to speak, the best to speak." He grasped Iscah's hand and led them briskly across the room toward the door.

As he approached a curtained hall, he tapped the wall with his finger. Instantly another, younger man was at his side, received whispered instruction and scuttled away.

Iscah twisted her head vigorously from side to side as they whisked by one wonder after another. Some doors were closed, but some were open; and she glimpsed more frescos, exotic tapestries and deep wool carpets. Then he opened a last door, and they were standing outside. She squinted briefly in the sun, immediately warm. Overhead was woody grapevine, growing from either side on thick, ancient, twisted stalks. It was held aloft by a lattice of reed. At this close inspection she could just see the tiny fruit beginning to form, each no larger than a grain of sand. He continued to pull her through the arbor toward an odd, round structure. She could not see inside, for it had no windows and was taller than she. A great jungle of vine grew above it and over it. She heard a distinct and delightful sound from within.

"My foolishness," he told Kittim, "my great pleasure." And he cautiously opened the door.

Before the door was opened, Iscah could hear the sounds. The enclosure was large, with two full-sized fig trees growing there, and a water pond dug in the center, flanked by every green thing, a virtual oasis. Iscah craned her neck; light blue shared space with the leaves of the vine to form a mosaic of earth and sky. Bright little creatures flitted in the expanse overhead, flashing their colored feathers and filling the air with their songs.

Iscah turned in place, open-mouthed.

Tutan began to laugh. "Splendid," he said.

And Madai was astonished once again.

Kittim held his hands clasped at his back, gazing upward, a look of pride. "Artistry," he murmured.

The door behind them opened, and their hostess appeared. Two servants followed, one with a low table and cushions, the other a tray of spice-smelling tea. She excused the servants and made the table ready herself with brisk efficiency. Then she sat upon one of the cushions, waiting patiently for her husband to finish.

She might have some long time to wait, for he had moved to the pool and sat upon a bench that was set amongst light green ferns which curled at their centers, softly furry. He gestured for her to join him. She obeyed with a grace that was to Iscah's estimation, like a queen's.

His eyes sparkled, looking at his wife, then he spoke again.

"And there," he pointed, "a golden fish of the East."

Indeed, several swam there. And tiny green frogs, with little padded feet. Iscah knew, for she had stooped and captured one. She opened her hand to look quickly, as it leapt with its miniature legs and splashed away into the water. She hoped the oversized fish would leave it alone to live. Then she glanced at the Lady again, in time to glimpse a nearly imperceptible suggestion of displeasure. Iscah flushed.

"However were they captured?" Tutan was asking, looking at the fluttering overhead.

"We began by use of the caravans," the great man explained through Kittim. "Many died. Though their colors were brilliant, it was a futility. So, I surmised it should be better with native birds. Such was my success, as you see." He bent to scoop a bit of grain from the ground and held it aloft in his hand. "Be very still," he urged.

A tiny brown bird fluttered straight into his hand. Her beak was twice as long as most, and her tail stuck straight in the air behind her. She rewarded him with a surprisingly loud and melodious song for one so small, then pecked the barley from his hand. She flew instantly back into the canopy, chirping an equally disarming farewell.

"Might I try?" Iscah whispered, brushing the frog slime from her fingers. Her tiny brown hand was a smaller target, but it was landed upon instantly, if not the selfsame bird, then one of identical markings. It cocked its head at her, warbled the same tune and stole the grain away. She was ecstatic. Another came, and another, until there were birds on her hair, in her hand, and on her shoulder. The Excellency had replenished his palm with grain, and another variety came to him, this one tiny and blue. Its cheep was short and bright. Iscah was afraid to move. He laughed, and they all flew away.

"You are pleased?" he asked her.

"Very pleased," she answered him in her own language.

His face warmed with surprise. "Child!" he exclaimed. "You speak as one of us! Then your kinsmen are near?" And then he looked embarrassed to have inquired after her great tragedy. He didn't wait for an answer, but asked kindly instead, "From where were you taken, child, do you know?"

She lifted her shoulders, "Sabeans," was all she replied.

He nodded, knowingly. "Brutes," he answered. "We shall look for your kinsmen."

His wife rose and took Iscah's clean hand. "Shall we take refreshment?" she asked, pulling Iscah away with her and leading them all to the little squat table.

Perfect delicacies of pastry lay under a cloth for them, as well as a warm tea, smelling of ginger. Iscah wondered how ever she could put more into her stomach; but with the first bite, she found the way. Tiny crumbs of pastry slipped secretly from her fingers to the ground just beside her cushion. She shared a side of the table with

Tutan, who turned her a wink before he joined the discussion of bird husbandry.

A deeply blue bird was currently pecking the dirt beside Iscah. It soon hopped to her lap, where more crumbs had gathered. She put her finger slowly down to touch its shining feathered head. It allowed her just a charitable moment before it fluttered away toward the pool.

"You must consider," his wife was saying, "what an honor is yours. Rarely do visitors enter here. Even myself." She voiced the last bit somewhat petulantly. "Certainly never the servants."

"It is my pleasure to tend them myself," her husband interjected.

She nodded, smiling demurely into her napkin.

"How have you come by them again?" Kittim asked.

"A local merchant," he answered.

His wife sniggered softly.

"And an old friend," he finished.

"My dear," his wife murmured, "she sleeps in the trees."

He chuckled candidly, "So she does, my dear. But only in season."

Madai, having formed an immediate disapproval of the woman, leaned forward, a roguish look on his face. "Ask him who this person is," he requested of Kittim.

"The daughter of an old friend, really," the Excellency answered. "Of many years. My benefactor of sorts."

His wife laughed aloud at this, "He was handsomely paid," she interjected.

He took her hand in his, holding it firmly at his side. "Began a camel boy with the caravans. At the end, a merchant himself. Most successful. His goods were the finest, the rarest, the most extravagant."

She drew her hand from his. "He was elegant," she interjected. "What was done, was done with a certain.... flair. Even his demise." She smiled at her husband blandly.

He coughed. "Yes, quite. A tragedy of incalculable proportions to me. A friend. He brought his adventures to this place."

Iscah grew indignant toward the Lady as she raised her eyebrows and tilted her head away from him.

"He brought me birds from Cush," the man continued. "It was these that did not live. So he determined, as did I, that a better result would be had with birds of the locale. And he devised a most successful way to capture them unharmed." His voice trailed, "It has been perhaps ten years... perhaps more ... since he fell."

"He thought it a great adventure," the wife said. "No, perhaps it was an economic pursuit. Certainly it would rouse the blood and draw many with a heavy purse."

They looked at her curiously.

"It was my sternest counsel that he abandon his folly," the Excellency offered. "But he was a wild one. Born to poverty and unworthy parents. He made his own way. He traveled from one foreign land to another and bought every exotic skin, every oil or spice, every cloth.... even men... though I chastised him for that... and brought them to this civilized place." He coughed, "Yes... well, a shining skin in a desert market place caught his eye. Well he knew the creature it was taken from.

They range here as well, and scavenge like dogs."

Iscah was immediately alert.

"He wanted to cage one, or, rather, to take an egg of the foul thing and brood it. If anyone might have succeeded it would have been he, had he not fallen... from the ledge. A tragedy."

"A winged serpent?" Madai asked incredulously.

"Precisely."

Madai shook his head, agreeing with the disagreeable wife. "What of the daughter?" he asked.

"It was the scales of the thing, you know," his train of thought continued, "beguiling. Such a thing might have enriched him. Though I think it would never have been tamed." He had a way of trailing off. He looked at Madai, "His daughter? Yes, nearly as wild as he. He raised her on the caravan." With his narrative turned to less disagreeable things, and more current, his voice brightened again. "We never knew the mother."

"He brought her from Cush with the birds," his lady offered mildly. "Not the wife, just the child. One never knew the mother. Perhaps there was not a marriage at all."

The Excellency acknowledged with a nod of his head. "Perhaps not, perhaps so. He did not speak of it but to say that she, Reenah's mother, had died."

Iscah took a note of the name, thinking perhaps one such as she, without a mother, might be a friend.

"So Reenah was a merchant-adventurer's daughter," he continued. "And she traveled the routes with him from the time she was three. She speaks other languages; has, in fact, tried to teach me. She has seen all the great cities, tasted all the strange foods, and has an eye for what will bring a profit."

His wife's lovely face had grown more aloof but was slightly flushed. She sat rigidly straight.

"It was she who painted the camels you saw as you entered," The Excellency finished.

"How does she sleep in trees?" Iscah asked, wickedly baiting the wife.

He laughed. "She does not, except just before the eggs hatch. She waits, making the mother at ease till they fledge and just learn to fly. Then she takes one, only one each, from many nests, and keeps some, and sells some. So, you see, they are, at the start, better acquainted with us."

Iscah nodded. It sounded sensible to her.

"Might we see her?" she asked.

The wife rose daintily from the bench. "My dear, we have left our guests sitting too long. Perhaps they need a rest from their journey."

He stood as well. "Forgive me. I am a poor host." His wife was already moving to the door. "There is so much more to tell and see. Things of the Almighty, His Name be praised. And things He has made and done. And more. But they may wait."

Servants came to remove the table. The Excellency's watchful eye guarded his collection of birds; and when their picnic was safely removed, he led his guests through the door. Other servants were waiting there to show them their resting places.

CRCR   CRCR   CRCR

Iscah was irritated. She did not want to rest. She wanted to watch the birds and let them perch on her finger, or she wanted to meet the strange, motherless girl who lived in trees. Very romantic. But she certainly did not want to rest - and she did not.

Instead, she crept barefoot to the door, pushing it silently open. It moved without effort, heavy, thick cedar on oiled hinges. The exotic rooms she had just glimpsed in passing were her goal, and she slipped with bare feet down the long wood-paneled hall. The first door that stood open was a sleeping chamber like the one given her, elegant and, quite thankfully, vacant.

To the next room and the next she moved, until she supposed all the rooms off this hall were private chambers. It was the sitting room or library that she wished to find, and the murals of snow-clad hills or forested gardens. Then her stomach lurched to her throat, for down the hall, coming her way, was the manservant, Sabta, he who had attended the Great Man when they had first arrived. Her body flushed, feeling that her unattended movements about the house might be ill-mannered. His glance was a thorough appraisal, from her unshod feet to her thrashing heart to her flaming earlobes. She perceived a sordid look in his eyes as they lingered ever so slightly too long. But he inclined his head and passed. She believed he had turned when he was past and watched her, though she would never know for sure.

Moving swiftly into the maze of the house, she took the next opportunity and turned down another long wing to still her heart. She thought briefly that she must be cautious to keep her wits so as not to be lost. She heard a faint movement inside one of the rooms and glanced in. It was the Lady, sitting before a fresco, her impeccable gown covered with a smock, a flat knife in her hand. Iscah froze, leaned back toward the opening and peered in again. The Lady was smearing plaster onto the wall and had not heard, so intent was she. Iscah stood in the doorway and waited, watching as a painting of the desert grew one knife of plaster at a time upon the wall.

After a time, the Lady seemed to sense her, and turned, still gracefully poised even in surprise. "My dear!" she exclaimed, "Why are you not resting?"

Iscah was tongue-tied. It was neither that she could not understand the Lady, nor that she could not answer, but that she was suddenly confused. How lovely the Lady seemed, alone in this room. Even kindly. It did not meet the unpleasant opinion Iscah had almost completely formed of her.

"My lady, I...I could not rest," she stuttered. "I am filled with," she searched for the word, "seeking."

The Lady laughed, a tinkling, light sound. "I understand," she replied and rose from her stool. "Come inside. See my humble pursuit. It brings me pleasure, none the less."

Iscah approached her slowly. She did not think the pursuit humble at all. Instantly she knew the hand of the Lady had painted at least one of the frescoes in the eating chamber.

"They are beautiful," she told her, not lying, for though they were not fashioned with the same zealous spirit as the caravan, they were faithfully true.

The Lady inclined her head demurely. "You are gracious," she answered, obviously pleased.

"You put those in the great eating room?" Iscah asked.

"Yes. I was instructed by a master. There are others in this house done by him. Do you wish to see them?"

Iscah nodded. The Lady put her pallet knife into the wet plaster, covered it with a damp cloth and smeared her hands on the apron. Then she removed it, smoothing her robe delicately. She took Iscah's hand into hers and led her into a long hall. At the end was a large, dark room. The Lady pulled back heavy woven fabric which covered a window open to the air. On the wall was another river scene. In the center of the river was a great creature - Behemoth.

"My Lord's favorite," she informed Iscah, "perhaps after my rainbow."

It was just as they had seen it on that day at the Pishon, leaving the river to graze in the meadow. Its long neck and smallish head were pointed into the room to look her directly in the eye. It was almost alive, though not the same color. Odd that it was a deep purple. More lovely, really, against a fading sky at dusk. The water rippled around its great legs, reflecting a pale violet sunset.

"My Lord's tribute to the Almighty God, praise His Name. He says this is the Creator's crowning achievement." She looked at Iscah, "But I think it is humankind, think you not?"

She nodded her head, looking at the great Lady standing in the sunlight, beautiful and calm, beside the mural of a crowning achievement. Iscah felt sudden compassion for her.

"You are lovely," she whispered, unable to contain the thought. A tendril of the Lady's hair was loose from what held it under the veil, ebony against her ivory skin.

The Lady laughed lightly and, as if to read her thoughts, touched Iscah's unruly hair. "Come with me," she insisted.

Iscah followed her back down the long hall and into another room, a sleeping chamber which smelled richly of spice and hyacinth. The Lady sat her in the center of the room and left her just long enough to retrieve a comb and a stone jar. She expertly untwined the braid and slowly, ever gently, drew the very wide toothed comb through Iscah's hair. Patiently, patiently, she took each tangle one by one. Though it pulled at her scalp and more than once brought tears springing to her eyes, Iscah did not wince or cry out. What was done to her was a kindness that reached into her very heart.

The Lady did not weary, standing so long pulling out a journey's worth of tangles. "You have a great mane, my dear," she informed Iscah, a horsey reference which Iscah did not find insulting.

"There," the Lady proclaimed at last, "I believe I have got it all. It is very curly, indeed." Then she took an object from a table behind her, a piece of well- polished bronze mounted with a handle. She held it up for Iscah. Her image was better reflected than ever she had had occasion before to see, though once she had glimpsed herself in the mirror of Hamonheb's first wife

What looked back at her were eyes wide and dark, skin not ivory, and speckled on her nose. And her hair was indeed a mane, standing away from her head in a billow of brown waves and passing behind her shoulders. The Lady took a strand and with a pleasant expression watched it coil round her finger. Then she took the stone pot, from which came a thick oil, to spread into Iscah's hair the sweet smell of hyacinth.

"Made of olive oil, and something which I shall not tell you to thicken it. Perfume of hyacinth and anise. A favorite of men," she told her, dipping into the pot several more times.

When Iscah's hair was saturated, it gently coiled, rather than sprung wildly around her face. The oil darkened it, drawing attention to her eyes, wide again with surprise.

"And this," the Lady said, her finger lifting Iscah's chin, "is a beautiful face."

Iscah loved her.

The Lady went to her closet. She drew aside gossamer curtains and inspected the contents. Then she sighed. "I fear there is nothing small enough," she said nearly to herself. "Though perhaps....wait..." she instructed Iscah, leaving the room in a flurry.

She was soon returning, holding a soft, grass-green gown in her hands. "My daughter's," she said, gleaming, holding it toward Iscah.

Iscah was stunned. The kindnesses were too great, and great tears filled her eyes. The Lady somehow knew, and waited patiently for her to recover.

"Do not argue," she instructed and left the gown on the bed. "I shall knock presently, for I believe it is almost supper."

Shortly after, Iscah heard a faint rap at the door. She squeaked her readiness, and the Lady returned. Her eyes widened. "You are less child than I thought," she whispered.

Iscah winced.

"Nothing to fear," the Lady assured her, reading Iscah's face. "Perhaps I shall braid your hair after all."

And as she braided it back into youthfulness, Iscah found herself confiding in the Lady her great tragedy and lost virtue. When both tales were complete, the Lady took her shoulders gently with her hands and said, "My dear, you are at heart a maiden still," and kissed the top of her head.

- 41 -

Supper was as sumptuous a meal as had been served before. The end of it was curd with honey, boiled bulgar, and dates, filling Iscah's stomach till it was uncomfortably taut.

"We are ever grateful," Tutan spoke first. "Your generosity..."

"What is mine is got by the Hand of God," the Excellency assured.

Tutan bowed slightly, "Just so," he affirmed. "Praise His Name."

"Praise His Name," Kittim repeated, then continued to translate for their host, as his learning of their tongue was difficult and imperfect.

"If it pleases you, there is a place I should like to take you," he began.

Iscah nodded enthusiastically.

But Madai cautiously replied, "I have been thinking of the great ship which you say may still be found."

"Ah," the man answered, a knowing smile. "Yes, I understand perfectly. It is, I fear, some distance further. Beyond Shinar. But the place of which I speak is a related sight." He studied Madai perceptively. "Though this is not your question - is it?"

"Excellency," Madai responded with respect, "you are a wise man, though, I suspect, not an Ancient."

At this, the man laughed. It was not a gentle laugh, but a release of true amusement. He looked at Kittim to speak quickly through him, "My young friend, you are short of years and excessively polite, which speaks well of you. I am esteemed by you all, this I know, and you may rest well that I am your friend. I wish it so.

"No, I am not an Ancient, and I am not an Excellency. I am Job, the farmer, lover of God, and blessed by Him, Praise His Name. But I am not your better, only your Elder..." he looked at Tutan with merriment in his eyes, "perhaps."

At this, Tutan laughed out loud.

Job looked back at Madai, if self-effacing, still in quiet control. "Tell me, who is this Ancient?" he asked.

Madai found them all looking at him. "I am persuaded by the common knowledge of this flood that it is true, in its entirety." He waited for Kittim to translate, "One who knew the great Nua face to face," he continued, "is an Ancient. One who, by Nua, has knowledge of the time of beginnings and truths of the Great God," he considered, then added very quietly, "should He live."

Iscah felt shame and looked down, plucking at the folds of her new dress. She had a curious impulse to excuse Madai but could think of nothing to defend his terrible blasphemy.

"Madai is one who must see with his eyes," Tutan interjected.

Save to translate, Kittim was silent.

"A pilgrim true," Job thoughtfully replied, then smiled shrewdly. "The deluge, it may yet be a deception, thrust upon men's minds long ago at the tower. What say you?"

His response surprised Madai. "My father's father remembered the confusion of tongues," he said. "This lore is true. I accept it as logic to believe the flood as well."

"I perceive you have believed without seeing," Job commented. Then he continued in an unperturbed and candid voice, "I suspect, as well, men live who knew Noah. I should begin at Shinar."

Madai was pleased, for he had retained the direction of the great ship: beyond Shinar. A convenience, if nothing else.

"You have spoken with an Ancient?" Iscah asked, hoping to draw Job's attention from what Madai had said.

Job shook his head, still calmly smiling. "Nor have I seen the great ship of Noah. There are those who have," he reiterated.

Kittim straightened his back. "You perhaps have not known Noah, nor seen the ship, yet you are wise and respected. I have purposed to bring Madai to you, to seek what you know of the Great God."

Their host stroked his beard, an unconscious habit, and looked a long time at the rainbow painted on his wall. "I know He is Maker of all that lives," he began. "I know the first sky was as a mirror of cast bronze, and the stars when first He flung them from His mouth sang back to Him. I know they speak with their patterns across the night sky even now, His good news, future news, that He Himself shall destroy the destroyer." Job's eyes misted, a thing which Iscah alone observed, "And I know that at the end of these days He shall stand upon the earth. And after my skin has been turned to rot, yet in my flesh I shall see Him."

Incomprehensible. They waited in silence. Job's wife sniffed softly and he looked at her, then at each of them, one by one. He waited a moment to calm the beating of his own heart, then turned back to the eyes of his wife, eyes that suggested he spoke of God with an untoward intimacy. He studied her another moment before turning to Iscah. "Perhaps you are tired."

Iscah shook her head, eyes round as the moon.

He saw it and bent forward to ask quietly, "Do you wish to see that which is related to the deluge on the morrow?"

"I do," she squeaked.

"Excellent!" he clapped his hands enthusiastically. The sound brought a servant scurrying into the room. "Sabta, show my friends where they are to pass the night."

The little man ferried them each to their own chambers, sumptuously provisioned rooms. Though the comfort was unsurpassed, each watched the ceiling long into the night.

Job

- 42 -

Tutan woke before the light, lying on the comfortable mat, face toward the painted ceiling he had already so well investigated, straining his ears for the morning's first sounds. His imagination's appetite was whetted. He could hardly contain his legs, wanting to leap from the bed and race into the new day. Just when he had thought his adventure complete at the mouth of the Pishon, here he was, inspired again.

Finally, some time later, he began to hear the stirring of the servants below him. The breeze, which had come chill and brisk through the night was still. He affirmed it to be a proper time to rise, dress, and wake his fellows, if they were not already up.

"Kittim," he rapped on his door, "Madai."

He had just called when each appeared, dressed, also. "There is stirring below," he whispered.

Madai led them to stairs attached to the outside of the house leading both up to a flat roof and down to the main rooms.

"I am eager to see the thing our host spoke of last night," Tutan said, following them.

Madai stopped at the last step. "I, too," he agreed. "But the ship of Nua..."

Kittim put his hand on Madai's shoulder. "We are only just here," he chuckled, "Let us inquire more of our friend, Job. I think there is much more to gain."

The kitchen door opened. "It is you!" Iscah exclaimed. "Come see what is being made for us."

The cook was at least one hundred, and as lean as a new foal, surprising as she had ready access to every delicacy. She was wrapping shriveled brown fruit and malodorous cheese, putting them both into the same sack. Iscah lifted another, bulging with spelt and barley bread. "Marisheba says we will just have time to eat a bowl of pottage before the Master takes us off across the fields to the river. Isn't it grand!"

"I have waited the long night for it," Tutan agreed.

୧୭୧ଓ ୧୭୧ଓ ୧୭୧ଓ

Five horses were saddled and ready when they finished their porridge of cracked boiled wheat with raisins. Iscah fairly danced into the waiting sun.

"There are only five," she stopped abruptly, looking at the animals. "The Lady -"

A servant lifted Job into his saddle, "My wife takes no pleasure at the river," he answered casually. "This day she will visit the eldest of our daughters. And should she stay overlong, Meira shall keep her the night, as well."

The servant Sabta lifted Iscah up, and he pressed his hand against her in an unseemly way. She cringed, leaned away and glared at him. She would not have done it, being a guest, but she had met him in the hall before and there was a very bad thing about him. Then she turned her attention away.

She had never before been astride a horse, they being reserved for masters and other great persons. They were also skittish and swift. But she would not betray her inexperience, loath to be left behind. This animal, however, was benign, being among the oldest of Job's herd; and Iscah became more confident as the solid stance of her horse assured her. She was excited to hold the reins in her own hands, to command such a great beast and look between its two ears instead of into Kittim's shoulder blades.

Tutan was well placed astride a horse, though this one was undeniably swifter afoot than his tired little pony. But the sorrel chosen for Madai could sense its rider's unease. This was a beautiful creature, not like his odorous camel. Madai touched the horse's warm, silken hide with a sort of wonder. And when he came astride the gelding, he felt its power, contained by the insignificant cords he held in his hands. The animal was well-trained and would do his bidding, if Madai would only manage his own nerves. The ever stalwart Kittim was as composed atop a horse as he was a camel, as he was when speaking a giant's tongue or that of a priest-king.

Job mounted a sleek and beautiful black. It had been purchased from the herdsmen of Havilah, a conspicuous breed with its slightly concave head, and named for the region. Havilah held his head and tail aloft, prancing in place, eager to carry his owner across the plain. He had done it many a time and knew just where they were going.

The familiarity of travel in the comfort of her fellows and the promise of more wonders to come congealed to an excitement Iscah could scarcely contain. Better still, the river was visible on the horizon, not some endless miles of plodding a great distance away. The horses all seemed to know what was expected of them and were taking their riders there without creating anxiety amongst the inexperienced. Job was speaking pleasantly to Kittim about his herds of beasts, and what grew here, and what grew over there, and what was planned for the season yet to come. Such ordinary dullery. So Iscah began to devise in her mind a picture of the motherless, fatherless Reenah, who was assuredly beautiful and brave. Iscah could not remember ever knowing a maid who was not owned by someone and could be sold away into a far land, never to be known again. 'Reenah shall live in her own house and have ebony hair and ivory skin, like the Lady,' she thought. 'But she shall not care about froggy hands; she shall scratch in the dirt for insects to feed her birds, and she shall splash in the river to get clean, and she shall be small as I, and – ' When Iscah had finished creating the triumphant Reenah, she was eternally youthful, audaciously brave, gallantly loyal, and decidedly consecrated.

Her mind was thus occupied as they crossed the distance to the river. It lay just before them, not visible, but hidden by the product of its life-water, a winding strip of forest. Sheltered there, a dwelling lay nestled beneath the shadow of those trees. Its precise form was obscured by the spatter of foliage that grew upon and about it. Or so it appeared, for as they drew nearer, Iscah saw that not all which traced a path across the mud bricks were living plants, but, rather, another vigorous mural of plaster and paint, somewhat faded by the sun. She was just discerning the colors and pattern when all the horses suddenly shied sideways, neighing frantically. At the same time, a great spotted cat appeared, screeching and spitting at them from the open door. All its hair stood bristling, as did its arsenal of spiked fangs behind curled and hissing lips.

It seemed prepared to leap at them atop the horses, when Madai released his hold of an arrow. Had his sorrel been more steadfast, it would surely have pierced the cat where it crouched. But the arrow struck the dirt, spitting gravel, and the cat shot away without a sound into the brush, a white and brown mottled streak.

Job was at the door of the cottage before anyone knew it, calling, "Reenah!"

Iscah's heart started to beat again, and she began struggling to dismount. Madai came alongside, pushed her back into the saddle and followed Job, arrow again at the string of his bow. Inside was dark, shaded by the forest, lit dimly with only one small lantern glowing atop a fire-pit made of rock. There seemed nothing amiss.

"Reenah," he called, more quietly this time, and turned to look at Madai. "I forbade her to keep that creature," he complained.

Madai put his arrow away. "The Lady keeps birds and wild cats, you say..." he began obliquely.

"Reenah," Job called again, leaving the cottage. "We shall have to find her now. I intended only to take wine with her and leave the horses." He looked at the forest behind the house. "Perhaps she is just at the..."

A woman came walking through the trees holding a smoking torch in her hand. A veil covered her hair and face. Iscah was immediately disappointed.

"Uncle!" Reenah exclaimed, her surprise evident. She clutched an earthen pot filled with a dripping honeycomb in her other hand. She dropped the torch and pulled the veil from her head, flinging her free arm round Job's waist.

Madai retrieved the torch from the ground. He rose to look into her delighted and delightful face.

"Reenah, this is Madai, my friend and guest," Job introduced, speaking with some difficulty in Madai's language.

Reenah's mouth creased at the edges when it turned up. Her eyes had not lost the sparkle put there by her uncle. They were midnight black and vibrant as a maid's, yet possessed a certain maturity, with little lines put there in the sun. Madai was entirely captivated. As fair as Ido had been, Reenah was dark, her hair purple in the sun. She wore it tied in a rope down her back, with stray tendrils at her neck, damp against her sand-colored skin. The pulse of her heart was beating there.

She lowered her eyes. "Peace to you, Madai," she said in his tongue, without a trace of accent.

"And this is Kittim," Job continued, drawing Reenah behind him. "This is Tutan, and Iscah."

Reenah was smiling at them all. "It is my humble pleasure to welcome my uncle's guests," she pronounced earnestly, leading them into her house. Madai followed last, still holding the smoldering torch.

She laid the jar of honeycomb on the table and resupplied the lamp with oil. Iscah retained her first disappointment only partially, for the inside of Reenah's house was an assemblage of marvelous things. Her walls were adorned in multi-hued paint, not demure replicas, but brilliant creations. Another caravan of camels climbed across the walls, perhaps the pattern of what graced the great house. A ziggurat stepped its way toward the sunrise. And birds of every shade and size were alive in plaster. Some were done in the same way as the caravan, their bodies formed and carved of clay, their feathers etched, ready for flight. Only the tiny idols set in wall niches dampened Iscah's admiration.

The interior was fastidiously neat, despite the collection of articles acquired in far-off places and a recently roaming cat. It glowed in the lamp-light, a golden tone reflected from its painted walls. A carpet of rich but muted colors lay across the brick floor. The only furniture was a low-setting table, inlaid with ivory and gold. Atop the table were little sculptures. The odors of this house were exotic as well, with incense burning at the fire-pit. And there were other rooms, closed from view by veils, each another color, each ornamented by gleaming beads and silver threads. Though this house was small, it was a place of no small value.

A movement near the ceiling caught Iscah's eye. A painting seemed to move, little and red, perfectly disguised amongst the clay ones. The bird flew from a niche in the bricks and fluttered to the top of Reenah's head. She brushed at it absently, sending it back.

"The leopard is still here," Job chastised her.

"Uncle," she soothed, pushing him gently onto a wood bench, take some wine." She poured from a glazed jug into six goblets taken from a cabinet of smoothly rubbed ebony.

Job took a sip. "It is always cooler here," he observed. He put his goblet down and looked at her. "I would show my guests the sand bar and wish to leave the horses here. Though I shall know of the leopard first."

"She was a mistake, I concede," Reenah answered. She turned to her visitors. "I bought her from a peddler on the caravan from Cush. She was too young, unweaned and filthy. Her brother was dead. What could I do?" she asked, eyes sliding to Job.

"Dispatch her," he answered coolly.

Reenah nodded compliantly. "Your foreign speech is improved." But he did not smile, so she continued, "I put her in the mountains months ago. She has come back looking for food. I think she has kits."

"So...she will be after my lambs."

Reenah nodded again. "Forgive me."

His face relaxed. "There is more than your leopard in the mountains," he conceded, picking up his wine again. "But she is a danger to you."

"Perhaps."

"Undeniably."

"Yes," Reenah finally assented. She went to the corner and brought a spear from the shadows. "She has got food here. She will come here again, and she will bring her kits."

Job nodded. "It shall be resolved."

Reenah put her spear against the clay feathers of a preening bird. "I am too old, Uncle, for such a folly."

"Yes, you are," he agreed.

"Excellent," she smiled at him triumphantly. "So - your friends?"

They had watched the exchange with undisguised interest, though Iscah was alarmed at the boldness this woman used to address so great a man as Job. She was beautiful, and her extravagant walls nearly redeemed the issue of her age; and she was brave, irrefutably. But she was, most assuredly, not consecrated. That was clear in her beguiling smile, which greeted each of the three men in turn.

"You are come for the sand bar," Reenah affirmed, an impish glance toward Madai. "Shall I be offended it is not to visit me?"

"We are here from a long way off," Kittim answered, insensible to her charm. "Madai is from a great distance west and Tutan, a great distance east."

Reenah looked closely at Tutan. "Yes, I see the East in his face." She smiled her brilliance at him. "A land of eloquence is the East.

"And you?" she asked, looking at Iscah.

Iscah was still indignant for Reenah's boldness and lifted a shoulder just to show her so.

"Hmm?" Reenah responded.

"Taken by Sabeans," Job explained, "some while ago. Madai and Kittim redeemed her from a village in Mizraim."

Reenah looked at her fiercely. "Sabeans are a scourge," she proclaimed, "and you survive. Indeed, you must be brave!"

But Iscah would not melt. "By the Hand of God," she answered.

The older woman's eyes glinted as she looked at Job with an affectionate smile.

He drained his cup and rose. "We shall leave the horses here, Reenah. Do you wish to come?"

She shook her head, still smiling. "I have a honeycomb to clean. Has Marisheba sent something?"

"Certainly." Job answered.

"Leave me to tend it, and I shall provide the honey and wine when you return."

৩৩ৱ ৩৩ৱ ৩৩ৱ

Afoot, they entered the forest behind the cottage and followed the river upstream. The walk was pleasant and cool, canopied from the sun by towering trees, branches spreading across the expanse, one to the next. The air was filled with birdsong, coming from little baskets hung in the branches, and clay pots, and flat rocks, all filled with grain. Iscah watched them flutter from one to the next, birds of every size and color. A trail of bright green grass grew under the baskets where the grain had sprouted, having been scattered by years of zealous pecking.

There on the far bank Iscah saw a spotted deer with her fawn, licking up kernels from a flat rock. The doe lifted her head, unperturbed, and continued her meal. Iscah thought instantly of the leopard, still savoring a critical disposition toward Reenah. The river was wide and deep, another world of itself. Iscah imagined It would be no surprise here to find the behemoth again.

690&2 690&2 690&2

Another apparatus spanned the river ahead. It was not small for birds, but long and meant for men. Tutan saw it before Iscah had time to say, "O! Are we crossing that?" She sounded a little afraid, with only a trace of excitement in her voice.

Tutan was not so glad. He had not had good outcomes on swaying bridges. It was woven of reed, as was the canopy above Job's garden of birds. It was picked up with the wind, an erratic sway, and looked near enough to the sky to be carried away.

As he had dreaded, their trail continued to climb and was proving something of an exertion. The banks seemed to rise, even as the river dropped below them. His heart was pounding as Job reached the bridge and took the two cords in hand on either side of an inadequate path of braided hemp. Even as he watched Job's face abounding with confidence, he felt the flutter in his stomach and an old, ragged wound. He closed his eyes to see again the last look of Enico's terrified face. It had imprinted itself in his mind when nearly all else of her had faded. He quickly opened them. Job was mid-way across, the bridge giving with the weight of his every step. Iscah followed him, as lithe as a squirrel in a tree.

If Tutan had been hoping he would gain confidence himself by their safe crossing, he would have been disappointed. He was, instead, feeling the flutters up his legs, so much that he was not convinced he could move them at all when it was his turn. He swallowed. It seemed to be his turn now. Kittim was just ahead, moving with expected ease. Then he turned around and looked into Tutan's face.

Tutan's legs were weighted like stone.

"Look at me," Kittim encouraged him. He stopped just shy of offering his hand.

Tutan looked up from the depths of the gorge to Kittim's face. There was no point denying his terror, but this was not the season of flood, and there were no score of frantic people stumbling to get across, or her, calling back to him in fright across her perfect little shoulder. Yet the old memory immobilized him.

"Keep your eyes straight ahead," he heard Madai's voice from across the gorge.

Kittim stretched his hand out then, and Tutan put his focus there. Then he looked up before he stepped off the parapet onto the bridge. His first step sent his stomach skipping as the ropes quivered. The bridge dipped and swayed with his every tentative step. He would certainly not look down again, and he commanded his mind to command his feet to take each and every step. And so he was surprised when Kittim finally grasped his wrist and pulled him back to solid footing on the other side.

He scarcely noticed their steady climb after that.

൪ഐ൙ ൪ഐ൙ ൪ഐ൙

They crossed a second rocky hill and came to its top. There lay below the wide waste of a valley. It was strewn with rubble, and boulders seemed scattered by careless hands. It sprouted clumps of wiry grass, and through its center snaked a trail of gravel and cracking earth. It looked like a dry waterbed, fed once by a forgotten stream. Job stopped, shading his eyes with his hand. Then he turned with an excited expression.

"There was a great river here once," he said, pointing to the corpse of the old waterway. "It fed all this valley and dug out a lake. Many flocks watered here." A breeze lifted his dark hair and swept it unnoticed across his face.

"I was a boy," he continued. "My father brought his herds here. And when I was just old enough to bring them myself, there was a great quake. It heaved up the earth and tumbled mountains down and changed the course of rivers; it opened up a cleft in the stone floor of this river and drank it dry. A great loss." He shook his head. "There were a great many more quakes when I was a boy."

"When the shaking ended, we came here to see what was done. We found streams moved, and great gaping chasms, and this water pouring back into the earth. It was a calamity to us all. Still... we found something." Job looked around at them, his face still marked with awe at what the quake had done... and with a knowing, secret smile.

"Do you see that?" he asked, pointing at a far spot where the bank rose up to form a rocky hill.

Iscah strained her eyes.

Job smiled again. "Come with me," he said.

They followed him as he descended into the bowl of the old lake. It was a long walk, difficult, across a forest of scattered stone. The bottom had become a bed of dry silt and struggling buffalo grass. But Job moved through the obstructions as though he had a map of the easiest route already rehearsed. He brought them right up to the edge of the bowl, where it was bounded by the uneven, rising hillside. Their closer inspection proved it to be the last great accumulation of rock and earth the mighty river would deposit with all its determined force.

It was a conglomerate of red, dried mud and stone, mixed and churned and hardened together. A lumpy mass. They could read on its face the ripples of the water as it had once ebbed and risen in season. They studied it, wondering what greatness Job might see in it, until slowly they recognized what it was. Jumbled into the mix was partially-buried bone, both great and minute, an ancient graveyard.

"When the water was gone, this came to sight," and Job gestured with his arm all along the heap of red clay. "Do you see now?" he asked. "See how they are twisted and tossed, like chaff at harvest." He bent over to run a finger across an ancient spine. He traced it along the neck to grasp a jawbone, still embedded with blunt, large teeth. "This is one beast and this another, all piled together - and so down the length of this rise." He extended his arms on either side of his body again. "A great disaster brought them here, you see, creatures of every kind, old and young." He pointed his finger at the ground some distance away. "I have dug bone from this hillside, heavy as bronze, and collected an infant, a behemoth, nearly entire."

He walked to the place where he had pointed. Laid there were thick, dark legs and disks of vertebrae and scimitars of rib, and one perfect skull, less the bottom jaw.

"It is a testimony," he explained. "A depository of the great deluge." His eyes were brimming with passion.

They each stood rooted in place, listening and looking at the hillside, minds racing. Madai could envision violent water, churning and gorged with the carcass of the first earth. He looked down at Job's behemoth, carefully laid out on the ground, the articulated bones of a mythical creature.

Madai knelt beside the behemoth calf. He touched it with his finger and circled the thick leg bone with his hand. He lifted it carefully, heavy as stone. Then he studied its skull, the slightly concave forehead and large eye sockets. He ran his hand around the curve of its rib. Then he looked up, back toward the jumble of bones embedded in the clay. "This was the effort of a powerful destruction."

"Are there people here?" Iscah asked, a sudden trembling in her voice.

Job looked down at her stricken face. "Forgive me, Iscah," he was quick to say. "I have looked upon this spot since I was a boy and it has lost its terror to me." He picked up a scrap of leg bone attached to a split hoof. "It is a historical pursuit to me now. Here, this is a swamp tapir," he said, handing it to her.. "I have come to believe that men were carried away first, upon the crest of the storm. And their bones that were not lost in the mud were light and disassembled, finally taken by creatures of the deep." His voice trailed, fearing his explanations had made it entirely worse. "No," he finished awkwardly, "I have found nothing of men."

She was perfectly still, listening to his explanation with wide, round eyes fixed on Job's face. She nodded once, and looked at the object in her hand. She touched it carefully with her finger.

"Remarkable," Madai announced to himself. "How are they made of rock?" He stood up from where he had knelt beside the skeleton calf and shuffled back toward the littered mound, watching the ground and kicking at pieces of stone along the way. He laid his palm flat against the ridge, where the top end of a smaller bone was unburied, the rest of it tipped into the hillside. Then with a sharp stone he began to unearth it. It was stained by the growth of water plants but entirely smooth when cleaned of dirt. It was not wrenched loose by a scavenger, or pitted and gnawed by a predator's tooth, but simply lost from its other parts.

"This is a heaping of creatures drowned by the deluge," Tutan mused quietly.

Kittim smiled at him.

Job was nodding, enthused he had found ones to appreciate the significance. "And," he continued, "there are bones of creatures I have never seen before. Skulls of things I do not know, nor wish to know, greater even than Leviathan."

Tutan's eyes were as big as Iscah's. "Leviathan?" he whispered.

Job nodded.

"Unknown creatures?" Tutan asked.

Job nodded again. "This place has brought me some of the most contemplative of days," he replied. "And I have mused with God, praise His Name, over what has been lost."

Madai's ears prickled. 'Musings with God.' It would shame him to deride the words of so good a man as Job, indeed, Madai felt curiously envious of him, though he busied himself at the hillside to hide it.

"Do others know about this?" Kittim asked.

Job went back to his constructed skeleton, moving a vertebra back into place. "Know and fear," he answered. "The shepherds, of course, cannot find water here, and the people of Ur..." he spread his arms toward the hill, "this is all a curse to them. The tangible signature of a rival God."

Tutan crouched beside Madai. He put his hand heavily on the thick leg Madai was now trying to exhume. "Think on this," he said quietly. "This creature may have been spoken to life by the Creator Himself. It lived on the first earth, and I am touching it."

Madai put his digging stone aside. "I am taking this back for my father," he said, "and my son, that there is this testimony of the deluge."

掁 掁 掁

Iscah was watching them. She had decided that a beast called Leviathan could not live here, as Job did not seem wary of him now. She squatted to dig at a smallish bone protruding near her feet. "O!" she exclaimed, "it snapped."

Job knelt beside her. "I have discovered by mishap that the ribs must be dug with special care."

She nodded at him. She turned the foreleg of the tapir over in her hands, scratched it with her nail. "How is it turned to stone, I wonder?"

"An interesting question," Job replied, smoothing his beard. He sat back on the rocky ground and crossed his legs. "There is a place in the mountains of Zoreb where I have heard it said there is a forest of stone, great fallen trunks, even some that still stand with roots of bronze. I have a piece of limb, I can show you; a trader brought it from the north. And still..." he looked at Madai who had stopped to listen.

"We may see the bones of a goat left by a jackal and scattered across the desert, white as snow. Light as chaff." He paused and gazed back at the dry riverbed. "Perhaps it was the water, or the earth covering over them. What dies now lays atop the soil, plundered by scavengers and wind. But the deluge - it would have been a sea of water and mud." Job looked back at Iscah with a sparkle in his eye. "Or perhaps they have been turned to stone by Mighty God just for you, that you may believe what He has done and see what He has made."

"I do believe," she insisted.

"I know you do, child," he replied with a hand on her arm. He patted her. "Only it may come, when time passes, that men will forget."

"Men do forget," Madai interjected.

"Don't be silly," Iscah quipped. It hardly seemed at times that Madai could possibly be her elder.

The corners of Madai's mouth turned up an imperceptible degree and he began to dig again. She watched him the merest of moments, thinking it was an unwieldy piece he was attempting. But it was getting hot, too hot to bother. And, besides, she had another question.

"So, were not two of every sort taken onto Noah's boat?" she asked, directing her question toward Job. "Why do you find creatures here," she pointed at the hill, "that do not live to this day?"

Job had a frosting of dust in his beard that made his face pale as chalk, all but his eyes that continued to sparkle at her. "Not enough to eat, I suppose," he replied. "A great change from the first earth was made in the second." He leaned forward. "But there is a great beast that lives on the river we have come up. Frightful. Leviathan."

It was worse than she thought. It lived in the river. "He is greater than behemoth?" she whispered.

"A greater danger than behemoth, though he hunts at the deepest parts of the river and lives amongst the cliffs and can be avoided."

She nodded, not entirely convinced.

Finally, in the end, they were all left watching Madai. He was still working on a... leg perhaps... larger than he had expected. Iscah thought he could have imagined that, seeing the baby behemoth. She was sitting cross-legged beside Kittim, getting hotter every second. She had already discovered what creatures could be discerned from the hillside, really grotesque shapes of a terrible violence: a tail joined to a great hip, or disks of a twisted neck no longer attached to a skull, or just the orphan of a leg. When she had thought about the cruelest of peoples being justly judged, she had forgotten to think about the animals.

ভেও   ভেও   ভেও

Tutan got up to walk along the top of the mound. He was searching the ground, bending and retrieving bits. He put some in his pocket and looked down the forgotten path of the ancient river. 'This might have been the Gihon,' he thought, 'draining off the flood waters.' He looked at the coiled shell in his hand, turned it over and dropped it into his pocket with the rest.

Reenah

- 43 -

It was some hours till dusk when they reached Reenah's cottage, grateful for the cool and the slight breeze that seemed to cling along the river. She was ready with water for them to drink.

Madai carefully laid his treasure on her table, spanning it crosswise. All their pockets were depositories of little fragments and spiraling shells of sea creatures, even one curving horn of a long-forgotten sort of thing.

The fruit, bread and cheese Marisheba had prepared were arranged on platters. Reenah had added to the fare her own cheese and honey. She brought them a pouch of goat stomach for their smallest treasures, amused by the significance they placed on them.

"You are tired and hot and dirty," she proclaimed after they had finished drinking. "There is a good shallow behind this house at the river. Very refreshing."

"Not before I eat," Job protested.

Reenah raised her eyebrows, her lips upturned in a lovely smile. Then she placed a large painted bowl on the wooden cabinet and filled it with water.

"Wash," she commanded.

Job chuckled. They all took their turns at the bowl. When they were done, a sediment of sandy mud rested at the bottom. She refilled the bowl and insisted. Iscah was only too glad to wash again. She waited for the men first, as she ought, and restrained herself from a bowl of almonds till her hands were clean.

Only after the washings did Reenah place the food on the table, though not before she removed the bone to the floor.

Iscah set about her portion with ravenous gusto, cheese and bread and lamb. The wine was cold and mild, watered, which she was glad of, being nearly plagued by thirst. Her hair was coiling in ringlets on either side of her face. Those she pushed behind her ears with irritation, taking a second piece of bread, this with honey. As Reenah sat at the far side, and seemed not so particular as Job's wife, Iscah did not mind the mountain's grime she had not quite scraped clean from under her nails. She took a piece of date and dropped it unceremoniously into her mouth. She grinned at Madai, a peace offering, as he did the same thing, but with two.

"Well done again, Marisheba," Job proclaimed as if the cook were present.

ભાજી ભાજી ભાજી

Tutan was the one who ate the least, in part because he was thinking of what was lost of the first earth. But it was also the woman, and not just to hear from her about the caravans. He felt startlingly aware of her - uncomfortably aware, in fact. It was, however, the merchant routes he inquired about with clumsy indifference.

"I am mostly finished in that trade," Reenah offered in answer to his question. "I sell a few birds yet." Then she looked up with a smile. "The caravan shall pass here at harvest."

Tutan nodded, aware of the smile. He had noticed her frescoes and accumulated wares; her fine cheekbones and able hands...

"Your honey is clean to perfection," he said instead. "You must show me the hive."

Reenah looked at him with a hint of charm. "Indeed, Tutan, thank you. It is in the hollow of a tree, at the river."

"A perfect cause to return another day," Job interjected. "As for this day, it grows late." He rose. "God's blessing upon you, Reenah. Perhaps you shall sup with us tomorrow? And bring a red bird for Iscah."

Tutan bowed from his waist. "Eminently delightful," he effused, "May your ways be blessed by the Holy One."

Having apparently spoken for them all, he followed Job through the door, as did Kittim. Madai was third behind them, after he had retrieved his bone and their other treasures from the floor. Iscah took a last look at the glowing room, noting as she did Reenah's kindly smile, and decided to allow her a second chance.

ભાજી ભાજી ભાજી

It was just dark when they returned to Job's estate. Sabta might have been a seer, for he stood ready with two servants to take their horses. He eyed Madai's excavated bone with what Iscah perceived a sardonic amusement before he led them inside. The same maids waited with water for their feet. Having spent the day in the hot sun at the dry riverbed in the dirt, they were in need of more than foot-washing.

The Lady had not stayed the night with her daughter but had returned and was waiting in elegant style for them.

"Iscah," she said as they entered, "come make yourself clean in my rooms." Her brows were lifted again as the men slipped past her, Madai with his leg bone, Tutan with their pouch of goat stomach, and Job with a smear of mud all across his tunic.

The Lady studied that intently as he walked away.

Iscah was pleased to find that it was not Lemmeri who waited on her, but the Lady's own maidservant. All her needs were provided for in a far gentler way. When she slipped into the water, she saw that already her skin promised it could be softer, her ribs less prominent.

Another fine garment was laid aside for Iscah to wear. It was the color of goat cream. It fit her as though she were the pattern its maker had used. And the Lady herself returned to see her to the night meal. Never had she been so well, nor so often fed, and she wondered whether her stomach could possibly hold more.

The food began to arrive with a glorious aroma and abundance. Iscah could scarcely recognize, amongst the sprigs of green and floating fruit, what she assumed to be lamb, but she found she could eat it all quite well.

Their conversation was of their day's adventure. The leg bone lay in front of the fire-pit on the floor, and their smaller discoveries were laid out singly beside it.

"I should suppose there are a dozen such skulls that I cannot recognize," Job was saying. "One has a great scooped chamber that rises like an antler from its head, most curious. I should think, as many years as I have had, I should have got more creatures laid out. But it is a difficult task, and there is little practicality."

"In truth," the Lady agreed quietly.

"It has proved to be another private pleasure of mine, there being no market for it. Though I have passed an interesting day there."

"I understand you perfectly," Tutan asserted. "A thing that lived upon the first earth, it is... momentous."

Job turned and looked at him. "Yes, it is," he answered. He took a sip of wine and was quiet for a while. "It has been no long time, really," he mused thoughtfully. "Yet evil has sprang up again full-grown."

"Precisely so," Kittim agreed. "I perceive rebellion rules the heart of man."

"No better example of it than Shinar," Job finished.

Sabta stood behind them, pouring wine. A certain malice passed his face at Job's remark.

"Thank you, Sabta," the Lady injected evenly. "I shall tend the wine. You may take your supper." She turned him an authoritative look; he bowed stiffly in return and was gone.

She leaned forward slightly. "He gossips," she explained. "And he is insolent."

"And an idolater." Job finished. "He will not be persuaded if we do not speak of it."

The Lady bowed her head and did not reply.

"Sabta was sold for debt in Shinar," Job explained. "Had I not redeemed him, his life was forfeit to the man who had claim upon him."

"An idolater?" Iscah could not stop herself. She had little sympathy for idolaters, having come at close quarters with them. What they envisioned as the needs of such gods - En-UtuAten of the temple, even Hamonheb with his little grotesque clay statues.

"For lack of instruction." Job asserted. "Does not every man merit the prospect of knowing the One True God?"

"Has he got his idols?" Iscah pressed, undeterred.

"He brought nothing with him; he was barely clothed," Job answered patiently.

She was barely satisfied.

෬෬   ෬෬   ෬෬

Madai watched them, thinking Sabta had a disagreeable look and was not likely worth the gold paid for him. But the mention of Shinar was important. It was the kingdom of the mighty king and the path to the ship of Nua and - birthplace of the

Spear.

"What do you know of Shinar?" he asked. He looked from one to the other, expectantly, waiting for Job to answer.

Again, the unconscious stroking of his beard, as the Lady quietly refilled his goblet. "Mind what you speak," she whispered.

He touched her hand as it held the pitcher.

"Sabta has his converts," she insisted.

He patted her hand again. "Nothing to fear," he answered, his words caressing her.

"Pray, do not distress the Lady," Tutan urged.

Job smiled at her affectionately; she took her place upon the cushion again, lifted her goblet to her lips and sipped it.

Job turned back toward Madai before beginning with slow, deliberate words, "At the lowlands to the North is a wide plain named Shinar. Upon this plain is a city of antiquity, named for its builder and king, Nimrod." Job glanced at his wife. "He himself is its god, the architect of all its vile practice." He took another drink of wine, seeming to have forgotten his meal.

Madai was surprised. He remembered what was said of a man called the Nimru: a mighty hunter, a warrior and provider. But he had met the farmer, Job, and respected him. If it was the Nimru adorning the temple walls of that abhorrent priest, if he was Shinar's king, then the old lore was untrue, in this matter, at least, a great disappointment. He looked at Iscah, whose eyes were trained on Job with stony calm.

"It is he who defiled what Mighty God has spoken through the constellations," Job continued, "and remade the villain of the deluge to be Holy God Himself." Job looked up as though to plead mercy at having uttered a blasphemy.

Madai listened with a sinking, finding in Job's words the tendrils of a corruption that had infected The Family. Of a sudden, he was stricken with the dire possibility that he had come to this far land only to find it mired in a similar chaos: deception and truth, and which be which...

"The Ancient I seek," Madai entreated, "surely such a one may live in an aged city."

"Or upon the plain," Job answered, "though it is no place for men of God."

Quiet spread around the table. Shinar was no enticement for Iscah, that place from where idolatry sprung. She looked with apprehension toward Madai, he who would draw Kittim away with him.

"I have seen great things here," she announced, eyes turned to Madai. "What do you need in a place like Shinar?"

Madai looked at her quietly, hearing the bite in her voice and knowing that Kittim held little esteem for cities. He was not at all sure how to answer her. A disruptive clatter sounded at the door; they, as one, turned to see Sabta standing there, a tray of fruit and cream in his hand, an odd mix of appeasement and reproach on his face.

The Lady rose, walked across the room and removed the tray from him. "Did I not release you?" she asked.

His bow was brittle as he murmured apologetically.

"I do not wish to see you more tonight," she sternly rebuked him, and he backed from view, bent at the waist.

"Pray, can you not discharge him?" the Lady implored when she was certain he had gone. "Others of the servants have been enticed by him."

Job looked at her with surprise; a deep line came between his eyes. He spread his fingers on the table. "I am charged by more souls than his," Job mused, nearly to himself, "though I had wished him to know the mercy of God. Who other of the house is defiled?"

"Those who keep the horses, every one," she was quick to reply, "and that maid, Lemmeri, whom I have sent back to Marisheba in the kitchen." She wished to say more regarding the maid but, minding the sensitivity of Iscah, held her tongue.

Job's face was first sad, then stormy. "How it spreads," he muttered. "I shall discharge him, or send him to tend the goats; none there to ruin."

The Lady did not look quite satisfied, but she held her tongue. She offered each a bowl of stewed apricots sweetened by honey and cream. This Iscah received quietly, disarmed by Job's countenance, and the Lady's, and the memory of Sabta's disagreeable hands lifting her up onto the horse.

"Treacherous is the heart of man," Tutan muttered.

"Fortunate, the rainbow," Kittim observed.

They ate their apricots as a vaguely uncomfortable silence stretched the evening. Tutan was feeling it and laid his spoon aside. He cleared his throat.

"Will you tell us about Noah's ship?" he asked.

Job looked up gratefully, a slow sparkle returning to his eyes. "It rests atop the mount of Ararat, beyond Nimrud Dagh. I do not know precisely, though such knowledge is easily gotten in the region."

"What say you, Madai?" Tutan asked him. "A great witness, I should say."

"Indeed so, Tutan," Madai answered the kindest of men.

The Lady

- 44 -

On the next day, Iscah escaped the confines of the house while the Lady was gone on errand with provisions for an Elder son, taking, indeed, a small caravan. She had with her five menservants, Marisheba's little kitchen maid, her maidservant, and two camels, well loaded. Within the packs, Iscah had seen fruit breads, crocks of cheese and three large skins of wine, garments of every sort and hue, as well as perfumes and oils carried upon the second camel. The Lady would assuredly remain till the morrow, as a feast was intended for the following day. It would be large, would last the week entire. That she could not be present to attend Reenah when she arrived was thus unavoidable.

Her husband seemed satisfied that Marisheba would do their luncheon without his wife. Iscah thought he seemed accustomed to the Lady's absence. But she would miss Job's wife. They were to follow on the morrow when all the preparations were complete, and Iscah would see all of the great Lady's sons.

But Iscah was not anxious for the feast, though it promised to be a splendid affair. She was caught by a sudden glooming apprehension. As well as she knew Madai and Kittim, she knew they would leave the feast toward Shinar. She had heard them speaking. And she, most assuredly, did not wish to return to the most wicked of places. Perhaps they supposed she would stay with Job. In any case, a parting was near.

She had asked Kittim to keep her not so very long ago. She suddenly felt her nose begin to sting and her eyes fill. She wiped them brusquely and, as she did, she glimpsed a figure in the distance. "Reenah," she hoped.

☙❧ ☙❧ ☙❧

Sabta did not appear at the door to assist their visitor. It seemed he had disappeared, for which Iscah was more than pleased. Instead, Job was there, and behind him, a young man with a bright expression. The young man, Lehabim by name, averted his eyes as he passed to take the reins of Reenah's camel. And then he crouched to the ground, offering his back for her step. Iscah was amused, knowing Reenah more than capable of dismounting for herself.

The robes Reenah wore were marvelous beyond even Iscah's imagination, a topaz and azure silk that reflected the sun. They made a swooshing sound when Reenah glided down from the saddle to light upon Lehabim's bent form.

"God be gracious to you," Reenah murmured with a broad smile before taking Job's hands. "Uncle! My eyes have taken their pleasure again at the sight of your face." She turned to Iscah with a flourish. "And your young guest." She looked behind him into the house. "Where is that insolent goat?"

Iscah was partly won. She chuckled. "Have you no fear? He may drop poison into your wine."

"Iscah.." Reenah chided.

"My wife could not abide his ways, and I am informed he had snared others of my household by his idolatries," Job replied "That I did not know. He is sent away."

"Excellent," Reenah approved. "Where is he gone?"

"To the stables, I suppose. He has the camel I brought him on. He wishes to return to the city of Shinar."

"He leaves better than he came," Reenah remarked dryly.

Job shrugged. "I cannot send a man to die on the way, even an idolater."

Reenah waited until Lehabim had led her camel away. "You do not know the ways of men, Uncle. What you let loose with generosity is made the more bitter. He will not thank you; he will all the more despise you."

And Iscah believed it true. She knew the skulking glances of slaves toward masters, and the enmity of eunuchs. She slid her eyes toward the stables with a chill. In the next moment she heard a twittering from behind Reenah's back. Reenah, having heard it as well, took from behind herself a little wicker basket.

"For you," Reenah said with a glimmer in her eye, handing the basket to Iscah, but looking at Job.

Iscah peeked cautiously inside. Sitting bunched at the bottom of the basket was a tiny red bird. Its beak was yellow, and its little black eyes blinked at her.

"Perhaps Uncle shall allow you to use his enclosure," Reenah teased.

At which suggestion Job's face molded to a hearty laugh. "So, you think I am greedy for your birds, Reenah," he chuckled. "No, indeed, Iscah, the bird is yours. Let it go in the garden, and whensoever you wish you may reclaim it."

Iscah smiled with them and started toward the enclosure. "Cautiously, Iscah," he called after her. "Do not let them all loose."

Reenah followed Job into the house, allowed her feet to be dipped and dried, then entered the main room where the other men waited. Madai was crouching on the floor, still tinkering with the bones from the sand bar. She was drawn to the youthful expression of adventure shaping his countenance. She thought she should like to mold it in clay. Tutan stood beside him, eagerly inviting her with his eyes to enter. It was long since she had been admired by the gaze of men...

"Delighted you are come," Tutan spoke first.

She inclined her head, not demurely, but with a subtle flair, as was her character. She knew how the vibrant silk woke the sparkle of her eyes. And the gilded bangles hanging in her ears were a merry addition. Lines etched round her mouth and eyes by the sun and the years were concealed with her ready smile.

"I am honored," she replied.

Madai looked up; her unfeigned liberty carried with it a strong attraction. Reenah could read their approval and could not deny herself a certain satisfaction, though she felt it a bit silly, having long ago perceived the character of men.

"Is Iscah with you?" Madai queried, looking behind her.

"She is brought a red bird," Job replied, "and is gone to my garden with it."

Madai was smelling the fragrances of the kitchen with anticipation. "I will get her," he offered.

ೞೞ ೞೞ ೞೞ

It was the first time Iscah had been alone since their arrival, and with permission to enter the most delightful of delightful places. She could feel the little bird's weight at the center of the basket and hear its sharp little chirp. She smiled. She would sit beside the water pool and feed it grain from her hand.

The air was still and cool under the arbor of grapevine. She hoped the door would open properly, and nothing might escape, that would be dreadful. But she did not want to call for help. She coveted a bit of time alone, where she would consider what it would mean when Kittim and Madai left for Shinar. And how she would beseech Kittim to keep her when they returned, for that they must. She would entertain nothing less. She had passed through the length of the arbor and just come to the tiny entrance when she heard the rustle of leaves beside her.

"Lady Iscah," a voice entreated her.

She had seldom heard him speak, and was not alarmed until his hand touched her wrist.

"I must bid you farewell," Sabta crooned.

She jumped slightly, catching her breath. He smelled of camel. "You touch me," she snapped coldly.

A sardonic smile twisted his face as he loosened his hold, though he still circled her wrist with his fingers.

"I wish only to speak with you," he replied, looking at her brazenly, studying her ear lobe.

She felt it burn; it was her greatest weakness. She wanted to bolt but for his hand around her arm. Instead she said, "I believe Madai is to help me with the door of this enclosure."

"Indeed," Madai's voice sounded behind them.

Sabta released her abruptly.

"Why are you still here?" Madai barked.

"Only to bid farewell and bless, by the hand of god, my benefactor these many months," He feigned. "I was passed by the Lady on my way."

Iscah felt her wrist sting where he had held it.

"He is occupied," Madai answered.

Sabta bowed imperceptibly and backed away from Iscah. "Pity," he remarked. "Perhaps, then, I shall just...."

"Be away," Madai commanded, finishing Sabta's sentence.

He shrugged, and bobbed his head again. Still, his eyes glittered as he turned ever so indifferently back the way he had come. They watched him take the reins of a young camel left chewing its cud beside the enclosure. He put his foot into the leather stirrup and swung himself up. Again he inclined his head, turned the animal, and reined it with haughty care toward the plains of Shinar.

Iscah felt a rush of heat surge into her body. "Vile," she snapped, trembling.

"You are beset by calamity, Iscah." Though Madai attempted a casual voice, it was edged with icy calm as he watched the man ride away.

She began to tremble in earnest. "I am saved by you now," she held up her hand, "three times."

He looked away from the departing form of Sabta and the camel to Iscah. "You had best stay with Job," he said.

They heard a racket at their feet, where Iscah had dropped her basket. The top had fallen off, and the little bird sat on the ground, unaware at first, of its freedom. They watched as though it were a monumental event when the red bird suddenly hopped two times and ruffled its wings. And then it flew away.

"I knew you would not take me," Iscah murmured, stricken now that it had been spoken aloud.

"Job has agreed," Madai answered quietly. "His wife is taken by you. And there is Reenah..." His voice was low.

She looked at him, a trace of defiance in her mouth.

"The city at Shinar is a wicked place." Madai insisted.

"Then why shall you go there?" she retorted.

Madai felt a hot flush climbing his neck, truly uncomfortable at her rigid will and the piteous distress on her face. He knelt down, toying with the little basket. "You know what I seek."

"Foolishness," she snapped.

He grinned, a bit relieved by her grit. "Maybe," he responded. "Still, wouldn't you like to talk to a wise and ancient one?" He colored, realizing what he had said.

'Well, yes, of course,' she thought, but instead she bored to the core of the matter. "You have suffered," she said aloud, recalling the tale of his lost family and surprising him. "Though Mighty God Is... you must know that."

"You speak of the God you imagine," Madai answered.

"I speak of the God of all humankind. What foolish men believe of Him does not alter it."

Her declaration startled him, and he looked up. Then he stood up. She was two heads below him now, flushed and young and indignant again. This child with her speckled nose and bristling hair would always defy him.

"Did I not just now save you?" he tried to laugh.

"By the will of God," she retorted.

"The very will that had you taken by the Sabeans?" he asked, then regretted it.

She lifted her chin. "When you believe in Him, you may ask Him."

She was maddening, intense and unrelenting. He wanted to ask how she could be so sure, and she but a most unlucky girl.

"When you were brought to En-UtuAten and sold to Hamonheb and taken by

Anak, by what sorcery do you suppose they bested your God?" There, he had said it.

Momentarily shocked at the suggestion of 'sorcery,' she glared at him. Then she was angry, that this wild man should take Kittim away. She answered coldly, "By Whose Hand was I held, do you think, when I lay in the dark? When I loathed the sound of his footfall? Pray answer that if you can."

He could not, for her eyes were raging coals and he was growing ashamed.

"Kittim said it was not foolishness to seek truth. I say it is wisdom to know when it is found," she proclaimed with lifted chin.

Her nose was suddenly burning, and her throat began to close. In her state, she must not weep before him. She bolted toward the house, feeling more the child than perhaps she was.

Madai was shaken. He watched her disappear through the door, then looked back at the empty basket on the ground. He had opened the private wound of her misfortune, and done it raggedly. Somehow, it had left him more bloodied than she. He followed slowly behind her into the house.

ଔଔ ଔଔ ଔଔ

There, penetrating the air, was that spicy aroma, for Marisheba was doing her utmost to please Reenah, a favored guest. It seemed there would be no lack of effort in that cause, as Tutan was energetically engaged in conversation with both Job and the beguiling woman. They did not notice Iscah arriving late, out of breath and out of sorts, except for Kittim, who called her to the seat beside him with a question in his eyes. She answered with a stiff little smile and took a sip of wine.

Marisheba served the food herself, just as Madai took his cushion beside Tutan. "You shall join us," Job spoke to Marisheba with warmth. "As once we were."

Marisheba's acceptance was evidenced by a rather wan smile. She listened, distracted, as Job thanked his God in his all-inclusive way and lifted his wine to his guests.

Madai, hungry as he was, ate with little enthusiasm. Avoiding a chance encounter with Iscah's eyes, training his own toward Marisheba and Reenah. Though Reenah was engaged and relaxed, Marisheba was uneasy, eating with a zeal no greater than his own.

But the meal carried on in an ordinary way until Marisheba set her cup down. There was at present a vigorous discussion of the most efficient routes to Nimrud Dagh and Ararat beyond. Iscah hadn't joined the conversation, which was curious in itself. Instead, she was distracted and even annoyed. At a normal time, Marisheba would have consoled her, for it was evident that the girl would remain behind. Not a dire prospect, as Marisheba perceived it. But she was beset by a calamity of her own, a thievery, and within her own domain, under her own watch.

She cleared her throat nervously. "Perhaps..." she began in a husky voice.

They turned her way.

"I am most ashamed to say..." she blinked twice. "I fear we are robbed."

Job's expression barely changed.

"The gold platter and carafe, and smaller of the precious wares. I would think it that worthless maid if she had not gone away with the Lady."

Job asked evenly, "You are sure?"

She nodded miserably.

He laid his glass on the table. "No doubt Sabta," he replied calmly. "Gold is of use in Shinar."

Madai stood unconsciously, instantly energized with the prospect of confronting the man again. But Job lifted his hand.

"Sabta will not be well served in that city. Let it be done to him as God wills."

"There may have been worse planned than thievery," Madai argued.

"What?" Job's voice rose in genuine alarm.

Iscah's face became whitish, with just a blotch of red flaming across her cheeks.

Madai glanced at her. "Iscah was approached."

A sound of infinite displeasure escaped Tutan's mouth.

"Job has rightly spoken," Kittim interjected. "Let it be done to him as God wills." He took Iscah's hand. "Are you well?" he gently asked.

Iscah nodded.

"Child," Job muttered, passing his hand down his beard, "I have brought trouble to this house."

"It was just a small thing," she replied immediately, seeing how the good man was distressed. "Easily righted by Madai." To whom she looked with a frown.

"Even so," Job continued. "The safety of my household is an obligation."

"He is gone," Kittim stated flatly. "What is past is done. It merely makes evident the need to keep Iscah safely here."

Iscah moved her eyes from Madai to Kittim, acutely reminded that her lot lay not within her own hands. It seemed, in truth, already decided.

Tutan looked at Iscah sympathetically. "Well I know the appeal of a quest to Ararat. Though I shall remain here as well." He looked at Job. "Our good host has offered his hospitality until a caravan passes, when I shall join it East."

Kittim looked warmly at Tutan. "We shall miss you on Ararat."

It was not until this moment that Madai was certain Kittim would join him to Shinar, for his companion was inscrutable. It surprised him to be so immensely pleased. Then he looked across the table at Tutan and Iscah. "We have come far together," he said, and said no more.

The night ended badly, as they each retired to their own sleeping quarters, not the festivity Tutan had anticipated in the company of his good friends - and the colorful Reenah. He had wished to inquire about her years with the caravans, and her paintings, as well. But a pall was cast over the evening, one which he felt acutely. He began to remove his outer clothes, hearing Madai pace and stir about in a room shared with Kittim and separated by just a woolen curtain from his own.

"The jackal has my Spear!" came Madai's stormy voice from behind the veil.

He burst through the curtain into Tutan's room, then back into his own, hunting his bow.

"Madai," Tutan called, following at his heel in his undertunic.

Madai had the bow in his hand when Kittim gathered the arrows into his own.

"Pray, what will you do in the dark?" he asked calmly.

"The pagan spear?" Tutan asked, coming alongside.

Madai looked at him, his lust for vengeance so great as to ignore Tutan's description of the sacred object. "The forged Spear," he answered. "Heritage of my people."

"And etched round by serpents and scorpions and such," Tutan pressed.

"A formidable weapon," Kittim offered. "But he cannot be pursued in the darkness. Moreover, we know where he is going."

"The city of Shinar," Madai affirmed.

"Precisely. Sabta will seek to buy favor of Nimrod with it."

Madai looked at the bow in his hand, and at Kittim, who did not seem to care whether or not they pursued the idolater. It was not only the thefts, but also what was intended with Iscah. Madai stalked around the room. "In the morning, then," he insisted.

"An ill-use of our host," Tutan argued.

"How is that? He is also robbed."

"He is better pleased by our company at the feast of his son," Tutan insisted. "Did he not release Sabta to the vengeance of God?"

Their two faces held Madai's gaze with aged reason. Madai knew what lay behind it. They did not wish to chase the Spear.

೮೩೪ ೮೩೪ ೮೩೪

The journey to Job's eldest son was made south, along the river. Kittim and Madai rode horses and led a camel each, gifts for their continued travels. Marisheba came as well, as she would help with the feast; but Reenah stayed behind, for the first fledglings of the season were expected.

It was midmorning when they arrived at the house of Job's son. They were greeted by an ebony-hued servant. Iscah stole a glance at his ear, happy to see it whole, and Madai studied his burnished skin with fascination. The efficient young man ushered them inside.

Though the main meal was meant for evening, Marisheba led them toward the rear of the house, she being well acquainted with the kitchens of all of Job's children. The Lady met them along the way, polished and elegant, but completely distressed.

"She has vanished!" the Lady cried, lifting her hands away from her sides. "At the day's light, she is not to be found."

Job reached her and took her hands, bringing them up to his chest. "Who?" He asked simply.

"Marisheba's kitchen maid. And the beast she rode. Beguiled by Sabta, you know."

"She cannot hope to find him," Tutan offered.

Job frowned, stroking his wife's fingers absently, "Perhaps this has been pre-arranged. Is there missing anything of value?"

Her hands flew to her throat. "I had not considered that."

She scurried down the hall then, Lemmeri instantly forgotten with the worry over something grand. An inspection of gold wares and the Lady's ornaments revealed nothing amiss. "Foolish maid," she harped, "escaped for desire of idolatrous vermin, and nothing more." Her face was awash with disgust.

But Iscah was suddenly afraid for the kitchen maid, Lemmeri, who was, in truth, little older than herself. If she had been haughty, it did not stop her being cruelly treated. It was not pleasant to think on the schemes of Sabta. Iscah shivered and suspected the captive was for profit as much as lust.

જીભરુ જીભરુ જીભરુ

The course of the evening was much as had been planned, though there was an undercurrent. For her part, Iscah's concern had turned to Kittim, that he would be taken away by a restless Madai bent on revenge as much as folly. And she could not understand what of Madai kept Kittim's allegiance. She would prevail upon them to wait, a day at least, but she knew they would not, not with this new thievery making a ready excuse.

And she was denied even the peaceful warmth of Job's gathering room after the foodstuff was removed to the kitchen. Lively voices filled the house. Even if she did wish to be cordial, Iscah could not retain their names nor properly converse.

Madai made no pretense of courtesy. He sat and then paced and stared out the open window. Kittim and Tutan alone displayed what grace was afforded by their little party.

As the evening carried on, Iscah felt the weight of her abandonment too grievous. The room, with all its chatter swum in wavy blurs as tears slid down her cheeks, too late to hide. Kittim had seen it.

So slight a touch it could have been imagined, Kittim took her hand. He navigated her past Madai and Tutan, leading them all into the cool darkness of the night. A place of calm, the quaint cheeping of crickets in the grass and frogs at the river all combined tragically enough to make her weep.

જીભરુ જીભરુ જીભરુ

Madai listened. He could understand. He remembered that he owed her his life and hoped she had forgiven him. And he was also pricked with sentiment, hearing her cry.

"You will return for me," she begged.

It was Madai who answered. "We will come this way again," he assured her. "And bring you news of a great ship."

At that, she lifted from Kittim's chest and turned her eyes to Madai, pools of glimmering unhappiness as large as he had ever seen of her. He might have taken her to Shinar at that look, had Tutan not gently patted her shoulder.

"I shall be here, Iscah," he soothed. "And we shall busy ourselves about. Perhaps at the river cottage Reenah will show us how to snare birds and tend honey bees."

She looked at him. Two times now she had wept, in as many days. "Thank you, Tutan," she whispered, trying to smile.

Tutan patted her again, feeling his own distress.

"You will leave at first light?" he asked them.

"No, we shall take proper leave," Kittim insisted. "Provision is made for our journey and he has given us horses, also." He looked at Madai. "In truth, we shall be swifter than Sabta and may well overtake him along the way."

Madai nodded, feeling oddly guilty at the moment. He had an affection for the rescued girl, and there was the gentle kindness of Tutan. He would miss them.

"We will save our God-speeds for the morning," Madai agreed. Then he bent and patted Iscah's head awkwardly.

ଔଷ ଔଷ ଔଷ

Indeed, the morning was not so difficult as the night. All were better rested. Job rose early, offering his wisdom in terms of the City Nimrod, his direction in terms of the ship of Noah, provision well beyond their need, and an entreaty to his God for their safe return. Tutan blessed them with all his hopes for a true ship and mount of Ararat. He assured manifest diligence in Iscah's regard. The girl herself did not appear.

Madai laid a scarlet bundle in Tutan's hands. "For Iscah, from the caravan," he explained. "I've carried it weeks with never the right time..." A shriveled, cracked wad of leather laced by a thin bone lay atop the silk. "From the spot the Anak found her," he continued. "If she wants it... "

Tutan took it from him. "She will be pleased. Perhaps she will wear it at your return."

Madai chuckled, thinking of the cap rather than the Eastern silk.

"Mind leviathan," Job added as Madai and Kittim mounted the horses, which were his gift. "Beyond Reenah's cottage and the river bridge, where the waters are deep, is his lair."

Madai nodded, anxious now that it was morning to be quickly away, anxious for Ararat, anxious for the King Nimrod and to know for himself the man who wore a ring of stars for a crown.

ଔଷ ଔଷ ଔଷ

Iscah stood atop the roof, watching them leave. She had had her cry, which was her farewell, long into the night and had no wish to do it again. She recognized her leather cap with a sharp prick when Madai put it into Tutan's hands; the scarlet silk she did not know. She trusted in Kittim to return, though much had proved false in her life. But she believed him in this matter and it got her through the whole of the feast.

ଔଷ ଔଷ ଔଷ

Kittim and Madai made excellent progress up the river riding their horses, while the camels, burdened only by provision, followed easily. They had reached Reenah's cottage to find her high in the branches of a tree, perched on a platform of bamboo. She was crouched there, patiently waiting at what must be the nest of a fledging brood. She did not risk the movement of a wave but pierced the air with her flashing smile. Madai lifted his hand in return, intently perceiving the gleam in her ebony hair.

Some distance beyond, the marks made by the kitchen maid's camel came to view and were quite distinct. Some little way further, she had crossed the camp of another, and the two were joined, putting a conspicuous trail in the earth along the length of the river.

"As Job instructed," Kittim mused, "we shall follow the river as well."

Madai's gaze passed across the landscape, following the tracks until they faded into the distance. "They lead us by two days," he worried.

Kittim disagreed. "He waited for the maid. And we will overtake them."

So, they continued on in a way that was slower than Madai would have desired. It was, by comparison to parts of their travels, a leisurely journey. The two were comfortably mounted, well fed and led by the visible guide of the river, under a drooping cool fringe of its trees. Even here, miles from the cottage and the lure of its scattered grain, the birds were plentiful, varied and hardly frightened of them at all.

"They would like it here," Madai commented, thinking of Iscah and Tutan.

"Indeed they would," Kittim agreed.

"She will be all right," Madai continued. "And there is Reenah to amuse them."

Kittim's face betrayed a touch of amusement. "No doubt. I perceive even the stalwart Tutan is beguiled."

Madai laughed at this. "Unlikely, Kittim. He bides on the wing of heaven - and her years are half of his."

"And twice yours," Kittim quipped with lifted brow.

෨౭ ෨౭ ෨౭

In the morning there was little doubt that they would catch the fugitive pair, for signs of frequent rests were scrawled in the dust. "Sabta may repent his taking her," Kittim observed ironically.

Madai thought so, too, remembering Iscah's stamina with pride, for she had never hindered their progress. In no little way further, however, the path was lost, veering into the stream to travel the other side.

"Why has he done that?" Madai asked, perplexed.

Kittim studied the crescent indentions in the sand at the river's edge. "Perhaps he knows we follow him."

"Shinar is east," Madai argued.

Kittim shrugged. "Thus, he shall cross again." So they proceeded, alert for the sign they had done just that.

They were now well past the river bridge, watching the water grow deep and strengthen its course. It sliced its way through a gully and beside a ridge that had thrust itself up on the far side. By afternoon, the west bank of the river was a towering cliff, and the wind whistled through the gorge, adding an eerie note to the sound of the rushing current.

This roar obscured the sound of a death throe. They were full upon the scene before becoming aware of it. Foaming white, the water was in tumult with the bellow of a camel, its padded hoofs thrashing at the air. Inside the dark river was a great beast, identified instantly by both men as Job's leviathan. Almost impossible to see, its plated body melded with the depths, all but a powerful, fearful head holding the ragged camel in its mouth. It did not appear the struggle could continue long. The water was scarlet, beaten to bloody froth at the banks. The animal's legs seemed to have stopped churning and had begun to twitch.

Suddenly the other beast rose fully from the water, the dangling, limp camel lifted like a rag in its mouth. A rushing trail of red flowed in the stream toward them, and the great beast leviathan shook its prey triumphantly.

Kittim spied the maid near the bank, nearly drowned, clinging to the rocks against the current. It was the fortune of unrestrained appetite that leviathan pulled the broken camel to the shore at the base of the cliff and ignored Lemmeri. It began to snap camel bones and sniffed its way to the soft belly, consuming rapidly all that was there, spraying blood when it finally emerged to breathe.

Madai was stunned by the sight of such efficient and complete ravaging. He had forgotten the drowning maid, though Kittim had not. Without heed to danger from either the creature or the river, he had somehow got across. Lemmeri's arms were wrapped around his head and were, in their frantic way, hampering her own rescue.

Leviathan lifted its head above the carcass, sensing their struggle. Another snort sprayed a red mist, and its nostrils twitched. Madai waved and called, but he could not be heard above the rushing water. The horses were going mad, inviting the plated beast to swing its dripping head round. At the sight of their pack camels and horses, leviathan curled back its snout and opened its mouth to taste their air. It put a foot on the half-consumed camel, sinking one long claw into its hide, and lifted its yellow eyes toward the cliffs. As though wary of some interloper, it heaved the carcass into the air, gripped it in its terrible mouth, and carried it as though it were no more than a rabbit. Without a look back, leviathan was gone, vanished to some inner cavern.

The beast's departure, however, did not settle the animals. They jerked and pulled away, their dark eyes ringed white, ripping the reins through Madai's hands and bolting back downstream like marmots for burrows. Madai started after them on impulse but remembered the maid, who might still manage to drown her rescuer. So he plunged after Kittim, immediately up to his chest in water. The bottom was sand, pulling his feet away so that he gasped down an icy mouthful.

Kittim had pried the girl off the rock and got her onto the far bank. He was carrying her down stream to the crossing Madai had chosen, and she was limp in his arms. Only when he tried to cross the river again did she come alive. She thrashed enough to drink in froth, then wrapped herself around him like a spare, spineless limb and buried her face.

Madai found his footing and met Kittim near to mid-stream. He could only steady his top-heavy friend, as Lemmeri seemed an enormous tick, refusing to let him go. Together, they made for the other side.

Kittim laid her down. Her eyes had been squeezed shut; but when she felt the ground, they snapped open with a wild, disoriented look and she started to shake. Kittim was on his haunches beside her, his head resting on a knee, teeth chattering.

Madai could feel the cold from the icy river crawling into his bones. He looked in the direction the camels had run, thinking all their dry clothes had fled on four padded hoofs. He was astonished to see his horse. The camels might have sprouted wings, but there was the steady gelding. The animal lifted its head as though it knew Madai had spotted it and blew a tremulous whinny through its lips. If Madai had not been so cold, he would have pronounced a blessing on the reliable beast.

ᘓᘒ   ᘓᘒ   ᘓᘒ

Madai was surprised to be surprised. Kittim had been cold, or seemed cold. Madai could not remember a time when Kittim had not been altogether... all together. He was eating the bread Marisheba had sent with them, the camels and all provisions having been quickly recovered. The girl was still slightly blue, asleep and naked as a skinned quail under the blanket she had pulled up to her nose. Madai had peeled off her sodden clothes, as he had been married before and assumed by some instinctive sense that Kittim had not.

They had decided to move a distance away from the site of the river that Leviathan hunted and were watching the sky turning orange, as orange as their snapping fire.

"Where is Sabta, do you think, in all this?" Madai asked.

"Perhaps he is eaten," Kittim suggested, turning to look at Madai. "The leviathan was rather quickly satisfied by the camel."

"So," Madai said with a thin smile, "it has been done to him as God wills?"

"Who can say?"

The maid opened her eyes, "He is not ate," she chattered.

"So!" Madai began, surprised. "You are awake."

She carefully sat up, having discovered the scratchy blanket on her bare skin. "I wish he was ate," she glowered, closing the blanket tight at her chin.

Madai had to smile, suspecting something entirely cowardly had happened. "Where is he then?" he asked, and extended a piece of bread to her.

"We were set upon," she explained and shuddered. "Lucifer himself! Would have dragged me to deep hades hadn't I slipped. The river washed me down, praise the gods and I took hold of the rocks - whilst Sabta run away." She took a bite of bread and immediately choked. "He might have stopped," she muttered. "There was time."

Madai felt a delicious righteousness welling up, thinking about Sabta and what could still be done to him. It even planted a thread of compassion in him for the unremarkable, stupid girl. She did look ghastly in the firelight.

"Sabta said, 'Meet me, Lemmeri. I shall wait above the mad whore's house,'" Lemmeri crooned miserably. "Job's woman."

Kittim stiffened and Madai's compassion snuffed out like a wet torch.

"'And bring a piece of gold,'" she continued. "So I brought myself to him. Only I was too afraid to bring the gold," Lemmeri was quick to add, casting them a wary look. She might not have revealed herself at all if she had not been so recently come from a deadly plight, and put aside at that, as they would learn, rebuffed.

"He said he loved me," she whimpered, then clamped her lips tight and hugged her knees. "But he said, " she continued with a trembly voice and despite herself, "he said... 'There is a remarkable lack of virgins in Shinar.'" Lemmeri would not say that Sabta had not spilled her maidenhood but would have gold for her instead; she would not say it. He would have had Iscah, she knew, because she had watched him watching her. Lemmeri put her face in her hand.

Kittim watched her sniffle. "You will return to Reenah's cottage," he insisted, with not a trace of pity.

"Surely, I can not!" Lemmeri cried, brought up by the command.

"You will," he repeated. "We must go a long way, and you can not come with us. Reenah is a day's ride directly the way you came. And you shall repent your accusation of Job, and you shall repent your idolatry, and Reenah will send you back to Marisheba."

"My camel is ate!" she protested.

"I give you mine," Kittim answered.

- 45 -

Reenah waited, still, still, as the mother warbler perched herself upon a thin branch and called her brood away from the nest. They were her perfect, identical, slightly miniature, images. The first, usually the largest, perched perilously at the outer edge of the nest, flapped its inexperienced wings. What was practiced inside a crowded nest of siblings became suddenly understood and useful, as it obeyed by command of the Maker its precise design. A little dip, a frantic flutter, a lift upon the air, and its first short flight was accomplished. Its eyes were bright with pleasure when it lighted on a near branch and gave a little dance for the Maker. Its first adult song would be to Him.

The second and third followed at the same command, until just the fourth remained. A soft hand encircled it lightly and removed it from the nest to the woven basket lined with grass. Its wings were frantic, not by fear, for Reenah had waited patiently there and her eyes were not foreign. But the call of the mother and the call of its own purpose made it beat its wings frantically.

This part of Reenah's business was the most piteous. As she listened, the mother continued to call, knowing the precise count of her brood. With a sigh of remorse, even after many a season at it, Reenah climbed from her platform to bring the fledging back. She would let it flap to its wings' delight, but inside her house. There it would grow strong and sing to her at night till she could finally sell it.

She reached the cottage. Placing the basket on her table, she opened the latch to set it loose and it emerged, fluttering wings immediately. "Good," she smiled. "He will live." And Reenah decided, as she did every summer, that it was her last year for it. She was sitting thus, watching him find the perches on her wall, hearing his grateful chirp answer that of another set free before him, when less fragile sounds were heard outside: the ill-humored huff of a camel and a cautious rap upon her door.

"Lady Reenah," a hesitant voice called.

She hurried to open it a crack. "Lemmeri!" she exclaimed, both surprised and slightly alarmed, "is there trouble at the house of Job?"

The girl merely stood there, pale and trembling.

Reenah slipped quickly outside, taking her firmly by the shoulders. "Tell me," she commanded. "What has happened?"

"Just I," Lemmeri quavered.

Reenah shook her slightly, exasperated and growing more fearful by the girl's demeanor. "Tell me!" she commanded again.

"Be merciful," Lemmeri pleaded.

"I shall thrash you if you do not instantly tell me what has happened!"

The girl grew whiter still, because she believed Reenah would do it and she truly feared a thrashing.

"No harm has come the house of Job," she frantically sputtered. "But Sabta is removed."

"That I know," Reenah answered with a frown. "His thievery."

The girl looked as though she would faint, her eyes widening, a damp glistening on her top lip.

"What, girl?" Reenah's voice had lost any hope of patience.

Lemmeri lowered her head, seeing only Reenah's feet in the dust. "I have come back in shame," she whispered, "commanded by Lord Kittim."

Reenah instantly calculated that the trouble seemed limited to the whimpering girl and felt a faint breath of relief. She eyed the top of Lemmeri's head, the scarlet tops of her ears, the white, wringing hands. She took her arm firmly and led her to the shade of the trees, cautious of her house and the newly captured nestlings there.

"Tell me now, from the start," she coaxed, mildly generous.

But the girl's face contorted and a gale of sobbing began afresh. Reenah tettered between vexation and pity, but she forced herself to wait, hoping the girl would spill the story after a cry and a break in the storm.

It took Lemmeri a sniffle or two more than expected, but she finally pulled her skirt up to wipe her face. "I followed Sabta," she whimpered. Her forehead, where it was visible, turned all shades of red.

This Reenah digested. She could imagine the rest, knowing Sabta's wiles and Lemmeri's penchant for absolute folly. But she softened despite herself, remembering the nonsense of youth - even herself. "Then it was not Job's house that was harmed, but you," she consoled.

Lemmeri raised her head involuntarily, startled by compassion, and she grew faintly emboldened.

"Rather, nearly ate," she announced with a trace of returning spirit.

Reenah lifted one brow, truly surprised. The girl simply nodded.

"Tell me."

And so the kitchen maid recounted her tale of the first appearance of leviathan, with its savage attack and consumption of the camel.

"Its great jaws would have me, too," she concluded, "but that I leapt from the saddle into the river, nearly drowned but for holding onto rocks." She rolled her eyes. "Oh, the tragic wail of my poor beast," she embellished.

"Job's beast," Reenah corrected. "And Sabta?"

"Deserted me," Lemmeri replied quietly. Her spark faded at this ultimate betrayal.

Reenah had a short length of pity.

"And your rescue?" she pressed.

"The Lord Kittim," Lemmeri answered, beginning to sniffle again.

"Ah," Reenah realized. "Precisely. They followed Sabta, no doubt. They passed here just two days ago."

The girl threatened to crumble into weeping. Reenah could not restrain herself. "Whatever made you follow that viper?" she asked, though it was as much to divert the tears as ask a question. She had the answer already.

Such was not the outcome. With a weary shake of her head, and without the coaxing skills of other women, Reenah let the girl have her cry before she took her into the cottage to find something to feed her and to lay her to bed for a rest.

C3CR   C3CR   C3CR

Iscah recovered her buoyancy, trusting as she did that Kittim would return. And she remembered Madai's proof of the flood, his bone of rock, which he would most certainly return for. She was satisfied by that, and they were comfortably astride Job's padded saddles and atop the gaily-bedecked horses, followed by camels not so heavily loaded as at the departing journey. The Lady was weary and actually reclined on a couch encircled by heavy curtain, carried by the strong shoulders of four servants. Iscah had seen it done in the city and knew it no great burden, as the way was both level and short, being a mere day's journey. Job led the procession, his great desert horse, Havilah, in his best finery and form. It was a stirring sight, really.

They had come nearly the whole way, Reenah's cottage coming visible amongst the trees in the distance. There was a quick stab in Iscah's heart, having come here last with Kittim and Madai. But she resisted the melancholy by the force of her will and began to plan the trips she would make here with Tutan. She intended to spend much time here, whatever the Lady would allow and was not ill-mannered. She glanced at Tutan beside her. His eyes were trained on the cottage, as well.

"Do you think we will rest here?" she asked him.

"Perhaps... "

Iscah nodded; her legs were sore. Then she glimpsed Reenah coming from the cottage. She was not alone. Iscah's young eyes were quick, perhaps the first to identify the kitchen maid.

"They have done it," Tutan whispered.

Reenah walked toward the little caravan, meeting them some distance from her house. She spoke to Job, who leaned down, listening quietly. The maid, Lemmeri, stood where she first had stopped, as stiff and still as a startled fawn. Afterward, Reenah turned and walked back to the house. Job lifted his hand in parting and they continued with barely a pause.

C3CR   C3CR   C3CR

As Iscah was compassionate by nature, she was truly conflicted by the excitement she felt seeing Reenah's cottage the next day. It was the hope of adventure that stirred her rather than the plight of the maid. She and Tutan trotted forward, just beginning to feel the breeze born in the shade beside the river. Iscah heard Reenah's camel call from its corral and watched the door open and Reenah step into the sun. She lifted her hand in greeting.

"Uncle has not come?" Reenah asked.

"He is making an offering for his children," Tutan answered, swinging from his saddle and bowing formally. "Good greeting, Lady Reenah. I pray the Fellowship of the Holy One upon you."

She approached him with polite amusement. "Indeed," she answered. She took his hands boldly, delighting herself and disarming him. "Pray, heed me less exaltedly. I am but a merchant, bred at Cush and carted the world round. I am only Reenah."

He bowed again, drawing his hands away. "As you wish."

She saw him cool. "Though your words do me honor," she quickly added.

He bowed yet again, allowing a smile to lighten his face, and turned to assist Iscah, which was entirely unnecessary. She was upon the ground, anxious to begin her own new adventure.

"Iscah!" Reenah delighted. "How is the red bird?"

"Escaped," Iscah answered as she smoothed her robe.

Reenah clucked her sympathies and scowled at the mention of Sabta. She indicated the interior of her house. "There is another of his crimes," she said, meaning the kitchen maid.

- 46 -

A familiar and rather unpleasant smell carried on the wind; camel and goat in concert, in concentrated form. And another scent mingled there also, human habitation confined in a profusion of haggard dwellings, these at the edges of what seemed a splendid city, larger by far than that of Hamonheb.

It became their misfortune to ride upon an indignant seller of wares who, by means of hurling camel dung, was scattering a flock of crowing, tattered children. A misfire struck Madai in the leg.

The merchant immediately flung himself down, face to the ground. "Pardon, pardon, my lords," he cried, dust settling on his hair.

The man on the ground was a curious sight to Madai. He had yet to see one quite so girthsome. They had been bowed to before, but that had been for the dragon. Perhaps this latest absurdity was for the finery of their borrowed clothes.

But Kittim was insensible to the man; he was watching the children, who took flight like sparks in a fire and disappeared into the maze of dusty huts. When he wheeled his horse back around to eye the man, he was still on the ground.

"Do you know the region?" he asked the merchant abruptly.

"Indeed," the man leapt up and grinned, a hopeful look in his eyes. He licked his lips and pulled his robe straight where it had wadded up on the ground.

"Ask him where travelers bide," Madai asked Kittim.

"We seek the mountain, do we not?" Kittim insisted, cutting Madai a stern eye.

"But Sabta..." he began.

Kittim's expression didn't change, but he lowered his voice. "Is your old talisman worth so much?" he asked, speaking of The Family's Spear.

Madai knew precisely what he meant. "There was more villainy done than just the Spear, Kittim."

Their horses began to paw the ground; their skin quivered in a ripply motion against the growing haze of insects. They tossed their heads, blowing back a spray. Even the merchant was growing tired of his subservient pose, his grin fading.

"Who were they?" Kittim asked the man abruptly, indicating the scattered children with a toss of his head.

"Just beggars, my lord," the merchant groveled, beginning to doubt his first expectations of the wealthy travelers.

Kittim studied the shabby dwellings. "Where do they live?" he demanded.

"Oh, my lord, you shall not find them. They live," he waved his hands through the air, "wherever they like."

Kittim's eyes darkened. "They are orphaned?"

The merchant's face twitched. "Unfortunate," he answered carefully. He turned his hands palms up in a helpless gesture. "Fathers are criminals, no doubt, or mothers."

But Kittim did not seem to hear, and Madai could not follow their conversation. He looked through the gate, less than confident of finding a fugitive thief. There was a growing crowd, all with ordinary faces. He moved from man to man; his eyes trailed across the dirty outskirts of the city, as Kittim was quite obviously intent on something else. He could see nothing of interest or assistance in any of the indifferent faces which chanced to stray their way. Excepting one.

Madai tensed immediately. He felt for his bow, energy surging into his fingers. And the man disappeared.

"He is here," Madai hissed.

Kittim looked up from the merchant, faintly bothered by the interruption.

"Sabta," Madai repeated. "He is here."

Kittim frowned.

"My lords," the merchant whined, his head carefully bowed, "I am your servant." By which he meant, of course, 'if you have no further need, there is a cup of wine waiting in the cool of my tent.'

Kittim turned back to him. "What sort of criminals?" he asked, as though the conversation were never interrupted.

The merchant shrugged miserably, "Thief... debtor... who knows? Perhaps a cult of other gods."

The deepening of Kittim's eyes began to frighten the man. He shuffled back a step. But Kittim reined his horse abruptly toward the narrow alleys into which the children had disappeared. Madai, caught by surprise, turned his horse to follow. The merchant, sweating and uncomfortable, scurried back to his tent and pulled down the flap.

Kittim directed his horse between the huts, scattering guinea fowl and dust.

"Do you know where we are going?" Madai asked him, catching up.

Kittim reined up his horse reluctantly. He looked down the lane where it twisted around in an unending string of dry-mud huts. "They are not my charge," he whispered faintly.

Madai was confused. "What?"

Kittim slowly turned his horse around and looked at Madai with an intensity so deep it startled him, "Do you still want the Spear?"

The question was so entirely unexpected that Madai couldn't answer. The theft was so small a thing beside Lemmeri and the leviathan. Beyond that, there was Nua's ship... and for the first time, the Spear did begin to feel like a talisman. Still, surely justice was required for Sabta's crimes...

'May it be done to him as God wills.' Madai heard the pronouncement again, as it had come from Job and Kittim both. It was a hard decree, an intangible verdict. He looked at Kittim again, who was waiting for an answer. Madai slowly shook his head.

"No," he said. "I do not need the Spear." Then he looked out across the hovels to the city rising white into the pale, dusty sky. "We have been warned of this city by Job," he finished.

Kittim's eyes widened. A smile flickered briefly across his face and he reached across the space separating their two horses. He grasped Madai's arm. "I am pleased," he announced.

"It has not saved me," Madai gradually realized, "From neither the fire breather, nor the winged serpent, nor the Anak."

"Precisely!" Kittim agreed. "Now we will seek an Ancient, shall we not?"

A creeping satisfaction buoyed Madai until he felt light, suddenly picked up by some mysterious breeze. They simply nodded and turned their horses in the narrow lane, back toward the plain, prepared to leave the legendary city behind. Then, without warning, they were surged upon by a noisy dozen men or so. The dust bloomed with them. And the most burly of the mob grabbed at Madai's camel. He pushed at the man with his boot as another hand took a grip on the horse's bridle.

Sabta.

The mob grew still. Sabta twisted his thin smile at them.

"There is one would like to see you," his oily voice proclaimed. "Your lordships." He chuckled, leering at Madai's lance. He straightened his shoulders, taking an important air, and led the procession toward the city's open gate.

Madai snatched at the reins, but Sabta had them firmly. So he reached across his back for his bow.

Kittim put his hand against Madai's back, resting it on the weapon. "It seems we are not done with him," he said in a restraining voice.

The burly man was growling at them, as well. Madai glanced down at him; a thin smile twitched across his face at the sudden reversal, not altogether unhappy to have another chance at Satba. His oak lance where it was still strapped to the saddle seemed to burn a place on his leg.

沂 沂 沂

The way near the gate was snarled with humankind. Merchants. Peddlers. Soldiers. Camels and asses. Ragged children. Caged and spitting panthers. A scrawny dog came careening through the street after a manic chicken and was dropped to his haunches by a hiss from the cat. It was a conglomeration of color, sound and smell.

At the gate, the shabbier of Sabta's mob seemed to drop away, till it was only the burly man and Sabta himself who braved the city. Madai guessed he and Kittim might have escaped, and left a fallen idolater in the effort, had a more imposing escort not come on the scene. Sabta bowed as though he would scrape his face on the ground if his body would only unhinge. His friend deserted him entirely, though not without a last covetous glance at Job's camel.

They were a dozen warriors, soldiers, if Madai had known the name for them. The leader was decidedly imposing, and he spoke to Kittim with the frank air of authority.

"Pray, forgive this rabble," he barked with an eye at Sabta. "The time is possibly near to cleanse them again."

"And we are not detained?" Kittim asked with a steady voice.

"Certainly, no! Though the Lord shall wish to amend this hostility toward you. He has been advised of you," the soldier answered, glancing at Sabta again. He reached out and firmly took the reins of Kittim's mount. "Shall we remove your horses? They will be tended."

The last appeared, even to Madai, an order rather than a question, though the commander of the guard left him his weapon. The tide had turned, and the circumstance was familiar, though not Madai's folly this time. He walked beside Kittim, not with fear, but with frustration. They were led and followed by an escort of serious and efficient men who carried daggers at their waists.

"What trouble do you think Sabta has arranged for us?" Madai asked, with the man himself near enough to smell.

"Whatever shall put him in good stead," Kittim answered.

Madai looked over his shoulder at Job's manservant, who did not appear in the least intimidated. He was dusting and straightening his robe.

෬෯ ෬෯ ෬෯

The city was all that the village was not: a vibrant, ordered place of commerce, a web of lanes down which the merchants brought their wares, where even the dung was removed, dwellings of brick, painted white, stacked and adjacent, the luxuriant version of Hamonheb's little town - an achievement of human effort and prosperity.

Citizenry flocked to a market that stood literally in the shadow of a miniature ziggurat, whose steep stairway was climbed, up and down by a steady stream. Women of dark and light hue hailed passing merchants. Exchanges were made on the steps with men in colored robes, licking their lips and wobbling after the women. Other, more pitiful creatures sat or lay along the outer margin of the steps, mostly old, undeniably ill. An odd assortment.

Beside the ziggurat, a like stairway and monolithic pillars rose to front a second building, in appearance, as imposing. It was here the regiment of soldiers brought them. Madai and Kittim followed up the stairway, only to wait on an over-arching portico. From this regal height and the cover of a shaded porch, Madai observed the vigorous city. They seemed all to thrive, and Madai was impressed. He only must ignore the cast-off ancients who littered the ziggurat steps.

The commander of the soldiers barked at the sentinel standing guard at the entrance. He in turn sent another scuttling inside, leaving behind the sound of his boots clipping across a stone floor. Madai listened till the sound faded somewhere inside, grateful for the shade, conscious of a certain honor being granted them from one whose domain was as grand as this. But he took his cue from Kittim, whose demeanor was as clearly unimpressed. Perhaps only a few moments passed till the courier returned, speaking to the stone-faced sentinel with a clipped few words, words which delivered them inside.

More than a score of assorted persons milled about inside the hall. They spoke in subdued tones; perhaps reverent would describe their appearance. They turned when Kittim and Madai entered, looking entirely foreign, watching with a note of curiosity. And, when they were ushered directly through the crowd, decidedly resentful. Madai's sandals snapped across the marble floor, a touch too loud, and he found he missed the convention of foot-washing here.

On towering walls a collage of plaster murals climbed toward an arching dome at the ceiling. There the muffled multitude of voices was trapped and echoed footfalls upon stone. The murals, which maintained a common theme, boasted a prominent personage: warrior, hunter, king. His proclaimed presence was everywhere.

They crossed the large chamber, past milling groups of citizenry, to a juncture where two halls met. Each sprawled a long way in opposite directions; and their guide took them left. Here the ceiling was not so high, and Madai's feet were boisterous and announced his every step. Oil lamps lit the way, as the far length of the hall left it dark. An aura ringed each lamp to reveal a dark and foreign wood, rubbed smooth and mildly scented.

Two massive doors, fashioned of the same sort of wood, stood closed at the end of the corridor and guarded on either side. Two unusually tall men opened the door to them. The officer took three steps into the room and fell to his knees. He dropped his face to the floor in an act of absolute submission, this proud soldier. Sabta fell in the exact posture, which left Kittim and Madai looking across their backs. At the far side of the room sat a large man, elaborately throned. A woman was seated beside him with a hawk-faced man behind. This standing person came rushing from the dais across the room, his silk robe flapping.

He struck Kittim, a stinging sound, and barked at him, to which Kittim replied as though it were a common matter to be launched at. Madai hadn't even the time to move; it was happening so fast and unexpectedly. He had the immediate perception it was because they were not face to the ground and rump to the air. He still had his spear, but there were giants at his back. He might have used it anyway, if not that Kittim seemed, even now, strangely in control.

The man on the throne stood. Madai had a full look at him. He was the giant in this room! His skin was oiled. It gleamed. He wore no sign of kingship upon his head. He had just his hair, thick coils to his shoulder woven with gemstones, a sparkling frame to a beautiful face. He had a nose that once had been straight, a common sight in dangerous lands, though this crooked nose enhanced him, lending the man an aesthetic both splendid and veteraned. His eyes were brilliant black, keen. He was smiling.

His vest was vibrant of color and opened at the front to make visible his significant strength. He wore a kilt that hung to his knees. Madai had considerable time to study the man, for the room was long and narrow and he approached them with ease, in no great hurry at all.

The King's eyes appraised them with a look of intelligence. "Namim," he murmured, "I pardon them. They are strangers here."

"Ah," he murmured, "Sabta."

The manservant did not look up.

The King then looked at Madai with an appearance of approval in his eyes. He stood quietly studying them both, Madai and Kittim, before he turned, crossing the room back to his throne, indicating as he passed that the two prostrate men should rise. He sat beside the Lady again and spread his lips apart in a smile of genuine benevolence.

"Approach," he insisted.

The officer led their way and took a stiff posture to the side, though not before he relieved Madai of his spear.

"So they have come as promised," the King addressed Sabta.

"Truly, my Lord."

"You are Madai?" he asked, looking into Madai's face. Though his name sounded odd on the man's tongue, it was discernible, and he nodded.

"And the banal Kittim."

Not a muscle of Kittim's face moved. "Nimrod," he assented. Kittim's eyes bored into the great lord's eyes with authority, which seemed more to amuse than to challenge him.

He casually turned to Madai. "I am told you are a great hunter, and a philosopher, as well."

"He is a Japhethite," Kittim offered.

"Indeed," Nimrod crooned. "You are a great hunter, I am told," he repeated in the Japhethite tongue of the continent.

"He has come far, across the Sea," explained Kittim dryly.

Unaffected, Nimrod spoke swiftly to his official, Namim, who abruptly left the room.

"I speak his tongue," Kittim continued.

Nimrod tried to wilt him with his eyes. "Perhaps I shall need a more... private conversation," he answered pointedly.

There was something in the exchange and in Nimrod's voice that was smooth, unpleasant. It crawled a bit across Madai's skin, a stark departure from the first thrill of honor. Madai watched the two, who seemed locked in a sort of silent impasse.

Shortly, Namim returned. With him was a young man, nearly as young as Iscah, his face as smooth and his head completely shaved. He walked with a decided limp on his right side. Namim produced him with an air of ownership. The youth sprawled immediately to the floor. He rose only after a nod from his master, with a cautious glance at Nimrod.

"My Lord," he murmured carefully.

How sweet was his voice, and his body tall and pale. Madai had the first impression that he was a maid instead.

"Tazek," Namim simpered. "This is a kinsman," he said indicating Madai.

The youth looked up, startled. Madai glimpsed a moment of hope in the young face. He noticed instantly the green eyes and the nub of red sprouting on his head.

"You shall speak my words to him," Nimrod commanded, beckoning Tazek and Madai to climb the dais.

Nimrod rested his arms on the elongated necks of two carved beasts, speaking in soft tones to the young man, Tazek. It was a discourse long enough to grant Madai a glance at the Lady, in appearance older than Nimrod. She was appraising him, as well, with a gleam of moisture on her parted lips.

Madai looked away. He trained his eyes at the back mural, suddenly feeling a sprouting of sweat across his scalp. In the fresco was a king with a long-bow, victor above a dragon. It was a perfect prompting, reminder of the murals in the temple of En-UtuAten. He knew he was at the birthplace of the legend. The Naru. He had arrived, and he was keenly aware of Kittim standing in the room behind them, knowing by experience what his stance would be - disapproval and predictable silent prayers.

By his posture, Madai was correct, though Kittim's prayer had already been made. Instead, his eyes were stark and burned, a look which caused Sabta to tremble as none else save Nimrod was able to do.

Tazek finally turned to Madai with a tremor in his voice, "My Lord Nimrod, is told of the dragon. He is...." the youth groped for the word, "My Lord admires courage... and strength."

Madai glanced at the lord Nimrod.

"You shall now inform us?" Tazek finished.

Madai was caught somewhat by surprise. He felt himself flush and was instantly annoyed by the vulnerable feel of it. Perhaps it was his imagination that Nimrod noticed and was pleased. But he began his tale, with a voice less steady than he would have wished. He told the felling of the dragon in an abbreviated form, stressing both the aid of Kittim and the bitumen. He told of the town and its celebration, its priest-king, at which Nimrod's eyes narrowed, though the story in whole did not displease him. Nimrod had a light in his eyes that was almost friendly when Madai finished. Nimrod leaned toward the guard who had brought them in and muttered a command.

The soldier nodded. He was still holding Madai's spear, and Madai briefly thought he might be restored it. But the guard did not spare him a glance. Instead, he stood just at his back, between himself and Kittim, even as he dismissed Sabta with an indifferent nod.

"We are honored at your visit," Nimrod asserted. "I shall wish to speak more with the Japhethite by you, Tazek. Kittim may go."

Madai turned to follow, not understanding Nimrod's words but only hearing Kittim beginning to leave. The officer gripped his arm. Madai would have tossed the man aside, or at least tried, had Kittim not spoken quietly and then walked away. Madai was both astonished and alarmed at the turn, watching the tall and composed Kittim walking confidently through the great wood doors, which swung shut with a soft swoosh behind him.

Nimrod

Lemmeri pleaded with them, infinitely afraid of the Master and his wife. She sat beside Reenah with a cup of honeyed tea, her eyes downcast, ashamed to be seen by Tutan and defiant before Iscah.

Tutan put his drink down. "What deceit was told you, child?"

The question, simple enough, soured a sour face even more.

"Lemmeri!" Reenah snapped.

The girl turned her wilted eyes toward Reenah. "No slave goes unpunished," she insisted, a petulant voice despite the trembles.

"Job keeps no slaves," Tutan protested.

To this she did not reply. "I shall be shamed," she answered instead.

Iscah was long ago vexed by the whining. "As you ought!" she interjected. "You followed him!" Which was, for her, past understanding. "Sabta follows false gods. "

Lemmeri fixed her with a glare.

"And still you are rescued by the One True God," Iscah finished with a glare to match.

"There is nothing more to be said, Lemmeri," Tutan interjected with finality. "You are summoned."

She lifted her chin. "So - you say I am no slave?" There was more than a hint of rebellion in her voice.

"You are a haughty maid," he answered. "And you owe a duty to the house of Job, who wishes only to restore you." This last he spoke a degree more gently.

"Of certainty, Lemmeri, you shall return. Old Marisheba cannot tend the kitchen alone," Reenah insisted. "We will have done with this."

The girl's eyes quavered again.

"I know a hurt was done you," Reenah added, which surprised them all. "But the best cure for that is a good, ready hand at work. You shall see." She turned her head away from the girl, ending the matter, and pushed back her hair with her hand. "Now, I am for a cooling at the river," she announced abruptly and stood without waiting for the others to agree.

The river was wide and moving slowly behind Reenah's cottage. There was, indeed, a shallow with a bottom of sand angling gently toward the center, where it was certainly deeper. Baskets of grain hung from the limbs of the trees, with scatterings as well on the rock, pecked and emptied of grain. Iscah noticed six little platforms set in the biggest, highest limbs.

Tutan studied the water with uncertainty, being modest of the maids, but of Reenah more. She was taking Lemmeri's sandals and admonishing her with a severe expression. The girl dropped her eyes before she waded slowly into the stream. Tutan watched her glancing down the length of it, as if looking for a great hungry monster. He couldn't help the sympathy rising in him for the disagreeable girl.

When Reenah looked at him, he felt himself flush. As she came across the sand, it was with her most potent smile. She extended her hand and said, "You may wish to see the honey hives, as once you asked."

"Indeed," he heard himself answer. "With the greatest of pleasure."

So she led him to the buzzing hollow in a great, old tree. It was wrapped around by gnarled bark and a wide wound like an open mouth, healed smooth in a crest around the edges. The mouth seemed to speak by the sound of its countless, busy little horde.

"You need not fear," she told him. "We will keep a safe distance."

"Have no concern for me. I am familiar with bees," he assured her. "I tended them in my family garden when I was younger than Iscah," his deep laugh rumbled in the still air, "and was rebuked by them on occasion."

He heard her laugh merrily in return and felt an odd prickling in his chest.

"Then have a good look," she said. She watched him carefully. "I would not have thought you were a man of the earth."

"As Adam?" he asked, thinking himself clever. But she didn't seem to understand the reference. So he added with as casual a tone as he could muster, "You have cleaned it perfectly."

"Hmm," she agreed, "the day you first were here. So... you keep the philosophy of Uncle?"

This surprised him. "You do not?" he asked before he thought. He was disturbed, uncomfortably so, at the prospect of Reenah's being a pagan. "I... I do not judge it... a philosophy."

She appraised him calmly. "No, indeed you would not."

He looked at her more closely, seeing an ironic look in her eyes, the first unattractive aspect of her appearance he had observed. She was tall and erect and exotic. Her blue-black hair was pulled away from her face, which was both angular and dark. He noticed, for the first time, a pattern etched upon the skin of her neck. Quite a lovely pattern, really, the color of henna, curling loosely toward her ear. He was suddenly alarmed by his dampened hands and knew he looked at her as he might once have looked at Enico. This was a horrifying insight, as he was struck with the realization that she knew it, too.

"Within my experience, and that is vast," she continued with a faint gleam, "those who keep a belief do not consider it a simple philosophy."

"No." He was fast to agree. "Though I had presumed you would serve the God of your kinsman."

She smiled broadly. "Quite naturally," she responded. "Uncle is a good man, though," she continued as she looked up at Tutan, "he is not a kinsman by blood, but rather by... sentiment."

Tutan didn't answer, but the talisman objects in her house were making better sense. He looked away toward the girls to collect his thoughts. Lemmeri was lying stretched out on the grass, as far from the shadow of leviathan as possible. And there was the still form of Iscah lying on a rock, swinging her feet in the water, the only sign that she was not asleep.

"You are finished with the bees?" Reenah asked.

He looked back at her and thought her self-confidence had somehow slipped, with a suggestion of fleeting loneliness in her eyes.

"I should rather wish to hear your philosophies," he answered kindly.

She began a casual walk toward the cottage. "My philosophy is to do no dishonor to any god."

"But surely, if One is true, then another can not be," he responded, scurrying to catch up beside her.

She stopped at that and faced him with her ironic smile. "Not all suppose there is but One, and I honor the god in whose land I dwell. There are many lands."

"You dwell in the land of Job at present."

"Precisely," she answered. "And his God has been good to him."

"His God is the One True God," Tutan insisted.

"That I do not concede, though He is the God of Job."

Tutan heard no hint of guile in her voice, or ambivalence. Her eyes were candid and decided and rich as her golden honey.

"You have learned the ways of many lands," he remarked.

"As have you, Tutan," she replied, slowly retracing their path. "I should like to hear."

She stopped again before they reached the girls and faced him. There was the lonliness again, and a parting of her lips. It set his face afever.

"When you have taken Lemmeri back," she continued with a look that plunged to the innermost part of him, "perhaps you will return before the snow and we may talk more of philosophies."

The thought pleased Tutan enough to make him slightly afraid. But he answered, "We, Iscah and I, shall deem it an honor," and he bowed from his waist.

- 48 -

"The Lord Nimrod is pleased by you," Tazek told Madai, who was still stunned by the sudden loss of Kittim. "There is much he would learn of the lands from which you came. And for what prize you are searching."

Madai listened with half an ear, reserving the best of his attentions for where they might have taken Kittim. There was hidden power in the man, Madai had no doubt, though should it sustain against a power so great as Nimrod? He wondered.

Tazek was talking again, with evident fear in his voice. Madai would have liked the sound of it, but for that, because it was like the strains of home. Then he felt a gaze and was drawn back to Nimrod himself, hearing Tazek speak his thoughts in a soft tone that could hardly differ more from the look in the eyes of the King.

"I have come far," he finally answered. "From lands to the west, beyond the Brine Sea."

Nimrod nodded at that, a first shine of interest on his face. He rendered words to Tazek that Madai could not understand.

"Lord Nimrod wishes to know your purpose here," the young man continued.

Madai considered his reply carefully, "I have come with my companion," he began vaguely, "seeking a mount - Ararat by name."

Upon hearing Tazek's translation, the lord's countenance abruptly changed. Benevolent supremacy was swept away. The visage that followed came from frosty depths; ebony eyes glittered viciously as he barked a short reply. Tazek trembled.

"Pray you do not seek that relic of Huwah," he soon repeated to Madai.

"I seek the ship of Nua - Noah," Madai replied.

Tazek did not speak the words to Nimrod, for the giant had risen. He stood towering on the dais; his expression did not change, even as he started to laugh. He snapped a sentence to the woman beside him. She, who had first trailed her eyes across the plains of Madai's body, was heated by another temper now as she nodded some shared secret. The change had come at the name of "Noah."

Tazek faintly quivered when Nimrod spoke to him again, only a short few words, adopting its former cajoling tones.

"It is our wish to speak with you more," he said through the boy. "Yet my judgement is required. There are others come waiting my service. You shall be my guest; Namim will see you away."

The great man turned his attention away. Madai suddenly thought he should need to support the boy, who was paler with every exchange. But it was Namim who reached out to him and led them both through an opposite door from where he had entered, and into a deeper part of the palace.

"Where is Kittim?" Madai asked Tazek quietly.

Tazek merely shook his head.

"Is he harmed?" Madai tried again.

"He is well away," the boy found his voice, glancing quickly toward Namim.

Madai was not afraid. There would come a time to escape, if that were necessary. Only he was keenly aware of the boy's cold terror, following Nimrod's man, and the guard a half pace behind.

Their route skirted the gathering hall, no chance to glimpse Kittim there, and moved into a narrow, dim corridor, which somewhat dampened Madai's assurance. As a result, his surprise was great when Namim stopped beside a high wood door that opened to what could only be described as sumptuous sleeping quarters. It seemed he would be a well-provided-for captive.

They entered. Directly opposite the door was another opening, visible past the soft fluttering of a curtain. Madai strode past Namim to inspect it. It opened onto a wide ledge that overlooked a clay brick courtyard many feet below. This courtyard was hedged by sheer brick walls - no easy escape, but entirely possible.

He heard Namim behind him, waited a moment and turned. It was a moment too early, permitting him a glimpse of what was to Tazek a dishonor, and to himself a telling of unnatural passion. This Namim did not attempt to hide. Rather, his lips curled in a slightly cruel smile, and he leaned to Tazek's ear, murmuring. The boy did not translate, his ears flaming red. Namim straightened, and brushed his robe. He let his eyes linger on Madai in a cold way that caused him no fear, though it may have been intended a warning. He grunted a word in his unattractive language, cast a last look at Tazek and left the room.

Tazek watched him go. He looked at the floor before he told Madai, "I am to serve you."

"Am I a prisoner?" Madai asked before the echo of the door's closing ended. Then he turned away from Tazek with both pity and distaste. As he turned, he was surprised to see that his lance leaned against the wall.

Tazek fidgeted. "I would say that you are an honored guest of the Great Lord Nimrod, the Shining Light of Heaven, were you not a kinsman." Madai was surprised and faced him again. "But I shall speak the truth that you are being tested, and you shall likely die here, if you are fortunate."

The boy's candor, spoken with a hint of courage, caused Madai a better opinion of him. But there was a distance in the boy, whether of fear or dislike Madai could not tell. He went to the balcony again.

"There is no escape," Tazek assured him bitterly.

Still facing the courtyard below, Madai surveyed the enclosure for any weakness. "How have you come here?" he asked casually.

He waited a moment, hearing only silence at first, and then Tazek's brittle chuckle. "I have come by way of a gift. " His voice spoke Madai's language with flawless cadence.

At this, Madai faced him. He could only be a remnant of The Banned, as he was quite without question of The Family, come here and made a slave. "What has become of your family?" Madai asked.

The boy hesitated. It seemed to Madai he wouldn't answer. He was flushed, though not with fitness. He was leaning to the right because of a weakness on that side. His eyes flickered with emotion, and then a coolness passed his face before he finally began to speak:

"I was not yet come to the making of men when my father and mother came with others from amongst The Family," he nodded at Madai. "The Family... to the land of Shinar, for the sake its gods. It was a terrible journey," his voice shuddered, "and a number half that we were remained at the edge of the Great Sea to tame it and make it theirs." Tazek's voice grew so soft Madai took a step nearer to hear. "But it was not the dwelling of the gods, so we came farther.

"I was young, and my sister." He waited a while before continuing. "We lived a time at Ur. This is my greatest..." He stopped.

Madai sensed a tragedy unfolding. Tazek walked to the balcony and looked into the little enclosure below till Madai was nearly afraid he would fling himself down.

Instead Tazek produced another bitter laugh, followed by another sound, one that was familiar, and Madai joined him on the balcony. It was a rumble, and menacing. Tazek looked up with a hint of pity in his eyes toward Madai.

"They are hungry," he said ironically, indicating the spotted cats below them. The leopards had begun to pace. Madai gripped Tazek's arm and pulled him back.

The boy's mouth quivered at the touch. "I am not so brave as that," he muttered. Then he looked at Madai with great, sad defeat in his eyes, so much that Madai released him and looked away. He had to grant the wit of his captor.

"You are the first I have seen," Tazek continued, as though his narrative had not been interrupted. "The first of my kinsmen, save Palapa. And I would rather have saved her from this."

Madai's opened his mouth to ask...

"My sister," Tazek answered before he could. "Gifts to the Light of Heaven. By which our mother and father have good favor in this city."

Madai was as still as Tazek, looking at the boy.

"She was brought for Nimrod. And I... for Namim."

A low grunt escaped Madai's throat. Such things were forbidden! He would not think about it. He thought instead of the long-ago threat to Ido. He remembered the sight of Iscah washing in the stream with tears on her face. All innocents, at threat from corrupt men. And he knew that as he had done to the Anak, he would do to the Light of Heaven.

The leopards made all the sound that was in the room. Madai and Tazek just looked at each other, and then the spell was broken. Tazek's glimmer of courage vanished and, with it, any strength of The Family. His eyes trailed the floor again as he backed toward the door with his right leg dragging. He nearly said something else, but he closed his lips and pulled at the door, which seemed a weight more than he could manage.

჆•჉   ჆•჉   ჆•჉

With Tazek was gone, Madai leaned back over the ledge. No less than three cats fought after miserly hunks of meat tossed at them from some place below. There was a slow rise in Madai as he watched the animals. He should be cursing the hot sand, measuring the distance to Nimrod Dagh. Instead he had lost Kittim, for the moment, had a trio of leopards below him and was without his arrows. There was never a doubt that he would escape, but he had certainly no intention of doing it alone. The problem lay in finding Kittim.

He considered the distance to the ground. Possible. "I cannot find him locked in here," he muttered aloud.

Shadows began to cast across the enclosure's brick walls, a startling development, as it harkened the day's swift passing. But Madai's mouth turned up in a half smile; for revealed as well were protrusions in the wall, irregularities with the bricks, perhaps sufficient to climb. He studied the niches and jutting bricks and mapped a path up the wall.

Still, there were the leopards...

჆•჉   ჆•჉   ჆•჉

Darkness began to claim the room, leaving no light save the rising moon. It was a good time to hide from the eyes of guards he could only presume were set to watch him. But the grass was high in the courtyard, and cats hunt by night. He would not be hasty.

There was suddenly a light rap on his door. He heard a gruff voice, then the scraping of wood, and the door opened. A maid stood at the entrance with a crock and a lamp in her hand. The owner of the gruff voice closed her in.

"My Lord," she spoke demurely, extending the crock in Madai's direction. "The Lord Nimrod regrets the oversight of your meal, and this darkness." She spoke in Madai's tongue, a thing that had ceased to surprise him. It might even suggest her origin.

As the light illuminated the room, it illuminated her face. Madai was struck as by a heavy blow. She was slighter still than her brother, though tall as The Family. Her hair was yellow and long to her hips, and her skin was light enough to remind him of the face of Ido. It was a reminder he had not endured since coming to this land of dark-skinned peoples.

"You are Tazek's sister," he muttered.

She nodded. He took the crock and smelled it.

"It is not poisoned," she assured him, and took a sip from a small ladle to prove it.

Her hands trembled slightly offering him the bowl and Madai could not miss the queer twitch around her mouth when she spoke. Any resemblance to Ido was lost when he remembered his wife's ready laughter. It was a thought that filled him with a tempest of unexpected pain. He took the food to hide it.

Eating with the miserable girl in the room was a distraction. The food might have been delicious; he couldn't tell. But it did fill a belly that had been a long time empty. He finished with a last scrape around the sides and extended the bowl to her. She took it and put it on the table. And she didn't leave.

Madai watched her, an unwelcome suggestion forming in his mind.

"I am Palada, my Lord," she whispered, "and I am at your pleasure."

Fear blanched her face, if it were possible to be paler than she had first appeared. Madai recognized the situation for what it was. But there was a standard etched in him, and she was as appealing as a salamander. He laughed. Leopards and a woman...

"I do not require you," he said, more unkindly than he should.

"My Lord," she hung her head. She dropped to her knees and put her hands on his feet. "Do I not please you?"

He moved his foot. The scent of her hair wafted up toward him, and he thought with a flash that it had been a long time, which, in turn drew a harsh rumble up his throat. He had been undone by that sort of thing.

"Have you no shame?" he asked ruthlessly. "You are of The Family."

She whimpered, unable to lift her face. "Give me just a corner for the night," she pleaded. "I will be punished."

He fought against the pity that was trying to surface. What he really needed was a plan, first to get past the leopards with only his spear, and then to find Kittim. Madai moved away, feeling her hands slip off his feet. He grabbed a blanket from the bed and wrapped it around his shoulders. Then he lay on the floor facing the open balcony and listened to the cats.

When he woke in the morning, a faint light shone through the open balcony - and she had gone.

- 49 -

"Palada has told me you would not have her," Tazek said. It was past first light, and Madai had been calculating the formula of his escape. "And yet I do not suppose you share the taste of Namim."

Madai looked up sourly. "Is there news of Kittim?" he asked.

Tazek seemed to shrink a little, "I have heard nothing," he answered. He went to the table slowly to sit down. "It is rumored you are here by design," he began again. "An insignificant has returned a sacred object to Lord Nimrod. It was got from your hand."

Madai guarded himself. 'This boy is dangerous,' he thought, 'with his lame foot and piteous story.' Tazek's mood was erratic and Madai would not suffer for it. Nor would he betray a mounting anxiety for Kittim, which was a weakness. Instead, he turned his face away toward the morning sun with as much indifference as possible.

"What advantage am I to Nimrod?" he asked coolly.

"In that you have kindly treated my sister," Tazek replied, "I shall tell you all that I know. Namim is quite indiscrete when we are alone." The boy's face reddened again. And then he changed, taking on a dark cast, a chronic fear. "Lord Nimrod's ambition is boundless," he breathed. His eyes darted toward Madai, unsure.

"What has that to do with me?"

The boy did not answer. He seemed to be calculating. "I know what little you think of me, but you should not suppose your strength will save you here. You shall be saved or lost at the will of one man. And he is a god."

Madai laughed aloud.

Tazek smiled disagreeably. "Laugh, kinsman. You do not know the Lord Nimrod."

Madai left the open balcony; he walked purposefully toward Tazek and sat opposite him at the table.

"What scares you, boy?" he asked unkindly.

Tazek jutted his face forward. "I was as you once," he breathed. He pulled his leg from under the table with his hand. "And got this."

Madai did not look at the leg.

"There is worse done to men here," Tazek continued, "to ones who serve Huwah."

It was the second time Madai had heard of the mysterious Huwah. "You are from The Family, Tazek. There is no god Huwah."

"You are correct, kinsman," Tazek replied. "His death has been accomplished. This is what I would tell you." Tazek pulled his leg back under the table. "Huwah was usurped by Nimrod at a great battle. He was killed atop the tower." He spoke with a tremor that suggested he believed what he was going to tell.

Madai was unmoved. "Who is the Huwah?"

"The God who struck the earth by water," Tazek answered simply.

Madai laughed again. "Empty deceit, boy. Man does not counter with God."

Tazek's expression was entirely serious. "You have not tasted Nimrod's power," he answered quietly.

The boy's terror was real. "Nimrod is no more than any other man," Madai asserted with a greater passion.

But Tazek shook his head, and Madai looked more carefully at him. His eyes spoke of fearsome memory. "This you would not say," Tazek warned, "had you better experience. Mind my words or no, but when you taste from his cup, you will know his power."

Tazek's fervency put a chill along the hairs of Madai's arms, and he was reminded of other powers, of those who sang new songs and crept away into the forest for other rites - and were able to intrigue him. Yes, he knew that power. Madai steadied himself; the power was false. Now he knew of certainty that Tazek was a danger. Surely the boy had lived too long here. He did not remember the sun, nor the true earth beneath his feet. He did not remember that all men bleed and die, even Nimrod. What sorcery was spilt upon his mind?

"I have killed a giant," Madai explained forcefully, "as great as Nimrod. His skin split by a wooden shaft. He spilt his life at my feet, and I took his own dagger to pierce his heart. I assure you, he did not expect to die that day. Nimrod is no more than he."

Tazek looked at him with sympathy. "Nimrod is more than a man," he repeated.

Madai continued to stare at him, expecting finally to see a rift in his certainty. But Tazek was entirely bewitched. "You know there is One God. No man will better Him," Madai insisted. And he did not feel like a sham saying it, because the boy needed to be reminded of who he had been, and The Family from whom he had come. It suddenly seemed terribly important to convince him.

But the boy would not concede it, and Madai leaned against the back of the chair, oddly disappointed. He looked out the window into the sky. "Tell me the defeat of Huwah, then," he asked. Perhaps it would be an advantage to know the tale.

Tazek nodded smugly. His thin mouth curved with rare satisfaction before he began. "Nimrod ascended the tower," he recited, "in the midst of a great storm, full of hail and darkness. Huwah was in the storm, and Nimrod met him and withstood him for murder, the weapon of water against the world.

"There was a darkness in this territory; the sun was wrapped up in a shroud. The people of the tower waited through the storm. Many perished by hail and lightening while Nimrod battled the Huwah."

Madai did not disguise a snicker, which Tazek ignored entirely, but to cast him a superior eye.

"The storm prevailed the whole of the day," he continued. "Till at evening, Nimrod descended. Not a hair of his head was lost, and Huwah was removed lifeless into the heavens by his few last servants." Tazek dared Madai to scoff with his own absolute belief. He continued in a low, droning voice, "So the spirits of heaven were free, and trusted their loyalty to the Lord Nimrod, as did the men of the earth. Those who would not were cast out and lost their souls and took the souls of beasts, which could not speak the tongues of men and scattered across the earth."

Madai chuckled openly. "An utter fable," he retorted. "Those who scattered were your kinsmen and mine. Had they the souls of beasts?"

As though Madai's logic were a very part of the truth, Tazek's energy grew and he pressed what seemed to him an advantage. "Yes, kinsman. And it was for this purpose we returned to the land of Shinar and the Lord Nimrod, though we did not understand it then. Those who return may redeem their souls from the Light of Heaven."

"Were you and Palada the price of your father's redemption?" Madai's cut was swift and cold.

Then he knew his folly. Tazek's eyes, which had wavered, steeled themselves to complete loathing.

"Only worship is required," he answered flatly.

Madai returned a steady gaze. Perhaps he should have salvaged an ally; perhaps it was too late already. "Tell me, Tazek," he asked instead, "by what marvel does Nimrod prove himself the Light of Heaven?"

Upon the asking of this last question, the door shook with the harsh thud of a guard's heavy hand. Namim's malodorous voice followed, and Tazek scurried to the door just as it opened. He bowed more deeply, as though Namim might somehow discern what blasphemy had been spoken.

"You are retained overlong," Namim indicted coolly. "I did not know your taste ran to swine." He reached out and ran his hand down the edge of Tazek's face. "Inform your kinsman," he pronounced the last word with dripping scorn, "the Lord Nimrod has requested his presence at the morning sacrifice - quite an honor."

Tazek had begun trembling at the first words from the man who was his master, and his voice was chilly when he translated the summons. The guard had stepped into the chamber with Namim, and there was nothing to do but obey. So Madai followed them in an opposite direction from that which he had come the day previous.

The corridor was lit by oil lamps, as no light of day penetrated the thick walls. Each pool of lamplight revealed a serpentine ribbon of painted figures embroiled in battle: beasts, men, spirits of heaven, perhaps. His swift march upon the tile of the floors forbade a closer perusal of the scenes, though he knew Nimrod was surely the victor, the impostor-god.

An opening of light shone at the end of the hallway, a door opening to their destination. They entered together, but Tazek did not speak to him again. Though it was a smaller room than where he had first seen the King of Shinar, this was large enough. No paintings decorated these walls. They were stark white, pristine, cold. But there was a dais. Upon it sat the man Nimrod, perched on another carved throne. Behind him five men stood, dressed in white from neck to hem, their heads shaved. Nimrod was covered this morning; gone was his garish vest, replaced by a robe of purest white, a stark backdrop for his great mass of coiled hair and burnished skin. All this was glimpsed in a flash, for Madai next realized that all but he were prostrate upon the floor. Madai maintained himself standing until a great crack sounded and a staff struck him against the back of his knees. It drove him to the ground, crumpling him in blind agony. He heard himself gasp and, for reason of the pain alone, laid his face upon the cool tile. A throaty bark commanded him in the tongue of Shinar, its meaning plain.

The soft triangle at the bend of his legs competed with the crack put upon the cap of his knees for pain. He feared he could not walk, should he be commanded, and from his bent posture he watched Namim rise with a sneer. The priest muttered something to Tazek before addressing his five subordinates.

Tazek suddenly insisted that Madai stand, a strident tone in his voice; and when Madai attempted it, he was grateful that he was not broken and did not belittle himself. He did, however, suffer the cruel discipline of the staff in rivulets of pain as far as the heels of his feet.

"You will not do that again," Tazek warned him.

Nimrod nodded benignly from his ornate chair and Namim came forward to stand just behind the throne, basking in the distinction. The five lesser men stepped carefully aside.

A long bench paralleled the walls of the room the full of its length.

Tazek bowed deeply before hissing at Madai, "Follow," leading him to sit on the end of the bench.

He remained standing, just behind Madai's ear. "This is a place of tribute, an honor," Tazek whispered. "You shall not cause me censure." Madai glanced up, perceiving that he was warned.

As at a silent command, a single line of other personages solemnly entered the room. Each planted his forehead to the tile floor. They were dressed in opulent finery, brightly colored and varied, men and women, young and old. Each seemed awed and pleased and important and afraid as they rose to greet the Lord with various prepared remarks. All, in turn, took their seats beside Madai on the bench. It was half filled.

It was just the turning from dawn to full light, early for such an assemblage of respected citizens. Madai felt cold, even as his hands dampened with sweat, but he kept his gaze casually set on the far wall. He heard rather than saw the approach of yet another group at the door. And then a rustle indicating they had prostrated themselves as well. He heard a slight scuffle, prompting a command from Nimrod, and looked up soon enough to see Kittim, standing alone amongst the flock of carefully bent folk. How it was managed, Madai didn't know, but it pleased him immeasurably that Kittim did not relent but simply walked to the bench upon which he, himself, sat, some twelve persons down. The simple audacity sent him chills and so joyous emotions to see his companion unharmed, he forgot the peril they now shared. He turned to catch the calm aspect of Kittim's eye, reading there a mutual feeling - and that steady confidence. Would they could speak.! The others, confused that Kittim was not punished, rose to their places, and the bench was filled.

Nimrod was darker yet, fury dissolving his man's features to something else, but he did not rebuke Kittim, nor did Namim. In a voice which was low, pregnant with contained ferocity, he commanded a guard standing at a door to his right. The heavy wood door opened with a sound of metallic release, and a huddle of large, partially clad men emerged. They were warriors, every one. This was evident to Madai though they had been robbed of their weapons. And this had not been done easily, for the wounds of a vicious battle were proclaimed on their bodies and marked each man at one part or another. Madai could not resist them; they radiated both power and disdain. One man was hoisted by his arms between two of his fellows; his head dangled. Another stood with his legs spread, blood dropping on the tiles between them, in stony calm. The man who glared into the face of Nimrod wore an expression of pure, remarkable hatred. A rip was torn in his flesh from his ear to his mouth. The blood trailed down his cheek and pooled in his hair. They were ten in all. Madai was proud of these men who were prisoners, proud of the strength that was not stolen from them.

Namim began to speak to the assemblage, his voice far less than dynamic beside the ten. Tazek, who stood behind Madai for purposes of translation, bent to quietly repeat the priest's words.

"These are the souls of beasts in the skin of men, and they are condemned for rebellions against the Great Light of Heaven," Tazek whispered. "The gods of earth and sky shall be fed by their blood on this day."

Those to whom this oracle applied growled in unison, giving no heed to the soldiers who handled their chains.

Madai willed his own strength into them, with an inexplicable desire to hurl himself at the guards for their defense. But he could feel the presence of Kittim through the twelve lumps of men who separated them. He could feel the restraint of his friend upon the impulse. He turned his head, hoping to read by his eyes what they might do to avert this massacre, but Kittim was veiled from sight by the line of men seated between them. The faces he saw upon the bench were masks of wary smiles. Sweat glistened on the skin of the man beside him.

Nimrod spoke. His words were clipped and loud, as though to pierce the prisoners, in whose direction he aimed his speech.

"Shemites," Tazek abbreviated Nimrod's rant. "Captured outside the city. They shall be skinned."

Madai shuddered reflexively. He glanced at the boy who had suffered Nimrod's whim to find no sympathy in his features for the prisoners. He thought of Kittim, wishing exceedingly to talk to his composed and careful companion, to devise a plan to free the brave captives. But the line of condemned men was being pushed back through the door, their judgment decided.

The friends supporting the unconscious man dropped him in the shuffle. He slumped to the ground with a moan and they hurried to lift him again, before the guards could react. Perhaps it was a diversion, but the warrior with the wound on his face hurled an invective toward the dais. Madai did not clearly hear it and could not have understood it if he had. But the man paid for the outburst dearly and, in the interim, the unconscious man was hefted through the doorway. Madai was proud of them all

When the prisoners were finally removed, an almost audible sigh was released from the audience seated beside him. Perhaps these worshipers of the Great Nimrod indeed had hearts of flesh.

There was another short speech from the ponderous King; Tazek explained it was a blessing; and these citizens, this honored 'court,' bowed their respectful gratitude as they each rose to leave, in part privileged, in part relieved. Kittim stood a head above them. He turned his deep eyes to penetrate the confusion of Madai's senses and put some calm there.

Bereft, Madai watched as his companion passed out of the hall once again. He heard Tazek's voice. He took a moment to control his face, and turned with a determined leisurely disdain, to find Nimrod smiling, calling him forward.

"Madai the Japhethite, welcome." Tazek translated frantically, "I am pleased by you. You will share the morning feast with me." He licked his lower lip slowly. "I am honored each turn of the moon to feed the gods."

Madai was not sure whether he meant to feed himself a sacrifice of Shemites - and his belly began to climb up his throat.

But a common food arrived. He watched a soft white sphere floating in cream come to rest before him, and a piece of flat bread, all of which it seemed he ate with a single bite. All of which, as well, carried no taste. Rather, Madai thought about Shemites, first sons of the second earth, and Nua. Great ironies of Madai's life, this was one.

And madness to be so close.

Above all else, Madai knew they must be rescued. Only it should take a god to find them and set them free. The One he knew did not seem to rescue His own. It was apparent to Madai that it would be done by human effort, if at all - and only upon his own escape, of course, and finding Kittim. Then he must discover where they were held. Perhaps Tazek would tell him.

All the while, Nimrod plied him with questions of The Family and what skills they used on the Brine Sea. What ships did they build? What beasts did they kill along the way? How great were their numbers? He asked after the beauty of their women, and did they match that of Shinar? Madai abandoned thinking about escape to answer Nimrod's questions carefully, walking a thin edge. He perceived Nimrod to be a man captivated by high tales and assuaged by flattery. The flattery

Madai could not quite bring himself to. Of high tales, he embellished quite a lot.

The morning seemed endless, with so much to plan, and he sensed that the Shemites' time was short. When Nimrod finally set his cup on the table a last time, Madai was greatly relieved, and sweating. Nimrod stood as quick as a swamp fly, with his attention shifted entirely. He seemed pleased by the meal, but required somewhere else.

"I wish another audience with my Japhethite friend," Nimrod said through Tazek. "Less formal, perhaps."

To all those present, it was a clear command and no simple invitation. He caught Nimrod's chilly gaze on the boy and vaguely regretted his own contribution to Tazek's trouble. Perhaps it was that he was of The Family, known now to Nimrod as admirers of Nua. Or perhaps it was only his relationship with Namim.

"You may attend the Japhethite in his chamber," Nimrod informed Tazek, though Madai did not understand. Tazek bowed stiffly in reply.

They all scrambled to stand as Nimrod left the hall. Namim cast a last look at the boy before following at his lord's heels.

ⰅⰒ   ⰅⰒ   ⰅⰒ

They were scarcely behind the heavy door of Madai's room when Tazek collapsed on the bed. He closed his eyes, his breathing so shallow that Madai bent to inspect him.

"It is well over," he said, intending to encourage the boy as much as speak to him.

Tazek opened his eyes slowly. "It is not well. And I am coupled with you now." He glowered at Madai resentfully.

Madai was not surprised. "This is then an unfortunate turn. Can not your Namim save you?"

Those of The Family can not disguise the rise of blood under pale skin. Tazek's blood rose rapidly. "Perhaps you do have the soul of a beast," he spat.

Madai laughed. "So you doubted it? Nimrod's spell was not complete."

Tazek shot a curse at him.

Madai laughed and went to the balcony. "Tell me about the Shemites." He insisted.

Tazek did not answer. So Madai turned to face him. The boy shrunk from the look on his face, but he rebounded when Madai picked up the lance, left so incomprehensibly in the room. Madai slowly raised it, resting it softly on the boy's chest, Tazek lifted his chin in defiance.

"Tell me of the Shemites," Madai repeated sternly.

Tazek's green eyes glittered. He seemed to consider the choices of skinning versus impaling... and began to speak with a voice that was cold. "There is a great company of them advancing toward Shinar. These were spies."

"What of skinning?"

"Does it offend you?" Tazek taunted. "The dragon slayer is afraid?"

Madai pushed the point gently into his skin, though not enough to draw blood. When the boy puffed his chest into the point, Madai was alarmed to consider that Tazek might prefer death. But the contest ended, Tazek's gaze fell, and he relaxed back onto the bed.

"They shall die at the change of the moon this night," he finally answered. "Rather, they shall begin to die."

Madai ignored the intended barb and repeated. "Where are they held?"

Tazek laughed, high-pitched, nearly hysterical.

"You are an attoyak," the boy cursed. "And that is worse than I am."

"Where are they kept?"

"Down there." Tazek jerked his head in the direction of the courtyard.

Madai withdrew the spear but took it with him to the ledge. It was midday, and the light was bright. The walls looked sheer and smooth.

"Where?"

Tazek rose from the bed. "All the holds open to the pit," he answered vaguely. "It could be any one of four."

- 50 -

Lemmeri was returned with little fanfare, though Marisheba kindly baked a favorite dish of sweets for the girl. The Lady was ill with the coming weather, taking to her bed and thus permitting a peaceful resolution to the entire affair. If Lemmeri sought the camel boys who venerated Sabta, it was not discovered. And she should have been disappointed in any case, for they had been sent to tend the flocks. If she resented her demotion to the kitchen, she did not show it. She quietly, if ungratefully, resumed her old position and cleaned the cooking pots, and the yams, and waited for the harvest when she would seed the grapes.

Job could not accompany them, as it was time to inspect the orchards and watch the clouds and pray that they would not spill their hail. But today the storms of harvest season seemed a distant and unlikely threat. Iscah was eager to return to the unconventional world Reenah had created at the river. Better prospects surely, without the sullen Lemmeri, though she felt a faint stab of guilt as they rode away, leaving Marisheba alone with the surly girl. A pleasant breeze soon blew even that away, and she chatted merrily with Tutan the whole distance.

"I am taking a real swim," Iscah pronounced as they neared the cottage. She drew a stiff piece of cloth from a bag tied at the saddle, "I have a garment special for it." She held it in the air.

Tutan smiled at her. "A good day to swim," he agreed. "Though I hope you shall not press me to join you."

"Why ever not, Tutan?"

He did not answer, and she looked up curiously. 'What have I said?' she wondered. She smiled uncertainly. "Was I disrespectful?" she asked aloud.

His eyes sparkled at her. "You are not disrespectful," he assured her, reaching to pat her hand.

"What will you do then?" she asked, "if you don't swim?"

"Study Lady Reenah's clay figures, perhaps," he answered, flushing slightly.

Iscah noticed the reddened skin and looked at him more closely, noticing his dark hair which was just slightly streaked with white and the lines at his eyes and mouth, which could be signs of sun and smiling, rather than age. She had seen flushed faces before, after all, but she would not consider it. How well she admired Tutan, loved him, with his devotion to the One God. No, she would not consider it.

σα σα σα

When they arrived at the cottage, Reenah seemed to be waiting. In truth, there was the aroma of bread freshly baked drifting from her open door. And she was standing there, a great fresh smile on her mouth.

"I hoped it would be today," she effused. She reached to take Iscah's bridle. "What plans I have made for us! All my work is finished for this season, and I have fairly reproached each day for its slowness." She laughed as she drew Iscah into the cottage. "Pray, you are hungry. This bread is just finished and," she smiled rather generously at Tutan, "this last honey is taken from the meadow. How is Uncle?"

It sounded to Iscah, watching Reenah flush, as if this last was said as an afterthought. Iscah put it down on a tally of regrettable flushes.

"He is testing and tasting the grapes," Tutan answered. "The caravans have not returned, and I suspect we shall soon learn the art of making wine."

Iscah abruptly uncrinkled her brow and suggested excitedly, "Perhaps Kittim and Madai shall return by then!"

"Perhaps," he agreed, "though you must not grow impatient. The ship of Noah must sit atop a very great mountain."

She put her finger in the honey, freshly annoyed at being left behind.

"It is a very high mountain," Reenah agreed.

"How do you know about that?" Iscah asked, looking up.

"I have seen it."

Tutan looked as surprised as Iscah felt. "Why did you not speak of it before?" he asked in a mildly perturbed voice.

"I didn't know they were seeking the ship!" Reenah retorted, sounding stung. "You spoke of ancients, or some such."

"Ah," Tutan replied more gently, "perhaps it was not discussed...."

"Why does it matter?" Iscah interrupted impatiently. "Tell us about the ship."

Reenah peered coolly at Tutan. "Very little to tell. My father took a few camels to bring relics, and I was with him. I was a child. We took some wood," she laughed. "To sell for good fortune. We might have spared ourselves the trip, for it could have been from any forest. But we packed it up and brought it back.

"Father later sold amulets made from more easily retrieved wood, but by then the want for it was gone."

"Tell us about the ship!" Iscah insisted, carefully ignoring the hint of fraud.

"Large, very large. I was a child, you know. And it was dark inside. My voice answered me when I called out."

"But it is there," Tutan insisted.

She turned dark eyes toward him, relenting slightly. "It is there," she answered.

Iscah had not decided whether she was pleased or angered by Reenah's tale. Certainly she was jealous, and Reenah so nonchalant. She, herself, would certainly have admired the ship for what it was. Iscah handily ignored her aversion to Shinar and grumbled again about being left behind.

Tutan smiled at her and gave her a warm crust of honey bread. Then he spoke a blessing over all company present, and thanks for the food. The honey was sweet on Iscah's tongue. She allowed her ruffles to quiet down and, after a time, forgot to be annoyed.

Tutan inquired after the honey again. A more tiresome topic Iscah could not imagine, and she imagined instead the moment of Kittim and Madai's return. It troubled her that she could not remember the faces of her mother and father; the dreams that brought her the sound of their voices had ceased nearly altogether. Moreover, Job had inquired, and her father's little band with their flocks was not known. There was only one family to which she belonged now, them who had saved her. She would follow them when they returned and she would be to Kittim whatever he desired.

෪෬ ෪෬ ෪෬

Tutan watched as Iscah nibbled her bread in silence. Her expression now was one he loved. No doubt she gained peace here at this cool spot on the river, this orphaned child. Perhaps solace was got here by their fellowship. His gaze wandered to Reenah. What a gloriously striking credit to the One who made her! He let his eyes study the black hair which waved loose down her back today. That design of henna was covered. And how agile were her hands as they lifted the cup to her mouth - which was where he stopped. He knew that should her eyes turn toward him they would witness the color which he felt hot on his face. Whatever was he thinking? He felt as he had when first he had admired Enico. And he an old man... or, perhaps not quite old yet.

Others had laid their rice at his door after the passage of a respectful time. But Enico's grip on his heart was eternal, and he had, with finality, pledged his life to the One True God. What mockery then, this - and Reenah a reluctant believer at best. More likely, a follower of many gods. He could not bring himself to think she worshiped them.

He refocused his eyes, for Reenah's face had turned to a blur. Quickly he looked down at the top of the smoothly rubbed table and began to chew his bread. But the honey she had liberally spread it with only brought him back to her. He hoped they wouldn't notice. Their happy chatter told him that perhaps they had not.

- *51* -

The shadows of the afternoon were long, and the air was chilled. Iscah glanced at the second garment she had brought for swimming, and wondered whether the water would be too cold. There was also the matter of Noah's ship. Should she swim, or should she talk? Conversation could be both boring and entertaining...

"I have remembered your shallow at the river," she began tentatively.

"Do you want a swim?" Reenah responded.

Tutan knew this was an activity he could not risk, and Reenah was turning toward him.

She gaily laughed. "Tutan looks as though he were putting his hand in a fire-pit." She pulled her hair into a ball and tucked the ends into the center. "Perhaps you are modest," she teased.

He quieted himself and slowly shook his head with a meek smile. "I fear the water is cold," he explained. "And my bones shall regret it."

Iscah studied him skeptically, knowing his bones did not complain. She had seen his face kind, had seen it tired, had seen it joyous - she had never seen it like this. So it was true. She would ask him to explain consecrated again.

"Perhaps it is over-cold," Iscah quickly amended.

Reenah smiled. "This day is for your pleasure," she assured Iscah. "Whatever you wish, it shall be. The leopard and her kits are gone; Uncle has managed that. Perhaps you want to visit the sand bar again, or we may climb to the platforms. The nests are empty, but the view is uncommon." She waited,

"Or perhaps we may shape creatures of mud, as on Uncle's wall. I find good pleasure in this, when the weather is close."

"Good pleasure is had by good companions," Tutan replied. "Iscah, it is yours to choose."

"Let us make creatures of mud," Iscah suggested, looking wryly at Reenah, "and speak more of Noah's ship."

Reenah grinned. "So we shall," she agreed, rising to scoop clay from a large stone jar set in a dim corner. "If you would stoke the fire, Iscah?" she asked. "I crave a cup of ale."

രുൽ രുൽ രുൽ

A rather lovely goblet was forming beneath Reenah's quick fingers, while Iscah pushed and pulled a great behemoth to life. Tutan tended the beer till Iscah urged him remove it from the fire and take a piece of clay. She was, in good time, delighted at his delicate ability and the graceful wings of his little bird.

"This may break in the fire," Reenah instructed, reaching toward the object in Tutan's hands. She took it gently, studying its every side. "Pity," she murmured. "It is beautiful. But it is too delicate."

He took it from her, touching her with his fingertips as he did. "Perhaps you are correct," he agreed. He took a small bit of clay and pressed it under each wing, smoothing it artfully into the body. It was not so fragile now, and the grace was not lost. "Will it hold?" he asked Reenah.

"We can only try," she answered, smiling. "It is only mud. If it is lost, we shall start again."

Tutan was unduly warm at the intimation of "we" and felt foolish. But he held her gaze until she looked away.

"Or we may continue our discussion of philosophies," he suggested cautiously.

At this, she shook her head. So lovely a day to spoil. "Indeed, or perhaps the ship of Noah, Iscah? What think you?"

"Noah. Certainly," the girl answered.

52

Tazek lay on the bed, asleep – or feigning it. Either way, Madai cared not at all. He was listening to the leopards. He was watching them pace and growl and spit, snarling over the last scraps of meat on just a very few bones. Nimrod liked keeping them hungry. There were three animals in the enclosure; the brush was dense, and the ground covered by tall, dry grass. An excellent place to hide

Somewhere, within those thick brick walls, Madai knew, ten men were imprisoned. The sun was not gone, would not be for many hours more, and so they were saved till then. Madai had devised a plan, one which held good promise for the luck of the irregular bricks scaling the far wall.

He felt obsessed by the Shemites. They were nobles, enemies to his enemy. They carried the name of the son of Nua and surely did not deserve the end with which they were threatened. He would search out the holds, if the cats would give him time. If Kittim were only here... Madai was suddenly struck with the wild hope that Kittim might already have planned a rescue. He had witnessed, after all, their valor, and knew their sentence as well as he did. Madai felt buoyed by the possibility. Kittim, who despised evil and was completely wise, had an uncanny ability at times.

Madai bent his knees, crouched to the ground and stood again, and repeated the exercise until his legs burned from the abuse of the soldier's staff against them. He was insisting by the strength of his mind that his legs do what he needed them to.

A scrape at the heavy wood door interrupted him as it pushed open with a labored groan. He would have groaned as well.

"You," Namim growled, "Japhethite." This last word Madai understood. Tazek sat up. So... he had not been asleep. He leapt from the bed and prostrated himself on the ground. Then he touched Namim's feet with an indecent intimacy.

"Do not discard me," he pleaded.

Namim was haughty, but he was also moved. His reply was not so harsh and Tazek scrambled up.

"Come," he commanded Madai. As they left the room, Tazek kept so close to

Namim they might have been a creature of two heads, and he avoided even a glance behind at Madai.

CℨCℛ   CℨCℛ   CℨCℛ

It was to be another appearance at Nimrod's command. Madai felt his heart racing, the day slipping away and the new moon coming nearer. And he was calculating the cost of refusing to bow. What would be the effect of another staff against his legs? Would they carry him safely off the ledge and then up the wall? Perhaps obedience would not be an act of worship, all things considered. Compromise was something he had done before, he finally decided. So he would do it again, for the greater good.

This chamber was entirely different. Gone were the trappings of nobility. In its place was a stark little cavity, nearly the quarters of a soldier, and Nimrod sitting at a rather ordinary table. The lord looked up as the door opened, his eyes widening in pleasure. Madai actually believed he was sketching a picture upon a wafer-thin parchment. Namim and Tazek crumpled to the floor and Madai was prepared to do the same. But Nimrod lifted a hand to him and spoke a mild-sounding few words. Tazek looked up, confused.

"I am well pleased to see you, Madai," he had said.

He turned the parchment on the table and pushed it toward Madai. There was the semblance of a dragon sketched on it; in truth, a well-done likeness.

"What do you think?" Nimrod asked. "Is it rendered as the beast you killed?"

Madai looked down at it, stretching the time, for the change in Nimrod's manner was disorienting. "Very like," he finally responded. "Only, there was a crest..." Madai put his finger on the crown of the serpent.

"Ah, interesting." Nimrod sketched again. "Yes?" he asked.

"No.... longer, from the head and a little down the back of the neck."

Nimrod altered the drawing.

"Just that," Madai confirmed.

Nimrod studied it for a moment. "A different brood," he decided. "The head is ridged above the eye in these that lived once in Shinar. Beyond that, they had a very snake-like head."

"Fire beasts in Shinar?" Madai asked.

Nimrod's mouth turned up at one corner in a friendly smile. "I am casting them out," he replied proudly. "They were grievous among the peoples here, mountain areas unapproachable. There is only a wild place that remains, a breeding ground which I shall lay waste before the snows." He looked at Madai with a winsome expression. "I should be inspired with you at my side."

Madai did not know how to answer. Was this the same skinner of men?

Ah, but the men, the Shemites. Very important men to Madai. He looked back at the king... dressed like a warrior with a quill in his hand. Madai nodded ambiguously, guarding his thoughts, and looked at Nimrod's dragon again. A detailed portrait created from the eyes of experience and close inspection. Nimrod was, indeed, a great hunter, as all the murals declared.

"What of the skin, its aspect and the color?" Nimrod pursued him further, noting and approving Madai's inspection of his drawing.

"Smooth scales, as a snake, yet stout enough to break my spear shaft." Nimrod was nodding as Madai described it. "My arrows were cast away as drops of rain."

"The color?"

"Green... gray... it shimmered in the light, like a rainbow. It had, I remember it plainly, a streak of red from its eyes to its nostrils. It might be called handsome."

Nimrod was pleased. "Beautiful and deadly," he agreed.

Madai nodded and studied Nimrod with a wary eye, only to see that his asking after the dragon's description was sincere. The King looked from the parchment to Madai's face with a certain comradely air and Madai felt himself respond to it.

This, Nimrod noted and he pushed himself away from the table to rise. His great size was striking as Madai stood at close proximity, certainly eight, perhaps nine feet in height. He was no less than a head taller than Madai himself. His arms were round as a young terebinth and lined with thick sinew.

"I wish to show you something," Nimrod said as he crossed the room.

Then Madai saw The Family's Spear, cradled in the antlers of a stag set upon the wall. Nimrod lifted it down. It was smaller in his hands.

"It was received from the hand of an insignificant who said it was got from a great man in battle, by name of Madai." Nimrod smiled derisively. "I do not entirely believe the account."

Madai looked at the Spear. It possessed the same straight, smooth shaft, carved round in the pattern of a serpent. It was fitted with the forged, five- pronged lance. It was deadly, especially in the hands of the one who held it now. Madai knew it had found the place of its origin, in a land of secret powers and darkness, as Job had warned. Suddenly, the Spear had assisted him in a way he would not have thought; for here in his private quarters, Madai was drawn toward Nimrod, Nimrod the hunter. The Spear had reminded him of Nimrod the sorcerer.

"Sabta is a thief who skulks about in the darkness," Madai replied.

Nimrod acknowledged the fact with an amused half-smile. "Though his account of the man from whom the Spear was stolen, was correct," Nimrod asserted, casting a respectful glance toward Madai.

The camaraderie once again. Madai could not resist the sharp prick of pride as Nimrod placed the Spear into his hands, a bold and unexpected gesture.

"Show me the secret," the lord requested.

Madai knew precisely his meaning. Without hesitation, he ran his finger along the grooved shaft and released the spearhead with a click. Nimrod smiled.

"That was done quickly," he admired. "Able craftsmanship." He looked from the Spear to Madai's face. "How is it made?"

"This I do not know. The skill is forgotten."

"Pity," Nimrod responded.

"Indeed," Madai agreed, handing it back to Nimrod.

The lord examined the Spearhead, pushed it back in place, and located the thin groove Madai had used. He ran his finger up and down it gingerly, then he released the catch. "It is the more dear if it can not be built again," he observed, casually replacing it on the wall. He turned to face Madai and spoke frankly. "We shall see to whom you pledge yourself. Then perhaps I shall return it to you."

Then Nimrod smiled - and it was sincere. Madai did not reply. The prospect was clear, as was the bait.

In the silence that followed, Namim cleared his throat. Madai realized they both had forgotten the priest. Nimrod glanced out the open window and answered Namim with a tone sounding, to Madai, a lot like irritation.

"I must prepare for the evening sacrifice," Nimrod told Madai through Tazek. "Much cleansing is required. It is a propitious occasion, as enemies of the gods shall be used. And if the signs are favorable, it may restore their souls."

He studied Madai's face. His own expression had gone vaguely sinister, a transformation of startling design, and Nimrod continued with a calculating voice, "This night's sacrifice is auspicious. Perhaps, should the gods approve, you shall be witness to it."

Madai did not flinch. He stood quietly and prayed that his face be vague.

"You shall be sent for," Nimrod instructed.

With that, the guard returned him to the comforts of his cell.

ଓଞ୍ଚ ଓଞ୍ଚ ଓଞ୍ଚ

Namim and Tazek had not left with him, and Madai was a jumble of perception and calculation: the placement of the cats, the depth of the niches in the far wall, the character of a changeable lord. He could hear the leopards fighting below as he waited in the center of his quarters, waiting for Nimrod's next summons - but alone at last. The Shemites weighed heavily on his heart, and he began to doubt his first hope, that Kittim was free and would achieve their escape. Somehow, being with Nimrod had robbed his optimism.

The Shemites were kept in holds facing the courtyard, if Tazek were to be believed. Perhaps Kittim was there, as well. Madai looked at the distance to the ground, and the leopards, determined to set about his plan. Whatever the outcome, he would not be witness to a slaughter. He could not restrain himself and should likely be skinned himself. And if he should fail at this, it would be to the leopards, a prospect entirely more tolerable.

Madai snatched the heavy wool curtain from the doorway. He took the lance and pierced the fabric through, then he wrapped it loosely around the spearhead. He assessed the drop and the position of the leopards. They were pacing, waiting for the next meal. He knew the distance could break his leg; when, indeed, the leopards would be fed.

As the shadows lengthened, he studied the walls beyond his balcony for the exact location of the uneven bricks. He gauged their depth by the shadows, deftly certain that he could do it, supposing he outwitted the cats. There was oil in the lamp, quite a lot. He took it to the edge and poured just a puddle of oil onto the curtain wrapping his lance and set it ablaze. The wool smoked but did not burst into flame, only just the one spot where he lit it first. He leaned over, and purposely aimed the lance at the ground.

He felt his heart thudding as the fire was almost snuffed out in the dust; but the oil revived it, and it came to life again. His shirt was wet. He bent his knees again, pleased that the pain was better. The leopards were in view, curious and looking up at him. But they had also smelled the fire and were cautious enough to remain where they stood. Madai lowered himself, gripping the ledge with his hands, and dangled his full seven feet, plus the addition of his arm's length, over the edge. He ignored the cats as they began to snarl in the background, for he was fully focused on the fall below him. He relaxed his leg muscles as well as he could and let go.

eenah had just put the clay creations into a fire-pit outside the cottage which had been designed for this purpose. "They shall remain the whole of the night," she informed them. "It is ever difficult to wait." She finished with a liberal smile. Then she pushed more wood into the mouth of the blaze, and rolled a clay lid into place, closing the fire in, save the air vents at the top. The night had chilled considerably; when they left the surround of the kiln to hurry inside, they felt it.

"It has grown late," Tutan observed. "I fear we have stayed overlong."

"Precisely," Reenah delighted. "I shall get us a warm drink and you must keep here tonight."

"It was not planned," Tutan argued. "Job will trouble himself for us."

She smiled and shook her head. "Job himself has remained the whole of the night occasionally, with his manservant, of course," she hastened to add, noting Tutan's surprise. "Indeed Uncle is exceedingly vigilant, lest he create even the illusion of misconduct. A reverence for his God, no doubt."

Iscah clapped her hands. "O, will we?" she pleaded. "It will only wake the house if we return."

Tutan looked at their two faces. Merriment was there, and he relented. When his eyes had just revealed the decision, a fierce gale suddenly blew upon the cottage from the desert, pelting it with the sharp edge of sand. It seemed providential, and he was rightly relieved that they would not venture out into the night.

"Ah," Reenah observed, "now, indeed, Uncle shall not expect you."

Tutan nodded, and Reenah began to put bread on the table again. She peered into a pot of boiling water and removed it from the fire to ready it for leaves of green tea brought from the caravans. She was so pleased that these two would share her table and warm her home this night. So many nights, when the winds howled, the solitude was nearly an ache. How she still mourned her father, the one person who had loved her, save Uncle. Not love enough for the whole of a lifetime.

"You shall tell us more of Noah's boat?" Iscah asked, never quite satisfied, "You have told me nothing, really, but that it is great."

Reenah left the fire to sit at the table, bringing the pot of water. She took the leaves of tea from a sack and began to gently submerge them. "Will you bring the honey, Iscah?" she asked as she covered the pot again with a round lid of forged tin and copper.

"The great ship," Reenah mused. "It was so long ago.... It had a distinct odor," she began to remember. "Odd, as I recall, for it was so long ago built. It was really dark. We came in by way of a small opening, very far up. These openings gave us our only light. There was nothing at all remaining upon the floor, no grass," she smiled, "no animal dung."

"What of rooms?" Iscah asked.

"No, not precisely, levels, rather," Reenah clarified, "though there might have been cages. I put my head through a break in the floor where a ladder might have been, though it was gone, while Father was hacking at the timbers. He soon called me back. Regardless, I could see not a thing in the dark. And that was all."

Iscah was hugely disappointed. "Were there people?" she dared to ask.

"Noah and his sons?" Reenah enunciated.

Iscah nodded timidly.

"Dear child," she murmured, "the sons were scattered, as was all humankind, and Noah, is certainly dead."

Iscah was mildly annoyed. Why should Reenah scoff, and call her 'dear child?' It sounded more patronizing than when it came from Tutan's mouth. She glanced at Tutan, finding him totally engrossed.

"I nearly wish I had gone with them," he muttered.

"I, as well," Iscah affirmed.

Reenah smiled as she poured their tea. "A great adventure," she agreed. "Though if the boat remains there this day, it shall be next year, as well."

Iscah did not wish to be easily assuaged, but Tutan nodded eagerly, taking his cup, reminding himself he did not need Eden to reach The One God after all... but he should like to see the ship of Noah, anyway.

They sipped their tea and listened to the wind howl. Iscah laughed at the monkey story Reenah told them and eventually forgave her the use of 'dear child.' She pried Reenah for a glimpse of the smells and wonders of the East and lay on Reenah's mat to hear them. Something about great, tall, black women clothed in splendid color was just about the last part of the story she heard.

Still, the sand blew against the cottage, the storm blotting out the stars in the heavens. Reenah lit another lamp, then came to sit at the table again, facing Tutan.

"Perhaps you are tired, as well," he began.

"I should rather speak with you more; little chance is had for it, above all, on such a ferocious night as this."

"How does she sleep in this?" Tutan asked.

Reenah looked Iscah's way and faintly smiled. "Do you not remember how simple it once was?" she asked him. "I sometimes wander about the cottage, even the river's edge, if the moon is whole, for want of sleep."

"There is danger in the night." he warned her.

"I do carry a torch," she assured. "And I do not go far. Cats see well in the dark."

"You are quite a fearless woman," Tutan remarked.

She felt herself blushing like a girl. "Perhaps," she laughed. "I was fathered by a fearless man."

"Just so," he agreed. "Whom you greatly loved, and greatly miss."

She nodded. "He was the grandest of men in my eyes. It was he who gave me the love of all things which fly. Even the le'abwat, winged serpent," she clarified. "It was a quest for this creature that killed him."

"So you pursue winged creatures of a gentler kind."

She smiled again, amused at his joke, though her eyes were tired. "Precisely," she agreed.

"Exquisite creatures," Tutan replied. "A testimony to His more delicate ability and His love for beauty in yet the smallest detail." He looked at the niche on Reenah's wall where the yellow little bird had come to perch out of the storm. "You know this better than I, how their wings flutter and they fly for the first time. The first time... Do you know what that means, Reenah?"

She looked into Tutan's animated face, certain she did not know what the dusky man wanted her to say.

"It means He put it in them, in their little bones and feathers, in their very beating hearts. They simply.... fly.... out of all they know into what they know not, because they are called," Tutan instructed earnestly, anxiously.

Certainly this had been the vein into which she had feared he would stray. "By this you speak of Job's God?" she asked reluctantly.

"Precisely. The Creator."

"There are as many creations as there are peoples."

Tutan scoffed. "I have traveled, too. The soul of man leaps from the mouth of a crocodile, or a great red frog from the murky Euphrates. What wisdom is that?"

Reenah shrugged, then laughed. "Rather ridiculous, perhaps," she granted.

Tutan was j encouraged when she added, "But can you tell me, Tutan, who has spoken with this God to ask how we were made, or why? And who can say that He is beyond and more than any other god?"

"Does not Job?" Tutan asked. He waited and watched her face to see if she lent Job enough credence to be believed. When he saw that she was not convinced, he was nearly persuaded to tell about his own interludes, the heavy, vibrant moments when the air itself was pregnant. But she stopped his tongue with a sardonic smile.

"He does," she answered, thinking of Job. "But men of the Euphrates are spoken to as well in such ways. Who is to tell them that the god they hear is not god at all?" She was watching Tutan with an uncomfortable glitter in her black eyes. "And why should Job not worship a God Who provides him so well? Why would he not?"

It was the first time he had heard her speak with even a hint of derision regarding the good man. In this, he knew a soul that did not commune with the True God was a vulnerable soul to all that is not holy. Her splendid beauty, her liberal spirit, her gifted hands which mirrored those of a Creator, her vibrant laugh - all a dangerous enticement. He suddenly wanted to touch her skin, not as a man with simple desire, but rather with awe of her beauty. She was the exquisite daughter of God... and she did not believe it.

Instead, it was she who reached across the table, sensing the emotion in Tutan's face, and put her fingers gently on his hand. A familiar loneliness was creeping upon her, and she wished to quiet it. "It is long since I have had a man through the night," she murmured involuntarily, and flushed, and hastily stammered, "O, Tutan...I do not mean in that way." She looked down, pinching off the prick she felt for a half- truth. "Only," she felt herself shudder, "this storm...I am glad I am not alone through it." She looked at him again. "And I do gain solace in speaking of such things as gods. We are... so alone on the earth... "

Tutan could feel the tops of his ears grow hot, heated by what she had first suggested and then withdrawn. Truth be told, it was a possibility that had briefly whipped his heart against his ribs. But he forced himself to listen to her words. It did what was necessary to tune his awareness toward her and her deepest need.

"I know I am forward," she stammered, seeing his first reaction, "and you are exceedingly modest." She stopped herself.

"No, Reenah. I am a man as any other. But there is a God in heaven. We are not alone on the earth."

Again the wind howled, like a hungry animal, and the constant scraping of sand against the walls of the cottage caused her to shiver again. She thought it a blow of such force as she had not heard before. She looked at the door to see if it were strong enough and back at Tutan, most unwilling to pursue the solitude of sleep. "Tell me how you know of such a certainty," she said with as much sincerity as her look suggested.

'Ahh,' he felt the relief of familiar footing. "I took the caravans merely to bring me here. It was providential that I came upon my three friends, for the caravan was slaughtered and plundered by marauders, giants. My purpose was to seek a place."

"Marauders?" she asked.

He tipped his hand at the air. "Yes, grievous. And I do not make light of it. But I was saved and come upon by Kittim and Madai to seek a great Truth."

"The ship of Noah?"

Tutan shook his head.

She frowned. "Did you find it, then?" she asked.

"Indeed," he answered. "I found it."

"What?" She asked as though she might believe him.

"The One True God," he answered with a wry smile.

Reenah stared. He believed it himself, but she was greatly disappointed to find that it was only words. Words from sincere lips, but only words. And it could not be 'a god' he had found, but it was 'the One True God.'

Tutan watched as her face fell nearly imperceptibly. It was a face of enormous importance to him. O, to prove her the truth. He thought about the Hsai writings with a surge of hope; she admired knowledge.

"You yearn for truth, do you not, Reenah?" he dared ask.

She felt a heavy weariness begin to fold itself around her and didn't answer. Indeed, the shadows fell across her face, deepening the darkness under her eyes in a way that aged her.

"Whose truth?" she finally responded.

He started to say something that likely would have sounded foolish in the growing atmosphere, but she lifted her eyes to his and looked afraid. "I feel it, don't you?" she asked.

He was stunned. "What?" he asked as quietly as she had spoken.

"The darkness," she whispered.

And when she said it, it seemed to swarm the cottage.

She trembled again and visibly shook herself. "Stuff of fable... I sound like a superstitious camel boy," she scoffed. Then she put her hands on the table, folded them and straightened her back. "I do not want fables tonight, or such things as cannot be known."

Tutan was mesmerized by her. He wanted to reach out and wrap her in his own certainty, to protect her from everything that haunted her. A futile impulse, he knew. Faith cannot be lent.

"Truth is important," he finally said, searching out a way to help her. "What else do we do with our years?"

He watched some thought cross her face before she looked away.

"Have you ever wakened from a dream, be it terrible or not, and believed it was true for a breath of a moment?" he asked.

"Certainly."

"Have you dreamed a dream so wondrous you yearned for the night to live it again? And then dreamt it... Only... does its lie carry you through the waking?"

"Then sleep," she suggested with a terrible smile.

"You of all people do not want to sleep, Reenah. You want to live."

She looked down; her smile evaporated. "Yes," she murmured. "So, I ask you again, how will truth be proved?" Her voice was a challenge.

"I say it may be concluded."

"And how is that?"

"Your mind and your spirit," he answered.

At this, she smiled in her flourishing way, and she tapped her finger on the table, "Did I not instruct that we speak no more of fables?"

"Your thoughts are not fables, nor are the spirits. And the spirits frighten you," he dared to add.

She lifted her brows slightly. "I said nothing."

Tutan answered as though he did not hear her. "There is what must be chosen at the end of all reason. It is God within us. Not so the beasts. It is reason alone which I may instruct you. At the end, the judgment shall always remain yours." He was suddenly aware of a throbbing, a drumming in his ears, as unrelenting as the storm outside.

"I agree, certainly," she answered. "One will not be forced; surrender in the face of force is just a pretense."

As he grew tired, she seemed to revive; and Tutan began to feel the difference of years between them. Perhaps it was not the night to press the Hsai writings upon her.

She went to the fire and lifted the tea. She brought back two cups and he was grateful, because he did not really want the night to end. She poured for him and drizzled in some honey. It was warm in his hands like a consolation.

"Tell me your adventures," he heard himself say, feeling an aggravated conscience that he was letting slip by a fragile moment when she might have been persuaded.

Her smile was the reward. "Yes," she agreed. "It is a noisy night with the wind, and too late for gods and such."

Reenah felt reprieved; the night would not end, and the differences between them were avoided. She sipped her tea and tapped her finger softly against the table, recalling the younger years and the daring roads.

"I had an excellent father," she began with a sentimental smile. "I traveled a great many roads with him, to far places. He was a lover of knowledge, as you, Tutan." She lifted her eyes in a disarming way. "I learned the languages of many peoples. There was a yellow-haired lady once, like Madai, who kept my father's bed for a time. She stayed with us a long time and I learned her speech. Father wept when she died, and so did I.

"I am told my mother was a Cushite, not wed to my father at all. I suspect Job's lady has a good deal to disapprove. But I did not suffer from want of love with Father. And the great adventures and grand peoples and marvelous places - It was a splendid time."

Tutan heard the beginnings of her story with mild shock, watching her eyes sparkle again as she recalled a childhood unmarked by any sort of acceptable behavior. He felt the difference between them grow as the distance between them disappeared.

"I was, enticed by the wonders, you see," Reenah continued. "And educated by societies of people. All the varied tongues, the names and habits of exotic beasts, both fiercesome and tamed; even the skill of making the marks of words upon clay at Shinar - everything was possible, everything. I believed that if I wished it, I might fly." She blushed. "That was, of course, a wild fancy. But my father, excellent man, made me believe I could do whatever I set about to do."

She put her hand unconsciously over his again. His hand was pulsing wildly.

"By which I was well served, as I knew no fear nor any foreign place. It was all a grand earth." She was wildly aware of Tutan, his hand with hers on the table. She nearly felt young again.

But he was devout, like Job, and her first budding joy began to shrivel. He had spoken of truth with such a certainty. He was truly an innocent, living a life of cloister and narrow margins. It angered her, unreasonably, and then, with an inexplicable chill, she decided to see just how much he really loved the truth.

She smiled, watching for the flicker of change in his eyes. "I was young, and gay, and rather comely," she announced, "when we met a young officer from Nimrod's army, a youth, really. Very beautiful and brave. Father admired him. So he shared our tent for a time. He and Father's lady." She examined Tutan's face.

"It is scandalous in your eyes, dear Tutan," she continued. "I loved him fiercely. And he, quite naturally, loved many a woman in many an outpost, and one day he did not return. I suppose he did not love me as well as I loved him. I don't know what came of him." She looked steadily at Tutan. "I have needed no man since, save a night or two. And when Father was killed, I proved it to all who cared to notice. I enlarged Father's trade and passed many a year amongst the caravans, collecting fat little gods from everywhere," she waved her arm to indicate the statues placed about on her walls. "I put aside a goodly amount of gold. And I never loved another man. Except, of course, Uncle, who was Father's great friend - though I do not know why." She paused, shocked by what she had said. "But Uncle built this house for me upon his own land when Father died and guarded my gold as long as I traded amongst the caravans." She finished the story with a rise in her voice, enough to cover the trepidation she felt at having told it all.

Silence filled the cottage at the conclusion of her speech.

"Then why are you here?" Tutan finally asked. "If it was a life you loved so much?" He felt decimated by her.

She smiled, and pulled her hair across her shoulders in a most alluring way, holding it in the light of the lamp for him to see its signs of age. "Do you see the silver?" she asked.

Indeed, it glimmered. It was uncommonly beautiful. Tutan looked at her eyes again. They seemed to dare him.

"I was wed," he suddenly declared. "It was in the first new spring of my own manhood...Enico...A poet and an artist, an exquisite maiden. It was arranged, and never regretted."

Reenah felt oddly chastised. It was not that he had wed and she had not; it was that she had hoped to hurt him and did not know why. But she was not surprised he had loved; had she not read passion in his face before?

A wry smile, still vaguely melancholy, bent his lips. "A flood," Tutan continued ironically. "She was killed in a flood, before my very eyes."

Reenah stroked his hand unconsciously. He was a poet too, she thought. She read the exotic East in his face and thought perhaps it was only this that charmed her. But she would be no fool. She knew he bent at the feet of a very jealous God.

- 54 -

It took no time for Madai to feel the ground strike his feet. The muscles of his legs strove to maintain him there, crouched but upright. He could not fall for fear of twisting a knee or sprawling in the dust, convenient for a hungry leopard. He quickly grabbed up his spear, still wrapped with the curtain that was now fairly engulfed in flame. He pointed the burning rag at the snarling animals. In his periphery was the first hold. A timber was simply laid across to bar it shut. Madai edged his way there, holding back the leopards with the fire.

His fingers touched a large timber. It would take both his hands. Still, in the face of bristling cats, he was suddenly unafraid. As when the hunt was on, he felt powerful, indestructible, suddenly free. And the hunt was not just for leopards; it was for brave, imprisoned Shemites somewhere behind these doors. Then he would find Kittim. He flashed his spear at the cats with a loud shout. They recoiled and he dropped the spear to free a hand and lift the bar in one motion. He pushed it open to a dank, tiny cell, no greater in size than five feet square. The waning light of the sun exposed every corner.

Escaping from the little place was an enormous smell, and huddled in the corner was a man of indiscernible age, shielding himself from the light. Blood stained his rotted rags with a red streak all down his front, starting at his mouth. Madai reached in for the pitiful creature, who shrieked at him from a sunken chest and babbled incomprehensibly. Madai looked at the wrist he held in his hand – a bone draped with mottled, brittle skin. He had a sudden vision of pulling at the man and taking away only the arm. The man's eyes rolled with terror, and Madai knew it was a hopeless cause. He had an unpleasant impulse to drive his spear into the fluttering heart as a mercy. Instead, he flung the door shut and barred it with the timber.

Cold sweat oozed from his skin. He was covered in the smell. The leopards smelled it, too, and were inching their way close again. He fled the hold in a few quick paces, gripping his spear with sweaty hands. The leopards were distracted behind him, spitting and snarling at the door that kept the shriveled creature alive.

The second door was secured in the same way as the first. Madai didn't turn his back to the cats this time, as they had circled, discouraged only for the moment by his fire. They had tested the first cell with its man-smell and found it impenetrable. He lifted the timber with one hand, his back to the wall. Doubly hard to do it that way, bracing against the wall and pushing up, but he finally had it and swung the heavy wooden bar around. Now with two weapons, he pushed back the leopards again. The door swung out. The cell was larger and reeked as much as the first, but it was empty. Had he taken the time, he would have seen the dark stains of blood on the clay floor.

The cats had pushed back into the tall grass. They had begun to stalk him the way their wild cousins did, in hiding. Their fear of his fire would not outlast their hunger, but they were nearly as anxious to kill as they were to eat. They would fight over him when it was over. He knew he would soon have to light the grass, though he wanted to wait as long as possible for that because the smoke would bring the guards. There were two more cells and he needed time. He moved to the third. Here lay a corpse.

He resisted the urge to run for the last door, knowing it would start the leopards after him. The biggest had just crept back within striking distance. Madai lunged at him, fire first, and a bit of flaming rag fell to the ground. The dry grass caught in an instant, traveling with a crackling sound toward the leopards. They bolted back with a shriek.

What advantage it gained him was quickly moderated by the other threat, that the fire would bring the guards.

Flames raced across the ground, tall, dry grass their ready tinder. The cats were running in angry circles. They still wanted Madai. But he was standing just beyond them, in the shadow of the wall, where the grass didn't grow. In the end, the fire proved to be more insistent than their hunger, and they ran to the center of the courtyard, where one ragged tree struggled to grow. The biggest leopard, in a last effort of frustrated disappointment, leapt at the cat nearest him, wrenching from it an indignant screech and a mouthful of hair. When Madai reached the last cell they had all found their refuge in the knobby limbs of the lone tree.

A cover of smoke soon blanketed the enclosure, trapped in the still air. Madai had not thought about the smoke nor foreseen the intense heat that was beginning to build inside the four confining walls. He was suddenly reminded, as well, of the poor, helpless man in the five-foot cell. Perhaps he would suffocate soon.

Free of the leopards, Madai released the bar from the last cell door. Empty. His stomach dropped into emptiness and he stood transfixed. He wiped a hand across his burning eyes to look again. Still empty. It could not be that he was too late! He looked up through the haze to see the moon had not yet appeared.

Maybe Tazek had lied. He cursed him.

He was immobilized by complete disbelief and abruptly realized how vital the Shemites' rescue had come to be, how he had depended on discovering Kittim. He was a dazed man as he backed away from the open door, till the heat scorched his back to remind him where he was. He turned to the adjacent wall. Like a path to the top were the hand and foot holds of irregular brick. They became suddenly his singular aim, as he rushed at them to take frantic hold of the first jut in the wall, within his easy reach. A personal guilt encroached on him again as he climbed away from the enclosure. He was deserting the cowering man of bones, which would haunt him, and he was leaving Kittim.

Fire reached the base of the wall. He felt the heat but did not look back. He pulled himself by the strength of his arms alone to catch a niche with his toe. Certainly, the encroaching fire and threat of cats propelled him and pulled him even farther away from the ground. His foot slipped from one brick, only to catch on another. And he could feel the sweat oozing from every surface of his skin, putting a slick film on the wall.

The leopards were starting to whine. He imagined the fire was likely burning the tree. Then he heard another shriek, carried on the air from outside the court-yard. He flattened his body to the wall, hanging there, scarcely breathing. At first he thought about the man left behind, but then he thought about the Shemites. Pray, let it not be! It was faint; it was human.

He felt a rise of bile in his throat. Another shriek and he wanted to cover his ears, but his hand's grip was slipping. He quickly repositioned himself and pulled up again. He tried to close out the sounds and started to feel sick. Maybe it was the smoke beginning to coat his lungs, but he felt his strength draining away. The niches in the bricks seemed to narrow. The smoke rose in a steaming pillar, careening into the cool night, up and over the walls in a deadly spiral.

Again the unbearable, human cry, seeming to crescendo in egregious agony, trail-ing into long, shrill, animal-like sounds. It set the cats to growling, for which Madai was thankful, as it masked the other sound. He drew himself up in panic. He began to pray that the executioner would slip with the knife and end the screams. But there were ten. It would take a long time.

He crawled like an ant up the side of the wall, making what seemed to him very slow progress. He started to tremble. He didn't know whether it was what was be-ing done to the Shemites, or the heat, or his own physical collapse. He only knew that he must reach the top soon.

A low whine began at the base of the wall and gradually turned to a growl. He tipped his chin down enough to see that the biggest of the leopards had descended from the tree and was leaping at him. The beast had an enormous vertical range, its claws snatching at the brick. Madai knew he could not afford to lose even an inch. He pushed up with his legs, preparing to grab at another handhold a few feet higher, but the brick crumbled under his foot. He was supported by only the toes of one foot wedged in the wall. He slid his dangling foot over the bricks, finding nothing to support his weight. Still the cat leapt, as the fingers of Madai's right hand slowly and painfully began to slide away.

"God in heaven!" he cried, scarcely aware that he spoke it aloud.

His toes caught on just the tiniest of outcrops, but enough. He clung there like a drowning man, then dared to grip a better hold with his hands. He was fastened to the wall in four places again and pressed his face against the clay bricks to still his heart, knowing he could not rest long before his strength gave way altogether.

His body was dripping sweat, and his legs began to quake again. 'Only a little more,' he promised himself.

When he finally pushed a last time, he pulled himself over the top of the wall and hung there, sucking in cooler air. He swung his long right leg over the top, followed by the left, and sprawled across the top. The wall was quite thick, wider than the tiny cell. He hugged it and listened to the men in the darkness cry out to their God. He wanted to weep, whether for himself or for them, he couldn't tell.

He gave himself just a moment more of rest and lifted his head. To his right, the palace rose another full story, dotted with open windows like the one in his chamber. He rolled his head to look beyond the wall and saw in the distance a great white temple, source of the cries and the sacrifice. He slowly realized the night was quiet.

'Terrible,' he thought. 'It will only start again.' But he made use of the quiet to gather his wits. He oriented the palace by way of the temple and wondered where Kittim was being held. Maybe Palapa would know. Madai suddenly knew he could not leave without him.

The howls of another man began, and he leapt to his feet to run along the top of the wall toward the palace and its open windows. He reached them almost before he knew he had risen.

He leaned on the wall, catching his breath. There, just above his head, was a great gaping hole, the way back inside. He glanced down into the courtyard and couldn't quite force himself to crawl through the window. Freedom was attainable. And what if Kittim was not in the palace? He shook himself, remembering how quickly Nimrod had produced him when the Shemites were produced.

"Kittim is inside," Madai whispered to himself. "Palapa will know where."

Still, it was a force of will that stretched Madai up to grip the window ledge and pull himself up to eye level. He strained his eyes into the darkened room. True sight was impossible, and he could hear not a sound, so he carefully pulled himself up.

Madai slithered through the window and crouched below it, listening. He was waiting for his eyes to adjust when he thought he heard someone breathing. In the aftermath of his escape and disappointment and, finally, the decision to go back, he believed it was indeed Kittim waiting in the darkness. His heart soared with enormous relief, though only a moment.

Someone laughed and gripped his arm. And another on the other side. There was a flicker of light as the men uncovered a lamp, and beside Madai stood the tall soldier who had guarded his door.

&#x3orz; &#x3orz; &#x3orz;

"Attoyak," the man spat and laughed again. Then they lifted Madai off his feet and started for the door. They dragged him down a corridor, scraping his knees and gripping his arms in a hold as tight as a new wineskin.

They didn't speak again; but Madai had seen the holds and was panicked, certain he would be flung into the cell with the man of bones or fed to the leopards, after all. But they stopped at an upper level. His senses were so nearly overwhelmed that he hardly noticed. The men dropped him like a rag and released the latch of a heavy, thick door. They kicked him inside.

He was sprawled across a stone floor and felt liquid on the stones. They were cool. The liquid was his blood. He closed his eyes, tired, beaten, only wanting to lie there. He could still hear the human suffering at the temple. Had he been more lucid, he would have known it was only his own wheezing lungs and terrible memories having a trick with him. He slowly rolled over to let the floor cool his back. He stared up into total darkness.

He did not believe he was a cruel man. He had wanted to save the Shemites. He had wanted to save Kittim. And he wanted Ido. But he was just a man, after all, and he had failed.

"If you are God," he cried into the air, "You might have helped."

He heard it echo in the still room and felt rebuked by his own voice. He would not cry out again for the men of Shinar to hear. Somehow, it seemed amiss to dishonor the God of his father here in such a terrible land. He would be silent.

There was a scraping at the door. He struggled to his feet, for he would not be found at a disadvantage. A light suddenly shone, illuminating a face.

Palapa looked at him with alarm, maybe even fear. "Madai!" she gasped.

He could not respond; it was impossible.

"He said you would be here," she whispered, her hand on her breast.

Madai was completely stunned. He could only look at her and try to make sense of human speech. "What?" he heard himself croak from a parched throat. "Where's Kittim?"

"I do not know Kittim."

He ran his dry tongue across his dry lips. It tasted of soot.

"Lord Nimrod said you would be here, but..." She slowly approached him with a look of pity and surprise in her eyes. She put the lamp on a table, took a cloth from a water bowl and carefully touched his face with it. He could only stand and stare and look at the cloth when she drew it away, red with blood and black with soot.

"Why are you here?" he finally asked.

"This is my room."

Madai shook his head as though to clear it. "Then why am I here?"

She blinked. She looked away. "You are being tested," she finally said.

Shock was slowly replaced by anger. The pitiful man... his own spear left in the room... even the Shemites? "Are the Shemites finished, then?" he asked in a low voice.

She took his hand, which was black and streaked with dried sweat. "In this you shall be pleased," she answered; "they are vanished."

He was jolted. "It cannot be. I heard the screams."

He felt her shudder. "Lord Nimrod will not be denied," she whispered as though Nimrod might hear. "It was the men who guarded them."

Madai felt the need to sit down. His legs were weak again. It was not quite joy that he felt, for all was not well, but he sank to the ground this time in utter relief. He stared at the stone floor.

"How did they escape?" he finally asked.

"It is not known," Palapa answered. "And it is not spoken aloud, though I am informed by Tazek. He says it was a spirit, for when the door was opened – they were vanished."

Madai smiled. So his first hope of Kittim at the aid of the Shemites had been granted. All that was full of dark and loss was suddenly altered and he was a muddle of confusion again, regarding the imponderable God.

- 55 -

She was awakened by the stillness. Lying curled beside Reenah, Iscah first heard the soft snort of a horse, then someone rapping at the door. She crawled across the sleeping woman toward the door and a new day and whoever chose to seek them so early.

"Marisheba." She had scarcely got the word from her mouth when the older woman's face crumpled.

"Marisheba," Iscah repeated, "you are here alone? What…"

Marisheba made her way to Reenah, who was just waking.

"Why, Mari, how early you have come," Reenah delighted, then stopped at the white and aged look on Marisheba's face. "Whatever is wrong?"

Marisheba drew herself up and restrained her trembling mouth. "A calamity is befallen the house of Job." Suddenly tears came to her eyes. "All is lost."

Tutan had lain awake since the first quieting of the storm and had heard Marisheba's horse. He rose quickly. He put his hands on her shoulders, turned her and quietly folded his arms around her.

"What is lost?" he asked gently, looking across Marisheba's white head to Reenah's stricken face.

Marisheba drew herself back. She looked at him, suddenly a very aged woman. "All," she repeated. "The flocks, the herdsmen," she stopped, scarcely able to squeak out the last, "all the children."

Tutan stood in stunned silence. "Certainly, this cannot be…" disbelief spoke the words.

Reenah rose to her knees and grasped Marisheba's hand. "This is a wicked rumor," she pleaded.

Marisheba did not answer. She sat upon the bed and lowered her head. Reenah heard the wail of mourning begin and knew it was true. "It cannot be all," she whispered to herself. "Uncle…" She leapt from the bed and began to snatch up her clothes. Iscah, first standing mute, turned to do the same, but Marisheba stopped them.

"She will not have you," she murmured. "I am sent to keep you here. The Lady will be alone with her grief."

"Uncle?" Reenah asked.

Marisheba only shook her head.

Reenah stood in the center of the cottage, her day clothes in her hand, insensible. "His God could not save him," she muttered, her eyes stricken.

Iscah was as still as Reenah. She sat at the table where the night before they had taken the pleasure of a world that is well. Then as Marisheba began to weep again, she found the purpose she needed. Iscah and Reenah came round her, each determining wisely to take the day piece by piece.

Tutan was forgotten. He was equally dazed. Certainly Marisheba was wrong. Job's herds were spread throughout the valley and his children lived in different houses. All could not be taken in a single day.

This resolve was a comfort to him, and he went outside to find his horse. The sand had piled up against the cottage, and the wind had broken the tops of some of the trees. But their horses were safely kept in Reenah's stable.

The animals turned their heads to look at Tutan as he entered, reassured by his presence against the raging night. Tutan laid his hand on his horse's rump to feel the warm sturdiness. He smelled the musty odor of horse and closed his eyes for just a moment before he dressed Cusah with the gaily ornate saddle and bridle.

Tutan was uncommonly aware of the creaking leather when he pulled up onto Cusah's back. As he bent to pass under the low door frame, he felt his back stiff from sleeping on the floor. But he began the ride across the fields that divided Reenah's cottage from Job's great house by half a morning. 'How,' he wondered, 'did Marisheba arrive so early? Assuredly she had left in the dark.'

His horse was uncharacteristically skittish, having suffered the howl of the storm through the night. But Cusah was stretching out his nerves and did not complain when Tutan urged him to a faster pace. Rider and horse seemed intent for their own differing reasons to cross the plain with speed. What Tutan could not mask in this dash across the fields was his own guarded expectations.

The call of a fox across the meadow did not bring him delight, nor did the morning's chatter of birds. He was intently fixed upon the destination. But the earth was well; all was in its place. He took this as an omen that no evil had befallen this land of Job.

All such thoughts accompanied Tutan as he continued to press his horse. He felt the animal slow, having run out its tension. He drew back the reins, patting the beast at his neck. "Calm, calm, Cusah," he soothed. His horse began to prance and blew froth from his mouth; steam rose from his overheated body into the cool morning air.

The slower pace was fairly torturous for Tutan. Though Cusah carried on at a trot, the horizon seemed to draw no closer. And when at last he glimpsed the great house, he could somehow not approach it. There seemed an inordinate stillness. It frightened him and he turned aside, toward the vineyard on the hill.

It was there he had first surveyed the bounty that was Job's. From there, Kittem had offered his 'man of renown' with great satisfaction. Tutan looked down at the vines as Cusah carried him up the hill. The storm seemed to have done some slight damage, but they were not destroyed. This reignited greater hope in Tutan that Marisheba was overwrought and, in this state, certainly mistaken. So with better spirit Tutan crested the hill and looked across the wide, fertile valley.

It was lovely and green, watered by the canals from the river. But it did not crawl with life as it had on that first day. Indeed, Tutan could see not a single ram. The valley lay still and quiet.

The slow realization filled Tutan with chilly alarm, for if the herds were gone, then perhaps the worst was true, as well. 'Though they may be beyond the hills,' he suddenly thought.

Tutan sat upon Cusah's back gazing at the quiet plain. He began to feel an unexpected hunger waking in his stomach. He leaned down toward a cluster of grapes, vaguely aware that thinking of food was peculiar at such a time. But the fruit was plump and ripe to harvest, and the air was edged with the first crispness of autumn. "This shall need tending," he mused, putting a purple orb between his teeth.

He ate a dozen, let the rest drop back to the ground, and watched Job's silent, still house a moment more, stretching the time before he should know. He slowly filled his lungs with autumn air and tapped Cusah's ribs, assailed by increasing dread. He let the horse carry him back down the hill toward the house. The nearer he came, the more still seemed the day. He did not smell the aromas of baking bread or meat roasting. 'Where is the manservant, Lehabim?' he wondered, coming near enough to see the door standing open. Still no one came to greet him and nothing moved. Instinctively, fearful of disrupting the quiet, he dismounted and left the horse to munch the grass at a distance. Still no one appeared. The faint odor of a prior day's cooking floated through the open door.

Tutan cautiously peered in. The interior was dark, unusual for the hospitable Job. The quiet was evidence enough. Then he perceived a dark form sitting at the long eating table. It was, in profile, a solitary figure. Hair slightly disheveled, hands folded, it was the spectre of an old man. Tutan had just entered when the man slowly turned his head toward the door.

Job did not acknowledge Tutan, nor did he weep, nor did he speak to ask Tutan to leave. He simply turned his head back to stare at the tops of his trembling hands.

- 56 -

Madai woke with a start. There had been screaming in the night. He hastily touched his arms. "A dream," he whispered aloud.

A great skeletal face had grinned at him, all the while plucking out his arms. Madai sat up to another jolt - Palapa, sitting like a pale ghost beside the bed. He suddenly remembered all. The Shemites were rescued by the hand of Kittim, who would not turn to bone in a dank cell after all.

"You slept badly," she interrupted his thoughts.

His mouth was like parched desert sand.

"You have sat there all the night?" he asked.

She rose, bringing him water. "No," she answered.

"You must get me news of Kittim," he insisted, taking the cup eagerly.

She did not respond regarding Kittim; instead, "There is little time," she said, rising to fill a large copper tub with water. He was amazed to see water flowing from the very walls. "The Feast of Inanna is near. He shall measure you for it."

Madai watched her silently, still slightly dazed.

"Come," she insisted.

He looked at the vessel of water.

"You are bidden by the Lord. You must hurry."

Palapa intended that Madai should bathe. But she was a Japhethite, if among The Banned, and she recognized now that he was one who kept the old ways. Recognized and approved. She put the robe he was to wear near the tub, then silently pulled her chair behind a curtain to wait for him. She heard the water splash against the copper sides, as there was nothing for him, but to obey.

"Lord Nimrod is in a generous spirit," she said from behind the veil. "He admires men of strength." She seemed less timid, hidden as she was. "He is pleased with your cunning. He wishes you to serve him. Great advantage can be had," she quickly assured him. "Even a house within the capital, and a wife - or many wives. Even I," she finished quietly.

She heard the water splashing as Madai moved. "Never," he replied harshly, "would I serve such a one as he."

She looked at her hands. "Just so," she replied, quieter still. "I shall be sent to the temple."

Madai could not hear above the noise he was making.

"I shall not serve Nimrod," he repeated.

"This I know," she answered more loudly.

"How does Nimrod feast while the Shemites are escaped?" he asked.

Palapa cringed, suddenly terrified that she had revealed what would do nothing but bring her trouble.

"You must not speak of this," she pleaded, her voice trembling.

Madai smiled as he watched the water turn black with soot. Certainly, Nimrod would not acknowledge the weakness. "Tell me about the feast, then," he insisted.

She was relieved by a safer question, pray he be done with the Shemites, "The feast of Inanna," she answered. "At the turn of each new moon, sacrifice is made for her."

"There is such a sacrifice at each whole moon?" Madai asked, horrified.

"Each whole moon," she affirmed. "To honor the virgin and bring forth the promised seed."

Madai stopped his washing. "What virgin?" he asked.

"The one spoken in the heavens. The Japhethites have this knowledge. The Virgin, Inanna, spreads across the sky, a stalk of corn in one hand, a branch in the other."

He sat immobile, putting the star story into the framework of Nimrod, remembering an account of The Virgin less profane. Remembering the way his father traced the forms upon the ox-skin star map.

"How shall he bring forth the promised seed?" Madai asked quietly. "Is that not accomplished by the wisdom and effort of Mighty God?"

"Certainly," she answered. "The Lord Nimrod. A new virgin is brought at each feast," she continued, "to take the seed of Nimrod, to bear the one who is promised."

Madai smiled again, a sardonic smile. 'To be god of such religion,' he thought. Aloud he asked, "Where then, is this offspring - the babe?"

Palapa was silent a long moment. She pressed her white hands into each other. "Lord Nimrod has great power, great... malice," she whispered. "And he shall soon become suspicious and discover what is done, and the Queen will perish." The girl was still, and so was Madai.

"I was brought a bitter drink by her maidservant," Palapa finally continued. "At the close of the feast, and each night of the month I shared the chamber of the Lord. It brought a retching sickness, and I did not sprout a babe. None other... "

Madai sat in the cooling water. Not even his most dread imagination would strike a babe in the belly of its mother. Of course, nor would it flay the skin of a living man. It was a worse snare even than he had first discovered.

"What does Nimrod want of me?" he asked gruffly.

"Your allegiance. You may be assured he greatly desires it."

"How will that be accomplished?" Madai asked.

"If it is not, he shall kill you."

It was an obvious assumption, and still he had learned nothing. Madai rose dripping from the water and dried himself with a cloth. The presence of the girl had ceased to trouble him, replaced by other, graver matters; and besides, she was behind the curtain. He absently pulled a delicate, embroidered robe over his wet hair. The cloth was soon damp at the shoulders.

He crossed the room to the window, which opened to what must be a bright blue sky. It was not an unobscured opening, but rather a weave of clay brick, allowing brick-sized shafts of light to pattern the floor. Palapa heard him and pulled her chair back from behind the curtain. She took a thicker robe from the cupboard and carried it to him.

"This is for you," she insisted, noting his silhouette.

It had a great opening in the cloth for his arms, and it covered him back and front. The cloth was smooth and finely woven, a sturdy garment. He ran his hands over his beard, squeezing water down the front of it.

Palapa admired his form. He was a great solid man, with a goodly red beard and thick yellow hair. Remembrance of The Family was comforting and pleasant. How long she had borne the indecencies of Shinar. This Japhethite - would that he preferred her.

"What do I next?" he muttered to himself.

"I shall bring you to Lord Nimrod," she answered quietly, thinking he had spoken to her. "And you must not speak of the Shemites," her voice pleaded.

He looked away from the window.

"Pray, be as genial as you may," she continued. "If you have been noticed, and you have, the Lord shall have his way. It need not be... entirely unpleasant." She smiled her best smile.

Madai nodded, watching her lips oddly twisted.

"Tell me about the feast," he asked again.

But she was conscious of the passing time. "Later," she whispered with a final approval of his appearance. She rapped at the door timidly; it opened by hand of the guards, with a scraping of timber. She led Madai through and to the left, down a great long hall. He was once again in the bowels of the palace.

He walked a long, soft carpet, an opposite direction from and distinct contrast to the night's corridor. It was flanked on either side by paintings, a mural of men and women, men and men, and his color rose at the long tangle of corruption. Palapa did not seem to notice, though, had he known her more, he would have felt the shriveling of her heart.

"Lord Nimrod has taken his meal," she whispered as they walked. "for he rises early. Something will be left for you to eat, after which you will be brought to him. Pray, drink nothing that is not water, and nothing which is bitter or smells."

Madai nodded.

"I am summoned elsewhere, but you shall be returned to my quarters at the end of day." She had no sooner whispered this last than a door opened before them. Palapa tipped her head slightly to the youth waiting inside.

Madai noticed that when he bowed, it was deep. Her standing, then, was not so low as he had presumed. With a hasty last glance at him, she scuttled away in the direction from which they had come.

ଓଡ଼ ଓଡ଼ ଓଡ଼

Madai surveyed the room to find it empty of any other soul. The youth did not speak his tongue, but guided him to a table of roasted meat and bread. He quickly studied the pitcher of wine, cautiously refusing it. He smelled the water before he drank, wondering where Tazek was gone.

The meat was tender, dripping with fat, and Madai was suddenly ravenous. So it was true: he was not yet out of favor. The youth stood fidgeting beside him at the table, glancing as he did toward a second door. Madai noted that his head was shaved, as was Tazek's, though the nub of his new growth was dark. Would that the lad would calm himself, for the meal was tasty and Madai needed it. But it took no great skill to realize this youth wanted him finished. Madai would have lingered, letting him fret, had he not recognized the terror in which Palapa lived and felt pity. And so, taking the last of the bread into his mouth, he stood, pushing back the platter - to the boy's utter relief.

The youth scurried across the room and through a second door. It revealed a man standing guard. The man did not speak, but called Madai with a gesture into the hall. And then he pointed the way forward with an insistent lance, down a different corridor, painted in an entirely different manner. The man was dressed differently. His feet were shod in stiff, thick animal hide; he wore no long robe, rather, a skirt of leather which reached the middle of his thigh. His breast was covered with the same hide as his feet, knobby, gray, thinly covered with short, bristly hair. Madai briefly wondered what animal produced it. This escort was a man of war, no doubt, for a thick purple scar ran the length of his left arm.

They moved quickly down the hall into other stately rooms, past closed doors and silent sentries, to finally come into the bright light of morning sun. It was an instant of pure delight to Madai. He felt the fresh coolness of the air, though he smelled in it a faint odor of burned grass. He glanced sideways at the guard, who did not appear to notice.

They were behind the complex of the palace, on the far side of the city and its temple. Had he his horse, Madai would have been able to ride away toward the mountains visible in the distance. Though immediately visible as well was a fully set and impressive army, huge men, dressed as the one bringing him. They stood in ranks stiffly, silently, waiting at full ready before the great lord Nimrod himself. The sight of his thin companion, Tazek, standing at the side brought Madai more relief than he would have expected.

Nimrod was an imposing figure, heading this army, though many that kept the ranks were as large as he. It was the set of his head upon great shoulders, a certain quality of boldness and conceit. He turned at their approach.

Madai had resigned himself to a show of deference, deciding it was a shrewd deception. But he tipped his head to the King, just short of a bow. His silent escort bowed more deeply, glared at Madai and approached his lord with brisk competence. Nimrod approved the man, spoke to him heartily and dismissed him to stand with his fellows. He welcomed Madai with a similar degree of approval, even pleasure, with pride gleaming in his eyes.

"You have arrived at an opportune moment, Madai the Japhethite," Tazek translated. Madai heard the coolness of his voice. "The Mighty Lord Nimrod highly regards your prowess."

Madai watched Nimrod's face, finding that Tazek had spoken truly. He was reminded again of the giant's deep and emanating power and the countenance that had once disarmed him.

"Tell him I am honored," Madai replied brusquely. "Tell him, too, I am pleased to have accomplished his test."

Nimrod laughed, and Madai was suddenly cautious, wary of a man who might understand more of a foreign language than he disclosed.

"You are proved able." Nimrod spoke the words with halting amusement.

Before he could tame them, Madai's eyes widened with surprise, which pleased the giant more. But Nimrod turned to Tazek then and used his skill from that moment forward to communicate. Madai watched the elegant mastery of Nimrod, to disarm, to intimidate, to cajole and to terrify.

The great, malevolent lord slowly turned his massive head to fill his eyes with a field of ready solders.

"A great army, no?" Tazek translated.

Madai nodded. "A great and terrible army," he affirmed.

Nimrod's lips parted with a smile. "They are ready for battle," he proclaimed. And then his eyes grew malignant as he turned back to look at Madai. Their darkness was complete. "I have enemies beyond the mountains. The Shemites shall be removed." He ran his tongue across his lips.

Then Nimrod's face lost even the semblance of a smile. He turned to his men and Madai heard the voice of a spectre rising up from the deep to command a massacre. The army was roused to cheer. Nimrod was stoic as he let their thunder sing to him. He closed his eyes, sweat springing up on his lip. Then he lifted his right arm to quiet them. He spoke again, a sort of oracle. The atmosphere pulsed and the army was engorged with the power that Nimrod lent them.

An efficient, brusque gesture of Nimrod's hand further charged the air and brought the army to a nervous energy. Nimrod clenched his fist, threw back his head and barked a command dispatching his army. They sprung into immediate action, some to the backs of their skittish horses, some to march in deadly ranks, shaking the very earth. They formed an efficient and lethal horde as they turned like a locust swarm toward the mountains. Nimrod's nostrils flared, attending a presence - a tangible, manifest presence.

Madai watched it all. He was thoroughly persuaded of a truth beyond superstition. And he actually shuddered when Nimrod turned his eyes from the distance to put his hand atop Madai's shoulder.

"You are a man of composure," Nimrod spoke pleasantly, through Tazek. The potent voice was gone. "There is a great lack of such men in these days, save men of discipline." He paused. "I am pleased by you." He began walking back toward the palace, directing Madai with his hand. "Man can be... corrupt in his flesh... unreliable."

Madai was disarmed again. He reminded himself of what he had just witnessed. It took an effort to let himself be guided by Nimrod's hand. He heard the words spoken ironically by Tazek, an incautious moment provoked by his own disaster, and Madai felt again a prick of pity for the boy, crippled in body and soul.

They reached the entry. A guard opened it to them, but Nimrod turned for a last look at his departing army. Then he led them through the dim hall like a pulsing animal, into a large room of murals and maps. There he stood in the center, visibly calming himself, face turned toward the East. Many silent moments passed before Nimrod finally sat down at a long, narrow table. A lamp was burning, fanning its light across the table top.

Madai was surprised. In the light of the lamp's flame, visible and beautiful, was an unnecessary aesthetic. It was a mosaic of shell and lapis lazuli, a winged dragon which coiled its long body, wings unfurled, brilliant turquoise. Its eyes were red sandstone, as was the breath flaming fire from its open mouth.

"I come here when I am moved," Nimrod muttered. "A King should lead his army."

Madai was as startled by his blatant candor.

"Though it is the Innana that keeps me here, the sacred rites," Nimrod continued. He then remained silent a long moment more. Madai and Tazek stood motionless. Madai found the vacant stillness of the room unnerving.

Nimrod eventually moved; he slowly began to trace the outline of the serpent. "I shall have another made," he suddenly proclaimed. "It shall be your beast with a crest."

Madai struggled, as the King's face began to relax. He had never known a man so unsettling as Nimrod, a chameleon. He watched as the lord ran his great, thick finger across the pink and white shells with a delicacy that defied the slaughter he had just commanded.

"Beauty pleases me," he said, looking up at Madai. Then he tipped his head, sending the four armed men from the room, leaving only Tazek. "I have removed the fire-breathers by my own effort and brought order to this land. My army shall soon finish it. Chaos is made by my enemies. Good is all I seek." He finished this last by laying his great hands upon the back of the dragon, fingers splayed. "For this end, I seek men such as you. You may sit."

Tazek was terrified at this last command. He looked cautiously at Nimrod and stood uncertainly as Madai drew another stool to the table.

"The fire was brilliant," Nimrod suddenly proclaimed. "And your strength at the wall was unmatched. I am told you opened the holds as well..." At this, Nimrod's eyes became calculating.

Madai looked across the dragon's wing into intensely cunning and changeable eyes. "The skinning of any man is abhorrent," he answered, knowing Tazek would soften the words.

The expression of his opponent did not change. "Admirable - both courageous and merciful. Though one who rules cannot abide rebellion. It creates disorder. But I do not expect this discipline of you."

Nimrod smiled faintly, analyzing once again. He became officious, drawing a weathered roll of leather from a compartment inside the table. "Speak to me of this," he quietly demanded, unrolling the skin.

Madai looked down at his own scroll. He found himself disadvantaged again, as Nimrod seemed ever able to produce something unexpected. "It is the star map of my people," he managed to answer with a steady voice.

"It is skillfully rendered," Nimrod asserted. "And accurate." He looked at Madai candidly, lifting his right brow. "Explain its meaning to me."

The request would have made Madai laugh aloud, as he was being asked the questions for which his quest was made. And did he know? He returned Nimrod's gaze with an uncertain look of his own, an enigmatic smile. "There lies the difficulty," he answered.

Nimrod nodded slowly. "Then what say your scribes?"

By scribe, Madai supposed Nimrod spoke of holy men. But he would not reveal The Family's conflict here, its weakness. He would recite the old lore as though there were no dissension.

"This," he answered, running his finger along the faded pattern, "is mother of a coming and promised warrior."

Nimrod's expression did not show surprise or displeasure. It did not change.

"If there is a warrior," he baited, "then there is a foe."

Madai held a steady gaze. "Do you see the Archer?" he asked.

"The Centaur," Nimrod corrected.

"Whose Bow is aimed at The Scorpion," Madai continued.

Nimrod laughed. "You are superstitious," he accused.

"Then it is a map of the sky," Madai replied calmly, without a pause. "With which to navigate the sea."

Nimrod's mouth turned up at one corner. He rolled the scroll and pushed it across the table. "I return it to you," he said, sitting back and folding his arms across his chest. He wore a coil of gold wound around his lower arm to his wrist, ending at the head of a serpent lying on the back of his hand. "Tell me of the seas you crossed," he asked. "Their danger."

Madai retrieved the roll of ox-skin, holding it loosely in his hand. "The Brine Sea," he answered.

"For this I have no skill," Nimrod replied. "Though I have seen the Great Sea. Aptly named; it touchs the sky in every direction." Nimrod rubbed the snake's head. "There are stories of sea beasts."

"They are true." Madai struggled to keep his eyes calm and tried to think what Nimrod's purpose might be. He could not imagine it was benign. "But they prefer fish," he continued. "It was the storms and the great expanse that held the worst fears."

Nimrod nodded. "Indeed. I honor your courage." He tapped the table absently. "Do you think others of your kin shall follow?" he asked casually.

"Others have come before me," Madai replied. "Tazek and Palapa and their kin."

"A trivial group of starving beggars," Nimrod replied contemptuously. "It was the generosity of Namim to take Tazek as his companion. And Palapa..." his smile was a leer. "I believe you have discovered her pleasures."

Madai was still, reminded once again of the man's cruelties. In such a moment Nimrod's utter darkness was betrayed, a darkness that lurked inside one who was the hunter of dragons. It could not be restrained. Madai was suddenly struck with a realization: if a malicious spirit inhabited a man, then might there not be...

"She does not please you?" Nimrod asked. "Indeed, I should have released her to the temple long since, a good honor. She may be eager for it, and if she does not please you... though she speaks your tongue." Tazek's translation of all such matters of Palapa were done in quick, low tones. The shaved head betrayed a spreading crimson.

"I am well pleased," Madai answered quickly.

And Nimrod smiled again. "Excellent," he replied. "I found her quite delicious." Which was the last said of her, to Madai's great relief.

"But you did not come starving and naked with your companion. I believe the thief said you came by way of a great land-owner."

"One who is content in his own lands," Madai was hasty to insert. "He does not admire cities."

"Pity," Nimrod murmured. "He is known." The lids of his eyes drooped slightly as he studied Madai's expression. "Though he worships the god of chaos."

Indeed, Madai could not control his surprise.

"I see you do not agree."

"I do not speak for Job's God," Madai answered cautiously. "Though a god of chaos is not what I should expect such a man to serve."

"Come," Nimrod demanded abruptly. "I shall show you chaos."

57

The lord Nimrod did not ride upon the back of an ordinary horse. This great animal was completely red and stood no less than four cubits at his shoulder. All that was not red were his great, rolling eyes. His hoofs were polished; his mane and tail were braided with scarlet cloth. His coat gleamed in the sun, and he outran them all.

Madai was given his own gelding to ride, the gift from Job. His bow and clutch of arrows were conspicuously missing. Four armed men accompanied them, confirming for Madai that, though he was perhaps not out of favor, he was entirely guarded. Tazek was quite accomplished on horseback and seemed, for the first time, to find pleasure in what he was doing.

A crumbling ziggurat rose before them in the distance. The top was high and looked utterly unstable. Nimrod's horse ran at his full speed, foaming up the dust back at their faces. Madai coughed, conceding the great figure they both made: Nimrod and his beast. Nimrod's black hair blew behind him, and the mid-day sun shone on the dark skin of his great, wide back. It recalled for Madai the Anak giant he had killed.

It was a wild diversion and a pleasure to race across the plain on his horse. Deceptive freedom, but Madai enjoyed it. It was shrewd that Nimrod required the guard, for they were needed.

When they reached the structure, Nimrod had already flung himself from his horse. The animal stood obedient where he was drawn up, sides heaving and nostrils flared. He followed the retreat of his master, snorting, shaking his mane, pawing the ground.

"Come up here," Nimrod ordered. He was already great strides ahead of them. Madai had a wild hope he might reach the rubble at the top and stumble off, for it was no small height.

Tazek had the most difficulty, dragging his leg. His breath was labored when they reached the pinnacle from which Nimrod looked out at the city gleaming white in the sun. He stretched out his arm. "It is there," he barked.

Madai looked where Nimrod was pointing. Behind the wall was another part of the city, a row of buildings and a tumble of charred brick.

"It was the army of the enemy. They would burn it all, slaughter man and beast... and the great temple of Inanna. That, we saved, and drove the marauders back." Nimrod turned to look at Madai with a stony glare more cold, more menacing, than Madai had yet to see. "Warriors of Huwah, god of chaos. Look at my city. Is it not grander than the plain? Better protected than the hills which trembled at the roar of dragons? Those I tamed, as well." Nimrod's eyes had grown wild. "And this!" He stomped his feet on the ziggurat. "A pinnacle of achievement reduced to sand, crumbling." He ground a brick under his foot. "Deserted for want of labor, all at the whim of that - " Nimrod spat a word into the air which Tazek would not translate. He whirled around to bore his eyes into Madai's face. "I give no place to the man who worships Him." The great lord was trembling.

Madai was silent, a hot feeling rising through his chest. When he finally spoke, he was surprised by himself, by his own daring. "I am told He is dead - at your hands."

It surprised Nimrod, as well. Where earlier he might have laughed, now his rage superseded every other thing. He answered, low and measured, "You are not superstitious, Japhethite." He put his mouth even with Madai's, breathing in his face. He spoke so quietly Tazek had to draw closer to hear. "I let them believe, to quench the old fables. And when it is needed, we quench the old fools, as well." He rose back to his full height and smiled with his splendid white teeth. "Such fools as Kittim."

Madai could feel the whiteness of his own face. He steadied himself with the knowledge given him by Palapa that the Shemites were freed, and by whose hand but Kittim's? It allowed him to keep Nimrod's gaze. "Kittim is a good man," Madai replied with a slightly shaken voice.

Nimrod merely lifted his brow. He brushed past Madai, near enough to push him from the edge. Madai steadied his footing, well aware of the danger so near the edge, but knowing full well that if the King wished him flung from the precipice it would already be accomplished. The giant stood at the edge with him, vulnerable as well. Jjust a push... But the soldiers knew it, too, and were trained on Madai. He watched Nimrod gather himself and slow his breathing, until the giant's countenance began slowly to forget him and Nimrod looked out at the hills behind his palace, smiling with secret rapture.

"My solace is there," he murmured. "Where His minions shall die. Would that I were present. With my own hand I would crush them; I should taste their blood." His own body was responding to the prospect, as though the battle were a woman.

He turned back to Madai with exhilaration.

"And now, my Japhethite friend," he effused, "I shall show you order."

ଓଃଙ୍ଙ   ଓଃଙ୍ଙ   ଓଃଙ୍ଙ

The ride back to the city was as frenzied as that to the ziggurat. Madai noted that Nimrod did not lead them through the gate which kept the rabble of peasants. Rather they entered by way of the palace gate, well guarded, arched and clean. He took them down a well-worn road which passed before great structures grander even than Job's, past a round water-well surrounded by some manner of red blooms, and to the enormous white steps of Inanna's temple. These they climbed, mindless of the cripples who begged for a piece of silver.

A scramble of pallid men dressed all in white surged from the temple's portico to meet Nimrod. They fell face to the hot stones to greet him. Nimrod's great, sweating body was a severe contrast to the unctuous men, Namim among them. Nimrod swept past in a flourish, "Come," he ordered Madai, as they, together, entered the dim interior.

There was a coolness that made steam rise from their bodies, and a strong, enveloping aroma, as well. It was silent and empty, unlike the palace where Madai and Kittim had first been taken. When his eyes adjusted, Madai stood in a place all of white stone, a cavernous space. Men were here, keeping to the shadows, mild and silent. And slaves. Nimrod was a wild bull, out of place. Every soul fell to the floor, and the great lord was pleased.

An aged priest was first to stand. It was his duty to greet the king and he did so with downcast eyes. Nimrod's restored humors brought the priest a gracious lord, which lifted the flaccid lines of his aged face. He called a servant forward to instruct him in a whispered voice. The servant scurried back across the hall and through a distant curtain.

Madai noted that the guards remained outside in the sun. A little rabble of priests had appeared. Theirs was a distinct honor, as was plain to Madai. An odor of incense and wine followed them, and Namim. This was his domain, his kingdom, which he granted Nimrod with distinction and charity. The lifting of Nimrod's one brow became a silent discipline to the high priest, and Namim immediately surrendered.

They moved through the marble chamber, following the clutch of priests into a second, smaller hall. This was also empty and narrow, lined with tall, thick pillars. These flanked numerous little alcoves set into the walls, draped by heavy, multi-dyed curtains.

A sound of women's chatter came from a distinct gold curtain at the end of this long room. It was toward this sound that Nimrod was steadily headed, and with such haste that the priests scurried to follow him. At the entrance they stopped as one, reverential toward the lord, bowing as he entered, aggrieved when he bade Madai follow him inside.

The air was pleasantly scented and a long pool of water was sunk into the stone floor. Beautiful young slaves, male and female, lingered at the edge. Informed in advance of Nimrod's coming and, well-sotted with the arousing herb tiamat, they rose unsteadily, bowing at his appearance, which delighted the King. The pupils of his eyes enlarged as he trailed them across the youthful bodies.

A stately woman dressed all in gossamer white came from some hidden corner. A priestess. She carried a small urn and came to present herself. She ignored Madai, turning instead to Nimrod, and poured an amber liquid into the pool. A sweet odor rose in the steam. Then she watched with parted lips as Nimrod removed his leather skirt and lowered himself slowly, ceremoniously into the water. All he wore was the coiled snake of gold. The priestess did not move as Nimrod held her with his eyes.

She watched as he cleansed his skin with the water, then she brought the urn, to trickle a stream over his hands, which he rubbed into his breast.

Nimrod did not invite Madai to this ritual cleansing; perhaps it was reserved for gods. Madai was relieved. The young slaves tittered beside the pool, and Madai trained his eyes away. A weakness had caused him shame once before; If it were another test of the Shinar king, he would not fail.

When Nimrod rose from the water, he glistened; and he turned himself to the best advantage as he dried, while the priestess gazed at him. He was draped with a robe, one identical to that of the priests. His face was severe as he looked at Madai, contained and impassioned, his eyes intense.

"This is order," he said through thinly parted lips.

Then he merely nodded his head, and every slave at the water's edge left the room; Madai stood alone with just Nimrod and the priestess. The woman led them with swaying hips toward yet a fourth room. Madai planted his gaze vacantly into space, not to entertain her form as she moved.

Lining the white walls of this chamber were a score of young women, Tazek, and a gilded throne. Upon the throne sat a tiny figure clothed in white, glittering with gems that circled the neck of her garment. Her eyes were dull. She scarcely appeared to breathe, nor dared she look at the giant, Nimrod. In the center of the room rested a great slab of stone, carved and smooth. Its surface was as reflective as a mountain lake. A second, identical throne sat at the head of the stone table, positioned opposite its counterpart, facing the little child.

Tazek came to Madai's side. He rendered Nimrod's words for him, "The priestesses of An are come to watch their god eat."

Then Nimrod turned to the one on the throne and bowed. "Exalted one," he murmured. Again Madai perceived Nimrod's passion. Surely his voice held more arousal than worship as he took his place and began to be served. Madai stood with Tazek at a wall opposite the women. They watched as the single priestess who had served Nimrod the bath brought him bowls of broth and wine. Something floated in the liquid.

The women gathered in the hall were absolutely silent. They watched Nimrod eat with rapt attention, certainly with desire. The priestess who served him, they resented. They were dusky of skin, with gleaming dark hair, save a very few. One seemed to stand apart from the rest, as though it were her intent. Her hair was hidden in a veil, and she looked not at Nimrod, but at Madai.

Nimrod drank the wine that floated with the crushed leaves. He drank the cup deeply, tipping his glance to the child on the throne. His body began to gleam with sweat, a curiosity as the temple was pleasantly cool with its stone walls. 'Perhaps it is poison,' Madai hoped. But Nimrod was not made weaker, and the priestess clearly did not want him dead.

Nimrod pushed away the bowl and cup to rise; his strength was evident, enhanced even, and when he moved away from the table he was not in the least impaired. Madai caught his gaze as he stepped forward; his eyes were dilated and he smiled wickedly at Madai, as if to bait him.

"He goes," Tazek whispered. "In this place he is god."

Madai glanced quickly at the doors through which they had entered; no guard waited there. As he swung back to the far side of the room he caught Nimrod's challenge again. Then the giant placed his great hands on the priestess. She led him to a curtained section of the room, where they could be alone.

"It is better guarded than you know," Tazek cautioned. "Do you think the Inanna is not secure?"

The women watched Nimrod's departure with disappointment. Tazek was called away and Madai watched him go. It was the voice of Namim from outside the gold curtain. Other priests removed the child from the throne, and in the transition, Madai began to assess the risk.

"Follow me." He suddenly heard and whirled around to see the very priestess who had stood apart from the others. He would not have obeyed had she not led him through the arched door that led toward his freedom. "And be no fool," she finished. It did not immediately strike him that she spoke his tongue.

They were at the inner hall, which housed the sunken pool. He followed her beside it when she grasped his wrist. "You are watched." Then she put his hand around her waist. "Follow me," she insisted, taking him back to the narrow outer room. He might even then have bolted, had he not glimpsed a shadowed form at the entrance.

She pulled him gently to the side, into one of the hidden alcoves. As she lifted the curtains covering the niche, he perceived only a small space with a cushioned bed. She drew him behind her upon it and let the curtain fall. "Be no fool," she hissed, and disentangled herself from him. "Palapa says you are a true Japhethite."

He struggled to sit up against the wall of the alcove. "What is this?" he demanded.

She drew away the veil which covered her face. "The vengeance of God is come," she whispered. "It shall soon arrive."

He heard a soft footfall cross past their hidden space. She put her hand against his mouth and sighed heavily. "There is some time," she whispered then. "Nimrod has taken tiamat stalk. He shall savor its effects a good while."

"How is the vengeance of God to come?" he demanded.

"That shall be accomplished. What is purposed for you is knowledge. You must know what is done here, for lies will come of it."

Madai stared at her. He felt his blood running hot against all that was Nimrod. He did not want to carry knowledge; he wanted a spear.

"Excellent," she whispered. "This is what I wish to see." Then she put her hand on his arm. "He shall be worse when he is dead. It will be... just the beginning."

He stared at her again, "Who are you?"

She was slightly annoyed. "I am a servant of 'Elohiym, the One True God. And I am putting you to use for Him." She waited to see if this would suffice. "And I have word of Kittim."

It was what she needed to say.

"He is well," she hastened. "A high servant of the One True God. He loosed our spies."

"As Palapa told me," he confirmed. "Has he spoken to you?"

She shook her head. "He can not," she replied. "I am a prisoner here as you are."

"How then..." he began.

"There are many ways within a secret court."

He waited.

"All take the stalk here, save a few. The Inanna so she may bear what shall be done to her, the consorts so they may be desirable, the high priestess so she may be pleasured." She paused. "But there is much to tell. You must know it all, and what will come of it."

"Tell me."

58

"Nimrod has painted the map of the stars," she began. "It is studied and recorded within great scrolls, measured against the night sky. He knows when the path of the sun shall cross the span of each constellation. He has assigned fables for each, and omens." She waited to see whether Madai had questions. When he did not speak, she continued.

"The favored constellation is The Virgin. This is her temple; he is her consort."

"And the child upon the great chair?" he asked.

"Nimrod shall take her at the end of four days. She is a virgin. If she is truly Inanna, she shall bear his seed."

"Though he has spawned no child yet..." It was a question.

The priestess smiled. "It is his perfect illusion. Do you think he does not know what is done by Semiramis? She would have none else bear his son, and he will not have her."

"She is no virgin," Madai asserted, recalling her indecent eyes.

"Indeed not. It is rumored that she was concubine to Nimrod's own father. She is more ambitious even than he, and bore a son, whom Nimrod does not claim. Moreover, she is host of a foul malady; sores rot her body - come by her many consorts, it is said. Why suppose you Nimrod insists upon virgins? Or these who are confined? He is their only hope of seed, and they each vie for it, hoping to be queen if they can not be goddess."

It made no sense to him. "Then he knows. Why would he permit the poison?"

"It is not precisely poison; very few are dead by it. Though it serves his purpose. For he does not wish a son. He wishes to be god of all, to Inanna, as well, over and over, each month till a babe is bred. Perhaps he believes he will never grow old."

Madai's mouth twisted out a curse.

"He is more dangerous than merely foul, for he has spread his religion to the borders of this kingdom and will spread it farther still. You are a means by which it shall be proved false."

Madai thought she spoke in riddles, though he was pleased to slit the lord's throat. "I am prepared to kill him," he assured her.

Her eyes widened with understanding. "I do not doubt that you are. But it is already planned. It shall be accomplished soon in such a way that his kingdom will be utterly destroyed." She waited for him to accept it, predicting his disappointment. "You know the truth of this place; you will witness his defeat and his death and make it known in the far land from which you are come. You will expose any deceit that may come from it. Semiramis shall use it to some end of blasphemy, or a high priest or someone else rising to take his place."

Madai heard her stubbornly, more than disappointed. The job should not be left to an unknown when he was better equipped. He started to protest and she knew it, because it was spread across his face in a hard line. She put her hand on his arm.

"It is all planned," she repeated.

He heard another passing guard. She did not flinch and he saw the courage in her eyes. She had endangered herself, but Nimrod had used a woman before...

"Why this ready bed, then, if Nimrod wants his women clean?" he asked, suddenly doubting her.

"Kittim said you would be cautious. This is a temple of the flesh. Inanna is a goddess of the flesh. People of this city may taste of it for a piece of gold."

The mention of Kittim did not persuade him this time, and he saw she was becoming impatient. "Suppose a seed is born that is not Nimrod's?" he asked.

Her mouth pursed slightly, for there was more she needed to tell him. "There is a select assembly, one that does not bide here, save the high priestess. These tempt him, but he is done with them. Palapa will share their fate soon enough; it is why you were given her. She shall die here, very young or very old, diseased and misused."

Madai was suddenly reminded of Iscah, young and alone at the hands of Hamonheb and En-UtuAten, even the Anak. "And you," he asked, prodding. "You are so used?"

"I am pure!" her words fairly struck him. "I do not use the stalk, and I do not display myself. The rest are better pleased that I do not vie for him." She calmed herself. "I was inserted amongst the rest when a child was dead at his hands, a young Inanna. They did not suspect, and he does not know us by our faces."

Her anger was genuine. He believed her again. "The god of chaos..." he began to ask.

The ferocity of her eyes matched that of Nimrod's. "Never use such words! He blasphemes and it will be avenged. His time is past; there will not be another Innana. For this and so much more, destruction will come. It is done," She arched her brow.

For the first time, Madai understood their vengeance would be surer than his, and he believed it would be soon. "When will it happen?" he asked.

"That is not for you to know. We would not have him read it in your eyes." Someone passed their alcove again, and the girl pulled Madai against her on the couch. She moaned, then whispered into his face, "You will know it when it comes, and you must escape. It will be possible then."

"And you?" he asked.

"I shall be upon the swiftest horse."

She rolled him off and disarranged her hair. "Nimrod seeks to replace Yah," she spoke the name with reverence, "The One True God. He seeks to remake the purpose of the great deluge and the confusion of tongues, to paint The One God ruthlessness. This fable must not spawn, nor the corruption of the stars. This is my only purpose." She began to pull away the curtain, but Madai grabbed her wrist.

"Tell me who you are," he insisted quietly.

She smiled at him proudly. "I am a daughter of Shem," she answered.

- *59* -

Almodad raised his arm. He waited for the precise moment when the enemy would be completely ensnared. He watched the sun glint off their coin-studded bridles and ran his left hand over the wound on his face. He thought of Abbidai and gripped his scimitar. He would not be too anxious.

The complication was the footmen. They lagged behind and were a swarm, though he must not wait too long and allow the first column to escape the wadi. So, with all but a few trapped in the canyon, he dropped his arm and the onslaught began.

He felt the Strong Arm.

He knew they would see victory today, and He would have it done quickly. Almodad dispatched arrows again and again. There was a deluge of them, stabbing the air like a storm, felling Nimrod's battalions till they were just a tangle of fallen men. The horses went wild. There was nowhere to hide.

But there was no King Nimrod atop his red horse, and Abbidai would not be safe. In a rage, Almodad called his yellow horse and sprung to his back. A company followed him. They galloped and slid the descent off the bluff, finding bloody purpose along the way - stopping Nimrod's remnant trying to escape.

- 60 -

Madai sat in the alcove. She had stunned him with her proud claim. A daughter of Shem! He could not believe it. He didn't know what to do next; she was gone and he was... sitting. He started to think about how they would do it, kill the man Nimrod and destroy so great a kingdom, an army. He was glad he had seen the Innana, and Nimrod, his passion exposed, because he had also seen the other Nimrod, the one who might have been better.

Somehow, sitting behind this curtain, it seemed things were lining up and he, witless, had stumbled into the very center. He felt a curious settling, even here.

Nimrod pulled the curtain back. "Madai!" he chided.

Madai jumped as he looked into the face of Nimrod - remarkable timing.

"I see your strength is sapped." Nimrod smiled. "I am pleased you have been served. I did not wish to doubt you." He lifted Madai bodily from the couch and set him to walk beside himself. Tazek had somehow reappeared behind them. "We shall yet produce in you a champion of Inanna," Nimrod laughed. "I shall have tiamat sent to Palapa tonight. You do not want to disappoint her."

Madai was saved a response. A loud disturbance sounded at the temple steps, drawing Nimrod's full attention. His good humor dissolved, and he stalked across the vacant hall toward the entrance.

"It is soldiers," Tazek whispered. They followed at a distance, stopping behind a pillar, watching just as Nimrod stood the first man up from his submissive posture.

"He is speaking," Tazek whispered again.

"I see that," Madai snapped. "What does he say?"

"I cannot hear."

Madai edged closer, hoping it was news of a great vanquishing, but Tazek would not follow. And then they both heard the roar Nimrod used to set the messenger quivering. Madai could see too well the unfortunate man's face. He was covered with dry blood, and wildly terrified. Before Madai could grasp the movement, Nimrod had gained hold of the man's scimitar and opened him from chin to groin. The remaining soldiers fell back, bent at the waist in absolute terror. Did they offer their heads? But no, Nimrod stepped over the dead man to leap across the steps toward his palace. He signaled one of the soldiers to follow, then barked another command at the rest. Madai and Tazek were gathered up and pushed forward to follow behind the raging giant.

They simply dumped Madai into Palapa's chamber and sent Tazek scampering to find his own way. It all happened at such a speed that Madai was stunned. He stood stock still in the room, wondering, hoping, trying to remember whether the daughter of Shem had said it would start today.

He took a drink. Could he save Palapa? Tazek? He would do what he could when the time came.

He waited a long time but heard nothing. When he tried the door, he found it barred. There was no sound of horses returning home, or armies or rampaging kings. But only silence. And darkness creeping slowly into the room. Madai looked between the bricks of lattice at the sky. The sun would soon touch the earth. It seemed a circumstance past enduring, until the door quietly opened.

He turned at the sound. Palapa entered her chamber hopefully, for she held the precious tiamat in her hand. If this were not favor enough, they were both called to Lord Nimrod's banquet this night. Rumor was whispered that one of the lord's own consorts had bedded a foreigner, an ally. She hoped it was Madai, though a part of her mourned the loss of the true Japhethite. But if he were won to Nimrod, then she might be saved. She entertained this notion with something akin to pleasure and put the tiamat carefully on the bed table.

"Palapa!" he exclaimed, relieved to see her.

At his pleasure, she was nearly certain. Her face was lit by hope.

"Tell me everything. The soldiers at the temple..." Madai asked.

And now she was confused. "Deserters," she answered blankly. She approached him timidly, putting her hand on his arm.

He started to tell her about the Shemite woman but remembered it was a secret; and there was something about her eyes, nearly as though... just when he was trusting her.

"Lord Nimrod is pleased by you," she murmured, running her hand down his arm.

He took a step back to look at her. "You have had the stalk," he accused.

She peeked up at him, hopeful again. "And some for you," she murmured, moving toward the table to fetch it. "There is time before the banquet." She looked up at him, lifting her yellow hair from her shoulders and arching her back. "It is said you have taken the flesh of the temple."

He grabbed her arms so roughly she grimaced. "You will quit this!" he demanded.

He shook her.

He pulled the weed from her hand, flung it to the floor and scraped it into the stone with his foot. He was angry to see the potion maneuvering her when he needed news. The pupils of her eyes enlarged and retracted and she started to weep.

"She shall not be punished," Palapa cried. "She shall be yours if you wish, for you are favored by the lord." Her chin quivered pitifully and she found herself pleading, "surely you do not love her."

He didn't know whether to laugh or to rage. It was an effective combination of both, and Palapa crumbled to the bed. Madai let her wail.

'How long does the tiamat last?' he wondered.

જ્રજ   જ્રજ   જ્રજ

It lasted till she awoke, for she had wasted herself with tears. It was completely dark, and no one had come to disturb them. When he heard her move, he dared to touch her shoulder.

"Palapa... you must be well," he commanded gently.

She opened her eyes, feeling nearly herself again. But tiamat does not distort the memory, and she was embarrassed. She rolled away from him. "I am well," she whispered.

"Excellent," he assured her, taking her shoulders to make her face him. "The banquet..." he urged.

She sat up as deliberately as she could and smoothed her dress. Then she scrambled off the bed. She would not look at his eyes but went to a polished bronze mirror to recover herself. She began to arrange her hair. She patted her face with water of anise and found her rouge. The worst had befallen her. The good Japhethite was lost and, in his fall, he still did not desire her. She dabbed herself with perfume, for she must not appear discarded. She would make of it the best she could. She would serve Madai faithfully and well and be among his household. She would lace his drink when he did not suspect, and bed him and be safe forever.

"You have pleased Lord Nimrod," she finally answered, turning back toward him. "Tazek has told me that he ever wished your service. And now that you have embraced the goddess," she waited for her pulse to calm, "there is all to gain."

"The banquet?" he asked again.

"We will be late, though it shall be excused," she answered him with her best bravery. "For Lord Nimrod expected..." She whispered the last. "We must hurry." Then she looked at his attire, still that of the ride to the ziggurat. Hastily she produced new robes from the cabinet and pulled her chair behind the curtain again as he changed.

- 61 -

Palapa was not entirely herself. She was gracefully lovely, her yellow hair combed down her back in waving silken threads. She knew her gown was not vulgar, as would be the dress of many a prosperous lady. Yet, it revealed her allure in a more delicate fashion. She was undeniably still a consort within the lord's palace. But it was not her appearance, it was her poise. She entered the hall clutching the hand of a kinsman, a man of strength she knew would become a man of power. He was known. Other men of power noted them as they entered. Ladies examined him with favor, and Palapa was resolved to become no public chattel at the temple. The high-born turned to admire her at Madai's side. Yes, that was better. She was carried by as heady a drug as tiamat.

Madai allowed her hand in his, knowing her timidity. She would be distressed at the faces that turned their way. He took her arm firmly and was assured of her gratitude by the look in her eyes.

They were directed to an empty space waiting at an enormously long table, where Madai found they were to sit on the floor with soft cushions. It was not so terrible as he had expected. There were no courtesans or dissipation or drunkenness. In fact, those at the table spoke quietly with one another, anticipating the King's arrival. But the room was not quiet; it was punctuated by the short, harsh calls of large, brilliantly colored birds, none as he had ever seen. A rainbow of color. Reenah would know...

The walls were draped with silk: crimson, violet and blue. Lamps lighted the room from golden stands, and sapphires were spilt on the table like common gravel. There was an incessant murmur of expectation in the air when suddenly a harsher sound trumpeted an arrival. Madai spun around to see a more beautiful creature yet. It walked upon its two legs, a bird of another sort, crested with drooping feathers of green and amethyst. They shimmered like the scales of the flying serpent; though entirely more benign. It dragged a long train of feathers behind it and twisted its shining head from side to side as it walked, the crest swaying and dipping. It was followed by another of its kind on the far side of the room. The crowd was delighted. The creatures began to call to each other and suddenly, lifted their magnificent tails.

They were high fans, standing, surely, five feet and as many in width, competing with each other and delighting their human audience.

Palapa was clapping her hands. She was giddy and Madai eyed her wine for floating leaves.

She looked at him expectantly.

"What are they?" he asked brusquely. Perhaps he could distract her.

Instead, she leaned against his chest and giggled. "You are so charmingly naive," she crooned, stroking his chest.

He sat her up with alarm. A lady opposite them smiled wryly and nodded to him as he held Palapa's wrist tightly at his side. "Do not make a display," he muttered, wondering where she had gotten more of the stuff. She was hurt again, because she fussed with her dress, but he could not be bothered now. She was, in the end, content to press her arm against him.

Two lovely slaves followed behind the birds. They were as dark as Nimrod, and wrapped in bright-colored cloth. They wore crests of feathers on their heads, fashioned from the birds, and held long thin cords which tied to the creatures' necks. The peafowl brandished their tails and strutted the full length of the hall, then unfurled their wings briefly to reach a high perch, on which they sat, attended by the dusky slaves and restrained by the scarlet cords.

A well- staged entrance, for Nimrod followed behind, the elegant priestess at his side. The surprise, really, and the delight of the guests, was what walked at his other side; confined by a leash was a black leopard. Nimrod held the cat firmly in command and smiled at his audience. Though the priestess was arrayed in a simple gown, Nimrod wore the dress of an army commander: leather skirt, scimitar and thick boots. The leather breast-plate, however, was missing. In its place was a covering fashioned of dragon-hide, the scales unmistakable. Madai was impressed. Nimrod was lord of a prosperous kingdom, its provider and protector. He was shrewd.

The birds were in a raucous panic at the sight of the leopard. They squawked and beat their wings at the air, to no avail as they were lashed to their perches. But feathers floated in the air and the leopard nipped at them, snarling at the frightened birds and nervous guests. A thick, dark man appeared immediately to remove him and tie the beast to a brass ring set in the stone wall. He did not leave, but stood at the back, beside the animal - just out of reach.

Nimrod laughed with delight as the birds slowly quieted. "Citizens," his voice was mellifluous when he finally spoke. "We are indeed graced by the gods; such beauty, such provision." He fanned his hands before them, indicating the enormous quantity of food. "I am delighted and honored by your presence."

The assemblage each bowed and muttered infatuated gratitudes.

Then Nimrod sat at the same table as Madai, at its head. He leaned on his elbow to partially recline against the priestess. She might be no more than a pose, but she was euphoric.

A line of slaves filed into the room, each carrying an urn to refill their goblets. Madai noted it was more wine and looked at Palapa with caution. She turned to him her most comely face and leaned toward him.

"It is safe," she assured him. "You are approved."

As if to underscore a truth, Nimrod nodded at Madai and smiled disarmingly.

"Eat, my friend," Nimrod commanded. The other guests noticed it, too, and determined to know the stranger.

Another noticed it, sitting at the far end of the room with the merchants. He could not maintain his place in their society much longer, for the gold platter was all that was left him. Sabta did not enjoy the profits he had hoped for. Surely the Spear should have brought more than it had. Who was the Japhethite that he should be lifted up? An ally of Job, no less, who denied the gods. Sabta would enlighten Lord Nimrod, if he were only given the chance. That there would be no chance, he regretted and resented. This banquet had cost him all the gold coins in his pocket.

The food was opulence. There were meats. There was fruit bursting with sweetness. There were breads and honey. A young flutist accompanied the banquet while all in attendance took more than their fill. And again, Madai could not enjoy the feast. He could not forget the daughter of Shem. He had watched for a sign that Nimrod's trouble was beginning, and he was watching for her. But she was not at the table; he had studied each lady's face, all unfamiliar, and found more than one willing to smile at him in return.

Palapa maintained her close presence at his side but did not attempt to caress him again. She was slowly deflating. Perhaps, too, the tiamat was filtering out of her blood, for she was becoming timid again. She would not think of all that she had said and done. She looked at Madai sidelong, through the veil of her hair. He was distracted, looking about the room. Was he looking for the prostitute? She was no more priestess than Nimrod was god.

A jealousy that might have spurred another to chase her passion brought Palapa only grief. Her grand ambitions were melting away.

Nimrod plucked the fruit from his plate to feed the priestess. The meat he kept for himself, absorbing its strength. He was a gigantic man, and able to take goodly quantities of food, but in this he was restrained, and finished his food in lieu of later pleasures. He had not yet drunk overmuch, as he had yet to address his audience before the rest of the wine and the anticipated tiamat. He found he was coming to need the drug; perhaps it was time the high priestess was replaced.

At a prearranged signal, one of Nimrod's army entered the chamber. He carried the sacred Spear. Nimrod stood up from the banquet, received it from the soldier and grasped it in his great hands. The diners quieted, looking up at him who was their host, and so much more.

"Citizens of Shinar," he began, "we have together enjoyed a night's provision in safety and abundance. It is not concluded; indeed, the best by way of drink and entertainment yet remains." He appreciated the scattered murmurs of approval for a short moment before continuing. "We are prospered by the gods. Indeed, as we feast, my army washes the earth with the blood of our enemies."

Instantaneous cheers erupted from the crowd.

Nimrod stood smiling and proud. "The goddess is revered and defended at this occasion, a mere three nights before the sacred marriage feast.'

Madai flinched, was then impatient, the assurance of the Shemite daughter starting to dim. He replayed the death of the messenger on the temple steps to cheer himself. But there was an abandon at this feast, and a confident King. Perhaps the soldiers were deserters after all.

"Our lands are freed from the fire-beasts," the King continued. "Our maidens are saved from the ravaging Shemites, and we are revered in the whole of the earth." Nimrod turned and looked directly at Madai. "Stand, my friend." He waited for Madai to slowly rise, the color of his face blanching first, then coming red as his beard. "This Japhethite is a mighty warrior. A worthy foe, but foe he is not. He is emissary of his people. He has traveled here for knowledge of the gods and to admire our prosperity. And he has returned an ancient instrument of war." Nimrod held the Spear in the air. "This Spear is endowed with all the secret art of the spirit world. There is power in this weapon that even we have forgotten. But it shall be reclaimed."

He looked at Madai with affection. "You may sit, now, Madai," he said quietly.

He lowered the Spear to address the audience again. "I knew you should wish to celebrate this high honor, the admiration of the earth and the final defeat of our old foes."

The room was silent. Then it burst into more thunderous applause. Nimrod's face was elegant with his pleasure. He returned the Spear to the soldier who remained behind him and sat back down. Tangled murmurs hummed on the air.

Another prearranged signal brought out more musicians with flutes and lyres and a flutter of veiled women who floated around the room, their movements an instrument of harmony. The wine goblets were refilled, and the citizens of Shinar reclined against one another to enjoy the amusement.

ങരു   ങരു   ങരു

But Madai watched the evening's progress with a sense near to depression. Nimrod sat within arm's reach, the very instrument of his death at the ready behind him. Madai studied the man holding the Spear. He was not young, and he was admiring the dancers, distracted. It would be quickly over... It would not be difficult, only allow Nimrod a bit more wine. Madai played with his drink, because he did not misjudge the giant's prowess or his strength.

Then he stopped himself from thinking like a boy. The Shemite woman had not said it would be tonight. No, he would not be foolish. If he had gained the mighty man's favor, there was time enough to wait. She had said there was a cause they hoped for him, to dispel a lie. He would like that, and he could kill Nimrod later, if the Shemites failed, and perhaps, still escape.

The music changed. It became a different quality, and a man and woman entered the hall. They were clothed only by strips of animal skin, remarkably few, at that. The coverings were not meant for modesty; indeed, they created a more suggestive appeal than had they been missing entirely.

The tall woman was coiled round by an enormous pale serpent. His head lay at her breast. His length must be ten feet, greater perhaps, for his great tail was carried by her partner and wound round the full length of his arm. They were powerfully strong, perfect specimens of humankind; they posed and stroked the snake and stroked each other. Then they carried the great serpent around the whole of the room, bending often to allow a nervous lady to touch his body. Her more intoxicated partner often reached out to handle the dancers rather than their snake, creating an uproar of laughter.

They passed the beautiful, noisy bird and the dark slave girl who held its leash. The man reached out, snatching at her costume in vain before passing by, stirring more laughter. The dancers and serpent even passed the mob of merchants at the back of the hall, pausing to twist and pose for their benefit. The snake constantly flicked his tongue at the air, lifting his head, then nestling amorously against the woman's skin.

The way the man and woman caressed the serpent, allowing it to roam the plains of the woman's body, was a sensuous exhibit. It was, for Madai, a mute testament of terrible allegiance. There was a serpent in the constellations and it was the enemy.

He watched the dancers with a bitter taste as they continued down the other side of the table, allowing its guests to admire their serpent, as well, until they neared the great man himself. The woman leaned toward Nimrod. He took her face in his hands; he stroked her neck; he ran his finger down her arm and smiled. Then he let her go and lifted the serpent's head and kissed it.

There was a silent moment, then an eruption of applause all around the room. The couple attempted to lift their serpent into the air for his last admirations, but he seemed too heavy and had grown increasingly irritable. The man uncoiled his arm by no small effort and attempted to remove the snake from his partner. But he was possessive of the woman and would not let her go. Evidently something more was to come, for the music changed again; but they had an unwieldy beast in their arms and the entertainment of the serpent was prematurely ended. Rousing applause followed their hasty retreat.

Nimrod leaned against the priestess and murmured in her ear. She was pleased. The music grew louder, the meter more rapid and the rhythm more intense. Madai grew ever more resistant. The atmosphere was telling, the mood was growing, and the expectations were coming clear. Nimrod lifted his head to look at Madai. His eyes were as lucid as ever. "If she does not inspire you," he murmured, indicating Palapa, "you may have your pick." He tipped his hand toward the dancers. Madai attempted to smile in return, drawing the wilting consort to his chest protectively and kissing her hair. Nimrod nodded and turned his attentions to the priestess, though he had taken note of a slim young dancer to his left.

The predictable tiamat was served on gold trays, carried by slaves who wore bells that jingled as they walked. Madai took those offered Palapa and himself. He crumbled them in his fist and waited for the crowd to drug themselves.

The guests drank and filtered away from the banquet table, Madai began to faintly detect a distant rumble. His muscles tightened, at immediate alert. He was seized with beautiful hope. He looked quickly at Nimrod, who had lowered his face to the priestess. The young dancer was there, as well, perched on his lap. As the priestess and the dancer vied for Nimrod's best attention and offered their goblets of wine, the rumble increased; Madai heard the unmistakable sound of horses. Nimrod heard it, too; he removed his hands and glanced toward the exterior doors of the long hall.

Every part of Madai urged that he leap up and take the Spear lying beside its sleeping keeper. None but Nimrod was yet alerted. As the sounds in the distance began to wane, even Nimrod, taken by tiamat, returned to his interest closer at hand.

Nimrod was just struggling to stand, fairly lifting both the priestess and the dancer as he did, to move them to a more convenient place, when suddenly the meaning of the distant sounds became undeniable - and less distant. Indeed, it was at the door. He pushed the women away from him, staggering slightly, for he was far gone with arousal. This he turned to his favor and roared in outrage. He leapt to the sleeping attendant, snatching up the Spear that had fallen to the floor.

In that instant, the doors burst open, shattering the air and filling it with terrified, shrieking guests. There was a trampling of citizens toward the back doors.

Madai leapt to his feet in expectancy. He pushed Palapa, who was screaming incoherently, behind him. "Run," he commanded her. The explicit directions of the daughter of Shem were immediately forgotten as he hastily scanned the room for a weapon.

Sabta was nearly crushed by the mob. He was pushed by its surge toward the exits, though he trained his eye on the tall, blond man at the far end of the room.

There was just a remnant of Nimrod's army still attempting the battle. Their horses were spent, and the men were every one wounded. But at the first breach of the city walls, the palace guards were alerted and swarmed the hall. There had been no wine for them, for the news of the unfortunate messenger, if not believed entirely, had been received.

- *62* -

A wild pandemonium of shrieking birds and shrieking women and a shrieking black panther splintered the air. The palace guards were stumbling across frantic slaves as they continued into the hall through a door to the south, rushing to secure the eastern doors as the Shemites pushed through them. Madai could hear Nimrod bellow; he saw him meet the enemy at the eastern wall, swinging his scimitar with terrible success, the Spear clutched in his left hand. There was nothing for Madai to grab. A surge of struggling men pushed against him; one of Nimrod's guards fell, mortally wounded. Madai stumbled as he snatched the dagger from the dying man's fingers, just as he heard one startled cry from a woman's throat.

He staggered, a sudden weight flung against him. Her arms flew upward as she threw her body against him; and she cried out again. It was then, her head slowly sliding down his chest, that he spied Sabta standing behind. The man's mouth was askew with frenzied hatred. Sabta yanked his knife from Palapa's back. As she slumped to fall across the scattered remains of the table, Madai met him with the soldier's dagger. He felt it slice off Sabta's nose at his first advance. Sabta dropped his knife, screeching in startled agony through bloody fingers, pawing his face. It was easy business for Madai to sink the dagger into the man's heart, a quick end to a forgotten foe.

It was not so easy to bend over the wounded woman. The abuse of her back would be mortal. He rolled her gently over and lifted her head. Her eyes were wide; she was warm, she was breathing.

"I told you to run," was all he could say. She could not answer at all. The length of the knife had perforated her through, and he laid his hand helplessly against the blood which was beating out across her chest.

Palapa felt nothing; indeed, she could move nothing at all. But she could see the face of the Japhethite, who held her gently and looked altogether undone. She was satisfied, for he was saved at least. She closed her eyes, feeling herself drift... and in the hum of blood which coursed past her ears and out the hole in her front, she heard the beautiful news that she was saved as well.

Madai laid her gently on the table.

ⲥⲅⲱ ⲥⲅⲱ ⲥⲅⲱ

The roar of battle was enormous. Men wrestled each other and dismantled each other. He was suddenly rushed by a Shemite, identifiable by his dress.

"I belong to the One True God," Madai shouted at the man.

The Shemite heard him and understood him and, in the haste of battle, accepted it as truth. They formed a battlement of two and fought across the tabletop toward Nimrod himself. Somehow, in the din of thrashing men, Nimrod heard his shout as well.

Madai was limited by the dagger, and pried a scimitar from a severed hand. It was impossible to tell whose cause the hand had served. He used ithe sword to slice his way across the room. His companion was fierce and fought with skill and presence enough to inspire even Madai. A wounded man fell across his path, one of Nimrod's. Madai saw him finished.

They fell into a battle against three of Nimrod's personal guards, known by the serpent's crest upon their shields. By this, Madai supposed they were nearing the front of the banquet hall, and the great King himself. The floor was slippery with blood; and though the enemy was weak from prior wounds, they still fought for their lord. The biggest of the three slipped; he caught Madai's blade with his chin, allowing him the simple task of a mortal thrust. The third man swung his scimitar singing through the air to take Madai while he was occupied with the first, only to catch Madai's sword under the ribs, spraying him with blood.

Still, more of Shinar's men poured into the hall from the palace proper to face the startling aspect of a man astride a yellow horse clattering through the eastern door and into the very center of the battle.

The man and his horse ignored the last squabble of men, shoving their way through to the very ground where Nimrod fought, a man possessed. The King was pushed back against the wall, yet surrounded by his most faithful guards. He held the Spear again, though he wielded his scimitar in his right hand and drove the Spear with his left. He was magnificent, and Madai marveled at him.

In that one mesmerizing moment, Madai felt the sting of a blade cross his back. His sword wobbled weakly as he quickly turned. The enemy was ready, grimacing with blood-washed teeth. Madai lifted his sword defensively and pushed away the heavy forward thrust of the man's long knife. The clash jarred his arms and he tumbled, off balance, slipping to the side. He lifted his sword, reading the signs of expected victory in his assailant's eyes. Then, as quickly as the danger presented itself, the man's eyes widened in surprise. Madai's companion took him from behind. The Shemite turned away immediately to engage again, and Madai scrambled to his feet lest he be caught unawares once more. But it seemed to be a battle with a forgone conclusion; the men of Shem were undefeatable, while the guards of Nimrod were confounded, even to fall by the swords of their own fellows.

ⲥⲅⲱ ⲥⲅⲱ ⲥⲅⲱ

When Madai looked again, Nimrod stood alone. He was facing the Shemite on the yellow horse. It was clear to Madai that the end was close at hand, and he wondered whether Nimrod knew it, too. He was startled when the King turned his way, for only an instant, to look him in the face. It was a look of ultimate rage.

The yellow horse reared high above him, pawing the air. Nimrod took the moment to heave the Spear at its great, powerful chest.

The horse was not killed straight away, though pierced through. It stumbled; and as it fell, Nimrod pulled back at the Spear. But its prongs had circled a rib, and held it there. He yanked it again and tried to twist it loose, then remembered in the instant that what made it deadly also held it fast.

It was his first panic and his last life's breath. As the horse fell to its knees, the man astride him brought his lance down into the giant's startled heart.

Madai watched Nimrod drop... bewildered... crumpled to his knees. Then the Shinar King bent at the waist. Inelegant death.

A silence followed. There were no pronouncements. Just a body empty of its power, no more than one of the fallen horde that stretched across the Shinar plain.

The Shemites roared and praised the man of the yellow horse. A raging purple wound trailed down his face. They allowed him the first approach to Nimrod. He tipped up the face with his boot to study it for life. Then he signaled his men remove it - as simple and final as that. The Shemites gripped Nimrod's feet and dragged him across the floor, trailing his blood. They pulled him down the stone steps and flung his body over the back of a horse.

The palace guards, scarcely standing, bloodied and disoriented, watched the dispatch of their king and were summarily finished.

ෆ⬧ ෆ⬧ ෆ⬧

The roar of clashing metal and the din of wounded men are the backdrop of war. It is as present as combat. But it is lost in the moment, only to be recalled in the stillness at the end. It was this stillness in the clamor of victory that made Madai remember what was lost. He looked across the banquet hall, over backs of fallen men, to where Palapa lay. He wondered briefly what would become of Tazek. What would the boy do without his sister?

He began the careful crossing of a field of bodies. It surprised Madai that the distance to Palapa was so short, for surely it had been an ocean's width only moments before.

He neared her reluctantly. She lay so disgracefully across the table, her gown a terrible crimson. But he was better by it; for when he reached her, he saw that her face was not pinched by misuse and disappointment, but was fresh and young again. It was graced by the only true smile he had ever seen of her.

ෆ⬧ ෆ⬧ ෆ⬧

"I told you to run," he heard the voice behind him. It was what he had said to Palapa.

"I did not remember it," he replied quietly.

"Come with me," the daughter of Shem demanded.

He followed her, still gripping the scimitar. "We are searching for Semiramis," she told him.

They picked their way along the north side of the room. The colorful birds were knocked from their stands, dying and dead. The panther, released somehow, had disappeared. A few of the citizens lay trampled amid the army.

"There is a woman behind that curtain," she said, drawing it back, "though I think she is not Semiramis." She looked at Madai for verification. No, it was not. A tall, slender form lay crushed within the coils of a yellow snake. "We killed the serpent," she finished, and dropped the veil with an imperceptible shudder.

"Semiramis was not at the feast," he told her quietly.

Then he followed her back through the jumble of bodies to the place where the blood of the horse and the blood of the giant mingled. The man who had wielded the blow stood beside his fallen beast.

"This is he," the girl said.

He looked up. "Madai," he said with a grim smile. He had been one of the ten Shemite captives. "There is one who is anxious to see you."

'Kittim,' Madai thought with relief.

- *63* -

The basket was heavy with fruit. There were no other beasts to carry it but their horses, saved from destruction by their absence on that day. Reenah called for Tutan; she did so quietly, even at this distance.

But he heard her and came to help her lift it with his ever-present kindness. There was, however, a graveness within him which she had not seen before the time of Job's trouble. She would have spoken to him, merely to make him smile, if not that Iscah called, her basket heavy and full, as well.

There were rows yet to harvest. But this would be the last basket of the day, for there were not horses enough to transport more. They would continue to pray that the frost would not come early. This fruit they would take to Ur; the morning was late, so they would likely remain the night there. This Iscah dreaded. The city sounds were disturbingly familiar, and they brought her dreams in the night.

Tutan fastened the last basket securely. "Good Cusah," he soothed, stroking the warm hide under the gelding's mane. He stretched his back, though it was by habit. The bending to get the bottom fruit and stretching to reach the top had made him fit and recalled harvest time in the fields of home. It was a superb day. His appreciation of that pleasure made him look back at the quiet house in the valley with remorse.

- 64 -

Madai's horse was swift and sure of foot, its path lighted only by the moon. They drove the horses quickly across the plain with care, wary of fallen bodies, man and beast, littering the way. Their group was small, just three and the daughter of Shem. Madai heard in the distance behind him the last assault upon the city of Shinar, as all that was not clay or stone was burned.

He heard the thud of horse's hoofs against the hard ground, and the creak of leather bound to leather, and the breathing of the horses. He also heard occasional shouts from the city, but these faded till finally he heard only their own sounds. Of the few he had known in the city, only Tazek and the little Inanna brought him pause.

He replayed the loss of Palapa; it would not stop. He felt the scimitar in his hand and the release it bought him. He replayed Nimrod's eyes looking at him, for what recompense it offered. And he remembered declaring, "I serve the One True God."

Madai was grateful for that moment, grateful he had cried out in the mayhem. A subtle turn, a creeping assurance, one he had not perceived until the moment his mouth spoke it. Perhaps it was why he had left the Spear behind.

In time, Madai was wooed by their steady pace and trusted his horse to follow the others. The battle was over and he was tired and would close his eyes... The night grew blissfully silent, his body's steady rocking a perfect, unconscious bearing with the gait of his horse; a pleasant drifting... Until a subtle shift of balance, or perhaps it was the daughter of Shem. He opened his eyes to tiny pinpoints of light in the distance as he heard the girl speak to him again. He looked at her with a start.

"It is my father's camp," she repeated.

At this he was fully awake, watching the campfires slowly grow larger. 'Kittim may be here,' he began to think again. The fires were enormous, a beacon in the night. He began to see shadowy forms walking in the distance; he began to smell burning wood.

It was more than an army camp. There was a sound of bleating sheep. And they did not fear an ambush, nor discovery by an enemy, as was proved by a friendly sentry. A large tent was erected in the center of many smaller ones, and it glowed amber with a light from inside. To this place they were steadily aimed; and when they reached it, he was forgotten. His escorts jumped eagerly down from their horses, even the woman, and flung back the tent's closure with abandonment.

"Father Shem!" they cried. "We are returned by the Hand of 'Elohiym – Praise His Name. The corrupter is dead!"

Madai dismounted his horse stiffly. He looked at the light streaming from the open tent and found himself timid to enter, as though he walked outside himself and all the battle forgotten. An overwhelming apprehension began to pound with his heart - fulfillment. An Ancient.

The voices quieted as he stepped into the tent. The daughter of Shem and his two escorts were standing at his left, and the woman smiled at him. Though he could not see her plainly, for the lamp was low, he expected it was a proud smile. He looked beyond her to four men sitting on a rug along the back of the tent, obscured by the smoky interior. There was a low table in front of them, and they held small cups of tea in their hands. It seemed ridiculously commonplace. And no one spoke.

The first man was older than Madai's father. The shadows of the tent found the long, deep furrows in his skin, reminding Madai more of an ancient shepherd than a warrior. Was it Shem? He would, by reason, be the eldest. The aged man simply smiled a silent greeting.

The second man, just to the right, was not so old. He appeared come from battle; a long dagger was lashed across his chest. His arms were large. His eyes were black; a great dark beard grew just below them, and the hair of his head stood up like a sheep's, ready to shear.

The third man was near the age of the first. His hair was braided and hung down each side of his face and was lined with gray. Indeed, this was a shepherd, for he wore a fleece across his shoulders.

And the last man sat in the farthest corner, in the shadows, as dark as the other three, with curling black hair and intense, piercing eyes. He smiled.

Madai was rooted to the ground by his pounding chest. He could not move. "Kittim!" The name slipped through his lips on the breath of relief and simple joy.

The sound broke the silence of the tent.

Kittim stood up and, with two quick steps around the small table, reached Madai. He clasped Madai's arms in his hands and kissed him on both sides of his face.

"God be praised," Kittim announced. "It has been a very long journey,"

It was a moment that spills itself over with untold emotion, questions and a need to tell. Madai could only nod and smile.

"His Strong Arm has brought you," Kittim continued, words meant specially for Madai.

CBCR   CBCR   CBCR

God's Strong Arm. Yes. The storm upon the Brine Sea, and the serpent, the Anak and the fire-beast. What lured him in Nimrod's eyes. Yes. He did not speak it aloud, that he was sure, though he saw Kittim's silent joy as though he had.

"Son of Ye'fet," a man spoke behind them.

They released each other and turned to face he who had spoken - the man in the center, the warrior, the tallest man Madai had ever seen.

"Madai," Kittim pronounced, "This is Shem, son of Noah."

- 65 -

They were interrupted at that moment by the sound of horses and the shouts of jubilant men, though it was only a backdrop for Madai, a meaningless din. He was staring from Kittim to the one he had called "Shem." It was a moment to be forever remembered, one that made the soles of his feet tingle, one he knew he would recount to Japhet in perfect detail.

The man named "Shem" was standing and looking out toward the noise, as intent on it as a falcon after prey. He looked at Madai, a penitent expression on his face.

"Shalom, kinsman. I praise Elohiym at your coming. But I must meet them; forgive me." He moved quickly outside, swept away by their triumph; indeed, had he not, Madai was quite sure they would have tried to enter, every one of them.

"The city is taken," Kittim became interpreter again.

The words brought Madai back to the enormity of what had occurred this night. "Yes," he replied. "And Nimrod is dead."

"They are discussing the body," Kittim told him.

"It's here?"

"The queen was not captured," Kittim continued, betraying distress, "The temple was empty. Semiramis and the priests have disappeared." Kittim listened to the scramble of words outside the tent. "The deception will live."

Madai remembered what was warned of Semiramis by the Shemite woman.

There seemed to be a disagreement. Many voices speaking all at one time, then quiet. Madai heard one man's voice, even and resolute. Kittim did not tell Madai the words till the speaker stopped and the clamor of voices raised again, this time to fill the night air with consent.

"They will cut Nimrod's body into parts," Kittim told Madai, "and take them in every direction to the cities he built to show them how much a god he really was. To remind them that Mighty God will not be blasphemed."

Madai was caught off guard by the grizzly plan. He had the immediate image of a body cleaved from breast to groin. And yet, the man was dead... what he had done to the living... Madai slowly nodded. "Will it persuade them?" he asked.

"Men are persuaded by many things," Kittim answered vaguely. "Shem is very zealous for his God."

He looked at Madai's arm where he had held it, and the front of his torn robe. "You did not heed Misha," he said abruptly.

Madai looked down; dried blood traced the lines in his hands and his tunic was black with it. He felt the tight sting of a wound on his back. "It was on me before…"

But Kittim stopped him and put a tight grip on his arm to lead him away from Shem's tent, toward another. All the while a man they had come so far to find was somewhere in a swarm of men and horses, just come from a great victory.

"There is a tent prepared for you," Kittim explained. "Shem purposed to take the city before the feast of Inanna, and you, as well."

Little fires dotted the plain, abandoned, as the camp congregated in front of their leader's tent. It was good that the fires burned, for they lighted their way to a small shelter of woolen rugs. There was no lamp burning inside, so Kittim took a branch from the fire to light it, illuminating a simple interior furnished with two sleeping mats, a low table, a water jug and basin, and Madai's bow. Madai ducked his head to enter behind Kittim, glimpsed the weapon and turned, startled with admiration.

"How do you accomplish such things?" he asked.

"By the Mighty Arm of God," Kittim answered again. He poured water into the basin. "You are covered in blood."

Madai began to wash it from his hands, his face. His beard dripped red.

"A woman was sent me," he began quietly. "A Japhethite." Madai looked at Kittim as he replaced the dirty water. "She took Sabta's dagger - meant for me." Madai pooled fresh water in his hands, thinking of Palapa, and splashed his face again.

"Nimrod kept many captives," Kittim replied severely. "Such was the mission of the ten Shemites; they were after their daughters."

Water dripped from Madai's nose. "And were they found?" he asked quietly.

"They were rescued by Misha as the battle began, in the first panic. She had been alerted." Kittim waited a moment, permitting Madai to digest it. "The Inanna, as well, daughter to the one who slew Nimrod, Almodad by name."

Madai listened as the tiny droplets of water drained through his beard into the basin. "Good," he answered, thinking of Nimrod, who would have ravaged her, so terrible, a changeable man.

"He might have been a better man, Kittim, maybe a great man."

"Yes," Kittim answered, taking a clean robe from the mat on the floor. He handed it to Madai; it smelled faintly of sheep. "A quality given him by the Mighty God. So have all humankind this making. Nimrod did not use it well."

Madai took the shepherd's robe, noting Kittim's modest sermon. He removed his tattered clothes. It seemed so long since they had been given him by Palapa. He piled them in a heap on the floor. Then Kittim saw his back.

"This should be tended."

Madai lay on the mat. "It isn't deep," he argued. "But I am tired."

He could hardly believe it just this day's morning that he had ridden behind

Nimrod to the ziggurat, and now everything had changed. There was the promise of an Ancient, Kittim was found and the dawn was near.

"It's good to find you," he told Kittim. The reminder that he would speak to the son of Nua in the morning was nearly an afterthought.

🙰🙰 🙰🙰 🙰🙰

Madai woke to a bright day and the clamor of bustling activity, remarkably, the bawling of sheep. He turned on his side, feeling the tight reminder of his back. He opened his eyes and the sides of the tent startled him. He reoriented quickly: the victory, the Ancient, his own expectations. He was awake with energy. The timing was perfect, as Kittim pulled the drape of the entrance aside.

"Good morrow, Madai!" he exclaimed. "The greater number of the camp has already packed up and are gone. They are returning daughters to their mothers." His voice was vigorous.

"How have I slept through it?" Madai asked as he rose, sorry he had not seen with his own eyes the rescued maids.

"With great intensity, Madai," Kittim answered in a good humor. "How is your wound?"

"Is Shem gone?" Madai suddenly asked with alarm.

Kittim chuckled. "He is waiting at his tent for you. There is chill in the air," he finished, handing a ram's fleece to him.

"This is the Ancient I hardly hoped to find." Madai was excited as he wrapped the offered pelt across his back and left the tent.

The camp was nearly deserted. Again there was the confidence of the Shemites; just a hand full of tents remained, and a gathering of sheep. The aspect of war had been erased in a night.

In the light of day, Madai could easily identify Shem's tent. It was the largest, to accommodate numbers. The tents were grayish, mottled black and white, made by the wool of the scattering flock. The air was cold and Madai invigorated, with expectations high.

He hardly noticed the distance they crossed to the warrior's tent. Shem was waiting for them at the entrance. The morning's impression of him was nearly the same as the night's. He was a tall man, heavily bearded, with severe dark eyes sheltered in thinly lined, weathered skin. His hair covered his head like a fleece, black, though in better light spattered with gray. When he smiled, his teeth were large. And his intense eyes wrinkled.

"Shalom," he greeted. "Son of Ye'fet." He bowed his woolly head and waved his hand toward the tent. "We have waited for you."

There were the two other Shemites, holding the little cups of tea. This morning there were hard loaves of bread, as well, the remains of an army's provision. Madai looked at the two elderly men sitting in front of the morning coals which heated the tent remarkably well.

"Shalom," the elders effused as he and Kittim entered, taking seats on colorful rugs.

Kittim received the tea, and Madai, also. Shem recited thanksgiving to his

God.

"The excellent arm of Elohiym, praise His Name, has recovered you here. For this I am greatly joyous," Shem said. "Kittim has made your purpose known. No better purpose is there."

Even the proximity of an Ancient could not quiet Madai's stomach as he received the cold bread. He looked at the men sitting on either side of Shem, clearly older. "I am humbled by you," he managed.

"You could bring me no better joy," Shem reiterated. "It is the intent of my years to speak the truth of Elohiym. There are few who wish it."

Madai watched the men take their tea. They seemed completely content - and he with a churning in his belly. He calmed himself and sipped his hot drink carefully. "What will become of Shinar?" he finally asked.

Shem studied the rim of his bowl as the lines of his face hardened. Then he looked through the door to the sheep still milling round. "Shinar..." he muttered. "Man will do what he will. Semiramis serves the enemy. She will increase; we did not discover her."

"Surely Nimrod's defeat is a triumph," Madai insisted.

Shem looked back at Madai with a thin, sympathetic smile. "Nimrod contended with Elohiym," he replied vaguely, "and did not prevail. We divided his body; it may dissuade some."

But Shem's disappointment would not diminish the accomplishment for Madai, nor his own purpose. Here sat an Ancient, the very son of Nua, and yet... Madai looked at the elders who sat on Shem's either side. He turned to Kittim.

"How is it that Shem is not the eldest here?" he asked his friend abruptly.

Kittim was smiling. "Ah," he answered. "The vigilant Madai, you have returned. But let me answer you; perhaps it speaks more of the first earth."

"What sort of answer is that?" Madai sputtered, as an evasive Kittim had returned as well.

"It is an answer better told by those who lived it," Kittim returned.

Shem put down his tea to chuckle outright.

"I am Hadorum, son of Joktan," the first elder replied. "What had my ancient father, Shem, to do at my years but enjoy the grace and bounty of the first earth and strengthen his arms fitting timbers?" Hadorum looked at Shem with a blend of affection and respect. "I have 224 years upon this earth and do not doubt that few remain. Look at my ancestor; there shall not come another who endures as long or as well as he."

"And I am Abimael, brother of Hadorum," offered the second man. "We keep the service of Elohiym, through the words of our forefather, and hold him up." Abimael chuckled, looking at Shem's sturdy form.

The three kinsmen laughed together and finished their tea.

"Madai," Shem said, standing, with a slight apology in his voice. "The snows are near. These herds must be moved to a near valley, and it can not be delayed. Your questions deserve proper answers. I wished to tell you myself, for I know your purpose, and that the way has been long. But it is only a short journey more." He recognized Madai's dismay. "One is there who is better able to restore, in words, the first earth for you."

Madai was instantly and entirely incredulous. He stood watching in disbelief as Shem and his ancient son's sons began to remove their belongings, and the activities about the remaining camp began in earnest. Younger men began to arrive and set about the removal of Shem's very tent. They folded the heavy rugs to pile upon the backs of their war horses while Madai watched. A more inconvenient activity there could not be for the man who had crossed the Brine Sea to find this Ancient, this son of Nua.

"Have we not journeyed far enough?" Madai asked Kittim as they watched the bustle. "Only a day longer... could he not remain a day?"

"Perhaps there is something better at the end of his journey." Kittim tantalized him with his vagaries. Madai was frustrated. Kittim saw it and finished the conversation as kindly as he could. "The Ancient you seek is not Shem," he counseled. "It is his father."

Rahabim brought them Havilah for fear that the Lady would sell him. He brought them himself, as well, and Lemmeri, for Job's Lady would not abide them any longer stirring about her house. It had become a silent and dire place.

Reenah's cottage, in contrast, was cramped and busy. Havilah was welcome, for he was another beast to carry grapes to Ur and to return with more wine pots. It meant, as well, that Iscah did not have to go to the city.

On those occasions when they were gone to sell the grapes, Iscah sat at the river, or she climbed to the platforms Reenah used for her birds. She even ventured once to the sand bar to dig at the bones of behemoth. This Marisheba forbade her ever again to do, lest she be eaten along the way.

Iscah allowed herself these afternoons to look to the east, waiting to glimpse the first dust of Kittim's horse, and Madai's. Had there been time enough to reach Ararat? Tutan warned there had not. He at least shared the longing for their return and tales of their adventures. When Tutan was at the end of day, his hands and legs purple with grape, they dreamed of the ship and their friends and imagined what it would be to put fingers and hands against the ancient timbers.

Iscah hugged her knees, feeling the wind bring a chill from the north, and thought about Kittim... again. Kittim, the beautiful man who had first calmed her fears, who loved Mighty God and saved her from Hamonheb. Kittim, whom she loved and longed after. She looked toward the eastern horizon and knew she would serve him in whatever way he desired.

"**H**is father? Kittim, you can't mean..." Madai's words trailed as he followed Kittim at a trot.

Kittim was already fixing their belongings to the saddle of his horse. He glanced across his shoulder with a tempting look. "You know who Shem's father is."

Madai reached his gelding, which was eating the low grass like one of the Shemite's woolly sheep. He took the halter and grabbed up his bow, so inconceivably retrieved by Kittim. He saddled the horse over one of the colorful Shemite rugs and quickly mounted. He gouged the horse's flank, more roughly than the animal deserved, and skittered up beside Kittim.

"The genealogy I know," Madai insisted. "What I don't know is how that can even be possible." The horses began to trot. "If I could only speak to Shem for a day..." His words rattled through his teeth as he looked at the far mountains.

And when Kittim only gave him a helpless shrug, Madai muttered, "Though I suppose there is the ship. How far is that?"

"Beyond Nimrud Dagh," Kittim answered, pointing to a mountain in the distance. "And then, very near."

'So you say,' Madai thought stubbornly.

Finally he had just to settle on his horse for the ride. In reality, it was a respite he could use. It had been a troubled journey to the city of Nimrod; things had been seen and done and left which needed some quiet unraveling. He looked at Nimrud Dagh, the mount which was yet a monument to the fallen King of Shinar, and rounded his shoulders.

ᏩᏋ   ᏩᏋ   ᏩᏋ

Their company no longer looked like an army. Cries of triumph were replaced by the constant bleating of sheep. Madai strayed his gaze to the dingy, shaggy backs, like one ever-changeable beast, remaking its shape each time an unruly ram led a knot of ewes astray. Ever-vigilant canines darted after the erring bunch to bring them back. He watched their busyness with mild amusement, even admiration. A remarkable achievement to so tame the beast that would by nature hunt the sheep.

By midday, the diversion of the herd had lost its distraction. Madai had settled into that familiar monotony which was learned in the long distance of the travel that lay behind him. There was nothing else to be done but to accept that Shem would not wait for his questions. He could scarcely imagine the prospect of finding Shem... yet, Nua? Certainly he had not believed the tale of long lives. He was bothered again with doubts; he recognized the feeling...

Even so, he trusted Kittim. And he began to consider what to do if there were to be found the forebearer, an unlikely prospect, certainly, but if it were true,,, There would be so much to ask the father of the second earth.

There came a whirlwind across the plain. It drove dust in a spiral, a steady churning, coming ever nearer. It was a persistent cyclone, aimed headlong at them, more than a capricious wind.

'I wonder who it is,' Madai thought, watching.

His horse slowed, a silent command from all the others of his kind, and Madai looked to the front of their troupe, at Shem, who led their woolly company. He had stopped, awaiting the approaching cloud as though he expected it.

"Warriors?" Madai asked Kittim.

Kittim nodded once. "Likely," he answered.

"Bringing news," Madai continued, and Kittim nodded again.

The little specks grew to become men and finished the distance quickly to come alongside Shem. They talked. Madai stood in his stirrups to watch and wondered after the news of the city for the first time. It seemed so long ago, with prospects of Nua or, more likely, his ship. He wondered if there were word of Tazek or Semiramis and thought again about the warning the Shemite girl had left him.

It seemed they would make a temporary camp, for a young man came to Madai and Kittim and began to erect a square of white cloth, under which he laid two thick rugs, and a third over the two.

Madai dismounted, not altogether sorry for an unexpected rest in the shade. He and Kittim drank water from their flasks and watched as the sea of sheep settled down to snatch a mouthful of grass. The men were still talking to Shem. Perhaps it would lend Madai a hasty conversation with him after all. Madai, shielded from the sun, soon recognized one of the men, him who bore the scar on his face. There were five men in total.

One of the group dismounted and began to make his way toward them. Madai soon grinned in recognition. He rose to greet her.

"Daughter of Shem," he smiled.

"Shalom, Madai," she responded as he led her back to his spot beside Kittim.

"You are better than when last I saw you."

Kittim rose to meet her. "The peace of Elohiym be yours."

"Yours as well, Kittim." She smiled. "I see you have restored Madai."

"The hospitality of Shem has done this," Kittim answered graciously.

Madai thought the hospitality of Shem had gotten him frustration. But he looked at the Shemite woman, recalling the one who wore silk and sweet fragrance, now replaced by one who dressed as a man and carried a scimitar. As she sat down on the wool rugs, she observed him observing her.

"Almodad's son will bring us tea," she continued calmly. She smiled at them. "We have made a great victory." She pulled the scimitar from her belt ,where its hilt dug into her side, and laid it on the ground.

She looked at him with wide, candid eyes, dark, flecked with amber, then she didn't flinch, even telling them, "We have delivered the head of Nimrod to Akkad."

"And the young Innana's?" Madai asked, as though it were commonplace to deliver heads.

At this she gave a genuine smile. "The young daughters of Shem are rescued," she answered.

A youth arrived with tea. "Thank you, Sheleph."

He did not linger; but he looked at her with undisguised admiration before returning across the little camp.

She held the cup in both her hands and briefly closed her eyes. She seemed suddenly tired. Madai wondered what was accomplished by her and the other four of her company. How far, he wondered, was Akkad, and what dangers had they found there as they arrived with the gruesome spoil? She opened her eyes to find him once again looking at her.

"I am happy you are restored," she said, "as you did not obey my instruction." At this, Madai perceived her less disapproving than her spoken word. "I am here at Abba's bidding," she continued, "to inform you what was done and to tell you that you shall make camp here. One will come to assist you. We must be brief, for my companions want to go farther still. I wish, as well, to learn what was the death of Palapa, who was a help to me."

Madai watched her face soften at the mention of the girl. Kittim asked, "Was there good achieved at Akkad?"

Misha shrugged. "Only hostility was done. They were shaken. Nimrod was a legend to them." She shrugged. "He is proved no god, at least." She looked at Kittim with a suggestion in her eyes that he would know the importance of what she said next. "We did not find Semiramis."

"Then she will increase," Kittim predicted.

Misha nodded slowly. "What was gained as Nimrod's queen will be her advantage." She looked at Madai. "You must renounce Semiramis when you return to your land. Expose the deception."

"The people of my Family do not know the name of Semiramis," he assured her.

"But you are come for that cause, are you not?" she asked, mildly confused.

He took a delaying sip of hot tea, then he looked at her, sorry for what he would answer. "Evil is there already," he confessed. "Corruption was brought in the scattering. It is my appointed quest to search out the truth."

Misha returned his look with a weary shrug. She took another slow drink of tea. "Well, you have seen him dead," she muttered.

Kittim put his hand on Madai's shoulder. "She is tired, Madai."

"Still, there is the corruption of the stars," she persisted, a rugged metal in her voice. "You must renounce that."

Madai nodded.

"And there is the father of Shem," Kittim encouraged her. "We are taking Madai there."

She looked up. "Father will take you to 'Ab Noach himself?"

Kittim nodded. "Does that surprise you?" he asked.

She finally shook her head slowly. "I thought only that Abba would wish to be alone when he brought the news of Nimrod."

"It will cause him grief?" Kittim asked.

Misha's brows lifted. "It should bring me no grief," she announced. "But my elder Abba shall mourn him." She passed her hand across her face, pushing her hair back. She looked at Madai with a shrug. "His years remember Nimrod as a son of his son."

Then she drank the last of her tea and put the cup on the ground. She ran her fingers across the hilt of her scimitar, and Madai could see that she was thinking of something else.

"Would it bring you pain to give me the telling of Palapa?" she suddenly asked.

Somehow, it was easier to tell her that than what was already said of spreading deceptions. "There is little to tell," he answered carefully, intending to guard the shame of the tiamat potion. "She died quickly, saving me."

It seemed to startle Misha, though she had seen Palapa slain. Madai explained the murder.

"And she did not suffer?" Misha asked after another assurance.

Madai remembered the true smile Palapa had left with him. "She did not," he answered quietly.

When Misha was gone, Kittim stretched out on his mat. "You have been patient," he remarked.

Madai lay on his back and smiled ironically, staring at the peak of their tent. "You are most eager to get me to this man," he answered.

"Shem's father." Kittim stated.

"Yes." Madai continued to look up. "I have wondered about him."

"Hmm."

"It's hard to believe, you know."

"Do you think you know so much about the earth?" Kittim asked him.

"Only that men do not live many hundreds of years," Madai replied, looking at him. "Those are myths."

"So what of Shem?" Kittim challenged.

Madai rolled to his side. "Is he the son of Nua?" he asked. "Not the son of the son?"

Kittim turned his head to look at him. "I have never deceived you. But, as with all things, you must judge that for yourself."

Madai stared at him, his unwavering face. He decided to change the subject. "You remember what Job has said of Nua's great ship?" he asked.

"We will search for it," Kittim responded. "It would be the proper tale to bring Tutan and Iscah."

"Yes it would," Madai agreed. "And The Family."

- 68 -

Reenah lay beside Iscah on the mat beside the oven. She listened to the soft breathing of sleep which came from those who now shared her cottage. It was empty no longer. Lahabim curled on a rug, Marisheba slept with Lemmeri in the room that had been Reenah's, and Tutan slept on a mat beside the door, where it was coldest. She could distinguish his breathing from that of all the others. It was deep and slow and dear.

She was bone-tired, though she could not sleep. Her back was stiff from the bending and lifting, and she could not fix herself in a comfortable position. Tomorrow they would finish the last of the wine and wait for a better time to bring it to Job. 'Uncle,' she thought. 'Deserted by the God you served so well. Ah, so it is... He is no God at all.' She was sad at the thought.

She heard Tutan turn in his sleep. It had been long since she had wanted a man or loved a man; indeed, her young soldier had been the last, though more had shared her bed. And that had been long ago, as well. The fatal blow to the deity of Job's God was heavy, indeed, for He was revered by Tutan - even now.

'I cannot share what I do not possess,' she thought, meaning faith in the One God. Tears trailed from her eyes, down the sides of her face.

ೲ ೲ ೲ

The cold night found its way between the door and Reenah's brick floor. Tutan pulled his robe tighter. He wanted to move nearer the oven, but it would be too near that other warmth. He could hear her breathing, she who was even more beautiful stained with grape. She who could not tame the hair around her face and bore the henna scroll. She who did not believe.

He turned his back to the door in a stubborn if fruitless search for warmth. And he asked God to remove the hindrance Reenah caused him. He asked as he had done countless times before, till he heard her turn in bed and wondered whether her back ached so much as to steal her sleep away.

- 69 -

A cold wind blew from Nimrud Dagh and caught Madai off guard at the approaching season; though perhaps it was known by the Shemites, for they had erected better tents tonight. The sheep scarcely needed tending, as they had huddled one against the other, not for want of heat, surely, but perhaps to brave the howling wind.

Misha had gone many nights ago with her companions. Madai hoped she would be saved from the weather and was not sure whether she had gone to her family or to the Ancient himself - for she called him 'Ab,' a title which meant father, as explained by Kittim. He turned to his side, adjusting the warm fleece, not knowing why he could not sleep.

He passed the night with his shoulder up into his neck, curled on his side, listening for morning. It came before light with the sounds of unsettled sheep. He pushed back his night covering and jumped up quickly to look through their tent flap. He was face to face with Almodad's young son, Sheleph.

"Shalom," Sheleph said quietly. "Father Shem will take you today, over the mount. He waits at his tent for you."

Kittim heard them and sat up.

"Ah Madai!" he announced. He clapped his hand on Madai's back, starting out of the tent. "You must be cheerful."

Thus was the prelude to their final day of travel in search of Nua's ship, nearly commonplace and without fanfare. There was no time for giddy nerves and little time for food. Just a bite of bread and cheese, and scorching hot tea.

Madai watched the shepherds lead their sheep into a wedge of valley as he and Kittim followed Shem toward the mountain.

‣‣‣ ‣‣‣ ‣‣‣

A huffy, dusty, annoyed man approached them on the back of an equally annoyed grey ass. He swatted his donkey's rump with a short stick and led a second. A trio of desert slaves followed him. Their shoulders were broad, and bent with heavy loads. As their procession drew near, the man seated on the ass barked at Madai and his companions. His invective caused Shem a wry smile and, when the man had passed, a laugh from the cavern of his great chest.

"He wishes us better fortune," Kittim explained, "than he has had."

Madai thought it was an odd thing to say and twisted in his saddle to watch the slaves follow after their master, stirring up the dust as they passed. The plump little man continued his mutterings, grumbling until they were gone from sight. Madai decided he looked like a merchant and was mildly encouraged, thinking there must be a settlement near. Then he glanced back around at what still seemed to him a complete wilderness.

Madai had been gauging their progress by a high mountain, which he had spied after reaching the crest of Nimrud Dagh. They had passed through a narrow valley and were now nearing the base of the mountain, which rose to even steeper heights. As Madai was dreading that their efforts must take them farther still, he smelled the unmistakable bite of smoke in the air. Straining though he might, he could see no human habitation. He did, however, see the smoke, coiling high into the crisp air, rising from the very grass of a small foothill. A campfire, nothing more. Perhaps the disgruntled man had left it burning. Shem made a straight line toward it, though the mound was set at an awkward spot for accessing the mountain, which rose to forbidding heights beyond.

Madai had no sooner begun to dread the climb than he recognized evidence of cultivation. An orderly, mature vineyard grew here, already harvested of its fruit. As they rode past it, he noted a stone wall, well-constructed, encircling a garden. A skillful hand worked here, tending and taming the earth. But try as he might, there was not a house nor a tent to see.

A little herd of strange creatures nipped at the grass beyond the stone wall. They lifted graceful, longish necks to watch the men ride past, chewing steady at a thing in their mouths. Madai had seen such eyes as they had before, eyes like a deer, large and dark with a long, curling fringe of lashes. The animals were curious, though slightly skittish, as they continued their chewing. They were nearly camels, though altogether more handsome and not so large. Their bodies were covered with soft, reddish wool that went toward yellow at their bellies. Handsome as they were, Shem rode past without a glance. Madai noticed he had hastened his pace, taking them in a deliberate straight path toward the smoky fire.

They were near the mound when Madai suddenly realized it was not a hill of dirt at all, but a human construction. It was a great and ancient stone building. And the fire had been no merchant's campfire, but smoke rising from a stone chimney. The entire huge structure was made of rock, topped, remarkably, by a meadow of grass. There was a large stone altar at the side, such as was used by The Family, where he had burnt thanks to the Great God with his own father, so far away.

Shem looked back at them over his shoulder. "We are arrived," he pronounced with excitement and total joy. He crossed the remaining distance at a canter, dismounted before his horse had stopped and bounding into the house, leaving the animal to stand looking after him, its breath heaving up a mist.

Madai and Kittim sat motionless on their horses. "It's a strange house," Madai vaguely muttered. His eyes trailed along its stone construction. It was large and high, overgrown with sturdy bushes and vines that crawled up the stone to finish their tendrils somewhere in the grassy roof. There were single, pointed blades of bright green sprouting up at the base of the building, dotted with splashes of color, red and amber. The stones were not hewn, but they were skillfully fitted, bound by mud or perhaps pitch.

His eyes trailed back to the roof. 'How does one make a covering of living thatch?' he wondered. 'And why?' He wondered about the rain, and did it drip mud? There were still meadow flowers sprinkling the green, making the illusion of a hill complete. If it was a curiosity, it was a charming one.

"Who lives here?" Madai asked Kittim.

"I believe it is Shem's father," Kittim answered wryly.

"Your Noah?" Madai chided him.

Kittim turned away from the building to look at Madai with a lift of his brow. "Did I not say that you would judge for yourself?" he asked deliberately. "Moreover, you shall not need my skills. Noah and Shem each speak the tongue of Japhet. Noah speaks many languages; his purpose these many years has been to proclaim the One True God with whatever speech is required."

Madai stared at his companion, feeling chastised again. In all their journey, Kittim had proven to be nearly without defect in regard to judgment. A thin shiver ran across his skin as he realized it; he looked at the house and considered who might have built it - a builder of giant ships?

The door swung open, Shem suddenly reappearing, "Abba is in the stable," he announced.

Kittim and Madai came with their horses behind Shem. He waited only until they dismounted before he started at a jog toward a second shelter, made in the same fashion as the house. When they reached it, Shem pushed back the heavy door.

Its interior was quite large. Already sheltered there were a small band of sheep, a few horses, and something rather bulky, like a wild ox.

What stood looking at the sheep was an extremely tall man, taller even than Shem, should you straighten his slight stoop. He did not hear them enter. He was dressed in a cloak of woolly skin. His hair was not entirely white, though nearly. At the back it was grey, the color of thunderclouds, and generously streaked with waves of silver. This hair had escaped from a leather strap and stood nearly on end. Even from a distance, and in the dim, Madai could see him; his beard was entirely white, reaching just below his chin, and very thick. His face was darkened by years in the sun.

And then there came a snort, Shem's horse, recognizing both the man and the stable. The old man looked up, his hair circled in a billowy white wreath around his head. He was surprised at first, before his face came alive, widening with round, wrinkly eyes and a great, merry smile. He lifted his arms, spreading out the cloak, creating the image of a gigantic woolly bear, though his eyes were keenly and kindly human.

"Shem, my son!" the man cried.

"Abba!" Shem was transformed into a boy. He reached the man in one quick, enormous stride. They wrapped their arms around each other in a mighty hug.

Madai watched. He felt greatly touched by the scene and thought about his own Patta.

Shem and the old father were laughing, speaking over one another with indiscernible words, stepping back to look into each other's faces, calculating that each was well. It was a moment of indefinite duration and familiar affections and allowed Madai a moment to catch his breath, to really study the man. Yes, he was the father. He had given Shem his curly hair, his nose, his bearing. His back was stooped now, somewhat, though not frail; and his voice was strong. Dark eyes glittered from an envelope of furrowed, leather-like skin. A man of many seasons, no doubt ... yet, indeed, not ancient enough.

Madai recognized the disappointment which betrayed what he had allowed himself - the tiniest of hopes.

He glanced at Kittim, confused by what could only be a lie - on someone's part, at least. But Kittim was watching the two, looking wholly convinced. Shem was talking, the father listening now, and it was a lengthy tale. Kittim did not break the moment by rendering the words for him, but Madai heard the name 'Nimrod.' Madai watched the father's face draw up, and he was reminded of what Misha had said, that her Ab would grieve. And, indeed, there was a grievous look of pain on the old man's face. Then his eyes slowly rekindled as he nodded once. Madai could understand that grim approval. The father asked something else, to which Shem replied with a nod of his own. A weighty look passed between them before Madai felt the atmosphere change; then he heard his own name spoken, and Ye'fet's and Kittim's.

The old man's face changed again, the last scrap of pain vanquished, replaced by surprise and delight.

"Son of Ye'fet!" the father exclaimed. He opened up his arms again, supreme joy adorning his face. "Son of Ye'fet," he repeated and took Madai up in a vigorous embrace, his arms remarkably strong. He smelled of the dry, sweet grass piled high in the stable. When he pulled back to look at Madai, he studied his yellow hair with curiosity and remained just that way for a time, thinking, perhaps, about another son. Then his eyes watered with a sheen of tears before he let Madai go. "Son of Ye'fet," he murmured again and turned to Kittim.

The father, taller than Kittim, inclined his head and kissed him on the cheek. His face was slightly reverent as he drew back, and he spoke to Kittim with respect unfeigned and undisguised. Madai watched his friend, listened to the tone of his reply, and recognized in it the flavor of authentic esteem.

Shem stood watching with an intimate smile, hinting of his youth. The smile lingered as he turned to tend his horse. "We shall keep the horses here through the night," he told them. " Abba says the nights have come cold." He removed the saddle and began to brush the animal's sturdy back.

The father led Kittim's horse to the trough. He forked in new grass, then folded his arms across his chest, enjoying the sight of his son, of them all, safely delivered.

Madai slid his hand across the gelding's back with a growing affection for the animal. He heard it crunching the hay as the wind began to blow and was suddenly grateful for the sweet-smelling stable. The father and son were talking again, a melodic language, purported to be the first. Madai would have liked to believe it, here at last, watching two very tall men who had a certain uncommon appearance. But it was altogether impossible. Even that Kittim believed it was not enough.

He was roused by Shem's father, suddenly talking to them, explaining in Madai's own language, with minor odd intonations, that he would like their help gathering up the little herd of silk camels; it was his rather indulgent name for the fawn-eyed animals. Madai had a growing perception that the older man had a giant place in his heart for creatures. And he was proved it mutual as the animals followed their old shepherd like children, vying for the chance to nuzzle up under his hands. He led them all back to the stable like a goose with her goslings, hardly needing their help at all.

"I am uncommonly fond of creatures," the father confirmed, having brought them right up to the troughs. He watched a moment to enjoy that his silk camels were satisfied with their fodder. Then he put his arm around his son again.

"Let's go surprise Zahab," he said with a twinkle in his eye.

Shem shut the heavy doors behind them. He didn't divulge that his mother already knew he was back.

ଓଃଜ ଓଃଜ ଓଃଜ

A wonderful fragrance of baking bread greeted them as they came inside - such a common and welcome domesticity. Though quite large, it was home to a simple family. Madai's eyes skirted the room to take in every sight, like a boy too amazed for calm. There was a hall at the far end, leading to other numerous rooms, and walls, and floors of stone draped by thick and ancient woolen carpets looking worn and heavy. Dry swags of bundled fruits hung from high rafters, lending their subtle fragrance to grasses and bulbs and wrinkled tubers. There was a wall fitted with spades for the garden, lances on another wall, and long-bows for war.

It might have been dark inside, the windows being shuttered, but that Shem's mamam had fires glowing in every conceivable form: in a fire-pit emanating substantial warmth, in the flame of oil lamps dancing in the corners and tallow candles lighting the top of a dark, long table. She was waiting for them, expectant, with the ever-present pot of steaming tea. There were four little cups of the strong stuff, and still there was the sense that her focus was only for her son.

"See who I have brought!" her husband announced, coming in behind them.

Shem's mother was once a tall woman, as her husband. But her back was bowed at the shoulders. Hers must long have been a merry face, for the multitude of lines crossed it in a sort of permanent smile. Eyes that were dark orbs set in nut-brown flesh spoke a vigorous mind as she chuckled at her husband.

"I see him," she answered in their melodious tongue.

When the father removed his cloak, he hung it over a peg set in the wall. He was exposed as a fit man, though stout around the chest and belly, dressed from the waist down all in animal hides. His breast was covered more genteelly in woven cloth, decorated by one who loved exuberant color.

His wife served him tea, and brought him another bowl, this of something white and warm. She put it beside the tea. She returned four other times with like bowls, and finally the bread which Madai had first smelled and salivated for.

Shem drained the bowl in a single slurp. "Thank you, Mother," he said, a new warmth in his voice.

"I hope there is more of this," the father chuckled, draining his bowl with equal speed and in the highest spirits.

His wife chastised him fondly, the way people long acquainted and comfortable with one another may do.

These parents of Shem had furnishings of wood, covered with fleece for comfort and warmth, covered over that with weavings. Certainly not fit for nomadic life. The wood of the table was dark, black really, the sort Madai could not identify, smoothed by years and many fingers. The mother filled their teacups again, looking energetic despite the hour. She finally sat down beside her husband.

She was beaming. "Elohiym be praised," she repeated again. "You are safe."

Shem reached for her hands resting on the table opposite him. Then she said no more with her mouth. It was the way her eyes rested on her son that caused Madai to recall his own mother on that last day, telling him God would keep him safe. It surprised him, that an Ancient should have a family as any other. Not gods at all, entirely human.

It also surprised him that he thought it, having decided before that Shem's father could not be "the" Nua. Which meant, of course, that Shem was not "the" Shem. Which meant, as well, that Shem had lied, and Kittim, also. It was something Madai could not reconcile with what he already knew of the men, or Kittim, at least. But there was a quality about the people, the place itself, as if they were guardians, as natural here as mushrooms in an ancient forest.

"Would I not be safe?" Shem was asking her. "I know how you entreat Elohiym." Their eyes smiled at each other, and then he said, "This is Madai, son of Ye'fet. And this is Kittim. They have come to see the ark, and Abba, for news of the first earth."

His mother's face was crinkling with emotion.

"Excellent," Shem's father announced. "Excellent. Bring us a pot of stew, Zahab. We shall begin tonight, for I am not young." Then he watched her go to the fire. He slowly turned, refocusing on Madai with a crooked set to his mouth. "But shall we contend first, son of Ye'fet, with that which is your first doubt?" His eyes twinkled. "You think I am addled, do you not?"

It horrified Madai that the man should think it, even if perhaps it was partly true. He couldn't respond, nor did Kittim soften the awkward silence.

The father nodded knowingly. "Addled to imagine I am the man of the ark." His expression did not say he was offended, not in the least, but rather amused, in fact.

Zahab returned with the stew. She sat it before her husband with a soft clucking sound.

"Consider Shem," he instructed, leaning in for a mouthful of stew, abruptly more serious, "He shall live but one hundred years more, by my count, if a wolf doesn't eat him; and you, Madai, only that and half again." The old man looked at his wife. "A vine withers in the sun," he said, "and Zahab has withered with me. And even our son, though the benefits of the first earth have preserved us. Our years shall be many more than those who follow us."

He found meat in his bowl and took his time chewing it. Then he lifted his hand above the table and held it there. "Do you see how it is still steady?" he asked. "And I the father of a son so old."

"It is a question Madai has of me himself," Shem offered.

The man looked at his wife. "Zahab? A mother knows."

The face so trained to smile looked at her son and answered, "He was one hundred years old when we came from the ark, some three hundred years past. But don't let my husband deceive you; he has the book of Adam and has kept it exact from new moon to new moon. He knows." She looked at her husband, shifting all the lines in her face as she lifted a single eyebrow.

"I was ninety-eight when the rain began," Shem amended. He watched his mother stand, knowing she was after the book. "The whole of my first years were spent at ark-building."

Zahab put the scroll on the table for her husband to open. "It will be Shem's to keep," she said, "when we are gone."

The father took the roll of skin in his hands as if it were holy. He gently peeled it open. Madai could see it wanted to rewind, with its top end curling back. He could also see it was an exquisite work of tanning, preserved with meticulous intention. It was covered in black marks, not like the ones Tutan had shown him, but with the same sort of aim.

"The Account of Man," Noah read. "From Adam, the clay of Elohiym.

In his 130th year, Adam begat Seth, living 930 years more.
In his 105th year, Seth begat Enos, living 807 years more.
In his 90th year, Enos begat Kenan, living 815 years more.
In his 70th year, Kenan begat Mahalalel, living 840 years more.
In his 65th year, Mahalalel begat Yared, living 830 years more.
In his 162nd year, Yared begat Enoch, living 800 years more.
In his 65th year, Enoch begat Mathuwshelach, living 365 years, and was no more, for God took him.
In his 187th year, Mathuwshelach begat Lamech, living 782 years more, til the year of the deluge.
In his 182nd year, Lamech begat Noach."

Noah looked up from the scroll. "I am not dead yet," he said. Then he continued to read past Shem's birth, and the birth of a son named Arphaxad, all the way to the name of a man "Abram," which was its last notation. The ending years of the 10 men following Noah had not been inscribed.

"It shall fall to Shem to record their deaths, and all the births after Abram," Noah said, "until his son shall take it up from him. It is a heavy honor."

Madai was intrigued, hearing once again common names from the bag of stones which hung around his father's neck. But he was still a long way from convinced. He could calculate the years roughly, centuries more than a thousand. And the world was full.

"There should be more names," he said.

Noah put his hand palm down on the scroll and threw back his head, his eyes open.

"Mighty Jah... I thank You!" he exclaimed. He seemed to chuckle with an unseen friend, a shining trail moistening the ruddy caverns made from the skin around his eyes.

"Precisely!" he proclaimed, looking back squarely into Madai's eyes. "But there is the Crushing Seed!"

Madai was utterly lost, thinking again, with a good deal of regret, that the old man might have a mind that had, indeed, dwindled over time.

"It is in the constellations, Madai. You retain their prophecies, I think." Noah's excitement was building. "There is just too much to tell!" he cried. "I must live past the night!"

His wife gently touched the scroll. She moved Noah's hand and started at the top edge to ease it into a soft roll. Then she put it in Noah's palm with a smile.

"What would you do if you spilled your tea?" she asked quietly.

Her words seemed to quell the frenetic energy that had taken hold of him.

He looked at her. "Yes," he said. He wiped his eyes. "Well, there is a very good story about the names," he explained. He leaned toward Madai, holding the scroll away from his cup. "There are men, son of Ye'fet, who will bear honored sons. And these sons shall bear sons who will one day bring the Crushing Seed, the One Who will take away this curse from the earth."

Madai's forehead wrinkled. "Of all the sons," he said, "how do you know who is the one for the scroll?"

Noah pointed upward. "He will tell us."

The old man could see that Madai was doubtful, at least. So he explained. "If it were not so, then this scroll would fill my house, and who could carry it? I do not know when the One will come, nor to whom. But I know through whom He will come. He will come from Adam, through Seth... through all the names on this scroll, through Abram, who was only just born. Serug brought the news to Arphaxad, who brought it to me. Perhaps the One is in the loins of Abram now, though he is but a babe."

"The Bowman, do you mean?" Madai asked. He was granting the old man not mad at the moment. "But, it is through a Virgin that the Bowman will come."

Noah's smile reappeared, and a trace of his first excitement. "Precisely!" he exclaimed again. "How will He do it? I do not know. I only know what I am moved to know, that the One will somehow come, and through the names on this scroll."

He settled himself down again and took a long drink of tea. He cleared his throat and said with an instructive air, "So you see, Madai, how we keep our years. They are all in here."

Madai had an image of his 'story pole,' painted red another stripe in autumn, and smiled.

Kittim was cleaning his bowl with warm bread. The father was watching Madai. Madai sat inanimate at the table, his stew cooling and untouched. It was one thing to see a thing in the heavens and know what it meant; it was another to think you hear from the very God Himself in these ages. He could hardly believe that. He looked away from Noah's eyes.

'Then how did he know to build the ark?' he suddenly wondered.

Noah watched the young kinsman's struggle. "The first age was much kinder than the second," he announced, in another vein entirely.

It startled Madai and was the second time, even the third or fourth. that he had heard mention of another kind of earth. Then he realized he had not shifted his position since sitting down and moved to ease out a stiffness.

"What do you mean, kinder?" he asked, nearly relieved to have something else to talk about.

The old man looked at his wife. "We have lived too long," he told her as though they were alone. "Don't you miss it?"

"The first earth," she prompted him.

He raised his unruly white brows and turned back to Madai. "Yes, my son," he answered in a lighter voice, "the first earth was very beautiful. It never stormed. It was filled with the gentlest and greatest of beasts. I am fond of beasts." He picked his cup up and drank. "And it was neither too hot nor too cold. It is boundless cold here; I can not get used to it. You would think I could." He drank again. "And a mist watered the earth..." He put his cup down, having acquired a slightly wistful expression.

And then the look was abruptly gone. "With all of that, it was not enough goodness for men." His eyes took on a fervor. "All that Elohym provided, and they, running after corruption - not creeping - running. Giving their own hearts to it. They would not listen."

Zahab took the scroll from his hand and rose to put it away. The house grew silent. Madai heard a log crumble in the fire.

"It was the raqiya," the old father continued, "the firmament. It cast back the sun's barrage, that which drinks water from flesh and turns it to buffalo skin." He tapped his hand. "It does not shake, but it is craggy as tree bark."

Shem laughed, which broke the spell, and the father looked at him with re-emerging vigor.

"These were not the hands of my father. Even when his years were many, even in the tomb. It was the air, thick at dawn." The old man looked away. "And the stars... silent now."

Madai looked down, closed his eyes and slowly shook his head, all involuntary and unwitting.

Shem's father was watching him with a twinkle in his eyes. "Yes, the stars sang at night. I can tell you they sang. Like a tribute, and He let us hear it, too. But you do get used to things - till they are gone."

Shem laughed again. "He can not believe you," he said.

The old man chuckled, well aware of it. "What you do not know of Elohiym can not be to your blame," he sympathized. "The first earth was... His perfect intent. We were blessed with it." Then he settled farther into his seat and cast an unabashed and solemn eye at Madai.

"When we first stepped from the ark, it was onto a mountain top, a height more than ever I knew of earth, and scorched with icy wind. How it roared! Know you, son of Ye'fet, that we did not know cold before?" He blinked at Madai as though it still surprised him. "'Tis true," he added, and finished his tea.

"I did not know Adam, nor Qayin, nor Seth, nor Enoch." He pushed back the empty cup. "But I knew Yered, and Mathuwshelach, sons of Enos... who knew Adam... who knew what Adam told them... " Noah closed his eyes.... He opened them. "But even then, my old Ab Mathuwshelach could not tell me what I wanted most to know: Elohiym, as Adam knew Him."

Madai was watching the man carefully.

"He could only repeat what his own Ab Adam had told him: that a man could not understand what was lost when Eden was lost... when Elohiym was lost ... and his own mortal self was changed. Ab Adam had no words for it. We only know that it was grievous. More grievous than the loss of the world." The old man's lips quivered. "No man can know what it was like before the serpent," he finished, trailing his words at the end.

Noah

- 70 -

Madai was rooted to his seat again. He felt the atmosphere change and his own doubt sound but a feeble call. He was conscious of the night creatures chirping through the shutters, and the fire and the wind in an otherwise silent room.

"Consider my years, son of Ye'fet," the father's voice came abruptly. "You had best ask tonight what you want most to hear." He indicated his wife with a nod. "They want to keep us young - impossible. So," he lifted his hand casually, "you never know."

"Noach," Zahab gently chastised him.

Madai was always surprised, listening to this strangely comical, decidedly confident man who shifted between vigorous and dilapidated. Through the steam still rising from his forgotten bowl of stew, he peered at the calm eyes of a man who was not mad. There was something about his 'Book of Adam,' even if Madai could not believe exacting word from a God in the heavens. And he calculated the number of an army that called his son "Shem," the Shem borne of Nua. In his depths, he knew he had changed his mind. He wanted to. He had chosen. Madai looked away from the billowy-haired man to Kittim and asked anyway.

"Is he?"

"I have not brought you here for less," Kittim answered.

The fire snapped, an animal in the forest called to a mate, the air was still in the house. 'Of course, an Ancient. What I've come for,' his mind told him. But Madai felt paralyzed, numb, physically tired. He took a sip of tea. It had gotten cold. The wind started to blow and sounded stormy. He listened to it as though it brought a touch of reality to the night.

'What do you ask the father of the second earth?' he wondered. 'Do I ask? Or do I just wait here for him to speak?' Madai decided to wait. He looked at Noah expectantly.

The old man's eyes were rimmed in red; he was tired. He was looking back at Madai, waiting, also. Madai was vaguely disappointed. He was looking at the face of an old man - more than only old - ridiculously old. And only a man. Still, he waited, till it was awkward, and Madai finally decided to ask a simple question. Trifling, yes, but one he had always wondered, a part of what had made the story seem nothing more than a high tale.

"How does a boat carry all the beasts of the earth? How did you do it?"

Noah's laugh burst into the quiet. "It is always the first thing they want to know." He ruminated, though he didn't really seem to mind. He leaned his back against the wall and folded his arms. "It was done with a great many years," he assured Madai. "And these arms, and the arms of my three sons, and the Arm of Elohiym."

It was not the sort of answer Madai wanted, though Noah looked pleased with it. "Just those three sons?" Madai persisted.

"And the Arm of Elohiym, praise His Name."

Perhaps it was a tweak from some mischief left in the man, because there was a twinkle in his eyes, but Madai was suddenly so seized with the need to know that he didn't care and he quit being afraid to ask. He was like a boy trying to dig out a badger. He wanted to know the size of the boat, how did the animals come? How long did it take, and how scary was the whole business? A terrible task, and the strength of only four men, plus a God.

But, where to begin? "It must have taken a long time," he prodded. "A ship big enough..."

"More years than you have lived," Shem offered the answer. "I was just a boy when Elohiym first commanded we begin to build. And nearly one hundred when the earth quaked and the first rains fell."

Madai was genuinely surprised; he hadn't imagined it would take so long. "One hundred years?"

"Almost."

Noah was watching, enjoying a private memory painted in his head of three sons at a common aim. "Do you want the number precisely?" he asked.

"Ah, yes, you do have it," Madai admitted. "The Book of Adam."

"And the line of the Crushing Seed," Noah repeated, "Eve's revenge - the seed."

He looked at his wife. "It was said that Eve was most sorely offended by the smells. I should like to have smelled it before..." his eyes strayed, "...before there was rot in the air." Noah touched the end of his nose.

"The Crushing Seed," he continued, nearly to himself and down an ambling path. "A good end told in the stars, Madai. Put there by the Word of Elohiym, the Head of Days."

"Yes," Madai agreed, if only to be courteous. Such unknowables felt suddenly burdensome. There was something uneasy about them, besides - too ethereal. Madai wanted the flesh on the bones of a legendary story. He could not stop himself.

"But one hundred years..." he persisted. "It's a long time to build a ship and wait for a flood. Did you never think you had got it wrong?" Madai knew men who would have quit - maybe even himself.

Noah leaned in a little more. His face lost its look of joviality to become starkly somber, old again. "My eyes remember the ways of the first earth," he answered. "Wonderful and terrible, and men with murder in their hearts from day's rising to dark."

Madai recognized the change in him again with a slight impatience, wanting a direct and thorough telling of the ship and all it contained. But there was a piercing quality in the old man's eyes that belied his suddenly sagging mouth.

"Do you suppose I begat only those three?" he asked with a demanding voice and yet a terrible tremble. Zahab touched his hand.

It stopped cold Madai's vexing over the boat. And he looked at Noah. He knew he would not attempt to answer the dreadful question, nor prod at it... but steer away. And he was ashamed at being impatient. It was like the night he overheard his father telling his mother sorcery had invaded The Family, and he hadn't wanted to know. There was much more to the story than the building of a great ship.

He realized in his depth that there was something worse than seeing a son dead, and he shuddered for Japhet, determined again to bring him home the truth. It was what had driven him across the Sea. How else might he face his son and tell him, 'Yes, there is a Mighty God Who has done all this. The God of the heavens.' How else would he wrestle his boy away from the power in the forest?

"One hundred years to carve an ark of gopher wood," Noah finally continued, "and to proclaim the Word of Jehovah Elohiym, with a warning. What of absolute love is so terrible?"

The old man was watching him... and not watching him. He seemed to be asking someone else the question. Well enough, because Madai would not dare answer.

"The decree of Elohiym," Noah finally began again, "one does not forget it. No, son of Ye'fet, one hundred years was not long enough. To build an ark, yes. To change a heart? Not long enough." He shook his head sadly.

An invisible, terrible intimacy filled the silence that followed Noah's speech. His face was melting from stony man to poor frailty. It was not what Madai had expected; it was more than he wanted to know. He sniffed and drained his tea, cold as it was.

"And you brought every beast of the earth to the ship?" he asked. The question sounded thin.

Noah lifted his white brows. "The beasts were called by Elohiym." He answered.

"Every beast of the earth?" Madai insisted.

"Is it too great a thing for Him to do?" Noah responded, beginning to revive. "Yet, it was two pairs of each that were unclean, and seven pairs of clean - of every kind of beast of the earth and fowl of the air."

Madai considered this was perhaps possible, though he did not know the number of all the beasts of the earth. But he instantly painted a picture of the close proximity of a ship, no matter its size. He thought about the fire-breast, and leviathan, and the mammoth, and the elk, and the behemoth. He thought about the lynx and the leopard and the great birds of Shinar....

"How did they not eat each other?" he blurted. "How did they not eat you?"

Noah's angst expelled itself in a gust of amusement. "They did not eat flesh," he replied, "before the deluge."

Madai had not considered this. "Leviathan ate grass?" It was astonishing, remembering the fierce teeth ripping apart a camel.

"There was an abundance of grass," Noah explained. "Though men were violent, beasts did not consume each other."

At this, Madai was silent. A hunter that ate the grass of the field was something he could not imagine.

The wind continued its low whine against the solid stone of the house. Madai was aware of it again, reminding him of another question, a fierce storm on an endless sea and helpless against it.

"It was surely terrible," he muttered. "Such a flood. Were you afraid? Were the beasts?"

Noah liked the question. It led him to tell the shelter of a wing, a peace that would not be explained.

"When Elohiym saw that the ark was complete, He commanded that we fill it with all that we would eat and the beasts that were to come, Zahab and I, and Shem and Ye'fet and Ham and their wives. And when that was done, He commanded that we enter, as well, to escape the waters which were to come. Still there were no beasts, those that we had provided grass for, those that we had prepared space for. Still we waited, and He brought them, those that He chose, and they came willingly to us." Noah sat perfectly still; just his eyes moved across the plains of Madai's face, looking as though he were the first man ever to whom Noah had recounted the tale. "Still the ark sat upon the green earth. There was yet no rain. Indeed, never in all the years of my life had I seen the rain."

Madai would not ask about that.

"All the waters of the deep heaved up," Noah continued, "the rain like terrible thunder; and the shaking earth, as though it would rend itself; and the dreadful roar – horrible - had we not Elohiym." Noah paused. "It was worst for us who were man."

"I understand." Madai said.

Noah nodded again, slowly, which was his oft and patient response. "Son of Ye'fet," he finally asked, looking for something in Madai's eyes, "have you ever known the presence of Elohiym?"

Madai was caught off guard once again, driven back to the depths of himself where so little was sure. "I don't know."

The old man nodded. "If you had, you would know."

It was like the smell of lightning in the air, and only those few words... not accusing, but only a pregnant declaration. Madai was brought back across the Sea to another time, as though the voyage had not been necessary at all. He remembered Ido, the last thing he would have expected. If he could tell her that here he sat with the very Nua of sacred song and it all was true, she would only smile with a look that said, 'Of course.'

'But then, you always knew.'

He felt his eyes slowly burn, until the table was blurred and everyone sitting around it. It was a rising emotion built of something so much more than pain.

"His Presence is… " Noah looked off into the room… "I cannot tell it." Then he looked back at Madai with an invading purpose. "Do you want to know it, son of Ye'fet?"

There had been that day swimming in the sea when Ido had told him of Japhet and she had lifted her hand and told him that Mighty God still walked with man, and the way her face had glowed… more than just the babe inside her; he knew that now.

"I had a wife," Madai suddenly told him, "who knew the Great God… " His voice trembled. "He was life to her… and she was life to me." He steadied his hands on the table and looked down. He struggled to control himself. "And she is dead," he whispered. He lifted his eyes, ignoring the overflow down his face. "Does the Great God know what that means? Does He mourn?"

Noah felt a great sympathy for the yellow-haired kinsman. And he felt nearly young again to touch an earnest heart, a bleeding heart, to see a son of his eldest son whom he had thought never to meet after so long a time. Noah emphatically nodded.

"Yes, He is grieved, son of Ye'fet, for you and for Himself, that none are innocent." The old man's voice was threatened again with passion. "Think, my boy, you were witness to the kingdom of Nimrod, and his felling. Nimrod, a mighty man made by the Hand of Elohiym, made with strength and courage and a skill to shepherd men. Nimrod was the son of my son's son - Ham, who laid his hand with mine to fashion the will of Elohiym in gopher wood." Noah's worn hand trembled, and he looked every year the survivor of a millennium. "Yes, it is absolute: Adonai mourns the corruption of sons." Noah looked steadily into Madai's eyes. "Ham is my son, whom I love. He is my enemy."

A terrible thing.

"None are innocent?" Madai asked, unable to believe it.

"You have seen just the shadow of the serpent," Noah answered. And then he shook his head firmly. "There are none who have lived, nor live now, who are innocent."

"Yet, you are saved," Madai insisted.

"By His mercy," Noah whispered, a tenacious strength holding him.

"Mercy?" Madai's heart felt dangerous again.

"When you have come from such a season of death," Noah continued, "to find the earth remade… desolate of life," he lifted his hands in a futile gesture, "swept clean… and watch it fill again with men who render their hearts for the serpent's seed… you will know it is by the mercy of Elohiym that the bow fills the sky after the rain. You will know that none are innocent. You will know that it shall take the Promise, that which He spoke to the prophets and wrote with the stars, to save us again."

Madai was exhausted. What he had come to learn, beyond imponderable singing stars, was that Ancients were no more than men... and assailed with every ebb and tide of feeling, with every sort of ecstasy and devastation. It was as though Noah's private griefs had entered Madai just enough to tear him asunder, to prove them both men of common flesh and common despair. He slept the length of the night as one at respite from a war.

He woke to the cold leaking through the stone. He pulled a fleece up over his nose and listened to Kittim's soft breathing. He wished he could look out the shuttered window to see if it was light, but he didn't want to brave the cold. And he shuddered for Noah's last words, that it would take God's mercy to save them. That was a thing Madai could not trust.

He lifted his hand out of the coverings to prod Kittim.

"Is it morning?" Kittim muttered.

"I feel the cold," Madai answered.

After a moment of silence, Kittim replied, "Take my extra robe."

Madai was glad his friend was awake, even if it had been his own doing. "No," he answered softly. "I mean the weather is turning. The snow will come soon."

Kittim pulled the blanket around his shoulders as he rolled over to face Madai. "We are here none too soon, then."

"I want to see the ship," Madai announced.

"Yes, of course." Kittim stretched and pulled his hand down the length of his face. "Yes, there may be little time left for it."

"The mountain is high."

"It cannot be already covered over with snow," Kittim argued. "We came only last night."

Madai considered the implications of snow-covered passes. "Do you think the weather will trap us here?" he asked Kittim.

"We should be here a long while, in that case."

"We have been away a long time already," Madai replied.

"Yes," Kittim smiled. "Iscah will be... vexed."

Madai chuckled, relieved to think about their friends. How Tutan would understand Noah, as he did not; and Iscah - it would be all about the ship. He was inspired again, and he missed them both.

They heard the wind faintly through the thick walls. "Perhaps Shem will lead us to the ark today, if it does not storm," Kittim suggested.

And then there was the smell of bread.

The stone floor was cold, and Madai was glad his boots were stuffed at the end of the bed where he had warmed them through the night. There was a rising urgency in him this morning, because the season was surely changing.

The light was dim in the house, but they followed the trail of aroma back to the main room, where he saw that they were the last to wake. Almodad, Sheleph and Misha had arrived sometime in the night.

The stone house was large enough to house many families, which had, in truth, been its design. Almodad's wife would soon arrive, and the daughter he had fought to rescue, the little Innana. Their numbers of herds and kinsmen had increased so that they no longer kept the same pastures, but each took a season with Noah and Zahab at the times of snow.

"Son of Ye'fet!" Noah happily greeted him, a revived man after a night's sleep. "See, my children have come."

Madai was a little befuddled, having slept past the rising of the old man. But he was glad to see Almodad again, and Misha and guessed Noah had been more so. They had likely brought him more news, as they still looked like warriors.

"We would like to climb to the ark," Kittim suddenly announced, surprising Madai with the boldness of it.

Almodad nodded to him with a knowing smile. "We all have wished it," he said. "It well may be the time for it. Winter is coming."

ଔଔ ଔଔ ଔଔ

The air felt new and light, refreshing, promising. There were birds, diligent to root out last morsels, and rock rats doing the same thing. They all smelled the clouds that had formed overnight. Madai smelled them, too. They hung over the northern mounts, looking too heavy to move.

It had been a day and a night up Ararat, dragging a donkey with wood for the fire and roasted goat. There were streams aplenty racing away from the upper regions before they could be caught by the coming season. The water was sweet, it turned Madai's skin a rosy, bright shade and made him feel new.

He didn't want to talk. He wanted to savor the trip, every sound, every stone. The day that followed his meeting Noah had been their first day ascending the mountain. He did believe him, but the ark would be irrefutable. He was anxious for the ark.

His first glimpse was of something like a great dark rock face, jutting upward, the prominence of a sheer cliff. It sat upon the crest of the mountain as immovable as any formation of stone, an up-thrust that was angular, with square corners and vertical planes. A falcon circled above it.

At its square pinnacle, revealed in shadow, were precisely spaced openings, of equal dimension. It looked intact, undamaged by the years or the deluge, and it was as black as tar. It rested on a slight incline, its nose tipping toward the mountain's peak.

In its stony silence, it proclaimed itself a fact.

Madai stopped below it, where it could be seen in total, where it had become like a part of Ararat. What had he expected? Madai hadn't stopped to think about that, but he knew it wasn't this. What the forebearers had used against the Brine Sea, what The Family built, were sleek vessels, fitted with sails and graceful. How was this colossus suspended upon the waters?

Madai let the others go ahead. Almodad had come, glad to leave his warring behind. Shem led them and Misha was trying to hide her own excitement. Kittim was his ever stolid and forbearing self. But Madai needed to be alone. He needed to look up at the granite mountain and the wooden mammoth that had come to rest there. It was the moment to chronicle such an event, if he were only better at song-making. He sat down on a flat boulder and crossed his legs. He watched the others reach the underside of the ship like miniatures of people in its shadow, and then disappear behind it.

What struck him first was how much it seemed at home, nearly a rock itself. The wind whistled through openings set at the top as though they were well acquainted. It was a chilly wind the ark had long endured... and stormy seas, and snow, and an earth's fill of life...

He needed to touch it.

Madai got up. He finished the distance, watching the walls loom higher above him the nearer he came. It was nearly frightening in size. He watched his own hand reach out and spread across a hewn length of timber coated with pitch. Black, but still a tree. It felt smooth. He ran his hand down to where the ship was coated with sea barnacles, sharp and crusted, like a second skin, and all the way to the ground, where the bottom-most hull was buried in what once had been sodden earth.

He stretched up, extending his body as far as it could reach - not a third of the way to the top. Then he backed away again, tracing the form from front to back, from top to bottom. He was fixing it in his mind, thinking about how to tell Japhet and his father, his mamam... The Family. He felt a gaping expanse in his chest, realizing that his quest was complete, and he was filled with the fertile promise of optimism.

He suddenly needed to find Kittim! It needed to be shared, this feeling. Every part of his story had a piece of Kittim in it. They would bring back this news to Job and Iscah and Tutan. He had just begun to follow the way to the others when Shem reappeared, crunching toward him on the shale.

"Well, Madai?" Shem called. "Is it all you hoped?"

Madai was grinning. "I don't know what I hoped," he said. "I guess it's really just enough that it's here." But, no, he realized it was so much more than that. "Do you imagine what it is like to hear a thing all your life...a legend..." he expanded, "and to see it with your eyes, to put your hands on it when it was only real in a song before? But this," Madai put his hand against the timber, "is more than a song."

Shem was smiling, too. He put his hand on Madai's shoulder. "Men forget," he answered. "I am glad to bring you here."

"This..." Madai continued after a moment, spanning his fingers across a beam. "I was born in a forest, and there were never trees so large."

"The first earth," Shem replied with a nod.

"But - they must have weighed - "

"You do now perceive the use of one hundred years."

"Even so..." Madai trailed his eyes across the planes of the ark.

"Are you familiar with a beast?" Shem asked. "Here, let me show you." He knelt on the ground, took a stick and began to draw in the shallow dirt: stout legs, curved tusks and long, undulating trunk.

"A mammoth!" Madai exclaimed. "You tamed a mammoth?"

Shem peered up at him, a wider smile on his face. "If that is what you call them," he answered. "Beasts did not fear man; we did not eat them. And they were very strong, tireless."

"I am amazed," Madai muttered, gazing down the long expanse of the ship.

"Thirty cubits high," Shem informed him. "Three hundred long and fifty wide." He paused. "You do wish to go inside..."

"I do," Madai answered quickly. "What is a cubit?"

Shem showed Madai a length of his arm as Madai followed, running his hand all along its three hundred cubits.

They came to the back side, where a jagged opening was gaping at them like the mouth of a cave. And, like a cave, it was dark inside.

"There is a door on the other side," Shem explained, "But it is closed up now. It was the door Elohiym closed and sealed before the waters came. By it the beasts entered and were released. Only it filled with snow, and we shut it up again. This," he said as he ducked his head to enter, "was made by searchers like you."

Madai rested his palm above the breach in the timbers. He put his head through the hole to get a first look. The air was cool and musty. The dark of the interior was broken only by slender wedges of light filtering in from cracks in the timbers above. A little scattering of stones covered the floor near the opening. He stepped inside.

"Shem..." Madai whispered, and was surprised at the sound of his own voice echoing against the emptiness. "There is an odor of the stable still here." His voice was nearly reverent.

Shem softly chuckled. "Forgive me for this, Madai," he answered, "but it is the rock antelope, curious creatures. They climb everywhere."

Madai chuckled, a bit embarrassed. "I'm as full of fancy as Iscah."

"Who is Iscah?" Shem asked.

"The child we brought from that most unworthy place," Madai explained. "Very excitable... and she will envy us this."

"Ah," Shem remembered, "the little slave you found at Mizraim. She follows Elohiym?"

"Furiously," Madai answered with a grin, "and our companion, Tutan, who came from the East."

"Then they will be glad to hear all you have seen," Shem remarked. He walked across the hollow space to a large ramp extending down from the ceiling to the floor. "We brought the largest beasts into this lower-most level, down that incline," Shem explained, pointing. He fanned his arms behind himself. "There were enclosures here, as well, though they have been removed."

"O?"

"Yes. We used them for the roof of the stone house which we built after a time." He chuckled. "Mother would not have them inside for the odor of pitch, though they make the roof fit against the rain."

Madai didn't bother asking how they might have gotten the gigantic beams down the mountain, being already convinced that Nua and his sons had accomplished the impossible. He listened to Shem telling him all about a complex construction of pens, and all the while it was like walking out a dream in the semi-dark. He smelled the closed space, with its rock antelope and pitch. He followed Shem across the massive planks of the ark's floor, planks that had ridden upon the surge of the waters. They were as sound and firm as the earth itself. Madai and Shem started up the ramp.

"There is another level, just like this one," Shem explained. "Elohiym had precise instructions for the ark: its size, the kind of tree, the alignment of windows and door, and three levels. We built it just as He said."

They used the ramp to reach the second deck, where the light was a little better. It filtered through the ceiling and the second incline. This level smelled of dirt. Remains of dung and grass had turned back to earth long ago; except for that, the space was empty. There was a half-wall partition at the farther-most end which Madai studied as though it were a mystery of the universe. 'What must it have contained?'

The others were on the third level. Almodad had lost his war face and was showing Kittim the way the timbers had been joined. Misha listened to it as rapt as though she were here for the first time. Windows some cubits' length in height were left unfinished at the top. From this, the afternoon light filled the space and showed Madai where The Family once had lived.

Dust floated in the air; he watched it filter down in rays from the windows and slowly turned in place. He touched the beams again, where the light showed them best. They were black, coated even on the inside with pitch, so thoroughly that the wood was smooth. There was something carved in it; he ran his fingers across them and found a whole gallery of markings. Some might have been writings such as Tutan had showed him.

Shem was watching Madai. "These are new," he explained. "Since I was last here." Shem traced an etching with his own finger. "This one is a symbol of sorcery."

Madai was startled. He pulled his hand back as though it were bitten and looked at the scrawl. It could have been a blessing for all he could tell, but the memory of Shinar was fresh, also older memories of what idolaters brought with them. In the intersecting lines there could be left some power. Madai took his knife to carve it out.

"It is only a mark, Madai."

Madai looked at Shem, mildly surprised. "It despoils this ark," he argued.

"This place is not holy, my friend. We are saved by the Hand and Word of Adonai Elohiym."

But Shem couldn't stop the son of Ye'fet as he attacked the symbol with a kind of violence. And Madai didn't stop till it was obliterated. He looked back at Shem with a wry smile.

"Nonetheless," he announced, "it is gone."

Shem nodded at him, and Madai put the knife away. Then he followed a single timber down the length of the ark, passing other etchings, wondering what they meant. He followed the walls up toward the ceiling, where the open places let in the light. A large, bulky nest of twigs filled all the space of one of the windows.

"How will we ever get her forgiveness, Kittim?" Madai asked "when Iscah learns where we have been?"

Kittim stood in the center of the cavernous space. He was in the path of a dusty ray shining through the window. "We shall have to embellish our story well," he answered with a smile.

"Take her a piece of plank," Shem suggested. "It is done by many. They make amulets of pitch. That is what sets Abba in a fury."

"The amulets?" Kittim asked.

"Do you remember the man on the donkey?" Shem asked them. "He came away with a bag of pitch and had the misfortune of asking Abba to bless it."

Madai chuckled, remembering the grumbling merchant.

"Sorcery?" Kittim asked.

"Commerce," Shem corrected. "But a piece of timber for a young servant of Elohiym is another matter."

"They will both be pleased," Kittim agreed.

Shem knelt beside the hatch-opening in the floor. He took a small ax from his belt, having expected to need it. "As this is a testament to you," he said, beginning to chop at the planks, "it has become a monument to others, and Abba its priest." He did not sound pleased.

"But it is a proof," Madai argued, "Noah is a proof."

He heard Almodad. "What is proof to a usurper?" he grumbled.

Shem glanced up at his nephew, "One does not reach Elohiym by possessing old timber," he warned Madai, "nor by the relic of an old man. If it were so, what would it be when Abba is no more? As well, this ark, which may fall away in a quake, or be buried with snow."

"You are correct," Kittim agreed. "What is just a witness of God must not be made god."

"Idolatry," Misha accused, standing with Almodad.

Then there was silence, save just the sound of Shem's renewed hacking at the wood. Madai thought a moment about helping him and decided his blade would accomplish very little against the ancient trees. And besides, there were dark clouds now visible through the windows, and still so much to examine and think about.

A little mound of rocks was set up in one corner. He pushed it over with his foot because it looked like an altar. Shem was right, setting up shrines was too much like idolatry. He could hear Misha and Almodad talking to Kittim. Their voices sounded hollow in the vacant space. Madai looked away. How must it have been? He craned his neck up toward the openings, knowing that all Noah and his family would have seen of their dying world was through those windows. He stretched up and gripped the bottom sill. He pulled himself up.

Looking through the opening, he could see beyond the ark to the mountain's rocky summit. The wind was getting colder, but he wasn't thinking about the cold. He was thinking about a stormy voyage, his own but a pittance by comparison, and what these eight must have endured. What a terrible knowledge of what was lost, and who was lost, with nothing but musty dark for...He realized then that he had not asked how long they sailed above the earth. He would have to find out. A pair of cliff kikes flew high overhead, catching the wind's updrafts. They swooped and spun and let the wind drive them backward. It looked to Madai as if it was just for fun.

"In truth, I am reminded of Ye'fet," Shem's voice echoed from across the length of the ark. He was watching Madai hanging from the window. "Though perhaps we were all the same," he grinned. "After the rain was gone we passed a good time doing just that."

"And tending beasts," Misha reminded him.

"That as well," he chuckled at his youngest daughter.

"It has been a lifetime ago," he mused. "There has been living since then, joys... and trouble, and many children. And I have forgotten a lot. But this one thing I remember. When I hung in the air, as you do now, watching the waves at the start when they were still fearsome - it made it all true. That nothing could live but what was kept in this ark."

"A terrible thought," Madai replied, dropping back to the floor.

Shem was silent a moment, crouching on the ground with his ax in hand. "There were many hopes," be murmured. "Within this, that the earth would be reborn." He looked up with an expression that was both stricken and resentful. "The rebellion was begun within us, Madai, Abba's very sons."

There was a falcon's call that seemed to emphasize Shem's angst, and a whistling wind.

"You are too mournful, Abba," Misha complained. "This place does it to you. You must remember what we have finished in Shinar. There will be more to come, and we will do it together." She knelt beside her father and picked up a piece of ark. "Will this make your Iscah happy, Madai?" she asked, sounding like she was ready to leave.

"Am I a dour old man?" Shem asked her.

She kissed his forehead. "You are my good Abba," she whispered, "who only needs reminding from time to time that the earth is beautiful again."

"So it is," he conceded. He looked at the clouds. "But the weather is changeable here."

"Time to leave," she announced.

It was a great shame, for Madai at least, but the wind was rising and it was cold, coming from the north. He watched the others start down the ramp and listened to the whine squeezing through crevices in the ark. He closed his eyes, hoping for The Presence Noah talked about. If there were to be a voice of God... surely here...

"Madai..."

He was startled. But it was only Misha.

ଓଷ ଓଷ ଓଷ

They heard the unmistakable baying of wolves as they descended the mountain, making just half the distance in what remained of the light. There was half the wood left, as well, carried on a donkey for the journey to and from the heights of Ararat. But it seemed colder on the way down, and the fire a trifle inadequate. Perhaps Madai had gotten lean since leaving the land of mammoths, but the wind carried the promise of snow in its bite as he wrapped himself in the woolen blanket. He was aware of Misha, the surprising daughter of Shem, sitting beside her father. And he remembered her valor in Shinar's temple. She smiled at him across the red flame.

They were all tired and cold, and warmed only tea before falling asleep. Madai huddled in his blanket, trying not to think. There was something coming at him, an unwelcome, resurrecting guilt. It was always just beneath the surface, like an eel sliding through the sea. He was not like these four asleep.

Who puts to earth the most loved of women, only to bed another? He had known it was not Ido when he came full awake. He had. There were no floods great enough to wash that away. It seemed most bitter, in fact, after a climb to so great a height.

Shem had warned that the mount was not holy; Madai could not help but think it was. And he was not seen of God after all, but only by the great Ark peering at him from the rocky top of Ararat.

- 72 -

Lehabim was making himself a real pest. Iscah could go nowhere that he was not. If she climbed to her favorite perch in the tops of the trees, he would wait below. He was helpful only when she wanted to go to the sand bar, for Marisheba would not let her go alone.

It was still warm in the sun's light, though not so uncomfortable as the day she had gone with Kittim and Madai. She had asked Tutan to take her, the work of harvesting grapes being finished. But he was occupied at the stable. And besides, there was something distant about him these last days. It made her sad. Maybe he was impatient for the caravans. They would take him back to his land in the East. She blamed Reenah. Tutan avoided the dusky woman - and wanted her. Iscah knew it as she knew what was vexing Lehabim. It was a troublesome reality, men. But she was glad Tutan did not abandon his vow to God. Reenah kept idols, after all.

Iscah glanced at Lehabim, who grinned at her hopefully. If he would but consecrate himself!

Dispirited, she straightened the bones of the infant behemoth Job had dug out and placed in the sand. It was a long time since she had seen Job. She did not know what had become of him now, or the Lady. So complete was their undoing. Lehabim had brought news one day, returning from Ur, that Job was covered with boils. The whole town talked about it. How terrible was his suffering!

She asked God for his relief, and she asked for Kittim and Madai's return...and for the jolly spirit of Tutan, which was her only comfort now.

It would soon be dark; this Lehabim warned her again. She got up to follow him back over the hill, but only because she was ready to leave. She knew Marisheba would scold them, having waited so late, and Lehabim without a bow.

They reached the swinging bridge, and though it was not yet dusk, the river was dark. It was angry today, swirling madly with an angry roar. There was something in the water, turning it red. She could not see it, nor hear a cry above the din of the river. Lehabim grabbed her hand and began pulling her quickly across the bridge. It was not a bridge for crossing in haste, and it began to swing wildly from side to side.

"Lehabim!" she cried. "We shall fall."

"It is Leviathan," he warned and pulled her more urgently.

They were agile, and perhaps God was with them, for they reached the safety of the bank. When she was on an earth that did not swing, Iscah craned her neck to see what was the trouble in the waters, afraid, yet curious enough to look. She thought she saw its eyes just above the water, and the back of its head and its thick neck in a rush of waters the color of blood. She would have watched a moment longer if Lehabim had not jerked her forward; she relented to follow but pulled her hand away from him.

- 73 -

They arrived just at dusk. Madai knew he had not imagined the small, white speck that had hit his face with a sharp edge, leaving a cold, wet spot. If it were just an early storm, perhaps they could still get away to the south. And if it were not, then he would have a winter to glean the particulars of Noah's lost world. Perhaps he would even come to believe in mercy, given the time. .

The stone house seemed uncommonly silent in the distance. Smoke was rising from the chimney; it was also rising from a smoldering hulk on the altar, but no one tended it. There was something amiss and Shem knew it. He tugged at the donkey, who had planted its front legs, at odds with itself so near the stable.

"Abba!" Shem called as they trotted toward the house. No one answered. He left the donkey standing beside the smoking altar and rushed inside.

The place was lit warmly by the ever-present fire. Even so, the room was empty.

"Abba!" Shem called again, and Noah appeared.

"In here," he answered and disappeared again.

Shem hurried toward the back room.

"Bring Almodad," they heard Noah call.

Madai and Kittim stood just inside the house, beside the clay oven. They were alone, and left to wonder what had put an edge of fear in Noah's voice. They heard muffled voices coming through the stone walls. Madai recognized Almodad's voice and recognized alarm in it, and then anger. Shem said something in a softer tone and reemerged.

"Sheleph has been attacked," he told them simply.

Madai and Kittim could only stand gaping.

"There was an ambush set from the edge of the forest," Shem continued. "He was next to Abba at the altar, and they struck him through his right breast. He is my height."

Madai knew what that meant.

"A second arrow struck the ground just beside them."

The fire crackled as a log fell into the ash. It was the only sound after Shem's revelation.

"How is the boy?" Kittim asked quietly.

"Very bad," he answered. "He cannot get his breath - a lot of blood." Shem's face was stern. "But his mother is here, and Almodad."

"Who was it?" Madai asked.

Shem looked at him, his eyes the color of coal. "We have not been left alone here," he explained. "Always there is the threat against Abba, who is a voice of Elohiym, and a proof that judgment was reined against the world."

"Who are they?" Madai asked again. "What will we do?"

"Men of Shinar."

"But... they were destroyed!"

"Not the priests, and there are assassins in their number."

"And Semiramis," Kittim finished.

"Yes."

Shem tugged at his beard as his eyes roved the room, coming to rest on his bow. "Our every move is visible from the forest," he muttered.

"They think they have killed you, Abba," Misha spoke from behind them. They turned, not having heard her enter the room. "Perhaps they have left."

"They will not be satisfied just with that," Shem answered her. "We have routed them; they will seek the same - the death of all that is Abba's, all that is mine." He went to her and put his hand on her arm. "You are not afraid..."

She shook her head, and certainly Madai believed her, for he had seen her fierce grey eyes before.

"But we are blind in here," she insisted, "and you are tired."

"Yes," he answered calmly, taking her hand, "we are blind in here."

She was about to answer when Almodad came like a lion from the sick room. There was a terrible look on his face, accentuating his ragged scar. He grabbed a lance from its niche in the wall.

"The grass grows high on the roof," Shem said abruptly, stopping him.

Still, Almodad took a step toward the door.

"Do you not want them dead, Almodad?"

Sheleph's father turned then. "What do you mean?" he asked.

"Do you think they cannot see? They are entrenched somewhere out there," Shem argued jerking his head toward the forest. "One at a time they will pick us off." He looked at Kittim and Madai. "Four of us."

"And Jah."

Shem nodded. "Yes. Let us use the sense He gave us."

Almodad's mouth tightened, as did his grip on the spear, but he stopped. He looked at Shem. "Then, what?"

Shem strode across the room for his bow. He ran his hand lightly down the tested wood. "We eat, then we climb to the roof," he said quietly. "There the grass is high; there we will see them and they will be watching the door."

Misha followed her father to the weapons.

"You will stay here," he told her.

She flinched. "But I have perfect aim."

'You do, daughter," Shem agreed. "And it may be needed inside."

"Certainly not!" she argued.

"Abba may need you." His reply was final.

Noah came from the back room. He had yet another look on his face that Madai had not seen before. There was a storm in his eyes, his wrinkly face become a craggy face, his back nearly straight.

"These are sorcerers," he barked. He looked pointedly at Madai. "No disguises here, but the serpent itself."

"We are going to the roof," Shem told him, taking a piece of flatbread from a crock on the stove. He handed bread to the others.

The old father nodded. He retrieved his bow from a cabinet and gave it to Misha, taking a second for himself. "The Strong Arm of Jah Elohiym goes before you," he declared.

After he had eaten, Almodad went to the window. He lifted a wooden timber to release the shutter, inviting in a cold wind. He looked once at Noah, as though to say, 'Keep him alive while I am out here.' Then the moment passed and he became an avenger again. He swung his right leg up and crawled through the window.

೧೪ ೧೪ ೧೪

Weapons strapped to their backs, they scaled the stone wall as though it were a cliff. Already it was lightly crusted with a clinging skin of snow. The light was fading quickly, the sun dropping into the distant forest where the assassins had hid themselves. Grass grew to a camel's knees and gave them nearly complete cover if they crouched. It shifted as they crawled through it, but the wind was angry and swirled it like a prairie storm. Only their eyes lifted above the thatch, scanning the forest for any moving silhouette. Everything was quiet, as though even the birds knew there was a presence in the forest, and nothing moved.

Shem rose on one knee. He pulled back his bowstring to send an arrow deep into the trees, hoping to flush out a yelp. Madai was amazed at his strength. He shot an arrow of his own, only to watch it fall short.

It got them something: an immediate rise of chanting, an ambiguous movement, followed by a sort of cackling call, like unnatural birds. A signal, certainly. The noise was like crickets – everywhere, with no discernible origin. And then it was still again; just the eerie whine of wind. Madai felt the surface of his skin prickle, thinking the grass an impotent shield and quickly spreading shadow the perfect cover for the enemy.

Madai heard Kittim grunt and suddenly rise up to his knees. He drew back the bowstring, pointed toward the mountain behind them. The arrow spun away at the rising cliff, followed by a sharp, brief and startled yelp. Madai had turned, scanning the mountain with rising alarm, thinking what a trap the roof would be with assassins above and behind them. There was a flicker of moving shadow, and Madai nearly bent his bow in half to send an arrow racing. It caught a man in the back.

The whine of another flinty missile struck the roof just at Kittim's bent knee. He swiveled on that knee and set his aim with uncanny perception, answering arrow with arrow. There was not a cry, but a crack of breaking brush as another man of Shinar fell, rolling over the edge of the rock-face. He was followed by a cascade of loosened gravel. Broken shale scattered at the base of the cliff. A last stone bounced, and it was quiet. They waited in silence, eight eyes trained above them now.

"I know the cliffs," Shem whispered. He slid toward the edge of the roof.

"We don't want to shoot you!" Madai hissed.

"You will not hear me or see me," Shem promised them, and indeed they did not... which was not all-together reassuring.

୧୨ଔ ୧୨ଔ ୧୨ଔ

As the night came full on, clouds crawled over the sky, eclipsing both moon and stars. It left them only their ears to catch a footfall or the soft twang of a bowstring drawing back. Madai was relieved to hear a muffled creak of leather as Kittim shifted his weight, and no foreign shuffle or broken twig, or even a night creature. He settled into the grass. The quick first volley of arrows receded and was replaced by vigilant waiting. A thinner cold seemed to come with the clouds.

Madai pulled his hat over his ears. He blew into his hands and looked out into sheer blackness. He could hear them in the forest. There was a rising croon; It was a spell, he knew. He had a fear of spells and pressed his hands over the flaps of his cap and watched for any sign there was someone creeping across the field at them. It was a miserable end to their climb for the ark.

When it felt as though Shem had been gone a long time, one tiny star opened a way through the clouds. It cheered Madai. 'What a lot of light comes with just one star,' he realized. It gave him the eyes to look toward his right side and the stable yard. He thought he had heard something move there - then remembered the pack ass deserted by Shem. He relaxed, only to feel the muscle in his thigh seize up. He eased down to his knees in time to hear a boot on stone and tense again.

" Abba... Misha," he heard the whisper from below, "it is Shem."

Madai heard the unmistakable scrape of a boot across the beam frame as Shem climbed back through the window.

He had come for word of Sheleph. Shem let the heat waves from the clay oven reach into his skin and bring feeling back to his hands.

"They were after the mountain," he told Misha, "but we took them as they climbed." He rubbed his hands. "I think they meant to take us in the presence of Mighty Jah, beside the altar...stunning confidence." He smiled thinly at his own joke. Steam was rising from his clothes. "The old serpent either does not learn or does not care."

"Who it kills it will replace," Noah muttered. "What is man, after all, but the image of God?"

"Well, there is still a band of them in the forest."

Noah's eyes glimmered. "They will freeze, then," he said. Then he glanced at the back room with a softening. "Sheleph lives."

Shem nodded once. "I must tell Almodad," he replied, starting back for the window. Then he turned to study his father. "Are you well?"

'Ab Noah grunted and Shem faintly smiled again.

"And you, Abba?" Misha asked.

"We are all well, and three idolaters dead."

"Take care you do not freeze," Noah insisted. "It will come winter tonight."

Shem nodded, severe again. "Fasten this behind me" he insisted.

ꚇꚉꞧ ꚇꚉꞧ ꚇꚉꞧ

Shem called up to them and scaled the wall. "It was only those three," he guaranteed.

"Sheleph?" Almodad asked.

"He lives."

"Jah be praised!" the father whispered.

"So, do we wait?" Madai asked.

It was Almodad who answered, "We watch here."

"Winter is coming tonight," Shem said "And they will come tonight, also, or not at all." He nodded at Almodad. "We watch here."

The cold was numbing. If Madai had doubted the first wisp of snow, he was certain now that it had arrived. A light dusting settled on his robe, only to lift in the cold wind and resettle in the grass or spill off the edge of the roof and swirl to the ground. His consolation was that the priests of Shinar were as miserable.

That solace, thin as it was, was short-lived. A tiny pinpoint of light began to flicker in the forest's dark, beyond the range of even Shem's arrow. Two others were lit, forming a triad, revealing the present location of the enemy, if not their precise number. Madai pulled the fleece over his head and tucked his chin. There was a certain insulation created by the woolly cloak. But Madai shivered nonetheless, till his jaw and shoulders ached, and watched the fires taunting him from a distance. He needn't ask how Kittim suffered, because he could hear the man shaking beside him. Still, they watched the forest.

He heard the chanting start again. Almodad spat, and Madai had a flashing thought of spit turning to ice on the way down. It helped him endure the eerie baying till it finally stopped again. The fires got bigger and Madai hunched himself lower into his coat.

Grey clouds finally grew less grey. They had sat through the night and Madai was numb. He might not have had hands or feet or nose at all. He knew they needed to get back inside, at least for a while. He had seen blackened toes before.

Kittim knew it, too. He crawled through the grass toward Madai, speaking to Shem and Almodad as he did.

"We must go down," he whispered.

Misha lay with her head on the table. Her shoulders rose and fell lightly, the bow lay across her lap cradled in her open fingers. Noah stirred the fire.

"Sheleph?" Almodad asked as he started for the sick room.

"His breathing is hard," Noah answered. "But he lives."

They huddled at the oven, beating their arms and turning to heat their backs. Almodad had forsaken the thought of warmth to see about his son.

412

"We took three," Shem announced. "There are more. Curses were cast in the night." His words were distorted by shivering. "The rest will be harmed by the cold," he added.

The heat of the room was not able to stop Madai's trembling. His teeth chattered and his bones hurt from shaking. Noah handed them each a cup of hot tea. It was the tea that did the most good. Misha woke, jerking her head up. She looked embarrassed, but only for a moment, before she asked about their vigil. Then she took a cup of tea to Almodad and didn't return.

Shem took his cup to the window and opened the shutters to watch the forest.

Their shaking had just subsided, when Almodad reappeared, bearing an inscrutable expression.

"He is a strong boy," was all he said in a flat voice, taking a spot at the fire.

"Elohiym gives us the advantage," Shem suddenly announced, opening the shutters wide to expose what was quickly becoming a blizzard. The wind was rising, blowing the snow sideways and coating the pasture with a blanket of white. It would be their sentry.

Madai opened another shutter facing the animal shelter to find no prints in the newly fallen snow there. Windows facing all the four directions showed the same. Then he joined Shem, looking out toward the forest. He smiled. He could see three smoking spots where the fires had been. One was still struggling to survive, being plied with brush and spitting sparks. Whatever their number, they would suffer.

Madai felt no pity for the men huddled in the cold. He did, however, remember the donkey that had carried their wood onto Ararat and then had carried the ark planks. He turned and left the window to see to the beast before it froze.

Marisheba opened the door of Reenah's cottage a third time in as many minutes. Her eyes searched the bank of the river frantically, watching for Iscah. Dusk had turned to nearly night, and she had not come, she and the boy, Lahabim.

It seemed there was nothing but worry now for Marisheba. How was her wise and good master now a ruined man? And Reenah, who had been to her a daughter, brought by that reprobate father from Cush, she carried a secret and silent grief. Tutan, whom she had depended upon to be strong, to see them through the storm, had become nearly always absent. And now Iscah, lost somewhere in the spreading dark. Marisheba looked into the dusky sky.

"Elohiym," she breathed.

Then her heart leapt, for nearly as His Name was spoken, Iscah appeared, hurrying up the path. She preceded Lehabim by several strides, reaching the door nearly breathless.

"Forgive me, Marisheba," she wheezed, "I dreamt too long at the sand bar... and at the river." Iscah's eyes, already round and bright, grew larger. "Leviathan!"

This last was more than Marisheba wished to hear. She gripped Iscah's elbow and pulled her into the cottage, followed by a winded Lehabim.

"The last thing I need is to worry over you," Marisheba scolded, and she shot Lehabim a look.

"The fault is mine," he quickly wheezed. "I shall take better care."

At this, Iscah cast him an annoyed expression, and he was crestfallen.

I snowed the whole day through. The shutters were long closed against the blowing. The small openings left at eye level for the purpose of keeping watch became channels for an icy blast. But Shem would not have them blocked, not at any of the windows. They all peered through the little open squares, scanning the surroundings in all directions till their eyes were red from the wind - and nothing moved. When Noah returned from the animal shelter - because he would not neglect his herd - his beard and even his lashes were frozen.

"It will soon take a tunnel to reach the stable," he predicted. He put a gloved hand on Madai's back and turned as Almodad came from Sheleph's room. His face was pinched at the scar, which traveled across it as a ridge of purple, and he moved with a heaviness made of more than only fatigue.

"By the arm of Elohiym he will live, or die." Almodad stated flatly.

Madai hated the look of the man who had ridden the yellow horse into Nimrod's banquet hall and brought the great giant down. The one who had roared his defiance when Nimrod bade him be skinned, and the one who had retrieved all the daughters of Shem. Madai watched as he crossed to sit at the table and take a cup of tea. He was just a worried father now.

Madai looked away. He remembered the lad who had brought him tea in the shepherd's camp and admired the daughter of Shem without concealment. A good boy. He was glad the assassin's fires were out. He had watched them flicker their last and was alert for any movement across the field toward them. It never came. They had either made good haste back to the city, or... Whatever had become of them, it didn't seem to matter.

Noah began to pray. He was standing behind Almodad and lifted his arms straight in the air toward the ceiling. He did not close his eyes. He moved his lips, but without sound. Madai was fascinated.

Noah looked like a white pillar standing that way, clothed in a white fleece, white hair standing at end. He was a solid, breathing, motionless pillar. Then Madai began to hear him, the melodic tongue, faintly audible, an intimate tone. And without understanding a word, Madai was envious. Noah was talking to God. Madai did not have a doubt of it.

He watched till Noah's face began to change. He seemed consumed by a peace. Something true, something mystical was happening. Madai would not look away. He felt a shiver travel down his back and thought that this silence spoke a louder claim than all the reminiscence of an Ancient, or even of a great wooden ark.

Noah's lips quit moving and still his arms were upraised. He closed his eyes. If it were possible, his face seemed luminous. He was yet a great, immobile statue, and no one spoke. Madai believed, in fact, that it would be somehow ignoble to speak - sacrilege.

By some unknowable sense, Zahab and Bethua had left Sheleph's bedside to wait and watch Noah. They watched as he opened his eyes. Madai still believed his face was glowing.

Noah looked directly at Bethua as though he had expected to see her, and he began softly to speak to her. He spoke in his own tongue, as he put his hands gently on Almodad's shoulders. Madai looked quickly at Kittim.

"The Mighty God has spoken," Kittim whispered. "Sheleph will live."

Bethua had begun to weep. Almodad reached her, laid his head on hers, and wept as well as she.

಄಄ ಄಄ ಄಄

They watched through the day, though all concern had been sucked from the house. What was left was an atmosphere of intense calm. Even Madai could feel it, for which he was grateful, though he knew he would not be satisfied again in the world without it.

And so, Sheleph's wounding brought with it... Presence.

76

*T*he wind blew and the snow fell that early winter till piles of it reached midway up the shuttered windows. And Noah was correct. They needed a tunnel to reach the animals in their stable.

When that first blizzard was finished, Almodad and Madai set off across the pasture. They found the spot where the assassins had made their fires. There had been five left, huddled together under the boughs of a large fir tree. Their faces were perfectly preserved in their tombs of frozen flesh. This flesh was marked with scarlet paint, their eyes darkened with black ash. Whatever spirit had been hailed by them in the night had not saved them.

He and Kittim had, of course, lost their opportunity to return to Job before the snow. It was like the winters spent with The Family, when Ashkinaz plied Madai with all sorts of pieces of learning. Madai came to learn that winter, in the home of a true Ancient, that Nimrod was a son of Ham, a mighty man who tamed the plains of dragons and loved the flush of beauty. He drew men to him by the allure of his own approval, and was a usurper who followed the usurper. What had made him make such a choice? Madai couldn't understand. But Nimrod had made an untrue religion of the stars and had detested the One Who formed them.

Madai learned the whole of a great world that was lost in the flood. He learned that a ring of patterns of stars circled the earth like a crown and spoke of absolute redemption, planned even before time itself, and certain beasts once roamed a succulent forest but could not survive what was resurrected after the founts of water. He learned a creature called ape flew through the trees with its tail and had little hands like men. He learned tiny dragons changed their hues to hide beside a scarlet flower or brown sticker bush. All was born in six days and swept away in forty.

He learned that what filled the lungs of men was rich and thick, healing... even so much as to make a brother's murder a violent, difficult business. Yes, he learned that a brother killed a brother for little more than envy - sons of Adam. Madai dwelt on that for a week and couldn't understand, for he had lost brothers and grieved them still, stolen away by a second earth of bears that ate flesh and quakes that still tore the rocks apart. He learned that a thousand years was a life-span once, and men walked with God. But serpents fell from heaven. He learned there was a great deal missing now: mists instead of rain, bronzed heavens instead of animal skins, fruit instead of flesh. If it were God's first intent, would they ever have it back? He was God, after all.

Madai learned how much had been forgotten, or never believed, or never known. But he had seen the ark, rooted at the top of a mountain too rugged to drag a carpenter's tools there; home of stunted, wind-blown trees, not gopher wood; not the home of tar - an ark lifted on waves and come to rest on a height too great to carry.

It was a profitable winter. It was a long winter.

77

Iscah pulled the curtain across the little space she shared with Marisheba and Reenah. It was early, and they were still sitting at the fire, speaking of the planting which would begin tomorrow.

She sat on the cot which had served as bed these many months. The winter had brought a good amount of snow; the snow melted and filled the river and made the earth ready for seed. But she was worried over the long absence of Kittim. If he did not come soon, she was afraid it would be Lehabim for her. What a dreadful thought!

Tutan still talked of leaving with the caravans. He was gone now, anyway, attending Job, when it should have been Lehabim, as it was his duty. Frustration brought Iscah's tears, for which she was immediately ashamed in light of what was suffered in the good man's house. Still, a tear rolled down her nose as she unloosed the binding around her chest. She had used it to hide behind, and perhaps it had spared her Lehabim's greater persistence.

She had planned her moment; when Kittim returned she would reveal herself. She would tend him as servant or wife. 'Only let him keep me.' She wiped her face and lay on the cot. She sniffed.

"I shall cast my lot before him," she whispered, making herself feel brave. It was only her secret self, her authentic self, that begged God for a happy end .

- *78* -

The God of Noah was kind and carried Madai through the winter with every hearty provision for flesh and spirit. And when at last the spring sun began to melt the morning mist earlier each day, Kittim and Madai began their preparations. Theirs had been a wealthy season at the fire of an Ancient, but they were restlessly drawn back to the West, and to the far West.

Noah felt their energy in kind. His voice would not preach to the farthest corners, but Madai's would. And there lived the sons of his son. The Ancient was not sorry to lift his hand in farewell; he was a preacher first. Zahab was mother to a tribe across the Brine Sea, and she was mindful of it. Even Sheleph, who was recovered and clasped Misha's fingers in his hand when he waved, was not sorry to see Madai go, if for another cause. Shem would tend his family and his sheep and press against the deceptions of Shinar till he was earth beside his father; and his would beget, one far day, a promised crushing Seed.

C3C2   C3C2   C3C2

This monotony was not the same as that in coming, for success had been found. Only it had been a long way through the pass of Nimrud Dagh not quite unfrozen; a hasty skirting of the crippled Shinar and a relentless passing of long days.

Madai had been thinking the river had a familiar look for a while now, but perhaps it was just an overzealous anticipation. For surely, there was a treasure to share. They rounded a bend - and he was sure. It had not been impatience; this was the place where they had rescued the kitchen maid - Madai was certain.

"Kittim," he called.

The man slowed his mount, and turned in the saddle. He raised his brow and smiled.

"I say we go the whole way," Madai suggested, suspecting Kittim had known a long time that they were near.

"They will all be asleep," Kittim argued.

"Yes," Madai looked at the distance. "Yes." He shook his head absently. "Iscah will be surprised," he pronounced, thinking about the plank of timber strapped to a camel, "and Tutan." He put his hand lightly against the leather pouch hanging from his girdle, to be certain that it was still moving.

"Indeed," Kittim agreed. He looked at the sun; the day was far gone. "I think we need a washing."

They rode down the river, past the keeping of Leviathan, and built a fire big enough to keep them warm after their bath. Madai knew Kittim was right; they both stunk and mud hugged him like an arm. The water was frigid. Only the thought of Job's beautiful house, and persnickety wife kept him in the river.

᠂᠂᠂᠂᠂᠂᠂᠂᠂᠂᠂᠂

Tutan knelt on the rich earth. The vines were budding. Little shoots of fresh, reddish leaves could just be seen. 'There is a season of rebirth, thank the Holy One,' he thought. He stood, stretching his back, which was still vigorous from the fall harvest. How much more alive he felt here. Too much, in truth, thinking briefly of Reenah. He shrugged. 'It is well that I be away,' he said aloud, 'with the early caravans.' He shielded his eyes against the sun, seeing the first caravan of the season in the distance. 'Though perhaps it need not be this one...'

Tutan began the descent of the hill before his brain quite registered it. Then he began to smile and to run. As he ran he began to wave, and to laugh. He was out of breath before he reached them, so he stood in the center of the field and waved with both his arms. The horses were galloping now, followed by jingling, puffing camels.

Madai leapt from his gelding and threw his bulk at the Eastern man.

"Tutan, Tutan!" he exclaimed over and over.

"Madai!"

They were laughing. Tutan pulled away, for Madai was considerably taller, and Tutan's face was buried in his coat.

"Kittim!" Tutan cried, turning and taking him by the arms. "Mighty God be praised."

They began to laugh again. "We have waited too long for this," Madai said, thumping Tutan on his back. "And come far." Then he stood back, taking stock of Tutan's face. "How well you are!" he proclaimed.

"Yes, yes... and you... and you, Kittim," Tutan agreed. He pulled at Kittim's arm, "Come, come! Job is with the Lady. What have you to tell?" He stopped and looked at them both. "No, let us be inside first. Iscah must hear."

But Madai was not restrained from the showing of the ark wood.

In their perfect joy, Madai did not note the quiet of Job's pastures. He followed Tutan into the stillness of the house, breathed the sweet fragrance of spring blooms on the table, and believed nothing ill of the world.

"Lehabim," Tutan called. The boy came at the first call, though he was not so much the boy as he had been. "Will you tend the animals?"

He opened the door and called, "Job! See who is come!"

Madai looked about for Job, wondering absently why it was Tutan who commanded the household. He just glanced down the long hall flanked by a colorful caravan in fresco, forgetting that his boots were coated with dust, and did not wait for the girl with the basin of water. He came eagerly into the great room, while Kittim untied the planks of ark and followed him inside.

A man was just entering the room from one of the Family chambers. Madai looked at him oddly. Who strode about Job's house with such familiarity? The man moved to the fire and looked at him with a gaping smile. It stopped Madai mid-step.

The man with entirely white hair extended his arms. "His Name be praised," Job spoke in a quiet voice. "Our friends have come."

Madai could not move. The great, hearty man was excruciatingly thin, and his hair was as white as the first snow. But his voice was merry, if it was low; and it was strong, though it was quiet.

Tutan and Kittim, each carrying one of the planks, followed Madai into the room.

"See what they have brought," Tutan exclaimed, perceiving Job as quite recovered and no longer alarmed at his appearance.

Job's eyes strayed to the wood. His face held a questioning aspect. "What is this?" he asked.

"Can not you guess?" Tutan's voice was rich with excitement. He laid the wood in Job's hands. "From Ararat," he whispered.

Job's dark orbs, all the more extreme in his thin face, widened, and his smile grew to astonishment. "This timber is hewn," he muttered, and looked up.

Kittim put his hand on Job's shoulder with a gentle touch. "The great ship," he affirmed. "Resting whole at the peak of Ararat."

"The ship of the deluge?" an astounded woman's voice asked behind them. It was the Lady, they saw on turning, though, indeed, as changed as her husband. For her hair was loose, as though she had been napping, and her robe was sturdy, for working. It did not appear she had been ill; she was quite robust and beautiful, as she had never quite been in her regalia.

The surprise quelled her decorum only briefly. She extended her hands toward them, smiling. "How splendid you are returned," she said, looking from Kittim to Madai.

Kittim took her hand, bowing over it. "The blessings of Almighty God be yours."

"And yours as well," she answered, and asked "My lord Kittim, the ship of the deluge...?"

He nodded, still looking kindly into her face. "It is a great size, a remarkable structure."

"Iscah," Tutan interrupted suddenly. "She must be fetched."

"Yes, certainly," the Lady agreed.

"A lambing, in the stable," Tutan explained.

Madai stopped him with a hand on his arm. "I will surprise her," he said. "Stay with Kittim. Ask him what you will," he added with a knowing smile.

ദരു ദരു ദരു

The stable was fairly dark; its windows were eastward and south. A torch lit the small circle of ewe and straw and little person. Iscah was squatting, murmuring softly with the tail of the sheep in her hand. She heard Madai behind her and lifted her other hand.

"Quietly, Tutan," she whispered. "She is a good mother... it is coming." Iscah turned to look over her shoulder and gasped. She dropped the ewe's tail.

"Madai!" she cried, if it were possible, in a hushed voice. But the mother recognized the change of her tone and lifted her head nervously. Iscah quickly returned to her task.

Her heart was thumping. "It is her first," she explained somewhat breathlessly. "All the sheep are birthing three at a time. There - it is just coming," she told him. She gently tugged at the little black hooves as they emerged, then let them go.

"Good," she whispered, looking back at Madai. "It is the same head as the feet." Then she went back to the new mother just as she bawled, and a sack of hooves and wet, black wool slipped onto the straw. The yearling mother twisted her head round to look at what had come out of her.

"I must not touch it," Iscah whispered. "Unless she does not know what to do."

Madai watched the homely little drama silently. Iscah was intent on her chore and the smell of blood on the straw was strong.

"It is vital that none be lost," she broke the silence, if barely.

Another wet bundle of lamb began to emerge. And she tested that the hooves belonged to the head sharing the canal, though with a less happy result. "It is his twin," she explained, as she tenderly pushed the tiny black nose back inside, whilst holding the slippery hooves of the other in her hand.

"Should I help?" Madai whispered.

Iscah shook her head. "She must do it alone, if she can; two of us is too much." She grinned at him, and the yearling complained as the second and third lamb tried to be born at the same time. "Sh... yashab qatan 'em... shh. It is well."

Pushing the nose of the third with her left hand, Iscah evenly pulled the hooves of the second. And it slipped out as quickly as the first.

"Job is blessed again of God, praise His Name," she affirmed. "Even the yearlings."

The last of the three began its short journey into the world. Iscah worried that its hooves be bent backward; but they came as they should, and, without her help, the latest of Job's herd was born. The mother laid her head on the straw and breathed out her relief. Her sides, greatly narrowed, softly rose and fell. Then, as though the gentle voice of Life explained her course, she picked up her head again, twisted her neck, and began to clean her babies with her soft pink tongue.

Iscah dropped back on the straw and closed her eyes. Madai noticed then that her face was covered with sweat. She drooped her head back between her shoulders, opened her eyes, and grinned at him upside down.

Madai came nearer and knelt beside her. He pulled a strand of dripping hair from her forehead. "We do not keep sheep," he explained, still whispering.

She flung her arms around him. "You have been away so long!"

Madai laughed. "There is a lot to tell you," he began.

The new mother bawled at them and she put her hand on his mouth. "Sh," she warned, and Madai remembered what she had whispered before.

"Why is it vital that none are lost?" he asked. "Surely Job has multitudes..."

She did not answer at once. It was so pleasant to rest her head upon the solid comfort of Madai's arm. Slowly, she pulled herself upright and looked squarely into his eyes, as light and blue as hers were dark. "A great trouble has come," she answered simply. "All his herds were lost," - she knew it best that she finish the calamity in one sentence - , "and his children as well."

His face did not quite register comprehension, so she nodded her head with finality. "It is true," she affirmed.

"The sons?"

She nodded again.

Madai watched her. Her eyes rimmed with red and that made it real to him. He looked away to the scene that had only moments before been so full. "All was not lost..." he insisted, a feeble argument.

"We harvested the vineyard and bought a small herd," she replied, compassionate for the stunned look in his eyes, and reminded him, "all the ewes have delivered three. It is a blessing from God."

Madai nodded once, feeling the threat against his fresh belief from a familiar enemy.

"Should I not have told it so freely?" Iscah whispered. She put her hand gently on his shoulder. "Madai?"

"How?" he asked.

"Sabeans took the herds, and a great wind collapsed the house of the eldest son. All Job's children were inside," she answered quietly.

Madai couldn't move.

"And Job?" he asked.

"He is well," she was relieved to answer. "And the Lady. Theirs is a peace now. We cannot understand it."

"Peace," he spoke so quietly she could only read it on his lips.

"Are you well?" she finally asked.

He nodded and brought his focus back to her face.

"I have decided there are questions for which there are no answers," she told him.

"Is that sufficient for you?"

He recognized the bright glow in her black eyes as she answered, "I believe we have had this discussion before. Have you traveled so far to return the same as you left?"

He felt her steady gaze no less than her hand on his shoulder. He hesitated; he tested his heart. "No," he finally answered. "I have not returned the same."

Her face relaxed, and she smiled. Then she leaned forward and lightly kissed his cheek. "I am glad for that," she assured him.

The voices of the new lambs called their attention. Only two had found their mother's milk.

"She may not suckle them all." Iscah observed. "There are four others already to feed." She looked at Madai with a lingering concern. "This blessing from God brings its own difficulties."

∞ ∞ ∞

When Iscah and Madai came round again into the house, they found Job sitting with a plank of wood resting on his knees. The Lady sat beside him, and Marisheba was serving them wine.

Madai crossed the room quietly.

"Madai!" Job called him with a smile. "You have Iscah. Come."

"I must wash," Iscah said quickly, and added, "three."

Madai didn't watch her go; instead, he inspected the white-haired man. "I hope you and the Lady are well."

Job chuckled. "You do not need to whisper, my friend. I am not fragile." He shrugged. "I have been ill, but I am recovered."

"Sit, sit, Madai," Tutan urged. "We have waited for Iscah. Now we shall hear all that you have seen."

"When she returns," Marisheba reminded him. "Remember Reenah, as well."

"Yes, yes," Tutan answered eagerly. "Lehabim is fetching her." His eyes blinked rapidly. "Tell us just a little."

The pouch at Madai's leg moved. He laid his hand over it as Tutan glanced down.

"What do you have, Madai?" he asked.

Madai pulled the pouch off his belt and put the bundle on the floor. It seemed to try to run across the wood, pouch and all. "Something I brought for Iscah. Bright as the skin of the flying serpent, but not so ferocious."

"Let us have a look," Tutan urged.

Madai held the bag up in the air, letting the creature drop to the bottom, and unknotted the top. Tutan and Job peered inside to greet the open-mouthed hiss of a colorful reptile. "What is it?" Tutan asked.

"Noah calls it a rainbow dragon, " Madai began. "A lizard as I have not seen before. It changes its color - "

"Noah?" Job was incredulous.

Madai smiled.

"Do not tell too much," Tutan started, holding up his hand.

"Noah as well as the ship?" The Lady interjected. "Is it possible that he lives?"

Madai carefully pulled the bag closed. He looked at the faces surrounding him, with their astonished expressions. "It has to do with the first earth," he said with a smile.

- 79 -

"Maybe Marisheba was right," Madai observed. Pulling the dusty tunic over his head, he caught a piece of straw in his hair.

"Hmm," Kittim replied, doing the same. "This is not just a bath, you know. It is to wait for Reenah."

Madai looked at him once before sinking into the warmed water. "I guess we did not do such a thorough job at the river." He immersed his head as he once had done at the bathhouse of En-UtuAten. There was so much to tell his friends, but much had happened here, as well. Job had not only been ill.

When they were dry, they pulled on the clothes the Lady herself had given them. She had led them to their old rooms. She had opened a cabinet and stepped back to reveal it full of folded clothing. She had touched the clothes gently and had let them take their choice. Madai remembered, running his palm across the weave made for a prince, that all their children had been killed.

"A terrible thing has happened here," Madai said as they dressed. "While you were with me at the ark." Madai's voice was full of remorse.

"What has that to do with me?" Kittim asked.

"You were sent to him by your Master, were you not? If you had been here..."

"I only said I sought a man in the East," Kittim answered vaguely. He sniffed the air and looked at Madai with a lifted brow. "Do you smell it?" he asked and followed the aroma down the hall.

A good and savory odor greeted them. They were all waiting at the table. Tutan jumped from his seat when they appeared and hurried forward to show them where to sit, as if they had been gone too long to remember.

"Lehabim has gone for Reenah," he said. "Job will have us wait for her before you tell us everything."

Madai looked from face to face. Even the Lady seemed agreeable. He looked at Job, thin, with the hair of an old man. Then Job prayed for their meal, a quiet prayer with a tone more modest than Madai had ever heard of a man.

Job looked at Madai when he finished, to find him watching. He lifted his cup with steady hands. "A long journey... and successful," he said before he drank with a wide smile outlined by a snow-white beard.

"By the Arm of God," Kittim affirmed and drank from his cup.

Iscah was quiet. She seemed nervous and looked at Kittim only once.

"A mighty thing has come of our affliction," Job suddenly announced, looking at Madai.

"There has been suffering. The loss of herds, and shepherds..." he stopped.

"Our children," his wife finished softly.

Silence filled the room.

"Sabeans took the shepherds and the herds," Job continued. "A great wind toppled the house where my sons were eating, they and theirs. And I," Job stretched his hand across the table, revealing deep scars, "was beset by boils." He leaned into the light where pit-marks were visible on his face. "But I would not have you think we were deserted." He looked at his wife gently. "What came of that trouble were ministrations from the Holy One, and instruction."

"And a new babe," the Lady supplemented, covering her belly with her hands.

Madai swung round in surprise to look at her.

"What instructions?" Kittim asked.

"What ministrations?" a grim voice asked from the doorway.

☙ ❧   ☙ ❧   ☙ ❧

Reenah stood in the entrance, with Lehabim behind her. The color of her face belied the calm expression she wore. She wore, as well, Iscah noted, her most handsome dress. Her abundance of hair was gathered artfully at her neck by a clasp of inlaid gold. The pronouncement of her ardent and effortless womanhood was never clearer. She was erect, dark and beautiful, though dark hollows haunted her eyes.

"Reenah," Iscah greeted her, rising, vaguely regretting the drab brown she wore.

"What ministrations, Uncle?" Reenah repeated. "Do you cling to your god even now?" she finished in a whisper. Remorse at her words, or seeing those newly arrived perhaps, bloomed in the color of her face as she smiled at Madai and Kittim. She held out her hands with that familiar flourish. "Forgive me, good friends," she murmured. "Certainly you are a cause for joy."

The Lady crossed the room to greet Reenah. "There is a place here for you," she said, taking her hand. She looked into Reenah's face and finished quietly, "You sound very much like me."

Reenah was stunned by the kindness. She surrendered her hand with surprise and followed Job's wife. She was brought to sit beside the Lady, which was a greater surprise yet.

"I am just telling what has befallen this house," Job quickly interjected. "And what good has come of it."

Reenah quickly removed what showed of her emotions regarding all that was Job's trouble, though her face was bathed with color. But her smile was true when she looked at Madai and Kittim. And when her eyes passed Tutan, she lingered just a moment and blushed more deeply. She sat and reached for her cup, filled with the wine they both had made.

"I cannot speak lightly of the grief or the loss," Job continued. "I confess, I do not understand. Though," he smiled faintly, recalling the moment, "there are things too wonderful for me to know,"

"Wonderful?" Madai and Reenah exclaimed in unison.

Job smiled at them. He picked up his wine and sipped the cup empty, then he folded his hands calmly on the tabletop. "You mistook my meaning," he gently answered. "I do not make light our suffering. By wonderful, I only mean..."

Reenah lifted her hand brazenly. "I will not hear it," she proclaimed.

The Lady's brows arched.

"As you wish," Job calmly replied.

Reenah, whose imprudence surprised even herself, looked at him tightly and sipped from her cup again.

Tutan studied her with a look that was commonplace now, one for which Iscah was indignant. The peace she had struck with Reenah had been silently withdrawn by the trouble she had brought the heart of a good man.

Job pushed back from the table, having forgotten the food before him. "Well, my friends, now you may tell us all your good news. I, too, have just the story of things past." He paused. "Dare we hope you have found a witness?"

Madai glanced at Kittim, and, like a familiar smell that brings with it a perfect memory, Madai's senses raced back across the miles and the winter to tell their story: the betrayal of Sabta, Nimrod's enticement, his malignance and his charm.

Sabta, they knew; but of Nimrod, who vaguely connoted evil, they were ignorant. Iscah would have the immediate telling of the ark, but there was something in the story of Nimrod that was still a puzzle to Madai.

"He was cruelty itself," Madai explained, "without mercy. And still... he was something more. He rid the country of dragons, and he loved a beautiful thing." Madai looked at Iscah. "There was a table, inlaid with shell..."

"And who is Nimrod?" Iscah asked, impatient.

"The King of Shinar," Kittim answered. "A man of uncommon power, unnatural."

Iscah's look at Madai struck him to his bones. Every suspect thing she had ever imagined of him raced through her mind and out her eyes.

"Builder of the great tower," he finished lamely.

"The confusion of tongues!" Job interjected. "You found its maker alive?"

"We did. Though it was Madai who contended with him," Kittim answered.

Iscah's tone was cool as she asked with lifted brow, "The King of Shinar?"

"He was a giant, Iscah," Madai answered. "And the very evil itself."

Her face was impassive as she slowly nodded.

"I admit," Madai continued despite her, "that his charm was potent..."

"But he served the new religion," Job proclaimed.

"He authored it," Madai answered.

Kittim's face was stony. "No," he argued. "It was authored by one more ancient - Nimrod was the tool."

Job nodded knowingly. "The maker of the tower lives," he murmured.

Kittim shook his head. "No longer," he corrected. "But the religion will spread.

His queen survived him, and her priests."

"He was jealous of power," Madai added, looking directly at Job. "Your fame was known to him, and resented. He would have extinguished all who did not bow to him."

"You did not bow," Job's Lady insisted.

Madai looked at his companion. "Kittim did not bow," he corrected.

"I have been to Shinar," Reenah suddenly announced.

All turned to look at her. She slowly stood, eyes turned away from them, and glided across the floor to the fire.

The Lady rose also, calling to the kitchen maid, "Lemmeri, will you bring more wine?" Then she followed Reenah and sat beside her. "It is more comfortable here," she affirmed.

"I have had dealings with the King of Shinar," Reenah continued guardedly, but with a hint of challenge. She looked directly at Tutan as they sat down. "An impressive man. It was on the last journey I ever took with my father. We brought trade from Ur. It drew the King's interest."

"You were not persuaded by his religion?" Tutan asked, aghast.

She turned to him placidly. "Did I not once tell you it is wise to give no offense to the gods in whose lands you travel?"

They were quiet when she said that, even Job's wife, whose new kindness had surprised them all and was being tested at that very moment.

"If you knew what we know," Madai announced, "you would not be tolerant."

Reenah looked away from Tutan's stricken face. "Perhaps," she agreed mildly. "We only dined with him."

Iscah twisted on the couch. Madai had redeemed himself, partially. Reenah had betrayed herself at last and still Tutan was looking at her with that look. Only Kittim held firm in her first estimations. Thank the High God for Kittim!

"Then I will tell you about Nimrod," Madai felt his blood rising. "Everything corrupt, even on my own shores, was started in Shinar. Nimrod turned the deluge on its head: Mighty God was the culprit. And the confusion of tongues was His act of chaos. The constellation stories were changed, hiding what God meant with them." He looked at Reenah; all her beauty reminded him of the tiamat and that reminded him of Palapa, and that reminded him of the child on the throne and what Nimrod would have done to her in the name of heaven. Every vile thing. "Nimrod brought peace to the lands as a slayer of dragons, and for that alone he was a champion. And he executed every lust for every power. He was host to the serpent, Reenah."

There was a glitter in her eyes. She looked away from Madai to Job, and then, with revolution in her eyes, to Tutan. "What is it that proves Nimrod's version is not correct?" she asked.

Iscah could not keep the gasp silent coming up from her throat and out her mouth. The Lady herself turned her new eyes of kindness at Reenah with stunned silence.

"Nimrod is dead," Kittim answered flatly.

Reenah was silenced by that, and as surprised as Iscah had, just a moment before, been with her - because she knew the great might of Nimrod. She knew his fortifications and vast army. She had been witness to the unnatural power he wielded.

"Did you kill him?" Iscah asked Kittim.

"Not merely killed," he answered, "vanquished, his army destroyed. Though not by me; by Almodad, son of Shem." Kittim looked purposefully back at the merchant's daughter. "In one single moment, without secret abilities or magic."

Tutan felt the icy cold in the room. He felt the current passing from Kittim to Reenah. He still felt the trouble in his own heart, and he rescued her from the moment. "The son of Shem?" he asked.

Madai nodded. "Almodad," he said. "Son of Shem, who is the son of Noah."

"Kittim and Madai have brought timbers from the ark, Reenah," Job inserted, looking at the dark woman.

Reenah nodded vaguely. "I have seen this ship myself."

"A ship of greater girth than I thought possible to sail a sea," Madai said. "Built of mammoth trees, trees of the first earth."

When she didn't react, Madai turned away from her.

"There was Eden," he said to Tutan. "Adam and his wife were driven away. The border was guarded by fearsome angels with blazing lances. Just as you said, Tutan."

"Border sacrifices," Tutan murmured.

"What is that?" Reenah asked.

Tutan eyed her. "A learning I acquired from a people in the East," he answered. "Of little importance beside this," he indicated the planks from the ark.

"It fortifies the tale of Eden," Iscah insisted coldly. She looked at Madai. "Continue."

An invitation he was happy for, and he said. "Noah did not know all those before the flood, Adam, Seth, or Enoch. But he knew the son of Seth, and he knew the son of Enoch. These men knew Adam in their days, and Adam knew Eden." Madai paused. He looked directly at Tutan. "And Adam talked to God."

The room grew silent. The silk of Reenah's impeccable gown rustled.

"Not as men do now," Madai continued. "I cannot imagine that... the Mighty God... but Noah swears it is so. And you were right, good friend," he said, looking at Job, "some way we will see God in our flesh, even those put to the earth." Madai stopped, thinking of Ido.

"Enoch..." Kittim prodded.

"You tell us, Kittim," Iscah urged.

"Shall we let Madai?" he replied, and Iscah blushed.

Madai cleared his throat. "Yes," he said. "Enoch, an ancient forebearer to Noah, a seer. Enoch did not die." He looked at them purposefully. "One day he only vanished. He left a prophecy that Great God Himself will put His foot on Eden again and bring His holy ones with Him."

Iscah looked at Kittim, who seemed in agreement with Madai. "What does that mean?"

"Ridiculous," Reenah insisted.

Madai had nearly forgotten her. Her reaction might have irritated him, did he not know that he couldn't understand it either. "Noah said..." he began.

"Who was this man?" Reenah challenged. "Do you know what they say of Noah's years when he built the Ark? Ten hundred." She pierced him with her tone, holding up all her fingers.

"Five hundred," Madai corrected.

She laughed. "An old man will not better two hundred," she announced with finality.

"It was the first earth," he explained. "Formed with a shield against the sun, the air heavy with dew."

"Precisely," Job agreed. "The sky was spread out as hard as a mirror of cast bronze."

Madai nodded brusquely. "It was this other air that gave men of that earth many years, and the giant trees and beasts. I saw those trees in the timbers of the Ark."

Reenah scowled.

"You saw the Ark," Madai insisted. "We saw the man. How can you doubt it?"

"It shall be a choice in any case," Kittim said abruptly, looking at her.

"Tell us about the animals," Iscah asked, impatient and without a hope of rescuing an idolatress and spoiler of Tutan.

Madai felt a righteous pounding in his chest, made the more so by the look of scorn on Reenah's face. So he turned to Iscah. "They all ate grass," he told her, ignoring Reenah, his face like a boy's, glad this time to be the one telling something hard to believe.

She blinked at him. "No, that's not what I mean," She shook her head. "How did they catch them all? How did they all fit?"

Madai laughed aloud. She sounded so like himself! "God told Noah to make a ship of gopher wood and coat it with pitch inside and out and build it with three levels. And then God brought the animals Himself."

Iscah opened her mouth to ask something else, then closed it and leaned against the couch, with a smile playing in her eyes. She nodded once.

"Does The Holy God still talk to him?" Tutan asked quietly.

Madai looked at the Eastern man. He had changed in less remarkable ways than Job, but he had changed. There was a vigor in him now, but restless. And Madai remembered that unnatural moment, the night of the great snow, and the promise of Sheleph's life. He remembered the illuminated face of Noah...

"He does, Tutan," Madai answered. "Kittim and I were there when God told him a boy would live. I remember it well."

"How did He sound?" Iscah whispered.

"God did not speak in words," he answered, not sorry for himself, for he had seen the moment, but sorry he must tell her that The Voice was not heard.

"So!" Reenah interjected.

Tutan, who had privately watched her, held his mouth in a thin line. What he admired of her, the liberty and daring, the independence, were now the obstacles. What he loved in her, the tireless duty and talent, the beauty, were his suffering. He scarcely heard Kittim repeat what had been his answer before:

"Indeed, yes, Reenah. God speaks, though to believe is still a choice in the end."

Iscah watched the exchange silently, and the play of emotion on Tutan's face. But she had not guessed the depth of Reenah's ruination. The woman was good in so many ways. Perhaps that only made it worse. It had ensnared Tutan, a consecrated man. Surely, after so many a blasphemy there was left no hope for her.

"Who are we?" Job suddenly asked. "We are vessels of dust. Do we contend against God to justify ourselves?"

Madai was instantly confused by the random turn, but Reenah's face softened even as its shade darkened.

"Perhaps you should," she answered quietly.

This, Job ignored. "Do I bind the Pleiades? Do I loose Orion's cords? Do I provide the raven its food, or count the months of the deer's confinement?" "Tell me, Reenah, is man so great as that?"

She only wet and pursed her lips.

"Do you know what art He used to lay earth's foundations, or give orders to the morning, or show the dawn its place? Have you this skill, Reenah? Is there a man so wise as that?

"He it is, adorned by glory and splendor and power, Who holds the cords of behemoth, even leviathan."

Iscah held her hands gripped in her lap. She watched Reenah's face exercise itself from generic objection to inexplicable rage and back to calm.

"You have spoken rightly of the Creator," Kittim responded.

Reenah ignored him. She stared at Job as she asked, "What has that to do with anything?"

Job lifted his arms away from his sides, palms up. "Well, everything," he answered. "The Maker has rights."

Her expression hardened. "For this answer your sons lay in the earth?" she whispered.

The Lady was jolted and, with her hand at her breast, answered with palpable hurt, "No, Reenah. They are with Him... where He is."

"And this suffices for you?" Reenah asked the Lady sitting so wilted at her side.

"It is a comfort," she replied softly.

Madai listened to the Lady's tender tone and would have thought he had not met her before, changed as she was. The suffering here was extreme. He would have thought more so even than his own, but that was hard to admit. Perhaps it wasn't true. He listened to the breathing in the room, to the disparate wars being fought, and recognized again his own. He reasoned that the righteous die, as do the wicked, an injustice that still chewed his bones inside. But it didn't seem to trouble Job, he who was now a small, slender man with a pocked face and white beard, a man, he had to admit, with peace in his eyes. Certainly an innocent man.

"How is it just that you, of all men, a good man, should have suffered this?" Madai allowed himself to ask.

The expression of Job's eyes changed.

"I tell you this, my friend Madai, with the earnest prayer that you shall receive it as true. There is One Who is good, and none other... God Almighty, Who endures us for love of us, and for naught that we have done, nor that we are. Hear this well, that you need not have it proved."

They were all startled by the passion of Job's speech, no one more than Madai, as it seemed a true warning. Job held him with a look and Madai felt a vein of ice run down his back.

Reenah was only glad the attention had shifted. She felt true remorse for her wicked attack on the Lady; still, she harbored for Tutan the highest regard, but dimmest of hopes. For his eyes had lingered on hers till then. The impediment lay not with his god alone...

"Pray answer me this," she asked in a meeker tone, finding that she needed the answer, "is your God proved just by the means of His power alone?"

"What has you by the gullet, Reenah?" Madai suddenly asked. She turned on him not the stormy expression he expected, but a look of sadness for which he was as perplexed by her as ever.

"Not just His power, child," Job answered patiently, "but perfect goodness, which none other can possess. But that is not your question... is it?"

She was shaken, first by Madai and then by Job, who had not called her 'child' in a long time. She did not want to answer, not with the room so full.

"Do you love your doubt so much?" Job asked, having mistaken her silence.

But it was a proper question, a safe question. "We are given minds, are we not?" she decided to ask.

Job smiled ironically. He leaned forward. "What is His to know is more than I have the wit to wonder," he said. "When I answer the riddle of His dullest wisdom, it shall be, beside Him, less than a clam in my pot." His eyes glittered. "Estimate the heavens if you can, or what dwells upon the earth, and have them do your bidding. You may then fathom God."

Reenah, for reasons more than only this, could not relent. "So your answer is that there is no answer?"

Job raised his snowy brows, setting a row of furrows across his forehead before he allowed himself a wry smile. "Man has his limits," he said.

Reenah's mind was a beautiful instrument, fashioned by a perfect Hand, and she had grasped Job's argument from the start, even as it satisfied not a whit.

"What you ask," she challenged, "is that I trust Him to be just."

"What I ask," Job replied, "is that you trust Him to know better than you what is just, and to trust that He is God and His wisdom is better than yours."

"Trust naively, you say?"

"As our friend Kittim is fond to say, it is a choice. What proof really is there that the ship to which you traveled with your father was the ark of Noah? Was it the assurance of your greatly loved father, that scoundrel Aubed? Could not the ship have been built to match the legend? To acquire the fame of an Ancient? Or to get relics for a piece of gold?" Job's voice grew ever more forceful.

"Do you tempt me?" Reenah asked.

Job's smile widened. "I bring you notice, my dear, that you have made choices by trust already."

When Reenah didn't respond, Job reached across the table and patted her arm. "Do you trust me?" he asked.

She slowly nodded.

"As I trust Mighty God," he finished. Then he took his wife's hand. "It has been dark very long," he added.

Reenah looked at the shuttered window with sudden alarm.

The Lady noticed it. "Reenah shall stay the night here," she proclaimed with her new voice.

- 80 -

Reenah lay on the bed, fully dressed. This bed she knew to be that of a son, dead not a year. This room, his as a child, into which the Lady of this house had brought her. And brought her kindly.

She listened as the house went to sleep, and she regretted that she would stir it. Lifting the latch, she quietly opened the door and creaked the floor boards as she moved down the hall.

All the sleeping chambers were on this wing, as the sons had been kept close. She knew the suite she sought, on the northernmost end. She tapped lightly on the door, as now she knew the Lady kept the bed of her husband.

"Uncle," she whispered.

He opened the door, fully dressed. "I have expected you, child."

Though it was a surprise, she let him lead her back down the corridor into the dining hall. The fire was low, but it was not cold. He stirred the embers.

"Marisheba has left us tea," he told her.

"How did you know?" Reenah asked.

"I know you very well. Did we not raise you?"

She would not concede this, being a mild affront to the diligence of her own father. Instead, she busied herself with the tea, only lukewarm. She went to the kitchen for honey and cream, a favorite treat from long ago.

"And bring some bread," Job called after her.

"I have questions," she told him, coming back with a tray. "And I do not wish to hear lofty speeches. Answer me plainly."

He took the cream from her. "Ask what you will," he answered.

She studied him across her cup. His face was so drawn, the face of the one she loved nearly as well as a father. It caused her a cutting grief.

"You do know me well," she began, sorry if she was about to make it worse. "You know the best... and worst. I have entertained merchants and sheiks. You know I have traded wares in temples and brothels. You know I have bedded soldiers and kings. You know I have served no gods..."

"Even still, He loves you," Job quietly insisted.

"Do not tell me this!" she looked at him with sudden brimming eyes. "Who is God? Is He the wind? Let me see Him!"

"My ears have heard Him, my eyes have seen Him, and I despise myself," Job whispered.

"What?"

"And I repent in dust and ashes," he finished.

"Do not tell me you are mad!" she cried with alarm.

"I am no more mad than you, Reenah. But you may not see God. He is too wonderful. You can see only what He has done."

"He has killed your sons!"

Job's eyes filled with tears and she was suddenly terrified to see him cry.

He did not, his bitterest grief spent long since, and the moment passed. "As Kittim has truly spoken," Job answered, "there is the enemy."

"The serpent," she chided. "Shall I believe this fable, as well?"

"It is no fable, Reenah. You know that; you have seen the wreck it leaves behind."

"Father did not believe such tales."

"Your father was a rogue. You know that, too."

Reenah quickly looked down as, to her great dismay, her hands began to shake.

"Then what has become of him?" She looked up, daring to ask the question. "He is no more, and only dust... is he not?"

Job looked at her gently, having always known the dread she kept for her father. "There was one before the flood," Job began on an unlikely course. "As told by Madai from the very mouth of Noah, he who knew. This Enoch, prophet of Mighty God, one who walked with God, one who did not die, but God took him. He spoke words of the end of time." Job let the room fill with silence again.

He looked at Reenah with eyes keen to her mood, and she looked at him. She knew that he was in greatest earnest, and that he believed what the mad prophet had spoken to the depths of his being.

"This I know, that when I am no more, yet I shall see Mighty God in new flesh upon this very earth. I shall come with the Lord, I and thousands of his holy ones with him. I shall be no pile of dust; neither shall your father, nor my sons."

It began slowly; her lips trembled, her hands shook all the more as she covered her face, and then she wept... bitterly.

"You cannot save him," Job whispered, laying his palm against her face. "His lot lies with God now." Job bent to look at her face. "I loved him, too, you know."

"He did not believe," she cried.

"We had talks. You and I do not know what he believed. Though you can not change the truth of God, even for his sake."

Reenah looked at her lap. "What of me?" she asked through desperate gulps.

"You are yet alive," he soothed.

"I have bedded such men... even..."

"You suppose this the most grievous of sins?" he asked. He lifted her red and dripping face. "Mighty God is holy. What man is innocent?"

She did not pull her face from his hands. She wished that he see her at her most pitiful, in her greatest despair, at her most true self - and she dared him to love her now. "Even Nimrod," she finished.

Job pushed all the hair from her face and, leaning forward, kissed her brow. "I know, child," he whispered. "I shall sacrifice a lamb and beseech Mighty God for you. You have only to ask it."

All the tears of her life could not match what was spent now. "But you have no sheep," she sobbed.

"Tonight I have become your father," he promised. "And your father has a lamb set aside for you."

- 81 -

Reenah left before first light, confident that Job would, indeed, beseech God for her and fearful of The Holy Presence. She rode across the field toward the cottage upon her horse, reaching home before the lamb was selected from the tiny herd, before the swift draining of its life-blood.

Tutan woke Kittim and Madai. Together they walked in the morning chill to the hilltop, there to sit in a newly budding vineyard. He told them of the fall and winter, describing their frantic harvest before the frost, their wine-making and its profits. He recounted the days at the river after the calamity, when all of Job's household was sent away to Reenah. He withheld his personal temptation there, for as such he viewed his affections. He described his return, finding Job's illness past, replaced by a veritable peace. He told with amusement of the heart-sick lad who pined for Iscah. With pride, he described her own ability with the little herd of sheep bought with wine in the early spring, and of the remarkable swelling of that herd by way of triple births. This was all told from their hilltop perch, watching Job at the stone altar preparing one of those lambs for the Mighty God.

"It is the only animal that does not cry out when it is killed," Kittim remarked, watching the swift crosswise slash of Job's knife. "It is for Reenah," he continued. "She has let go her false gods."

"She served no god," Tutan corrected quietly.

Kittim looked at Tutan with flat assurance. "Men have gods," he said.

Tutan slowly nodded, almost imperceptibly. Then he looked back at the altar, at the fire which was beginning to ignite the lamb.

"We have word of Eden," Madai offered. "It was as your writing told."

Again Tutan nodded, watching the smoke from the altar rise like a saber toward the sky. He was reluctant to look away.

"God walked there."

Tutan looked at him skeptically.

"Indeed," Madai assured him. "As you or I. His steps were heard."

"Is that possible?"

"It was, but no longer," Kittim answered, bearing a note of sadness.

Tutan studied Kittim a moment, knowing him to be unfailingly honest. Then he looked back at Job. They were silent, watching the scene below. Job stood before the altar, obscured by smoke, with his arms upraised. Kittim smiled faintly, and they watched until the lamb was consumed.

Their morning meal was waiting when they returned. Iscah chatted in her own merry way; Kittim, eating little, kindly engaged her. Job, in the highest of spirits, conversed quietly with his wife. Madai ate voraciously, and Tutan did not appear at the table.

- *82* -

Cusah, the little Arabian, carried Tutan with speed. Her muscles cried with pleasure, the open field before her, an able rider on her back. The way was known, a familiar destination. She smelled the river. The horse is a beast of intellect, brave and willful. It carries man with perception, knowing when he is uncertain or capable, fearful or eager. And her good master, Tutan, was eager. He held the reins lightly, not to bruise her mouth, and he let her go. If he did not restrain her, she would reach the river soon.

Though he did not prod her, Cusah carried him with brilliant speed. Tutan gave the decision over to her, for he was fearfully conflicted of spirit, feeling both afraid to reach the cottage and anxious for it. He would not think of how he would do it, but he would do it. It was only his horse that perceived his rightful condition. She felt it in his steady hand and determined knees. Tutan was bent upon the prize.

His first sight of the river cottage showed a great fire blazing in the dust in front of Reenah's door. It seemed dreadfully close to the cottage, fueled by debris from the winter storms and parchments that filled the air with stench. Tutan came at a distance and was first afraid she had set fire to her house... but, no. She came through the front door, blinded to his approach by the smoke, with a great armload. She dumped it into the fire and disappeared back inside. He slowed Cusah to decipher what it was about. But she did not come out again.

When he came to the side of the cottage, he skirted the blaze to stand at the open door. He peered into the dim, watching Reenah, her back to him. She held a mallet, and she was banging away at a clay relief on her wall. Her hair had tumbled from any semblance of arrangement. It and her robe clung to her, drenched with sweat. She was frantic in her efforts, and exhausted, as her scraping brought only clay fragments breaking away, dissolving in a cloud of red dust. He quietly entered the room, hearing her labored breath, punctuated by foreign speech and an occasional gulping sob.

He came quietly beside her. He took the mallet, wrapping his hand around hers. She jumped, startled, a cry escaping her throat. His eyes took full sight of her in the instant, flushed and damp with sweat, smelling of smoke. Her eyes were wide, and a tiny trickle of blood ran from a scratch on her hand. In that instant, he understood it was the goddess of Cush she was pounding off her wall.

The lovely, forbidden woman stood upon her parade of gods who were partly crushed and ruined, pounded to dust. The soot on her face was etched clean in a trail from her eyes to her chin. And she was stunned motionless. He slowly lowered the mallet she held, his hand over hers.

"Let me finish it," he said.

His attack on the clay was less frantic than hers, and more effective. It left the gaggle of gods rightly at their feet. And when he was finished, he looked at her through the dust floating in the air. She did not smell of perfume, but smoke, and her hair was not silken. Her olive skin was alive with color brought up from a pounding heart.

"You do not know me," she whispered.

"There is time for that."

"Such things I have done." She began to weep quietly. "You are... good."

He looked at her face and cleaned the soot from her cheeks with his thumb. "Did you not hear the words of your Uncle?" he asked. "There is One Who is good."

She steadied herself, conscious of where his hand had touched her. "Is it done?"

"The sacrifice?" he asked, and she nodded.

"It is done."

"It was accepted?" her voice trembled.

Tutan put his hands on her arms. "I watched the smoke rise to the heavens," he answered. "I watched until the lamb was consumed. It is accepted."

He watched himself in the irises of her eyes as she dared believe what he said. He watched her face slowly relax and wanted desperately to stroke it.

"We should return to Job's house," he told her. He was not afraid now. "I am bent upon you."

His face turned crimson as he uttered the words and slow understanding crept through her.

She collected herself gradually, watching him. Then a characteristic flourish began to ignite in her eyes and she could not keep from straightening her apron. She brushed the wet awkwardly from her nose, and then she smiled. She had never been more lovely.

- 83 -

Another lamb dropped to the straw. The last of them was born. All the ewes of Job's new flock were delivered, and all their young were alive, save what was given for Reenah's sake. The air was filled with their bleating and suckling. Kittim held a skin of milk to the urgent mouth of a tiny lamb, as did Lehabim and Madai and Iscah, even Lemmeri. Marisheba was busied filling the skins. Job kept his wife inside, guarding her own belly.

They were covered with milk and slobber. It was no small business to satisfy twenty-one thirsty newborns. They scarcely had a moment to wonder after Tutan. Iscah's gaze strayed toward Kittim again, kneeling in the soiled straw, his hand cradling the lamb as he fed it. She loved his hands, and she kept her own budding hopes, a conflict of fear and purpose, for she knew her young womanhood would not be concealed. Great damage had been done her before, at the hands of wicked men, but Kittim's hands were kind and good. She suddenly felt heat climbing to her face and looked away, afraid of something more - that he would not want her.

Her own lamb satisfied, she returned it to its mother, careful it did not lose her smell. The triple births amazed her. Never had her father's flock been so fertile. She took another. The lamb sucked her finger into its mouth and began to pull on it with a determined tongue. Madai chuckled as he brushed past her, coming for his second.

"How often must this be done?" he asked, stopping to sit in the straw beside her.

She pulled her finger out with some difficulty and replaced it with the skin of milk. "Often," she replied.

He was curious at her tone. "There are so many," he complained.

She suddenly looked at him with awful understanding. "You wish to leave," she whispered.

He was caught unexpectedly at the hurt in Iscah's voice, and at what she so easily perceived that he himself had not. Milk dribbled from the side of the lamb's mouth, and it bleated that she had let the nipple drop away. Madai watched in shock as tears suddenly filled her eyes and spilled over her face.

"But we have only just come," he argued.

"You will leave..." she accused him, and turned away.

He sat on his haunches watching her, utterly confused. It seemed she was finished speaking, an inexplicable change of moods. He watched her hands, capable and efficient, coax the lamb to take the nipple again. He heard her sniffle, remembered the times before that she had wept, and was wholly baffled.

"I will just get another," he muttered. "Which one?"

"Find one that is crying," she answered.

So he left her and shortly scooped into his arms a wobbly little lamb that would not stop bleating.

He settled into the task, keeping watch over Iscah, who would not look up. He started to wonder where Tutan was gone. Marisheba collected their skins, brought them back filled, and did it all again. His back began to ache, all bent over.

Lehabim seemed for the second time or more to edge near Iscah. She turned him a stormy face and Madai frowned. He remembered the night he had found her at the stream. She had not been a child then, and months had passed. He should talk to Job about it; Lehabim would bear watching.

All this about Iscah, the changeable mood, the unwelcome attentions and his squirmy sheep passed the time till he was aware at last that the noise of hungry lambs was quieting. There was only one bleating lamb left. Were they finally finished? He looked for the last complaining little mouth.

"There is bread on the table," he heard Marisheba announce, "when you have all washed."

He smiled. She would not fail to provide them food and command them be clean. He wondered what time had passed, considered as he did, that this first crop of Job's new herd needed their four hands, his and Kittim's. He wondered vaguely how long till weaning. Perhaps Iscah was right, after all, that his aim was to leave when they could be spared.

Certainly she would want to stay. Surely she did not suppose they would deny it. Maybe that was the trouble. She wasn't their slave, after all. And he was a little indignant that she doubted them. More likely she still doubted him, and that made him sad. Curiously so. She was a changeable girl with a family likely dead, but she would find a home in a good house such as Job's. He knew it. And they should not come this way again, nor Tutan. He would miss them. Then he thought about Kittim, his friend who would go back from where he had come, surely. And Madai was suddenly a lonely man.

He was the last to leave the stable, and not disobedient or even reluctant in the washing of sheep slobber. He found Job and Kittim, even Lehabim and Marisheba, scooping humus with their bread, a gathering of people who have done a day's work well. Only the Lady and Iscah had not come, and Tutan, still not found. It was growing late in the day. This would likely be their night's meal. He reached into a bowl of dates, glancing at Lehabim as he did. The color in the boy's face deepened, and a peak of red crowned each of his ears. Madai felt a frown scoot across his face.

"My dear!" Job suddenly exclaimed, rising to meet his wife. She flushed as she reached her hand to him. She was dressed in a gown of sapphire silk, and she was lovely.

Iscah came behind. She caught Madai's notice, and then his breath, as she was wearing a garment familiar to him. The crimson silk of the caravan, patterned with gold and white orchids, retrieved from the pack of a dead camel. Wearing it well, though she was awkward, uncomfortable. She fixed her gaze on Kittim as she entered, color climbing the planes of her face, inflaming the flecks of brown that sprinkled her cheeks.

"A celebration," The Lady announced. "All the ewes are birthed, friends are about us, my husband is well again..." She smiled as she sat beside him.

They spoke of Job's growing prospects, his swelling herd of sheep, the camels which were straying back across the desert. The Lady pressed her hand gratefully across her belly. Still, the house was quiet, and Job began to speak of his house servants, planning to bring them back when his fortunes allowed. Madai listened as futures were discussed.

The provision of food was sufficient, though not superfluous, and was soon consumed. Only a portion of bread was saved for Tutan, set upon his plate. They heard the sound of Cusah on the brick courtyard. Madai looked at the door as it opened to the entrance of both Tutan and Reenah. Their faces were adorned with the paint of joy, and he was astounded at his own dullness. For it was now all quite obvious.

- 84 -

Madai sat alone with just the fire for a companion. It had all been told of Tutan and Reenah, that she cast aside her heresies, a good end for his friend, the exotic woman. He smiled.

He was waiting for Kittim, gone into the night, as was his custom more often of late, in fact. Madai was feeling a fresh longing after his isle of lakes across the Brine Sea. It relieved him to have a passion for home. He had something to bring with him, something of infinite value. He wanted to confide it to Kittim and to find what his companion would do. He paced the room, fueled with the sort of energy that makes sitting impossible, and he re-stoked the fire.

It popped at him with a smell that hinted of mammoth on sacred altars. He could nearly have been there at this moment for the clarity of remembrance. It shot a river of nerves down the length of his core, as if he were fifteen again and waiting for his first mammoth hunt. His heart was suddenly pounding, reaching all the way to his belly, when he heard his friend's footfall at the door. He turned, both excited and anxious to see what Kittim would do, only to see there Iscah, even now wearing the silk.

It was a shock to him, unnerving, as if she were some sort of unworldly creature, out of place. His mouth went curiously dry. "Iscah!" the name escaped his mouth, in part a resolution of his own surprise. "What are you doing here? You should be in bed."

'What are you doing here?' she thought, a more likely question, as she had come looking for Kittim and here was Madai, the very one who claimed Kittim's first loyalty. Madai was restless, she knew, and he came from far away, so far that he looked like no one else on these shores. If Kittim would follow him there, then she would never see him again - unless he would take her. She closed her eyes, being so close to her purpose here, and steadied herself. That Madai had returned from Shinar with great tales and a new belief was secondary, if it was good. That he would rob her of Kittim was first on her mind.

Madai watched her eyes snap, and he grinned despite himself. She might be dressed in finery, but she was still Iscah.

"As should you," she answered, pacing past him to the window. "I am waiting for Kittim."

"I, as well", he returned.

She looked across her shoulder at him, both disappointed and annoyed.

"He has gone into the night," Madai continued, his amusement with her being replaced with... "You won't find him. I've looked before."

"I may wait here, in any case," she replied. She looked at him steadily, color beginning to climb her cheeks.

He nodded and she turned back to the window. He knew she was going to be stubborn tonight, and... she was remarkably comely in that dress! He looked at her looking out at the night. She was still and stiff, her back straight and thin, almost childlike. He remembered the little maid they had rescued. He remembered her nut-brown face turned up to Kittim with all her hope and fear.

"You want to go," she accused, still looking out the window. A cricket had made a home in the stones of the floor somewhere and chirped. "But you will stay till the weaning," she insisted.

He couldn't answer, knowing, of course, that he would stay to help. He was silenced by what she was inferring – that she would not come with them - and though he had only just today thought it was a good plan for her, disappointment and a feeling of severest loss was claiming his heart.

"You want to stay here, of course. Understandable," he began, even as her eyes darted him with ire.

"At the will of Lehabim?" she spat.

"No!" He heard the violence in his voice with surprise. "You are still... too young for that. I will talk to Job."

At which she laughed.

It was no part a merry laugh.

"We have come a long way together," he ventured quietly to cover the distance suddenly blooming between them. "You and Kittim and I."

He waited for her answer. "Yes, Madai. Many great adventures." Her own words slowly thawed her, looking at the sunburnt face of this yellow-haired foreigner who had been a part of her rescue and was, all his folly aside, surprisingly dear.

"And Tutan," he continued.

"Consecrated," she muttered, and chuckled despite her prickly mood.

He laughed with her. "Besotted," he corrected.

"Yes." She glanced at him again, and then away. She began to twist her hands, holding them lightly in front of herself. She looked around the room and began an aimless pace, suddenly shy. "The rainbow dragon is nice," she added, glancing at the doorway.

"From Noah," he reminded her, and she nodded.

She looked at him again, a little ashamed, glad he couldn't see into her thoughts to know how churlish she had become, jealous of Kittim.

He had the impression that it was the first time she had really seen him tonight. He glanced at her worried hands, and he remembered them stinking of onion. He remembered the waif hiding in a cloak too big, her turtle shell, that scruff of curly hair.

"We will miss you," he said softly, authentically sad.

She looked as though she had been slapped. She squared her shoulders before she moved away from the window, her grievance instantly restored. It was both a graceful and deliberate advance across the room. She smoothed away an invisible wrinkle from the silk gown and sat on Job's exquisite couch.

"If we will each wait for Kittim," she said carefully, "we may at least spend the time profitably." She was perched with a straight back, looking like the Lady in her posture, and Madai would have chuckled if he'd dared. "Tell me more of Eden," she demanded, cupping her hands under her chin with chilly eyes.

But he would not be cowed by her, as he finally, slowly, recognized the feeling she awoke in him. Her in her woman's garb and beautiful. It reminded him of taking Ido's hand, so long ago. He knew he was not hiding it from his face, that Iscah would see a shadow of old grief if she were only to look, a hint of guilt. But Ido was good at loving, and she would not blame him for wanting Iscah or want him starved of life.

So Madai carefully began to talk – of Eden, a subject most dear to his heart. He would speak of the other later... when it was time.

Iscah was watching him, watching more than she listened. She saw the light come to his face and heard the words of God and garden spoken without a trace of bitterness or doubt. 'So, he has found Him,' she thought. She turned away to look out into the night again and watched the way the stars trembled in her tears.

"They sang, Iscah," he said, seeing her turn. "The stars."

She blinked, unwilling to be caught unguarded again. "And beasts that talked to men?" she quipped.

"So, now you are mocking me," he said with humor in his voice.

"You have finally found your truth," she replied, ignoring the accusation.

"Yes."

"You will take it back from where you came," she continued.

"Yes." He stood up, and this time it was he who walked to the window. He thought of his village somewhere west beneath these same stars. "Do you remember what Job said?" he asked.

"He says very much," she replied.

The night air was growing chilly, but it smelled too good to close the shutter. He savored it a moment before he continued, thoughtful and quiet, "Mighty God walked the earth of Eden, Iscah. His steps were heard." Iscah's silk rustled on the couch behind him. "Tutan was right," he said, turning slowly. "Adam was cost everything when God drove him out of Eden... And perhaps they did try to find Him again... behind the blazing lance, at the border," He scratched his beard, feeling suddenly in need of another wash. And he thought how it was... not to be seen of God...

"I've seen the depths of myself, Iscah. I've looked into the eyes of a ruined man, and I've stood on a tower with corruption by my side." The night seemed full of unexpected emotion. He felt himself nearly pummeled, straying down an unpredictable path. He felt himself brushed by a manifest hopelessness. "Do you think a lamb is enough?" he suddenly whispered. And he thought about mammoth, too, of better worth than a sheep, and wondered even about the mammoth.

"There is a great trouble, Iscah." He gathered himself and turned to her with intensity. "Adam could come no more to Eden, where God walked, and still – this is the trouble – Job said that we would walk the earth with Him in our flesh – and Enoch – that holy ones would come with Him." He looked at her. "Are we the holy ones, Iscah?"

She couldn't answer, but only looked at him, struck by the subtle shift in his eyes.

"I hope it is us," he whispered. He came to sit beside her. He felt alone again, chilled by that glancing blow he had just suffered, that accusation. He gripped her hand, which steadied him. "But how will He do it, do you think?"

She was taken aback by him, by the question that was so much more than she would have expected of him. "Walk the earth with us?" she asked.

"No," he said, looking into her round brown eyes. "Not that." He thought of all he had done thus far in his life, and the worst outweighed the best. Yet there must be a way. "No, Iscah, how will He ever, even God, make us holy?"

The cricket continued its song. Madai was holding her fingers too tight. He thought he might be hurting her hand, and he let it go. But she laid her fingers lightly on his again. She leaned against him absently, peaceably. Madai felt her beside him.

He knew then. It raced at him like a flood, passed into his heart with a great fullness. And he also knew that what Iscah wanted of Kittim was not what she thought. She was, he knew, more a hatchling affixed to his friend than a lover, because Kittim was not like other men, somehow, and he would go back to his master.

Madai let himself breathe in her nearness. He knew she would sail with him in his boat and they would cross the Brine Sea together. They would bring tales from the Ancients back to The Family. And she would love him, by then, or later. He could wait.

Her fingers on his hand told him all of that.

About the Author

Kathy Frias lives in east Texas with her husband, Robert. Kathy is a graduate of Harding Christian College in Searcy, Arkansas. When asked, Kathy says her greatest achievement is the good character of her 3 sons, and that was accomplished only by the Hand of God and the help of her excellent husband.

Rumors of Eden is her first published book.

Bibliography

— To learn more about the Border Sacrifices and Chinese symbols, read:

Kang, C.H. and Nelson, Ethel, The Discovery of Genesis, Concordia Publishing House, 1979.

— To learn more about the constellations, read:

Bullinger, E.W., The Witness of the Stars, Kregel Publications, reprint of 1893 ed.

Seiss, Joseph R., The Gospel in the Stars, Kregel Publications, 1972.

— To learn more about ancient cultures tracing their geneologies to Adam, read:

Cooper, Bill, After the Flood, New Wine Press, 1995.

Other related books:

Baugh, Carl E., Ph D., Panorama of Creation, Creation Publication Services, 1989.

Morris, Dr. Henry and Whitcomb, John, The Genesis Flood, P & R Publications, 1961.

Oard, Michael, Frozen in Time, Master Books, Inc., 2004.

The Holy Bible, New International Version, Zondervan Press, 1988.

Texts: Genesis, chapters 1 - 11

Job 19:25-27 and Job, chapters 38 - 42 and Jude 1:4

— The Gilgamesh Epic is the poem Iscah recites to Kittim and Madai about Noah's flood. There are flood stories in many cultures from the earliest of times.